Canal Town

A NOVEL

SAMUEL HOPKINS ADAMS

PEOPLES BOOK CLUB EDITION

Published by

CONSOLIDATED BOOK PUBLISHERS

Chicago 1944

This is a special edition published
exclusively for members of the
Peoples Book Club, P.O. Box 6570-A
Chicago, Illinois

THIS IS A WARTIME BOOK

IT IS MANUFACTURED UNDER EMERGENCY CONDITIONS AND COMPLIES WITH THE GOVERNMENT'S REQUEST TO CONSERVE ESSENTIAL MATERIALS IN EVERY POSSIBLE WAY.

Manufactured in the United States of America

To the Memory of

DEACON ABNER ADAMS

who did his bit, made his pile
and left his name upon a section
of the Big Ditch, this book is
piously inscribed by his
great-grandson.

Foreword

THAT *vast, Clintonian enterprise, the Erie Canal, brought with it to Western New York not only progress and prosperity but unforeseen upheavals. The peaceful countryside was beset by an alien irruption. Disease and social laxity marched with economic expansion. The early days of the Big Ditch saw the minds of men broadened and their morals loosened. From old, half-forgotten records and family legends the author has attempted a reconstruction of an American phase not of sufficient intrinsic importance to have found a place in history.*

In writing a historical novel devoid of historical characters, he has avoided the irksome necessity of justifying his personages. If any resemblance to individuals once living be found in the story, it is more by luck than art, though the author would be happy to think that it was so.

To the fair and peaceful village of Palmyra, apologies are herewith tendered for sundry liberties assumed in the matter of its history and topography. For Palmyra, as herein treated with fictional license, is to be taken less as a corporate entity than as the prototype of those old, sturdy, up-state communities which maintained their essential individuality and local character through the turbulent years of the 1820's.

The fantastic episode which wrecked the "Latham" family (the real name is widely and honorably known throughout the nation) may be found by some readers difficult of credence. Such skeptics are referred to the Albany Medical College in whose museum the evidence, in the form of the corpus delicti, is preserved behind glass.

To many persons and institutions I am indebted for help, advice and correction. My heaviest debt is to Walter D. Edmonds, whose novels of the Erie Canal are now classic, for his generosity in turning over to me his invaluable notebooks on the construction of the canal, thus saving me months of laborious background research. Special acknowledgments are due to the following:

To two former classmates of my Rochester school days, Norman Mumford, who, many years ago, suggested to me the subject of the novel; and Beekman C. Little whose family records underlie an essential part of the plot.

To Mrs. C. A. Ziegler and Mrs. N. F. Benjamin of Palmyra for a wealth of local data.

To E. Donaldson Clapp of Auburn, N.Y., and Joseph D. Ibbotson, of Hamilton College, whose scholarly editing has saved me from embarrassing errors.

To Dr. Howard L. Prince of Rochester, N. Y., and Dr. T. Wood Clarke of Utica, N. Y., for valued advice and assistance on the medical side.

To Harold G. Metcalf and Mrs. Robert W. Messenger of Auburn, N. Y., for expert help on technical points.

To R. W. G. Vail of the New York State Library, for guidance and suggestions.

To Dr. John A. Boone of Meggett, S. C., and the library of the Medical Society of South Carolina; to the New York Academy of Medicine, and to the Albany Medical College for medical data not elsewhere available.

S. H. A.

Wide Waters,
Auburn, N. Y.
April, 1944.

Part One

1

A new Young Gentleman came to Town today. He has a very Serious Asspeckt.

(ENTRY IN THE DIARY OF MISS ARAMINTA JERROLD)

GRAY mists overhung the stream called Mud Creek, and the sun stood clear above the earthy thimble known as Winter Green Knob. On every side for miles around similar protuberances jutted up from the level, all sloping gently from the south and dropping in clifflike abruptness at the northern end. It was a landscape the geologic like of which exists nowhere else upon the face of earth.

The young man on the wagon seat did not appreciate this. Nevertheless, he was interested in his surroundings which he surveyed with an observant eye. Here was a countryside very different from the Oneida Hills of his birthplace with their harsh acclivities and turbulent watercourses, a region more suave and friendly. Palmyra village, too, as he approached it from the east, was comfortable to the apprehensions of a stranger about to make his venture in life.

No fewer than three church spires thrust upward into the scented June air. The main thoroughfare along which his mare daintily picked her way was a generous five rods in breadth. The crude log cabins of the environs had been succeeded by trim frame houses, white with green shutters, topped by brick chimneys and gay, gilded weathercocks brave in the slanted sunlight. Beyond these, the stores and mills stretched in ordered array, substantial as fortifications. A prosperous town; an up-and-coming town. His Scottish grandmother would have had a word to put to it. The word was "couthy."

"Hospitality, Clean & Decent, for Man & Beast" announced the

Eagle Tavern in red letters picked out with white against a background of true blue. "L. St. John, Prop'r" was authority for the promise. Above, the symbolic bird spread gleaming pinions.

"Come in. A good morning to you."

The stranger looked up into a seamed and ruddy face.

"Good morning," he answered pleasantly.

"Are you for breakfast, sir?" inquired the host.

"Yes. And accommodations for the night."

"You come none too soon. By evening we shall be full-taken. Not a room will be vacant and we shall be charging two shillings for standees in the halls."

He pointed to a newspaper advertisement affixed to the posting board.

June the Twenty-sixth, 1820.

Upon this Evening and the Following,
a Superior Theatrical Entertainment
will be Presented in the Great Ballroom of this House.
The Lyceum Dramatic Company
in the Moral Tragedy
GEORGE BARNWELL,
or the London Apprentice.
To be Followed by the Comic Glee,
Dame Durden.

Saturday Evening, *The Spectre Bridegroom.*

Admission, 50 Cents—Children, Half-price.

The new arrival gave it an incurious glance.

"What is your charge for a chamber, by the week?"

Mr. St. John conned him with shrewd appraisal. "A dollar a day," he said boldly.

"Surely that is very dear."

"My dear sir, consider the character of my house," returned the host warmly. "The Eagle is the regular victualing-stop for all stages. You can be sure of your fare here." He reflected. "I've to keep your animal, too. Make it six dollars the week, and no more said."

"Very good. What's for breakfast?"

"A pork pie, fine and hot. Tender-boiled steak. Sausages. Eggs to taste. Flannel cakes with honey. Well-burned coffee, all the way from Albany. Will you have a dram of liquor?"

"No. I'll have a wash."

He went to the pump in the yard. Mr. St. John watched with surprise as he took from one pocket a horn toothbrush and from another a stick of chalk which he rubbed upon the bristles, preparatory to cleansing his teeth.

"Proud pertickler, ain't he!" commented the host to himself. He was not sure that he approved such extreme measures. They served, however, to whet his interest. Presently he drew a chair to the table and seated himself opposite the guest.

"Where you from, Mister?"

"Clinton Settlement in Oneida County."

"Quite a piece of travel. Got a tetch of the Western fever, huh?"

The other smiled. Food had ameliorated his reserve. "I find the region interesting."

"If you were minded to take up land, you couldn't find better. Rich soil and easy to subdue. Once the trees are cleared, it'll grow anything. Thriving commerce. Look at our mills. Look at our stores. Look at our asheries."

"I intend to."

"Are you farming, then?"

"No."

"What is your business, make-so-bold?"

"I am a practitioner of physic and surgery. Horace Amlie, M.D. Certified by state and county boards."

"Likely you'd pick up a bit of practice by exhibiting a card on my post-board. All the township consults my post-board. Half a dollar to you, since you are a guest of the house."

"Not too fast. I must look about me first."

A formidable voice bellowed, "Taproom! Taproom! Bar, there! Can a man get a drink, by God? Or is this a temperance house?"

"Coming. Coming," cried Mr. St. John, bouncing out of his chair.

A moment later Dr. Amlie heard the robustious tones demanding, "A fipsworth of the ardent, and don't scamp the brim, old cock."

Having made a satisfactory meal, Dr. Amlie returned to the veranda. His mare had been taken to the shed. Where she had been tied, four sturdy horses stood with their night blankets of oilcloth still over their flanks. A legend, gaudily painted on the side of the wagon to which they were hitched, read:

JED PARRIS. PALMYRA TO ALBANY.
Merchandise Teamed. Prices on Request.

The man himself came out wiping his lips, a heavy-bearded, jovial ruffian of thirty-odd. To the proprietor who followed, he was saying with a grin, "Thirty cents a gallon for your whisky? You may keep it to rot your own fat gut. I can buy my wagon full in Schenectady for two shilling."

"Prices are up," grumbled the other. "There's no profit in anything. What do you make on your drawing?"

"One hundred dollars the ton on the through haul," replied the teamster with satisfaction.

"Wait till the canal comes through," said Mr. St. John with a gleam of malice. "You'll touch no such price then."

"The canawl! The canawl!" jeered Jed Parris. "I'll spit you all the canawl you'll get." He ejected a welter of tobacco juice over the rail and lifted a hoarse basso.

> "Clinton, the federal son-of-a-bitch,
> Taxes our dollars to build him a ditch.
> Bury old Clinton so deep in the mud . . ."

A metallic peal cut him short. The door swung wide, revealing the slim and elegant figure of a man in his early twenties. His handsome, hawkish face was framed in luxuriant side whiskers, sprouting upward to meet the long, silky hair that wholly screened the upper part of his ears. He wiped the mouthpiece of a shining bugle.

"Who sings that weevily, Bucktail ditty?" he demanded.

Jed Parris bristled. "I do. And what's that to you?"

"An offense," returned the other coolly.

"Mr. Silverhorn Ramsey is a canaller by trade," put in the host.

The bulky teamster seemed struck by the name. "Mr. Silverhorn Ramsey?" he repeated.

"Captain Silverhorn Ramsey," corrected the other. "A hot rumbullion for me, if you please, my worthy host."

"Just the same, this here canal talk is east wind in a man's belly, as Scripture says," blustered Parris.

"This gentleman might tell us otherwise," said the innkeeper, interpreting the stranger's wise smile. "He's from a county where it's already operating—Oneida."

"Is he a boatee, too?" asked the teamster disgustedly.

"He is a practitioner of physic and surgery," explained Mr. St. John with respect.

Silverhorn Ramsey lifted wet lips from his glass. "Young Æsculapius, eh?"

"What do you know of Æsculapius?" asked the other curiously.

"Oh, I tried my hand at the pellet-and-bolus trade. Not good enough," said the canal man negligently. "Have you a sure medic for the pox?"

Horace Amlie, M.D., stiffened. He held a high and prickly regard for his chosen profession, the more so in that he was so new to it. His look measured the other steadily.

"Do you seek a professional consultation, sir?"

Silverhorn cackled with arrogant mirth. "Not I! But I could put you in the way of a thriving trade, so be you could warrant a three-day cure as the almanach promises. The turnpike coffee taps are no better than fancy kens, and the teamers still have money in their pockets."

"I am neither an itinerant nor an almanach healer," said the young medico coldly.

"You could do no better than sport your shingle here," averred Mr. St. John with conviction. "Our commerce increases daily. We are the nation's center for the mint industry. Our hemp establishes the market price. Our ash, both pot and pearl, has no superior. Mud Creek teems with traffic. When Governor Clinton's waterway is projected here and beyond, Auburn may swallow its pride and Geneva and Canandaigua wring their hands over lost glories, for we shall indeed be the Golden Emporium of the Growing West."

"I read it all in the newspaper," said Silverhorn. "Hunca-munca to your Palmyra, say I. The canal's the thing."

"The canal will establish Palmyra at the very heart of the new prosperity," declared the local man. "The day the first boat comes, I enlarge my accommodations."

"You may rent them to the chintzes for all the good you'll get of the ditch," snorted the teamster.

"No man ever found a chintz in my beds that he did not bring there himself," said St. John, reddening.

"Why are you so assuerd that the boats will not come here?" the physician asked the teamster.

"Boats run on water, don't they?"

"They do."

"Can water run uphill?"

"Did you never hear of a lock?"

"Aye. And seen 'em, too. And the pent water breaking through their ruinated sides. It's agin nature, so it is. You can't go agin nature. Water seeks its level and God help what stands in its way," said the teamster, using the hackneyed argument of the opposition.

"It is true that defective locks have broken through," conceded the physician. "They have been rebuilt. The commerce goes on. Mr. St. John will do well to enlarge his facilities in advance."

The big teamster spat on the sanded floor. "If you know as little of physic as of traffic, you may eat your own boluses or starve." He lifted his nail-studded boots, one after another, and examined them critically, sole and heel. "These bottoms must last me to Fort Plain," said he. "I charge off a pair against profits for every trip. Four miles to the hour and but one mile out of ten on the wagon seat. My poor pads! I shall take them to the barber on my return. He calls himself a medic, too. Will you trim my corns cheaper than him, Doc?"

"Dr. Amlie to you," said the young man rigidly.

The teamster made a vulgar noise through his pursed lips.

"Buy you a boat, Jed, and you can sit on your own deck and trail your corns in the water," the innkeeper taunted him.

"That dithered lunk on the canal?" interposed Silverhorn softly. "There's not a spavined nag from Albany to Rome that wouldn't kick his fat bum off the towpath at sight of him."

This was too much. Parris let out a roar and pushed back his sleeves. To Horace Amlie it seemed probable that the impudent bugler would presently have need of medical attention, for his opponent bulked to nearly twice his weight. But Host St. John popped nimbly forth with a hickory bat in hand.

"Outside for your settlements," he ordained.

"Wait a bit," said Silverhorn. "Is that a fly on your wall?" There was a swift pass of his hand. A gleam split the air; a thud sounded. The knife quivered in the basswood boarding. "Missed him, by God!" said the young man with a pretense of incredulous discomfiture.

Mr. Jed Parris, though a bold enough fighting man, left the room peaceably. He was convinced that to push the difference further would be unprofitable. Unleashing his nigh lead horse, he clucked his four into movement and was off, stretching his legs in the steady rhythm of the "dust-eater" with his fifty miles to do by sundown. Silverhorn, stepping to the porch, looked after him and yawned. He polished his mouthpiece on his sleeve, pressed it to his full lips, and sent after the departing equipage a beautiful, clear, ringing note, as vainglorious as the crow of the victor in a cockpit. Indeed, thought Horace Amlie, he had all the virility and vanity of a cockerel, and with it, something of the menace of coiled steel.

The innkeeper polished and replaced his glassware. "Why not take a look around our village, young sir?" he suggested. "You will see much to please you."

A young lady, making the turn from the inn corner, craned her graceful head, affording Horace Amlie an advantageous sight of a delicate, serious face of pure contours, from which dove-gray eyes looked out in shy appraisal. Silverhorn assumed a rakish pose.

"A bene mort," he commented, caressing a side whisker.

"None of your gyppo lingo for the likes of Miss Agatha Levering," the tavern keeper rebuked him.

"The Leverings of the asheries," Silverhorn was obliging enough to explain for the stranger's enlightenment. "They hold their chins high."

"And why not?" said Mr. St. John.

"True for you," conceded the canal man. "They're crumey with bank-rags. But does that righten her to look down her pretty nose at a man that's had better than her and left 'em when done with 'em?"

Horace was both amused and disgusted. Evidently this young sprig had flaunted his manly charms in vain before the gray-eyed beauty. The caneller expertly twirled his bugle on his thumb, restored it to the buckle on his belt and swaggered to the door, bidding Horace farewell with an airy flirt of the hand.

"We'll meet again, young Æsculapius."

"Who is he?" Horace inquired of the host.

"A rouncher. A real rouncher. His family were well thought of, down Jerusalem way. He's the black sheep. Had his turn at smuggling on the lakes. If you can believe the talk, he was with the New York mob that operated a bogus two years ago; I've been nicked with the false money of their coinage and be damned to it. Nothing proved on him, though. He's slick as a mink. Since then he's swung his tiller on two canals, and now he's for this one. Very much the gentleman when he chooses. It's good blood with a bad turn to it. Are you for a stroll of inspection, sir?"

Dr. Amlie looked ruefully down at his feet. "I shall have to get my gear mended first, or go barefoot as an urchin."

"Nothing easier. Decker Jessup is your man. At the Sign of the Red Boot."

The village had not yet waked to business as the physician walked down the street, but the door beneath the swaying emblem was open. Within, a pale, corpulent man sat wheezing at his bench, which was fitted with neat shelves for his awls, punches and hammers, a shallow leathern pouch for remnants, stretchers for the strips of hides and, over all, a palanquin-like roof.

"You work early," remarked the caller.

The cobbler peered nearsightedly at him. "When fools are still abed, the world is to the wise," he croaked. "What's your will?"

The doctor pointed to his boots. "Can you repair these?"

"Stand steady." Decker Jessup picked one foot from the floor as if it were a horse's hoof, set it down and repeated the process with the other. "You go shod like a mincing miss," he pronounced. "Nothing to be done here."

The young man was annoyed. "What kind of craftsman are you that cannot mend sound leather?" he demanded sharply.

"A very good craftsman. An excellent craftsman. But not in such a matter. Your gear is better fitten for a ball-floor than for road service. Delicate leather, but not worth the cost of repairs. Cast 'em to the rats and let me make you a serviceable pair."

"By declining to mend my shoes you hope to better me in a trade, I presume."

"I better no man. Value given is my rule. Will you be shod with the true preparation? One dollar."

The visitor regarded his feet uncertainly. "I should like to save these. Waste I cannot afford. Few things are beyond repair."

"You tell me that, who are a learned doctor?"

"How do you know that?"

The cobbler's round shoulders shook with self-satisfied mirth. "When you turned, a blind man could see the Latin print on the certificate perking from your pocket. Come, young man, let me turn you out a pair of boots, factored from the true preparation, such as will do honor to your feet. Ready by sundown. A dollar will nor make nor break you, to judge from your fine clothes."

"Will you take it out in trade?"

"What! Physicking? I don't hold with doctors. I medicate out of the *Masonic Almanach* and save the costs."

"You look it," retorted the customer. "You've bile in your eye to be scraped with a knife. Your skin is yellow as cowslip and the cat could borrow your tongue for a tail."

"Hoity-toity and hale-you-to-jail!" said the astonished cobbler. "What cockerel have we here? I've done well enough for forty year without your opinion."

"What's that at the turn of your jaw?"

The craftsman fingered the protuberance with tenderness. "What would you say of it?"

"*Cynanche parotidea.* Or perhaps *caries dentium.*"

"English will do for my jaw. It's no more than an overgrown tooth."

"As I said. Let me examine."

Hypnotized by the other's masterful touch, Cobbler Jessup permitted his head to be tilted back and his eyes covered with his own neckerchief.

"Open," said the young man in an authoritative tone. "Wider. Ah!"

"Ow!" yelled the patient.

Having lifted from their appointed place the cobbler's own pincers, Dr. Amlie had tweaked forth the tooth in one powerful jerk.

"There!" said he. "Didn't hurt, did it?"

"Yes."

"You'll sleep the better for it this night. Wash out your oral cavity with whisky. *Extractio dentis,* one shilling."

"You charge high for a small matter," grumbled the other, caressing his jaw.

"Skill and education are worth their price," returned the sententious physician. "Deduct it from the cost of my boots."

The patient grinned. "You will go far, young man."

Dr. Amlie looked out upon the street, now burgeoning into activity. "Perhaps no farther than this," he murmured.

"Are you opening a consultation room?"

"I must make a start somewhere. Why not here?"

"I know the very spot for you," declared the cobbler. "Genteel lodgings at a fair, living price. A most respectable lady. I should know, she being my widowed sister. Let me conduct you there."

Putting aside his leathern apron, he led the way around the corner of Canandaigua Road to a small, pleasant dwelling. Mrs. Martha Harte presented a lugubrious countenance, a clammy hand, and an air of discouraged patience, but admitted to having a ground floor which she might be willing to rent.

"Ten shillings the week, and I'll victual you well, though I'd prob'ly lose money on it," she said with a snivel.

Dr. Amlie privately thought this prophecy unlikely. The house was roomy and well-placed, the chamber stoutly furnished, if a bit musty, and the price little more than he had intended to pay.

"I am obligated to the Eagle House for a week," he explained. "After that I will advise you of my decision."

Bidding them good morning he turned back into Main Street. To the casual eye he would have appeared a young gentleman out for a pleasurable stroll while smoking his after-breakfast segar. But the eyes beneath the fashionably curved hat-brim were alert and observant; the brain back of them busy with estimate and appraisal.

The clock in the window of J. Evernghim stood at eight. The street was already astir. Downwind was borne a spicy tang, new to the nostrils of the outlander. He doubtfully identified it as spearmint, though he did not locate the prosperous still which produced the principal supply of the tincture to the candy, the medical and the perfume trade of the nation. A sharper, more acrid odor exuded from the tannery on the creek bank, and with it mingled the sour, sturdy aroma of the two asheries which faced one another across the stream, and the festive breath of mash, fermenting to whisky in the corner distillery. Along the waterfront sawmills buzzed, gristmills clacked, and fulling-mills clattered in choral contribution to the happy clamor of prosperity.

The stranger paused beside a vacant lot giving a long view down Mud Creek, that legally established traffic-way between Macedon to the westward and on to Lyons in the other direction. A barge toiled against the sluggish current, laden with cord from the ropewalk two miles downstream, product of the local hemp-fields which commanded their price of more than two hundred dollars per ton in any market. Two lean Indians were paddling a canoe, across which was balanced a fine buck, ready for dressing into venison. Back of them, and slower of pace, two batteaus moved to the impulsion of oars; the men sweating at the task, while the womenfolk, gay with finery, anticipated a day of shopping in the superior emporia of Palmyra.

Already the windows erew setting forth the temptation of their wares; the Cheap Store exhibiting its bonnets, shawls and bright kerchiefs from Albany and New York; the provision shops their viands both dry and wet; the smithy, ringing out its metallic music; the tailoring establishment flaunting its dandy apparel for man and boy; Drake's Wagon & Sleigh place its equipages; strong and graceful furniture by Bezabeel Fornum, the cabinet factor; ironmongery for all uses and to every taste; the butcher, the baker, the candlestickmaker all smiling a welcome to the early trade.

As young Dr. Amlie stood in interested contemplation, a bent and crabbed dyspeptic emerged from a doorway, bearing an ornate sign under his arm and dragging a chair in his other hand. Stepping upon the seat, he carefully swung his board to two wrought-iron hooks, thus proclaiming to the world that O. Daggett, gilder, painter and sign-factor was ready for business. The young physician cast a desirous eye on the splendor above him. He hesitated in balance between his ambition for a similarly alluring professional announcement and his consciousness of depleted funds. A squat, brisk fellow was chaffering with O. Daggett.

"How much for a sign, this style?"

"How many words?"

The customer counted them on his fingers as he enunciated jerkily:

"T. Lay—Buys Everything—Fair Dealing to One and All—Highest Prices—Custom Solicited. Thirteen words."

O. Daggett occupied himself with his own fingers. "I make it fourteen."

"You wouldn't charge a man two words for a name as short as mine, would you?" protested Mr. Lay, aggrieved.

"Make it three dollars."

"Three dollars is a power of money."

"Take paint and I'll do it for two. This is the costliest gilt in the market."

"It shines like gold. I like it. Three dollars, then. Barter?"

"Cash from you, Trumbull Lay."

"I got no three dollars cash. Where would I find three dollars cash? There's little money going in this town. Take whisky."

"Don't drink."

"Twist?"

"Don't chaw."

"Black-salt?"

"Don't shoot. Got no gun."

"Fresh meat and vegetables daily for your table then," appealed the other.

"Got no digestion, neither. Bring me cash or good bills or save your breath and my time." O. Daggett turned to survey the stranger. "Anything in your line, young sir?"

Dr. Amlie returned a regretful negative, and resumed his stroll. Before spending he must begin to earn. An elderly black man limped toward him, smiling and knuckling at his sparse white forecurl.

"Give a po' slave a shillin', Your Honah."

"Whose slave were you?"

"Massa Helms's, on Great Sodus. He daid, praise God. A hahd man. Give old Unk Zeb a shillin', sah. Zeb's hungry."

"No. I won't give you money. But if you come to the Eagle late this afternoon, I'll treat your eyes." The ex-slave's vision was blurred with trachoma.

The Negro bobbed in gratitude and hobbled on. From an open window a reedy and pious refrain came to the ears of the wayfarer. A hunchback was operating a lap-organ with busily pumping elbow, while he hummed the refrain of "Bramcoate" in rehearsal for the morrow's service. Facing him a woman wove a fine straw hat with delicate and careful art.

"Plat you a hat, young gentleman?" she asked, seeing him pause.

Everyone in town, it appeared, was after his or some other person's trade. He liked that. It betokened an alert and active community. Presently he would have something to sell to it.

"How long does it take you to finish a hat like that?" he asked, admiring the handiwork.

"Nine days. I sell for six dollars and find and cure my own straw." She sighed. "I make out to gain our living while he"—she nodded indulgently toward the musician—"pumps his little wheezer and lines out the hymns."

A stern-looking personage in black stopped before the place. "See to it that you keep truer measure than last Sunday," he admonished the hunchback.

"The Reverend Theron Strang," said the woman respectfully, as he left. "A kind man until the dyspepsy takes him. Then he's a powerful hell-fire exhorter and death on backsliders. Weekdays he conducts the Register newspaper, where you see him climbing yonder stairs."

"And I'm his devil," put in the hunchback. "Tom Daw, the parson's devil."

The rattle-and-plunk of a handpress gave evidence that the reverend gentleman was his own printer. A specimen of his job-work made appeal to the eye in an adjacent window.

EPHRAIM UPCRAFT
the
Honest Lawyer.
Uncurrent Notes Bought.

The explorer winced. In his weaselskin reposed sundry paper of the Ontario Bank which was decidedly uncurrent, that institution being in a state of coma if not actually defunct. Elder Amlie of Utica, the young man's uncle, had offered him twenty-five percent of what he could realize on the $150 face value of the notes. Without some return from them, his immediate outlook was skimpy.

Where two churches marked the end of the business section, as it abruptly thinned out into stump-studded fields and heavy copses, he crossed over to retrace his journey of inspection on the opposite side. The farther he went, the more was he impressed by the number and quality of the establishments. He passed a timberyard, a store displaying splitwood chairs and baskets, a maltster's location, a second inn, the Exchange, rather dingy, and a barber shop, "At the Sign of the Streaked Pole; L. Brooks, M.D." The duly certified practitioner indulged in a private sneer. What sort of M.D. would debase himself from the forceps and lancet to the shears and razor?

The enunciation of his name, in this town where he was unknown, startled him. It was only Decker Jessup summoning him from the door across the thoroughfare.

"I've something to show you," said the cobbler as his new acquaintance approached. "Keep your eye on that door."

The indicated spot was the side exit of the Eagle. Presently there appeared a sleek, tall figure, glossy-hatted and heavy-bearded, dandling a silverheaded cane.

"Our medical faculty," said the cobbler. "Dr. Gail Murchison."

"He makes his visits early."

"He takes his dram early. He'll have another at eleven."

"I should like to meet him."

"Nothing easier." As the doctor came near, with a slow and dignified pace, the cobbler accosted him. "Dr. Murchison, good morning, sir."

"Ah! The worthy Jessup. Good morning, good morning."

"Make you acquainted with Dr. Horace Amlie, late of Oneida County."

"Doctor? Did you say doctor? You profess medicine, sir?"

"As a tyro, only," replied the newcomer modestly.

The older man peered out from beneath lowering brows. "Ah, so! You're not thinking to settle here, are you?"

"My plans are not yet matured," Horace evaded.

Dr. Murchison waved a hand, every nail of which was outlined in sable. "A cruel, healthy place," he bumbled. "And penny-pinching—oh, my soul! Our health is notorious. A practitioner finds little to do, and for that little is paid in thanks. Had you thought of Rochesterville?"

"I have visited there."

"A fine, feverous town," said Dr. Murchison with enthusiasm. "No better opening for an ambitious young medical man."

Decker Jessup coughed, gazing with intent upon the well-rounded belly that distended the flowery beaverteen of the speaker's waistcoat.

"Yes, yes, a starvation calling," sighed the other. He brightened. "But we serve a purpose, sir. The dignity of the profession."

An exploring bee, thinking favorably of the Murchison breath, became entangled in the luxuriant whiskers. The doctor clawed angrily at it.

"Damn that young Crego!" he spluttered. "His pests should be banished the town."

Two little girls, tripping along the sidepath, stopped and viewed his antics with mirth.

"Giggling goslings!" he muttered under his breath. "Oh, 'tis you, my dear Wealthia. And our little Araminta. Two of my young patients," he explained to Dr. Amlie.

Having exorcised the bee, he bowed to the alien and passed on. The children lingered, listening to the music of Tom Daw's lap-organ, now dispensing a lay which never derived from the hymnbook. The taller of the pair, who looked to be on the verge of womanhood, swayed her lithe body and moved on frisky feet. Her companion, a couple of years younger, lifted an impertinently cocked nose between two large and very blue eyes, and shook her strawy pigtail back over her shoulder.

"That's a dicty pretty tune," she said in lilting tones, and essayed to follow it.

The cobbler gave them good morning, to which they responded civilly. They clasped hands and danced on along the walk.

"Now, if you could get their custom away from Old Murch," said the cobbler, "you'd have a start."

"Who are they?" asked Dr. Amlie without special interest.

"The older one, with the comether in those brown eyes of hers—though she might not know it yet—she's the only child of Genter Latham. T'other one's an imp of Satan. She's from the stone mansion on the slope, the Jerrold place. Fine gentry, too, though not as rich and solid as Genter Latham. A neat penny Old Murch makes from the two houses. All our prosperous folks doctor with him."

"And the poor? Where do they doctor?"

"Not with Dr. M., to be sure. What would he gain from them?"

"Experience."

The other chuckled. "Not his line. If you're seeking experience, you'll find a free field here."

"I'll look about," said Dr. Horace Amlie.

-2-

Palmyra is a very Hospittible Place but not nessarily to Strangers.

(DIARY OF MISS ARAMINTA JERROLD)

MR. CARLISLE SNEED was a bit of a nighthawk. Seldom was he abed before nine-thirty. On mild and sleepless nights he might be observed (by hoot owl or whippoorwill) strolling the streets as late as eleven o'clock, thinking up tomorrow's jokes for the delectation of the coterie at Silas Bewar's smithy. Mr. Sneed was the village wit.

If a late light shone, he might drop in for a chat or, luck being with him, a quaff of home-brew. On this night all Main Street was darkened except for one window where Constable Mynderse sat up with his boils and would therefore be no fit associate for any man. Passing the place, Mr. Sneed was gratified to see a figure moving leisurely along in front of him. Here would be company. He did not at once identify the late pedestrian by his bearing. A stranger, presumably. As no passenger had disembarked from the mail coach, this must be the young physician from the east who had arrived in his own rig. Mr. Sneed set out in pursuit.

The young man's easy gait was accompanied by a soft and musical whistling. He pulled up beside a refuse heap, stirred it with his cane, bent above it, and stood, pondering. A little farther along another collection of muck engaged his attention. Rummaging in this, he extracted the remains of two skinned muskrats discarded, not too recently, by some casual trapper. The stranger seemed to be sniffing. Singular taste in odors, reflected Mr. Sneed. He coughed loudly. The stranger turned with a pleasant, "Good evening."

"Evenin' to *you,*" returned Mr. Sneed with the proper emphasis of the townsman on his own ground. "You must be the young doc they say is settlin' amongst us."

"Do they?"

"They do so." The time was come for introductions. "Name's Sneed."

"Glad to meet you, Mr. Sneed."

"Kinda smellin' around?"

"Yes."

"Like it?"

"No."

"You don't haffta smell it if you don't like it," pointed out the citizen, slightly huffy.

"It's my line of business."

"I *see,*" said Mr. Sneed, who did not see at all, but was interested. "Kinda nosin' around for trade, as you might say?"

"You might," allowed the other.

"What do you think of our town?"

"I've smelled sweeter."

"Huh! I guess we don't stink no worse'n any other town in the wet heat. You'd oughta smell Rochesterville. Or Lyons, when the rains wash out the sheep pastures." He paused and added thoughtfully, "I've knowed a man's smeller to get him into trouble. Mostly by pokin' it into other folks's private business."

"I'm not interested in other people's private business."

"Didn't say you was, did I? As to that"—he pointed to the reeking gutter—"you can always report to the village trustees."

"Thank you. Would it do any good?"

"Not a bit. But I'd admire to see you try. See that speck of red up there?"

Dr. Amlie looked in the direction indicated. The glow of a segar-tip moved deliberately along a slope on a rise near the street end. He nodded.

"That's a trustee. That's Genter Latham."

"I've heard the name."

"Guess you have. You'll hear more of it if you stay here."

"He keeps late hours."

"Don't think it's his conscience keeps him awake," grinned Mr. Sneed. "Hain't got any. More likely than not he's schemin' to nick some friend out of his dollars. Or waitin' for—no, it wouldn't be Sarah Dorch. Not any more."

"Romance in the moonlight?" asked the other, smiling.

"Might still be, the old goat! Takes whatever comes his way, and never a thank-you—women, money, or the shirt off'n your back." The emerging moon displayed what Dr. Amlie at first thought to be a glare of peculiar malevolence, until he perceived that its one-sided fixity was due to a poorly matched glass eye. "If you want rich smellin', hang your snoot over the brook that comes down from his house."

"I'm walking that way. Will you come along?"

"Not me!" declined Mr. Sneed with emphasis.

The small, red spark checked for a moment as Horace Amlie approached the spot where a small culvert carried off what little water was moving, then proceeded upon its patrol. Below the investigator a semi-stagnant pool lay, iridescent with scum. Tracing the water-course, the observer could see that it flowed directly beneath the impressive cobblestone mansion, for which it served as drain. Beyond the road, it meandered through a meadow.

The red light was approaching now. Horace Amlie looked up to see a formidably built, bearded, handsome man who removed the segar from his lips and stared silently.

"Good evening, sir," said Horace.

"What are you about?"

"Looking around."

"At my property?"

"I took this for a public thoroughfare."

"So it is. But it's my property you're overlooking."

"I mean it no harm, Mr. Latham."

"So you know me by name. I asked you before—what are you about?"

"I was wondering where the outflow of this brook went," said Horace pleasantly.

"Into Red Creek."

"And from there into Mud Creek, I suppose."

"Quite a geographist," said Genter Latham. "It does."

"Isn't there a settlement on the bank?"

"If you call the Pinch a settlement."

"So, all this matter eventually discharges there where people bathe."

"Bathe? The Pinch folk?" Genter Latham laughed.

"Or, worse, get their cooking and drinking water."

"What of it?"

The young man peered down. "There's a chicken's head in that eddy. And what looks like fish-cleanings in the weeds. And worse."

The man above observed him intently. "The next rain will wash 'em away."

"Into the source of water supply for people below."

"What of it?" repeated the owner.

"Disease, I should say."

"Newfangled folderol. What are you? A scavenger? Where's your pick?" proceeded the great man, pleased with his fancy.

"I am a doctor of medicine," said Horace Amlie.

This was no news to the other. He had heard of the day's arrival. "Do you doctor folks or ditches?" he demanded.

"I'll doctor your ditch, free gratis."

"You'll come on my premises when you're bidden, not before," returned the householder, but without rancor. "Do your scavenging downwind of some of the canal camps. They'll find that prowling beak of yours."

"I had it in mind."

"And be careful some of the diggers don't take you by the scruff and heave you into the ditch."

"I'll bear that in mind, too," said the young man so composedly that the magnate accorded him a reluctant respect. "Good night."

The stranger sat his saddle lightly, contemplating the brisk and laborious scene beneath him. He had ridden three miles westward from Palmyra village in the cool of the morning to watch the great ditch being driven, east and west, to its slow completion. A hundred men and a score of horses sweated and strained in the cut, dragging dredges, plucking out recalcitrant stumps as a dentist plucks a broken root, plying pick and shovel, prying with bar and bough at obstructive boulders, fashioning the towpath on one side, the berm on the other, toilfully embodying the dream of De Witt Clinton, the pride of the Empire State, the longest, broadest, deepest, mightiest canal in all history.

All this Horace Amlie had seen before, in the rocky Herkimer gorges, the steamy Rome swamps, the feverous Montezuma marshlands. It never failed to stir his pulses. For already the Erie Canal was a classic of American achievement, a future artery through which would flow the lifeblood of a new commerce, the inspiration of a stronger, more cohesive national sentiment. It was to be a solvent, ameliorating the narrow partisanships of county and state lines, clearing the way for a closer-knit patriotism.

For youth it had a special appeal. Odes were written to it, songs composed, eloquence dispensed in the forums of government. The haughty press of London, so contemptuous of all that was "Yankee," had begun to note its progress with grudging interest. "Who reads an American book?" Ah, but those snoot-in-the-air foreigners were watching an American triumph of traffic-building which they could never hope to equal!

A gang of barrowmen, trundling the new Brainard or "canal" wheelbarrows back to the sheds, lifted rough voices in the song of the ditch.

> We are digging the Ditch through the gravel;
> Through the gravel and mud and slime, by God!
> So the people and freight can travel,
> And the packets can move on time, by God!

Horace hummed the dogged refrain under his breath. "So the people and freight can travel." A saying of his old mentor, the wise, robust, irascible Dr. John Vought, merged with the measure. "The mainspring of human progress is the itch of restless man to be otherwhere than where he is." There beneath him was the surge and pressure of that invincible desire. It was a vision of expanding America. And it was threatened, as Horace Amlie well knew, by a subtle and unpredictable enemy.

Hitching Fleetfoot to an ash, Horace walked down the hillside. A whistle shrilled. The men knocked off work and gathered for instructions from a grizzled Irishman who removed his willow instrument from his mouth, substituting a richly foul briar.

"Mr. Shea?" asked the visitor.

"William Shea," confirmed the smoker. "Old Bill. Have a hearty?" He poured a hooker of raw rum into a tin cup.

"Your health, sir," said Horace.

"Health," grunted the overseer. "I'd wish my men more of it. A pinin', pindlin' lot. Who might you be, young sir?"

"Horace Amlie, M.D., from Oneida County."

"Lookin' for trade?"

"I wouldn't have far to look, I expect. Much fever here?"

"Not yet. Gripes and woolywambles a-plenty. No shakes so far. Smells aguish, though, don't it, now?"

Horace took a deep inhalation and promptly regretted it. The effluvium from the adjacent open latrine which drained to the creek when the rain flushed it, struck to his brain-core. A stone oven, flanked by a rude shack, smoked near by. The cookee emerged from the shack.

"Stinks, huh?" he remarked genially.

Horace gave an unqualified assent. "Is that where the men eat?" he inquired.

"That's it," answered Old Bill. "Tavern fare, liberal whisky, and fifty cents a day. Live like kings. Yet they're always sickenin' and growlin'. A pack of daffydillies," he added disgustedly.

A few rods away stood the log bunkhouses. A huckster's chant came to their ears.

"Pennyroyal! Fresh and fresh. A royal dozen for your penny. Pennyroyal!"

A dark, lithe, handsome lad with a wicker on his shoulder rounded the angle of the nearest building.

"Peddling charms against the shakes," Shea explained. "I don't hold with it, myself. But it keeps the gnats off. Hey, you!"

The boy came over to take the overseer's penny. Horace, also, invested in a pennyworth, crushed the aromatic leaves between his hands, and rubbed them against his face. At least the effluence mitigated the stench from the drain. The vendor thanked them civilly.

"I'd give something for a true charm against the damn fever," said Old Bill gloomily. "I had a gang on the Big Marshes last season and they was rotten with it. D'you think it'll hit us here?"

"It's the right, low-lying land for it. Plenty of night-mist rising?"

"Ay-ah. All through the valley." The Irishman peered through his protective smoke screen at the visitor. "You hold with this myazzama notion?"

"The best authorities believe that fevers are caused by miasmatic exhalations," answered the young man evasively.

"We gotta dig where we gotta dig," pronounced Shea. "There ain't no way as I know to keep the mists from risin' and the men from breathin' 'em."

"Did you ever think of moving the living quarters to high ground?"

A hoot of derision answered this suggestion. "Ask Genter Latham to spend money on such didoes."

Horace said, "I sell medical advice to those who can pay for it. I don't give it away where it isn't wanted."

"Latham ain't your market, then. He's doin' fine on this stretch, or was, till the gangs took to sickenin'. Stands to make a pot of money out of it if we can hold 'em to the work. You might talk to Squire Jerrold, though. He'll listen to anything. Fine gentleman, the Squire."

"Is he Mr. Latham's partner?"

"Not exactly. He's got the next reach west, up through Macedon. Latham had it first and passed it over to the Squire. Maybe he suspicioned there was quicksand and shifts there and maybe he didn't, but Jerrold stands to lose his money if things don't go better'n they have." He stared meditatively through his pipe smoke. "There don't many cuckoos lay their aigs in Genter Latham's hat," he observed. "Well, drop around and see us," he went on as the caller rose. "There might be some bellyache trade for you, even allowin' that the fever don't strike."

Horace thanked him and rode back to the hotel to sleep over his unsolved problem. He had still to make himself acquainted with the populace. Having been raised in a small town, he knew that there is no place like the blacksmith shop to give the flavor and trend of a community. He did not need to make occasion for going there since, after the long journey from Oneida County, his spirited mare's hooves needed attention. Late in the afternoon would be the best time. Then the informal town meeting would have gathered for that exchange of unfettered opinion which is the rural American's privilege and pleasure.

At four o'clock he rode Fleetfoot down Main Street, tethered her before the smithy, and went inside. From the silence which fell, he guessed that he had been the subject of discussion.

Silas Bewar, the bulky, bright-eyed Quaker blacksmith, glanced up from his task of rounding out a dog-wedge, and resumed it. Of the dozen men strewn about on boxes and barrels, none spoke articulately to the newcomer. Some nodded, a few grunted, others merely spat thoughtfully. Among these was the cadaverous and glass-eyed Mr. Sneed. He had no intention of recognizing this interloper and thus inferentially sponsoring him, until he had proved himself. Knowing the type, Horace, on his part, made no sign. He respected the other's caution.

The atmosphere was not positively unfriendly. Rather, it was that of sagaciously suspended judgment, neutrally expectant.

Having set aside the finished wedge, Silas stretched his hairy arms, shouldered his way between Cassius Moore's span of oxen, waiting to be shod, picked up a beetle-ring, and on his way back to the forge stopped before the stranger.

"Give thee good day, friend. What's thy pleasure?"

"Shoes for my mare, if you please."

"Where has thee left her?"

"Outside."

As at a signal, every man in the place rose, hunched his trousers, and followed the smith out for inspection. In the common interest of man toward horse the fetters of speech were loosened. Billy Dorch, the baker, delivered the initial opinion.

"A likely lass."

"Well-paced, I'll warrant," confirmed George W. Woodcock, who developed town lots for sale to the expanding population. "Look at those shoulders."

T. Lay, who trafficked in anything and everything vendible, passed an expertizing hand over the smooth hide. "Too light in the barrel for my taste," he pronounced.

"A man would take a desperation chance, offering more than a hundred for her," opined Jim Cronkhite, the political office seeker.

Carlisle Sneed spoke up.

"Got paper proof of ownership, Mister?"

"Yes."

"What's her price?"

"None."

"Not for sale, huh?"

"No."

"Say!" The questioner winked at his fellows. "If words was notes, you'd never start a bank."

Loud guffaws greeted the witticism for which the group had been waiting hopefully. The smith lifted his head from examination of the mare's feet and addressed the stranger.

"Shilling a hoof."

"When can you do it?"

"Soon as I finish the oxen. Come thee back in and set."

The assemblage trooped back and settled down to smoking, chewing and thought. Dr. Amlie found a chunk of wood for his heat. Silas Bewar tapped a keg against the wall, drew two beakers of a pale and beady liquid, handed one to the young man, and held the other aloft. Dr. Amlie touched it with his own. Both drank.

A quiver ran down the young man's spine. His stomach gave a start of surprise. His throat contracted. Tears rose to his eyes. He had drunk hard cider before, plenty of it. But this fermentation, aged to the verge of applejack, laced with raw corn whisky, sweetened with molasses, and hotly flavored with the local distillation of mint, was new to his system. Nevertheless, not a cough, not so much as a catch of breath, marked the passage of the astonishing liquid to its destination.

"Your very good health," said he pleasantly.

"D'you like it?" grinned Carlisle Sneed.

"A very mild, tasty brew," said the stranger judgmatically.

Thus far he had scored two points: he knew a good horse and he could take his liquor. Every man in the place was cognizant of his name, his profession, his purpose in coming to Palmyra, and a number of other things about him, some of which were true. But to give any indication of this knowledge would be a solecism. The smithy was sitting in Committee of the Whole to determine of what quality the stranger might prove himself.

"Hep! Jenk!" cried the smith.

A large, ungainly dog got to his feet, whined once in protest, mounted the treadmill and set himself to his duties with a pathetic air of boredom. The treads clacked, the bellows filled and poo-ooffed, the forge-cinders glowed redly, and Silas applied himself to the feet of the oxen.

Desultory conversation followed in which there was no effort to include the alien from Oneida County. It touched on politics, the price of wheat, the personal animosity of the weather toward the farmer, the progress of the canal, last Sunday's sermon—Elder Strang had preached four hours without pause, to the general admiration—the snakebite which had prostrated Miller Bundy's daughter, and the pro and con of the theory that a witch could ride best on a stolen broom. This was apropos of a charge that Quaila Crego of Poverty's Pinch had stolen Mam Cumming's hearth whisk. Someone observed that all the folks in the Pinch were thieves. Someone else said that there was sickness there again.

"We all got our griefs," said Mr. Sneed philosophically. He addressed Billy Dorch. "How's your gatherin's?"

"Bad again," answered Billy. "Both rumps."

"Why don't you quit your silly doctorin' and get Witch Crego to fix you up a mess of herbs?"

Jim Cronkhite, who was sitting next to Amlie, said in explanation, "Carly Sneed is inveterate against doctors."

"They tell me you're a medico, young man," said the humorist, slanting the good eye at him.

"I have that pretension."

Mr. Sneed delivered with unction a popular couplet of the day.

Doctor, doctor! Fetch out your simples.
My old woman's covered with pimples.

This gem, though familiar to all his hearers, was received with unrestrained glee. Horace regarded him gravely, waiting for the mirth to subside.

"Why not?" he said. "She lives with you, doesn't she?"

The grossness of the implication hit the public taste. The laugh was now against the humorist. Cassius Moore jogged him in the ribs.

"One for you, Carly, my lad," he sniggered.

"Aw, sandpaper your nose," growled Mr. Sneed. "Talk's cheap, but what do the pillslingers know? What do they do to the poor ninny-hammers that pay 'em good money? Bleed, bleed, bleed; purge, purge, purge. If they ain't opening you at one end, they are at the other. Man is a leaky vessel, but do they plug the leaks? Not them! Why, after your family M.D. is done with you, a moskeeter could drill into the juiciest steak on your behind and come away thirstier than a tee-totaller in a taproom. Ain't that so, folks? Ain't it?"

The bent form and shriveled countenance of O. Daggett appeared at the entrance. He addressed Amlie.

"So here you are. Hear tell you're thinkin' of settlin'."

"News flies fast on a windy day," observed the young man cheerfully.

"You'll need a signboard. Come to my shop."

Mr. Sneed leaned forward. "That green stuff under your feet—that ain't grass, is it, Ollie?"

Horace laughed with the others. He saw no occasion for handicapping himself with enmities at the outset of his career. The humorist, appeased, said patronizingly as Horace departed with the gilder,

"Not a bad young spark. Maybe I'll give him my custom. Got more gumption than old Murch, I'll warrant."

"A likely blade for the woman trade," hummed Daw, the hunchback.

The smith delivered his opinion. "Steel," said he. "Slender and hard of temper. Thee will get no change of a false shilling out of him."

"The town could do with another doctor," contributed Woodcock. "Murchison birth-charged me two dollars for my woman's seventh."

"Sell him a town lot, Woody," suggested Sneed.

"I got the very spot for him. If he could go to twenty dollars an acre on four acres." He set out upon the trail.

Passing up the street, the physician and his companion were hailed by Decker Jessup, who appeared in his doorway waving the new boots. Horace went in to try them on. They were serviceable rather than beautiful, but the young man, feeling the supple fit and judging the firm, well-cured leather, was content with his dollar bargain.

"Have you been bidden to the seats of the mighty for supper yet?" queried the cobbler.

"The mighty?" repeated Horace. "Who would that be?"

"It might be Genter Latham. Or it might be Squire Jerrold. Even it might be Dominie Strang if you were so minded to sit under him. Either way, you'd best mind your p's and q's."

"They'll put you on the block and estimate your price," added O. Daggett.

The young man smiled. "I thought the Act of 1817 abolished slavery in this state."

"Tell that to old Latham," cackled the sign man. "He's got half the township under his thumb with his twelve percent loans and his fifteen percent indentures. He and a few with him can make or mar a young man with his pockets to line."

The young man with his pockets to line did not appear unduly impressed. "I see. A non-political junto. So I am to curry favor with these gentlemen as the price of their forbearance or approval."

"Will it hurt you to be mannerly to them?" argued the cobbler. "You, a younger man, for all that you're a scholar?"

Horace perceived that they meant to be helpful. "Thank you both," said he. "But suppose these gentlemen do not favor me?"

"Then you'd better move elsewhere," replied the gilder bluntly.

A slow color rose in the keen, young face. He was about to say something, thought better of it. Decker Jessup proposed a drink and brought out a wooden flagon of wild-grape wine. The door swung to admit the spare form of George Washington Woodcock, who was invited to "set and share." As he drank, he eyed the stranger with a benevolence so flagrant that it would have stirred suspicion in the most innocent soul. He began with a beaming smile.

"Have you become acquainted with any of our young folks yet?"

"On the trail," said O. Daggett to the cobbler in an audible aside.

"No," answered Horace.

"You should meet them. There are no fairer and more modest maids between Albany and Ontario water than ours," pursued the other poetically.

"I am sure of it," was the polite response.

"I shall make it my interest to make you known to some of them."

"That is very kind of you," said Horace.

"Dan Cupid Woodcock, here," explained the cobbler, "buys timberland, clears it, and sells town lots. If so be he can get you married off, he hopes to sell you one."

"One hundred dollars for four of the finest acres in the township," said the unabashed exploiter, venturing an outrageous price on the offchance of having found a sheep to shear. "I'll take you to the spot now, where you may judge for yourself."

"You will not," interposed O. Daggett, his dyspepsia snarling in his tone. "The young man is coming to my shop to command a dandy signboard."

Horace ordered the signboard. He suffered a financial qualm at the thought of three dollars expended for this official display. But the pattern which O. Daggett sketched was a fine and tempting sight: gilt lettering against a sober, sepia background, with a beaded rim.

It committed him, for better or for worse, to the new venture.

If the social junto of the village turned thumbs against him, so be it. He was a free American citizen, and where he set his foot, there would he build his life. Independence forever! Cock-a-doodle-do!

3

When I grow up I shall be a Star in the Furmament of the Dramma.

(DIARY OF MISS ARAMINTA JERROLD)

"WHAT are we going to do about Dinty?" asked Archibald Jerrold.

"Araminta," sighed Mrs. Jerrold, "is an enigma."

"She's got the devil in her," said the father, and chuckled.

"I have taught her all that I am able at home."

Square Jerrold, fingering his elegant neckcloth, privately reflected that this would not be very much, but was too gentlemanly to say so. He was three times the age of his third wife when he married her, thirteen years before, and the advent of Dinty, after a varied brood of half-brothers and half-sisters had wedded and scattered, was a surprise to him and a shock to his eighteen-year-old consort, who, pale, willowy and torpid of mind and body, had had her stubbornly maintained sentiments and preferences of virginity rudely dislocated by the event.

"These Larrabees are said to be both genteel and pious," observed the Squire, consulting a neatly printed singlesheet before him.

It set forth that Prof. & Mrs. Larrabee had opened a Polite Academy for the Young of Both Sexes, who could there find skilled instruction in Spelling, Ciphering, Parsing, Geography, the Single and Double Rule of Three, Gain and Loss, and the Square and Cube Root with exercises from the English Reader and the Columbian Orator. Latin and Greek would be afforded the advanced pupils; French and Musical Instruction involved an extra fee. Piety would be inculcated as well as Elegant Deportment, and there was specific promise that "the manners and morals of pupils will receive careful attention and discipline." Also there was Special Medical Attention.

"Discipline," commented Mr. Jerrold, arching his delicate brows. "Our domestic efforts have not been crowned with invariable success."

A troubled silence followed. Both minds were uncomfortably reviewing an episode of the previous week. Dinty had observed at table, apropos of nothing in particular, that she did not see why there had to be a Hell. Worse, she undertook to argue the point with her mother. Upon Mrs. Jerrold's tearful insistence, the father had earled his child to the woodshed and undertaken to correct her heresy with the family strap. Under this *force majeure* Dinty recanted, but in bitterness of spirit. Imprisoned in her room on the bread and water of repentance, she brooded all day and departed through the window and down the trellised wall at fall of dark. After a night of anguished and futile search, the Jerrolds were choking over their breakfast when a diminutive and travel-worn figure appeared in the doorway.

"I should like my porridge," said Dinty.

There was dust in her hair and her hands were blistered. First caught to the family bosom, and subsequently threatened with further and direr penalties, she enunciated her declaration of independence in terms of the improving literature upon which girlhood was reared.

"I am your loving and obedient daughter and I owe you all duty and respect in which I trust you shall never find me wanting" (thus far, from *The Pious Child, by a Minister of the Gospel*: Dinty was blessed with a retentive memory), "but if you whip me again I shall run away and this time I'll stay. And I don't want to believe in Hell, but if you want me to, I'll try, and I hope a lot of people I know will go there."

Mrs. Jerrold shrieked in horror. Squire Jerrold, after a struggle, broke down and laughed with indecent abandon. Thus was Dinty's sore spirit saved from further humiliation, and her sore person from added stripes.

In due time she was informed of the plan to send her to the Polite Academy where she would learn the deportment of a little lady. She considered this mistrustfully.

"I'm not sure I want to be a little lady," she decided.

"What a child!" cried the despairing mother.

"What would you prefer to be?" inquired the Squire. In spite of misgivings and incomprehensions, there existed between the two a mutual sympathy unshared by the mother.

"A treasure-seeker," Dinty announced.

Her father took one of the little paws in his grasp, turned it over and examined the tender palm, where remnants of nocturnal blisters were still discernible.

"Oho!" he said, and Dinty blushed.

"Is Wealthy going to the new school?" she inquired.

"So I understand," replied her father. "In point of fact it was Mr. Genter Latham's suggestion that first turned my attention to it."

"If Wealthy goes, I'll go."

She was self-appointed maid-in-waiting to her local Majesty of the Court of Girlhood, Wealthia Latham. Two years older than Dinty, the motherless heiress to the Latham fortune accepted this worshipful fealty as of royal prerogative. In her early teens, she was already an object of warm speculation to the enterprising youth of the village. She was dark and lithely made, with lustrous eyes, bold curvature of mouth, and a proud little head, full of golden opinions of herself and of the world which afforded her everything that she demanded of it. Her austere father adored her and pampered her to an extent that would have spoiled a less naturally amiable disposition.

Wealthia's patronage of her admiring little henchwoman was tempered by a sensible recognition that Dinty was cleverer and more spirited than herself. She did not mind this. In her sunny self-satisfaction there was little room for envy.

On her part, Dinty was supremely unself-conscious, having far too lively an interest and enjoyment in the exterior world to bother about herself introspectively. This extended even to her personal appearance. When her father teasingly called her "Snubnose" she accepted it unresentingly as one of the prevalent disabilities of her years, like not being permitted a cushion in church and having to perform the lesser household chores. The overheard remark of a visiting half-sister, that those blue eyes were going to make trouble for somebody one of these days, left her incurious. She thought that the reference was to her exploratory habits of looking into whatever specially interested her, which included most matters within her ken.

The two children were deposited at the door of the academy by their respective fathers, who went on to the Eagle for a morning dram. Dinty hailed her friend.

"'lo, Wealthy."

"'lo, Dinty."

"You going to like coming here to school?"

"I don't know. Are you?"

"If I don't, I'll run away."

"Oo—oo! You'd get whipped."

"Then I'll run away again. I'll keep running away and running away and *running* away till they get tired of chasing me. Wealthy, did you ever dig for buried treasure?"

"No."

"It's fun."

"It must be. I saw a play about it once."

Dinty sighed with envy. "My ma says actresses are wicked Deli-actors and actresses?"

"Yes. In Albany."

Dinty sighed with envy. 'My ma says actresses are wicked Delilahs. She cried when she saw Pa talking to one once."

"I don't care. I'd like to be one."

"I went to a popet show once. It was called Punch and Judy."

"That isn't a drama," said the elder disparagingly. "There's one here tonight, though."

"Oh-h-h-h-h! Where?"

"In the Eagle ballroom. A moral tragedy. I don't like moral tragedies specially," went on the hardened playgoer. "I like laughable farces. There's a laughable farce to follow."

Dinty's breath quickened. "How I'd admire to go!"

"It's twenty-five cents."

"I haven't got twenty-five cents," said Dinty, despondent. She brightened. "I've got eighteen cents, though, in my missionary fund box."

Wealthia's dark eyes rounded. "You'd go straight to hell."

"I s'pose I would." Dinty weighed the chances, pro and con, and decided that it was not worth the risk.

"Why don't you get your pa to take you?" asked her friend.

"Pa might say yes. But Ma'd pout, and then he wouldn't."

The other girl had an inspiration of generosity. "I'll ask my pa to take us both."

Her friend's raptures were cut short by the peremptory summons of the bell.

Fourteen children trooped in and divided themselves by sex on the wooden benches, six boys and eight girls. They represented the aristocracy of the township: the prosperous agriculturists, the millers, distillers, factory owners and professional men. As the school had been open a week, there were no initiatory exercises, but Prof. Larrabee made an effusive little speech, welcoming the two new pupils.

He was a brisk little wisp of a man with a straggling chin whisker, a loose, benevolent mouth and sore eyes; a competent pedagogue of the standard branches. His wife, large, placid and slow, had charge of the elegancies and accomplishments. Their joint instruction was well worth the eight dollars per term with extras which they charged.

Besides the new pupils, the early enrollment was made up of the Fairlie twins, Grace and Freegrace; Bathsheba Eddy; Mary Vandowzer, whose father, the maltster, though wealthy and well-considered, still spoke both the high and the low German better than he did English; Jane Eliza Evernghim; and "Happy" (christened Happalonia) Vallance, these on the distaff side; while across the aisle sat Marcus Dillard, scion of the big peppermint still, exuding a pervasive bouquet of the trade; the two Evernghim lads, George W. and De Witt C.; Jared Upcraft, son of the Honest Lawyer; little Arlo Barnes of the ropewalk, a hardy stripling who paddled to town in summer and skated or walked in winter; and the handsome Philip Macy, youngest of the brood of Col. Gerald Macy, whose scientific cultivation of hemp along Red Creek had made him a comfortable fortune.

The morning procedure comprised an announcement from Prof. Larrabee, delivered with pardonable pride, that his was the only school in the Americas which included medical supervision as part of the curriculum, and he had the privilege and honor of introducing Dr. Gail Murchison, a certificated licensee of physical and chirurgical science.

Dr. Murchison beamed benevolently upon his "little friends" as he called them in his purring, professional accents, while he smoothed his patriarchal beard with fingers none too clean. Medical practice, he imparted to his hearers, was a high calling to be pursued in a spirit of helpfulness and sacrifice and not in expectation of earthly gain. He, himself, strove to be a friend to the poor and helpless without reward. (This would, indeed, have been news to that element of the populace.) He hoped that each of his little hearers would regard himself or herself as a little angel of mercy, seeking out the needy, sustaining the sick and weak, and reporting to him such cases as they found.

Dinty nudged her bench-neighbor, Freegrace Fairlie. She sensed possibilities in this. It combined good works, variety and adventure in pleasing prospect.

The speaker would now, gratis and at no charge, individually examine each little pupil. The examination was brief. The good physician cast a sapient glance at the protruded tongue, felt the pulse, with his head cocked to one side like a thoughtful blackbird, asked one question about digestive processes which brought a resentful flush to Dinty's cheek. She considered her intestinal timetable a distinctly personal matter. The speaker made entry in a ledger, adjured one and all to be good little boys and girls and to mind their kind teachers, and withdrew.

Dinty would have liked to consult him as to methods of charitable visitation but lacked opportunity. Her immediate concern was so to impress the master and mistress of the school with her smartness that she might have the same lessons as Wealthia, which they would study together. As she was precocious in all that concerned books, whereas her older friend took only a languid and mechanistic interest in learning, her preference being for dress and amusements, this was not difficult. Prof. and Mrs. Larrabee congratulated themselves upon these newest accessions, on the grounds of Wealthia's prettiness and popularity and Araminta's manifest cleverness. They added to the *bon ton* of the establishment, said Mrs. Larrabee who taught the higher aspirants French.

Hours were from eight-thirty to noon, and from one to four. At recess Dinty was so full of excitement that she could hardly eat her dinner. Assuming that this was the stimulus of the school, her parents questioned her at length. Do what she would to satisfy the parental interest, the child's mind was on a higher, starrier world. She did not dare broach the dangerous topic of the evening's theatrical entertainment as yet. First, Wealthia must see whether she could prevail upon her saturnine father to include the small friend in the evening festivity.

Happily Mr. Genter Latham was in fine humor that afternoon. Through a combination of business acumen and political influence, he had taken over a contract to excavate ten miles of the Erie Canal, on the Western Section, and it was now progressing so rapidly that he was able to estimate a minimum profit of fifteen thousand dollars. The usual chilly gray of his deep-set eyes warmed when they rested on his daughter.

"Ask Araminta Jerrold?" he repeated. "Why not?"

"Oh, Pa! Aren't you sweet! I do love you! But I'm so scared they won't let her go."

"Pooh! Stuff and nonsense! Why shouldn't they? I'll go there with you and put it to them. There's a matter which I wish to talk over with Squire Jerrold anyway."

To give importance to the mission, Mr. Latham ordered out his gig, to which he drove his pair of roans, tandem. In any other resident this would have been regarded as hifalutin, but with Genter Latham, nobody had the temerity to remark upon it. People respected his wealth, his power, and, above these, his black temper. He brooked no impertinence, as one corner wit who had ventured a derisive commentary upon "nose-to-tail drivin'" learned at the cost of having a well-directed whiplash cut a weal across his cheek from a distance of seven yards.

The Jerrolds welcomed the Lathams with polite warmth. Inwardly Archibald Jerrold considered them as one of the very few—possibly half a dozen—families of the township entitled to social equality with himself. Apart from this, he felt no special attraction to Genter Latham. Few did. The visitor, over a hospitable glass of genuine French brandy, came at once to the point.

"How would you like to undertake a further transaction with me, Squire?"

"I might consider it," was the cautious reply. Transactions entered into with Mr. Latham were not invariably profitable to the party of the second part. The Squire was beginning to doubt whether he would come clear on his present canal project.

The younger man knew that the Jerrold fortune was waning. Wool-raising was less assured than it had been in the days when Archibald Jerrold had founded his fortunes upon the high prices occasioned by the depredations of the swarming wolves, now pretty well killed off. Furthermore, the hard times of 1817 had hit him, whereas Genter Latham, having funds set apart and waiting opportunity, turned the crisis to good account, buying up rich bottom lands at seventy-five cents an acre, selling the timber, and planting the clearings to hemp, mint and grain. Men said with awe that he must be worth close on to one hundred thousand dollars, that there was no time when he could not, at need, touch as much as ten thousand dollars, cash. Of no other in all that region could as much be said, except of the Geneseo magnates, Squire Wadsworth and Col. Hopkins. Secured loans at twelve percent and conservative investments at ten kept the Latham income at a high level.

Jerrold asked, with affected indifference, "What is the nature of this venture?"

"A sizable contract east of here is in the market. The present contractor is in embarrassments. You and I might pick up a pretty penny there."

"I'm sickening of the damned canal," said the Squire gloomily. "There's nothing but worry in it. What does it bring to any locality that it invades? Fever and disease. Lawlessness and rapine and immorality. Conflict between the respectable citizenry and the wild Irish. Corruption of the lower classes and unsettlement of trade."

"And money," grinned the financier. "Don't forget the money, Squire."

Drawing to him a sheet of paper and a pencil, he began to cipher. Men said (and often with rueful conviction) that Genter Latham could make figures perform the magic of Mesmer. With fascinated eyes, the Squire watched the swift development of the proof.

So many units of labor at fifty cents per day per man, or twelve dollars and found by the month, to remove so many cubic yards of soil. Log houses for shelter to be cut from ownerless timberland. Provender? Flour, potatoes and all vegetables were at bottom prices, while for meat there was pork, pickled fish and game. Wild fowl and venison could be had almost at the price of the powder. With a quart allowance of whisky on Sundays the working force could be kept hearty and happy on one dollar-and-a-quarter or less per week. Get a good, rough-and-tumble overseer at three dollars a day and the backer could sleep through the contract while the balances piled up in his favor.

Squire Jerrold had heard it all before. Nevertheless he could not help but be impressed by the confident voice, the slick array of numerals.

"Ah, well," said the tempter, tossing aside his pencil, "give it your leisurely consideration, Squire. I leave it to your recognized business judgment. Tasty brandy, this. Excellent!"

They took another glass, lightly tempered with water, after which they joined the ladies. Genter Latham brought up the matter of the play. Jerrold's eyes lighted up.

"I might join you, myself," he said.

"Very pleased," said Mr. Latham politely.

"Oh, Archibald!" protested his consort in a dying voice.

Perceiving the prospect of tears, Squire Jerrold sighed. "Very well, very well, my dear. But there can be no objection to our daughter attending a performance endorsed by press and pulpit."

Dinty danced out of the parlor on air, to dress up in her church-best.

That evening was an experience of more than mortal exaltation. Seated between Wealthia and Mr. Latham, the child clutched first one and then the other as if to preserve herself from being lifted bodily into the air and floated away upon the tumultuous tide of emotion. She sobbed over the woes of George Barnwell's ill-fated lady-love; she shrieked aloud when the misguided young man's dagger pierced the rich uncle's heart; she shook from head to foot when the miscreant was led forth, exuding moral precepts at every step, to meet his gallows-doom. In vain did the sophisticated Wealthia, herself somewhat shaken, point out that it was not real. Dinty continued to shiver with horror long after the final curtain fell upon the last tidbit of moralization.

Then what an uplift to the stricken spirit! Part II was pure delight. Could this merry wight who sang so entrancingly the excruciatingly comic ditties of "Dame Durden" be the same actor whom she had but now seen racked with his impending fate? Yes, there was the name: Mr. Archbold. And Mr. Clarendon, who was so pitifully old and feeble as the slain uncle, dancing like an amiable goblin as he convulsed his audience with the risible sayings promised in the program. Miss Gilbert, too, how gay, how arch, how bewitching she proved to be, all her woes forgotten! And another charmer, Miss Sylvia Sartie, whose genius had been all but smothered in the part of the maid, now enticed the hearts of all, as the program had truthfully foretold. "Dame Durden," for Dinty's money! She would have liked to see it all over again.

The clear treble of her delight rang infectiously. She seized every opportunity for furious and prolonged applause. Her enthusiasm brought an unforeseen and incredible reward. The dainty, the vivacious, the lovely nymph who played the soubrette part was singling her out for her nods and becks and wreathed smiles. (Dinty remembered that line from the hymn book. Or perhaps it wasn't the hymn book. It didn't seem quite hymnal.)

"Did you see?" she breathed ecstatically in the intermission. "She was singing right *at* us."

"I noticed it, too," agreed Wealthia, enraptured.

Mr. Latham's Mephistophelian chuckle dispelled the roseate dream. "Not exactly, I fear," said he.

"But, Father!" "But, Mr. Latham!" the two childish voices united in protest.

"I saw her," said Dinty.

"I heard her," said Wealthia.

"She almost winked," said Dinty.

"Doubtless." He lowered his voice. "There's a handsome young man in the seat back of us," he murmured. "I suspect him of being the object of the young lady's attentions. Eyes front!" Mr. Latham had served in the militia.

The admonition came too late. Both children had twisted around. A soft-breathed "Oh!" of recognition came to their lips. It was the young gentleman of "serious asspeckt" whose arrival Dinty had entered in her diary.

Their disillusionment was assuaged by the chaste delights of Part III. They contorted themselves with mirth over the comic song, "Cherry-cheeked Patty." They wept unashamedly at "Robin Adair," rendered by Mr. Wilshire, the heavy, in a tremolo baritone that quivered in their heartstrings, and they went into final collapse over Mr. Archbold's Scotch dialect in his inimitable double characterization of the two ridiculous lovers, "Watty and Maggy." Finally it was over, and—crowning glory!—Mr. Latham was offering them sticky-sweet ebulum in the tavern parlor. As befitted so fine and public a place, they sat up, very ladylike, and conversed in esoteric references, intended to leave any eavesdropper unenlightened.

"Oh, Wealthy! Don't you *dote* on Mr. C.?"

"I prefer Mr. A. He's so romantic."

"But Mr. C. is so witty."

"What lovely whiskers Mr. W. has! And such a—a throbby voice."

"Do you think they're real? I've heard that they put them on."

"So they do," said the experienced Wealthia. "And they paint their faces. That's what makes them so beautiful. I'm going to be an actress. Like Miss S."

"I think she's a bold hussy," said Dinty. "Making eyes at gentlemen she doesn't know."

"You can't tell," said Wealthia sagely. "Maybe he frequents theatrical associations."

"Oo-ooh!" breathed Dinty. "Could he be a desprit rakehell? Oh, look!"

The charmer and the stranger passed the door in close communion.

"Let's peek," whispered Dinty, shameless where her curiosity about the ever-interesting human race was enlisted.

Opportunely Mr. Latham had gone across the parlor to speak to acquaintances. The girls scuttled into the hallway, stopping before a small room near the outer door. A murmur of voices warned them to go carefully. Dinty was first to project a cautious head.

The fair Miss Sartie was seated in a chair, her face uplifted in invitation to the young man who gazed adoringly down into her eyes. Such, at least, was Dinty's interpretation of the tableau. The immediate sequel dispelled it. The stranger opened a black bag, took out a bottle, poured a few careful drops of liquid into a small container and applied it, first to one, then the other of the lady's lustrous eyes. The two small spies uttered a simultaneous squawk as a firm grip retracted them from their observation post. Mr. Latham was grimly amused.

"Taking private stock of our new doctor, I see."

"Is that what he is?"

"Certainly. And an enterprising specimen, I judge. Did you think you were witnessing a Romeo-and-Juliet passage? Haven't you had enough drama for one evening?" He rubbed his chin beard thoughtfully. "That young man loses no time," he observed.

Dinty bobbed a curtsey. "Thank you, sir, for a pleasurable and instructive evening."

The Lathams drove her home, then returned to their own large and gloomy mansion. Genter Latham was well pleased with his day. His cleverly devised appeal to the avarice which, by his theory of human nature, was the mainspring of men's motives, was working favorably upon Archibald Jerrold. An honorable man, the Squire, but not over-keen in financial matters. If Jerrold took the bait, it was his partner's plan to keep the stretches of hard soil and the lock locations for himself—there was good money in lock-building—and turn over to his neighbor such sections as might develop "soft" areas. Let Jerrold take the risks. If all went well, he would make a fair profit. If not, it was no skin off the predatory Latham nose.

Mr. Jerrold was smoking and reading in his library when Dinty danced in, eager to tell him all about the wonderful evening. He could be relied upon to be a sympathetic and amused listener. First she pulled off her network mitts and breathed tenderly on her hands. He smiled at her.

"Sore paws again, little daughter?"

"That's from clapping so hard." She examined the palms. "The blisters are almost healed." She launched into excited panegyrics of the evening's entertainment and the actors for five uninterrupted minutes, after which she considered her hands again. "Pa," she said confidentially, "do you believe that treasure is always found on a south slope?"

"Which hill?"

"Sampson Farm rise."

"That's a good three miles from here. A long distance for a little girl alone at night," said he gravely.

"I wasn't alone. Tip Crego took me."

"That halfbreed!" said Squire Jerrold with displeasure.

"Tip isn't a halfbreed," returned Dinty warmly. "Not even a quarter. There's only a teeny bit of Indian in him. Just enough to make him Chief of our tribe."

"Tribe? What tribe?"

"The gold hunters. They're all from Poverty's Pinch but me. They dig in the dark of the moon. Tip's been promising to take me ever so long, but I wasn't to tell anyone. So you mustn't peach on us, Pa."

"I won't. But I don't like you to associate with those ragamuffins and cheapjacks from the Pinch."

"I don't believe Tip is a cheapjack. He wants to find gold so he can go to college and be a learned scholar of the sciences."

"Indeed! Well, little daughter, you go to bed and don't dream about treasure. We shall dredge our new fortunes out of Mr. Clinton's ditch, not out of a hillside. Nobody's found gold there yet."

"Maybe I'll be the one," she said brightly. She added with an effect of profound conviction, "You never can tell till you try. That's my motto. I write it every day at the top of my exercise."

"People who take that for their guiding principle get into plenty of trouble," warned her father, smiling.

"I don't care," said the child stoutly. "They have fun. And how else are you going to find out about everything?"

"I don't know," admitted the Squire.

He drew her to him and kissed her good night, a manifestation of affection generally frowned upon as tending to spoil the young.

4

A Beautiful and Tender Girl full of the Purest Sensabilities and Holiest Feelings of which our Nature is Susseptable. That is what we should Strive to be. It must be Awfle.

(DINTY'S DIARY)

YOUNG Dr. Amlie slept over his decision and, in the morning, found it good. His first patient, the little, blowzy, coquettish soubrette who had so enchanted the two small girls, had paid him sixpence ("Discount to the profession," she coyly murmured) after a winning smile and a sidelong shot from the eased eyes which suggested that there might be other and less commercial reward for his services. Dr. Amlie brought to mind with an effort the grave admonition of the State Board of Medical Examiners.

"A physician's personal character should therefore be that of a perfect gentleman and above all be exempt from vulgarity of associations, depravity of manners, habitual swearing, drunkenness, gambling, profligacy, or any breach of decorum and from contempt for moral rectitude and religious practice."

At the moment it struck him as an infringement of personal liberty. Caution intervened; he must consider his professional reputation. He took his sixpence, gave the fair patient a healing lotion, and retired to virtuous if not untroubled slumbers. Undoubtedly his proper course of conduct, he decided, would be to marry and settle down when a suitable match presented itself. Any irregular relation with one of the raffish calling of the stage would be a false start.

After a leisurely breakfast he strolled around to inspect his prospective quarters. The pleasant front room would serve him as an office. There was a closet for his skeleton, a professional extravagance which had cost him a cool eighty dollars, a convenient corner for his cabinet, a dusty carpet on the floor, two splitwood chairs, and a semi-alcove with a day couch where he could make shift to sleep. Upon receipt of a month's rent in advance, Mrs. Harte was agreeable to his putting in shelves for his equipment, which he had brought carefully packed in his wagon.

Having unloaded, he drove to Main Street, bought some planed whitewood boards, a hammer, a saw and nails, and exhumed from his piled-up library a second-hand copy of that invaluable sixpenny guide, "The Carpenter's Assistant, or Simple Instruction with Saw and Hammer." Opening all the windows, he set resolutely to work.

Notwithstanding explicit diagrams in the book, he was having trouble with an angle when he became aware that he was under observation. Two little girls were standing on the sidewalk, contemplating him in solemn silence. He gave them a polite good morning which they returned in kind, and continued with his task. Presently the smaller girl said, in a clear-carrying voice obviously intended for his ear,

"When I had the fever, our doctor bled me until I fainted."

The other responded, "I had ten leeches."

After this interchange, there was a silence. He heard the gate swing complainingly on its hinges. The pair were in the yard. One of them was coughing significantly. Patiently he turned around.

"I am Dinty Jerrold," said the smaller girl. "This is my best friend, Wealthia Latham."

"How do you do?" said Dr. Amlie.

Dinty gave critical consideration to the work in progress.

"You could hire a good carpenter for six shillings a day," she observed.

Dr. Amlie removed two nails from his mouth and said, "To what do I owe the honor of this visit?"

"We heard you hammering and stopped to make your acquaintance."

"I'm afraid I'm not prepared for callers."

"Then we'll sit on the fence."

They climbed up, disposing their skirts with propriety. The larger girl said in a soft, throaty voice, "I used to live in this house."

"Did you?" said the doctor with no great interest. "When?"

"When it was new. I was born here."

"That was before her pa got so rich," explained Dinty. "He is awfly rich. Richer than my pa. It is nice to be rich," she added complacently.

"I daresay." The young man resumed his work.

"What are the shelves for?"

"Books and medicines."

"Then I don't think you are doing it right."

"What isn't right about it?" he demanded.

"You're setting the plank flat. When a medicine bottle tips over, it could roll off. But if you slope the plank in, the bottle would roll against the wall."

Dr. Amlie looked at the small wiseacre, glanced into the printed "Assistant" and tossed it into a corner.

"Dinty's cruel smart," said her admiring companion. She stood up on the fence to peer in at the cluttered floor. "What a lot of books!" she admired. "Have you read them all?"

"Yes."

"You must be cruel learned."

"I endeavor to keep abreast of my profession," he said modestly.

"I'd like to read 'em," said Dinty.

"They are not for little girls to read."

"She reads everything," put in Wealthia. "I don't see why."

"How else are you going to find out what you want to know?" said Dinty. She eyed the littered floor disparagingly. "What a mess!" she commented. "Don't you want us to clear it up?"

"Would you?" he said gratefully.

They flopped joyously to earth and made such a rush for the door that, half way through it, they tripped and sprawled. Still sitting, they addressed one another in a mock antiphony.

Dinty: "Ask your pardon."

Wealthia: "Grant you grace."

Duet: "Hope the cat'll spit'n your face."

Thereupon they went off into gales of imbecile laughter, sobered suddenly, jumped up and set about their task with diligence. Amidst the welter that strewed the floor Dinty came upon a scroll which she hung upon the wall, the better to read it. It was inscribed,

HORACE AMLIE, M.D.
Certificated in Physic & Surgery,
New York State Board.

FEES

Bleeding	12½ c.
Leeching	12½ c.

Purging	12½ c.
Cupping	15 to 25 c.
Emesis	15 c.
Reducing fracture	Arm, $1.00; Leg, $1.50.
Administering quinine or bitters	12½ c.
Extraction	12½ c. per tooth; 3 for 25 c.
Surgical attention to corns	7 c. per corn.
Home visits	day, 25 c., night, 50 c., double for cases of a malignant or catching nature.
Consultations	$3.00 for first; $1.00 thereafter.

Medicines Extra. Terms Cash.

Wealthia whispered to her companion, "What's emesis?"

It was not in Dinty's nature to confess ignorance. "Having a baby," she replied in the same tone. "The doctor fetches it and you pay him fifteen cents."

"That's cheap," said Wealthia admiringly. "Let's get our babies from him. Maybe they'd look like him. Don't you think he's cruel handsome?"

"Mm-mm-mm, yes," said Dinty. "But I'm not going to have mine till I'm married."

They pursued their toil until the last item was dusted and placed. The young man thanked them and produced a box from which he dispensed a lollipop to each. Taking this as dismissal, they bobbed their curtseys in well-schooled unison and departed.

Said Squire Jerrold to his wife at breakfast, "There's a new young man in town. A physician."

Dinty looked up from her mush-and-milk. "I know him," she volunteered. "Dr. Amlie."

"Oh! You know him, Mischief." The Squire's attitude toward this child of his old age was one of perpetual entertainment. "What's he like?"

"Nice," said Dinty reflectively, "but violent. He said"—she looked sidelong at her mother—"a bad word."

"I'm often tempted to say it, myself, when you're at your didoes," said her father. "What were you doing to him?"

"He was putting up a shelf all wrong and I told him so."

"You would!" said the Squire. He turned to his wife. "Young Amlie attended Hamilton College under the learned and pious Dr. Azel Backus, as did my third son. He is doubtless a young gentleman of culture and parts. We must ask him to supper. Another physician would be no bad thing to have in Palmyra."

"I am perfectly satisfied with Dr. Murchison," said Mrs. Jerrold with a martyred air. "He understands my sufferings."

"We must have a few of our representative citizens to meet him," pursued the Squire.

"It would be nice for him if I was there," said Dinty complacently. "He knows me."

"The place for little girls is in bed," said her mother.

"I hadn't contemplated inviting any ladies, Poppet," said the Squire. "But we'll see."

Upon receipt of Squire Jerrold's polite note, Dr. Horace Amlie dressed himself with particularity, set his neckcloth with his best cameo, polished his boots to a fine gloss, imparted a touch of oil to his hair, scented his handkerchief, took his silver-ringed cane in hand, and set out. He had passed the test of the smithy with reasonable credit. Now he was to face the judgment of a higher, though perhaps no shrewder, tribunal. To say that he was nervous would be to misprize the Amlie courage and self-respect. But his color was perhaps a shade higher, his lips set a bit firmer than was his wont, as he mounted the railed steps and lifted the lion's head which formed the knocker of the elegantly oak-paneled door.

The knocker did not fall. The door was drawn quickly and quietly open. A small hand caught his wrist. Dinty Jerrold, with the finger of caution pressed to her lips, drew him within.

"I wanted to tell you first," she said in a breathy whisper. "Be very polite to my ma. Listen to my pa; he admires to talk. Laugh at Lawyer Upcraft's funny jokes even if you don't think they're funny. Neither do I. And whatever you do, don't let 'em see you're scared of 'em, specially Mr. Latham," she went on anxiously. She added in a loud and grown-up tone, "Why, here is Dr. Amlie! How do you do, Dr. Amlie? Pray come in, Dr. Amlie; my dear parents are expecting you."

The Jerrolds, husband and wife, gave him a pleasant greeting. Deacon Dillard, faintly scented with the mint whose distillation was making him one of the rich and respected men of the region, nodded stiffly to him from a rosewood sofa and resumed his conversation with Lawyer Upcraft. From the other corner Genter Latham gave the newcomer a quick glance in which there was no acknowledgment of recognition. Mr. Van Wie sat, straight-backed in a straight-backed chair, making noiseless estimates with his lips. The host presented the stranger in handsome terms. The Rev. Theron Strang, he explained, was unable to attend as he was wrestling with his Sunday discourse, which would probably be a riproarer.

"Why Mr. Jerrold!" said his wife in tittering reproof.

A peach brandy was served and the company went in to supper. The Jerrolds lived sumptuously. Silver, glass and napery were of the best and there was a sound French wine of the rich vintage of 1814. Watchful from her observation post at a small stand set in the window embrasure, Dinty marked with approval the young man's moderation as the bottle passed. The other guests were less cautious. Presently they were plying the stranger with questions, all but her father who sat back quietly smiling, and Mrs. Jerrold who sipped elderberry brew in a ladylike manner and said nothing, as was expected of her. Dinty did not approve of the persistency of the interlocutors, Lawyer Upcraft leading like a cross-examiner in court. She deemed it less than polite.

But she soon felt pride in the way in which her protégé stood up under the fire. To all questions pertaining to his attainments and career, he returned frank and full answers. The little listener, her ears fairly wiggling in her eagerness to miss nothing, gathered a pretty complete biography.

Young Amlie had graduated from Hamilton College in the class of 1818 just before his nineteenth birthday.

"With honors," smilingly interpolated the host. "I took the liberty of examining the report for that year."

"Who did you ride with?" asked Upcraft. As Dinty knew, he was appraising the other's training, gathered from the experience of "riding with" some knowledgeable practitioner.

"First with Dr. Swift of Schenectady."

"Did you find his instructions satisfactory?"

"No," said the young man bluntly. "I wasted my time and my two-hundred-dollar fee. He had no apparatus, no specimens in *materia medica* or anatomy, nothing but a damaged skeleton, a cabinet of purges and emetics, and a copy of Thomas's *Practice* with three chapters missing."

"I have heard," put in the Squire, "that few practitioners ever open a book after they are established."

"That is not true of those who attended Fairfield Medical College, where I took the course after quitting Dr. Swift," declared Horace loyally. "Most of them were earnest students of the science. Still less would it apply to the learned Dr. Vought with whom I finished my riding."

"Book learning, book learning," croaked Mr. Van Wie. "A skilled midwife brings my children into the world, and I'll warrant you she never read a book nor needed to."

"Vought? Dr. John G. Vought?" sniffed Deacon Dillard. "Our Dr. Murchison declares him little better than an experimenting quack."

Dr. Amlie flushed to his youthful forehead but held himself under control. "Medical men differ in creed and opinion as do the clergy and the bar," said he.

"I have heard that Dr. Vought neither bleeds nor purges," boomed Lawyer Upcraft with the fervor of one on the scent of heresy. "How otherwise can the body be voided of its evil humors?"

"Dr. Vought does not discard these methods. But he deplores their excessive use which depletes the patient's strength. There are milder expedients."

"A steamer," barked Mr. Van Wie. "A sweater. Is that your school?"

"Yes," put in the lawyer with a side glance at Latham. "Define your craft and practice. Are you Sangradorian, Morrisonian, Thomsonian? Do you profess the magnetical art or are you learned in the erudition of the herbist or florist? Are you phlogistic or antiphlogistic, a purger or a puker, a bleeder or a stimulator? Do you follow the diluters and Dr. Hahnemann? A doctor must stand to his creed."

Horace Amlie turned his deceptively ingenuous smile upon the legal light. "I perceive that you have been recently pleading a medical action, sir."

"I have. And I prevailed against the Medical Society of the State of New York, young man," bragged Upcraft.

"Then I should be bold, indeed, to submit myself to your cross-examination," said Horace blandly. The lawyer blinked.

"Perhaps you hold with no one school," smiled Squire Jerrold. "Still, you must have your own ideas."

The other hesitated. "Care of the body," he said at length. "Cleanliness. Healing medicaments as needful, administered with care and in moderation. Aiding the system to throw off its ailments and detriments."

"You'll gain a thin living here on that program," stated Genter Latham. "We expect more for our money."

Upcraft returned to the charge. "This Dr. Vought—I am told that he administers corrupt matter from sick cattle under pretense that it cures the smallpox."

"Prevents, not cures," corrected the physician.

"Do you hold with that?" asked Deacon Dillard.

"I have specimens of the kine-vaccine in my medicine chest. I would not be without it," said the doctor stoutly.

"It ought to be prohibited by law," averred the man of law.

"It ought to be compulsory by law," asserted the young man hotly.

"Would you give physicians authority to rub a foreign substance into a patient's blood, willy-nilly?"

"I would. For the protection of the general health."

Genter Latham folded his thick arms and glared across them with a look like the bristle of steel over a parapet. "Lord help any doctor that laid pox-knife to me or mine, without my consent!"

"I wager Sarah Dorch wishes she'd got vaccinated before it was too late," piped Dinty importantly.

At the mention of the name an uncomfortable stir was apparent to the stranger. Squire Jerrold shot a swift, covert glance at Genter Latham. Lawyer Upcraft coughed behind his hand. Deacon Dillard and Mr. Van Wie began a hasty conversation about nothing. Mrs. Jerrold said in a strained, shocked whisper,

"Dinty!"

Foreseeing that she would soon be squelched and with the laudable design of imparting information whilst there was still time, the child addressed Dr. Amlie.

"She used to be so pretty. The smallpox went to her face and now she's awful. I'd rather be cow-poxed any time than look like poor Sarah."

"To bed at once, Chattertongue," snapped Mrs. Jerrold.

Dinty cast a look of appeal at her father. Perceiving no support in that quarter, she rose with a martyred air.

"I'm sure I don't know what I said," she sighed. "Anything I say, I seem to talk too much. Good night, all."

Dr. Amlie was the only guest to return the exile's melancholy farewell.

The investigating committee now proceeded with an inquiry into Dr. Amlie's personal circumstances and condition. Was he married? He was not. Betrothed? No. Intentions? None. What was his religion? His political affiliation? His opinion of Governor Clinton and Andrew Jackson? How did he feel about the Grand Canal? Did he belong to the militia? Was he a Mason? What were his financial expectations?

He answered or parried the questions as best he was able. Checking up afterward, the inquisitors decided that they had got little more out of him than he was pleased to let them know.

Deacon Dillard, Mr. Van Wie and Lawyer Upcraft left early to attend a trustee meeting. Upon their departure, Genter Latham addressed the young outlander with an air of intending to get at the truth and being satisfied with nothing less.

"Now then, young sir, what fetches you to Palmyra?"

"The canal."

"You believe that it will bring prosperity?"

"I do."

"So you follow it. To get the dollars, you go where the dollars are. A sound principle," approved the great man.

"I have my living to make," said Horace Amlie frankly. "I am interested in the canal on that side, but for other reasons, also. Wherever the canal goes, fever follows. In the marshes it almost stopped the work."

"We—that is, Mr. Latham and myself—were considering a contract there," said the Squire. The magnate scowled. He disliked having his business affairs discussed with outsiders.

"Risky," said Horace.

"Folderol-diddle!" barked Genter Latham. "You don't know what you're talking about. Where's the risk?"

"Another such epidemic might drive away the workmen and imperil the whole project."

"Pooh! We've had no trouble getting diggers around here."

"Not yet, perhaps. The miasmas set in with warmer weather." He meditated, then continued, "I have some ideas about checking the malaria before it spreads too far. It would be a national calamity if the great work were hampered."

"A patriot," jeered Latham. "A Clintonian patriot. We're all Clintonians while the contracts fatten our weaselskins. Eh, Jerrold?"

"It is the only faction for a gentleman," pronounced the Squire. "I consider our young friend to be in the right. It is a national duty to see the work through to a magnificent completion."

"The fevers will never stop it," declared Latham. "What is fever? It comes and goes. Nobody knows why. Do you think you know, young man?"

"Not yet."

"Then let the hare lie in its hollow. You get your living from the sick, don't you?"

"Yes. But . . ."

"Then what call have you to meddle with keeping sickness away?"

"It's part of my professional duty."

"A looby profession, then. If men fall sick, they die or get well. If they die, others step in to take their places."

"Mr. Latham, do you know how much the canal has been belated, coming through the marshes?"

"What of it? It's coming through, ain't it? And it's going on."

"Nearly three-quarters of the workmen were laid off at once on some of the worst stretches."

"I take a contract," said Mr. Latham flatly. "I pay men to dig. No work, no pay. What's the fever to me?"

"While your men are off, you're at steady expense for rentals of machinery and keep of animals," argued the other. "Don't you reckon in the accrued interest on the money tied up? The fever is your liability."

Genter Latham grunted. But he was impressed. This young chap had a practical side to him.

Mrs. Jerrold, who had left them to their man-talk, now returned with a pouting complaint that the gentlemen were monopolizing Dr. Amlie, and that she would like a word with him, herself. The Squire issued a humorous warning.

"On guard with Mrs. Jerrold. There's Quaker blood in her veins. She'll get something for nothing of you if she can."

Mrs. Jerrold's still pretty face twisted itself into a momentary grimace. "My husband will have his little jest," she complained to his departing back, and immediately justified his forecast by beginning, "I am worried about my little daughter, Dr. Amlie, lest she fall into a decline."

"She seems healthy enough," said he, privately reflecting that if anything ailed the child it was too much rather than too little vitality.

"I thought you might tell me," pursued the mother, "speaking as a friend" (rather rushing the acquaintanceship, this! thought the young man) "is it good for her to take so many baths?"

"How many?"

"One every day. I cannot break her of it."

Dr. Amlie assumed his most judicial expression. "I do not forebode that it will impair her health," he pronounced, "if she uses plenty of soap."

The mother sighed. "A strange creature. I hardly know her for our own. Another untoward habit, she will not sleep in a room that has not a window open to the night air winter or summer."

"Some authorities hold that fresh air in moderation is beneficial."

"But, night air," protested the mother. "Surely it is perilous to breathe the night air."

"What else is there to breathe at night?" he inquired mildly.

Mrs. Jerrold giggled. "I never thought of that. The almanachs all warn against night air. Which almanach do you prefer, Dr. Amlie?"

At first he did not get her drift. "One is as good as another, I should suppose. The stars in their appointed courses . . ."

"But they differ so widely in their advice."

"Advice? Oh!" He was enlightened. "Medical advice, you mean."

"Yes. The *Temperance Almanach* contradicts the *Masonic*, and the *Arbiter of Health* in the *Family* sometimes says quite the opposite from the *Household Guide* in the *Friends*. Oh, Dr. Amlie, do you think that oaken ashes in old cider are as efficacious as Lee's Anti-bilious Pills for gripes?"

Dr. Amlie was wearying of this. "I should consider one as useless as the other," said he.

She misinterpreted. "I think so, too. I frequently administer both. You would hardly believe it, Dr. Amlie, but my husband says it is all stuff and nonsense. Setting up his opinion against our wisest writers! I call it almost sacrilegious."

"Isn't Dr. Murchison your family adviser?"

"Yes. He's very sympathetic. Sometimes he talks to me about my symptoms for hours. But my daughter positively dislikes him. So I am often reduced to medicating her myself."

"Out of the almanach?"

"I have my own selection of favorite cures," she answered smugly. "Would you care to look at them?"

She led him to a glassed-in porch whose shelves, intended for winter growth of plants, were ranged with half the advertised quackeries of the day. After a panegyric on her special favorites among the panaceas, the hostess went off on another tack.

"Araminta is inveterate. She reads day and night whenever I take my eyes off her. Don't you think, Dr. Amlie, that too much reading dulls one's interest in life?"

"I hadn't noticed it in your daughter's case," he said dryly.

"Perhaps you would come with me and admonish her against this dangerous habit."

Between amusement and annoyance, the young man followed his hostess, wondering how much further she would push her endeavors to get medical advice at the price of a supper. She called out, "Araminta! Dr. Amlie is here." She opened the door.

Dinty was propped on her pillows, with a slender magazine in her hand. A taper, floating in a bowl beside her, dispensed a steady light. The eyes which she turned upon the invaders of her privacy were consciously angelic. The observant physician noticed a nervous motion of her left knee, close to which, beneath the bedclothes there was a slight protrusion. Mrs. Jerrold spoke. "Dr. Amlie will tell you that reading in bed is injurious to health."

"You've only one pair of eyes, you know," said he. "How would you like to wear ugly, steel-rimmed spectacles for life?"

"I'd like it. People who wear spectacles look so wise."

Squire Jerrold's voice sounded from the hallway, summoning his wife. As she excused herself and left, Dr. Amlie bent forward to make out the title of the magazine which the reader had laid down.

"The Bower of Taste," he read. " 'Edited by Mrs. Katherine A. Ware, for the Improvement of the Mind, Morals and Manners of Old and Young.' Is this your chosen style of self-entertainment?"

"Yes, sir," cooed Dinty. "Sometimes I read *The Whole Duty of Woman,* and sometimes I con my hymns and texts."

"Very laudable. And what is that under the sheet?"

A convulsive and involuntary motion of the leg threw a protection over the concealed object. "Sometimes I take my doll to bed with me," said Dinty.

"A square doll?" He threw back the covers and took out the book.

"Snoop!" she said. "I hate you."

He turned the volume in his hand. The title leapt to his eyes: *The Fatal Effects of Passion, or the Spanish Grandee.*

"Hymns and texts," he observed.

Dinty wept. "Go and tell Ma. *I* don't care."

He set the book down. "I'd rather see you reading this than the magazine."

Lips and eyes widened in surprise. "Why?" she breathed.

"It's better print."

"Then you won't tell Ma?"

"No."

"I love you," said Dinty.

"Nevertheless, I shouldn't read too much in bed," he advised.

"I won't any more. When do you move in at Mrs. Harte's?"

"Tomorrow." He had made a composition with L. St. John on his hotel reservation.

"Let me come and fix up the room for you," she wheedled. "Wealthy and I. We'd admire to do it. Even Ma allows that I'm a clever house-hussey."

"Mrs. Harte is looking after me very nicely, thank you."

"Mrs. Harte! Pooh! She's a sluttish housekeeper. Men are so dumb! They don't know when a room's tidy and when it's messy. Old Murch's office is a pigsty. You don't want to be like him. Do you know Old Murch?"

"I have met Dr. Murchison."

"I wish you were our doctor instead of him. He puffs and he snuffles. He says, 'Protrude the unruly member' when he wants me to stick out my tongue. Silly!"

"Little girls should not judge their elders."

"Oh, deary me! Are you going to be like that? I'm disappointed. Ma says I must be respectful toward you. Must I? I'd much rather be your little friend."

Horace struggled with a twitching lip. "Your mother knows best. But you may keep your specially respectful manners for Dr. Murchison."

"Do you know what Old Murch said to Ma about you? He said you could find plenty of practice for your queer theories in Poverty's Pinch. Have you got queer theories, Dr. Amlie?"

"Some people might consider them queer."

"Are you trying them on the Pinch?"

"I don't know much about the Pinch yet."

"I've got a friend there, Tip Crego."

"I heard that name, Crego," said Horace, trying to recall the connection.

"I love Tip. He's teaching me things about birds and beasts and plants and flowers. He knows more about the woods than anybody in the world. Did you know that a fresh poultice of joe-pye weed will draw the poison out of a snakebite? Tip's aunt taught him that. Do you think she's a witch?"

"There are no such things as witches."

"So Tip says. He says wicked people call Mistress Crego a witch just to put a bad name on her. I've watched our broom when she came into the kitchen to sell herbs and it never twitched a bit. That's a sure sign. Unk Zeb Helms lives at the Pinch. You fixed his sore eyes, didn't you?"

"How do you know that?"

"Unk Zeb told me. He says you're a kind young Christian gentleman. You look kind." She peered shyly up into his face. "Would you do something kind for me, Dr. Amlie?"

"I wouldn't wonder a bit, Dinty."

"Tip got his hand hurt. Would you go down to the Pinch and fix it?"

"Certainly. I'll stop in when I go to see Unk Zeb tomorrow."

"Old Murch wouldn't. I asked him. He makes speeches and says we ought to succor the sick and poor. But he only succors the sick and rich. There's always fever at the Pinch. Mr. Latham says it would be better for Palmyra if the fever took off every soul down there."

Horace frowned. "Who made Mr. Latham judge of what people are fit to live?"

Dinty beckoned him nearer. "They're waiting in the parlor," she whispered.

"Who?"

"The youth and beauty of our fair village," said she romantically.

"What are they waiting for?"

"You, of course. Don't be so *dumb*. Ma sent for 'em. There's Miss Margaret Van Wie and Miss Thankful Upcraft and Miss Agatha Levering."

"I've seen Miss Levering," said he incautiously.

"I s'pose you think she's bee-yootiful. All the young gentlemen do. She's awfly uppity with them. Now you must set your neckcloth straight and unrumple your hair and go out and let them see whether they want to marry you or not."

"God bless my soul!" said the startled young man. "You go to sleep, you little owl."

"Tomorrow you tell me which you like best, and I'll tell you whether you're right or wrong," said Dinty. "Good night respectfully, dear Dr. Amlie."

Mint juleps perfumed the air as Horace rejoined the two men, Mrs. Jerrold having retired to her room. Serving the newcomer, Squire Jerrold brought up the subject of his wife's pet nostrums, with which, it appeared, she habitually dosed not only herself but her daughter.

"Sometimes I wonder whether it's good for the child," reflected the father vaguely. "What is your opinion, Dr. Amlie?"

"Half of the stuff is unmitigated bilge and the other half diluted poison," replied Horace, whose inwards were warming to the potent julep.

"Do you tell me so! What would you do with the stuff?"

"Set the bottles up for a cockshy," said Horace, accepting a refill of his tall tumbler.

"A sporting proposition," declared Genter Latham. "Twenty paces distance and sixpence a hit."

Although he had not expected to be taken so literally, Horace was game for the test. They heaped a clothes hamper full of the cures, carried it out back of the barn where there was a convenient stone pile and set up their impromptu gallery. Rendered expert by four years of snowfights at Hamilton, Horace exhibited prodigies of marksmanship. At the end, not a bottle was left unshivered and the stranger was five shillings to the good when he went in to make his manners to the waiting young ladies.

In process of moving his belongings next day, Horace was accosted by the Squire who was on his way to the tavern for a morning dram.

"You shy as neat a rock, sir, as I ever expect to see," said the gentleman. "But my wife is not speaking to me."

"And to me?" asked Horace.

"I shouldn't try," advised the Squire earnestly.

Horace had made an enemy.

-5-

It is our Christian Duty to Love and Cherish the Poor. They smell.

(DINTY'S DIARY)

GANARGWA CREEK narrows and shallows a quarter mile above Van Wie's sawmill. On the south side gathered the lower stratum of the local populace, the lees and detritus of prosperity, crowded in the huddle of huts, shelters and tents termed Poverty's Pinch. Here lived the casuals of the vicinity, practicing odds and ends of outdoor labor for an occasional pittance, picking up bounties on furred or feathered vermin, fishing, grubbing for sang, saxifrage, snakeroot, henbane, mandrake, horsegentian and other salable roots, easily fed and comforted in the long, soft summers, wretched refugees from the bitter winters. In the hot months, the populace was augmented by degenerate whites, runaway apprentices, escaped convicts, newly freed Negroes, and crossbreeds of various degree.

Here dwelt Unk Zeb Helms, Horace Amlie's first charity patient. He hobbled forth from his miserable lean-to to welcome the kind doctor. Horace treated his eyes and asked for young Crego. Oh, yes, the old Negro knew the boy well—a smart boy, a kind-hearted boy who had been good to po' ol' Unk Zeb when he was sick and helpless, had fetched him fish and birds and wild fruits. Tip's hurt came from the side-slip of a tree which he had been helping to fell. Unk Zeb was of opinion that it was mortifying.

He conducted Horace to a rough but comparatively clean shanty, before which a cooking-fire smoldered in a well-constructed stone oven. An aging and haggard woman sat near it, cleaning a mudfish. A boy of thirteen approached, dragging a bit of firewood with his left hand. Horace recognized the vendor of pennyroyal to the canal camp.

"This Tip Crego," said Unk Zeb in his elliptical way of speech. "Show yo' han', boy."

Tip loosed the injured member from its rope-and-rag sling, disclosing some aromatic-smelling leaves which swathed badly swollen and discolored flesh. The physician manipulated the fingers gently.

"Does it hurt much?"

"Some."

"Who put on the dressings?"

The woman looked up from her work. "I did."

"These fingers must be reduced."

"I tried to set them."

"It is no task for a layman," said the doctor austerely. "Do you wish me to undertake it?"

The woman hesitated. "We got no money," she said sullenly.

Horace Amlie nodded. "This will be painful," he warned the patient.

As he set to work, the boy's lips compressed over grinding teeth. He drew one deep, tremulous sigh, then submitted to the agony, silent and motionless.

"You are brave," said Amlie when it was over.

"It's his Tuscarora blood," said the woman. She went into the hut.

"Is she your mother?" Amlie asked the lad.

"No. She's my aunt. But when I say that in the village, folks laugh," he said gravely.

Amlie considered his patient. He was thin of frame, but hard-muscled and hard-weathered. For all his stoicism, the face was surprisingly fine and sensitive, the dark-hued eyes wide-set, intelligent and thoughtful to match the quiet voice.

"You've had schooling," said the doctor, interested.

"What I could get."

"I must see that hand again soon."

"She told you—there is no money."

"Have I asked you for money?"

"Dr. Murchison did. I wanted to pay him in barter, but he turned me away."

"What kind of barter?" asked the doctor, curiously.

"Simples. I gather them for my Aunt Quaila. She blends them into—" he hesitated for a moment—"into medicaments."

Wondering what he had intended to say, Amlie asked, "You know the local plants?"

"Oh, yes!" Tip was speaking with eagerness now. "I know where to find them all. I know their uses, too. Red birthroot that stops nose-bleed. Cocasse for canker-sore. Evans root that stays fluxes. Cuckold-leaf for the evil disease. Gorget to soften and discharge ulcers. Arsesmart for the making of blisters. White elivir ointment that allays the itch. Lungwort for cough and . . ."

Laughing, Dr. Amlie checked the flow of plant lore. "The lad has swallowed the pharmacopoeia. Are you a budding medico or a botanist?"

"I hope to study and go to college and become a naturalist," replied the boy seriously.

"You have made a good start."

Like so many country doctors of his day, Horace Amlie was an ardent student of nature. It was men like Amlie who, almost alone, broadened the boundaries of science in the new world, keeping alight the fires of enthusiasm until the arrival of the specialists. But for their extra-professional devotion, science in the Americas would have lost a century of advance. With the sympathetic intelligence of his kind, Amlie perceived in the boy a fellow spirit, however callow and undeveloped, and resolved to keep an eye on him. But what of the "aunt"? Had not one of the loosetongues of the smithy given her an evil name?

"Bring me some of your simples," said he kindly. "That will be my payment in full."

Now that he was in the Pinch, he might as well look around. The largest of the buildings was a rough log cabin, windowless, chimneyless, and with no door in the low orifice giving entry and exit. At least three generations appeared to be in possession, the oldest representative being a withered crone who rocked in the broad sunlight, sunning rhumatic bones and dipping snuff to her gums with a peach twig while keeping an eye on an idiot urchin in his teens. On the shady side hunched a girl of eighteen with a vacant, happy face, giving suck to a bear cub. Unk Zeb explained that she had lost her love-child the week before and had returned from night wandering in the forest with this queer nursling. From the next shack a man with a demijohn made signs to her to join him, tipping the mouth enticingly, but she shook her head, brooding downward at the cub. An urchin with eyes inflamed to blindness groped his way toward her and fondled the animal, which growled. An itinerant blade-sharpener in the last stage of grinder's rot coughed and spat blood.

Close to the verge of the creek, a patchwork tent had been pitched by a bevy of vagrants from Stone Arabia on the hills back of the far Mohawk. Throughout the state the Stone Arabia folk had a name as treasure seekers. Their picks and spades were neatly stacked, together with the wands which dip when gold lies beneath their sensitive tips. Over their fire a groundhog was roasting.

Only one evidence of productive industry was manifest in the little, straggling community. A shaped cypress log showed a blackly charred hollow along the center; it would presently be a dugout. A stolid aborigine stood near it, silent and contemplative. He was not really interested in the craft, being able to fashion a better one, himself, but he hoped to be able to steal something from the tent if the aliens relaxed their vigilance. A rod downstream, a lusty Negro wench rinsed her shift in a backwater, using potato-skin soap and singing softly the refrain of "Free grace, undyin' love." Amlie thought it a dubious environment for such a youth as Tip Crego.

"This Mistress Crego, now," he said to Unk Zeb. "What does she do?"

"Oddments," answered the old man after some thought.

"Is that all?"

The Negro made a sign with his hand. "Folks talk," said he. "There is broom-witches. There is fork-witches. Some say one worst, some say other. Fork-witch fly in dark o' moon. I see a broom at Mistress Quaila's oven. I never see no dung-fork." He shook his head, repeating the finger-sign. "What I know? Po' ol' niggah."

A three-year-old with running sores lolled in a leaky batteau, picking at his face. From some unidentified spot came a sound of wheezy groaning. A fever-red woman staggered to the brink to dip a bucketful of the foul water which she emptied over her head, repeating the performance several times. There would be plenty of practice in the settlement for any medico interested enough to undertake it.

A pungent spice drifted to his nostrils from Quaila Crego's fire. The reputed witch was selecting herbs from a hamper and dropping carefully measured proportions into a simmering kettle.

"What is this for, Mistress Crego?" he inquired presently.

"Fever," she answered readily enough.

"Here at the Pinch?"

She shook her head wearily. "There's no pay from the Pinch folks. I pick a penny here and there in the camps."

"Has the fever broken out there?"

"It will, when the black moskeeter stands on her head."

He smiled with kindly condescension. "What has the black mosquito to do with it?"

"She fetches the fevers."

"Gypsy lore."

"I'm no gyppo," she retorted. "But there's things known in their tents that folks under roof lack. They call the moskeeters fever-birds."

He refrained from correcting her vagaries. Let her dispense her decoctions. They would do little harm.

"Thank you for being good to my boy," said she in a low tone, and concentrated her attention upon her brew.

If any failing could be imputed to the gentle and proper Miss Agatha Levering, it must be that of being a bit of a sluggard. On this sunlit and fragrant June morning, she arose at the self-indulgent hour of eight, looped aside the coarse, stiffened-paper shades that defended her maidenly modesty against intrusive eyes, and yawned delicately. She shook the mixture of powdered cinnamon and sassafras, discouragement to possible though not probable "chintzes," from her bedsheets which she then vigorously flounced, preparatory to hanging them out for airing. Humming lightly a hymn which dealt in a minatory spirit with sin, death and fiery torments, she made her toilet.

The day stretched before her in pleasurable prospect. First would come those daily ministrations to the poor which always imparted a warmly charitable sensation to her conscience. At eleven o'clock there was a meeting of the Palmyra Township Female Domestic Missionary Association, whose official purpose it was to speed the spread of the Gospel among the Heathen in our own Midst. With the prospective augmentation of the populace through the expected canal construction gangs, opportunities and demands along these lines would broaden. The P.T.F.D.M.A. was girding its loins for the spiritual fray.

Parallel with this endeavor ran the efforts of the newly founded Society for the Promotion of Temperance, whose initial experiment in making a roster of the town's drinkers of alcoholic beverage had met with disconcerting resentment. Agatha was already enrolled in the Ladies' Branch and had worked a sampler, an art wherein she excelled, displaying the exemplary motto, "Shun, O! Shun the Fiery Bowl." For the evening, there would be the Presbyterian Bible Class meeting in the Levering parlor.

Agatha was more given to good works than might have been deduced from her good looks.

At her late breakfast, aristocratically served by a young hired girl who, contrary to village custom, did not eat with the family but in the outer limits of the kitchen, the fair daughter of the Leverings reflected upon the fact that, at the age of nineteen, she was still unmarried. This long-maintained spinsterhood she could afford to regard without rancor, since it was certainly not for lack of matrimonial opportunities. Yet the fact was not to be ignored that twice already she, the eldest girl of the family, had jigged to the rhythm of drumming kettles when two of her junior sisters had married at the appropriate ages of sixteen and seventeen respectively. Among the bitterer element of her rejected swains, a word passed that she was a Miss Betsy Uppish.

Never had the fair Agatha felt undue pulse-stir at the amorous approach of the opposite sex. Indeed, any such inner perturbation would have overwhelmed her with shame. That rakehell, Silverhorn Ramsey, had once insolently told her to her scarlet face that her veins were filled with milk and water. This was after a barefaced solicitation of her virtue at a church festival to which she had mistakenly invited him with the worthy, if offchance design of saving his soul.

Notwithstanding her virginal frigidity, the Levering eldest was not insensible to the social advantages of marriage. Each time that she gently spurned a suitable applicant, it was with the qualm inevitably attached to the prospect of one day being stigmatized as an old maid. Yet she had not been able to bring herself to a receptive view of domestic relations until she met Horace Amlie.

If her blood was not quickened by the town's newest accession, her interest was. Upon first acquaintance she was favorably impressed by the gravity of his bearing, the eminent propriety of the sentiments expressed in his general conversation and cultivated voice, his correct apparel and manners. At the meeting in the Jerrold parlor she had learned that he liked Palmyra, was minded to remain there, that he was addicted to books and music, that he was a Presbyterian in creed and an admirer of Governor Clinton in politics, that he was familiar with such innocent pastimes as 'jump-the-broomstick, hunt-the-squirrel and snap-and-catch-'em, that he preferred coffee to tea, that the increase in the price of necessities was a scandal and something ought to be done about it, that he believed wholeheartedly in the Erie Canal, that he had felt no pangs of nostalgia for the fair ones of Oneida County, and that (anyway and again) he liked Palmyra very much.

To have invited him to pay an evening call would have been premature if not actually forward. In any case, considering the developing social activities of the village, she was certain to encounter him soon again, that very morning perhaps, as she went about her errands of convenience and of mercy.

Carrying a well-victualed basket which represented Christian Charity, Agatha strolled down Main Street. Shop windows enticed her eye. The emporium of Stone-Front Sarcey, opposite the Eagle Tavern, was brave with tartans, both Scotch and Circassian, flanked by a fresh and fashionable consignment of cassimeres direct from New York, true Morocco shoes, French silk gloves, calicoes, bombazettes and pelisse-cloths, Canton crepe gowns, and a breath-snatching display of gros d'Eta dress kerchiefs. Further within was an assortment of the newest Cortes headgear, bonnets of silk and straw, and a fine showing of high-toned Leghorn flats. Pious though the spirit of Agatha was, she could still thrill to the lusts of the flesh in their more innocent manifestations. When the pickle money which her mother lavishly allowed her should have mounted a little higher in the jar, she would choose delightfully among these vanities.

At the Sign of the Streaked Pole, where L. Brooks, M. D., was dressing a customer's beard, she paused to read a placard announcing a return engagement of the Archbold Dramatic Troupe in *How to Die for Love, or Plot & Counterplot,* at the Eagle Tavern. But the theatrical performance was quite beyond the pale for a young damsel of her upbringing and professions. Moreover, she recalled uneasily, there had been some loose talk about a female member of the company openly essaying her wiles for the beguilement of young Dr. Amlie. Agatha was sure that he would have rejected any such bold advances with proper scorn. Still, one could never tell about young males. Doubtless he would be the safer and better for the restraining influence of chaste associations.

Turning north at the Presbyterian churchyard, she took the grassy sidepath toward the Pinch. The green shadows of the elms invited her. From the corner of a meek but observant eye she had discerned a well-set masculine figure ascending the slope.

Behold now Miss Agatha Levering, lost in sweetly melancholy meditation amidst the placid dead, a pretty picture in her soft, gray gown, with her soft, gray eyes contemplative upon a graven headstone and her mind not so abstracted as to be wholly unconscious of the artistic effect thus produced. The inscription which invited her gaze was an unpleasing design of skull and crossbones, framing the name of the deceased and the date, 1794. Below was jaggedly lettered a stanza, presumptively the composition of the defunct:

MY DAYS ARE SPENT
I ROT CONTENT
FOR WHAT CARE I?
SINCE I IN CHRIST
SHALL HAVE A HOIST
UP TO THE SKY

Alert to earthly concerns though she actually was, she managed a sufficiently convincing start when a pleasantly deep voice broke in upon her reverie.

"Good morning, Miss Levering. I hope I do not intrude."

"Law! What a start you gave me, Dr. Amlie! Good morning to you."

"A beautiful day."

"Beautiful, indeed! Yet how brief, how fleeting!"

"Dare I hope," said Dr. Amlie, maintaining with a slight sense of strain the lofty level upon which the colloquy had been established, "that your path coincides with mine? I am on my way back to the village."

"And I to visit my poor at the Pinch."

"I have just come from there, but I should esteem it a privilege to return if I may have the honor of accompanying you."

"I should be gratified, Dr. Amlie."

Smiling up at him, she was really a very pretty sight. Horace Amlie was about ready to forget the misspelt and blotted missive received by post-coach that morning, twenty cents unpaid and due, from the sprightly Miss Sartie, soubrette of the Archbold Company, apprizing him of her prospective return.

He took up his companion's basket and they made the rounds, dispersing what seemed to Horace a rather pallid selection of viands. The last parcel went to a hovel near the water's edge. The front door was inscribed with a roughly scrawled warning:

SMALL POCKS
KEPE OUT.

Horace frowned. "Have you visited this hut before?" he asked.

"I did not go inside."

"I hope not, indeed! Your life is too precious to risk. And your beauty," he added boldly.

She blushed daintily. "Oh, Dr. Amlie! What is beauty, even if I possessed it, in the face of such affliction!"

Having no answer pat for so fine a sentiment, he repeated his insistence upon her departure.

"What shall you do?" she inquired.

"Wash my hands in vinegar and examine the sick person."

"Isn't it very dangerous?"

"I have been vaccinated. Have you?"

She shook her head. "No. Do you think I should be?"

"Most certainly. At once."

"I will ask my father," she promised. "Good-bye. I think it is noble of you."

He glowed. "There is a sacred choral at the Eagle Big Room on Thursday evening. They sing 'The Christian Martyr.' Might I have the honor of escorting you?"

"I should be pleased," she murmured with modestly downcast eyes. She raised them. "Promise me that you will take no needless risks of the dreadful pest."

"I promise," he said fervently.

The patient, a quarter-breed woman of fifty, was already on the mend. Evidently the case was a light one. Dr. Amlie gave such treatment as was indicated, and offered to vaccinate the granddaughter who shared the hut, then and there, free of charge. A whispered colloquy between the two females followed, after which the hag on the bed made her proposition: for fifty cents cash or its equivalent in whisky—she held out a tremulous hand—the strange doctor would have her leave to put the fancy powder into Lena's arm. Horace left in helpless dudgeon. But first he sent Tip Crego about to notify the residents of the slum that Dr. Amlie would vaccinate such as were unable to pay, free of charge, at his office.

On his way back Horace found his mind reverting to Quaila Crego's confident prophecy about the coming of the fever. Superstition and folk myth, of course. Yet hadn't Dr. Vought once discoursed profoundly before his class on folklore, warning his hearers not to be carelessly contemptuous of what might be the stored and mysterious wisdom of age-old experience? But—mosquitoes! Standing on their heads! Absurd! Wait, though. What was that he had read about weak spots in the miasmatic theory of fevers? Hadn't that article vaguely hinted at some connection with the insect kingdom? He must look that up when his library was once more properly shelved and ordered.

A glimpse of Agatha Levering as she emerged from the minister's house and the flash of her smile relegated science to a far corner of his brain.

-6-

I will Speak my Mind, dear Diary, about my Loved and Revered Teacher. He is a Big Stinker.

(DINTY'S DIARY)

PROTRUDING a small, pink tongue, Dinty, who disliked mathematics, wriggled as she strove with this problem:

> Suppose a gentleman's income is 1,836 doll's per year, and he spends 3 doll's 49 cents a day; one day with another, how much would he have saved at the year's end?

Having worked it out four times to four different conclusions, the pupil let her mind stray to the lighter view. Her dreamy pencil set down in the blank-book lines but vaguely collateral to the income of the suppositious gentleman. In vain did her neighbor, Happalonia Vallance, nudge her. She was oblivious to the warning, until vengeance descended and she was yanked to her feet by a harsh grip on her ear while the rest of the Polite Academy raised fascinated eyes from their studies.

"What folderol is this?" demanded Prof. Larrabee's acid tones.

"Nothing," faltered Dinty.

"Versification!" he snorted, peering nearsightedly.

"Please, sir, I didn't mean anything by it."

He flourished the offending book. "We have a poet among us. Miss Araminta Jerrold will read aloud to us her latest effusion."

Desperately Dinty racked her memory and brought forth a forlorn hope. Pretending to read from the page, she recited in meek and uplifted accents:

Oh, may my broken, contrite heart
Timely my sins lament,
And early with repentant tears
Eternal wo prevent.

"Is that what you wrote, Miss?" demanded the baleful voice.

"I was going to write it," she quavered.

"Liar! Read what you have already written." He thrust her nose down upon the text. In a dying cadence she faltered out:

Multiplication is vexation.
Division is as bad.
The Rule of Three
Doth puzzle me,
And Fractions drive me mad.

"Fine sentiments!" snarled the little man, working himself into a passion of outraged dignity. "A noble expression of contempt for learning! To the platform."

This was the prelude to public castigation. Dragging the unresistant form along the aisle, he heaved it up on the dais and reached for the ruler.

Let Kindly Silence (wrote Dinty in her diary, freely plagarizing a half-remembered poem of the day) veil the Shameful Scene.

Which seems no more than fair.

White, tearless and inwardly raging, she trotted along Main Street. She had been dismissed for the day with a note to her father, prescribing that, for high crimes and misdemeanors duly specified, she be soundly chastised and kept abed until she exhibited signs of repentance.

Dinty decided that if this were done she would run away and never come back. She had had enough!

As she reached the corner of Canandaigua Road, a faint, metallic creaking arrested her progress. Swaying in the breeze, the gilded handicraft of O. Daggett advertised to the public that Medical Science waited within in the person of Horace Amlie, M.D., ready to bestow its ameliorations upon human suffering from eight to eleven in the morning and three to five in the afternoon. At other hours it was available for home ministration. Supplementary information of a more temporary character was imparted by a sheet of paper nailed to the door.

BACK IN ½ H'R

Horace was enjoying the fellowship of the smithy, to which he had been admitted on the strength of his first favorable impression.

The notice on the panel did not deter Dinty. Nor did the fact that the door was locked. She scrambled in at the window. Before going home with that damnatory note, she yearned for consolatory companionship.

Much ground may be covered in thirty minutes of diligent endeavor. Dinty started her investigations in the cabinet above the desk. First she tried to focus the microscope, without satisfactory result. The lancet box attracted her. She opened it and cautiously tried the edge of each blade. Passing from this, she examined the forceps, clamps, splints and bandages with awed interest. She puzzled over the stethoscope which she surmised to be a variety of ear trumpet. Her shin struck a sharp edge and she looked down into a tin-sheathed oblong, nearly full of water, in the murky depths of which languidly wreathed several small, obese forms. Dinty shuddered. She had been leeched for most of childhood's ailments, and each time the obscene bloodsuckers had turned her stomach.

A metal box caught her eye. She opened it gingerly, lest it contain other unpleasant fauna. A dated label was lettered: "Genuine Kine-Pox Matter; J. Vought, M.D." She regarded it with awe. Tip Crego's aunt knew a lady who, after being vaccinated, grew horns and gave milk. Perhaps, though, that was from an overdose. If Dr. Amlie believed in it, surely it was all right. It must be terrible to be like Sarah Dorch. Deacon Dillard said it was a judgment on her for the levity of her conduct.

Books! They were all about her in seductive array, such books as never before had she known of; strange, enticing titles, suggestive of unknown regions to be explored. What a feast for the inquiring mind! Where should she begin?

There was Hooper's *Medical Lexicon*, *Whytt on the Nerves* (her mother had nerves; maybe she could find out something helpful about them), *Blackall on Dropsy*, *Gregory's Physic*, with an impressive London mark on it, Hamilton's *Diseases of Women and Children*, *Burns on Abortion*, *Dorsey's Surgery* (she peeked into that and set it aside for its startling pictures), *Huxham on Fevers*, *Bayes on the*

Bones (who cared about bones!), Vought's *Treatise on Bowel Complaints* in manuscript (she could tell Dr. Vought something about those), *Denman's Midwifery, Cheyne on the English Malady* (What on earth was the English malady? She had heard one of the ladies say something at a sewing bee about the French malady and all the rest had hushed her up), *Conversations on Chemistry,* a *Medical Repository* in twenty-two dull-appearing volumes, a file of *Medical Magazine,* and many, many others. What a wondrously learned man Dr. Horace Amlie must be!

Dinty made a selection on a purely pictorial basis and settled down to enjoy herself. Soon her perky little nose was hovering close above the page. Her blue eyes rounded with wonder. Her mind moved, entranced, in alien and fascinating realms. She was deaf to approaching footsteps.

Horace Amlie advanced quietly to the window and leaned his arms on the sill.

"Improving the mind?" he inquired.

"Oh!" said Dinty. "You're not cross with me, are you, for coming in while you were away?" she asked politely.

"No." Such had been the loneliness of his professional quarters in the week since he had opened office that he was glad to see anybody.

Encouraged, she said, "This is a funny book. What's abortion?"

He craned his neck. *Burns on Abortion*—the extremely explicit Burns! "That book is not for little girls," he said hastily.

"I don't see why not. I like the pictures. Won't you tell me what abortion means?"

"It's a—a physical condition."

"Do ladies have it?"

"Yes. No. Sometimes."

"All the pictures are ladies' pictures." She spread the volume open to a full-page illustration. "That's a lady's inside, isn't it?"

"Yes. Let me have the . . ."

"Wait." She whisked *Burns* beyond the reach of his intruding arm. "Are everybody's insides like that?"

"Not at all."

"Are yours?"

"No!"

"I don't see why you should roar when I only want to know things," protested Dinty. "Why do people put things in books if they don't want other people to know them? I think it's very unfair. Will I be like that when I grow up?"

Dr. Amlie uttered a faint groan, which failed to chill his visitor's ardor of research. She set her finger upon the drawing.

"Her stomach looks like a miller's grist bag. Why does it look that way?"

"Never mind."

"There's a doll curled up in the bag. That's funny, too."

"Araminta, close that book at once," he commanded.

She sighed. "I will if you bid me to," said she meekly. "But I do think you might tell me. How did the doll get inside the lady?"

Dr. Amlie mounted the steps, let himself in through the door, laid violent hands upon *Burns* and relegated him and his too revelatory illustrations to a far corner of the upper shelf.

"These are my office hours," he said. "Go home."

Dinty's eyes became as those of the stricken doe. "Aren't you going to cure me?" she quavered.

"What's the matter with you?"

"I think it's prob'ly hydrophobia. I can bark like a dog."

"Well, don't," said he unsympathetically.

"And look at my hands."

She spread them, palms up. The flesh was wealed and blistered; in one spot it was laid open.

"Digging again?" he asked. He had heard of that escapade.

"No. My teacher spatted me. That isn't the only place he tried to spat me." She rubbed the other place. "Right before the whole school," she said in a voice dolorous and shamed. She cheered up suddenly. "He didn't spat me but twice there. I bit him."

From the contents of several sweetly odorous jars Dr. Amlie compounded an ointment over which her nostrils expanded appreciatively.

"Mm–nmm," she murmured.

"What devilment were you up to?" he inquired, applying the salve.

"I wrote a poem instead of my lesson." She recited it. "It was a silly lesson. Is your income one thousand, eight hundred and thirty-six dollars a year?"

"It is not," he replied, reflecting with a qualm that it was not likely to be, within reckonable time.

"If it was, would you spend three dollars and forty-nine cents of it per day?"

"Now look you, young lady," said Horace Amlie. "I am not here to do your sums for you."

Dinty's lips quivered. She raised piteous eyes to heaven. Her face became a picture of woe.

"You're mean to me," she accused, a heartbreak in every soft syllable.

It was just a little overdone. Yet, so skillful was the pathos that, in spite of his suspicions, Horace was moved. Those forlorn, upturned eyes of childhood; if he rejected her, they mutely asked, to whom, in a cruel world, could she turn for aid and comfort?

"If your problems are too much for you," he began uncertainly, "surely your parents . . ."

"No," said she mournfully. "Ma says figures make her head ache. Pa only teases. You could help me with my sums and I could redd up your room. I'd admire to be your little housewife. I'm a clever good housewife. Even Ma will tell you that. I can bake and fry and air the linen and sew a seam and put up fruits and everything."

"I daresay. But Mrs. Harte does well enough by me."

Dinty cocked a critical head. "Pooh! There's dust on the top of the shelf where I found the book. The framed motto on the wall doesn't hang straight. One of the buttons on your broadcloth coat dingle-dangles. And look up there in the corner. A mud-dobber's nest! I'd be ashamed!" She folded her hands virtuously. "How much is your bill, Dr. Amlie? I haven't got much."

"Nothing. That's for friendship."

"Am I truly your friend?" she crowed. "Then I'll come to see you every day if you'll let me. I'd admire to know all about the medicines in the bottles. Will you tell me about them?"

Horace conned his array of cures, liquid, powder, pill and wafer, with affection. Many of them he had garnered and prepared himself, for he was an enthusiastic botanist. Here, bottled, boxed and classified, were the concentrated essences of healing. Unimpeachable authority, crystallized in the books overhead, vouched for their virtues. Practically every known ailment was matched by its cure. For fevers there were bloodroot, spikenard, dragonsfoot, mallow and maidenhair. Rhubarb would take care of all but the "deep" rheumatism; the more potent pokeberry tincture in brandy was cautiously recommended for that. Slippery elm corrected constipation and spleenroot, incontinence. Alkanoke was specific in yellow jaundice; white birthroot in hysterics. Balmwort could be relied upon to comfort the distended stomach. Elivir powder miraculously eased catarrh internally and the itch externally. And, if all else failed, there was that sterling panacea, cow parsnip, to fall back upon in any crisis resisting less formidable and comprehensive remedies.

His visitor was spelling out the label on a jar, *Triosteum perfoli.*

"What do you give this for?" she asked.

"That's feverwort. It cools and dispels fevers."

"I know something about feverwort you don't know. You can dry the berries and roast them and they're as good as coffee, almost." She examined a smaller vial. "What's this?"

"Henbane."

"Isn't it poisonous?"

"Not when employed with discretion. It stimulates the liver."

She explored further. "What's tafsilago powder for?"

"Scurvy and humors of the blood."

"Does everything cure something?"

"Yes." It was a broad statement, but it rested on the best authority. If the learned writers of all those books did not know, then there was no wisdom in the world.

"Isn't that wonderful!" She meditated. "Then why do people die?" she propounded.

Dr. Amlie frowned. Contemplating that formidable battery of scientifically warranted medicaments, he had been hard beset to explain to himself how there could be disease, let alone death, left in a world so impregnably defended.

"You are too young to understand."

"No, I'm not," she denied brightly. "I know. It's because they don't come to you to be cured."

Reluctant to discourage so flattering a theory, Dr. Amlie endeavored to look sagacious.

"Do other doctors know about these?" She waved her hand toward the embottled pharmacopoeia.

"Yes. Certainly."

"But not as much as you do."

"Some know more," said he modestly.

She shook her head. "I'll never believe that." She pounced upon his trashbasket and brought forth a fur. "What's this?"

"Nothing," said Horace shortly.

It was, in fact, a fee, the only one he had taken in two days. Four applicants from the Pinch had availed themselves of his offer of free vaccination, one of whom, an Indian, had surprisingly proved to be a pay patient. After the inoculation he had blown gently upon the scarified spot, fumbled under his jacket, laid upon the practitioner's desk a well-cured raccoon skin and stalked out with no comment.

"Willful waste makes woeful want," said Dinty through the pursed lips of virtuous disapproval. "You shouldn't throw things away."

"What use is a coonskin to me in June?"

She examined it critically. "It's a summer hide, of course. But T. Lay will buy it. T. Lay buys everything. Haven't you ever read his sign?"

Professional pride bristled. "Am I to huckster whatever my patients may choose to bring me in the way of rubbish?" he demanded.

"Will you let me do it?"

Receiving a grudging assent she departed with the pelt. There was an air of triumph about her, and a trove tight-clutched in the pudgy hand when she came back. She set forth the transaction.

"I said two shillings and he said sixpence. I said eighteen cents and he said eight. I said fifteen cents and not a cent less and he said ten cents and not a cent more, you little harpy. So then, of course, I knew I could get a shilling, and here it is. What will you do with it?"

"What would you advise?" asked Horace gravely.

"Buy a pretty for Miss Agatha Levering."

"Why should I do that?" he inquired, successfully repressing a gulp.. (This child knew too much!)

"Aren't you sparking her? You took her to the Sacred Choral."

"Don't be so inquisitive," returned Horace.

"Nineteen is dismal old," she observed reflectively.

"You haven't to worry for some years yet," said he.

"I wasn't thinking of myself." As he did not fill the pause which followed by asking her of whom she was thinking, she continued, "I hope I shall be married long before then. Nineteen!" She shook her head. "But, then, you're very old, yourself. Has she promised to work you a sampler yet?"

"Who?"

"Miss Agatha."

"No. Why should she?"

"I got a prize once for working a sampler." She slanted her eyes around to take in Dr. Amlie, but he was not looking at her. "Shall I work you one?" she asked. "A pretty one. To hang in the bare spot." Dinty indicated the far wall whence the mud-wasp had been evicted.

"What sentiment would you use?" inquired Horace grimly. " 'Multiplication is vexation'?"

Dinty wriggled. "Now you're being mean to me," said she, sorrowfully. "Never mind. I'd like to do a sampler for you. I've got my wool all spooled for it. Do you want to know what my motto for the sampler is?"

"Yes, I'd like to very much."

"It's all printed out on your certificate. Such lovely letters! I copied it. You don't mind, do you?"

"Where did you see it?"

"In your drawer, when I was setting it to rights." She produced a square of paper from her school bag and read from it:

" 'I, Horace Amlie, M.D., do solemnly declare that I will honestly, virtuously, and chastely conduct myself in the practice of physic and surgery, with the privilege of exercising which profession I am now invested; and that I will, with fidelity and honor, do everything in my power for the sick committed to my care.' "

"That would make a long sampler," said he.

"Not too long. I can do fine lettering. I think the sentiment is noble," she declared warmly. "How do you ever think of such elegant words?"

"God bless the child! I didn't invent it," said he.

"Didn't you?" said she, disappointed. "It says 'I, Horace Amlie, M.D.' "

"It's the New York State Board medical oath," he explained.

"Oh! Don't you think it would look lovely in purple and green worsted? With a border of roses," she added, warming to her artistic forecast.

"Very pretty," agreed Horace, suppressing a shudder.

The wide-set blue eyes beamed with happiness. "Then I may do it? I'll get Miss Agatha to letter it out for me. . . . No, I won't. I'll do it all, myself. Every bit."

"I'm sure it will be very nice the way you do it."

Dinty's restless mind took another angle. "I wish I could be a doctor. Don't they ever let females be doctors?"

"Certainly not," said Horace, horrified at the thought.

"Then I'd be the first. And I'd promise"—she refreshed her memory from the slip of paper in her hand—"to honestly, virtuously, and chastely conduct myself in the practice of physic and surgery. And I'd read *all* your books."

A series of clear, beautifully modulated bugle notes sang in the air, to be answered by the long, brazen blast of the eastbound coach. Dinty jumped up and down.

"Silverhorn Ramsey! Silverhorn Ramsey!" she caroled. "The coach is coming, too."

A robust baritone chanted:

> In summer skeeters bite your nose,
> In winter nose and toes get froze.
> Oh, who, in any time or age,
> Would travel by the poxy stage!

"It's a canaller's song," explained Dinty excitedly. "It makes the coachees bitter mad. Then he offers to fight 'em. Let's go out and see."

Curiosity strove with Horace's misgiving that attending public brawls hardly comported with the dignity of his profession. His small companion was tugging at his wrist. He obeyed the double impulsion. But Dinty was disappointed. There was no fight.

The musician was limping toward the corner, his face, in spite of the habitual devil-may-care expression, pinched and pale. Dinty dropped him a curtsey.

"Hi, poppet!" He chucked her under the chin. "How's my little sweetling?"

"Nicely, thank you, sir." She lifted a worshipful gaze to his face.

"And young Æsculapius? I was coming to see you, Doc. Lay your peepers to that."

He loosened and drew up his left trouser-leg. Below the knee, the empurpled flesh puffed out, taut and globular. Horace gave it but one look.

"Come around to the office," he said.

At the door, Dinty was dismissed, a most ungracious proceeding, she considered. Seated in the patient's chair, Silverhorn exposed the wound for exploration.

"Lucky for you that he was a young one," commented the physician, working busily.

"How do you know that?"

"From the small punctures. They're close together."

"Not such a fool as you look, are you, Doc?" said the patient graciously.

Dr. Amlie straightened up. "Civility from you, sir," said he firmly, "or out you go."

The patient closed his eyes for a second. "I'm not feeling up to a fight," he admitted. "So civility's the word. What can you do for me, Doc? It hurts like hell."

Dr. Amlie neatly lanced the wound, criss-cross, pressing out the blood, though he knew that the poison was already well disseminated. He then put on a dressing of opiumized ointment, and bound it in with cooling plantain and wilted cabbage-leaf.

"Tell me about it," said he.

"I was riding over from Macedon where I've got an old uncle. Down by the tamarack bog I stopped and went in to you-know-what, when this fellow up and let me have it. Must have been lying under the log. Didn't even wait to rattle. Might have been in a worse place, huh?" He grinned.

"How much did you drink?" asked Dr. Amlie suspiciously.

"All I had with me. Short of a pint. It stopped the pain and gave me the notion of playing myself to town before I died. Will I die, Doc? Will I die and be shoveled in the cold, dark ground, as the song says?"

"Not of this. You'll die if you drink a pint of raw rum often enough."

The patient stared insolently. "Now, by the guts of Goliath! What have we here? Are you telling Silverhorn Ramsey what he may and mayn't do?"

"Do you want to live or die? It's nothing to me, you understand, one way or the other."

"I want to live to be a hundred."

"You're making a poor start. How old are you now?"

"Well-turned of twenty."

"You'll be worn out by thirty."

"What if I am? I'll have lived, won't I? There won't be much I'll miss. I'll have seen more and done more and drunk more than you could do by the time you're forty, old cock," bragged the other. "Made my little pile, too, and spent it as I made it. Wine, women, and song. Say, Doc, if you've got any likely looking young females coming along, just let young Silverhorn know. I keep an eye on 'em, watch 'em filling out." He made a grossly offensive gesture. "That filly of old Sharkskin Latham's now—she's beginning to have a look in her eye already. And your little poppet of a Jerrold rib; give her a couple of years."

"That's enough," said Horace, revolted.

Silverhorn laughed. "Mealymouth, hey? How much does your little job come to?"

"Half a dollar."

"Dear money, but worth it. Don't forget about the gals, Doc.

Hi, dandy, derry-O!
I had a little fairy-O!

Here's your four bits. So, fare ye well, my bonnie young lad, for I'm off to Fiddler's Green."

Gazing with disaffection after his departing caller, then with affection upon the first cash fee of his office practice, Horace felt like framing the small, handsomely engraved note as a momento. He might as well have done so. It was "Niagara money," the issue of a bank which had passed peacefully away six months before.

-7-

We should Always lend a Helping Hand. This is our Christian Duty; sometimes it is Fun.

(DINTY'S DIARY)

MIASMAS hung, soft and dank, above the valley when Horace paid his second visit to the labor camp. He found Old Bill Shea making his evening round with a smudge-box dangling under his chin. The hollow log, stuffed with damp leaves and sodden chips, exuded a protective cloud of smoke against the teeming insect life of the night. The Irishman was in sour humor.

"Six of my men quit me yesterday," he said. "The rest are grumblin' like bears with sore bums."

"What's wrong?"

"They claim the place is unchancy. Just because a few weaklin's are sick."

"How many?"

"I don't exactly know," said the overseer, coughing in the fumes that wreathed his head. "Take a look for yourself."

Horace went into the nearest bunkhouse. Two of the occupants, groaning with dysentery, got up and staggered out as he entered. An invalid who had just taken a long pull at a bottle of fiery Jamaica Ginger set it down and said sullenly, "It's the grub."

The cook's head popped up. "You're a goddam liar," he yelled. "The Eagle, itself, don't serve no better."

"It's good enough to the taste," admitted the sufferer. "What I say is, something's poisonin' us."

"It rips the guts out of you," confirmed another.

A chorus of voices detailed painful symptoms with unpleasing particularity. Shea withdrew, taking his guest with him.

"What can you do with a passle like them?" said he disgustedly. "Poison, my rump!"

Inwardly Horace considered the complaint probably well founded. He had his own notion of the nature of the poison. Last year in the Great Marshes he had seen dysentery run like a raging flame through the camps, always worst where conditions were foulest. He was committed in his mind to the revolutionary and unpopular theory of a logical connection between filth and disease, promulgated by the erudite if heretical Dr. David Hosack of New York.

He walked over to take a look and a sniff at the weltering latrine, then paced the distance to the nearest eating table. Less than seven yards. With the wind in the right direction odors would be borne across—and how much more than odors? Or were the stenches themselves a form of miasma, pullulating with disease? He did not know. Nobody knew. But it might well be so.

He advised the overseer to lay in a stock of blackberry brandy and balmwort.

The depth of Shea's honest concern for the contract was proved by his hinting that there might be an arrangement to pay the young doctor something. However, Horace did not anticipate getting rich out of it. He would do well if, at the end, he were not out of pocket for the cost of his medicines, as he already was at Poverty's Pinch.

Having sat out his office hours in loneliness the next day, he visited the Pinch late in the afternoon. He was not the day's only messenger of mercy to the submerged populace. A self-recruited band from Miss Agatha Levering's Bible Class was on the job. They called themselves the Little Sunbeams Cluster. Dinty Jerrold, Happalonia Vallance and Wealthia Latham were the leading spirits. A close-knit, determined and predatory trio, they ranged town, country and waterway, seeking whom they might succor. In their first week of official activity they rescued a wounded deer from Ganargwa Creek, adopted two families of destitute kittens, restored Bill Simmons, the town drunkard, to the bosom of his unreceptive family when all concerned would have preferred to let him sleep it off in the ditch, released a dozen fur animals from as many traps, to the righteous wrath of the trappers (Happalonia got bitten by a coon in the process), got into trouble by harboring in the Latham smokehouse a runaway apprentice for whom there was an advertised reward of six cents, and by various endeavors established themselves as ministering angels in their own eyes and pesky nuisances in public opinion.

As there was always somebody hungry, destitute, sick or fugitive at the Pinch, it was a port of call for the Sunbeams whenever they happened to think of it. Somewhere Wealthia had picked up the rumor of smallpox, and, upon her communicating it to her fellows, the little band was off to see about it.

The warning on the door gave them no pause.

"It don't mean us," said Dinty confidently. "Heaven protects the bearers of mercy. We've got a motto on our wall that says so."

All three entered. The sick woman's attendant had gone out, leaving her in a semi-stupor.

"Look how red her face is," said Happalonia.

"I think she ought to be bled," opined Dinty. "If I had a lancet I could do it. Or a leech. You girls go and catch some."

They demurred. They didn't like leeches, horrid, squirmy things. Wealthia was all for medicines, and opened up the basket which contained their surreptitiously acquired stock. Dinty went over them.

"Iron phosphate—I wish I could remember what that's good for. . . . Seneca oil—they gave me that once, and I had an awful pain. Powdered vetch—that's for hydrophobia, I *think*. But maybe not. Anyway, she hasn't got hydrophobia. . . . Squills—those are for the rattles. She hasn't rattled once, or even coughed. . . . Treacle and sulphur— My Ma says nobody was ever the worse for taking treacle and sulphur. . . . And feverwort. I'm *sure* she's got a fever. You lift her up, Happy. You hold her nose, Wealthy. I wonder how much water I ought to mix with it."

The struggle with the half-unconscious sufferer was still indecisive when Horace Amlie arrived.

"What on earth!" he began.

"We're ministering unto her," explained Dinty.

"Get out of here," commanded Horace. "All of you. Wait for me outside."

The three Sunbeams withdrew in good order. After ten minutes the physician emerged with a grave expression.

"Is she going to die?" asked Happalonia in awed tones.

"No. Stand over there and answer me." He ranged them in a correctional line against the wall. "Can't you read?" he demanded pointing at the door-sign.

Dinty brightly explained that they were under special angelic protection. Horace muttered so shocking a disparagement of the angels' prophylactic power against smallpox that Happalonia shivered.

"Have you been vaccinated?" he snapped, pointing a monitory finger at Dinty and letting it swing like a muzzle upon the others.

"No," said Dinty.

"No," echoed Wealthia.

Happalonia looked terrified and snuffled.

"I shall vaccinate all of you at once," he declared.

Happalonia uttered a loud wail.

"I don't care," said Dinty.

Wealthia shrank back. "Pa wouldn't like that, without my asking him," she said uncertainly.

"Where is your father?"

"Gone up to look at the Gerundigut canal cut."

"My Pa went with him," put in Dinty. "Ma, too. They won't be back till tomorrow."

"Tomorrow may be too late," said Horace decisively. "This is no case for delay. Get into my wagon."

He drove them to his office. Seating them, he took a small, bright lancet from his box. At the sight of him testing the edge upon his thumb, Happalonia rose, and, with a strangled yelp, bolted through the door and down the street.

"Pooh!" said Dinty. "She's a cowardy-custard. I'm not afraid." She bared her arm, quaking.

"That's my fine girl!" said Horace and brought the blood.

Wealthia watched the process with protruding eyes. Sensing her apprehension, Dinty said in a resolute quaver, "It didn't hurt a bit."

Nevertheless, the older girl, when her turn came, fainted dead away and must be brought around with a burnt feather and a whiff of ammonia.

"Wealthy's so ladylike," said Dinty, proud of her friend's delicacy.

Wealthia went home, but her companion lingered.

"Mistress Crego says you're destined for great riches. She read it in the leaves. She's named a mandrake root after you and keeps it over her door for your good fortune. She says the canal is coming soon and bringing sickness to many and luck to one, and you're the one."

Dinty's eyes began to rove about the room, and fixed themselves upon a vacant space above the desk.

"My sampler's half finished," said she. "It would look elegant right there." She solicitously rubbed her arm. "I'd better hurry and get it done before I'm too sore to work."

Quaila Crego's reading of the tea leaves stuck in Horace's mind.

Perhaps his luck did lie with the canal. In any case, it promised more than his home practice, which was practically nil. He fore-shortened his dates and made his third camp call on a Thursday.

"It's here," said Old Bill at sight of him.

Horace followed him between the files of bunks. Twenty of the diggers were bed-ridden, burning with the fever or shaking with the alternate ague. The chattering of their teeth made a dreary and familiar sound in the murk. To those who would take it, he administered the approved remedy of Peruvian bark decoction in brandy which, alone of the medically advised cures, he had found reasonably efficacious. When he had finished, Shea invited him into his tiny hut for a drop of the ardent.

"Genter Latham'd better get me some more men," said he grimly.

About to reply, Horace halted the tin cup in mid-course to his lips, staring, with transfixed attention at the wall beneath the hooded candle.

There, at a right angle to the boarding, a black and swollen mosquito stood "on her head," as Quaila Crego had put it, in the singular posture of the anopheles, not for many years yet to be scientifically determined as host and bearer of malaria.

8

It is Foolish to tell a Lie and Foolisher to get Found out.
(DINTY'S DIARY)

Two little girls with sore arms reported at the Polite Academy on Monday morning. Though yearning to exhibit her honorable wounds, Dinty refrained lest the news spread and involve Wealthia Latham in trouble at home. For her friend had immediately enjoined secrecy upon her.

"Pa would be cruel mad," said she.

"At you?"

"Oh, no! Pa's never mad at me. Or, if he is, he gets right over it," purred Wealthia, conscious of her power. "But he might get awful mad at Dr. Amlie and do something terrible."

"What would he do?"

"I don't know. He horsewhipped a man once for doing something he didn't like."

"You'll have to tell him, though. He's sure to find out," warned Dinty.

"I'll tell him a bee stung me," said Wealthia.

To Dinty's disgruntlement, Wealthia's spot was more inflamed and interesting than her own. Horace, after examining their arms two or three times, told them that everything was proceeding satisfactorily, and dismissed the matter from his mind. He assumed that both had informed their parents, and that there would be no trouble over his taking matters into his own hands. Dinty, indeed, had owned up to her father under injunction of secrecy; she did not want her mother to know.

When the pair, playing in the Latham back yard, saw their medical friend approach the front door of the mansion, they were dismayed. They might have saved their fears. Dr. Amlie's mission was only remotely medical. He was there upon Decker Jessup's insistence that, for business reasons if for no others, he ought to identify himself with one of the local congregations.

"Genter Latham is the man for you," the cobbler had said.

"What church does he represent?" Horace had not been impressed with any special religiosity in the great man's make-up.

"Any and all," was the cobbler's reply. "No dollar rolls in this town but that cashhawk must try to turn it into his own pocket. He's a factor-of-all-trades, religion included. Medicine, too, if you could show him a profit on it."

"I don't understand how . . ." Horace had begun when his mentor broke in,

"The Baptist church wants a bell to its steeple. Where's the money to come from? Genter Latham. The Episcopalians need new pews. Genter Latham's money will cost them only ten percent, for the sake of dear religion. The Presbyterian roof must be mended. Make out a note to Genter. For security the churches gives him a lien on their pews, and he pockets the rentals until principal and interest are paid off, and credits himself with a mortgage on Heaven into the bargain for abating his usual twelve percent moneyhire. Don't let him nick you for a fancy price."

Horace found the financier on the side veranda of his elegant, matched cobblestone mansion, in conversation with Lawyer Ephraim Upcraft. Mr. Latham listened, nodded and briskly rattled off his quotations: a well-placed pew in the Baptist Church, seven dollars, Methodist or Episcopalian, six-fifty, Presbyterian, eight. This did not strike the applicant as conforming to the law of supply and demand, since he knew that both Methodist and Baptist congregations were larger than the Presbyterian. Mr. Latham gravely explained that the latter comprised more of the leading people of the community and therefore commanded a higher rate.

"However, the Episcopalian edifice is specially draughty in winter," he observed with a shrewd twinkle. "Perhaps you'd prefer that creed."

"I fail to perceive the precise denominational significance of a draught," said Horace.

"Monday colds," said Mr. Latham tersely. "Money in a doctor's pocket."

"It's immoral and irreligious to expose worshipers to such risks," declared Horace.

Lawyer Upcraft said austerely, "Would you not trust to the protection of Heaven, young sir?"

"Not for heating purposes," replied Horace with a grin. "I've always understood that to be the specialty of the other locality."

Genter Latham cackled. "One for the devil. Come to think of it, though, Murchison has got the Episcopalians and the Baptists sewed to the lining of his medicine bags. You'd better try for the Presbyterians or the Methodists. Didn't someone tell me you were a Presbyterian member? Will you take a pew from date? I have an excellent one at disposal. It directly adjoins Mr. Levering's," he added in smiling afterthought.

"The Rev. Theron Strang is a powerful and uplifting exhorter," said Mr. Upcraft. "You will profit by his discourses."

Horace paid over his money with a qualm for his diminishing store of cash, and took up his beaver when his host detained him.

"You've been visiting my camp."

"Yes. Did Shea tell you?"

"You pumped him full of notions. He's after me to make changes. Changes cost money."

"So does sickness."

"You said that at Squire Jerrold's. I thought you a windy young fool. Now I'm not so sure."

Horace waited.

"Have you visited Jerrold's camp?"

"No. I hear two of his men have died. Bloody flux. You'll be lucky if you don't fare worse. Your camp isn't fit for humans to live in."

Instead of the expected outbreak of wrath, Horace found himself under a thoughtful regard. Genter Latham said, "Half of Jerrold's men are looking for healthier jobs. That sort of panic spreads. I don't want it among my loafers. Will you take five dollars a week, medicines included, to look after the men?"

It was a close bargain. But it meant at least the backbone of a reasonable subsistence. Horace accepted without undue elation. Professional conscience impelled him to give his new employer fair warning.

"You're in for a bad time with the fever, I fear, Mr. Latham."

"Why so?"

"The miasmas that rise every night from the valley."

"I've heard enough of that trash," barked the magnate. "You're after me to move the buildings," he charged. "Is that it?"

"It might save a great deal of sickness."

"Well, I won't do it, and be damned to your crazy ideas! You stick to your own line. Physick 'em when they're sick; get 'em on their feet and back to work; that's the way to earn your wages."

Horace said quietly, "I don't believe I'm the man for you, Mr. Latham."

(Now, he thought, it's all over. Five dollars a week tossed over my shoulder, and where am I to find any other chance as good?)

Mr. Latham took it calmly. "Independent, huh? Well, I'm not unfriendly to independence—when it doesn't go too far. Just you dose your patients and leave the running of the camp to me. We'll try it out for two weeks. At the end of that time, if you don't suit me, I'll pay up and no harm done. Eh?"

Horace stepped high as he walked back to his office. The dull room looked brighter, more homelike to him. It took him a moment to see why. Dinty's sampler hung on the wall, giving the whole place a touch of life and color that was like the reflection of her young vitality and mirth. That the purple-pink-green scheme was pretty garish he had to admit to himself, but the wording had dignity and was calculated to inspire his patients with a fitting sense of confidence and respect.

Where were the patients?

At the end of his first month's practice, Dr. Amlie entered in his day-book a disheartening computation. His total takings figured out to eighteen dollars and forty-eight cents.

That shrewd man of affairs, Decker Jessup, dropping in of an evening, supplied one reason for the scanty returns.

"It's your charges for treatment."

"Surely I am moderate," protested Horace. "Would you have me dispense my medicines at a loss?"

"You ask cash. Specie is scarce as hen's teeth in this region."

"I ask cash and get excuses," answered the young man sadly.

"Take what you can get," counseled the cobbler. "In winter the easiest-moved barter is gunpowder, prime pelts, cordwood up to what you need, and goosedown, but be sure it's goose. For this season, flaxseed, wheat, oats, or rye, and cheese. Don't take butter or vegetables, if you can help it. Whisky, rum, or brandy you can move any time. How much cash have you taken in this week?"

Horace reddened uncomfortably. "Less than five dollars."

"So! And part of that on the Bank of Whistleforit, I'll warrant you. Where's the profit in that?"

Reluctantly Horace crossed out the footline on his fee-list, substituting:

Barter Accepted at Current Rates.

Two patients had been steady in their attendance, both in the non-profit category. Dinty and Wealthia brought in their arms for inspection. Dinty's was healing nicely, but her friend, less docile to orders, had kept picking at the scab, and the area around it was still fevered after two weeks. Thus it happened that, overtaking his daughter in the garden as he came home to his noonday dinner, Genter Latham was surprised to have her wince away from his affectionate grasp on her arm.

"Hello! What's this?" he demanded.

"Nothing," she lied glibly. "A yellowjacket stung me."

"Let's see." Ignoring her objections, he examined the angry area with concern. "We'd better have Murchison take a look."

"Couldn't I have Dr. Amlie?" begged Wealthia. "Dr. Murchison is so snuffy and stuffy."

"That young man has yet to prove himself," returned her father with the good humor upon which she could always depend but never presume, since it did not interfere with his having his own way. "I'll send for Murchison."

The bearded practitioner responded with alacrity to the summons of his most important patient. He inspected the arm with narrowing eyes.

"Kine-pox poisoning," he pronounced. "Who performed the vaccination?"

"Vaccination?" roared Genter Latham. "What's this, Wealthy?"

"Please, Pa, dear, don't be mad with me. I couldn't help it." She recounted the episode, naturally casting the responsibility upon Dr. Amlie.

The father turned slowly from red to purple. Struggling for self-control, he asked the old physician, "Is there any warranty for the fellow's procedure without consulting me?"

"None at all, Mr. Latham," lied the physician. "Not the slightest. Most unseemly, sir. Medically most improper." He knew better, but here was his opportunity to discredit the young upstart.

"Can you do anything to relieve the arm?"

"We can bleed. The poisonous matter must be eliminated from the system. How long that will take depends on the amount of the rotted matter introduced into the veins," answered Murchison with malignant satisfaction.

"Don't let him do it, Pa. Please!" begged the girl. "It's getting better. Truly it is."

But it was not getting better. Poor Wealthia was soundly bled, purged, and puked, night and morning. Her father sent for Ephraim Upcraft, the self-stated Honest Lawyer. As was his custom in dealing with this autocratic client, Upcraft sounded him and then told him exactly what he wished to be told. They went to court together.

Timothy Mynderse, the constable, pinned on his badge, took his staff from the corner, and served the warrant of arrest upon Horace Amlie, M.D.

"What for?" demanded the astonished young man.

"It's all in the warrant. Atrocious assault on a minor child. Ten years in Auburn, I wouldn't wonder. Got any bail?" (Timothy hoped that the answer would be affirmative, as the jail was a casual affair, requiring constant official supervision to keep any prisoner so minded from kicking down the door and going about his business.)

"No. What bail? Where could I get bail?" asked Horace wildly.

"Ain't you got any friends?"

Horace thought of Squire Jerrold, but abandoned the idea. How could he know that there would not be a second charge on behalf of Dinty? There was Decker Jessup. The cobbler might be willing to help. He went to see him, accompanied by the official.

"Easy," said the cobbler. He put up a fifty-dollar bond with the magistrate. "Demand a jury trial," he advised. "The circuit won't be around for a month. That'll give us time. We'll diddle old Latham yet."

The arrest of the new doctor on the procurement of Genter Latham was the main topic of conversation at the smithy assemblage next day. Opinion was practically unanimous that the young sprig was done for. Best thing for him to do would be to skip his bail, saddle his nag, and dust off the highway. Only Silas Bewar, the blacksmith, took exception.

"Don't thee be too sure," said he. "That young man has a clear eye and a good conscience, or I miss my guess. He'll not be easy to drive."

Horace's situation was parlous. There was no other lawyer than Upcraft nearer than Canandaigua. Legal fees for his defense would run to twenty-five dollars and expenses. How could he afford so great a sum? Particularly as his remunerative employment at the canal camp was now irremediably lost.

One bit of evidence in his favor was that Dinty's arm was completely healed. Now, if Happalonia Vallance would only be so obliging as to come down with the smallpox, thus proving the effects of the exposure, his case would be sound. Though a humane and conscientious young gentleman who wished harm to none of God's creatures, Horace could not encounter Happalonia on the street without an irrepressibly avid scrutiny of her complexion. It remained dishearteningly pink, white and unblemished.

Poor Wealthia was having a bad time under the ministrations of Dr. Murchison. Her system, weakened by his potent measures, did not permit the arm to heal well. Moreover, the old fox was pursuing a strategic method of his own. Wealthia's legs broke out into an angry rash from the knee down, and the doctor, with a long face, told Mr. Latham, "I greatly fear that the disease, itself, has taken new hold."

"Will she die?" asked the distracted father.

"I will save her," promised Murchison. He had the best of reasons for confidence that she would not die. "I will save her," he repeated, "if she can be saved by the best resources of Science."

Gossip of the smithy passed a new tidbit from mouth to ear: Genter Latham had oiled up his pistol and sworn that he would kill young Amlie if little Wealthia died or if the poxes went to her face.

The source of this, it appeared, was Aunt Minnie Duryea, Wealthia's babyhood nurse, who had been called in. So Decker Jessup, alarmed, reported to Horace.

"Could you arrange for me to see Mrs. Duryea?" asked Horace.

"Surely. She's a cousin of mine. She don't like old Murch any too well."

They met secretly at the cobbler's shop. The old lady was vehement and voluble. Dr. Murchison wasn't doing the child any good with his drenches and squills, and now it was leeches on her poor, little legs to take down the swelling.

"Great, big, ugly, yellow blotches," she said.

Horace pricked up his ears. "What's that? Blotches?"

"Kind of muddy yellow. Filled with water, like. The leeches won't touch 'em."

"That isn't smallpox," said Horace positively, "nor pox poisoning."

"Don't look like it to me," agreed Aunt Minnie. "Looks like some kinda skulduggery to me."

Horace recalled the case of a Paris Hill boy who, having been exposed to smallpox, fooled the medical faculty for a time by breaking out into great, itchy weals, quite unlike the typical pustules of the disease. The experts believed that they had found a new manifestation, until the true nature of the ailment was discovered. This sounded suspiciously like the same thing.

"There's no rash on her face, neck or arms?" he asked.

"No. Only the vaccination spot. I noticed the Doctor rubbing her legs one day before they broke out."

"Before?" said Horace quickly. "You're sure it was before?"

"I'm pretty sure there wasn't anything there."

"Did he wear gloves when he rubbed her?"

"Yes, he did, now that you speak of it. I thought he was afraid of catching the smallpox."

"Will you do something for me, Aunt Minnie? I want you to prick two or three of the blisters and bring the liquid to me. You'd better wash your hands well after doing it."

She was back in a few minutes with some of the exudation in a small vial, reporting that the patient's arm seemed easier, but her legs itched her cruel.

Right here Horace badly needed a medical witness. The nearest approach to it in the village was the dubious personage who presided at the Sign of the Streaked Pole, and called himself L. Brooks, M.D. Of his professional title and knowledge, Horace was extremely skeptical. However, in as simple a matter as the present purpose, he might do.

Carefully anointing the inner side of his forearm with the serum taken from Wealthia's blisters, Horace waited. Soon the flesh began to redden. Presently it itched angrily. Blisters formed and slowly filled. At the end of three hours the arm presented a fine, typical appearance. It's owner took it to the Sign of the Streaked Pole.

"I have a rash," said he, rolling up his sleeve. "I should like your opinion upon it."

The barber looked and grinned. "That ain't no rash," he pronounced. "You been handlin' pizen oak. Soak it in sugar of lead and don't scratch to spread it."

"You're a better doctor than some in this village," said Horace grimly. "I'll have a shave."

But when Horace broached the subject of his coming trial and asked L. Brooks to testify as an expert witness, the barber turned pale.

"Put myself forward against Genter Latham? You must think I'm a booby. Why, he'd ruin my trade as soon as spit. He'd fetch another hairdresser to town, and where'd I be? Not me! I got a family to support."

"They're a spineless lot in this town," Horace subsequently complained to Decker Jessup.

"Well, I dunno, I dunno," demurred the cobbler. "Genter's a hard man to brook. Many a stout fella he's run out of Palmyra. They deserved it, I guess, by and large, but that wouldn't make any odds to him. Cross his path and his purpose, and he won't endure to breathe the same air with you. There's only one man's stood up to him, far's I know."

"I'd like to meet him and shake his hand."

"You met him. Silverhorn Ramsey."

"That young scalawag!" Horace smiled. "What was wrong between Latham and him?"

The cobbler lowered his voice. "Sarah Dorch."

"The young woman who had smallpox?"

"She didn't always have smallpox. You ought to have seen her before." He smacked appreciative lips. "Um—ah-h-h-h!"

"What's the connection?" asked Horace.

"We—ell, Genter Latham's a lusty widower and Sarah Dorch is —was—a mighty sightly gal who liked gewgaws and pretty duds. I reckon that side door of the Latham house got its hinges oiled pretty often so's they wouldn't creak at night. Then, one evening, Latham walks into the Eagle parlor like he owned the place, and there sits Sarah and Silverhorn smiling across two glasses of flip. Latham stood there staring, till the gal saw him and gave a cackle and scuttled home like a scared pullet.

"Next morning our young buck was swaggering down Main Street, dandling his bugle-horn, when Latham took him by a shoulder and shoved him into the ell of the building. You can bet, nobody came near to eavesdrop. What was said exactly we'll never know. But Latham was black as thunder's self when the young fellow slipped around him with a laugh. Silverhorn lifted his trumpet and blew his ta-ra-ra-ra. The folks came, a-running.

" 'Oyez! Oyez! Oyez!' says he like the court crier. 'I've a public word to say. Mr. Genter Latham prefers my room to my company. He'll have me clapt into quod as a ne'erdoweel and a vagabond if I show my cabeza again in town. So says he. But hark ye, friends. And hark ye, Mr. Genter Latham. Lay me by the heels and you'd best keep that little wren of a daughter in a locked cage, for, so help me Almighty God and the American flag! the next band of tenkers to wagon it this way will take her where you won't see her again. Or, if not the next, some other company. So sandpaper your nose with that!'

"There was a kind of sickish silence. Everybody knows that Silverhorn, for all that he's an educated scholar, has truck with tenkers and gyppos and horse-copers and the like. Mr. Latham's face was like death and murder. But he only gave a kind of croak in his throat and went away, walking blind and brushing folks aside like so many straws."

"What happened to the girl?"

"Sarah? Oh, she kept on with Latham. All this was a year ago. Then she caught smallpox, and he hasn't laid eye or hand on her since. They say he's afraid to."

Horace shook his head. "There would be no danger of contagion now."

"It isn't that. He's afraid of what he might see. Right, too." The cobbler shuddered sympathetically. "She's an awful sight, poor lass, let alone what pain she suffers."

"Suffers?" said Horace. "Physically, do you mean? That shouldn't be."

"Her face never healed since."

"Who is treating her?"

"Murchison was till her money gave out."

"Send her to me," said Horace.

"You're a kind young fellow," said the cobbler. He sighed. "I used to be kinda piney on Sarah, myself."

Casting about him for any possible help, Horace wrote to his old preceptor, Dr. Vought, now in Rochesterville, stating his predicament. Reply was received by the next coach from the fiery old gentleman.

> Stick to your post, my boy. I'll come up and help you at the trial. I know your precious lot. Genter Latham is a bully. Gail Murchison is the bastard offspring of a skunk mated with a rattlesnake. Upcraft is so crooked that if you threw him into Ganargwa Creek he would float upstream. All Palmyra is a hotbed of smug Federalism and aristocracy. Let them catch their small or any other pox and die and rot of it for all of me. But you are too good a lad to be beaten by them. Count on me. Draw on me, too, up to a hundred if you need the ready. I was young once, myself, and still have a fight left in me.

Sarah Dorch, veiled and timorous, added to his list of free patients. The cobbler's statement of her condition was not exaggerated. But what most shocked Horace in her appearance was that there was no occasion for it. An eczema which followed the pitting had been grossly aggravated by Murchison's inept or careless treatment. Horace compounded a bland ointment of beeswax, honey and boric acid for the open sores and arranged for the patient to pay him daily visits. She was wretched but grateful.

After mulling over the case of Wealthia Latham, Horace committed an inexcusable breach of ethics by visiting surreptitiously another physician's case, having persuaded Aunt Minnie Duryea to smuggle him into the Latham home while its master was absent. Under strict injunctions of secrecy, he examined Wealthia and treated her poisoned legs. In two days she was up and about.

There was now but a week to go before court convened. Lawyer Upcraft stopped Horace in the street.

"I have a message from Mr. Latham."

"What is it?"

"He stands ready to withdraw his criminal charge."

Horace's heart bounded. The hardshell magnate had relented now that his daughter was well. His hopes were promptly dashed by the lawyer's next words.

"On condition that you close your office and quit town within a week."

Horace's face grew white, then red. In reverse order these colors mean surrender, in this order, fight.

"Your answer," pressed Upcraft.

"What would you think it would be?" said Horace grimly.

"I warn you, young man. It's that or jail."

Horace turned and left him.

That night Horace lay awake long considering his plight. An expedient suggested itself. It was theatrical, sensational, perhaps cheap; but for that very reason it might be successful. Genter Latham's vulnerable point was his love for Wealthia and his pride in her budding beauty. From this angle Horace plotted his attack.

Pocketing his pride, he went to the Latham place. The mogul was sitting on his veranda, enjoying an after-dinner segar.

"Mr. Latham."

The formidable brows drew down. "Well, sir?"

"I have heard it said that you are a fair man."

This was a judicious mixture of speculation and flattery. Being anything but fair in his dealings with his fellows, the town great man would probably pride himself upon the very quality which he most signally lacked.

"I am a just man," said Genter Latham coldly.

"Mr. Upcraft delivered your message."

"You have six days left."

"Will you come to my office at four o'clock this afternoon?"

"Why should I?"

"It concerns your daughter."

The hostile eyes bored into his. "In what way?"

"I can explain only at my office." Horace plunged. "If you then insist upon it, I will quit my practice."

The smile that thinned Latham's lips could hardly be said to soften the menace of his expression.

"Very well. I'll humor you so far. Four o'clock."

At a quarter before that hour a veiled young woman turned into Canandaigua Road and mounted the Harte steps. Dr. Amlie seated her, half facing the door, and made his inspection.

"There is an improvement already," he pronounced. "Doesn't it feel easier?"

"It doesn't itch me so cruel," said Sarah Dorch.

He busied himself with the dressings. The girl sat rigid, mute and patient. At the end she asked wistfully, "Shall I ever be sightly again, Doctor?"

"You'll be free of the itching. So much I can promise you."

"There's someone coming," said she, and stretched a hand for her veil.

"Do you mind leaving it off for a moment?" he asked gently.

Genter Latham entered. At first he stared without recognition at the shocking visage.

"Gent—Mr. Latham," she murmured.

"*Sally!*" He backed slowly away from her. She sobbed once.

"Tomorrow at the same hour, Sarah," said Horace.

She rose, swathed her head in the black, obscuring folds, and crept out. Genter Latham's eyes, slow in a rigid face, followed her until the door closed.

"Is there anything to be done for her?" he asked hoarsely.

"Not very much."

"Do what you can. Send the bill to me."

"Very well, Mr. Latham."

The magnate lingered. He asked in a strained voice, "If Sally had been vaccinated . . ."

"Well?" prompted Horace.

". . . would she have escaped—that?"

"Probably."

With a painful effort Latham said, "She came to me for the money to take her to Canandaigua for the treatment."

"And you refused her?"

The man's face was ghastly. "I didn't grudge the money. It wasn't that. I thought the whole thing was damned foolishness."

"God forgive you!"

"Do everything you can for her." Still he did not leave. Finally it came out. "Wealthia," he stammered, "would she have been—like that?"

"Nobody can tell," answered Horace honestly. "She might have been."

With a desperate gesture, Genter Latham stumbled to the door and out.

Dr. Amlie wrote gratefully to Dr. Vought that there was now no need of his proffered help. At the behest of the complainant, the criminal charge had been withdrawn.

-9-

Who would Think, dear Diary, that Holy Writ could get a little Girl into so Much Trouble?

(DINTY'S DIARY)

It was Horace Amlie's habit to supplement his reading, Scriptural and profane, by scribbling notes of passages which he deemed specially applicable to himself. Dinty came upon one of these bits of paper which fluttered to the floor under the vigor of her dusting, and read it, first to herself, then aloud to her companion.

" 'Wisely has St. Paul said, "It is better to marry than to burn." He is the most human of all the Saints.' "

"What does it mean?" asked Wealthia languidly.

Dinty's brow furrowed. "Something," she answered. "I don't know just what. I could ask Doc." In conversation with her trusted friend she derived a reckless thrill from the use of a term which she would never have ventured to use to the gentleman's face.

"Maybe it's private," suggested Wealthia.

"Scripture's never private," said Dinty. "I'll take it for my text on Sunday."

"Without knowing what it means?"

"If I sit down and think hard about it," responded Dinty with that sunny confidence in herself which was seldom lacking from her approach to a subject, "I'll be sure to find out. If I don't, Miss Agatha will tell us."

At Miss Levering's Sunday afternoon Bible Class for the Young, each pupil was expected to present a text and offer a brief commentary thereon. Usually the selection was performed by the parents who also supplied the interpretation. Not for Dinty. She preferred to rely upon her own erudition, which was considerable, as she constantly explored recondite portions of the Scriptures, stimulated thereto more by curiosity than piety.

Several members of the class had droned out their short and innocuous offerings, when Dinty took the floor.

"My text," she announced, "is, 'It is better to marry than to burn.' "

Miss Agatha gave a maidenly start. "Do you think you understand the subject, Araminta?" she asked apprehensively.

"Oh, yes, Miss Agatha! I've thought it all out."

"Then you may proceed."

"There was a young man," began Dinty, "and he got a young lady into trouble."

"Araminta!" cried the teacher faintly.

"What kind of trouble?" put in Freegrace Fairlie, who had a thirst for information.

"Just trouble," answered Dinty. "I don't know what kind." Miss Agatha breathed a sigh of relief. "I heard my mother talking about a girl that got into trouble once, but she snapped my ear when I asked her how. It's got something to do with getting married, though." She resumed her exposition. "So the young lady's brothers came to the young man and said, "You've got to marry our sister or we'll burn you at the stake.' "

"Was he a witch?" asked Happalonia Vallance. "I thought they only burned witches at the stake. Were there men-witches? I thought only women could be witches."

"There is no instance in Holy Writ of a man being a witch," said Miss Levering. "I think, Araminta, that we have heard . . ."

"Anyway," broke in Dinty, quick to forestall a quietus on her further discourse, "he didn't want to marry her at all. So the young men arose and wound him up and carried him out, and when he saw the fire, he cried in a loud voice, 'Leave me loose! It is better to marry than to burn.' And so they were married and lived happily ever after, and the last state of that man was worse than the first."

"Araminta," said her teacher, "do your parents know about your text?"

"No, Miss Agatha. I got it from Dr. Amlie."

The effect shocked her. Miss Agatha turned so fiery a red that even the dovelike gray of her eyes caught a spark of it.

"Dr. Amlie?" she repeated in a failing voice.

"Yes, ma'am. Well, St. Paul, too, Dr. Amlie wrote it out and it fell on the floor. I thought it must be all right if it was from the Bible. Isn't it?"

"You are a wicked little minx," cried Miss Agatha, and adjourned the class.

Worse was to come. Dinty went to Dr. Amlie for enlightenment and comfort. She got neither.

"You told Miss Levering that *I* wrote that text?" he demanded, turning almost as scarlet as had the young lady.

"You and St. Paul," faltered Dinty.

"Go home!"

"Yes, sir," gulped Dinty, trying to restrain herself short of the weakness of tears. "I'm sorry. I'll go. But, please, Dr. Amlie, won't you tell me just one thing about what you—St. Paul, I mean, meant?"

"No!" he thundered and she staggered out, stricken.

Dinty's revelations forced upon the maiden mind of Miss Agatha Levering matters from which she had always withheld her thoughts. After the Bible Class session, though she retired to her bedchamber to blush unseen and there took refuge in cold compresses and delicate whiffs of Millefleurs and Florida water, she could not rid her brain of its perturbations. The conviction that Horace Amlie was burning for her would not be exorcised. What the nature of that flame was, she shrank from conjecturing. Surely no modest virgin could be expected to understand, much less respond to it. "Better to marry than to burn." Is *that* what men married for! The very idea that she had inspired such an emotion horrified and flattered her.

Yet the maiden was mistaken in her assumption. The immediate inspiration of the Amlie-St. Paul collaboration lay not in her charms (although she had her part in it) but in those of another. The sprightly Miss Sylvia Sartie of the Archbold-and-Clarendon thespians had written him again to say that, owing to financial complications common to the profession, the return engagement in Palmyra was postponed, but that the troupe would surely be there in late October. She was, so she wrote,

> . . . looking foreward Eegerly to seeing you and Renewing our Friendship. You were so Kind to me that I am boldened to say that I mite be Kinder to you. And I remane
>
> Your obed't servant
>
> Miss Sylvia Sartie of the Lyceum Company

Certainly Dinty's Bible Class exercise had painfully complicated the budding relationship between the two marriageable young persons. Consciousness of an awkward situation abashed Horace. As for Agatha, when next they met, at a Wednesday afternoon church sociable, she regarded him with a furtive and timorous surmise, such as might have been bestowed upon a domestic animal suddenly run rampant with alarming symptoms. Their conversation was formal, guarded and neutral.

Among those present was Dinty Jerrold, who observed it all with perturbation. Would Dr. Amlie ever forgive her?

Always for the direct and human approach, she gathered from the tamarack bog a great nosegay of the lovely white polly-whog blooms, which she interspersed with stalks of the pure-blue chicory (her Pa said her eyes were exactly that color) and carried it to Dr. Amlie's office in his absence, lifting the window to admit it. What she saw within shocked her soul. Everything was in musty disorder. A little shower of dust, dislodged from the sill, spattered the slip of paper on which she had written in a disguised (but not too much so) hand,

"With Love and Duty from
A Well-wisher."

Three hours later, dressed in her primmest, even to gıay net gloves borrowed from her mother, she walked around to Canandaigua Road toward the close of office hours when she was sure that nobody would be there. Probably nobody would be there at any time, she thought pityingly.

Dr. Amlie was seated at his desk, reading. He lifted his head. His regard was uncompromisingly hostile.

"Consultation, three to four P.M.," said Dinty in a small resolute voice.

"Consultation?"

"My heart hurts."

"Nonsense!"

"It does, so. And I have spots before my eyes."

"Indeed?"

"My pulse is funny, too."

"Anything else?"

"My blood is sluggish, and my lungs act queer, and my skin is febrile," said Dinty in a rush, her memory doing very well by her in the matter of earlier surreptitious medical research among the Amlie volumes. "And—and—and it's all your fault," she ended on a catch of the breath, abandoning literature for life. "You're mean to me."

"Stand here," directed Dr. Amlie in his professional tone.

Dinty placed herself before the desk. His sinewy hands gripped her shoulders. He shook her till her teeth chattered and her eyes popped, then picked her up and set her on the desk with a bump that jarred her to her toes.

"There!" said he. "That will teach you, young lady." He kissed her soundly. Dinty beamed.

"I knew when you got mad at me, you'd get glad again," she said sweetly. "If you hadn't, I'd have died."

"Just the same, you're a meddlesome imp and a limb of Satan."

"I don't care. Now may I clean up?"

"Yes."

"And have you missed me?"

"I have so," he admitted.

Dinty, sweeping dustily, borrowed a phrase from the Rev. Mr. Strang. "I trust that the Lord has been prospering you in your chosen calling."

"Not specially," answered Horace with a grimace.

"I think folks are *mean!*" scolded Dinty. "If they weren't so dumb they'd know how wonderful and wise you are and nobody'd ever go to any other doctor."

"I don't know how they're going to find out," said Horace glumly.

The light of a great thought gleamed in his little friend's eyes. "I do," she murmured. Unfortunately he paid no heed at the time.

Though the townsfolk withheld their patronage with the conservatism which distrusts all that is young and new, outlying custom began to come in. By word-of-mouth communication, the good news had spread among the scattered clearings that the new doctor knew his trade and was not so hard a dealer as Dr. Murchison, who would often be too busy to answer a call where payment was doubtful or slow. Rough, lean, hard-bitten farmers, hunters and woodcutters appeared at the Canandaigua Road office, with ax-wounds, tree-felling bruises, and snake or wild-animal bites. Sometimes they brought their womenfolk.

Too often there were tragedies. Not until they were in desperate case would these wilderness wives abandon their household duties and spare time and money for a visit to the doctor. They came to Horace, swollen with cancer, wasted with fevers, or worn bone-thin by the cruel privations and hardships of the struggle for existence on the fringe of civilization. For, even in prosperous Western New York, the frontier was anywhere and everywhere a mile back of traveled highway or traffic-bearing stream.

Patiently the young physician sought in his well-stocked library for treatment that would aid his sick. He met with contradictions, asumptions, evasions that all but wrecked his faith in science. Remedies which had wrought miracles in the text failed utterly in his hands. Yet he had conscientiously followed the directions of the most eminent authorities, as far as he could make them out. One line of practice was easy to adopt, the depletion method which had come down the ages as an all but universal gospel. He had bled, he had cupped, he had purged, he had squilled. In spite of all, his fever-shriveled patients from the wilds went home to die. Probably they would have died anyway. But where, then, were the boasted wonders of medical science?

Heresy and rebellion ran hot in his veins. For a fip he would have thrown those learned and lying volumes out the window.

In one department, at least, he could give full value of his services. Childbirth was no guesswork, and he was a competent obstetrician. Demand for such skill was limited in town since the upper-class ladies deemed it more modest to employ a midwife, while the poor relied upon home obstetrics and the good offices of the neighbors. In the outlying districts, however, Horace began to build up a far-flung practice when it became known that no journey was too arduous for the new Doc to undertake in case of need. For some of these calls he was paid as high as two dollars, though seldom in cash.

After an all-night vigil, terminating in twins, at a young trapper's shack near the headwaters of Red Creek, the physician returned to town with his fee tethered in the box of the wagon—three yearling shoats who, as the equipage entered town, lifted their voices in the Exile's Lament for Home. To young Dr. Amlie's painted self-consciousness, it seemed that the entire populace was out on Main Street that morning.

Queer wagonloads were too common for notice, but the spectacle of the dignified young physician in his beaver hat and skirted coat acting as jehu to a trio of vociferous porkers aroused the primitive sense of humor among the inhabitants. Small boys ran, whooping, alongside the equipage. Groups formed on corners to goggle and giggle. O. Daggett thrust his head out of the window, with jaw dropped and eyes staring. Genter Latham accorded the outfit a grim smile. Carisle Sneed supported his reputation for mordant wit by shouting,

"Takin' your patients home with you, Doc?"

T. Lay ("Buys Anything") bawled, "Give you six shillin' for the lot."

Other humorous-minded citizens raised the bid. Stimulated by the clamor, the nostalgic pigs lamented their rapine in lugubrious chorus, with a popular response of grunts, snorts, squeals and hog-calls of *"Peeg!*—Peeg-peeg-peeg!" Yes, Palmyra was thoroughly enjoying itself.

So was not Dr. Horace Amlie, close-lipped and hot-eyed in his seat.

Nor was Miss Agatha Levering, who emerged from the Cheap Store with a tasty pipsissiway lozenge under her tongue, and straightway lost all zest for it. Averting her face from the shameful sight, she hastily withdrew.

A solemn-eyed little damsel appeared at Horace's office on the following morning.

"It was awful," she began. "I could have *cried.*"

Horace agreed that it was awful.

"You mustn't let it ever happen again."

Horace had no wish that it should ever happen again, and said so explicitly.

"It won't do any good to swear," said Dinty. "You must have a gig."

"A what?"

"A nice doctor's gig. Like Old Murch's."

"Gigs," Horace pointed out, "cost money."

"Thirty-five dollars," said Dinty.

"I haven't got thirty-five dollars to spare."

"Mr. Latham would let you have it, I'm sure," said she. "Pa always hires money of Mr. Latham when he's short."

"I've never been in debt and I never mean to be," asserted Horace. "Besides, I've got a little money put by with my uncle in Utica," he admitted waveringly.

Dinty's eyes sparkled. "How much?"

"A hundred dollars. Maybe a little more."

"How much more? Fifty more?"

"No. And besides . . ."

"Twenty more?"

"Yes. About."

"A hundred-and-twenty," she cried triumphantly. "Send for it."

"All of it? What for?"

"To get you up, fine and pompous, the way we want you to look. Wealthy and I, we've got it all planned out for you."

"Oh, you have, have you! Well, let me tell you, young lady . . ."

"No, please, Doc—I mean Doctor. Wait till you see Wealthy. She's out getting prices and samples from the shops."

Though Dinty was the guiding spirit of the pair in all other enterprises, in social matters Wealthia took undisputed lead. She arrived presently, her great, dark eyes lustrous with anticipation, her dainty hands clutching samples and bits of paper.

"Now," said Dinty, "let's pretend you're our brother and our parents are dead, so we have to look after you. You tell him, Wealthy."

"We think," said the older girl with the confidence of one on her own special ground, "that your wardrobe needs replenishing." (The phrase was borrowed from an advertisement in that week's *Sentinel.*)

"What's wrong with it?" demanded Horace uneasily. He felt suddenly shabby.

"Everything," was the firm reply.

He struggled feebly against the items put forward for his consideration by the two small invaders, but finally surrendered with a wry acceptance, which was partly anticipation. Horace found himself committed to the following outlay:

14 yards velvet in three colors for pantaloons at 6 s, 6 d. yer y'd.
¾ y'd linings at 3 s.
3 skeins silk at 6 s. 2 d.
Thread, 4 d.
Twist, 1 D.
3 y'ds black supercloth for coat, $17.50.
8 y'ds shirting for common wear at 1 s. 3 d. per y'd.
6 y'ds shirting for church and social gatherings at 2 s. 6 d.
Thread, 1 s. 3 d.

Not until the bills came in did Horace realize how few dollars would be left in his reserve fund.

So be it! At least he would be living up to his position, while the position lasted. And if his hopes collapsed, he would go down with colors flaunting, three pairs of velvet pantaloons, a skirted coat to challenge anybody's eye, and a tartan neckcloth with brooch, not to be equaled short of Albany.

"Besides," said Dinty with an assurance which should have set him on guard, "you're going to have heaps and heaps of calls pretty soon. Isn't he, Wealthy?"

Wealthia giggled and agreed. Horace muttered that he hoped so but saw no signs of it.

He saw them soon enough. What amounted to a near-rush of trade set in. If it was not precisely the type to which his ambitions had looked, if none of the important inhabitants sought his skill in that first, inexplicable wave, if the cases were minor ailments at first, nevertheless the encouragement warmed Horace's hopes. Hardly could he believe his eyes when he looked over the record of that first rush-day business.

Item: Sammy Dorch had a sty. Lanced. Item: Linzy, the maltster's apprentice, wambled in with his throat bound in red flannel and goose-grease. Cupped. Item: Bub Jones, horse-boy at the Exchange Hotel, brought for inspection a ripe black eye. Leeched. Item: O. Daggett's two nieces, having overstuffed at the Methodist Church festival, were constipated. Purged. Item: Sally Moore, hen-hussey for the Leverings, came weeping over a felon on her finger. Opened and dressed. Item: Mindus Adams had a toothache but shrank from an extraction. Ether-paint. Items: sundry slivers, scratches and scarifications from Poverty's Pinch where anything that broke the skin was typically followed by inflammation. Salved, patched and bandaged. All of it fell short of a lucrative practice. But, if continued, it would give the young doctor enough work to do to keep him from brooding, and enhance his first-hand acquaintance with the ills that flesh is heir to, which, as Dr. Vought used to assert, was the better fifty per centum of medical education.

The second day was even better than the first. After dismissing the last patient, Horace walked down to the cobbler's shop to tell him of the improved status.

"That's the way to get 'em!" approved Decker Jessup.

"What way?" Horace failed to understand.

"Advertise."

"Quacks advertise. I'd scorn to do it."

"Say!" Decker Jessup jeered. "D'you see anything the matter with my eyes?"

Horace felt the first, faint stirrings of uneasiness. "What have your eyes been seeing?"

"You wait here till school's out and you'll see it with your own peepers."

Persuasion could get nothing more out of him but a series of deep chuckles and a reference to O. Daggett being a dab at a quick job.

Horace had not long to wait. Far down Main Street he saw a horse shy and move hastily over to the curb. The cause hove in sight. Down the middle of the highway marched four of the little Sunbeams, two-

and-two. They bore, upright and extended, a placard boldly lettered in O. Daggett's most flagrant style. At first the script danced before Horace's vision, but presently took on form and legibility.

"Hey!" said Decker Jessup, alarmed. "What's the matter? Took sick?"

Horace uttered an anguished yelp. This is what he read:

Are You Sick or Ailing?
COME & BE CURED
by
DR. AMLIE M.D.
The Best Doctor in Town.
No Cure No Pay

Horace struggled manfully against a devastating fury which, he told himself, was as unreasonable as it was futile. Plainly this was Dinty's doing, poor Dinty whose intentions were always of the best.

He went forth to a bloodless victory. The parade was dispersed without disorder. Dinty did not understand, but one look at her adored doctor's face apprised her that the occasion was unpropitious for protest or question. She scuttled, and after her scuttled the other Little Sunbeams.

-10-

I know Something I won't tell.
Doctor A. and Aggie L.

(DINTY'S DIARY)

BEHOLD now a new Dr. Horace Amlie, illumining the sedate streets of Palmyra with his splendency. The high-wheeled gig, decorously drawn by Fleetfoot, was a glowing spectacle with its dark-blue caduceus against cream-yellow—O. Daggett had outdone himself for friendship's sake—its crimson running gear picked out with white, and its slender, beribboned whip curving in the socket. At the side of the occupant his saddlebox was strapped to the iron seat-stanchions by the thongs whose normal use was to hold it to the saddle when he mounted Fleetfoot for such excursions as took him upon paths not negotiable by wheels. It was fitted with twelve featherglass vials for the tinctures, eight tin canisters for powders and pellets, and, in the opposite compartment, his obstetrical outfit, dental forceps, lancets, probes, and stethoscope.

Emotion swelled Dinty's bosom thus to see him in his glory. For, was not this her handiwork; hers and Wealthia's? She felt within her the ineffable thrill of creation. Dr. Horace, in his full regalia, was, indeed, she proudly told herself, a pompous sight.

Dinty's was not the only heart to be flustered by the pleasing apparition. Miss Agatha Levering, passing on some worthy errand, observed, blushed, and took a decision. Dr. Amlie was invited to the Levering mansion to supper. Thereafter, in rapid sequence, Dr. Amlie became a regular caller, and was presently installed as the Levering family consultant, vice Dr. Murchison, dismissed. There were phases of the young man's character which fell short of Levering standards, to be sure. In religious matters, he was a loose, if not a free, thinker. He had explicitly declined to take the Total Abstinence pledge. It was known that he raced his mare, believed in free education, and, though a sound enough Clintonian, admired the rabble-rousing scoundrel, Andy Jackson. But he was obviously a Rising Young Man. And Daughter Agatha was going on twenty.

The maiden's attitude toward her suitor—for, as such, the village now regarded him—was one of modest and flattering deference. With docile eyes she consulted him on a wide variety of lay problems, from the spicing of preserves to the hue of a hair ribbon. In a score of subtle ways she made him feel his masculine superiority. But if he so much as essayed to hold her hand, she quivered away with a look of panic.

Horace tingled with frustration. The painfully extreme propriety and restraint of courtship on so elevated a plane was rasping his nerves. What ailed the girl? Wasn't she human? If ever he did marry her, he grimly warranted his soul, he would resolve that chilling correctitude. Or could he? Or any other man? Still—it was better to marry than to burn.

Fires by no means hymeneal cast their heat ahead from another quarter. Horace saw, in his copy of *The Register,* the announcement of the Lyceum Company's deferred engagement, to be fulfilled on the last three evenings of October, but a fortnight away. The vision of Sylvia Sartie brightened with unseemly radiance in his mind.

Horace's twenty-second birthday was on the nineteenth. There came to his office on the anniversary morning a package tied with festal ribbons and bearing the inscription, "Friendship's Offering." Within was a sampler in cool colors, pink and pale blue, worked by Miss Levering's own fair hands. It was beautiful craftsmanship. The motto which it presented was impeccable in taste and morals, and garnished with a Scriptural text which had no connection with St. Paul. Such is the froward and irreclaimable spirit of man that, when he had hung it on his wall opposite Dinty's similar gift, he found himself preferring the amateurish to the expert performance. Notwithstanding, he wrote Agatha a letter of gratitude, embellished with recondite verbal elegances and apt quotations.

Though unable to divine why Dr. Amlie had taken so amiss the Little Sunbeams' attempt to improve his financial circumstances, Dinty and Wealthia had deemed it prudent to keep away for a few days and let his wrath simmer down. When Dinty estimated that the cooling-off process ought to be sufficiently advanced for safety, she presented herself at the office, bearing as peace offering a basket of herbs and simples which she and Tip Crego had gathered the night before.

"In the full of the moon," she informed the recipient.

"That gives them special virtue, I suppose."

"Of course. You must always cull herbs in the full and hunt treasure in the dark of the moon. Everybody knows that."

"Are you still up to those night-wandering tricks of yours? What would your parents say?"

"Oh, they'd have conniption fits. What they don't know won't hurt 'em."

"Is that honest, Dinty?"

The small, plump face took on a pathetic cast. "If I didn't get to go out once in awhile I'd *bust.* Mistress Crego told Tip I had gypsy blood in me, and when the night calls, the blood has got to answer. Don't you ever feel that way? Didn't you ever run on All Hallowe'en?"

"When I was your age I suppose I did."

"Hallowe'en's different, though. That isn't like woods-running. All the boys and girls come out then and some of the grown-up folks. You must hang a candle-punkin or a colored glass ball in your window for a witchguard. Wouldn't you like to come out with us just a little while?" she coaxed.

Horace declined politely. He had an engagement which he did not deem it necessary to mention to his young friend. Hallowe'en would close the local run of the Lyceum troupe, and Miss Sylvia Sartie would be free till the following morning.

Had there been a local item column in the press of the day, it would have chronicled that Dr. Horace Amlie was a first-nighter at the rendition of *The Spectre Bridegroom,* a second-nighter at the presentation of *How to Die for Love* and a third-nighter at the *gala* performance of *The Road to Ruin.* Had there been a gossip column (as there was, not so much later), it might have reported that a Certain Young Medico was seen supping with a Dainty Daughter of Thespis after the drop of the curtain. The consistory of the blacksmith shop, where such news was canvassed, avidly discussed both reunions and recalled the former acquaintance between the young people. Whatever the effect upon Horace's reputation in more lofty circles, among these avowedly virile citizens it was enhanced. They approved him as a rollicking blade. They recalled and recounted their own amorous adventures in personal experiences of which the zest was equaled only by the inventiveness, until the Quaker spirit of

Silas Bewar revolted and he bade them either curb their tongues or befoul some other air than that of a decent smithy.

The unquenchable Carlisle Sneed started an appropriate ditty:

> The woodpecker flew
> From his nest, in the night
> And the red on his noddle
> Was shining and bright—

when an ominous movement on the smith's part caused him to complete the air by whistling.

Nine o'clock was bedtime for the respectable except on social occasions when the hour might be extended to ten. Eleven of All Saint's Eve had struck on the tall clock with wooden works in the Jerrolds' stair-embrasure, when the mistress of the household raised her head from the pillow and pushed an elbow into her husband's ribs.

"Hark!"

A whippoorwill was sounding its impatient, insistent call somewhere very near.

"Whatsa matter?" grumbled Squire Jerrold.

"It's on our roof."

"What if it is?"

"Oh, Archibald! Don't you know it's a sign of death to someone underneath when a whippoorwill sings on the rooftree?" she quavered.

Her husband turned his better ear to the window. "Kiss the cow good-bye, then," he said. "That bird is on the barn." He settled down. "Go back to sleep," he grunted and set the example.

In her chamber below, Dinty slipped from her rope bed and put on her shoes. Otherwise she was fully clothed. After listening for any sign of vigilance above, she let herself down from the low window.

"I thought you were *never* coming, Tip."

"It wasn't easy, giving the slip to the others."

"Where are we going?"

"Presbyterian churchyard."

"Oo—oo—oo! Aren't you scared?"

"What of?"

"Ghosts. Witches. It's almost midnight."

"I'd like to see a ghost," said the boy seriously. "That's what we're going for. Besides, we'll be ghosts, ourselves."

He brought out their regalia, a pair of head-sized pumpkins, two hop-poles, and two sheets ravished from the clothesline of some unwary housewife who had forgotten that it was a night of license and depredations.

"If you aren't scared, I'm not, either," declared Dinty more stoutly than truthfully. "You'll have to do the talking if we see one," she added in prudent afterthought.

They took position in an alder copse to await the mystic hour when some unresting spirit might elect to return to earth. Tip was for old Capt. Jabez Wheeler, a Lake Ontario skipper whose profanity was so awful that it was credited with bringing on the gale in which he and his crew had perished. Dinty's selection lay beneath one of the ancient skull-and-bones granites, an ill-reputed Dame Mitchin who was suspected of having poisoned in rapid succession her husband's dog, his pig, and himself, and known to have died later by her own potion. It would be interesting, though terrifying, Dinty thought, if the old miscreant would rise up and make confession.

The watchers did not have to wait for midnight. Two dark figures materialized from nowhere among the graves. Low voices reached their ears. Shivering, Dinty clutched her companion.

"It's them!"

"Those aren't ghosts. They're folks," whispered Tip.

"Who?"

"I can't see. It's too dark."

"Let's run."

"No. I'm going to haunt 'em if nothing else does."

Horace Amlie was talking, low and nervously, to the girl at his side as they entered the silence and darkness beneath the trees. He was not feeling very comfortable. If not wholly inexperienced, he was no libertine, no practiced Don Juan. But the pressure of Sylvia Sartie's arm in his, the soft warmth of her body were stimulating. He wondered whether he dared try to smuggle her into his rooms; how she would receive such a suggestion. His whispered broaching of the subject was halting and equivocal.

There was nothing equivocal about her kiss. Nor about the welkin-rending shriek that interrupted it. Miss Sartie's soprano may have been heard to better advantage but never in fuller volume nor inspired of more emotional stress. A white and wavery apparition had risen to monstrous height before her horrified eyes and was advancing upon her and her companion. Frantically tearing herself from his embrace, she sprinted for the lights of Main Street and the world of the living as fast as a pair of sturdy legs would bear her.

Horace, startled and angry, made a grab at the ghost. The hop-pole dipped. The sheeting shimmered to the ground. Tip Crego's dismayed voice said,

"Oh, Dr. Amlie! I didn't know it was you."

Wondering how much the boy had seen, Horace said lamely, "I was escorting Miss Sartie to look at the tombstones."

"Did we scare her?" asked Tip.

"You apparently did," answered Horace grimly.

The second ghost sidled up. It said in Dinty's most demure manner,

"Good evening, Dr. Amlie."

"Good evening."

"He was showing Miss Sartie the tombstones," explained Tip.

"I think that's very nice and hospitable of him," said Dinty.

Horace glared at her. In what little light there was, her uplifted, innocently admiring face seemed to bespeak a guileless soul, incapable of sardonic suppressions.

"You ought to be in bed," said he shortly.

For once Dinty was meek. "I'll go if you say so," she murmured. "Come on, Tip. We've got to put the sheets back. Yours is pesky muddy."

All the ardor had oozed out of the adventure for Horace. Inclination pointed him homeward. Gallantry, however, prescribed that he should make at least the motions of following up his inamorata. He set out for the Eagle. As he approached, there came from the open window of an upper chamber the high-pitched whoops of hysteria. Dr. Gail Murchison brushed past him and hastened through the doorway. Horace turned his steps to his lonely bed in Canandaigua Road.

Timidity in human relations had no place in Dinty Jerrold's make-up. Nevertheless she approached her daily errand of neatness at the Harte house with some misgivings the next day. Would her Doctor cherish resentment toward her for last night's prank? He entered while she was conscientiously, albeit unenthusiastically dusting Miss Agatha Levering's sampler.

"Well, young lady!"

So that was all right! She had been afraid he was going to call her Araminta. She said courteously (having rehearsed it for the best effect),

"I trust that Miss Sartie is none the worse for her alarms."

"No thanks to you." As a matter of fact, he did not know. The daughter of Thespis had left town early in the Conestoga troupe-wagon, without vouchsafing him so much as a message of farewell.

Horace was, indeed, rather relieved over the turn of events. The salvage of his virtue was not so much in his mind as his extrication from an entanglement by which, prudence warned him, his reputation might and his exchequer certainly would be gravely compromised.

For the fair and frail soubrette had already nicked him for free medical services, a vial of Paradine's Complexion Water, and a new Leghorn flat from Stone-Front Sarcey's. This at a time of financial stress when he was still, in the current phrase, living down to his shoe thongs.

-11-

Getting affiansed does not Improve some Folks.
(DINTY'S DIARY)

AFTER the first impetus of the Little Sunbeams' advertising died out, Horace's practice flagged. Partly the diminution was due to the young doctor's own restrictions. Free treatment he could afford to give, but not free drugs. Sorely though it went against the grain to turn away those in need of his ministrations, he was forced in self-defense to weed out his list. But for the Levering patronage he would be running behind his bare living expenses.

Old Bill Shea staggered into his office one August evening with a load of liquor on his breath. But Old Bill was not drunk. He was shaking with ague which he had been trying to counteract by the popular corrective of hot buttered rum. Horace filled him up with wine-and-bark and put him to bed at the Eagle. In the morning he insisted on returning to his job. He begged Horace to accompany him.

"We're rotten with fever," said he. "Come out and help us."

Horace hesitated. "Genter Latham booted me off his payroll."

"He wishes he hadn't, only he don't know how to say so without ownin' he was in the wrong."

"Did he send you?"

"No. But I told him I was comin', and he let it pass. That's further'n I reckoned he'd go."

"He'll have to go further still if he wants my services."

"Well, to hell with him! I need you. Some of the boys are liable to die on me if I don't get help. Somethin's got to be done."

"I've told Mr. Latham what to do."

"Move camp? He hain't come to that yet."

"He'll never get rid of the fever till he does."

"It ain't fever alone. The dysentery's bad, too."

"Will you spend some money on an experiment?"

"If you say so."

"Buy a dollar's worth of quicklime. I'm going to sweeten up that stinkhole of yours."

"Then you'll come?"

Horace nodded. It was the kind of appeal which he could not resist. Besides, he liked Shea. Furthermore, it would bring in a bit of money and fill up his idle time. Anything was better than sitting in the office, watching the leeches wriggle with hunger.

Camp conditions were about as he had expected to find them. A little worse perhaps. The malaria was not of the extreme type. But he was hampered by the fact that several of the sick rejected his wine-and-bark, disliking the bitter tang of the quinine and the consequent ringing in the ears, and preferring to drink out the chills on the time-honored prescription of unlimited booze. The dysentery was severe and disabling. Five of his best workers, Shea said, claimed that it left them too weak to lift a pick, and quit cold. And look at the job!

Horace looked and got a shock. Almost no progress had been made since his previous visit. Not more than half the force that he had originally seen now made up the gangs, and that half worked with languid indifference.

"They've been advertisin' my men away from me," explained the overseer.

"Who?"

"Them Montezuma contractors. Advertisin' no chills, no fever, no gripes; work with your feet dry and make seventy-five cents a day. The lyin' sons-o'-bitches. Lucky most of my Irishers can't read or I'd have lost them, too."

Horace strewed a portion of the lime where it was most needed and gave instructions for the disposition of the rest.

"If that doesn't ease up the dysentery, I miss my guess," he said. "But you won't be rid of the fever till cold weather comes."

"Why cold weather?"

"They say it kills the miasmas," answered Horace after hesitation.

"Well, I seen 'em risin' so thick in November it was like fog. But I never seen no fever in November," argued the Irishman.

Nor had Horace. It had troubled him before, that discrepancy. Where was it that he had read that article casting doubt upon the miasmatic origin of malaria and the other low fevers? And the one about the flies and mosquitoes? He must remember to look them up.

"Are you much bothered with mosquitoes now?" he asked Shea.

"Not in the daytime. You can see for yourself. Evenin's, it's hell. You go out without a smudge-box and they'll eat you alive."

"Do they stand on their heads?"

The Irishman stared. "How the hell would I know? They light on my tail. That's enough for me."

It was all very confusing and discouraging. Then Shea said,

"Squire Jerrold's worse off than we are. But Geneseo Martin, up beyond Macedon, ain't had hardly no trouble to speak of, so I hear tell. I dunno why. Why'n't you ride up there and see him?"

Horace accepted the suggestion. But before he found Martin at his project, he had the solution, and it was one that bolstered his faith and raised his spirits. No habitation was to be seen anywhere in the bottom-lands. He waited around for the boss, who readily explained.

"This is a small contract and I've got mostly natives working on it. They won't sleep or eat in the damps. Say it's unhealthy and they can't stand the skeeters. So we put tents up on the hillsides. Even got the grub shack up there. No, we haven't had much of any fever. A little belly trouble, here and there, but that's all. We're keeping ahead of our contract time."

On the way back, Horace took a look at Squire Jerrold's area. A handful of men dolorously dragged themselves through the motions of work. If that were the measure of progress elsewhere, Governor Clinton's ditch would never be dug! Horace continued his ride to where Old Bill Shea was striving to speed up his force. The overseer listened to the report on the Martin project. He cocked an eye at Horace.

"Goin' to tell Genter Latham?"

"I don't expect to have any communication with Genter Latham."

Shea grinned. "You will have, though. He'll be comin' to see you."

Horace doubted it. But the Irishman was right. The great man thrust his bulk into Horace's office and said without preliminary greeting,

"Hear you've been out to my camp again."

"Good afternoon, Mr. Latham. Sit down."

The caller grunted. "How did you find things?"

"There's more sickness than there ought to be."

"Still got your crazy notions of moving the camp away from the work, huh?"

"I still believe that's the thing to do. Geneseo Martin's camp is healthy."

"Well, you won't get me to do it."

"Suit yourself. You'll have more fever."

"That's my lookout. Nobody tells *me* what to do. I tell them. Want your job back on those terms?"

"Yes," said Horace placidly. "I will report to you in a few days. Good day, Mr. Latham."

"I haven't gone yet."

"Is there something else?"

"Yes. My daughter."

"Have you any cause to be worried about her?"

"Nothing special."

"No further symptoms?"

"No, it ain't that." With an effort he said, "Her ma died of lung fever. I'm scared all the time she might go the same way."

"Oh! If that's all. Wealthia is an unusually sound and healthy child. You need have no fears on that score, I think."

The father's face warmed. "You're a sensible young chap in some ways," said he and went out.

Horace had the understanding to perceive that this represented the Latham substitute for an apology.

Prosperity seemed to be coming Horace's way; it cast a glow of hope before it. What economic status might be regarded as sufficient for matrimony in Palmyra? Young Fort, the school teacher, had married on his ten-dollar-a-month salary. But the Forts lived straitly on their little garden and the trout and sticklebacks that he caught in Red Creek; and in winter, he set traps. To ask a luxury-reared girl to share such an existence would be absurd. On the other hand, the Rev. Theron Strang had buried two wives and raised a brood of nine well-nurtured offspring, imminently to be increased to ten with the connivance of his third consort, on his stipend of five hundred dollars a year. Such rewards were not too distant a vision for a hopeful young M.D. How much did Murchison take in from his firmly established practice of twenty-five years? Sixty dollars per month? Possibly. Out of that he must pay for store-drugs and instruments. Figure as optimistically as he might, Horace could not foresee himself equaling that amount in the current year. Nor could he trust to any permanence in the renewed deal with a man of Latham's temper. Nevertheless and without undue conceit, he felt that if he spoke, his suit would not be rejected.

It was the sign of an expanding community that young people married on bold assumptions.

Horace was in a tentative, Agatha in a receptive mood on that unseasonably warm Indian Summer night of early November when he made his regular Wednesday call. The young lady, seated in the parlor, looked daintily cool. Horace found himself wondering whether she ever, in any imaginable circumstances, could be anything other than cool. Through the open window floated the tang of burning leaves and with it a heavier incense which his trained nostrils identified as the effluence from the Leverings' private drain, pursuing its fragrant course from privy to creek. There was also a definite suggestion of the family garbage heap in which a couple of stray, nocturnal pigs were rooting. Horace inwardly rebuked himself for allowing his attention to be diverted from his fair companion by such gross details. The Leverings' way of life was not different from that of their prosperous neighbors. Why be finicky? Well-bred folk ignored such things.

Several left-over mosquitoes were present at the interview. In spite of himself Horace could not control his eyes from straying to the rose-papered wall to see whether any of the pests assumed that grotesque right-angled posture. Two did. He wasted precious moments, after the worsted was duly balled, killing them. The maiden coyly rallied him on his interest in so insignificant a pursuit.

That precipitated the crisis, as was possibly intended. Before he knew quite how it had come about, Horace found himself an engaged man, had implanted a chaste kiss upon the marble brow of his betrothed, and was back holding a second skein of yarn. Agatha stipulated for the unconscionably long period of a year's engagement. She might be a willing, she was certainly not an impatient, fiancée.

Horace went home, telling himself with determination that he was the happiest man in the world.

Agatha now assumed a sweetly proprietary attitude toward her fiancé. With her mother acting as chaperon, she visited his quarters, where she proved herself gently critical. The place was not properly kempt. His books lacked orderly arrangement. (She opened one and clapped it shut with a hot blush.) Dinty's sampler attracted her unfavorable attention. The colors were gaudy, the workmanship crude, the sentiment too professional. Would he mind transferring it to his bedroom? Again she blushed as she uttered the intimate word.

Horace's next unofficial visit was from his two youthful friends. They sniffed around suspiciously.

"You're awfly redd up," commented Dinty.

"Mrs. Harte must be getting particularer," said Wealthia.

"It isn't Mrs. Harte," said Horace.

"I know. It's Miss Aggie."

"Her name is *not* Aggie. She does not like to be called so."

"Miss Agatha, then. Are you going to marry her?" asked Dinty.

"I am."

"You'll be sorry."

"You'll be cruel sorry," added Wealthia.

"I am not aware of having solicited your opinions," said their host haughtily.

Dinty regarded him with compassion. "She's too good for you," she asserted.

"I am proud to admit it."

"You'll have to go to church three times a week," said Wealthia. "You won't like that."

"And sign the pledge," supplemented Dinty. "You won't like that, either."

"And never go to see a laughable farce because it's sinful," pursued the other tormentor. "You'll hate that."

Dinty now addressed her chum. "She'll make him all over different."

"He won't be half as nice," agreed Wealthia.

"He won't be nice at all."

Two little hornets. Who would have expected that sort of grinning malice from them? Horace said through compressed lips,

"You are an impudent and interfering pair of young baggages."

"Oh-h-h-h! Listen to him, Wealthy." Dinty began a grotesque step, singing,

Doctor's mad
And I am glad,
And I know what will tease him.
A bottle of wine
To make him shine . . .

Dance and song stopped simultaneously. The singer's eyes were focused upon an empty wall-space.

"My sampler," she breathed. "Where is it?"

Horace stated the obvious. "It's gone."

"Where?" she demanded. "My sampler that I worked so hard at and pricked my thumb till it bled awfly."

"Miss Aggie took it," surmised Wealthia. "Didn't she?" she challenged Horace.

"No, she did not."

"Isn't that hers on the other wall?" asked Wealthia. She considered it with upturned nose. "I think it's pockish," she said. "All wishy-washy. Like—somebody we know."

Dinty of the dogged purpose insisted, "Where is my sampler gone?" It was almost a wail. The stricken-doe expression had come into her eyes. Horace looked away. She was a pesky brat, but he could not bear to hurt her.

"Someone must have put it away," he said weakly.

"Where Miss Aggie won't have to see it when she comes," said the malignant Wealthia.

Dinty gathered her dignity about her like a shroud. "I presume," said she in high, affected tones, "our services are no longer required."

"Well, you see, children, the fact is, my betrothed and her mother have kindly offered to look after my little place."

Extending a hand to her comrade, Dinty said, "Come, Wealthia. I guess we know when our room is preferred to our comp'ny. Good day, Dr. Amlie."

"Good day, Dr. Amlie." An echo from the other visitor.

Two little queens stalked haughtily forth to exile.

-12-

It is Safer to think as other Folks think and do as other Folks do, but What is the Fun in that?

(DINTY'S DIARY)

MID-November brought the premonitory cold snap. Any day now winter might lift an icy hand in the stop signal. Rod by rod the Ditch pushed its way toward Palmyra. In a strong west wind the townsfolk could hear the lusty Song of the Canal, with its tang of challenge and defiance:

We are digging the Ditch through the mire;
Through the mud and the slime and the mire, by heck!
And the mud is our principal hire;
Up our pants, in our shirts, down our neck, by heck!
We are digging the Ditch through the gravel,
So the people and freight can travel.

And, in softer antiphony, the rich voices of the black gang, ex-slaves from the lake ports:

Methodis' an' Baptis' jus' gone along
For to ring dem chahmin' bells.
Singin' freegrace, undyin' love
Freegrace, undyin' love,
Freegrace, undyin' love,
For to ring dem chahmin' bells.

Ague died out. Dysentery became sporadic. In place of them came chillblains, "putrid sore throat," and the dread peripneumony. Dr. Amlie's practice increased as the prophetic Dinty had foretold. He lost three lung cases in the first severe cold, and Dr. Murchison openly charged that it was because the opinionated young squirt had refused to bleed the patients. Old Murch himself wielded the lancet early and late. Of his patients, drawn from the town and less exposed than the canallers, he lost only two and bragged loudly of it.

Winter fell early in December with a crash of gales and an avalanche of snow. All canal work stopped except on the locks, where the half frozen masons held on for a few rigorous days. Stump engines, cranes and dredges were stored or abandoned to the drifts. Most of the men returned to their homes. Others took to the frozen turnpikes, itinerant job-hunters, a few of them to vanish until the spring opened and they were found by some casual trapper or marauding bear, long dead beside their long dead fires. Perhaps a quarter of the entire number wintered-in at Palmyra, bringing to the peaceful village its first foretaste of prosperity, confusion and sin.

The rum trade took a jump. Two new ginneries and a coffee house of bad repute, established by an ex-convict from Herkimer, opened up. Several of the womenfolk who arrived to join the new populace brought no marriage lines with them. There was singing in the streets at night, sometimes after nine o'clock. The *Palmyra Register* reported that "a French Hell has sprung up and is flourishing on the outskirts of our fair village," sourly inquiring what the authorities proposed to do about it.

The authorities did nothing. Since the "moral pox-spot" (the *Register* again) was beyond the confines of the village, the fathers washed their hands of responsibility, and the two sorry drabs representing the "oldest profession" were unmolested of officialdom. To protect the threatened virtue of the community, several of the enterprising ladies organized the Palmyra Society for the Suppression of Vice & Immorality. Dames and damsels flocked to join, provoking from that hardened cynic, Carlisle Sneed, the observation that, "You can feel 'em shakin' in their pretty little shoes for fear they'll hear something they hadn't oughta, and hopin' to God they will." Agatha Levering was a charter member. Horace joined perforce. He could find no way of avoidance which did not put him in the position of *advocatus diaboli*.

Being affianced to Agatha, Horace discovered, involved more obligations than privileges. Although she seldom proffered a direct request, he was expected to be at call to beau her around to such blameless entertainments as she frequented, for the most part of a devout or eleemosynary nature. Rarely did he find himself alone with her. On such occasions the most he ever got from his advances was a frustrated nibble at the corner of shrinking lips. And this was to continue for a year. A weary wait!

Surely Agatha was worth waiting for. She was gentle and sweet. She would make a model wife. . . . Did he want a model wife? Of course he wanted a model wife. Above all, he wanted a wife. "It is better to marry than to burn." Say! What kind of saint was St. Paul, anyway! How did *he* know so much?

Horace had acquired a new interest, the Crego boy. It came about through his treatment of the "gathering" in Quaila Crego's ear, following Dinty's appeal, an ailment which had resisted the sovereign home remedy of cotton batting heated in rancid oil and sprinkled with black pepper. Here was proper occasion for the lancet, and Horace employed it successfully. It seemed a favorable opportunity for speaking to the alleged witch about the nocturnal jaunts on which her alleged nephew still took Dinty.

"The child is getting too old for that sort of thing," said he. "You ought to forbid Tip taking her on these silly ventures after treasure that isn't there."

"Treasure!" echoed the witch-woman with scorn. "That's but a makeshift. It's the running in the night, the sweetness of rain on your face, the sounds and smells of the quiet forest. Don't I know!" She began to rock herself back and forth. "Leave them be," she muttered. "What good to harstle 'em with forbiddances that they wouldn't heed! If the child did not run with my Tip, she would with another, or alone. Leave be! There's no ill in it. I knew another girl child that had the night in her heart. Her folks penned her behind bars to wear it out. The blood withered in her and she went mad. No, no, you science-man! This is a thing beyond your book-knowledge. I have made a charm for the girl against all dangers of the dark. Let her run free. She will outgrow it." The seamed face saddened. "I doubt she will ever be as happy afterward."

Impressed in spite of himself, Horace said, "Tell the boy, then, that I hold him responsible."

Quaila Crego inclined her head, accepting the charge. "The boy," she said. "A good boy. I hope great things for the boy. You're a college-reared gentleman, Doctor. Could my Tip go to college? To your college?"

"To Hamilton? I don't know why not. He has the love of science in him."

"Schooling, too," she said eagerly. "I have swinked and sweated to buy him books when there was little to put in the kettle. He is good at his lessons."

Horace said hesitantly, "Later I might be able to help him with a small advance. Has he Latin?"

"For his age. And the mathematics. Well-read in religion, too. But not the Greek."

"I could tutor him."

Quaila exclaimed at his generosity. But Horace was no more than acting in the spirit of his time. Among young men of culture there was a missionary fervor to find and cultivate proselytes to learning; a sort of permanent evangelical ardor which burned, not as flashed the spasmodic religious outbursts in volcanic upheavals of righteousness, but with a clearer and steadier flame.

Thus it was arranged that, through the winter, Tip should report to the physician for instruction three evenings a week, and pay his scot—the Cregos insisted on this—by bringing in furs and game. Dinty was ecstatic over the arrangement. She came in specially to thank Horace. Her manner was exemplary, but her eyes kept roving from the chaste example of Miss Levering's needle-art to the vacant space whence her own sampler had been dispossessed.

"When are you going to be married, Dr. Amlie?" she inquired with her best social intonation.

"Next fall. Or perhaps summer."

"That's a long time," said Dinty brightly. "Lots of things could happen." The light waned from her expression. "I won't see you much after that, I guess."

"Nonsense! Why not?"

"She doesn't like me."

"You shouldn't say such things. Certainly Miss Agatha likes you. She likes everybody," he concluded lamely.

Dinty shook her head. "I wish you were my uncle," said she with apparent irrelevance.

"Do you? Why?"

"Oh, just because." She elaborated after reflection. "I did have an Uncle Horace once. He drank and played cards for money and blasphemed. So when he went out west to hunt for furs and the Indians scalped him, Ma said it was a judgment on his sins. Couldn't you be my Uncle Horace?" she asked hopefully.

"Would I have to drink and play cards for money and blaspheme?"

Dinty twisted herself in mirth over the delicious joke. "I didn't know you could *be* so funny," she gurgled. "I used to think you were awfly solemn."

"I'm very particular about how my nieces behave," he warned.

"Then you will be my Uncle Horace!" she crowed. "That's just lovely. Now she can't keep us apart."

"Dinty! I shall be angry in a minute."

"I don't care." Joy made her reckless. "I don't see why you had to put my sampler that I worked so hard over in the other room just because you're going to marry her."

"It's where I can see it every night and morning," said he weakly.

She was not appeased. "I don't see why people fall in love," she said, wagging her head in despair over the insoluble mystery. "Wealthy's in love with Wittie Evernghim. It's so silly! I don't think you're silly, though," justice impelled her to add. "Is Miss Agatha silly?"

"Certainly not." There was a hint of a sigh in his response.

"I'd like her better if she was. I don't believe I'll call you Uncle Horace while she's around. She might not understand it. It'll be our secret. Good-bye, dear Uncle Horace." She bobbed at him and left.

Shortly after the New Year, Genter Latham, who had developed his money-brokerage to the dimensions of a one-man bank, made Horace an offer to finance his home-building. This was not alone a business proposition; it was also, in the Latham fashion, a final composition of the quarrel. Horace thanked him but demurred.

"I have never liked the idea of going in debt."

"Sound business is based on wise debt," said the financier sententiously.

The prospective groom asked for time to consider and brought up the top that evening with his financée.

"It would advance our marriage by months," he said ardently.

Her hand went to her breast. "Wouldn't it be wiser to wait until you have the money, yourself, Horace?" she fluttered. "Of course, whatever you think right is best," she added, assuming in advance the role of dutiful spouse. She rose and went over to poke the fire in a great Dutch oven. "Only—would it be *very* soon?"

He resolved to take up Mr. Latham's offer. Before going to bed that night he read a chapter of De Weese on *The Nervous System of Females* with painful misgivings.

Normally winter was the slack season in Palmyra. This year trade quickened. The mere expectancy of becoming a canal town stimulated business. New building was projected. The brickyard advertised that it would have five hundred thousand bricks for sale in the spring. One harbinger of new fortunes now took to making frequent visits. Dropping in at Dr. Amlie's office, Silverhorn Ramsey encountered in the hallway the fair Agatha, lingering modestly on the threshold while her mother indulged in a gossip with Mrs. Barnes of the rope-walk. He swept off his glossy beaver with elaborate gallantry. The maiden shrank away from the quondam insulter of her purity.

"What!" he ejaculated, in nowise discomfited. "Does Beauty tarry in the inclemency of winter while fusty Science pores over his books within? We shall remedy that."

Raising the bugle to his lips, he delivered a ringing note, then held open the door as might a herald for his queen. Chin aloft, Agatha stared at blankness, desperately hoping that her demeanor expressed the proper loathing while her nerves thrilled. Horace thrust forth a grinning face.

"Be off with you, you oaf! Come back when . . . Ah, Agatha! Forgive me. Come in, my dear."

"Wounded in heart as well as hand," said Silverhorn, waving the bandaged member and with the languishing glance which he never spared any pretty woman. "I return anon."

Tactfully awaiting the departure of the ladies, Silverhorn returned.

"I've got a little account to be settled with you," said Horace, and grimly presented the uncurrent and unredeemable Niagara note.

Silverhorn stared at it with well-assumed surprise. "Well, by the left hind leg of the Lamb of God, d'you mean to tell me . . . ?

"No blasphemy," said Horace sternly.

"Is that the note I gave you?"

"It certainly is."

"Put it on my next bill."

"Your next bill will be paid in advance."

"Well said, my merry Swiss boy. Hard coin's the ticket. Patch up my sprained thumb, and then I've a word to say to you about the Ditch."

"Say your word," said Horace, loosening the bandage and setting to work.

"Have you figured when it'll be finished at the present rate?"

"Not this year, I daresay. Nor next."

"Not in ten years, by God! And that means never. The people won't go on paying the bills. The politicians will sicken of it. The whole thing will go flat as a flounder."

"What is that to you?" asked Horace curiously.

"I've got a stake in this canal," returned the young man. "There's capital waiting to build me a boat. I'll be my own owner and captain; I can make my pile, knowing what I do about the traffic. You'll see me a millionaire-man before I die." He dropped the braggart tone and talked shrewdly and sensibly of the project and its difficulties. Horace was surprised and impressed. "There's just one thing that can beat it and is beating it—the fever," continued the caller. "It'll be back on us next summer, won't it?"

"Probably."

"And worse than this year. It gets worse every year. Doesn't it?"

"Some authorities so hold," said Horace cautiously.

"I *know* so. I've seen it on the Santee and I've seen it on the Dismal Swamp. What do the weevily contractors know or care? All they look to is their poxy contract profits and Old Horny may stick the canal in his pants pocket. But you and I know that sick men can't dig."

"You seem to have given thought to it," commented Horace.

"Didn't I tell you I've got a stake in seeing it go through?" retorted the other impatiently. "I hear you tried to get the Latham camps moved to the high ground. Why?"

"To get the men out of the miasmas." Horace was becoming more and more interested.

"What's a miasma? What do you know about it?"

"Not very much," Horace admitted.

"No, nor anyone else. The medical blueskins spout and lather about miasmas, but all they really know about 'em you could stuff into a gnat's eye without making him wink." He fixed Horace with his keen and meditative glance. "Ever hear that gnats carry the fevers?"

Horace sat up sharply. "Have you?"

"There was an old fusty who lectured on it once at—well, where I was. The students egged him."

Horace was becoming excited. "I've been all through my medical books looking for that very thing. It isn't there. Yet I know I've read it somewhere."

"The old Johnny-come-lately had an article in a magazine to back him up," said Silverhorn. "The *Medical Repository*. Something like that."

Memory settled into place with a brain-click. Horace swore softly. "*Medical Repository!* I've got a file in my trunk."

His visitor rose and stretched with feline abandon. "On the rang-dang last night," he yawned. "Well, young Æsculapius, I guess we're together on this. If there's any fighting in the wind, straight, cross, or rough-and-tumble, call on Silverhorn Ramsey. And so good day to you, my bonnie blade, for I'm off o'er the heather with a hi and a ho and a gallant cock's-feather to flaunt as I go."

Hardly waiting for the door to close after his strange ally, Horace hastened to rummage among his old publications. Here it was, the file of the *Repository* back to 1816. He leafed feverishly through the pages. Eureka! A leading article in the 1818 file. The author boldly advanced the revolutionary theory that fevers did not inhere in the mists and miasmas, but that "moschettoes and perhaps other insects" were the cause of them by "importing deadly molecules" from the marshes and communicating them to the human species by their bites or by merely carrying the disease-agents adhering to feet or wings.

Horace sat, bemused, staring at the page. The "fever-birds" of the gypsies. Witch Crego's word—"when the black moskeeter stands on her head . . ." Folklore. What was it that the wise pioneer of his Fairfield days, himself a bold skeptic, used to tell his classes? Horace could recall the very words.

"Gentlemen, all that we know of disease, its causes, its courses, its cures, is a nodule of dew in the Atlantic of what remains to be discovered. Therefore it behooves us to receive with open minds the lore of the ignorant and untaught, which may have it roots in forgotten wisdom."

The thesis set forth in that careful and moderate magazine treatment had been obliterated from the minds of men. They had rotten-egged Silverhorn's lecturer, the instinctive mob response to disturbing innovation. Horace had a foreboding that the theory would not be more hospitably received in Palmyra.

13

Reverend Missionary Eaton says that ½ the World does not Know what the other ½ is doing, and Pa says Maybe it is Just as Well.

(DINTY'S DIARY)

It is the unique indiscretion of the stern science of Economics that Vice should so often march in the vanguard of Prosperity. The two poor mopsies, whose humble start called forth the righteous journalistic wrath of the Reverend Editor Strang, waxed fat as Jeshurun on their earnings and gathered to them others of the ancient sisterhood. They acquired a tumbledown log cabin beyond the Pinch, cleansed it, had it put in repair, outfitted it with furniture, and formed a business organization under the leadership of a stringy, shrewd-eyed, trade-minded Welshwoman from Olden Barneveld called Gwenny Jump. The place became known to the bated breath of public scandal as the Settlement. In one respect it was a pioneer institution; the rule of the house was money down.

It was the first strictly cash business in local retail trade and, as such, was a considerable though unacknowledged factor in commercial readjustment. The Rev. Theron Strang preached three rousing sermons upon the resort, choosing as his text, "She painted her face, and tired her head, and looked out at a window." Of the final blast Carlisle Sneed admiringly declared that you could smell the stink of brimstone from Macedon Lock to the ropewalk.

Soon after the opening for business, Gwenny Jump came to Dr. Amlie's office. One of her girls was coughing and spitting blood. She had called on Dr. Murchison first, she frankly admitted, but had been told that he wanted none of her trade. If Dr. Amlie felt the same way about it . . .

Dr. Amlie did not feel the same way about it. Certainly he would come. As soon as office hours were over. Miss Jump was grateful. She would pay extra. Everyone charged her girls double rates, so why not Dr. Amlie? Horace explained that his charges were fixed and bore no ratio to abstract or concrete morality.

There was little to be done with the unfortunate patient. Horace tried the "displacement" method, though with small faith in its efficacy. This consisted in attempting to transfer the focus of the disease, by drugs, cuppings and blisterings to some other locality where it could be more effectually treated. The books—those authoritative volumes which crowded his shelves and in which his confidence was dwindling day by day in the light of experience—cited brilliant examples of driving "a consumption" out of the lung into the armpit, the groin, even the great toe, whence it was presently eliminated to the admiration of the patient and the greater glory of medical science. To Horace it was suspiciously reminiscent of a more ancient process along the same line, the exorcism of devils. He never had any luck with it.

Though his success with the unfortunate Millie's case was impermanent and palliative only, his natural kindliness and conscientious care impressed these women, accustomed as they were to abuse and neglect. Before he knew it, he was installed as unofficial consultant to a brothel. It was profitable, for Gwenny paid on the nail, but Horace knew his Palmyra well enough to foresee trouble. He would have liked to abandon the whole thing. Conscience and human sympathy forbade.

It did not take long for the conversational junto at the smithy to learn of Dr. Amlie's new connection. Opinion was divided as to his wisdom. Some held that all was and should be fish that came to a new doctor's net. Others considered that he was foolishly compromising his good name on a line of practice which probably wouldn't bring in much, anyway.

"Maybe he takes it out in trade," sniggered Carlisle Sneed.

"A foul tongue for a foul mind," said the big smith in grave rebuke. "The young man does his duty as he sees it."

Lawyer Upcraft told his wife, and Mrs. Upcraft carried it over to Mrs. Jerrold, thereby insuring general currency to the gossip, for what Dorcas Jerrold knew, the town knew as soon after as might be. One of the first recipients of the information was Mrs. Levering, who deemed it a duty to pass it on to her daughter. Agatha paled, wept and refused to believe that Horace would have any traffic, even professionally, with Those Creatures. Mr. Levering said leave it to him; he would speak firmly to the young man about it. At the following Friday evening call, he put on his black and churchly coat and made a stage entrance into the parlor where Horace was awaiting his fiancée. After a preliminary haw and hum, the father opened proceedings.

"I wish to speak to you, my young friend, about a matter reflecting upon your good name, and so of deep concern to me and my family."

Horace's brows narrowed. "Professional or personal?" he asked. He thought he knew what was coming.

"You may claim in your defense that it is professional."

"I'm not aware of being on my defense," said the prospective son-in-law calmly. "Who's accusing me?"

"Well—er—ah . . ."

"It's about the Settlement, I suppose."

"It is, sir. A most unpleasant rumor has reached my ears."

"Yes, I heard that some of the town clappermaws were freighting gossip around the streets concerning me."

"Gossip? Then it is not true?"

"It is certainly true that I attend the sick in the Settlement as I would anywhere else."

"Sick with *what?*" asked Mr. Levering with tremendous accentuation.

"It doesn't matter what. If a patient is sick and needs medical care, that is all that concerns me. The case I am now attending is a consumption."

"Suppose it were an affliction of another nature," suggested Mr. Levering with delicacy.

"My duty would be the same in one case as the other."

"Have you no duty to my daughter, sir?"

"Suppose you call her," said Horace.

Mr. Levering clawed at his luxuriant whiskers. "Would you submit her to the humiliation of such a discussion?"

"Mr. Levering, Agatha is going to be my wife—the wife of a physician. She will understand that she must not interfere in any way with my professional actions. Nor," he added gently, "must any other person."

"You confound me, sir," cried the father. "You would come from the bedside of shame and pollution into the presence of a pure, young maiden?"

"What would you have me do? Let a patient die, untended?"

"Why not? The wages of sin is death."

"That's no business of mine," returned the young man doggedly. "A sick woman is a sick woman just as much in a brothel as in a church."

A long sigh and a gentle thump sounded from beyond the closed door. Both men rushed to the spot. There in a pathetic heap huddled Agatha. She had quietly fainted at the appropriate moment. Horace propped her in a chair and restored her. Her lids fluttered. She opened moist and grievous eyes upon her lover.

"I will pray for you," she breathed.

Her father tenderly helped her from the room. Mrs. Levering, who had also listened in, took a less sentimental and more practical view as she put her daughter to bed.

"You'll lose that young man of yours if you're not careful, Miss," said she with asperity.

That acutely receptive pair of ears which lurked beneath Dinty Jerrold's curls, caught echoes of the gossip, one of them a giggling reference at a sewing bee to "Dr. Amlie's fair and frail unfortunates down at the Settlement." Her notions as to the establishment were of the vaguest. She had read the newspaper paragraph about the "French Hell" and speculated on it. The French for "hell" was *l'enfer*. That she had from her lessons at the Polite Academy. But when she asked Mrs. Larrabee wherein a French hell differed from any other, she got in return a repressive scowl and no satisfaction.

"Fair and frail unfortunates." That sounded as if someone were in need of help. It was an opportunity for Good Works. The self-appointed investigating committee, Happalonia Vallance, Wealthia Latham and herself had not been very active of late. Dinty rounded up her fellow Sunbeams and they set out to succor the supposed needy with a well-filled basket. The prime mover had not thought it necessary to mention their plan to Dr. Amlie. In fact, she guessed that it would be wiser not to. Since the episode of the smallpox his attitude toward the efforts of the Cluster had been tainted with suspicion. Just as likely as not he would tell them they couldn't go. Dinty's curiosity, once roused, drove her inevitably forward. There was nothing prurient in it; it was simply the expression of a consuming interest in her fellow creatures and the riddle of the painful world.

At noon of Saturday when the helpful trio arrived, the log cabin which housed the denizens of the local underworld was just stirring into life. The day was unseasonably warm. The sun shone; great gobbets of snow slid and plopped from the slanted roof. A young slattern appeared in the door, yawned and stretched. One of the cold avalanches came down on her neck. She said a word which Dinty had heard only once before when a freighter was rebuking his horse for stepping on his foot.

"Let's go home," said Happalonia who was inclined to be timorous.

"Yes. I don't like it here," Wealthia supported her. "I don't believe they're nice people." She had the self-protective instinct of budding maturity.

Dinty, the intrepid, was not to be diverted. "You go down by the creek and throw snowballs at the teegle-ducks," she suggested. She assumed that expression of piety which masked, not always successfully, her spirit of adventure. "I shall not be wearied in well-doing," she proclaimed, and took over the basket of charities.

The blowen in the doorway kicked a carpet slipper from her left foot, examined the big toe with solicitude and thrust it into the snow. She uttered another word less familiar than the first. Dinty advanced.

"Good day," she said.

The other looked up. "Hullo!" she said hoarsely. "Whatcha got in the basket?"

"Some sick-room dainties," said the Little Sunbeam.

A gleam of interest shot across the sleep-sodden features. "Got any good, ole red-eye whipbelly rotgut?" she inquired hopefully.

"No-o-o. Elderberry wine, though," she proffered hopefully.

"Slops!" commented the girl. She wiggled her toe. "Hell!" she said.

"What's the matter with your foot?" Dinty was alert at once.

"It's sore."

"Let me look at it."

The girl stared and laughed. "Ain't she the young vixen!" she remarked. But she thrust forward the member for examination.

"There's a splinter," Dinty diagnosed after careful scrutiny. "It's all hot and angry." She delved into the basket, brought forth a housewife which was part of standard Sunbeam equipment in case charity mending was needed, and selected a penny needle.

"Hey!" said the girl. "Whatcha think yer doin' with that?"

"Taking out the splinter."

"Like hell!"

"Don't you want it out?"

"It'll hurt," said she distrustfully.

"It wouldn't hurt much if I had some ether-paint to put on, but I haven't." Noting the other's hesitancy, she summoned up her medical lore. "If you leave it in, it'll fester and matterate and spread and bite into the bone, and first thing you know your toe'll drop off and . . ."

"Hey!" said the girl, pop-eyed. "Wait till I get me a slug of comfort. Then you can go ahead."

She vanished within, and reappeared, her breath reeking. Dinty passed her the needle. "Lick it," she directed.

This was formula, folklore prophylaxis. The patient understood. "That's for luck," she observed, moistening the steel liberally.

Dinty set vigorously to work. Before she finished she had heard more language than in her whole previous life. But the sliver was out and the foot washed.

"Now," said the operator proudly, "take me to the fire and I'll make you a nice, hot bread-and-milk cataplasm to take out the fever."

The door was pulled open. Gwenny Jump appeared.

"Bob save us!" she ejaculated. "What's all this? Who are you, littling?"

"How do you do?" returned the always courteous Dinty. "I'm Araminta Jerrold."

"You hadn't ought to be here," the manageress told her.

"Why not?"

"It isn't a fitten place for little girls. Go away, little girl."

"What about my toe?" demanded the sufferer. "It's all tore open. She's goin' to fix it."

Dinty explained the virtues of the cataplasmic dressing. She must have heat in it. Gwenny, puzzled but obliging, offered to fetch out some coals in a firebox. Dinty wondered why it wouldn't be simpler to let her go to the fireplace. As the door closed behind the woman, a deep, male voice from the interior boomed out the start of a popular ditty:

"My Daddy is a Roarer, O!" A sound of coughing followed. Then, "Fetch me a drink, Donie."

The girl half-turned her head. "Shut your pan, you little punk!" she yelped.

Dinty asked in surprise, "Do gentlemen live here, too?"

"They come here. When they got four shillin's."

"Do they have to pay? Like a theatre?"

Donie giggled. Like so many of the sisterhood, she was hardly more than a halfwit. "Theatre, huh? That's a good one!"

"Then what's the four shillings for?" queried the information-seeker.

Donie leered at her. "Ask your ma. Where do you think you came from?"

"Shut up, wench!" Gwenny had returned, bearing firebox and linen swatch. "What you don't know won't hurt you," said she to Dinty, shortly but not unkindly. "Do your job."

Dinty did it very much to her own satisfaction. The bandage was one that she would have liked her Doctor to see.

"Fresh and hot every hour," she directed importantly. "And stay in bed as much as you can."

Donie sniggered and said, "That's my business," whereupon Mistress Jump bade her shut up and get inside.

"I hope for the pleasure of meeting you again," said Dinty in urbane farewell.

Gwenny addressed her with a furrowed brow. "Do you know what kind of a house this is?"

"No, ma'am," said Dinty. "But I think it's very nice."

"You go straight home," said the woman earnestly, "and don't you ever, ever come back. You're a sweet little girl and you mean well, but you ain't got the sense God gave a straddlebug. Good-bye and my thanks to you for what you did for Donie."

Somewhat downcast, the missionary rejoined her companions. To them she imparted that there was something queer about the place, but she didn't know quite what it was. She would ask Dr. Amlie about these ladies and why folks thought they were unfortunate.

The effect upon Dr. Amlie was as bewildering as the rest of the affair.

"First it made him laugh, and then it made him mad," she reported back to her comrades. "He told me unless I wanted my ears boxed off my head, not to say anything about it at home. So I guess we all better keep mum-mouth."

The adventure into the half-world might well have been without sequel had not that young, fair and sprightly Englishwoman of letters, Miss Frances Wright, visited Palmyra in her quest for American impressions. That she should have taken a fancy to the bright-eyed, nimble-witted Jerrold child was nothing extraordinary; most people did. After a formal round, committee-escorted, of mills, tanneries, breweries, asheries, mint-stills and ropewalk, the traveler may have caught a gleam of sympathy in the clever young face, turned admiringly upon her, for she addressed Dinty, over restorative tea and caraway cakes, as a fellow spirit.

"I am weary to the bone of being bear-led and supervised like visiting royalty. Is there anything really interesting in the locality?"

Dinty meditated. "There's Poverty's Pinch."

"What a delightful name!" The lady smacked her lips over it with literary gusto. "Who lives there?"

"Poor people. Gypsies and tenkers and wagonfolk. There's the Settlement, too. That's interesting."

"It doesn't sound so. What is it?"

"It's a house where a lot of ladies live, and gentlemen pay half a dollar to come and call on them."

Miss Wright had made a career of broadmindedness; she allowed nothing to shock her or balk her curiosity.

"Let's run away and go there," she whispered.

Upon her departure from Palmyra, the lovely chronicler of Americana assured the committee that she had found their village of unusual interest, though she did not go into explanatory detail. That was furnished by the loose-tongued halfwit, Donie, who was soundly thumped for her indiscretions by Gwenny Jump, but not before she had, in the phrase of the day, spilled the nosebag. A horrified Palmyra buzzed with the news that that Awful Child had actually taken the distinguished visitor to see Those Women, ". . . and, my dear, she's sure to write it in her book and disgrace us forever." Dinty was easily Prime Enemy of the Republic.

The day after the storm burst, Horace Amlie, stamping the wet spring snow and mud from his feet, opened his door upon Dinty, sitting in a dejected attitude, her cheeks mottled with woe and her network schoolbag crumpled on the floor. At sight of him, her housewifely instincts momentarily eclipsed her grief. Darting upon him, she pushed him back into the hallway, dabbing at him with the hearthbroom.

"Aren't you awful!" she cried. "Take off those dirty boots!" She fetched his carpet-slippers. "Put these on." Sorrow rolled in upon her again like a wave. "Alas!" she said.

"Hullo!" said Horace. "What's the matter now?"

"I am desprit," said his caller. "Alas!"

"Stop saying 'Alas!' and tell me about it."

"It's all because I tried to be nice to Miss Wright," she said, weeping.

"I heard something of that. What did they say at home?"

"My mind is all anarchy and confusion," said Dinty. "My soul is harrowed. To what lengths my despair may carry me, I know not. Ma spanked me. Alas!"

Casting about for the key to this singular conglomerate, Horace perceived the lumpy form of a book which the caller had failed to conceal in her bag. He extracted it and read the title: *Coquette,* a *Novel Founded on Fact,* by a Lady of Massachusetts.

"So this is where you get your alases," he observed. "What kind of reading is this for a child like you?"

"It's Wealthy's," answered Dinty. "She got it from the new two-penny-loan library. It is very sorrowful. Alack!"

"If you don't stop that nonsense, I'll bleed you," threatened the doctor. "What if your mother did spank you? A spanking never killed anybody."

"That isn't the worst of it," said Dinty, weeping afresh. "Ma told Pa he ought to send me away to schoo-oo-ool before I did something to bring his gray hairs in sorrow to the grave."

"It might not be a bad idea," said Horace, with what seemed to her an inhuman callousness.

"You don't care," she mourned. "You wouldn't care if you never saw me any more. Prob'ly you won't. I'll go away and never come back to see you or Wealthy or Tip or M-m-m-marcus."

"What's this? Who is Marcus?"

Dinty smoothed her lap. "Marcus Dillard," she said complacently. "He's in love with me. He squeezed my hand in dancing class and sent me a poem about the tender passion."

"Ho!" commented Horace. "We're growing up."

"He's awfly grown-up," continued Dinty. "Not old like you, Uncle Horace. But he's going on fifteen and he's almost got a whisker and if the mint crop is good next season his father is going to build him a boat to go on the Grand Canal and he's going to take me out in it."

"So this is love."

"I guess so. But I'd rather go birdsnesting with Tip." Her face fell. "There'll be nobody to take me to the woods in their nasty old school. I'll hate it."

"When do you leave?"

She brightened. "Not till next term. Lots of things can happen before then. Maybe I'll die," she said hopefully.

No symptoms of an early demise manifesting themselves, Dinty instituted a campaign of being unnaturally good, on the theory that thus she might escape the penalty of her misdeeds. She was assiduous at her lessons. She let pass no opportunity of helping her mother at the housekeeping. She kept her father's boots greased, his clothes spot-free, his shirts supplied with buttons; she even made spills to light his pipe. Her appearances at the Bible Class were edifying. Agatha Levering, to whom she had been an object of distrust if not dislike, confided to Horace that the child seemed really to be undergoing a change of heart. Horace, who knew her better, reserved judgment.

Dinty had one arrow left in her quiver. Through the days she had been building up her structure of impeccable behavior, as an appeal to her parents' better nature. On Easter Sunday she came to breakfast with a look of seraphic meekness that would have done credit to Miss Agatha, herself. She bowed a reverent head to her father's grace, then rose, folded her hands before her, and recited in touching accents a poem which she had carefully selected and conned as suitable to the occasion.

My father and mother, I know
I cannot your kindness repay,
But I hope that, as older I grow,
I shall learn your commands to obey.

I am sorry that ever I should
Be naughty and give you a pain;
I hope I shall learn to be good,
And so never grieve you again.

But for fear that I ever should dare
From all your commands to depart,
Whenever I'm saying my prayer,
I'll ask for a dutiful heart.

Squire Jerrold choked over his coffee. His wife glared.

"Please don't send me away from my loved home, dear parents," said Dinty in imploring, if somewhat specious accents. "Please!"

The voice of doom spoke through Mrs. Jerrold's delicate lips. "Your passage is booked on the Tuesday morning coach. Let that be an end of it."

Dinty said "Damn!" with all the fervor of a lost soul, and fled the room.

Providence intervened. The Aurora Academy for Young Females was full to overflowing and could admit no more pupils until fall.

Besides, Squire Jerrold's indignation had been weakening. The thought of his household, bereft of Dinty's liveliness and laughter and love was too much for him. He put her on probation. As long as she kept out of mischief, the sentence to Aurora would be suspended. One more misstep, though, and off she should go.

It was a respite. In her soul Dinty doubted that it was anything more.

-14-

I hope it is not Sinful to say it, dear Diary, but Sometimes Church is as Exciting as the Play.

(DINTY'S DIARY)

WITH the first purpling of the spears in the great mint meadows which vied with the hemp fields as the village's chief agricultural industry, the black mosquitoes once more assumed their gymnastic posture on the walls of the canal shacks. Fever should now appear, Horace reckoned, if Quaila Crego's lore and the theory of the *Medical Repository* were well founded. As science knew nothing of the incubative period, he naturally expected to find malaria following close upon its insect cause.

He rode Fleetfoot down the valley on an inspection tour. Medically it was a disappointing trip. Not a case of the shakes did he find. Was the mosquito theory just another superstition? Dr. Murchison would have told him so, with appropriate derision. The old boy would have cited authorities to prove that fever was, itself, a disease; that all fevers, whether scarlatina, spotted, typhous, bilious, or malarial were really varieties of the same fundamental and specific ailment. Physicians of the conservative school still clung tenaciously to that belief.

Horace's exploratory visit was not entirely profitless. Old Bill Shea welcomed him and took him to the bunkhouse where several of his workers were groaning over their distended bellies. The re-opened latrines had exuded their foul breath, the flies had gathered, and the withers of men were wrung with the inevitable dysentery. The doctor prescribed medicines for the men and demanded lime for the drains. Under the urging of Old Bill, Genter Latham grudgingly authorized the outlay and even winked at a weekly expense allowance to "that young science-monger" as he termed Horace with good-humored contempt. He offered to loan him to Squire Jerrold, but the Squire balked at the cost, slight though it was.

The Jerrold project was going badly. It was losing men and money daily. In fact, all up and down the line, except on Geneseo Martin's short and busy stretch and where Shea's men were driving hard toward the village bounds of Palmyra, performance was growing slacker, progress slower, and desertions more frequent. Clinton's Ditch was getting a bad name.

The Governor's political enemies fostered the fears. Wherever the canal went, they charged, it carried with it disease and corruption, physical and moral. Agues shook the countryside like earthquakes. Miasmas, lurking in the decayed vegetation, were stirred up, dispersing fevers among the defenseless citizenry. An intestinal epidemic in the Clyde region raged with such violence that young children were carried off in a day. Whispers of the Black Plague went abroad. It might be a judgment of God upon those who, unsatisfied with the lakes and streams constituting His natural waterways, undertook to supplant them by the puny and impious hand of man.

A proponent of this gospel, the Rev. Philo Sickel, was preaching powerfully in the non-canal towns, which were both fearful and jealous of the prosperity so lavishly promised by the Clintonians, and already proving itself where the traffic was in operation. Exhorter Sickel, the Scythe of Salvation, as he exploited himself, was now projecting a tour along the line of the work-in-hand, to deliver his already famous discourse on the Seven Plagues of Erie. These he listed as Harlotry, Blasphemy, Bastardy, Drunkenness, Rioting and (counting them as two to fill out the number) Chills and Fever. He made out a pretty good *ex-parte* case.

The Exhorter was a follower of the furious Finney, whose hellfire fulminations were then cowing the sinners of New England. Like his master, the disciple held a pessimistic view of humanity's chances; his baleful prognostications of the race's future gave pleasurable thrills to those assured of salvation and herded backsliders into the fold through the dire impulsion of terror. He was specially effective with impressionable children even to the extent of inducing mild hysteria. His personality was dankly formidable: a gaunt, lowering face, old for its thirty years, a ponderous form, always draped in black, and a voice that had been known to loosen putty on church windows.

Perspiring mildly in the early July heat, the Rev. Theron Strang sat at the editorial desk of his weekly, conducted to the greater glory of God with little reference to the news, and sighed over the Local Item which he was penning.

> Our Brother in Christ, the Rev. Philo Sickel, will visit our village in the near future and conduct a series of Revival and Temperance meetings. He will also inspire a refreshment of piety among our Presbyterian young people by personal visitation and wrestlings of the Spirit. His first service will deal with the Curse of Strong Drink, in which he will be assisted by Kumoolah, the Reformed Cannibal from the Sandwich Islands.

From Parson Strang's viewpoint, Exhorter Sickel might be a Brother in Christ, but he was also a Thorn in the Flesh. For the path of his gospel was strewn with factional dissension and the bitterness of creed against creed. In his innermost heart the old clergyman revolted from conversion by terrorization. He was a stern and rock-bound theologian, but he could not exclude mildly charitable allowances for alien sects; he had been heard to express the hope that the righteous of soul among Baptists, Methodists, Episcopalians, and Congregationalists might find salvation in the eternal mercy of God, and even that Romanists and Universalists of spotless life might escape total vengeance. Beneath his austere crust of creed and observance lay a submerged tenderness and abiding charity for all men. The Finney or hellfire presumption of damnation for all failed to enlist his approval.

By all means, let the Scythe of Salvation slash at the Demon Rum. It was a safer topic than the Seven Plagues of Erie. Indeed, he had written to the Exhorter, temperately suggesting that unless the spirit moved potently in the direction of martyrdom by egg and turnip, he would be well advised to shun the explosive topic of the canal.

The revivalist pair were housed, upon arrival, with the Levering family, much to Miss Agatha's gratification. For the maiden was troubled in soul over her betrothed and perceived in the coming services a chance of salvation. She realized that Horace was what is known as a drinking man, though perhaps not in an immoderate degree. Exhorter Sickel's widely praised discourse, "Hell's Brew, or the Spawn of the Serpent within our Entrails, with Examples" had arrested hundreds on the very threshold of destruction. Might it not turn the young physician against the Temptations of the Taproom?

Horace was bidden to supper at the Leverings', where he observed with covert disfavor the assumptions of the two proselytizers. Contrary to her usual maidenly custom of modesty and silence, Agatha perked up to the extent of relating instances within her own experience of young men for whom the first swallow had been the prelude to ruin. One was a third cousin on her mother's side.

"Every morning of his life," said she in hushed tones, "he drank a tot of hot buttered rum. He ended by becoming an actor on the stage and falling into the *lowest* associations."

This was a double-edged thrust aimed at Horace who contented himself with saying, "Indeed!"

All that was most respectable and representative in Palmyra was present in the Presbyterian Church that Wednesday evening, augmented by a liberal representation from the town in general, for the news had passed that something unusual and entertaining was in prospect. Could Horace Amlie have foreseen how generously he was to contribute to the public's entertainment, he would have stayed away.

Early to arrive, the affianced couple found the aisles already filling up with chairs, stools and milk-benches in anticipation of an overflow. They were lucky to find two seats in a rear pew. Looking about him, a practice reprehended by Agatha as savoring of worldly preoccupations, Horace noted some faces unfamiliar in that environment, among them Sarah Dorch and, more surprisingly, Silverhorn Ramsey, clad in mundane elegance and with the inevitable bugle bulging beneath his coatskirts. As the girl had not been a church-goer in the days of her beauty and of the liaison with Genter Latham, Horace surmised that she was now seeking the consolations of religion to compensate for the lost satisfactions of the flesh. But Silverhorn! What brought him there? Pure, cussed curiosity, by Horace's guess.

Further forward he descried Genter Latham's massive back, and the nodding head of Carlisle Sneed. Near by sat that master of equine invective, Jed Parris, meek and subdued in his Sunday blacks.

The Rev. Mr. Strang rose to announce that the services would be divided into two parts: Part I, the Edifying Illustrated Temperance Discourse by Brother Philo Sickel, the Scythe of Salvation, assisted by Brother Kumoolah, the Converted Cannibal from the wild jungles of the Sandwich Islands; Part II, a soul-searching of sins with a view to the chastening and redemption of the sinners, conducted by Brother Sickel. It struck Horace that Parson Strang's announcement had an undertone of distaste. Could it be for his Brother in the Faith?

Tom Daw's lap-organ wheezed and whined and the congregation, rising, blended pious voices in the hymn which the sardonic Dr. Vought had once named "Old Cathartic" from the opening lines of the second stanza:

> Blest be the men
> Whose bowels move.

When the Exhorter's robustious baritone rang out that beatitude, Horace Amlie giggled like an urchin. It was, perhaps, the beginning of his downfall.

The Scythe of Salvation opened by introducing his aide and disciple, Kumoolah, who rose and bowed, revealing himself as a sleek, dusky youth, thick of lip, limpid of eye, kinky of hair, and robed in apostolic white. Under the leadership of his rich basso, the gathering bade musical defiance to the Demon Rum.

> Ha! See where the wild-blazing Grogshop appears,
> As the red waves of wretchedness swell,
> How it burns on the edge of tempestuous years,
> The horrible Light-house of Hell!

Exhorter Sickel then spoke briefly for an hour and a quarter, after which he yielded place to his associate. After relating in sorrowing accents a number of titillating tales about wild and naked orgies in his far-distant home, the dark outlander unrolled a canvas brilliant with color, which he held up before the fascinated eyes of the audience.

"Stum-mack of a confirmed drunkard," he announced.

Horace gave an outraged grunt. From that point he exhibited increasing symptoms of uneasiness and resentment. Inbred in him was the scientific devotee's hatred of error. Ignorance and assumption were bad enough, but the deliberate lie was poison to his spirit. But for his companion's light hand on his arm, he would have risen and marched out in disgust, thereby creating a minor scandal and saving both of them a major one.

For when the Scythe of Salvation resumed charge, it was to announce an illustration of how the deadly fire of alcohol possessed itself of the very blood of its victims. All present knew our erring brother, William Simmons, who was—he stated it with grief and pity—a confirmed slave of strong drink. (Bill Simmons blushed humbly in his seat.) In his contrition over his most recent lapse, Mr. Simmons had allowed himself to be blood-let of a pint. Would their respected fellow citizen, the eminent Dr. Gail Murchison, rise and bear witness? Dr. Murchison stood, holding up to view a vial.

"I certify that this blood was drawn by me from the veins of William Simmons at 2 P.M. today. The said Simmons was under the influence of intoxicants," he stated.

Exhorter Sickel handed the container to his assistant.

"Brother Kumoolah will now demonstrate the awful effects."

The outlander came forward in his flowing robes, bearing a brass bowl. Into this he poured the contents of the vial (or of *a* vial; Horace thought that he had discerned a lightning-swift pass of the hand toward a capacious sleeve). He poised a lighted taper above the receptacle.

"Now," said he with a flash of white teeth, "we shall sssss-ssee."

He lowered the taper. There was a *plop!* A flame sprang. It burned waveringly, throwing off a dingy smoke. A great sigh of wonder arose from the people below. The smoke drifted out across the congregation as Kumoolah hovered, spritelike, above the unholy fire.

Horace got a sniff of it. His wrath, too, burst into flame. Agatha made an unavailing clutch at his arm as he rose to his feet, his face white but resolute. He pointed toward the bowl.

"This is a fraud," he said.

Dr. Murchison popped up, fuming. "Do you accuse me of fraud, sir?"

"No, I don't." Indignation had not supplanted Horace's instinctive fairness. "I don't doubt that you bled Bill Simmons. But not of the stuff in that bowl."

"What, then, do you claim it is?"

"Seneca Oil." He made a gesture of comprehensive and dramatic invitation. "Smell it!"

Noses sniffed audibly. A murmur succeeded. The odor of the illuminant was too familiar to be mistaken. Kumoolah leant to his principal's ear and whispered rapidly. The Exhorter came forward, extending a damnatory forefinger at Horace.

"Young man, I solemnly exhort you to cease doing Satan's hellish work and supporting the cause of strong drink," he boomed.

"I'm not supporting the cause of strong drink," retorted Horace in equally emphatic tones. "I'm supporting the cause of science against lies. Look at that picture of yours! It's no more a man's stomach than it is a pig's ear."

"And that ain't Bill Simmons's blood, neither," shrilled the indignant voice of Bill Simmons's wife.

Above the rising mutter of dissent and doubt, rose the dominating voice of Genter Latham.

"There's one way to settle this. Bleed him again and let's see."

"Not by a damn sight!" said Bill Simmons.

Profanity in the house of worship! A scapegoat was thus opportunely provided for the swelling emotions of the people. The blasphemous alcoholic was rudely hustled out. When quiet was restored Agatha Levering was observed to be weeping privately. Beside her Horace sat bolt upright, his chin at a militant angle. Kumoolah had unostentatiously retired. The Exhorter, quick to sense the tendencies of his public, abandoned his intention of passing the plate, and launched into Part II of the evening. This, he stated, was under the auspices of the Palmyra Society for the Suppression of Vice & Immorality, which had done the spadework and dug up some lamentable instances of total depravity.

Before considering these he would (consulting a slip of paper) bespeak the prayers of the congregation for the sinful souls of Ephraim Upcraft (who bowed a meek head), Bezabeel Fornum (who bobbed a self-conscious acknowledgment), the family of Deacon Dillard (who lifted pious faces to heaven in unison), the Fairlie twins (who had played truant from Sabbath School and were in deep disgrace), Carlisle Sneed (who gave his wife a venomous glance), Jasper Ramsey (that was a facer for Silverhorn!), Araminta Jerrold (aftermath of the Frances Wright episode) and, at the end of a considerable roster of self-or-proxy-confessed malefactors, Sarah Dorch. The girl's convulsive start apprised Horace that it came as an unwelcome surprise to her.

Passing from the particular to the general, the speaker embarked upon an indictment of Palmyra which would have been extreme as applied to Sodom or Gomorrah. Every count against the developing town was set forth and dealt with in scathing denunciation. The saloons got a five-minute blast, the taverns another five, the Settlement, twice the length with notable attention to detail. The Pinch was held up as a picture of Divine wrath. The sins of the rich and the offenses of the poor received well-apportioned attention. The godless crew of canal laborers was called to a proper accounting and the Great Ditch held chiefly responsible for the town's parlous state. For one solid hour the golden voice proved that Palmyra was an anteroom to perdition and that its inhabitants marched with the legions of the damned.

There followed a pause for digestion of the unpalatable outline.

The orator shot his cuffs, set his broadcoat, replaced a shock of shining hair maladjusted by the fervor of his eloquence, and boomed forth his first sub-text.

"The lady goes gaily, brave in what she hath not spun, fed fat with what she hath not sown. Her feet take hold on hell and the vengeance of heaven followeth in her steps."

He leaned out across the Bible stand. The compelling eyes beneath the shaggy brows swung hither and thither, searching, probing until they settled in a steady stare.

"Rise, Sarah Dorch!"

The unfortunate girl gave a gasp, clutched at the back of the seat, turned her head to and fro, hopelessly seeking an avenue of escape.

"Rise and stand forth!" thundered the Exhorter.

Mesmerized by the power of that inexorable summons, Sarah edged past the knees of her neighbors until she reached the exposure of the aisle. There she halted, lax, loose-chinned, terrorized beneath the fascinated regard of the congregation.

"Lift the veil from that face from which a just Judge hath stricken its carnal beauty and bear testimony to your adulterous sins."

Bending as before an irresistible wind, the girl lowered the impugned face instead of raising it and covered it with her arms. She sobbed, a choking, retching gulp of shame and terror. Her knees gave beneath her. A childish voice pierced the rapt silence.

"I don't care!" it pronounced passionately. "I think it's *mean.*"

Dinty! The rash challenge galvanized Horace Amlie into action. He forced his way along the aisle to where Sarah Dorch's form lay, crumpled. Another figure reached the girl at the same time. Silverhorn Ramsey and Horace together lifted her to her feet.

"Hale her forward," said the Exhorter.

Silverhorn laughed. "What's the Doc's orders?" he asked Horace.

It reminded Horace of his capacity as a physician. "Got a flask?" he asked.

"Certes." The silver gleamed in the dim light. Horace moistened the pale lips. They parted in a sigh.

"Don't make me go up there. Don't make me go," the girl frantically whispered.

"You're not going," said Horace. "Got her, Silverhorn?"

"Strong liquor," said the implacable voice from the pulpit. "In the house of God. Pray, ye people! Pray that the destruction of Nineveh and Tyre fall not upon us."

Silverhorn turned his impudent, mirthful face over his shoulder and delivered what was known in canal parlance as a gardaloo.* A murmur of horror ran through the assemblage. The trio gained the door.

"There pass three lost souls," declared the revivalist with the terrible impressiveness of utter conviction. "Leave them to their doom."

There was a moan from the Levering pew. Agatha had toppled forward in a swoon.

"Your gal's flummoxed out," Silverhorn informed Horace. "Want to go back?"

"No," said Horace between set teeth.

"What'll we do with this one?"

"Get her home."

Between them they got her to her room. Silverhorn sat by while his companion brought the patient through recurring hysterical onsets. When it was over and they were back on Main Street, Silverhorn said,

"What about the other one?"

"What other one?" asked Horace absently.

"Your fair lady-love. Have you forgotten her?"

"You mind your own business," snapped Horace.

The canaller laughed. "Good night, young Æsculapius," said he and swung away, weaving a strain of tenor melody as he went.

> She bade me to her leafy bower.
> Hey, nonny! No! No! No!
> The eglantine was full in flower.
> Never believe a woman's No.

Agatha must be faced. The sooner, the better. Late though the hour was, Horace was sure that the Leverings would be in council over his behavior. They were. The Rev. Philo Sickel was also there.

The family greeted him after the manner usually reserved for funerals. The Exhorter's welcome was even chillier. He immediately led in prayer, an invocation which presently passed from general terms to a specific consideration of the misdeeds of one described as "our erring brother." It was painfully evident to the subject that some agency, presumably the Palmyra Society for the Suppression of Vice & Immorality had been doing some intensive research into his brief past. Nothing was omitted from the Scythe's review. He touched upon Horace's alleged addiction to strong drink, his visits to the Soiled Sisterhood of the Settlement (the Exhorter was incurably

* This term appears to be closely akin to the modern raspberry or Bronx cheer.

alliterative) upon which the worst construction was put, his association with the profligates of the smithy, his solicitude for the erring sister, Sarah Dorch, with a strong intimation that it had its roots in an earlier relationship into whose nature the petitioner would not too particularly inquire ("You'd better not!" muttered the accused) and such minor offenses as betting and cards.

At the close, Horace, whose neck was bristling, controlled himself to a desperate calmness as he said to Mr. Levering,

"I should like five minutes alone with my affianced."

"No!" cried Mrs. Levering, evincing, by her horrified accents, a maternal conviction that the least Agatha might expect if left to this dreadful creature would be rape.

"Very well," said Horace. "What am I expected to do about it?"

The Exhorter took upon himself to reply. "Present yourself at tomorrow's meeting and humbly beseech the pardon of God and man."

Horace said, "I'll see you in hell first."

Agatha sobbed. Mrs. Levering shrieked. Mr. Levering chattered, "L-l-l-leave this Christian abode, sir, and come back only upon your knees."

Horace took up his hat, his cane and his gloves. He addressed the Rev. Philo Sickel.

"Would you step out with me for a moment?"

The Scythe regarded him mistrustfully. "I have said all that is needful, sir," he replied.

Horace sighed and made his respects to the others, being answered by a stony silence. He felt that he needed a drink.

Nearing the Eagle taproom, he recognized a richly accented voice, upraised in song. He entered. Kumoolah was holding forth to an admiring circle. It was evident that he and the Demon Rum had come to a composition. As he sang, he danced, but the evocations of his performance, though unmistakably Southern, were not of the South Seas. The Converted Cannibal was, in fact, rendering a good, old Alabama hoedown. He was subseqeuntly returned to that state and to slavery, leaving behind him a considerable deficit in the Sickel-Kumoolah treasury. The Exhorter had been not an accomplice, but an innocent dupe.

One drink sufficed Horace. On the homeward way he spied a light in the Strang study. Conscience stirred within him. For the austere and upright Dominie he had a solid respect. He knocked and was admitted. The parson received him with sorrowful reproof.

"I am pained, Dr. Amlie," said he in his deep tones. "Sorely pained by the levity of your conduct. You laughed aloud in church."

(Was that all? thought Horace, relieved. Nothing about Sarah Dorch?)

"I am truly sorry, sir," said he with sincerity. "I couldn't help it."

"Ah, well!" said the old gentleman. "Youth, youth!"

"There is something else," said Horace, and gave a succinct account of the interview and of the Exhorter's demand. At the conclusion his reverend listener's eye gleamed with a fire which was not that of piety. He leaned forward.

"Did you kick him?" he asked.

"No, sir," answered the startled Horace.

"Ah, well!" sighed Mr. Strang. "I am glad that you did not kick him."

"Do you think I should resign from the fellowship?"

"Certainly not," replied Mr. Strang with emphasis. "Let us lay it before the Lord in prayer."

The prayer was a supplication for release from violent and wrathful thoughts about one's fellow man. It struck Horace that the reverend gentleman had himself, the saint, quite as much as Horace, the sinner, at the core of his mind. Encouraged, he ventured to put in a word for Dinty, the other violator of the sanctity of the occasion. Mr. Strang smiled his gentle smiled.

"I fear," said he, "I gravely fear that I concur in her sentiments."

At home Horace found the note. In terms of superior and elegant grief, Agatha informed him that All was Over between them; their engagement was dissolved; she would always be concerned for his Welfare in this World and the Next, and would pray for his Repentance and Salvation, and she was, Sorrowfully and Respectfully, Agatha Levering.

With a deep-fetched sigh, the recipient prepared for a vigil of sleepless misery and vain regrets. As he buttoned himself into his long flannel shift and settled his peaked nightcap in place, he made a horrifying discovery.

He was whistling.

-15-

I do not care if I am a Wayward Soul. Nobody likes to be Prayed at.

(DINTY'S DIARY)

BANQUETING was the favorite indoor sport of the day. Any occasion sufficed. Self-appointed committees acted for the community. Speakers were selected, toasts apportioned and drunk; it was a poor and meager evening when they did not run to at least a dozen. When Horace Amlie was put on the list of regular guests, it was a recognition of his status as an established Palmyrian.

Two members of the powerful Canal Board having announced their intention of inspecting the local works, it was a matter of course that they should be feted at the Eagle. With them came the famous New York City physician, David Hosack. To Horace's mind, this was a bad sign; it meant that the commissioners were informed as to the prevalence of disease. A childbirth at Poverty's Pinch disappointed his expectations of attending the festivities, but he reckoned on finishing up in time to meet the noted doctor before the breaking-up hour.

A worse sign for Palmyra was that both visiting commissioners kept sober at the table. To the outpourings of local pride and optimism over the canal they responded charily. They were not pleased with the progress of the work and made no bones of saying so with a frankness which dampened the spirit of festivity. Did the local contractors, they inquired pointedly, think that they had ten years at their disposal? Why could they not keep their men up to schedule? Where was their boasted public spirit? What steps, if any, were being taken to check the fevers? Did they not realize that contracts could be abrogated for non-performance?

By the time half a dozen lifeless toasts had been drunk, the dreary affair was over and the diners had broken up into glum groups, who stood about discussing the problem over unofficial drinks. Such was the situation when Horace got back from his delivery. He sought out Dr. Hosack.

"Amlie? Amlie?" repeated the famous man amiably. "I've heard my old friend John Vought speak favorably of you."

"I owe much to Dr. Vought, sir," said Horace modestly.

"We all do. You've had opportunity of observing the local fever, I presume."

"More of it than I like."

"Is it the Montezuma type, think you?"

"Graver. We are having deaths."

"Bad! Bad! The commissioners take an unfavorable view. Abandonment of the work, even temporary, would have a very damaging effect upon public opinion."

"It may come to that, sir. It would mean ruin to the village."

"To many villages. It would be a catastrophe, Dr. Amlie, to the prosperity and pride of our great state. In your opinion, are the miasmas hereabouts heavier than elsewhere?"

"No. Less heavy and less frequent than in the marshes." Horace summoned up his courage. "Do you necessarily attribute the malaria to the miasmas?"

The distinguished visitor's eyes narrowed upon his junior. "What have you in mind?"

"Fever-bearing insects."

"It may well be so. I, myself, have pointed out a connection between filth and jail-fever. Filth can be disseminated by insects, and so disease."

"I believe that to be the case."

"Have you propounded your belief locally?"

"I have suggested it and been laughed at."

"Yes, yes, of course. I am an old man, Amlie. I have seen much and thought much and believed little except upon due proof. I have observed miasmas where there was no fever and fevers where there were no miasmas.

"Have you seen fevers without flies and mosquitoes, sir?" asked Horace with intent.

"Not the canal fevers. Not the malaria. But"—he waggled a warning finger at the other—"not proven, my young friend, not proven. Our medical pundits will have none of it. Propose it at peril of your professional neck. They'll skin you alive and hang your pelt on the fence."

"Then you advise me to hold my tongue?"

"Nothing of the sort," said his senior sharply. "I only say, go slow. There is for the skeptic and questioner in our profession an *odium medicum* harsher than the *odium theologicum* of the pious." He peered searchingly at the young man. "But you are of those who must speak as they believe. I see it in your face. Good night, my young friend, and God be with you."

As Horace thanked him, Old Bill Shea approached.

"Mr. Latham wants to see you."

The magnate was seated at a small table in the parlor corner with a glass of rumbullion before him. One glance told Horace that he was in a black humor. His "Sit down," was a direction, not an invitation. He did not even extend the courtesy of a drink as he bent upon the other what Dinty called "Mr. Latham's money-look."

"What am I paying you for?" he growled.

Horace silently enumerated the bones and nerves of the great toe, an exercise which he had found more useful in controlling a naturally lively temper than the classic practice of counting ten.

"To look after the health of your camp," said he.

"Do you think, by God, you're doing it?"

Trying to provoke a quarrel, was he? On the occasion of an earlier meeting with the autocrat, Dinty had warned him against the Latham bullying.

"I'm doing what I contracted to do," he replied quietly.

"Like hell you are! Shea, here, tells me half the men are laid off."

"Not half," protested the overseer. "I never said half, Mr. Latham."

"Well, plenty. Flat on their backsides with what they call fever. A passel of scrimshankers," he declared.

"They're not scrimshanking, Mr. Latham. They're sick men."

"Why don't you cure 'em, then?"

"As soon as they're cured, others will come down."

"And that's the best you and your college learning can do!" Genter Latham pounded the table-top until his unfinished drink slopped over. "How's the work to get on? Am I to sit here and watch my profits leaking away through laziness and incompetence?"

"I've told you what ought to be done, sir," said Horace passing that insult up. "Take it or leave it."

"You mean that God-damned nonsense about moving the men where the bugs can't bite 'em?"

"Ask Geneseo Martin whether it's God-damned nonsense."

"He's gettin' two to our one of work, with half as many men," put in Old Bill.

Mr. Latham consigned Geneseo Martin to the lowest depths. "A labor-coddler," he snorted.

Horace took another tack. "When you pay for medicines, you take them, don't you?"

"What if I do?"

"You're paying me for advice," Horace pointed out.

"Wasted money."

"Wasted, indeed, if you won't take what you've paid for."

"That's business, Mr. Latham," said the overseer respectfully.

"Business! What does this young sprig of science know of business?"

Foreseeing that he would some time have to face that challenge, Horace had prepared for it. He took from his breast pocket a neatly penned sheet of paper and laid it before his employer. Mr. Latham glowered.

"What's this?"

"A rough estimate of your day-to-day loss through sickness."

Figures commanded Genter Latham's respect where humans did not. The flushed anger of his visage was replaced by cool, shrewd contemplation. After studying the columns, he tapped the paper with his finger.

"Not ill-reckoned," he conceded. "But you've left out something."

"What?"

"The cost of moving camp."

Horace concealed his exultation. "Shea can give you that better than I."

"It won't cost us so much," said the Irishman. "We're nearin' the village; the work is too far from the camp now. When we move, we might as well pitch on high ground as low."

"Give me an estimate tomorrow," commanded Latham. He turned to the physician. "There'd better be no lay-offs in the new quarters," said he threateningly.

"I make no such promise."

"Then what the hell is this about?"

"My undertaking is that disease will be lessened—no more. For every man restored to work"—he tapped the paper in his turn, looking the other straightly in the eye—"you save computable money and time."

"Well, well," grumbled the great man. "Have it your own way. And have a drink, both of you."

The evening was not yet done for Horace. On his way to the door, he was intercepted by Carlisle Sneed who had been allaying his resentment for the affront to local pride by quaffing his toasts double.

"Doc, me boy-hoy," he hiccupped, "your eye is wuh-hiped."

"How is my eye wiped?" demanded Horace.

"Wuh-hiped dry. Dry's a bo-hone." The humorist warbled,

> Wreathe the willow and the rue,
> My sweet love has proved untrue.

"Didn'cha hear Misser Levering freighting the news around?"

"I did not," replied Horace. "What did he say?"

"Aha! Bow yer head, me bucko. Miss Agatha, fai-hairest flower of Palmyra's bloo-hooming maidenhood, is betrothed in ma-harriage to that canting son-of-a-bitch, the Rev. Exhorter-Snorter Sickel-scythe and may their first brat be born with a wooden halo."

"Amen!" said Horace.

He felt like a jail-delivered man.

Lacking a definitive period of mourning for a broken heart, it was expected of the lorn swain that he should exhibit a properly melancholious mein in public until time should have healed the wound. It was no more than what was owing to the lost love; to do less would be a reflection upon the lady's charms. But a new alignment on her part released the obligation. Horace's behavior had comported with the requirements of the case. He had gone about, clothed somberly and (except when it slipped his mind) with a creditable effect of woe. Now his penance was over.

Of deeper concern to him than any personal considerations was the new experiment. He did not expect miracles. There were still a few cases of malaria in the Martin camp, as he knew. This troubled him. It seemed to exculpate the mosquito as agent of the disease. Well, he could only give it a fair trial and hope for patience on his employer's part.

Nobody knew better the lay of the land in the township than Tip Crego. Horace set the boy behind him on Fleetfoot and they made a tour of exploration. Out of several locations which seemed suitable to the physician, his companion advised a site a mile west of the village on one of those singular and abrupt earth-knobs, later to be known to marveling geologists as drumlins. The valley spread out some fifty yards below.

"The night mists don't rise this high," said Tip.

"I thought we were agreed that it isn't the mists but the mosquitoes," objected Horace.

"The black mosketeers come with the evening mists. They only fly after dusk. Haven't you noticed that?"

Horace had not. He confirmed it by observation and set it down in his notebook.

The new buildings were rushed to rough completion in five days. Here young Crego further proved his usefulness by ridding the grub-shack of what flies survived the lime treatment, by a simple expedient. In door and window he hung great bunches of the tall, abounding sweet clover, the scent of which no winged insect can abide, suspending other festoons above the table.

Within a week after the transfer, the health of the camp was showing so marked an improvement that Old Bill Shea talked of putting on night squads to make up for lost time. Tip shook his head.

"They'll get bitten and they'll get fever," he prophesied.

"What about your pennyroyal?" asked the overseer who had come to have a solid respect for the youngster's knowledge.

"If you can make 'em use it."

Adapting the method used in the local mint-stills, Horace and his aide pressed out a supply of pennyroyal extract which was supplied to the workers at cost. At the physician's suggestion, Genter Latham issued an order, prescribing its use. He knew that there was still some fever in the camp. Horace had been quite frank in saying that he could not explain it. The great man was not captious. It was enough for him that his project was now showing better speed than any other in the valley.

The Irish workmen, an independent and fractious lot, were at first skeptical of the preventive virtues of what they regarded as a fad, and inclined to disregard the order. But when they discovered that the spicy-odorous oil protected them from the stinging pests better than the cumbrous neck-smudges which were the standard resource, they accepted the relief gratefully, all but a few old hard-shells who disdained to mollycoddle themselves. More than half of this number developed the shakes, to the great satisfaction of their physician who duly noted it for future submission to a medical journal. He tried to obtain data from other camps, but except at Martin's the overseers were surly and uncommunicative. They were doing badly. Squire Jerrold's project was one of the hardest hit.

With the approach of the excavation to the village, local spirit rose to meet it. Early and late Latham's diggers toiled, wielding their tools by the light of flares and fires, while the goodwives brought them coffee and the tavern keepers contributed a sturdier liquid to spike it on rainy nights. Bonuses for extra dirt-removal were increased. Rivalry drove the work forward at record speed.

They crossed the boundary line of Palmyra Village at two o'clock of a fine September morning. A cannon was fired, the churchbells pealed, and the populace turned out. All the men knocked off work. Genter Latham, aided by the village ladies, had prepared a mighty outdoor feast for which the fires had been lighted since midnight. The central feature was a Gargantuan potpie. Each simmering five-pail kettle held thirteen fowls, sixteen squirrels, ten rabbits, accompanied by liberal chunks of beef, mutton, and venison, with potatoes, carrots, turnips, parsnips, onions and cabbages to fill in. For side dishes there were baked beans, stewed squash, and peas boiled with pork. In the house ovens, pumpkin pies two feet across ripened. Liquor flowed like water: whisky, rum, hollands, hard cider and a choice of brandies, peach, plum, cherry and blackberry or all of them. The robust harmonies of canal song rang through sedate streets more habituated to the meter of the hymn book, culminating in that swift-paced chorus which was largely popular because it was supposed to represent some recondite and occult smut.

> Singsong, pillywinkle, snipcat, sootbag;
> Singsong, Polly, woncha guy me-O!

Overnight Palmyra became canal-conscious to an almost frenetic degree. Hitherto the more respectable and conservative element had regarded Governor Clinton's mighty venture with mingled expectancy and distrust. With the palpable evidence of progress under their noses the populace enthused over a new maritime prosperity. The tempo of the whole environment was quickened.

Converts hotly prophesied "Rochester to Albany in the spring." Warehouses, put swiftly into process, began to fill up with produce and goods before the roofs were shingled. New thoroughfares were laid out and named: Chapel Street, Jackson Street, Fayette Street, and, of course, Canal Street. There was a new tannery, a new ironmongery, a whitesmith's establishment, ground was broken for a stoneyard, two saloons sprouted where one had sufficed before, and there was optimistic talk of building a public library and improving the jail. Wages skyrocketed until carpenters were earning a dollar a day. Real estate boomed. Building lots doubled and redoubled in value. Genter Latham put up a building for his banking operations. People said that he would be a millionaire-man one of these fine days. The community went mildly and happily mad. Exhorter Sickel coined a sour locution, Eriemania.

The Scythe of Salvation was now embarked upon the second phase of his endeavors, a sort of Children's Crusade. He laid out a schedule of visits to the young of the Presbyterian flock, to test the armor of their faith for chinks into which Satan might enter, and to fortify their orthodoxy by prayer and admonition. In ministerial courtesy he invited the regular pastor to participate. The Rev. Theron Strang accepted as a painful Christian duty. He did not like the Sickel ways.

High on the Exhorter's list stood the name of Araminta Jerrold. This was no compliment; far from it; it was due to an appeal from Mrs. Jerrold, not participated in by the Squire, who tried vainly to persuade his better half that Dinty would do well enough if only her mother would let her be.

The mother was not content to let the child be. She was, she told herself, responsible for this immortal soul which she had, by a process which still left her dully bewildered when she considered it, brought to being. Dinty was not the only phenomenon which contributed to poor Mrs. Jerrold's obfuscation. Most things confused her. She found refuge from the perplexities of an enigmatic world in a groveling religiosity, expressed in dreary texts and the type of hymn which proclaims the singer to be a poor worm of perdition. It bored her worldly husband extremely.

In this crisis, Dorcas Jerrold found the support of the Rev. Philo Sickel profoundly comforting. The Exhorter guaranteed to rescue Araminta's soul if it was still salvageable.

On a crisp afternoon when she would have preferred to go hickory nutting with Tip, Dinty reluctantly put on her white frock and went down to the parlor where the two reverend gentlemen, black-garbed from toe to neckcloth, awaited her. After the greeting, which was in the form of an appropriate text, Elder Strang formally and mildly questioned her upon vital tenets of the denomination which both professed. She came through creditably on predestination, original sin, conviction of depravity, and salvation by faith, and was looking forward to an early release, when Exhorter Sickel took charge along more personal lines.

"When and where were you baptized, Araminta?"

"In Canandaigua, sir. When I was two years old."

"You then renounced the world and all its follies?"

"Oh, yes, sir!"

"So that, when you breathe your last, expiring breath, you can die in the hope of salvation?"

"Yes, Mr. Sickel."

"What would be your sad fate should you die, unbaptized?"

Dinty knew the answer to that one but did not like it. She temporized.

"I'd be in trouble," she said.

"You would be in hell," snarled the Exhorter.

"Yes, sir," said Dinty without enthusiasm.

He eyed her with stern suspicion. "Do you doubt it, Araminta? Are you tainted with the deadly poison of heresy?"

"I hope not, sir," said Dinty, troubled.

"You know that you are a sinner?"

"Yes, sir."

He intoned,

> Sinners shall lift their guilty head
> And shrink to see a yawning hell.

Dinty caught the cue and shrank. "Yes, sir," she quavered.

He gave out ten minutes of concentrated exhortation and commination and, at the end, pointed a bony finger at her.

"And now," he demanded, "are you willing to be damned for the greater glory of God?"

Dinty wriggled. "Please, sir, I'd rather not," she said.

"Answer me! Yes or no."

Her lip trembled. "I don't see how it would help God."

"That is not for you to say, lost soul that you are," thundered the Exhorter. "Yes or no?"

"No!" said Dinty desperately.

She would not cry! Not before this nasty sourface. She hated him. It wasn't fair. It was cruel. If she said she was willing to be damned, Mr. Sickel would probably tell God and God might take her at her word. She turned a piteous face to Parson Strang.

"Why do I have to be damned?" she whimpered.

A strange thing happened. The stern, gray pastor came over and put his arm around her quivering shoulders. His face was pale and strained. He said to his brother of the cloth,

"Are *you* willing to be damned for the greater glory of God?"

"Yes," answered Mr. Sickel with a meek and smug smile.

"Then, sir, you ought to be," returned Mr. Strang with such bitterness as Dinty had never before heard from his mouth. "Come, Araminta, my dear."

With that gaunt, protective arm still about her, he marched her out. The sound of Mr. Sickel's supplications followed them. He seemed to be asking Heaven's pardon for both of them in exasperated accents.

Before dark it was bruited about town that a devil of unrighteousness had issue from Dinty Jerrold and excited Elder Strang to insult the Rev. Sickel and balk him in his efforts to save the child's soul. Mrs. Jerrold wept purposefully all night and, in the morning, delivered to her husband what was as near to an ultimatum as she dared go; Dinty must be sent away. Squire Jerrold, heavy of heart and exhausted in patience, assented.

Full of woe and perplexity, the child sought out her trusted friend and counselor.

"Uncle Horace, do you think I'm a damned soul?"

"No. Why should you be?"

Dinty folded her hands, the unfailing concomitant of piety on her part, and recited,

> Soon as we draw our infant breath,
> The seeds of sin grow up for death.
> The Law demands a perfect heart,
> But we're defiled in every part.

"I had to repeat that a hundred times yesterday."

"Whose idea was that?" asked Horace, frowning.

"Exhorter Sickel's."

Horace muttered something so uncomplimentary to the Scythe of Salvation that Dinty gasped with horror and delight.

"Oh, Uncle *Horace!* There's such a lot of things they tell you to believe that I hate to believe," she went on meditatively. "Do you believe everything you ought to, Uncle Horace?"

Horace's eyes wandered to the shelf-row of infallible authorities; the cocksure claims and autocratic dicta of the discordant pundits.

"I'm afraid I don't, Dinty."

"Then maybe you're in peril of damnation, too."

"I'm liable to be, before all's said and done."

"If you can't believe, you can't, can you!" said the little philosopher summing up the despairing problem of saint and sinner.

"We're rebels, I expect, you and I," said Horace. "Born to trouble as the sparks fly upward."

"Is it very bad to be a rebel?"

"Perhaps it only means being born out of our time." He was talking more to himself than to her now. "A rebel has no contemporaries."

"How do you spell it?" asked Dinty with her diary in mind.

Horace laughed. "Never mind, little Dinty. You stick to your guns and don't let them scare you."

"Just the same," said Dinty, "alas!"

"Oh, no!" he protested. "No more of that."

"They're sending me away. To school at Aurora. Really, this time. Will you come to the coach to see me off, Uncle Horace?"

"Of course. I'm sure you'll like your school."

"I'm sure I'll hate it," she returned with a reproachful quaver. "If I do, I'll run away. I'll write to you when I get there. Will you write to me?"

"Perhaps," he said. Then, seeing her dolorous look, he kindly amended it to, "Yes, of course I will."

A small and sorrowing group assembled in front of the Eagle to bid the departing traveler farewell. Wealthia Latham was there in tears, Happalonia Vallance, the Fairlie twins, Grace and Freegrace, with several other schoolmates, and Marcus Dillard bearing a farewell token of an improving book selected by his mother. Dinty looked about in vain for Dr. Amlie. He was nowhere to be seen, being at the moment in the saddle and pushing Fleetfoot through the forest to reach a woodcutter who had, by a misstroke, half severed a foot. It was a desolate child who huddled into the corner of her seat, peeping out from damp eyes upon a wet and patchy landscape through the long day's journey to far away Aurora. She thought that her Uncle Horace had forgotten her.

Something awry with his office impinged vaguely upon Horace's consciousness a few days later. He presently identified it as a change in the decorative scheme. To his questioning, Mrs. Harte responded by tossing her head and avering that she didn't meddle where she wa'nt bid, but she couldn't warrant as much for that smudge-eyed imp of mischief, Wealthy Latham. Let him ask her.

Horace intercepted the girl on her way home from school. She was escorted by two boys, both considerably her seniors, one carrying her books, the other her bag.

"Have you had a letter from Dinty, Wealthia?"

She assumed an air of astonished admiration. "Aren't you cruel clever, Dr. Amlie! How ever could you know that?"

"My right eye told my left ear," said Horace dryly. "It was you that put back the sampler. Why?"

"I thought it looked prettier there."

"No suggestion in the letter?"

Wealthia dimpled. "Would you like to see it? I'll show you the last page."

Horace read the carefully inscribed words, evidently written under the still potent influence of the style of *Coquette*. It began with a broken sentence.

> ". . . see Marcus Dillard tell him I am thinking of him, and I read in his Book daily. You must visit Dr. Amlie's office, now that I am no longer there, and see that it is Clean and Neat. Mrs. Harte will negleckt him if not Watched. Please Wealthia do Something Important for me. Put my Sampler back on the Wall in Dr. Amlie's office. Somebody who shall be Nameless took it away. I think he would Like to have it There. I think it would Remind him of One who is Absent. I do not wish him to Forget me. Please do this for me, dear Wealthia and think Ofttimes of
>
> Your Loving and Afflicted Friend,
>
> A. Jerrold.

"What shall I tell her about the sampler?" asked Wealthia.

"Tell her I'm glad that it's back."

"She'll be glad, too. All right, all right, I'm coming." This to her two swains who were showing signs of impatience. "They're going to treat me to a brand-new beverage," she told Horace importantly. "It is called soda water and is said to be cruel tasty. Good-bye, Dr. Amlie."

"Good-bye, and thank you, Wealthia."

Some days later the mail coach brought him a communication of typical Dintyism, faintly qualified by the elegancies of the Guide to Genteel Correspondence.*

> Dear Uncle Horace:
>
> You may guess with what a heavy heart I was helped

* For the pattern of this letter I am indebted to the Wells College Library and Miss Louise Robinson Heath, whose great-grandaunt was the afflicted schoolgirl.

into the stage that was to convey me to this Detestable Nunnery, which I perfectly hate the Sight of. I want to take a little Rest in the Morning for I like to sleep as well as usual. I have to be Disturbed by a Rattling old Bell and when we go to bed at Night we might as well undertake to talk without mouths as to talk without our Mistress hearing. She will Poke her Head in at the door and tell us what is No News that it is against the Rules to talk in our rooms.

I have finished my Complaints and will now try to be more tame. They lock us in at Night but soon I may not be able to sustain it any longer so if you hear an Owl hooting on your Doorsill, rise up and let it in for it will be me—I; grammar.

Tell Tip I miss him and the Woods. If I do not Die of Loneliness and Abbandonment I will see you all next Vacation.

It seems Centuries away.

Your Loving,

A. Jerrold.

Post Scriptum. Sometimes I think I am God's Orphan Child and nobody loves me, and if you had been Mad with me about the Sampler I would have Died.

-16-

I knew all the Time my Doctor Amlie Would not let me Die.

(DINTY'S DIARY)

THAT fall saw the metamorphosis of Dr. Horace Amlie. Relieved from the cramping Levering influence, he developed into a bit of a gay blade. He became active in the Light Dragoons. He joined the Horsethief Society, meeting on Thursday evenings to devise ways and means of combatting a new and lively industry with which the constituted authorities were impotent to cope, while consuming the contents of Mine Host St. John's social bowl. He became a fire warden with beribboned staff, sworn to discharge the duties of that honorary office which had little to do with the devouring element directly, but were more of a police function to correct the widely held theory that a fire was a heaven-provided opportunity for the neighbors to augment their household equipment.

A ninepin alley had been established in the cellar of Mr. Hurd's new inn. Thither Dr. Amlie repaired two evenings of the week, to consort with such gaudy characters as Silverhorn Ramsey, Jed Parris and the more prosperous among the canal laborers. Going further in dissipation, he joined the sporting element of the smithy in laying out a quarter-mile straightaway racetrack on the eastern outskirts, where weekly trotting contests were held to the accompaniment of shameless and open wagering. Of a Saturday afternoon the rising young physician might be seen, fashionable in a suit of the gay London Blue with white silk gloves, acting as judge or, on occasion, competing on his mare, Fleetfoot. It was reputed that he had won twenty-five dollars from Ephraim Upcraft on a single heat.

The Palmyra Society for the Suppression of Vice & Immorality passed and published resolutions declaring that "horseracing is the box of Pandora from which issue more and greater mischiefs than ever man counted or measured," and accepted Horace's resignation without a dissenting voice. Exhorter Sickel, the society's new president, asserted that Palmyra was rapidly going to hell and Horace Amlie was going with it. If so, the wayfarer was patently determined to enjoy himself on the downward path. Thanks to the loan from Genter Latham, he was now established in his new residence, in connection with which another scandal attached itself to his besmirched name. With his cronies of the smithy he held weekly revel in his luxurious quarters where, it was darkly whispered, they played at fipenny loo.

Whatever the effect of these debaucheries upon his private repute, they did not impair his professional practice. Through that winter it steadily increased. Moreover, he was making social hay. His slightly rakehell reputation did not seriously prejudice him in the eyes of local spinsterhood. Only a few rigidly moral households such as (naturally) the Leverings', the Van Wies' and the Deacon Dillards' closed their doors to him. So impartially did he distribute his attentions, however, that he gained a name for baccalaureate caution. Dinty wrote him,

> Everybody wonders ~~who~~ whom you are going to marry and why you dont. Dont you think my grammar is improving?

Late in the winter the coach discharged a chilled but joyous Dinty whose first social call was upon Horace.

"What fetches you back?" he inquired. "School isn't out, surely."

"It's closed because so many of the girls took sick with throat fevers. One died."

"Throat fevers, eh? That's bad. But you're all right, aren't you?"

"Oh, yes. I'm all right."

"And how do you like your 'detestable nunnery' now?"

Dinty had the grace to blush. "I get along better," she admitted. "I miss you, though, Uncle Horace. Have you missed me?"

"Why, yes, I believe I have, a little."

"Only a little?"

"Well, quite a lot, if you insist."

"That's nice," she purred. She started to climb on his knee, but for some reason thought better of it. "Who are you sparking now?" she asked.

"Nobody."

"Then your life *is* blighted. Poor Uncle Horace! Are you cruel unhappy?"

"Never felt better in my life," he asseverated.

She looked about her, admiring the splendors of the abode. "What a dicty house! You built it for Miss Agatha, didn't you? I'm glad you're not going to marry her. She isn't right for you and never would be. She's too good."

"You told me that before."

"Well, you know what I mean. I mean too good the way you don't want folks to be too good when you love them. Was she jealous of Miss Sylvia Sartie?"

"Certainly not. There was no reason to be," said Horace with dignity.

"Oo!" said Dinty, wagging a sagacious head. "I'd have been." Horace reflected uncomfortably that this child had peculiar intuitions. "Remember what you wrote about St. Paul?"

"Never mind what I wrote."

"You're bound to marry somebody. I only hope it's the right person," said Dinty with undisguised pessimism.

"Thank you!"

"You needn't be pernickety about it. I'm only wishing for your own good. My ma says that being a doctor is a very gentlemanly calling, but a doctor's wife might as well be an owl. Why don't you marry Wealthy?"

Horace laughed indulgently. "Wealthia is a very young owl."

Dinty shook her head. "Don't you ever know when girls grow up? She's beautiful and she's going to be rich. It would be greatly to your advantage."

"Little Miss Worldly Wisdom. Now, what book is that from?"

"It isn't from any book. It's from my heart. Because you're my friend and so is Wealthy. She likes you awfly. She thinks you're well-favored and very dandy. Only thing is, she's in love with someone else."

"Blighted hopes," grinned Horace. "Which is the favored boyswain?"

"None of 'em. They're all in love with her—except Mark Dillard and maybe Arlo Barnes," she interpolated complacently. "But she has eyes for one alone. Guess. Three guesses. One for sight, and one for right, and one for cross-your-heart."

"Don't keep me on pins and needles," besought Horace.

"Now you're fooling. I don't care. I'll tell you. It's Captain Ramsey."

"Silverhorn!" Horace stifled a startled oath. "That unprincipled rip! How comes she to know him?"

"She doesn't exactly know him. But she saw him on Main Street and he smiled at her so romantically! Next time he passed her, driving in the country, he blew his bugle to her. So she wrote him a letter. I helped write it. It was full of passion and sensibility."

Horace swore, outright this time. "I'll have a talk with young Mr. Ramsey."

"No fair," she expostulated. "You mustn't. It's a secret. If Mr. Latham ever heard, he'd try to kill him. I'd never have told you if I thought you'd be so mean."

"Then you must tell her not to have anything further to do with him," warned Horace.

For several days he did not set eyes on his child-friend. Then, at the butcher's he met Mrs. Jerrold who purposely failed to see him, having regarded him as practically nonexistent since the destruction of her panaceas. She was talking with Mrs. Van Wie.

"Oh, yes, thank you, Mrs. Van Wie. The child is doing nicely. Dr. Murchison assures us that there is no cause for worry. We are fortunate in having a physician with his wide experience and learning." This with a contemptuous glance over her shoulder at Horace, who was pretending to be absorbed in a pickled loin. "We shall have her up in a day or two."

Horace made for the Eagle where, as he had hoped, he met Squire Jerrold, emergent upon the world after his morning's dram.

"Good morning to you, Amlie," said the fine gentleman genially.

"Good morning, Squire. How is Dinty?"

"Hearty, hearty," answered the Squire absently. "That is to say, a touch of sore throat. Natural at this season, eh? She will do well in bed, Murchison tells me."

"Sore throat?" repeated Horace uneasily. "Fever?"

"Murchison supposes a mildly typhous condition of the body. Nothing alarming." (Horace swore under his breath.) "He administered the tar-water treatment, bled and purged her, and reduced the swelling of the throat glands with a poultice of hops and vinegar. Mumpish. Nothing more, he assures me."

Horace said, "It was not mumps that killed her schoolmate at the Aurora Academy."

Mr. Jerrold started. "Kill—I know nothing of this. You think there might be danger?"

"Not having seen her professionally I am in no position to render an opinion."

"I wish you might. Murchison is all very well, I dare warrant, but sometimes I think him old-fashioned in his notions. What is your view of Murchison?"

"Since he has the case in his hands," said Horace, as in ethics bound, "I have no doubt it will be competently treated."

The other's eyes squinted. "You don't believe what you're saying. Murchison is returning this afternoon. If she is not improved, he will bleed her again."

"Doubtless," muttered Horace bitterly. He knew the accepted technic with the lancet. Too often he had heard veterans of the old school quote with approval the Sedgwickian dictum, "In the case of a child under fifteen, bleed until the patient faints."

Poor Dinty would have her veins tapped again. Then, for a wager, there would be calomel and castor oil, followed with emetic doses of squills and syrup of onions. Anything to "weaken the fever," ignoring the fact that the bodily vigor would be weakened proportionately and perilously.

There was nothing that he could do about it. The two men parted with sober visages.

No further tidings came that day. Horace was at his breakfast next morning when light, quick footsteps in the hallway, followed by a nervous rat-a-tat-tat on the door, interrupted his meal. He dropped a knifeful of beefsteak pie and hurried out. Wealthia Latham stood there, her velvety eyes hazed, the color gone from the rich darkness of her skin.

"Oh, Dr. Amlie! Come! Come, quick!"

"What is it?"

"Dinty."

He said, through a constricted throat, "It is not my case. I cannot interfere."

Wealthia sobbed once, a rending sound. "She's dying."

Horace consigned the code of medical ethics to hell.

"Is Squire Jerrold at home?"

"No. He went downtown before she started to choke."

"Find him. Hurry. Bring him back home. I'll be there."

He caught up his saddlebox and made speed to the Jerrold mansion. No one answered his violent tattoo on the brass knocker. He ran around to the porch door.

From within he could hear Dinty retching, bleating, pleading, "I want my Dr. Amlie. I want my Dr. Amlie."

Then the soothing tones of Aunt Minnie, the nurse, "There, my lambie! That's better. That fetches it up. Try again."

The door was bolted. Horace shook it, then hammered upon it imperiously. This was no time for considerations of dignity.

"Let me in! Let me in!"

Mrs. Jerrold's vain, pretty face, contorted with rage, confronted him.

"What brings you here? Get out of my house! Go away."

With a single swing of his muscular shoulder he battered loose the bolt. Dinty stretched out weak arms.

"Oh, Uncle Horace! I'm awfly sick." Then again the racking struggle for breath.

"Lie back," said he gently. He bent over to examine her.

A frantic grip on his shoulders pulled him away. "You shan't touch her," shrilled the mother.

He took her by the arms and, though she snapped at him like a mad thing, thrust her outside the door and wedged it with a chair. For a moment she battered at it. Then they could hear her yelling to the hired man in the garden.

"Fetch Dr. Murchison. Fetch Dr. Murchison."

The nurse whispered to Horace, "It's the rattles, Doctor. God help the poor mite! Two of mine went that way."

Anyone should have known it from the first for the dreaded croup, thought Horace bitterly, scanning the suffused and fever-swollen little face. Carefully he depressed the tongue. The appearance of the throat was dreadful. Already the terrible, pale membrane was forming.

He dipped into the saddlebox for a vial.

"Get me a feather," he bade the nurse. "A long one."

A duster stood in the corner. From it she plucked a slender partridge plume. Horace dipped the end, held the girl's mouth open, and delicately brushed the swollen channel through which the difficult breath came and went. He had the satisfaction of seeing part of the pallid scum dissolve. Dinty retched feebly. More of the membrane came up, and he cleared it away. Momentarily she breathed easier. But sad experience told him that the fiber would re-form time and again until the waning strength could no longer expel it. Silently he cursed the treatment which had already sapped the vitality of that sturdy body.

Now she was quieter. And now there were heavy steps outside and the bumble of a pedantic utterance giving forth something about the necessity of cleansing the system from its evil humors. Cleansing, indeed! Dearly as Horace would have liked to bar out his colleague, his professional conscience forbade. Already he had trespassed further than any medical board would condone. He stepped over and opened the door.

Dr. Gail Murchison stalked in, followed by Mrs. Jerrold. Ignoring the presence of another practitioner, the senior stepped to the bedside and laid a hand on the burning forehead.

"The fever increases," he pronounced judicially.

"Is—is she in danger?" stammered Dorcas Jerrold.

"What says the learned Dr. Hosack?" replied Dr. Murchison oracularly and answered himself, "That fevers are the greatest of all outlets to human life." The mother shuddered. "The case we have before us, Mistress Jerrold, is anomalous. Anomalous," he repeated. Any form of illness which he found complicated or unpromising, he catalogued as anomalous, thereby exculpating himself in advance for a possibly unfavorable outcome. "Did you offer a remark, sir?" he said sharply to Horace.

"No," said Horace who had merely grunted.

"If she is worse," said the mother with a malignant glance at Horace, "I lay it to him. Nobody knows what he has done to her."

"Have you presumed to interpose in my case, sir?" grated Murchison.

Horace recognized his right to put the query. He answered, "The child was choking. I cleared the throat with nitrate of silver."

"A dangerous procedure," said the other solemnly. "I hold you responsible."

The swollen eyes opened. "Don't let them vomit me again. Please don't let them, Uncle Horace," begged Dinty and was racked once more.

"Quiet, my dear." Horace caught the groping hands. His touch soothed her. She sank back.

"Don't leave me. Please don't leave me."

"I won't. I'll be right here." But he wondered how long he could maintain his ambiguous position.

Dr. Murchison appeared to be about to say something, but closed his jaws with a snap as he opened his lancet case. It was too much for Horace's good resolutions.

"What are you going to do?"

"That, sir, is not for you to inquire." He selected a blade with care, thumb-testing its edge.

"Do you intend to bleed her again?"

The other condescended to reply, "If you were a practitioner of experience, sir, you would have observed that the fever mounts. It must be checked."

"By God, you shan't!" said Horace.

The thump of hooves sounded on the lawn.

"Praises be!" exclaimed Nurse Minnie. "Here's the Squire's self."

For a moment Horace thought that his colleague was going to use the keen steel upon him, so furious were the eyes that glared into his.

"Ss-ss-sso!" hissed Murchison. "You cozen my patient's father into calling you upon my case and without due notification. A patient-snatcher! You shall hear of this from the censors, sir."

Horace knew that the threat was well founded. At the moment it mattered less than nothing to him. His whole thought was for that small, huddled figure on the bed.

Squire Jerrold hurried in. His wife ran to him, caught at his hands, pushed her crimson face up to his.

"Turn this young upstart out," she shrilled. "He has forced himself in here without warrant, and shut me from our child's bedside."

"Look at your daughter, sir," said Horace quietly.

The Squire passed to the bedside. Dinty did not know him. She was babbling. When he turned, it was not to Dr. Murchison but to Horace Amlie. There was terror in his eyes.

"Is she going to . . . ?" He could get no further.

Horace pointed to the lancet, still in his rival's fingers. "If she is bled again, she won't live an hour."

"And I tell you," blustered the other physician, "that unless blood is let the fever will burn her out before nighttime."

Mrs. Jerrold beat her hands together. "Will you listen to a young nincompoop like him against the experience and science of our own physician?" she cried.

"I will listen to both," said Squire Jerrold.

Dr. Murchison did not lack for cunning. He shifted his ground.

"If this is a consultation," said he smoothly, "I shall be happy to consider my young colleague's views before proceeding."

But Horace was not heeding. His anxious ears had caught a sound which meant another crisis approaching. Again he inserted the acid-tipped feather. But now the orifice was smaller, the effort to dislodge the choking barrier greater. There was audible to his practiced hearing the beginning of that moist clacking which gave the disease its vulgar name of rattles. When the paroxysm had abated, he rejoined the two men.

Dr. Murchison said weightily, "I recommend a sinapism for the soles of the feet."

(Great God! thought Horace. Not that it mattered; the mustard plaster could do no harm or good, and Dinty was beyond feeling its sting.)

"As the next step we should perhaps exhibit pyroligneous acid," continued the elder.

"Pyro—what for?" demanded Horace.

"To allay mortification of the tonsils."

Horace closed his eyes and prayed for patience. Dr. Murchison bumbled on.

"There is also *polygola seneka* to be considered. I have found it useful in similar cases of exasperated mumps."

The patience which Horace had besought was not vouchsafed him. "Do you still diagnose this as mumps?" he asked balefully.

"Do you differ from my opinion, sir?"

"Here is too much talk," broke in the father. "Doctors wrangle and my daughter lies dangerously ill. What are her chances?"

Dr. Murchison cleared his throat. "I consider her in a soperose state."

Horace said bluntly, "She is near to death."

The nurse lifted a pinched face, calling to Horace, "There's another attack comin' on, sir."

He returned to the bedside. Mrs. Jessup was bowed above the pillow, shutting out the free air for which the lungs were panting in agony. He set her aside, went to the window which someone had closed, and threw it open.

The small face below him was darkening. The terrible problem now was simply to keep the breath passing through. No longer would the feather serve. Horace reached for his forceps and began gently to loosen and draw the encroaching film. Someone behind him closed the window. Without looking he drove his elbow backward, shattering a pane. Now he took the next step, the insertion of a steel distender to hold open the channel for the desperate breath.

Slowly the paroxysm subsided; the flush of fever succeeded to the leaden hue of asphyxiation. It would come again, that dire struggle, and again and again until . . . He must not think of that. Concentrate on what slender hope remained, and be ready for the last desperate, necessary measure. He bathed the hot face with cooling vinegar and water, rubbed the parched and cracking lips with a soothing amalgam of honey, beeswax, and sweet oil, and was rewarded with what he fondly believed to be a flicker of consciousness.

Morning wore slowly to noon and passed into afternoon. If the condition grew no better, it was at least no worse. The temperature was stationary at 105½. But the pulse labored and flickered. It was difficult to keep Dinty quiet when the delirium beset her; yet every sound forced through the straining throat was so much essential strength expended.

For a time the problem of keeping the passage clear enough for breath was simpler. This did not deceive Horace with undue hopes. The disease was the most treacherous of all the enemies he was called upon to confront. It lurked and struck.

Dr. Murchison left at three o'clock to make his rounds. Horace overheard him promising to send a glazier to repair the sash.

"If you do," he threw over his shoulder, "I'll put my boot through it."

"I will return at five o'clock unless summoned earlier," said the departing physician to Mrs. Jerrold who was imploring him to stay.

That hour found Dinty's condition unchanged. But with the fall of darkness, the fever rose again.

"Night air," said Dr. Murchison glaring at the window. "Deadly! Deadly!"

As if to bear him out, the figure on the bed shivered all over and stiffened. The choking set in. Strive as he might with forceps and probe, Horace could no longer keep the narrowed channel from clogging. Dinty began to gasp. The cyanotic blue showed on lips and fingernails. In her face the red of fever was supplanted by the dreaded lividity of slow strangulation.

Horace dropped the forceps and caught up a blade from his lancet box.

"Aha!" snarled Murchison triumphantly. "Now he bleeds her. Pray God it be not too late."

"Hold her head back," Horace directed the nurse. "Farther. So."

"What are you going to do?" gasped the Squire.

"Tracheotomy."

"What is that? What does he mean?" cried Mrs. Jerrold.

"He's going to cut her throat," roared Murchison.

"Murder! Murder! Murder!" Mrs. Jerrold's shrieks rang through the house.

"Keep her off me," warned Horace as she rushed at him, only to be caught and pinioned by her husband. His face was agonized as he whispered to Horace,

"Must it be done?"

"She's dying. Smothering. Can't you see? Now let me alone."

He made the small, neat, perpendicular incision as he had once seen the great Vought do it over the protests of a group of consultants—thank God for that remembered lesson!—fixed a tube in the orifice, and heard the air rush, in great, life-giving gasps to replenish the flaccid lungs. Slowly the face changed from a leaden mask to the similitude of human flesh. The spasm-strained muscles relaxed. The head was eased back upon the pillow where it lay quiet, no longer twisting and turning in the anguish of breath denied. And all the time Murchison was bleating like a distracted sheep, "Tracheotomy is not recommended. What says the learned De Weese? Tracheotomy is not recommended."

"He has cut our daughter's throat," sobbed Mrs. Jerrold wildly. "Who will mend it?"

That would be a later problem for Horace to meet. The immediate crisis was still acute. After midnight came the first real change. Almost imperceptibly the pulse abated. The fever dropped. Only a degree, to be sure, but it was hopeful. Horace got some warm milk with a few drops of brandy into the stomach. Dawn found him still at his post.

"I think she'll do now," said he unsteadily, and gulped the spirits which Squire Jerrold held out to him. Horace was still very young. An older and more experienced practitioner would not have put so much of himself into any case.

He gave the nurse instructions and went home to wash face and hands in hot vinegar. Most of the authorities concurred in the theory which Dr. Murchison had aired, that croup, rattles, cynanche trachealis, cynanche maligna, call it what one might, was "epidemic and not contagious." It was caused by uncomprehended climatic conditions, or perhaps subtly poisonous exhalations from the decaying earth. Horace had his heretical doubts.

They were strengthened when, a few days later, seven new cases appeared in the village, one of them Marcus Dillard. Dinty's swain recovered, but two children died.

Horace made a deft repair of Dinty's wound and anticipated, having done so well, being called in on some of the other cases. He was disappointed. By hint and innuendo Dr. Murchison, working so cunningly that the evil report could never be traced to him, spread the rumor that the new doctor had cut a hole in Araminta Jerrold's windpipe, despite the tears and entreaties of her mother, and that the poor child would never speak again. That she was alive after the experience at the hands of so reckless an experimentalist was a mystery which Dr. Murchison could not explain, but covered by his familiar formula,

"Anomalous, anomalous. A thoroughly anomalous case."

He awaited only the appearance of Dinty in public to bring in his indictment to the medical board. But the girl upon her release from the sickroom talked as much and as briskly as before.

Dr. Gail Murchison preserved his complete notes of the case for future use.

In his care of the convalescent, Dr. Amlie made certain observations.

"How old is Dinty?" he asked the father.

"Fourteen. Why do you ask?"

"Why, she told me last year . . ."

"Yes, yes, I know." Squire Jerrold smiled. "She's a strange child. She has always resented having to grow up. So she pretends to be younger than she is. I would not say but what her mother has abetted her in the harmless deception."

Horace suffered an inexplicable pang. Dinty growing up! He felt as if he were threatened with the loss of something precious.

-17-

My Uncle Horace is a Hero. And I was not Scared much, my own self.

(DINTY'S DIARY)

WINTER broke early that year. The gangs, reinforced, attacked the ground before the frosts were fairly out of it, Genter Latham's being the earliest. Local advertisements called for two thousand pairs of knitted woolen gloves against frostbite, and many a weary housewife burned her bayberry candle to the click of bone needles, earning pin money for her summer furbishings. The Latham squad, with lusty song, pushed the cut through the village, west to east, between the turnpike and the creek.

"Rochester to Albany in 1822," exulted Elder Strang's weekly organ which, in a burst of local patriotism, had changed its name to *The Western Farmer & Canal Advocate.*

Horace Amlie surveyed the foul mudholes formed by natural seepage with a morose eye.

"We shall have disease," said he to Genter Latham and Squire Jerrold, as they sat on the Latham porch.

"What kind?" asked the Squire uneasily.

"Dysentery and diarrheas certainly; fevers probably."

"We've always been a healthy village, uncommonly healthy," protested Mr. Jerrold.

"So have the others, until the canal came," returned Horace. "We learn nothing from their mistakes. See how sickness follows the canal. Rome fever, Montezuma malaria, Schenectady shakes. Our turn is coming unless we take action."

"Move the village away, I suppose, like you moved my camp," grinned Genter Latham.

"I'd like to. Our worthy citizens have been using the ditch as a convenient dump-heap, drain and cesspool," said Horace. "I could show 'em some things."

"Show 'em to us," said Genter Latham.

"Come to my office and I will."

With the first warm weather Horace had been collecting from the fouled accumulations of water, flies, mosquitoes, and other insects and preparing slides from what he found on their feet. One of these he fitted to his microscope while his two visitors stood, expectant.

"Take a look, gentlemen," he invited.

Genter Latham applied his eye to the barrel. Knowing him to be anything but an impressionable person and expecting little from the exhibit, Horace was agreeably disappointed. Mr. Latham was so impressed that he vomited.

"Fetch that contraption of yours to our meeting tomorrow," said he after being restored with a tot of brandy. Both he and the Squire were village trustees.

"We'll make it a public hearing," added Mr. Jerrold. "Let 'em all hear what you've got to say."

The Big Room of the Eagle was well filled with representative citizenry when, on the stroke of seven, Chairman Levering's gavel descended. Rather sourly he announced that there would be a discussion of the town's state of health. For his part, he couldn't see but what they were doing well enough. Those things were in the hands of Divine Providence, so why go out to meet trouble before it arrived? With which ungracious introduction Horace was invited to take the floor. He spoke briefly and modestly, citing the course of the fevers which had so hampered and delayed the canal's progress. Would it not be well for the village to take measures in advance?

"What sort of measures?" asked Trustee Van Wie.

"Well, cleaning out some of our filthy dump-heaps and cesspools."

"Is this young gentleman from the Oneida wilds implying that our village is filthy, Mr. Chairman?" inquired Ephraim Upcraft.

"You've got a nose," said Horace shortly. "Use it."

"I don't poke it into other folks' backyards."

"You might try your own. Your cesspool is surface-full. I can smell it in my office when the wind sets that way."

Carlisle Sneed, who had been patiently awaiting a chance to be funny, now saw and seized it. "Move we appoint Doc Amlie privy counselor to the town," he giggled.

The laugh apprised Horace that he was on the wrong track. A

man's privy was his castle to every true American. He tried another angle.

"There's a compost heap at the bend of the creek that ought to be cleared away," he said.

"Dot's my doomp-heap," said Simon Vandowzer in his heavy, Dutch drawl. "Vot's de madder of it?"

"It breeds flies and mosquitoes."

"Vot off id? Vot's de madder off flies and mosgeedoes?"

"They're not healthy."

"Hunca-munca!" snorted Dr. Murchison. "Mr. Chairman, does my college-bred young friend insinooate that there is any harm to humans from the innocent winged creatures of the air?"

"Ever sit on a bumble bee, Doc?" interpolated Mr. Sneed.

"I do," said Horace, answering Murchison, "mean just that."

"Maybe you hold that bugs carry disease. Is that it?"

"You once quoted the learned Dr. Hosack to me, sir. Are you aware that he held filth responsible for jail-fever and dysentery?"

"We ain't in jail," retorted his opponent. "And where's your dysentery?"

"It will come," replied Horace boldly, "just as sure as present conditions are left unremedied. I'll stake my professional reputation on it."

Old Murch got out of his seat and paced the floor, stopping before his young competitor and thrusting a long and not-too-clean finger at him. Under the stress of excitement and resentment, the old fellow's medical polish dissolved. His voice became a throaty caw.

"Git back to your fevers, young man. Now, you tell us a canal fly catches canal fever. Huh? And passes it along to human folks. Huh? Is that it?"

"Mosquitoes rather than flies."

"Oh-oh! Moskeeters! And how do the moskeeters do it, young fellow? Tell us that. They catch it, says you. Did you ever see a moskeeter with the shakes?" He beamed triumphantly about him. The grin said that he guessed *that* would settle the young jackanapes's hash.

"It is believed that they carry fomites," replied Horace, reddening.

"What's a fomite?"

"I don't know precisely, but . . ."

"I warrant you don't. Nor nobody else."

". . . but it is supposed to be a microscopic molecule that disseminates the disease principle which it absorbs from swamps and filth."

"Listen to him, gentlemen! Listen to young Dr. Wisdom! Flies carry the gut-wambles. Moskeeters catch the shakes and carry 'em to you and me. Bats fetch around the yellow jaunders, I wouldn't wonder, and jaybirds scatter the itch. Ever hear that the doodlebug's bite gives you vapors on the brain, young fellow? Sure you ain't been bit by one, yourself?"

"Giving the town a bad name," growled Mr. Van Wie.

Discontented mutters arose in support of the complaint. Horace found himself confronted by the smug conservatism of settled and self-satisfied prosperity which resents any suggestion of change as a threat.

"Mr. Chairman," said Dr. Murchison, resuming his canonical air, "may I offer an eloocidation of the problum?"

"We shall always be honored to hear from a gentleman of Dr. Murchison's wisdom and special knowledge," said the Chairman pointedly.

"Thank you, sir. My young colleague"—he waved a patronizing hand toward Horace—"is a sad example of what the Hymn Book terms 'learning's redundant part and vain.' Let me first put him right on the nature of fever. All fevers are one and the same in essence, whether they are intermittent, remittent, bilious-remittent, lung fever, gut fever, or brain fever. They manifest themselves in different symptoms and stages. There is the simplex stage, the typhous stage, the depressive stage, the inflammatory stage and the malignant or putrid stage. The cause, my friends, is not in any silly bug-bite. It is in decaying matter, such as leaves, plants and rotten wood which exhale gases, humors and dangerous miasmas to be absorbed by the human system. All this talk of bugs and fomites is so much huncamunca and folderol-diddle-de-day. No, no, my young and fancy-minded sir! Don't try to meddle with the laws of nature and the privies of your fellow citizens. When the fever comes—*if* it comes—we'll handle it with the true-blue, old-style medicaments."

Squire Jerrold's suggestion that the Board examine Dr. Amlie's microscopic slides was swamped. The meeting adjourned. Outside, the Squire said not unkindly to Horace,

"You'll never make a politician, my boy."

"Nor do I want to," said Horace.

"That's all very well," put in Genter Latham dourly, "but you'd better get your disease-bugs working for you. Unless there are epidemics of bellyaches and hot foreheads around here pretty soon, they'll laugh you out of town."

"Wait till it warms up a little more. I doubt if they'll feel like laughing then," returned Horace tartly.

Nature came to the aid of the trustees. Steady rains covered the bed of the canal, drowning out the worst breeding places of the flies, and muddying up the water beyond the tolerance of even the hardiest anopheles larva. Intestinal diseases made their appearance with July's heat, but not worse than in other years. Malaria was sporadic.

Even among his pals of the smithy, Horace lost face. They regarded him with easy amiability as a well-meaning but discredited faddist. Having no clue to the reasons for the population's immunity from the expected illnesses, Horace was threatened with a loss of faith in himself, which, for a physician, is the beginning of the end.

As embodying the spirit and hope of progress, a marine apparition, trim and shapely, took form in the stocks back of Palmer & Jessup's Basin. "The elegant and superb Packet Boat, *Queen of the Waters*," announced Editor-Preacher Strang's paper, "will plow the waves ere autumn paints our fair land with its rainbow palette."

Not all the traffic now plying the canal sections from Rome to Albany so fired the patriotic souls of the Palmyrans—for, after all, to nine-tenths of the populace these far-off events were only hearsay, whereas seeing is believing—as the birth of the first craft to which Palmyra could point as its very own.

The work was rushed. Earlier than the time set by the fervent prophet, the packet, beflagged and beribboned, was played down the ways by the Palmyra Light Dragoons band in full uniform, into fourteen inches of what might by courtesy have been called water, while the populace cheered itself purple in the face.

Their acclaim was premature. The fifty-fifty composite of mud and water, after deepening to a foot-and-a-half, dwindled to ten inches, whereupon the regal craft turned on her side like a sick fish and there wallowed, in Carlisle Sneed's regrettably coarse words, "as flat as a slut on her bum in a puddle." The *Queen* crawled back on her perch under cover of kindly night.

Malaria broke out. Horace reported a dozen cases to Genter Latham who was unimpressed and quoted the proverb about the single swallow. His men were now working east of the village and pushing ahead at top speed. But back of his project, the work still lagged. Squire Jerrold's camp, and several others were, as Old Bill Shea informed Horace, "rotten with the shakes."

A hard frost early in September saved them, and the village as well, from a more disastrous epidemic. Every time that Horace met

Dr. Gail Murchison the older man animadverted upon the disappearance of the malaria and inquired solicitously whether his colleague was "still taking the pulse and temperature of your patients, the bugs."

That fall saw the marriage of Miss Agatha Levering and the Rev. Philo Sickel, to which Horace was magnanimously invited, and the establishment of Genter Latham's bank which the Reverend Mr. Strang editorially mistrusted as "a combination of the rich vs. the poor, a moneyed corporation whose power is a menace to free institutions." Some of the older inhabitants felt uneasily that Latham was acquiring too much power and employing it too arrogantly for the town's good. The great man went his way, disdaining hostility or, more often, ignoring it. Seldom did it take form in opposition. He was too powerful along too many lines. He had few friends and no intimates except Squire Jerrold. He cared for nobody but himself and his daughter, in whose burgeoning, darkly radiant beauty he took an inordinate pride.

The patronage of the Lathams now operated to Horace Amlie's professional advantage. To have two such conspicuous young maids as Wealthia Latham and Araminta Jerrold officially under his care was bound to give him a certain cachet, though both were now away at school, Wealthia at the Albany Academy. Through the winter he prospered, financially and socially, notwithstanding the detriment to his reputation as a medical prophet of evil.

Dinty Jerrold, home for Christmas, surprised him in a new uniform, resplendent with silken sash and a cocked hat with tricolor plumes. He had just come back from the noon drill of the Light Dragoons. She was rapt in admiration.

"Aren't you pompous!" she cried. "Who are you beauing now?"

"Nobody," answered Horace.

"Of course you are! Didn't you take Margaret Van Wie skating on the canal?" she demanded, checking the items on her fingers. "And didn't you escort Eliza Evernghim on the party to improve the minister's woodpile? And who was it that invited Dora Macy twice to learned lectures? And wasn't Sarah Ann . . . ?"

"Stop it! The child has swallowed the catechism."

She gazed at him pensively. "Don't you like me to ask you questions?"

"I'm flattered by your interest," he replied sardonically.

"Pa says curiosity killed the cat. Ma says I'm nosy. D'you think I'm nosy, Uncle Horace?"

"Ahem! I think you exhibit a certain interest in other people's affairs."

"Because I *am* interested. That's just my mind standing up on tiptoe to see better."

"Who's your local informant? You seem to have kept yourself current?"

"Tip Crego writes me about things. You never write me any more. Did you weep at Miss Agatha's wedding?"

"One more question and I'll dose you with jalap. You look a bit bilious, anyway."

"I do not," she denied indignantly. "I never was better in my life. Mark Dillard says I look nicer than anyone he knows, even Wealthy."

"Is Mark Dillard the favored one?"

Dinty looked noncommittal. "I don't know," she drawled affectedly. "There's Philip Macy and Ethniel Craddock and a new boy named Page—his father has something to do with the canal. I like 'em all awfly, but . . . Oh, I don't know! I don't believe it's the tender passion. Do you, Uncle Horace?"

Horace grinned. "I hardly feel myself competent to judge."

"Sometimes I speculate a lot on the tender passion," mused Dinty. "It's very muddling. D'you think there are some unhappy maidens that it never comes to, Uncle Horace?"

"I think you might better be speculating on your mathematics," said he, brutally touching upon her weak point.

Dinty was not to be diverted from the superior interest. "Haven't you something about it in your learned library, Uncle Horace?"

"Certainly," said Horace and handed her a treatise on Quaternions.

"I don't mean that," said Dinty, thrusting it aside loftily. She lifted another volume from his desk and dropped it as if it were hot. It was the revelatory Burns whose text, with illustrations, had been the topic of an earlier and unforgotten interview. Acutely conscious of her shamed face, Horace reflected uncomfortably that this was a changed and more informed Dinty.

A caller in the heavy woolens of a woodsman relieved the embarrassment. As he entered, Dinty tactfully withdrew to the inner apartment. She overheard an indistinguishable dialogue, then Horace's brisk query,

"How far?"

"Not more'n five mile."

"Can I get there on runners?"
"Most of the way."
"As soon as my footwarmer is heated I'll start."
The man left, mumbling his thanks. Dinty, reappearing, said, "Oh, Uncle Horace, take me!"
Horace hesitated, peering out the window at the gray threat of the sky.
"I'll be as good as pie. You've always promised to take me on a country call. Do it for my Christmas treat," she wheedled. "It's almost Christmas."
Tip Crego, now installed as office boy and bill collector while he studied the classics with the doctor, was not at hand, so there was an empty seat.
"Get your warmest clothes," said Horace, "and come back here."
She was on hand, clad in her heavy coat of otter, by the time he had the warmer packed with coals. The case, he explained to her, should not take long. It was a "putrid" wound of the hand, not difficult to treat unless gangrene had set in. For some five miles they traveled the fairly level Canandaigua Pike, then turned off on a rugged woods road where they bumped and slewed and Fleetfoot picked her way distrustfully. A few rods short of a clearing with a bare log cabin in the center, they pulled up, the yard being impassable with stumps. Dinty wrinkled a delicate nose.
"Pee-*yoo!*" she sniffed. "What's that awful smell?"
"Assafetida," Horace explained. "They sprinkle it on the snow to keep the wolves away from the sheepfold."
"Are there wolves around here?"
"Not with the wind as it is," he reassured her. "They won't come near. You'll be snug as a bug in a rug."
He blanketed the mare, tucked his passenger warmly about, and threaded the stumps to the door. Happy at being back in her beloved wilds, Dinty burrowed down for a catnap.
When she woke, dusk was already glooming. She saw Horace plowing his way through the snow. His face was cheerful.
"Is it all right?" she asked.
He nodded. "We'll save the hand. Were you afraid?"
"Of course not! I talked with a snow-owl for awhile, and then I fell asleep. Tell me all about the case."
They were in sight of the turnpike when a faint and dreadful cry, borne downwind, interrupted the recital. Fleetfoot pricked up her ears. Dinty began to quake.

"What was that?" she whispered.

"I don't know." He eased the mare to a halt.

"Maybe it's the wolves."

"No. It was only one voice. It sounded human." He put the reins into her mittened hands.

"What are you going to do, Uncle Horace?" she asked apprehensively.

"I'd better have a look. It might be someone in trouble."

"Who could it be 'way out here at night?"

"Somebody could be lost."

The ghoulish, wordless wail was repeated, a little fainter this time, a little less like anything known to earth.

"Nobody could make a sound as awful as that," she breathed. "Let's go home."

"Not until I've investigated." He jumped out.

"You haven't even got your gun."

"I'll take a lancet."

Suddenly she leaned out and clutched him. "I know what it is. It's a painter. You shan't go."

He tried to soothe her. "I don't believe it's a panther. Be my brave Dinty now."

"I'm not afraid for me. I'm afraid for you," she wept. "You'll be killed and eaten."

He felt less assurance than he had expressed. Once before, when a sophomore on College Hill, he had heard the hunger cry of the great, stealthy cat, and in the morning had found the mark of the broad pads on the snow. Again the air quivered to the meaningless and grisly ululation.

"Listen to me carefully, Dinty," he bade her. "If I am not back in fifteen minutes, you go to the cabin for help. Keep your head now. And hold the mare firm."

For a moment he thought that she was going to defy his authority. She wavered and sank back. Her head drooped until her nose was buried in the fur of the robe. She sobbed desolately. He patted her shoulder and turned away.

Sounds in the winter woods are deceptive. Pushing through the snow, knee-deep in spots, Horace paused from time to time to amend his direction, A clear, insistent call from the rear checked him.

"Hoo-ee-ee! Uncle Ho-race! Hoo-ee-ee-ee!"

The voice was more than excited; it was jubilant.

"What do you want?" he shouted back.

"It isn't a painter. Fleetfoot would go crazy if it was. She's quiet as a lamb."

Horace admitted to himself a surge of relief.

"Good child!" he called back. "You're a better woodsman than I."

The outcries from the forest sounded fainter and less terrifying now. There was a small watercourse somewhere in the vicinity; possibly a wayfarer had fallen into that and injured himself. A broken leg, perhaps. Death would not be far away in the falling temperature. He toiled up a small elevation and, on the farther side strained his ear to the wind. A desolate whimper rewarded him.

At first he saw nothing but the snowy forest, a felled ash, and its raw stump, bristling with splinters. A dark blob on the snow, hardly identifiable as human, was almost hidden by the trunk beneath which it was pinned. A dull, hurried babble rose from it.

"Oh, bress God! Bress my deah Saviour! He done ansah mah prayer. Bress His name!"

"Unk Zeb!" cried Horace.

He floundered to the side of the aged Negro. A glance told him the nature of the accident. The white ash, most treacherous of trees, had sprung at the last ax-stroke and felled the feller, driving him down into the snow until he was pressed against the hard earth beneath, and inextricably wedging him there by wrist and forearm.

In his youth Horace had accustomed himself to the ax. Attacking the tree-bole as near to the prisoned form as he dared, he hacked through it. Happily the severed lower end did not settle further, or the victim's arm would have been crushed beyond repair. Cutting three saplings, Horace carefully inserted them to form a rough rollway, and with a fourth gently levered the trunk. Slowly it eased away, slid, half-turned, and old Helms was free. He blessed his Maker again in his quavering basso, and fainted.

Working to revive him, Horace saw outlined the record of the grisly and brave tragedy, the almost hopeless struggle for life, determined for every last, slender chance in accordance with the woodsman's ritualistic and grim tradition. With his free right hand, Unk Zeb had scooped and packed the snow about his body for warmth. The best he could do for his legs was to burrow a little. Horace judged that both feet would be frozen, as well as the vise-gripped left arm. Within easy reach, the keen utility knife, without which no veriest tyro ever ventured into the wilderness, was driven beneath the rough bark. Had the tree been a smaller one of pine, hemlock, or whitewood, its victim might have tried a race with death, cutting through it. Against the iron toughness of the ash the blade was futile.

It was there for another purpose. When no hope of rescue remained, when cold and the ebbing strength imperatively called for the last gamble, forest lore prescribed the desperate venture. The prisoner would first cut strips from his clothing which he would place beside him in readiness for application. Minutes, even seconds, would count now. For his one chance was to hew through the elbow joint, severing the arm. How effectually he could staunch the spurting blood by ligature of the cloth strips, bound hard with hand and tooth, would determine whether he died on the spot. If he survived that ordeal, he must pit his last remaining powers against cold, night, and mortal weakness in the struggle to gain the public road where there was just a chance of being found in time. Such cases were not uncommon. No settlement was without its one-armed or single-footed victims. But the graveyards held most of them.

To carry the bulky form through the drifts would have been an overstrain for Horace Amlie's supple strength. With bandages from his pack he lashed together saplings to make a pole-sledge, bound the half-conscious old man upon it, and, supporting the ends upon his shoulders, dragged his burden to where the cutter stood. Dinty ran to meet them, carrying the flask. Together they got the old man up on the seat.

So close were they to the turnpike that it seemed best to make for town rather than take the nearer course to the forest cabin. Horace set his companion to rubbing the Negro's arm and wrist with snow while he urged the willing mare to her best speed. They made the Pinch in thirty minutes.

Summoning the Cregos to build a fire in the hut, he examined his patient. Both feet were frozen as well as the left arm. But there was nothing beyond repair. A few days of care, and Unk Zeb would be about again.

His account of his mishap was simple and commonplace. For the fall and winter he had turned his hand to his old, slave occupation of woodcutting. Only the hardwoods fetched a living price by the cord, so he located sections of unpre-empted oak and ash, not too far from some highway and cut systematically. After felling and portioning a tree, he would "rope-snake" the logs to the nearest road, pile his tiers, and either sell on the spot or dicker for an ox-team to drag them to market. Being skillful, though slow, he managed to keep himself in food and clothes. The usual practice for the industry was for the cutter to leave word with his family where he would be working that day. But old Helms lived alone; there was none to mark his comings and goings or to care. He would certainly not have been missed before morning, by which time he would be either dead or a one-armed "white-ash man."

"Who heah me fust?" he asked Horace.

"Miss Dinty."

The old fellow rolled back his eyeballs in pious ecstasy. "Bress her sweet soul! I knewed it. I knewed it all de time."

"How did you know it, Unk Zeb?"

"When de debbil in de ash st'uck me down, my sperrit floated in de air. I see a li'l white, shiny angel ovah me an' I heah her say, 'Po' ol' Unk Zeb! He in trile an' tribbleation. Go git his perishin' body.' Den I knewed he'p is comin' an' I call till de speech lef' me an' I can on'y hollah."

From the time of his recovery the old Negro appointed himself Dr. Amlie's retainer. Manifesting unexpected aptitudes, he became cook, house-hussey, groom to Fleetfoot, and man-of-all work. Invariably he prefaced breakfast by asking whether Marse Horuss had heard from "de li'l angel," who had now returned to school where her reputation did not answer precisely to that description. He dictated to Tip Crego hifalutin messages of gratitude, few of which reached their object, postal rates being what they were.

At first Horace found the ex-slave a responsibility, then a convenience, and finally an essential contributor to his ease of life.

-18-

Sometimes it is Nice to feel Grown Up. Sometimes it is Horrid. Other Times I do not know Which.

(DINTY'S DIARY)

To profess faith that the canal would be open for traffic in the spring now became the touchstone of loyalty to Palmyra. The *Queen of the Waters* was re-calked and fresh painted. Tactfully forgetting the episode of her earlier retirement from the life nautical, the community prepared for a second celebration. April found the trim craft, proud-pied and decorated, poised on the verge of the cut, all dressed up and no place to go.

For nature turned sour on Palmyra. The normal rains withheld. The sun blazed, day after cloudless day. The meager trickle of waters, feeding the gash in the earth, was absorbed as fast as it mounted. The only maritime enterprise visible was a toy sloop which Tip Crego had fashioned with his ready knife, as a gift to Dinty when she should return. The town went into mourning, as after a disastrous defeat.

Dinty had written to her Uncle Horace, hinting that she might be coming home before long (she hoped that it might be in time for the Canal Fete, now indefinitely postponed) because of some trouble at school. The exact nature of it Horace could not clearly make out from the smudged lines. (Tears?) There was a minister's son involved, and references to the Beauties of Nature and what they can Teach Us if Properly Appreciated. Also resentful reflections upon the severity of Miss Marriott's discipline.

He said [wrote Dinty without identifying the pronoun—the minister perhaps] that my Conduct was unworthy of the Brutes that perish. But Nobody would have known if Morris had not awakened the pesky Watch Dog. When I am Dead, some folks will be Sorry they were so Mean to me. And if they send me far away to Albany, I will Die and you will never again lay a Sorrowing Eye on,

Your loving and respectful,

Araminta Jerrold.

Post Scriptum. Morris was whopped in the Woodshed and howled like a Highena. They could not make me cry. P. S. 2—If they do send me Home at term's end I hope I can come by the Grand Canal.

Reading between the lines and with his knowledge of Dinty's propensities for a guide, Horace guessed that the call of the wild had once more proven too much for her resistance and that she was in disgrace for having taken a nocturnal outing with Morris, presumably the son of the denunciatory parson.

Her hope of canal traffic was unexpectedly borne out. For just as the Palmyra churches were about to combine in a service of lamentation and contrition for the sins implacably punished by a rainless heaven, the drought broke. A mighty thunderstorm heaved its mass out of the western horizon, spread, and discharged, ushering in a two-day downpour.

Ten thousand trickles raced down from the conical hillocks to contribute to every little heights-born stream, pouring its swollen volume into the muddy excavation. Inch by painful inch the water gained. The sun came out and so did the hopeful townsfolk to line towpath and berm and exultantly watch the descending floods. By evening of the third day, success was assured. The leading citizens of the place could be observed, boot-deep in the sludge, anxiously consulting the notches of their yardsticks. At nine twenty-five, the Rev. Theron Strang stationed opposite the upper basin, lifted a jubilant voice.

"The Lord hath prospered us. Two foot full, and still rising. Praise we the Lord!"

"And De Witt Clinton," supplemented Genter Latham. The cheers were impartially distributed.

Eager hands laid hold on the waiting *Queen* and propelled her bulk into the swirl of dark-brown, viscous fluid which fulfilled the function of water sufficiently to buoy her proudly up. A cannon from the War of 1812 fired a salvo. Two school squads, organized by sex, formed up on the south side. The boys were headed by a banner inscribed "Village School" on one side, and "Science" on the other. The girls, led by Wealthia Latham, supported the twin sentiments, "Clinton & the Canal" and "Internal Improvements." Squire Jerrold delivered the toast of the occasion, with gallant empressement:

"The Erie Canal, opening an Intercourse between the Interior and the Extreme Parts of the United States; it will Assimilate Conflicting Interests, impart Energy and give Durability to the National Compact."

A bit premature, perhaps, considering that the western section, joining up with Lake Erie, was not yet dug and that the extent of local navigation to be expected was a possible thirty miles.

However, there was indubitably that harbinger of marine trade, the *Queen of the Waters* and, from farther afield, a couple of freight Durhams from Lyons and Pittsford. If the full four feet of medial depth was not yet attained, at least there was plenty of water to buoy up any craft that wished to ply. Horses appeared, tandem, on the towpath, hauling the craft busily back and forth between the two terminals, but, as there was no great occasion for local transfer of freight, their most profitable trade was carrying parties of exultant sightseers.

By order of the Commission, the towpath was sacred to hauling. Horace Amlie, however, presuming upon his privilege as a medico, often found it his most convenient route to or from a call. Returning early in the evening from a visit to a measled household, he was astonished to see in the distance two mounted figures on the forbidden strip. The riders were moving at a slow pace; Fleetfoot's leisurely amble soon brought him near enough to perceive that they were ladies in full rig of long skirt and feathered hat. Presumably strangers in town. Certainly this was no place for them. If a tow appeared now, they would be subjected probably to insult, and certainly to arrest and fine. He hailed them.

"Ladies! Don't you know that you're on Commission property?"

The horsewomen pulled up. A gay young voice inquired pertly, "Are you the pathmaster?"

"Good Lord!" said he.

"Hello, Uncle Horace," Dinty greeted him, and Wealthia Latham added more demurely, "Good evening to you, Dr. Amlie."

"Good evening," returned Horace. "But you've no right here, you know. It's a five-dollar penalty."

Wealthia tossed her head. "My pa would make nothing of paying it. Besides, who's going to peach on us?"

In his mind, the doctor paraphrased an earlier Horace: "Oh, daughter, more arrogant than your arrogant father!" The pair had reined aside to let him pass on the narrow parapet.

"I'll ride along with you," said he.

The glance which passed between them told him that his offer met with no favor. What did this mean? Had he cut into a rendezvous? What sort of rendezvous, two young girls on this rough waterfront? Tip Crego, perhaps. They were moving in the direction of Poverty's Pinch. There was no harm in Tip; he was trustworthy. Was it not time, though, that Dinty outgrew her nightfaring? And Wealthia? And the horses and costumes? Horace revised his guess. This was no innocent nature outing.

A delicate thread of music, high and clear, thrilled along the air currents, note upon silvery note, to be lost in the far silences. Wealthia Latham twisted in her saddle.

"That's for the lock," she said.

"They'd better be brisk, hadn't they!" said Dinty importantly. "They'd better not keep Captain Ramsey waiting."

"Captain, hey?" said Horace. "Has Silverhorn made good his boast to return on his own deck?"

Wealthia, her face intent and absorbed, answered absently, "It isn't his yet. He's captaining for the owner."

"You'd both better get off the towpath," suggested Horace.

Wealthia's dark eyes flashed. "I wish you'd go away," she cried. "Make him go away, Dinty."

Dinty was sufficiently versed in Horace's expression to know when tact was indicated. "I don't believe I could, Wealthia," said she. "Maybe we'd better go home."

"An excellent idea," approved Horace.

"I won't! I won't! I won't!"

She was staring eagerly over her shoulder. Red and green, the sidelights of the boat appeared around the distant bend. The clear strain pierced the dusk once more.

Wealthia whirled her mount. Quick as she was, Horace was quicker. His grip on the curb brought the horse's head down. Wealthia slashed with her riding crop at the face, drawn close to hers, then folded her arms across her eyes and sobbed furiously. The bugle sounded again, an exultant summons. She shivered all over.

Carefully Horace guided Fleetfoot to edge the puzzled horse down the declivity and across the field, Dinty following. At the turnpike he checked the little cavalcade.

"Wealthia! How far has this dangerous nonsense gone?"

"You're not my pa." Her face was mutinous.

"Luckily for you."

"We just happened to ride down this way."

"Perhaps you can persuade Mr. Latham to believe that."

"You're not going to tell Pa!"

"Oh, Uncle Horace, you wouldn't be so mean!" put in Dinty.

"If you won't tell Pa, I'll promise not to do it again," said Wealthia with a sidelong glance.

He had his doubts as to how much such a promise would be worth. "Don't you realize the risk you're running? Have you been seeing Ramsey on the sly?"

"I've only seen him twice since last year."

"That's when I should have spoken to him. It won't lose anything by waiting, I promise you," said Horace grimly.

"I don't see why you can't 'tend to your own affairs," she complained, adding, under her breath, "Meddling old neversweat!"

The Latham mansion was dark. Mr. Latham was away. The two girls dismounted in the barnyard.

"I'm spending the night with Wealthy," Dinty said.

He gave her no response. Under his watchful eye the pair unsaddled and stabled their mounts. Dinty lingered, curling one foot around the other ankle uncertainly, but he only sat his saddle like a disapproving statue. There was the suggestion of a slam about her closing of the door behind her.

The lamplight went on. An interval. It went off. Fleetfoot, under guidance, moved quietly into a shadow. Horace was not taking any chances. He waited.

After a time, the side door opened cautiously. With a shock he identified Dinty's slight figure. Not as he expected. Worse! The girl called softly,

"Uncle Horace!"

He neither moved nor spoke. She was testing to ascertain whether the coast was clear. Once convinced that he had left, she would, he assumed, pursue her assignation with the dissolute canaller. So it was Dinty, not Wealthia. What precocious depravity! He was shocked to the core of his being.

"Uncle Horace!" she called again. Then, "I know you're there. I can smell your horse."

Tip Crego's tutelage again, teaching her to use her senses. He walked out to meet her.

"Where were you going?"
"To find you."
"If you hadn't found me?"
"How mean you sound!" she complained. "I'd have gone to bed."
"Where you are supposed to be now. Are you telling me the truth?" he demanded searchingly.
"Of course I'm telling you the truth, Uncle Horace."
"You weren't going back to meet Silverhorn Ramsey?"
"Who? Me?" Her astonishment was so candid that he drew a breath of relief. "Why, I hardly know him to pass the time of day."
"That's too much. And you'd better not be abetting that silly fidget in her flightiness. Does the little fool think she's in love with him?"
"She says she's mortally stricken, but perchance 'tis but a passing fancy, light as a fleeting cloud."
"Perchance, eh? I see you've been pursuing your extra-curricular reading while at school."
"I don't know what that means, but it doesn't sound nice. Uncle Horace, you're not going to tell her Pa on Wealthy, are you?"
"I shall use my own judgment as to that."
"If you do, I think you're a pesky sneak."
"Don't speak to me that way, Araminta," he snapped.
"Araminta, indeed! Aren't you ever going to stop treating me like a child?"
"What else, in heaven's name, do you think you are?" said the exasperated Horace. "And a very froward and high-minded one, into the bargain."
"Good night, Dr. Amlie," said Dinty with an air of resentful dignity, and withdrew in good order.
To make certain that all was safe, Horace rode to the lower lock. Yes, the keeper said, the *Firefly,* Captain Silverhorn Ramsey, had leveled out at nine-fifty on her eastward way. Silverhorn had blown a terrible blast for the lock and had cursed him, the lock-keeper, with every villainy in the canal language for being slow. He was in a foul humor. Horace chuckled with satisfaction as he cantered home to bed.
Passing the Fashion Store on the following morning, Horace Amlie was beset and seized by a darting figure.
"Come inside," invited Dinty.
"What's the matter now?"
"I want your advice on something extremely important." She pulled him to a mirror where she adjusted upon her jaunty curls a Leghorn flat at least ten years too old for her. "How does that set me?"

"Not at all."

"Oh, dear! What a disappointment you are! Men never know anything about styles."

"Let the styles go. You're not looking well," said he severely.

Dinty assumed the air of meek martyrdom with which she received rebuke or criticism. "It's that plaguey school," she averred.

"Nonsense! It's an excellent school."

"Not for me," she denied. "They never take their eyes off you. If *you* couldn't sleep nights for hearing the woods call you and loving and longing for them, what would you do?"

"I wouldn't run away with the minister's son."

"I had to do something. I think I'm going into a decline," said Dinty, observing herself with mournful attention in the glass, then setting the Leghorn at a fresh angle with renewed interest.

"I think you're not," returned Horace. "You tell your father to send you to me for a thorough going-over, from head to foot."

"From head to foot?" she breathed. "All over?"

The tone of dismay annoyed him. "Of course, all over. Why not?"

"I—I don't want you to."

"Oh! You don't want me to. Any special reason?"

Dinty's eyes slid sidelong away from his. She poked at a floor crack with the toe of her boot. "I'm too grown-up. I don't think it's delicate," she murmured.

"Delicate! Good God! I'm your physician. You're no more to me than a cadaver."

"If you think that's nice!" said poor Dinty wrathfully. "Ma wouldn't let me, anyway. She says you're no better than a Goth and a Vandal."

Horace grunted. "Your mother would do better to quit dosing you with her panaceas."

"I'm so grown-up," said Dinty, reverting to that line of thought, "that Pa has promised to take me to the Canal Cotillion for a little while. Are you going to be there?"

"I suppose so."

"I know how to dance now, Uncle Horace," said she hopefully.

Horace had other matters in mind. "If I were the committeemen," he said, "I'd wait awhile before celebrating the canal."

Dinty sighed. "Good-bye, Uncle Horace."

By proverbial complaint of the medical profession some woman always went into labor on a party night. This time, it was a rope walker's wife, two miles out. It was eleven o'clock before Horace could get home, put on his uniform, and hurry to the Eagle. Dinty had already been harried home to bed, protesting bitterly, but Wealthia Latham, more privileged, was there, the center of an eager circle of callow youth. With uneasiness Horace remarked Silverhorn Ramsey, not of the circle, indeed, but watching the fair fledgling from a corner. He was a gaillard figure in his captain's blue-and-gold, with a tiny packet-boat woven upon the lapel of his supercloth broadcoat, as he lolled gracefully.

To Horace, Wealthia was still the little girl friend of the other little girl, Dinty. He preserved his attitude of protectiveness toward both of them impartially. It stirred anew as he observed Silverhorn moving forward to join the group of swains. Had she signaled him? As he bent over her hand, Horace thought that her expression was one of apprehension as well as fluttered and flattered delight.

Shortly before midnight, that happened which was a frequent concomitant of such festivities. A careless dancer knocked over a candle. A curtain flared. Some fool shouted "Fire!" The damsels present screamed daintily. Rising heroically to the test, their swains rushed forward. All was over in five minutes with small danger but great excitement. Horace, who had been foremost in the rush, now disengaged himself and started for the taproom for a refresher.

On the way, he passed an alcove hung with portieres, from behind which he heard Wealthia's rich contralto, already deepening to womanly timbre, raised a little in tremulous excitation.

"Oh, Captain Ramsey! I wouldn't dare."

"Nobody would know. She's such a pretty boat."

"I know she's dicty. But how could I get away? Oh!"

"What is it, little darling?"

"Someone outside. I heard them."

Horace had coughed. Wealthia darted past him, her face mazed, her eyes heavy. Silverhorn sauntered after with a careless nod for the involuntary eavesdropper.

"Looking for something, young Æsculapius?"

"You'd better be careful, Ramsey."

"Free advice from a medico?"

"I'll be treating you for bullet in the belly if Genter Latham hears of this."

"How would you like a knife in the ribs for yourself?"

"Are you trying to scare me?"

"I've scared bolder. Peaceable ways first, though. You'll make more trouble than you can mend if you flap your jawbone about this.

Think that over in your sleep." He passed along with a mock salute.

Horace had no need to think it over. At the outset of his career he had taken a resolution never to meddle in the private and personal affairs of any patient. That way lay infinite complications. But what he would not do directly might be achieved through an agent. He re-introduced the subject with Dinty when he saw her next day. She fetched a cavernous sigh.

"Wealthy is cruel unhappy," she informed him in her most impressive manner. "She's desperate enamored."

"Childish infatuation," barked Horace.

"This is different. Captain Ramsey has stolen her young and tender heart. She sleeps but to dream of him; she wakes but to thoughts of him; she breathes but to . . ."

"Children ought to be barred from the hire-library," broke in Horace in exasperation. "I never heard such balderdash."

"Sometimes," breathed Dinty, "I wonder if a great and blinding love will ever come to me."

"A great and blinding box on the ear will come to you in a minute! Now, see here, child; I want you to keep watch on Wealthia and if she makes any further attempt to see that scoundrel, I want to know it."

"Would you have me turn spy on my best friend?" cried she, striking an attitude, and immediately adding, "I'd love it. I'll get Tip to help me."

"A sound idea," Horace approved.

He was about closing shop on the following Monday when he heard a lightsome male voice trolling a ribald parody of the pious Watts.

> "When I can aim my rifle clear
> At pigeons in the skies,
> I'll bid farewell to beans and beer
> And live on pigeon pies."

The imitator of the hymnologist pushed through the entry. Silverhorn Ramsey made the mock sign of benediction.

"Hail, sucking Galen! Are you at call professionally?"

"At your service."

"I'm feeling seedy. Been a bit careless, I guess."

More explicit indications were unnecessary after a brief examination.

"You have," confirmed Horace.

"Those damned road wenches!"

"You've had a drink, I observe."

"I've had three. What the hell is it to you?"

"No more liquor, if I'm to take your case."

"And no more women, I presume," jeered the other.

"You should know that without my telling you."

"All right! All right!" said the caller impatiently. "How long to clear up this little matter?"

"Uncertain. To be thorough and sure involves a slow regimen."

"Give me a notion."

"Three months minimum."

"Too long. Halve it and we can deal."

Horace shook his head. "Minimum, I said. I can give you the full strength cubeb-and-mercury treatment, but it is severe. It might keep you off your run."

"Cholera wouldn't keep me off the run. I'll take your embolics and like 'em if they'll do the trick."

"I should advise the slower treatment, however."

"None of your pinchgut potions for me. I'll swallow the whole damned armentarium if it will fix me up the sooner. There's a special reason." His grin became sardonic. "In the sacred confidence of our noble profession . . .

"Not *our* profession," Horace corrected him.

"I was a sucking medic for three months. Know the Hippocratic oath as well as you do."

"Anything that passes between us here is safely secret, if that is what you're driving at," said Horace stiffly.

"I know your kind," returned the other. "Conscience hag-rides you. That old bitch never bothered me much, though I can see her usefulness in others. Now, but for your conscience I might not risk coming to you."

"Spare me your philosophy. I can't minister to a diseased soul. Sit down."

Horace was ensconced behind his broad, new consultation table, upon which at the moment, stood four learned tomes, an instrument box, his microscope and a half dozen bottles of featherweight glass containing various liquids. The patient took the chair opposite. There was wafted from him the dainty odor of pomatum, shining on the long curls which rippled across his temples and draped downward to meet the luxuriant side whiskers. Notwithstanding his disability, he bore himself with that air of blithe self-satisfaction which was part of his charm.

"Well, here it is," said he. "I'm figuring to marry. Maybe you guessed it."

Horace stared blackly at him. "Not—not . . ."

"That's it. The Latham wren."

"By God, you shan't!"

"By God, I shall!" retorted the canaller with perfect good humor. "What's to stop me?"

"Her father. He'd strangle you first."

"Who's to tell him? Not you, I guess. Not on that oath of yours."

Horace groaned. "For a fip I'd put poison in your dosage."

"Too bad you can't allow yourself that pleasure," sympathized the other. "Just cure me up and keep your mouth shut till merry ring the marriage chimes. You aren't sweet on her, yourself, are you, my bucko?"

"That's no affair of yours."

"You well might be. Ripe fruit. I don't know that I'd go so far as the altar," he added carelessly, "except for the rhino. To be quite open, I need it."

"Do you flatter yourself that you'll ever touch a penny of Genter Latham's money?"

"Yes, yes, my boy," was the genial response. "He's dotened on the little flibbertigibbet. And you don't know my powers of persuasion. I've got a special use for the ready, and soon."

"Have you?"

"There's a sweet little freighter on the market. Owner dying of a consumption. Cost a round thousand, and can be taken, horses and all, for a cool eight-fifty. But where would I find eight-fifty, outside the honorable estate of matrimony?"

Horace rose. "Well, I'm not going to throw you out, much as I'd like to." Rounding the table, he stood above his patient. "Open your mouth. Wider."

He set a hand on either side of the jaunty head, tilting it for the advantage of the light. His left hand, pressed lightly against the side of the skull, communicated a message of something peculiar, something lacking. His arm was struck smartly up. Silverhorn was out of the seat, his mouth drawn in a snarl, his eyes feral.

"What do you think you're doing?"

Horace returned to his place. "Take your seat," said he quietly.

The caller obeyed, but his every muscle was tense.

"Any trouble with your hearing?" Horace made the tone as casual and professional as he could. He knew that he had a hair-trigger sitution to deal with.

"No. Why should there be?"

"You never can tell with this kind of thing."

The patient growled something beneath his breath, but it seemed to the observant physician that there was a sensible relaxation. Drawing to him one of his bottles which contained a transparent liquid, he toyed with it for a moment.

"You're something of an expert," he said presently. "You know what aqua regia is, I assume."

The canal man grinned evilly. "You'd like to give me some, wouldn't you? How would you rid yourself of the body?"

"Oh, no, no!" said Horace mildly. "I'm merely mentioning it as illustration." He lifted the vial, weighed it in his cupped hand. "Hydrochloric and nitric acid," he remarked. "A potent mixture."

"What of it?"

"You have something like it in your system," said Horace with deliberation. "If it is neglected or exasperated by indulgence, it could burn through you as this compound could burn into the bone, eat out your eyes, dissolve the very gold out of your teeth."

"Rawbones and bloody head!" sneered Silverhorn. "Trying to scare me, Doc?"

"Who cropped your ear?"

Silverhorn's hand jumped to his waist. His face was gray with fury. "Why, God damn you!" he snarled.

"Don't draw that knife."

"I'm going to cut your bloody heart out."

Horace poised the bottle. "I can't miss your face from here," he warned.

Silverhorn, half out of his chair, quivered like a snake's head.

"Sit back," advised Horace. "You might kill me before the acid worked. And you might come out alive. But you wouldn't have any face left to speak of. No eyes, certainly. Don't you think you'd get the worst of it?"

The other made a mighty effort. "You're a cool one," he muttered.

"Let's both keep cool. Talk it over like sensible men. Where did you study your medicine?"

"New York. College of Physicians & Surgeons." But there had been a moment's hesitancy.

"Sure it wasn't the University of Pennsylvania Medical?"

"What if it was?"

"Ever deal in cadavers?"

Silverhorn twitched. The sound in his throat was hardly a response.

"Three years ago several Penn medics were surprised body-snatching. A mob caught two of them and operated on their ears before they got away and disappeared. I could find out their names."

"Find out and be damned! I got my ear chewed off in a rough-and-tumble."

"Not that ear. I could feel the clean cut."

Silverhorn breathed hard. "What are you after? Hush money?"

Horace ignored that. "Mr. Latham will be advised to put a guard on his daughter until your record can be investigated."

"Why, you false invoice! I'm your patient. This is on your confidential oath, God blast your soul!"

Horace allowed himself a thin smile. "You have not consulted me about your ear. That is not a medical but a police matter."

There was an interval of silence. Then Silverhorn said, "So you want me to bow off the girl."

"I do."

The handsome face became a leering mask. "Suppose it's too late?"

"I'll know that, too. I am her physician."

Another side of the incalculable blackguard showed itself. "Well, it isn't," said he. "Not but what I might have, I warrant. But I played a different game this time. I'm half-dozened on the little witch, to tell truth," he added ruefully.

Horace wanted nothing now so much as to be rid of him. "I'll send your medicaments to the boat. Keep your undertaking and I'll keep mine. Remember, if there's any attempt on your part to see the girl, I go to Mr. Latham and the prosecuting authorities. Act like a decent man, and I'll keep quiet."

The canal man said sorrowfully, "Silverhorn Ramsey, slacking his towline for a puny punk like you. By the loins of Levi! It isn't reasonable."

"Report back here in a week's time. Take the medicine as directed. Good day to you, Captain Ramsey."

"Good day to you, Dr. Punk."

He retrieved his bugle and swaggered forth.

Horace dropped back in his chair, sweating freely with relief. That he had been very near to death, he had no doubt. His throat was dry. He uncorked the transparent vial and let the contents trickle down his throat to the last grateful drop. As he set it back, he heard a gasp. Silverhorn Ramsey stood in the open doorway, with protruding eyes.

"Jesus!" he whispered.

Horace grinned at him. He knew that there was no longer anything to fear, once his rage had subsided.

"Distilled water for microscopic use," he explained.

"Nicked!" said Silverhorn lamentably.

"What brings you back?"

"Your fee. I forgot it."

"I, also. Sixty-five cents, medicines included."

"Lawful money," said the patient, laying down the sum.

"Thank you. Mind my advice. No liquor. No women."

"What a life!" said Silverhorn Ramsey.

-19-

My Uncle Horace says "What's a nose for?" and Ma says "To keep out of Other Folks' business."

(DINTY'S DIARY)

NATURAL seepage, it became only too evident, would not suffice to maintain a dependable depth in the new channel, even for the strictly localized traffic. Some of the small hill streams were now diverted. Together, the several sources brought the level to a point where shallow craft would float.

No engineer had considered the possible effects of pressure in the vicinity of the banks. Quicksands developed, resulting in leakage which ruined some adjacent farmlands. Squire Jerrold, whose project comprised the most porous part of the terrain, was plagued with threats of lawsuits. Within the village limits, breaks and faults in the geological structure caused cellars to fill and noisome pools to gather in depressions. The resourceful anopheles mosquito availed herself of these golden opportunities for egg-laying. Horace found a number of specimens, displaying their gauche and familiar attitude against inner walls. Having once suffered the discredit of the mistaken prophet, he was chary of playing Cassandra a second time. He waited.

Results were not long in showing themselves. On the third Sunday of a humid July spell, Dominie Strang, after preaching for less than two hours and with much still to expound, toppled across the pulpit in collapse. It might have been a signal, so prompt was the response from his flock. A dozen of them were down that evening. Other congregations fared no better. Within a fortnight, ten percent of the populace were alternately burning and shivering. It was an epidemic.

"Every house its own earthquake," quoth Carlisle Sneed between chattering teeth.

Palmyra had lived through onsets before and expected to survive this one. Happily it was a disabling, rather than a virulent type. But a new factor was present, an economic threat more disconcerting than any physical woes. The place was getting a bad name. The evil word, "unhealthy," was attaching to it. Wiseacres from the regions around surmised that the pestilent miasmas of the Montezuma Marshes had blown westward on prevalent winds and settled down upon the valley. While the affliction was at its height, flies reinforced the mosquitoes and contributed their quota of befoulment with the result of adding the gripes to the shakes. Palmyra was an unhappy town.

In this, its hour of travail, Rochester (now, in its expansion, having discarded the belittling "ville"), allegedly envious of its neighbor's prosperity, dealt it a foul blow. The *Rochester Telegraph* published a headline, "Palmyra Plague." The local organ came back with a red-hot editorial, stigmatizing Rochester as "a nest of scandal and an emporium of mud, disorder and outcasts." Palmyra it roundly declared to be "the fairest, the most enlightened, the most prosperous, the healthiest and lawfullest community between Hudson River and Lake Erie, and this statement we challenge malice successfully to confute."

Once hatched, the malignant phrase gained currency with the traveling public. Coach passengers manifested a tendency to avoid the local inns and bed down farther along the line. Custom at the Eagle fell off by a round quarter. New money ceased to flow into the village. Several projected businesses, including a chandlery and a storehouse, delayed construction. Worst of all, the danger loomed that the canal authorities might abandon their announced plan, upon which the village was capitalizing, to establish a local pay-office with all the consequent influx of ready money, and to make the two basins, soon to be enlarged to three, the chief loading port for the whole locality. And now possibly to lose this! With the warehouses already bursting their walls with waiting produce! What a blow to local pride and prosperity!

Attack of an unforeseen nature followed. Broadsides appeared in the various camps, cunningly worded to play upon the reputation of the valley for unhealthfulness. Work could be had under better and safer conditions in the Montezuma region. No fevers. No ague. Good wages. Good fare. Liberal liquor allowances. Generous prize offers. Work for one and all. Another bid issued from the vicinity of Lock Port where work was under way on the Western Section.

"Dig, Dry-shod and in Comfort," invited the contractors. "Why Risk your Health among the Miasmas?"

Squire Jerrold's men deserted, almost in a body. Genter Latham lost two sub-foremen and many of his best diggers. Not an employer in the stretch but suffered from the specious representations. The village trustees appealed to the Canal Commission. How was the work to be completed if these pirates were allowed to lure essential labor away with false promises? The Commission did nothing.

"Treason!" editorialized the *Canal Advocate* which had conscientiously rejected the proffered advertisements. "What kind of patriotism is thus displayed? These miscreants care nothing for our State's most glorious enterprise."

At a meeting of contractors and sub-contractors, the question of an increased wage-scale was mooted. Genter Latham, the largest employer, vehemently opposed it.

"No digger is worth more than four shillings a day and damned few of 'em that much," was his dictum.

Nevertheless Squire Jerrold sent out a call for one hundred and fifty men at sixty cents a day, almost precipitating an open quarrel with Genter Latham. Lock Port raised its bid to seventy-five cents, and was followed by a like raise in the Montezuma area. Palmyra was threatened with paralysis. About this time, Editor-Pastor Strang, sorely afflicted in his bowels and with recurrent shakes to boot, retired from journalism, turning over his plant to a pair of energetic young men, Messrs. Grandin and Tucker, who immediately initiated a save-Palmyra campaign and set about organizing the citizenry.

Carlisle Sneed had been heard to say of Genter Latham that "no moskeeter with a fipsworth of sense in his noodle would risk breaking his beak on the old sharkskin." Nevertheless the great man looked yellow and seamed as he lumbered into Dr. Amlie's office. Horace reached for his thermometer, but the visitor waved him back.

"I ain't sick."

"You don't look well."

"You're nothing to brag of, yourself," retorted the other with a weak grin.

"I don't get much rest, these nights," admitted Horace, whose practice had increased beyond normal endurance.

"We're calling a town meeting tomorrow evening," said Mr. Latham.

"About time, too."

"That's as may be. Will you come with your microscope?"

"If the Board invites me."

"They'll invite you. And they'll listen to you this time."

"They'd better," gritted the medico. "I'll give them something to bite on."

The gathering, with the village trustees on the platform, had more than a touch of the grotesque. Nothing short of impending catastrophe could have dragged so many of the leading figures from their beds of pain and uncertainty. Chairman Levering, blinking out upon a sea of pallid faces, poised a tremulous gavel and, with a chittering jaw, proceeded to "c-c-call this m-m-m-m-m-meeting to orrrderrrrr." Simultaneously two trustees raced for the door with identical expressions of anguish and foreboding. Dr. Murchison in a front-row chair, bent over a stout cane, his skin of that unsightly hue termed "puke" except in the daintier prints which refined it to "puce." The old man, with a temperature which Horace Amlie expertly guessed to be at least 102, was game.

Horace, himself, was gaunt as a ferret from sleeplessness and overwork. Several times during the proceedings he was called upon to escort tremulous gentlemen to their distant goal. Palmyra's claim to be the healthiest settlement along the canal was not being well supported.

After a general discussion focusing on the dastardly threat to the town's growth and prosperity, Mr. Genter Latham (temperature 101½) moved that Dr. Horace Amlie be invited to express his ideas. The motion was seconded by Trustee Van Wie (twelve pounds underweight). Horace, who had fallen asleep on his bench from exhaustion, hauled himself to his feet and surveyed the assemblage with sore and uncompromising eyes.

"Well," said he, "how do you like it?"

A mutter of discontent answered him.

"You don't like it. Neither do I. You're getting just what you asked for."

Up rose the Honest Lawyer, shivering like a leaf. "Are you presuming a lay upon us the blame for a visitation of Heaven?" he challenged.

"It's a judgment of Heaven, I agree," said Horace. "But for what?"

"Our sins," said Deacon Dillard piously.

"Just so. Filth is a sin. And sickness is the judgment."

The Rev. Theron Strang, apologizing for a preliminary fit of active nausea, felt impelled to dissent mildly from this heterodoxy. Filth and flies were of Beelzebub, he admitted, but there was no Scriptural warrant for attributing disease to them, as his young friend implied. Dr. Murchison, for the medical faculty, concurred with the parson. Tenderly rubbing his distended abdomen, he repeated the time-honored theory of miasmatic poisoning. Horace stepped to the platform.

"Those of you who are queasy or incontinent had better leave," he warned. "I'm going to make you sick at your stomachs."

"Not me," announced Carlisle Sneed. "I got no stomach left to be sick at. I'm quitting." He tottered out followed by several other sufferers.

Horace extracted a covered fruit jar from his tail pockets and set it down on the table with a bang. It was half full of dark blobs, some of which appeared to be in a state of fermentation.

"Flies," he said. "Collected from local premises. Would anyone like to smell them?"

Mr. Van Wie volunteered, and was obliging enough to gag violently.

"Anyone else? Dr. Murchison? Mr. Upcraft?"

The Honest Lawyer shook his head. "What if they do stink?" said he contentiously. "So does a skunk. But a skunk's juice is healthy. It's good for a rheumy cold. Ain't that correct, Dr. Murchison?"

"A skunk," said Horace, "is a cleanly and respectable creature beside a fly. So is the dirtiest hog that ever wallowed in a swill-pile, or the foulest crow that ever scavenged in carrion. I'm going to tell you something about the flies that light on the food you eat."

With simple directness that brought out every point of disgust and nausea, he gave a five-minute character sketch of the local *muscae,* their breeding and feeding habits, their capacities as freighters of filth, and the human ailments which, in the opinion of enlightened science, they bore with them wherever they alighted. He then passed to the hardly more appetizing mosquito. When he sat down the hue of the faces below him was greener by several degrees. Maltster Vandowzer swallowed a brace of pills from the palm of his hand and broke the uncomfortable silence.

"Vell, vot do ve do? Vot doos de yong man vant?"

"An appropriation for quicklime."

"Vot you do vid it?"

"Lime every drain and cess in town. Scatter and lime such compost heaps as yours."

"Do you warrant that to cure our gripes and fevers?" asked Upcraft.

Horace was not thus easily trapped. "I'll warrant the dysentery will lessen," he replied. "Give me more money to treat the mosquito-breeding pools and I'd almost warrant the fevers."

"I maintain that there is insufficient evidence against the accused insects," insisted the always lawyerlike Honest Lawyer.

Horace had begun to tell them of the experiment at Shea's camp, when Deacon Dillard interposed the objection that they were dealing with conditions in the village, not out in the wild country where it might be quite different. He sat down, surrounded by the reek of mint juice which clung about all who worked in the minteries. It gave Horace an idea.

"Deacon, I've heard that you boast your workmen are the healthiest in town."

"It's true, too."

"Do you know why?"

"Because I pay 'em well, treat 'em well and feed 'em well."

"That's well known." Horace was not above currying favor by discreet and honest flattery. "But it isn't the whole story."

"What's your way of it, then?"

"Are you bothered with flies in your distillery?"

"No, siree!"

"Or mosquitoes?"

"Never see one of the dum things. The smell of the good mint keps 'em away."

"There's your evidence, sir," said Horace, turning upon the Honest Lawyer. "The Dillard establishment stands near insect-breeding marshland. Nevertheless, no flies, no mosquitoes; hence, no fevers."

"Post hoc, sed non propter hoc," growled Upcraft. "That ain't proof."

"It's flub-a-dub-dub," declared Murchison.

Chairman Levering joined the attack. "You say the canal breeds disease?"

"It does. The fevers have followed its course."

"Then you would do away with the canal, would you?"

"That's it," broke in Jed Parris. "Blow up the poxy Ditch and go back to honest teamin'."

Genter Latham was on his feet, his face aflame, his eyes brilliant with fever, but his mind under cool control.

"That's what it might come to, fellow citizens," he said with forceful quiet. "That, or as bad. If the present excavations are abandoned, if the canal is carried northward to the lake, east of us as the anti-

Clintonian busybodies would have it, do you know what it means to Palmyra? Ruin!"

He sat down. An apprehensive murmur passed through his audience. That might all be so, somebody grumbled, but was it any reason for giving this young medical upstart the town's money to spend on bug-fights? The economy argument was stressed and backed by citations of householders' rights. Dr. Murchison heavily ridiculed the younger man's "fairy-tales with flies for hobgoblins." Chairman Levering's personal enmity for Horace inspired him to an attack upon the young doctor's professional ability.

On the other hand, what Squire Jerrold called the *"argumentum ad nauseam"* had made an impression. Deacon Dillard swung to Horace's support. Decker Jessup, O. Daggett, Silas Bewar and others of the smithy coterie were there to back up their fellow member. When, after sundry threats of personal violence had enlivened the proceedings, the question was put to general vote, the clean-up forces were found to have won decisively.

Horace went to work. In three days he made himself the best-hated man in Palmyra. With twenty-five dollars' worth of lime and a corps of volunteers, he invaded barns and outhouses, found offenses in the gardens of such respectables as the Leverings and the Evernghims, scattered Simon Vandowzer's maggot-breedery, and substituted the pungent tang of the chemical for the more familiar and homey odor of the hot-weather latrine. Lawyer Upcraft, scenting possible business among the new smells, tried to stir up some of his clients to suits for trespass. It came to nothing, because Genter Latham announced that he would bring the best legal talent of the state, at his own expense, to defend Dr. Amlie and his "limers."

At once the dysentery tapered off, presently dying out. But the fever was more obstinate. While new cases were fewer, the incidence was still above normal provided by the comparatively inconsiderable breeding places of the creeks, now supplemented by the canal pools. Both Latham and Jerrold warned Horace of the impracticability of obtaining a grant for draining these latter. Stoutly though he had spoken for it, the proponent of the mosquito theory realized that his case was neither proved nor proveable. If only he knew more about the mysterious "fomites." Read as he might, all procurable data—and these were preety scanty and scattered—left him with a disturbing modicum of doubt at the back of his brain. If the fomites were, indeed, microscopical agencies of disease lurking on the person and in the clothing of the afflicted as well as inhabiting the unhealthful swamps and marshes, then it was only reasonable to believe that flying insects could and did transport them from place to place, from sick man to well man.

Unfortunately no microscopist had yet succeeded in identifying a fomite. If Horace could have produced a sketch of a horrendous crawler, bristling with horns, fangs and stingers, what a telling argument he would have had for the general public! Lacking such concrete evidence, he was prudently inclined to go slow after the initial clean-up. The taunt of "bugs on the brain" had hurt. He had a natural distaste for his growing reputation as a gratuitous busybody, a medical neversweat. Anyway, he had accomplished one good. Palmyra smelt sweeter than before.

-20-

If my Uncle Horace is not my Uncle Horace any More, what is he?

(DINTY'S DIARY)

JUSTICE befell the siren-voiced labor-stealers of the Montezuma district. Mysteriously quiescent for months, the fever returned there in exaggerated virulence. Half the working force was laid off. Several deaths were reported. Lock Port and the Western Section still held out their lures, but there, too, malaria appeared. Palmyra deserters began to drift back from both directions to their old jobs. They found the village almost free of sickness. Horace Amlie was doing a good job.

Not without opposition, however. Lawyer Upcraft threatened him with the law. Crabbed old J. Evernghim menaced him with a blunderbuss. T. Lay barricaded himself within his brookside privy and announced that if any man tried to interfere with his rights, he'd squib him like a fowl. Mr. Levering, himself, in spite of his official position, mounted guard over the assorted fragrance of his backyard compost heap, and Horace was obliged to level it at dead of night and in careful secrecy. All of which did not add to his popularity.

"How would you like to be appointed special constable?" asked Genter Latham.

"What for?"

"To give you official authority."

"I'll need it."

"Don't overdo it. You're getting yourself disliked already."

"So are the flies," grinned Horace.

Only the fact that they had suffered so bad a scare induced the grudging trustees to make the appointment. Thus Horace Amlie, M.D., became the first public health official in the United States. Genter Latham lent him prestige by permitting a dam across his noisome brooklet, since it was no money out of the Latham purse.

Dinty, hearing the news, wrote from Albany where she was not too happily settled in school.

> Will you wear a uniform? And carry a staff? I shall be more afraid of you than ever. Do hasten with your old canal so that Wealthy and I may come back on it soon. This is a plaguey fine city, the home of Culture, Refinement and Fashion, and there are many Estimable Young Gentlemen who are admitted to pay their respects at the Academy, on the occasion of our Social Saturday Evening. But the forest is far away, Hudson's Raging Waters roll between, and the Night Watch stalks abroad.

Golden prophecies to the contrary, there was no prospect of any better method than that of the coach for the accommodation of the two little exiles. Still the progress of the canal had become almost normal again. Of the hundred and fifty men sought by Squire Jerrold, more than one hundred answered his call, and Genter Latham was compelled to raise wages to a parity with the rate paid by his neighbor, which he did with a very ill grace. To the east, around Lyons and Clyde, the work still lagged, but the reaches along Ganargwa Valley steadily deepened and leveled.

Inspectors arrived, representing the Canal Commission. Palmyra held its breath. Rumor solidified into authentic good news when the *Canal Advocate* abandoned its basic principle of printing nothing of local interest to announce that the waters would be let in simultaneously from the Genesee River, Thomas's Brook, and the Canandaigua Outlet, and that, before the end of September the eyes of the citizenry would be gladdened by a nautical pageant, followed by a banquet and a ball.

It was a great day when the *Queen of the Waters,* painted and ribboned like any tavern-hussy, took its first charter party of merry-makers to the Gerundigut Embankment and the marvelous aqueduct across the Genesee, built by convict labor from Auburn State Prison. Work was rushed on a dozen other craft in near-by towns and news came from Pompey of a steamboat which was to plow the waves at the incredible speed of ten miles per hour. It never did, because the Commission inconsiderately put a five-mile limit on all canal craft.)

Full of patriotism and pride, Genter Latham, who had been to New York City on a business trip, stopped at Albany to pick up two joyous young creatures, freed for the occasion from scholastic trammels. Both were objects of marked attention from several of the male coach-fares, to Mr. Latham's surprised enlightenment and their own manifest satisfaction. He had not bargained for chaperonage to a brace of maturing spinsters.

They arrived in time for the girls, very much bedizened, to take part in the pageant, Dinty as the Spirit of Erie, Wealthia as the Muse of Transportation. The banquet which followed was the most elegant in the history of the town. Squire Jerrold, the toastmaster, struck the keynote in his initial proposal, "Palmyra, the Beacon City of Internal Improvements."

"Westward the star of empire takes its way," he proclaimed. "I venture to assert without fear of successful confutation that Divine Providence has appointed our community to become the metropolis of the western region and eventually a second capital of the Empire State."

Twenty-two toasts were responded to, and, as appropriate and usual, the guests got patriotically tipsy and helped one another home.

Horace Amlie stayed sober, not from lack of community spirit, but because he had a busy morning in prospect, including an operation for the stone which would be agonizing for the patient and a corresponding nerve-strain for the surgeon. He finished it, successful but limp, and was about to restore himself with a needed dram, when the note of Silverhorn Ramsey's bugle warned him of that flamboyant person's imminent arrival. The young captain was in town for the festivities, Horace surmised. The door was pushed open and the graceful figure lounged in.

"I've come for my bill of clearance."

Horace caught a whiff. "You've been drinking," said he.

"Now, by the bowels of Beelzebub! Can't a man take a single nip without being scathed for it?"

"How can you expect favorable results if you don't follow directions?"

"Damn your directions, you harping Hippocrates! I'm cured."

"I hear you say so. We'll see."

Horace went over him carefully. "You're improved," he admitted.

"Fit for the merry wedding bells and the parson's blessing," insisted the young blade.

"Not yet." Horace leaned forward to touch the other on the knee.

"Make no mistake as to my meaning what I said about that, Ramsey," he added sternly.

"Oh, the rib! Don't worry. I've got other projects," was the careless reply.

"As many as you like, so they don't include marriage."

"What's that to you? It's not your patient, I tell you. Our agreement covers only her. Isn't that true?"

Horace was constrained to admit it.

"Then keep your damned hands off!" He laughed. "Oh, well! Don't look so sour over it. Shall I tell you what ails you, young Æsculapius? You're carrying other people's consciences on your shoulders. Where's the profit in that? What do you get out of it?"

"Nothing that you'd understand."

Silverhorn looked about him. "They tell me you've got the witch's bastard from Poverty's Pinch in tow."

"I've taken on the Crego boy as my apprentice."

"Going to make a sawbones out of him?"

Horace looked hard into the derisive eyes opposite. "Take these powders as directed, Captain Ramsey. Come for further examination in ten days."

Silverhorn declined to be squelched. He pocketed the preparation, slid a half dollar across the table and observed,

"The brat ought to take kindly to medicine. That old she-wolf knows some useful things."

Gossip to that effect had already reached the physician's ears. "Such as what?"

"Ask the Settlement girls."

"I'm asking you."

"Going to try and put her in jail, too?"

"I'm going to put a stop to any illegal practices that I discover."

"Blueskin!" commented Silverhorn and followed it with a resounding "gardaloo" which, from his full lips bore a particularly rich measure of contempt. "You won't discover it from me. If Quaila helps a poor girl out of trouble once in a while, where's the harm?"

"You've had medical education. You should know."

"Phutt to you and all your blue-nosed kind! I say she's a good witch as far as that business goes. It's a line of practice I thought of taking up, myself, if I'd finished my medics."

"I'll live to see you hanged, yet," said Horace hopefully.

"Maybe. But I'll have had my fun, which is more than you will, old sourgut. I'll be singing in hell when you're itching in heaven."

"Don't let me keep you from your occupations," said Horace politely. "Is the *Firefly* tied up here?"

"No more *Firefly*. Haven't you heard?"

"No. You're not quitting the canal?"

"I'm captain and owner now. The *Jolly Roger*. She's a Durham, clipper-built. Makes her five miles against wind and current. Drop around this evening at Palmer & Jessup's Basin for a dram, and if you don't admit she's as trim a craft as ever took water, I'll be a hoggee and dust the towpath."

Curious as to the change of fortune, the physician accepted. At the basin he had no difficulty in picking out the *Jolly Roger*. The skull and crossbones of blatant piracy flew at the forepeak. Although but a freighter, she carried all the style of a packet; a cedar deck, two reflecting lamps at the prow, boat's name and owner's name in colors, fore and aft, a carved tiller-bar; every appurtenance in the whole seventy-foot length shipshape and of the smartest.

"You've got a boat there!" said the visitor admiringly.

"Twelve hundred dollars as she came off the ways."

"Didn't hit the grand lottery, did you?"

"Easier than that. I borrowed the stake against my marriage."

Horace frowned. "Must I tell you again . . . ?"

"Sheer off," the captain interrupted. "You're my doctor, not my parson. You jammed my tiller with the Latham rib." His face darkened; his eyes looked angry and hungry. "Let that content you."

"Who is the lucky bride?" asked Horace grimly.

"A widow lady from Utica. A cut above you, I expect," answered Silverhorn with a patronizing smile. "Thirty-five if she's a day, and seamy as a toad's pelt. But moneybags, my boy, moneybags!" He smiled. "I'll be sleeping in a berth more often than in a bed when through navigation opens. Well, keep your weather eye peeled and your towrope taut. I'll see you at the ball, later on."

Horace stared hard at him. "You're going?"

"Why not?" was the bland reply. "Silverhorn's a good little boy now. Fit for any society."

I was no fault of Dinty's that she had not seen her Uncle Horace immediately upon her return. On the pretext of a small and assiduously cultivated pimple on her rounded chin, she had twice visited his new quarters. Both times he was out. On her second call she elected to wait, but vainly. Admitted by Unk Zeb, she inspected the premises with a critical eye which observed dust in places beyond male discernment. Plainly her attentions were needed. To her satisfaction, the sampler worked by her youthful hands had a place of honor on the office wall, between the Hamilton sheepskin and the State Medical certificate. The more interesting of his medical books, however, as she discovered to her resentful disappointment, were under lock and key. Now that she was growing up, there was matter in some of these volumes, she felt sure, that would be profitable for her to know. It was mean of Uncle Horace to keep them segregated.

On the day before the cotillion Horace had his first conversation with her. She was sitting in the bay window of the Jerrold household, as he came in sight on Fleetfoot, having attended an accident at the ropewalk. She had been reading Gilpin's *Monument of Parental Affection,* a most improving treatise but not her habitual choice in literature. This might mean any one of several things, the most likely being that it was an imposition of penance for breach of domestic discipline. Upon catching sight of the doctor, she flung Gilpin into a corner and rushed to the door, yoo-hooing in what her mother afterward stigmatized as an unmaidenly and hoydenish manner.

Horace vaulted out of the saddle, leaving Fleetfoot "hitched to the grass," and went to meet her. It was cleaning day and, although the Jerrolds kept a living-in, seven-day hired girl, the daughter of the household was expected to help, wherefore she was still in apron and kilted-up skirts, and looked to Horace but little older than the Tilly Tomboy who had first amended the Widow Harte's frowsty housewifery. She hurled herself upon him.

"Oh, Uncle Horace!" she bubbled. "I *am* so glad to see you! Am I much changed?" She preened herself, expectant.

"Not a bit, thank Heaven!"

"You wouldn't notice, anyway," she pouted. She felt for the pimple, but it was, unfortunately, gone. Her skin was like the inner curve of a roseleaf. "Are you going to the ball?"

"I hadn't given it much thought."

"Do," she urged. "Think about me, too. You could invite me to dance."

"Wouldn't that make young Mr. Marcus Dillard jealous?" he teased.

"Oh, Mark!" She tossed her head. "Two young gentlemen from Albany of the highest respectability have come up on purpose to attend Wealthia and me," she said complacently.

Picturing the highly respectable young gentlemen as callow schoolboys, Horace smiled indulgently.

"You will come, won't you, Uncle Horace?" she pleaded. "I've got a mint-new frock, all frills and fluffs and flounces. It's as costly as Wealthy's. You'll see her, too. Maybe you'll become enamored of her. She's more beautiful than ever. There will be many a shattered heart in the path of those dainty feet."

"Dinty," said Horace earnestly, "if you don't quit talking like the poetry corner in the *Advocate,* I'll smack you."

Dinty pouted. "I worked so hard at school on Elegant Conversation, and now you don't like it. You're mean to me, Uncle Horace. Anyway, you must wear your elegantest coat to the ball. I do think you look so nice when you're dressed up in your dinktum best."

Accepting her as his social arbitress, Horace arrayed himself in the lastest masculine confection from the shop of Tailor Burr Butler, paid his half-dollar at the door, and entered the specially decorated Big Room of the Eagle. His first impression was that the assemblage was portioned into two groups of masculine youth. The one nearest the door centered upon Wealthia Latham, of whose dark, imperious and animated beauty he caught a glimpse as he passed. The other circle, quite as large and equally devoted in attitude, opened up to disclose Dinty Jerrold.

She waved a languid fan at him. He proceeded to the platform to pay his respects to the Lady Members of the Committee. A young stranger, detaching himself from Dinty's entourage, approached and stood, waiting for Horace to finish his polite and weatherish conversation with Mrs. Macy. He was not at all the callow youth of Horace's expectations, but a fine, upstanding young elegant with a promising whisker, in the glittering uniform of the Albany Riflemen.

"Are you Dr. Amlie, sir?"

"I am."

"My respects, and I am instructed to say that Miss Jerrold would like a word with you."

Misunderstanding him, Horace looked about in surprise. What could Mrs. Dorcas Jerrold want of him? Was this a gesture preliminary to peace between them? And where was she?

"I don't see Mrs. Jerrold present," said he to the messenger.

"Not Mrs. Jerrold. Miss Jerrold."

(Miss Jerrold? *Miss* Jerrold. Well, good God! *Dinty!*)

Horace composed his face to solemnity.

"My compliments to Miss Jerrold and I will have the honor of waiting upon her shortly."

Upon his arrival Dinty gave him a smile which she had been rehearsing all afternoon before her looking glass.

"I thought you were never coming," said she in her best party accent.

Horace said, looking about him, "You seem to be pleasantly occupied."

"Well enough," she answered complacently. "Aren't you going to offer me refreshment? Why are you looking at me so queerly?"

"Nothing," said Horace hastily. "I mean, I'm not. Refreshment? Yes, by all means. What shall it be? Shrub? Lemon syrup? Prepared soda water?"

"I should prefer," said Dinty with decision, "a glass of the elderberry wine punch."

Rising, she took his arm with the aplomb of a dowager and passed through the lowering circle of youths. There was a commotion at the door. A rough voice vociferated.

"I ain't a-goin' to pay no four shillin'. I want Doc Amlie."

"Here," called Horace.

The woodsman, in his crude and stinking leathers, pushed past the pay-table and strode up to them.

"Sam Bowen's been clawed by a she-bear."

"Bowen up on Paddy's Nose?"

"Yes. How quick can you git there?"

Horace hesitated, glancing at his partner. "Is it bad?"

"His belly's ripped open."

"I'll be there inside the half-hour."

"Oh, Uncle Horace!" Dinty was a little girl again. She looked as if she were going to cry. "Do you have to go?"

"I can't leave the man to die, Dinty."

"No. It wouldn't be you if you did." Not so much the little girl now. "Will you come back?"

"As soon as I can."

"I'll wait till the last candle."

The last candle was long snuffed out when Horace left the dead man's bedside and wearily remounted Fleetfoot. He had made a good fight for it, but Sam Bowen was too badly mutilated. The best he could do was to assuage the pain of the passing. He was profoundly dejected. Not yet had he achieved the immunity to emotion which is the armor of the experienced physician.

The darkened windows of the Eagle contributed to his gloom. What could he expect, he asked himself reasonably. Here it was, three o'clock in the morning; for a ball to continue after midnight verged upon indecency. Dinty would have been long abed and asleep.

Dinty. Confusion beset his tired mind at the thought of her. She had left for Albany, a stubby, chubby hoyden, little different from the child who had broomed out his dingy office, traded his barter fees for him, marched beneath that ghastly placard which blatantly advertised Dr. Amlie to be the best doctor in Palmyra. And now, this bewildering changeling, fined down to gracious slenderness, flushed and laughing and lovely within the crescent of her admiring swains.

Horace's peculiar reaction was dismay.

-21-

Passion is a Hidyous Monster but cruel Interesting.
(DINTY'S DIARY)

BECAUSE Dinty wished a redwing's plume to furbish up her bonnet, Tip Crego took her on a daylight prowl. First they climbed the hillock behind the Latham pasture lot, where from the hollow of a dead white-oak the boy brought forth his small-game equipment, a six-foot, hollow reed, fashioned as a blowstick, with a half dozen darts, steel-tipped and daintily feathered.

By this form of venery he added to his small income; blackbirds, crows, and woodpeckers, being reckoned as vermin, fetched a two-cent bounty. The marsh on the far side of the rise yielded five birds, a satisfactory day's return, before the young hunters rounded the hill and took a short cut to the crest. As they skirted the brink, Dinty's shoulder was sharply gripped.

"Hist!" warned her companion, in a dramatic whisper. "The foe!"

This was formula, a familiar signal of the woodcraft wherein he had tutored her. Dropping flat on her stomach, she writhed noiselessly forward to the brink, parallel with his stealthy movement. Peering out and downward she could see a figure, a few rods below. It was Wealthia Latham, walking along the dim trail on feet that hastened. And coming to meet her, with swift, springy step, was Catpain Silverhorn Ramsey. The pressure of Tip's hand across Dinty's mouth stifled her gasp.

Wealthia moved straight and silently, like a creature fascinated, into Silverhorn's arms. When she lifted her face from his kiss, it was so mazed, so lost, so heavy with frightened passion, that the eavesdropper flushed and shivered. It was a revelation which made her, in some mysterious and ugly fashion, feel shamedly older. The canaller's gay voice said,

"Little darling! I knew you'd come."

"I couldn't help myself."

"Now that I've got you, I shan't let you go."

A strangled sob was her answer.

"What is it, my sweeting?"

"That woman! The widow. They say you're going to marry her."

"Listen, little one. Say the word and I'll hand her the key to the berm tomorrow." Seeing that she did not comprehend, he laughed and explained, "That's what we say on the canal when we jounce a man out of his berth. It means I'll give her the mitten. It's you I want to marry."

"Oh, Captain Ramsey!"

" 'Captain Ramsey,' " he mocked. "Wait till you're Mrs. Ramsey!" He drew her back into his embrace. His voice became tender and impassioned. "Nobody ever comes here. We're safe." The rest was a whisper.

She swayed back from him, her hands pressed to her breast. "I couldn't! Oh, I wouldn't dare!"

He answered her with a confident laugh. "There's nothing to be afraid about. Witch Crego will tell you what to do. And when I come back next week, everything will be settled and we'll cut our twig and be married."

Her head drooped in helpless surrender. He was leading her toward an alder thicket a few paces away. At that the spell of terror and distress in which Dinty was bound, broke.

"No!" she screamed. "No, Wealthy! No!"

The couple sprang apart. Silverhorn's hand jerked to his belt. His face was dark with fury.

"God damn you for a sneaking little bitch!" he snarled. "I'll strangle you."

He started to claw his way up the shifting, sliding rubble, clutching here at a bush, there at a fixed rock. Pausing for breath, he raised his head. Tip Crego stood above him.

"What do you want, bastard?"

The boy made no reply. He set the mouthpiece of the blowpipe to his lips.

Silverhorn let himself slip slowly back to the level. Well enough he knew the deadly accuracy of that weapon in the hands of an expert. He had no wish to lose an eye. Wealthia stood, tremulous and poised as for flight.

"Don't be frightened, little darling," he bade her. He made a gesture to the others. He had mastered his rage without apparent effort.

"Come down," he invited smoothly. "We'll parley."

Dinty jumped and coasted under escort of a small avalanche. She rushed upon her friend and clasped her. Tip had picked an easier descent and now stood apart and on guard. Dinty panted out,

"Oh, Wealthy! You mustn't. He's a wicked man. Uncle Horace says he's bad."

"Uncle Horace, eh?" put in the canal man's suave accents. "That'll be the conscientious Dr. Amlie. You'll go to him with this, I reckon."

"Yes, I will," replied Dinty defiantly.

"If you do—if you ever say a word of it to anyone, *any*one on this earth, I'll never speak to you again," cried Wealthia passionately.

"I'll do better than that," said Silverhorn, speaking quietly. "If you tell your doctor friend, what will he do? Go to Genter Latham."

"I hope he will," declared Dinty.

"You'd better not. Because if he does, I'm going to kill him."

"Kill him? Kill my Uncle Horace? You—you wouldn't dare. You couldn't." Her eyes were great with terror.

"Wouldn't I?" Silverhorn smiled. "Ask your half-breed chum there."

"He's a killer," said Tip dubiously. "He knifed a man to death on the Lakes."

"In fair quarrel," qualified the canaller. "I'd scorn to kill any other way. But I never miss."

Wealthia began to sob. "I want to go home. I want to go home."

"So you shall, little darling," said Silverhorn in so tender a voice and gentle that Dinty almost stopped hating him.

The pair drew aside for a moment, whispering. Silverhorn waved a hand, and slipped into the thicket as snakily as Tip, himself, could have done. His voice came back to Dinty's ears,

"Remember—Silverhorn never misses."

All the way to the village, Tip walked back of the girls, vigilant for an ambush. When they reached the Latham gate, Wealthia asked her companions inside. In the safe retreat of the garden, she turned to them and said,

"Let's make a swearing,"

"What about?" asked Dinty.

"You know."

"Silverhorn?"

The older girl nodded, looking fearfully about her. "If my father ever knew, I don't know *what* he'd do to me. And if you tell Dr. Amlie, Captain Ramsey will kill him." Dinty shivered. "Will you swear never to tell about today?"

"Yes," said Dinty.

"Tip?"

"Yes," he replied.

All of them knew the formula. One after another they repeated it with uttermost solemnity.

Swear by earth;
Swear by sky;
Cross my heart and double-die.

As they parted, Wealthia whispered to her chum, "I'm scared, Dinty. I never want to see him again."

"It's a good thing you're going back to school," said the sage Dinty.

Driving westward, the canal was now draining the local labor camps of all but a few spademen who remained to do patchwork and occasional repairs. When, at long last, the Middle Section was joined to the Western for through traffic and the roystering fellowship of the towpath flooded the towns, replacing the labor squads, Silverhorn Ramsey was heard of here, there and everywhere, a leader in the frequent battles which broke out between the townsfolk and the brass-buttoned captains, swollen with pride and their princely wage of fifty dollars a month.

Now was decreed the mightiest glorification in Palmyran history. There would be a water pageant; there would be a platform in the Square with eloquent speakers exhibiting orations; there would be a banquet, and finally there would be a ball which, for splendor, was to outshine anything previously attempted in Western New York. Two of the Canal Commissioners had signified their gracious intention of being present. In view of this honor, the committee, under the chairmanship of Mr. Genter Latham, met to consider an innovation. Would it not be well, in order to conserve the dignity of the occasion, that attendance be restricted to a carefully winnowed list?

Such was the contention of Squire Jerrold, Mr. Levering, Deacon Dillard, Col. Macy of the hemp fields, and the rest of the element which felt bound to uphold the tradition of aristocracy. Mine Host

St. John, who saw his ballroom profits menaced by such limitations, headed the opposition. Representatives of the smithy democracy backed him up on broader grounds.

"Is this America, the land of the free and the home of the brave, or ain't it?" demanded O. Daggett.

Horace Amlie made a temperate speech supporting the broader basis. He got unexpected backing from the chairman.

"What about the canallers?" asked someone.

"They'll be soft as boiled pease, with the commissioners looking on," returned Mr. Latham confidently. "Any that ain't will be taken care of. There'll be no trouble."

Ten days before Canal Week, he had reason to doubt his judgment. Three captains swaggered into the Eagle taproom where he was talking over details of the cotillion with L. St. John. All were of the rougher element. The hefty Bull Horgan pounded on the bar, ordered a round of drinks, and thus addressed Host St. John.

"Heard tell you was talkin' of barrin' the canal from your shindigs."

"No," said the host.

"Lucky for you. We'd-a tore your goddam shack down." He turned to the quiet figure at the end of the bar. "Jine us," he barked. It was more a command than an invitation.

"No, thank you," said Mr. Latham civilly.

"Too high an' mighty, huh?"

The other looked him over with a cold eye. "That's it," said he.

"Think poxy well of yourself, don't you!"

"Mind your manners, Horgan," warned the proprietor.

"Don't you?" persisted the captain, edging along the rail.

"Yes," said Mr. Latham.

"Well, who yeh shovin'?"

The thick shoulder, thrust smartly at the quiet man, was not intended to hurt, but merely to show who was who. It met nothing. Swerving lithely aside, Mr. Latham caught the assailant in a grip only less powerful than a bear's. With two motions he ran the astonished mariner across the floor and heaved him through the window. He landed on a manure heap, stunned and cut.

"Bill me for the glass, St. John," said Mr. Latham, dusting his hands.

The two others, after a hesitant consideration of Mr. Latham's alert readiness and the baseball bat which had materialized in L. St.

John's nervous hands, decided upon the part of discretion, went after their fallen champion, and lugged him away to Dr. Murchison for repairs. His last word was a yelp over his shoulder,

"I'll be back."

Being on a short, neighborhood run, Captain Horgan reappeared in public after a few days, but without overt menace to the peace and stability of the community. He did nothing worse than parade Main Street with that blowzy belle of the Settlement, Donie Smith, conscientiously treating her to drinks at decorous intervals. Their romance was the talk of the waterfront.

Horace had it from Unk Zeb Helms. Long enamored of the burly captain, Miss Donie had received only the most transient patronage from him until she repaired for aid to Mistress Crego. The reputed witch compounded a love potion of widely bruited efficacy, which the girl secretly administered to her hero. The results were all that could have been anticipated. Abandoning the promiscuity of his attentions, Captain Horgan thereafter cleaved only to his wench and bought her a four-dollar Leghorn flat. Mistress Crego's reputation and trade were notably enhanced by this success.

"Evva month," said Unk Zeb, rolling his eyes, "dat gel pay Mis' Crego a dollah. Dat gel put de witchery in his drink unbeknownst an' now she got dat big man hitched to her skuttstrings lak a calf to a tent-peg."

Encountering the pair on the street, Horace noticed that the canaller's wrist was still swathed. To his practiced eye, the bandage looked foul. If that was Murchison's doing, it reflected little credit upon his medical standards.

The great fete was a three-day celebration. On the last morning schools closed, merchants shut up shop, Main Street emptied itself toward the canal, and the populace lined bank, lock and bridge, cheering and firing small arms. At ten o'clock a blare of military music floated downwind. Along the towpath pranced two mettlesome steeds. Plumes tossed on their heads. Beside the lead horse their hoggee marched like a drum-major, his beaver decorated with the national colors, his very whiplash gay with a braided rosette. One hundred feet back the elegant and superb packet-boat, *Western Trader,* clove the waters, followed by the *Starry Flag,* the *American Spy* and the *Gypsy Maid,* with three of the humbler Durham freighters in their wake. On each foredeck a captain stood stiffly to the salute, his gilt buttons gleaming in the sun. Abaft, the helmsman, heavy with the responsibilities of his position, gripped the tiller and kept his weather eye alert for emergencies.

The *Queen of the Waters* was next in line, followed by a jostling fleet of small and various craft. Bringing up the rear, an honorable position, swept the dainty pleasure boat, *Genesee Rover,* which Deacon Dillard had presented to his son and heir, Marcus. On her raised deck sat a group of young females in ladylike attitudes, forming a court circle about Miss Wealthia Latham and Miss Araminta Jerrold, elegantly arrayed.

They honored Horace Amlie, who had a reserved place on the bridge across the waterway, with painfully social smiles. He saluted with becoming gravity. Being on the Arrangements Committee, he was committed to attendance upon the formal speechifying of the afternoon and the brief banquet at four o'clock, and so did not encounter them again until the evening festivities.

These were of extreme magnificence. Not only were the youth, beauty, culture and fashion of Palmyra there, but representatives of Rochester, Geneva, Phelps, Geneseo, Canandaigua, Lennox, Jerusalem, Auburn, Utica and Lock Port were present. The canallers turned out in full nautical garb, and well-behaved to the last degree. Caution, not choice, dictated their urbanity. The commissioners wielded autocratic power over water, berm and towpath; a breach of decorum might involve painful penalties. Some of the captains even brought their wives as guarantee of correct deportment.

Lavish refreshments were provided. There were three varieties of brandied punch and one milder brew for the ladies. In the floral decoration there was nothing mean or common such as the vulgar bloom of garden or field; the flowers being all hand facture of artistic design and high cost. Cloth butterflies added a touch of realism. From the fiddler's rest resounded the basic harmonies of Tom Daw's lap-organ, the sawings of Manchester's dance-fiddler, and the zoom-zoom of Carlisle Sneed's double bass, paced by Decker Jessup's snare drum, as they dispensed the latest measures.

Early on the festive scene, Horace made an official inspection and was well satisfied. He led the two commissioners to the dais of honor. Presently Wealthia Latham entered, attended by her usual court of youth. But when Dinty Jerrold followed, Horace got a surprise. An even larger following than Wealthia's surrounded her. Horace found himself frowning. Why? He would have been hard put to it for an explanation of his displeasure. As between his two young protégées he had always been partisan to the junior. Yet, for some undefinable reason, he was not pleased with her too manifest popularity. Possibly this had something to do with her gown, which he deemed much too old for her, though he was bound to admit that she filled it quite satisfactorily. She tripped across the floor to him.

"Oh, Uncle Horace! Isn't it exciting!"

"Apparently it is for you," he replied, noting the roseflush of her cheeks and the butterfly poise of the morocco-shod feet.

"Have you seen Wealthy's new spark?"

Horace nodded. He had observed the dark, high-spirited, serious young South Carolinian who, in the course of the now fashionable Northern Summer Tour, had stopped over at Palmyra, met Miss Latham, and straightway canceled the balance of the trip. Dinty bubbled,

"He calls Wealthia and me 'ma'am.' Isn't that dicty!"

"You don't seem to lack for admirers of your own," observed Horace.

"Why should *you* be cross about it? Aren't you going to ask me to dance? Or are committeemen too important to dance? But perhaps you're not a dancing man."

"That's an absurd supposition," he returned tartly.

His pride was touched. Why should she doubt his possessing the commonest accomplishment of a gentleman? That one brought up in the civilized County of Oneida, a graduate of cultured and elegant Hamilton College, should be ignorant of the art Terpsichorean (unless, of course, he were a Quaker or a Methodist)—absurd, indeed!

"How could I tell?" said she defensively. "You're so solemn. You're solemner than ever this evening. Has anything happened?"

"No."

The denial failed to convince her. She cocked her head at him shrewdly.

"You've seen Captain Ramsey here and you don't like it," she guessed.

"No, I haven't. Where is he?"

"Over yonder, half behind that curtain, watching Wealthy. He's never taken his eyes off her."

"That won't do," declared Horace with decision. He left Dinty without so much as an excuse-me (Still treating me like a child, thought poor Dinty) and walked across the floor to touch Silverhorn's shoulder. The face that was turned to him startled him, so haggard and lined it was. Could it be possible that the profligate young rake was genuinely in love with the girl? That would only make matters worse.

"Good evening, Captain Ramsey," said Horace formally.

The canaller's features twitched, then swiftly composed themselves to their customary expression of insouciance.

"Hullo, Æsculapius."

"Is Mrs. Ramsey with you?" inquired Horace meaningfully.

"Mrs. Ram . . . Oh! We're not married yet. The lady has been ailing."

"Will you take a bit of friendly advice, Ramsey?"

Silverhorn twinkled at him. "Advice from my guardian of morals is sure to be sound. That doesn't say I'll follow it."

"I'm not your guardian. But I'm on the Ball Committee. Will you take a bit of *official* advice?"

"I'll take a drink, if you offer one."

"That, also, can be arranged. Come to the bar."

The navigator ordered and sipped a sangaree, bowing in courteous if faintly ironical acknowledgment. He had put on his best manners with his best clothes. Both were unsurpassable.

"Let's have your advice, my dear feller," he drawled. "Though I know in advance what it will be."

"There will be no trouble if you confine your attentions to other quarters," Horace assured him.

"That's a pretty strong hint."

"Call it a request."

"I've paid my four bits at the door. That should entitle me to equal privileges with the rest."

"You know what I mean. Genter Latham is here. If he sees you with his daughter, he'll throw you through the nearest window."

Silverhorn smiled. "It's never been done."

"Have you heard what happened to Horgan?"

"That clumsy ape! By the way, I don't see him here."

"It'll be quite as well if he doesn't come."

"Oh, he's coming. I saw him at the Exchange bar. He's beauing his sweetmeat, the buxom slewer from the Settlement."

"He mustn't bring her in here."

"Tell it to him," grinned Silverhorn, "but be ready with your fisties."

Horace had no desire for an altercation. There was enough bad blood already between town and canal. Arlo Barnes, at the ticket-door was a stout enough young blade, but no match for the ruffling Horgan. Declining Silverhorn's suggestion of another round, Horace hurried to the entrance and none too soon. The bulky captain, cash in hand and the much dressed-up Donie on his arm, was strutting down the hallway. At the door he proffered his four bits. Arlo Barnes looked around at Horace, who said civilly:

"I'm sorry, Captain Horgan. The doors are closed."

Donie flushed unhappily. "I told you, Bull," she muttered. "Come away." She tugged at his arm.

He wrenched it away, thrusting forth his freshly shaven chin at Horace. "Closed, are they? Since when?"

By good fortune, it was a few minutes after the hour. Horace exhibited his silver turnip. "Since eight o'clock."

"Ay-ah?" The big fellow smirked evilly at him. "How long do you figger they'd stay closed if I up-and-hollered 'Lo-o-o-ow bridge!' Huh?"

"Don't do that," said Horace quickly. The slogan, delivered with a certain prolongation of the first vowel, was a call to battle for the ever-willing canallers. Main Street, he knew, was full of them.

"Which'll it be; money or fight?"

It was a time for diplomacy. "Excuse me if I have a word with the lady," said the committeeman with careful courtesy.

"What's that for?" demanded the suspicious swain.

"Leave be, can't you, Bull?" complained Donie. "I guess the gentleman can speak with me if he likes."

The other growled but made no further objection. It was not the first meeting for the Settlement girl and the young doctor. Soon after her joining the household he had successfully treated her for a tetter which, owing to its location, was a commercial detriment. She was grateful and more than willing to listen to him. He came at once to the point.

"You don't want to go in there, do you?"

"Not if they don't want me," answered the girl stoutly. "I got my pride."

"Good for you! Can you handle your man?"

"Slick as a mink. I got him hawg-tied."

"Take him away, then. I'll make it worth your while."

"With what?" Donie might be appreciative of past help; she was also practical.

"Five dollars," said Horace recklessly. Peace came high, but surely the committee would be willing to reimburse him.

"Five dollars!" Donie was a four-bit girl; the amount named was princely. "*Five* dollars?"

"Cash," affirmed Horace and produced the evidence of good faith. She clutched it.

"Come on, Bull, dear," she called. "I don't hanker after this rout. It's got no sperrit. Dr. Amlie says I'm fevered. I wanna go to bed."

Not having been born on the previous day, Captain Horgan was skeptical. He indicated it in a labial and definite manner. But the girl's claim of her hold upon him was no idle boast. He glowered, cursed, argued, but weakened.

"I'll go," he grunted at last. "But not till we have a drink. And this young blood'll pay for it," he added in a tone which implied, "or I'll know the reason why."

"With pleasure," assented Horace.

At the bar the mariner consumed two killdivvles in quick succession, and was lifting a third toward his capacious face when the long-drawn howl of a pent-up and resentful dog sounded from the mews below. He set down the drink.

"That's a death sign, they say," he observed.

"Not me!" said Donie. She averted the evil with two fingers to her forehead.

"Anyways, it's a sign of trouble," he grinned. "You be about your business, me lad," he said to Horace, and, to the girl, "You wait here for me."

"What are you goin' to do, Bull?"

"Take the air for a bit." He turned at the door with a flash of yellow teeth. "My gel and my money not good enough, huh? I'll show'm," he promised.

Every tavern kept a dog as a matter of course. The Eagle's guardian was a small, chunky, senile mongrel of confiding disposition and so nearly blind that he must be tied up at night, the one cross in an otherwise satisfactory canine existence. Hearing strange footsteps approach, Bowser first growled, as in duty bound, then thumped the wooden walls of his house with a thick and strong tail which suggested pointer blood somewhere in an indeterminate ancestry. The man addressed him soothingly, drew a knife, and, to his intense delight, cut him free. This was a friend, indeed! Bowser came forth, gamboling and fawning. The stranger fondled him.

Instinct stirred within the canine brain, but too late. He was gripped and held. He snapped, caught the man by the wrist, but the place was protected by a bandage, and his teeth too feeble to hold. The powerful knees pressed him between them. He whimpered, then screamed as the keen knife did its work.

Shriek upon shriek of uttermost animal anguish followed. The music coming through the open window a few feet above faltered and stopped. So did the measured feet of the dancers. The next moment their own outcries were added to the clamor, as the unfortunate creature hurtled through the window and darted in mad circles around the floor, spattering blood from the stump of his amputated tail upon the dresses of the ladies and the trousers of the gentlemen and snapping at the hands outstretched to intercept him.

One after another, a dozen susceptible fair ones crumpled to the floor. Others leapt upon chairs and benches, clutching for support at the shoulders of their escorts and crying hysterically. A light dragoon bethought him of his musket, fetched it in, and fired a shot, which, by God's grace, hit nobody, least of all the dog. Around and around spun the agonized animal until he collapsed from loss of blood, and was mercifully dispatched with a club from the bar.

The drink-empurpled countenance of Bull Horgan appeared, triumphant, in the frame of the window.

"Shut me and my gel out, will yuh?" he bellowed, and went down under the weight of a wave of infuriated dancers.

The attempted war-cry of "Lo-o-o-ow bridge!" was stifled in his throat. It would hardly have saved him, in any case. Even the hard-shell canallers were shocked at the brutality. There was no movement of protest when word came back that the battered perpetrator had been lodged in the new jail.

Urgent demands kept both Drs. Amlie and Murchison busy for a half-hour, reviving deflated femininity. The evening bade fair to be ruined and the town disgraced. Horace took a minute off to apologize to the guests of honor and to rally the musicians. With more tact than would have been expected, the captains paid their respects to the committee ladies and took a prompt departure. All but one.

Last of Horace's charges to recover was Clarissa Van Wie, a high-strung little redhead who came belatedly out of her swoon only to lapse into hysterics. He had her taken to a chamber above stairs where he left her in the charge of two of the ladies. On the way back to the ballroom floor, he saw a door cautiously opening. Wealthia Latham was stealing out from a small parlor. She was alone. Her face was that of a person undispelled of a dream.

"Wealthia!" he called sharply.

She whirled about, both hands to her breast. "Oh!" she gasped. "You scared me so."

"Where have you been?"

"Nowhere."

"Who was with you?"

"Nobody."

He held her under a skeptical regard.

Outside, fine and high and clear rang a bugle-note. The swift color flashed into the girl's face. She said hastily,

"You haven't asked Dinty to dance."

"Dinty is well provided with partners of her own age."

"Of course she is." She added something under her breath which sounded to his incredulous ears much like "Ninny!"

"What did you say?" he demanded.

"Nothing. You'll hurt her feelings if you don't ask her."

"Nonsense!"

"Oh, very well!" The velvety eyes regarded him with an expression highly unbefitting a child of her tender years toward a gentleman of his mature age. "If you won't, plenty of others will."

"I can see that for myself."

"You needn't be huffy at me." She turned a shoulder to him with languid grace as she moved away, not without a Parthian shot. "Dinty's right. You *are* dumb about some things."

She lifted a smiling face toward young Hayne, the handsome Southerner who was hastening down the hallway to regain her.

Horace, his dignity somewhat ruffled, followed more slowly to the dancing floor. It was all folderol, what Wealthia had said, a patent subterfuge to divert him from the suspicion of her rendezvous with Ramsey. Still—if she was right about Dinty, certainly he did not wish to hurt the child's feelings. She was queerly sensitive about some things, an attribute peculiar to her time of life, he surmised. Anyway, there could be no harm in his offering his arm for one number.

The music was taking a rest as he approached the group around her. She signaled him with a consciously coquettish flutter and smile, rose at once and, amidst a hum of protest from her swains, detached herself from her entourage and attached herself to his arm.

"I thought you were never coming."

"You don't appear to be suffering from lack of attention."

"Oh, them!" She shrugged in an adult manner. "They're different."

He did not press for a definition and she remarked mincingly that she would appreciate a refreshing drink. Once free of the crowd and seated at the table which he found in a secluded alcove, she abandoned her ballroom manners and reverted to type.

"You're worried, aren't you, Uncle Horace?"

"Yes, I am."

"Don't you think it would take your mind off things to dance with me just once?" she inquired with eyes of limpid candor.

"I was going to proffer that request."

"And now you've made me do it. That's very unladylike of me. D'you mind my being unladylike, Uncle Horace?"

"I can stand it."

"You don't know how much nicer you look when you smile," she observed.

Carlisle Sneed, as caller-off, was announcing, "The next musical selection will be the slow and measured valse."

"Do you elbow-valse, Uncle Horace?"

"Yes. Or, for that matter . . ."

"That's all they allow here. The other isn't considered proper by the fusty old Abigails. I like it better, though."

She stood, billowing out her skirts, flexing her rounded arms. He cupped his hands beneath her elbows. They revolved solemnly.

"You do it very nicely," she approved. She looked about. For the moment the room was deserted except for themselves. "I don't care," she murmured and slipped into his arms.

Her cheek brushed his, a flower touch for lightness and fragrance. The supple young body pressed to him. The rhythm of the music took and swayed them. Everything around him seemed to be slipping away. She leaned back from him, her lips upturned.

"It's funny," she murmured.

"What's funny?"

"You. Me. Us."

"I don't see anything funny about it." (Funny! A feeble characterization, indeed!)

"Even your voice is funny."

"Dinty! Dinty!"—from without.

"That's Mark, searching for me."

"Mark be damned!"

She drew back, one slender hand trailing to his wrist and lingering there. "Why do you want Mark to be damned, Uncle Horace?" she whispered.

"*Do* you have to keep calling me that fool name?"

"It doesn't seem to fit any more, does it?" she mused.

Standing a little away now, as Marcus Dillard appeared at the entrance, she smiled upward. As he pondered upon it afterward—and he gave it an amount of consideration quite disproportionate to its ephemeral existence—it seemed to him a strange smile, difficult of interpretation; a smile alien to the Dinty of their former relationship; an over-sagacious smile; an absurdly adult smile; a smile of guile with an obnoxious suggestion of condescension, as if she were enjoying some recondite knowledge occluded from his duller, male comprehension. No, damn it! Not condescension. That would be too much.

There was another quality inherent in it, too. It came to him with a shock. It was—yes, by God! there was no other word for it—it was unscrupulous.

-22-

It was a Gallant Combat. Wo is me that I should not have been Present at the Stricken Field.

(THE WAVERLEY INFLUENCE UPON DINTY'S DIARY)

PORTENTS of trouble were abroad on the ill-fated night of the ball. Four canal boats, frugally avoiding basin charges, had moored to the berm in the widened area below Poverty's Pinch. The crews had gone to town, leaving one man in charge of each craft. The *Anna Maria*, salt-laden from Salinas, was guarded by her captain, Job Gadley, who, incapacitated by a humor beneath his knee, sat on his afterdeck, somberly chewing his plug. At his most amiable, Captain Gadley was no pattern of sweetness and light. His affliction enhanced in him a tempermental acerbity unworthy of his scriptural name.

Half asleep, he was roused by a sense rather than a sound of someone moving along the catwalk.

"Who goes there?" he challenged.

"Me. Mistress Crego."

"What's your business on my deck?"

Quaila was making the rounds with her basket of curatives, hoping to find some trade and pick up a few pennies. She launched into her formula.

"Herbs and simples for the humors. Seng for heated blood and aching head. Bitter willow for a lazy bowel. Sleep potions and love potions and proven relief from the gulping dyspepsy."

"And witchcraft for silly brains," he grumbled. He half believed in it. Had her foot so much as touched the planking, in her silent descent upon him? He doubted it. Witches floated. Doubtless she had dropped overboard the poker whereon she flew, where, notwithstanding that it was iron, it would float until she reclaimed it.

"White magic," said she in her deep, persuasive contralto. "White only. What ails your leg, brave captain?"

"I got a gathering," he admitted, "but I don't know how you twigged it."

"By the stars." She had the information from a canal-rat whom she fed when casual jobs were insufficient to keep him alive. "Let Quaila see, brave captain."

Muttering, he drew up his trouser-leg. By the light of a candle which she fired with tow from her flint-and-steel box, she examined the sore.

"A soothing poultice," she pronounced, "which I will prepare over your fire. First we shall expel the evil."

Setting down her basket, she gave the ulcer a hearty squeeze. With a yell, the agonized captain kicked her clean overside. It was involuntary muscular reaction rather than intent, but, having gone so far, he hurled her basket after her and added a string of imprecations for good measure. The profanity died on his lips. For Quaila, rising from the mud and standing, armpit deep in water, overmatched him with an output of objurgations beside which his choicest vocabulary was but a thin, diaconal piping.

Without pause for breath she cursed him, his boat, his crew, his cargo, and his horses. From that she passed to the adjacent craft, cursing each by name, together with its entire personnel and equipment. Rising from the particular to the general, she cursed the canal, lock, berm and towpath, from Hudson flow to Erie Water, from Governor Clinton to the meanest hostler in the local relay stable. She then (so Captain Gadley asserted to his dying day) spat a flame at him and waded ashore. His leg burned with all the fires of hell.

Before morning all four boats rested on bottom.

In spite of appearances, this was no magic, black or white. It was the very practical experiment of a practical mind. Jim Cronkhite, the local politician, had taken over the Welcome Lantern Coffee House, toughest of the new taverns, and was having financial troubles. Several of the captains, as well as lesser canal folk, were indebted to him for bed, board and drink, a reckoning which, as he judged from former disillusioning experiences, was likely to remain on the slate indefinitely, unless settled while hot. The debtors, it was whispered, were casting off at sunrise. After consideration of the problem over a mixture of his own drinks, Host Cronkhite borrowed an auger from a carpenter who was sleeping it off behind the woodpile, crept unnoticed into the water, and bored four neat holes, fore and aft, through the sheathing of each boat. Whether all four of them belonged to his debtors he could not be certain. It did not matter. The more boats tied up, the better for trade.

Loud and bitter was the outcry in the morning. On the basis of Job Gadley's report of his interview, public hostility focused upon Mistress Crego. Captain Job whetted his sheath-knife and declared his unalterable intention of slitting the witch's weazand if he swung for it. First catch your witch. Quaila's friendly rat brought her warning. She flew away, presumably on her poker, to wait for emotions to calm down. When the auger holes were identified, Captain Gadley's version lost support. What would a witch be doing with a bit-and-brace, cooler heads asked. Quaila reappeared and offered an alibi. Nevertheless there were many who looked askance at her. There was no doubt of her having cursed the canal and all its works. Henceforth anything that went wrong with the traffic would be likely to be attributed to her supernatural ill-will.

Such as chose to twist evidence to a preconceived text, found further proof in what befell Captain Horgan. The "Bull" was left to languish in durance vile for a day of meditation and perhaps contrition. In the evening, the jailer called at Dr. Amlie's office.

"My prisoner's havin' a fit, Doctor," said he.

"What kind of fit?"

"I dunno. Spasms, like. I wisht you'd come."

"Horgan is Dr. Murchison's patient. Call him."

"He's sittin' up for a baby and won't come. I wisht you would, Doctor. I wouldn't want him to die on us. Folks might blame me."

Unwillingly pursuant to his rule of never refusing a critical case, which this might well be by the evidence though he suspected nothing worse than delirium tremens, Horace went with the official. The jail was a trim and stout little edifice with a heavy, oaken door and a high window, heavily barred. More attention had been paid to the exterior than the interior. This consisted of a single room with no other furnishings than a twelve-inch-plank bench.

On the floor groveled and twisted Bull Horgan. His face was gray, his breathing difficult.

"We've got to get him out of here," said Horace.

"What'll I do with him?" asked the perturbed official.

"I'll take him to the tavern. Look up a trustee and get a release. I'll be responsible."

Late-faring residents were edified by the spectacle of their young and respected physician trundling a patient through Main Street in a Brainard barrow, for want of other conveyance. Having got his man into bed, Horace, something at a loss, bethought himself of Donie Smith. She came at call.

"Oh, Bull! What is it?" she wept. "What ails you?"

"It's witchings, that's what it is," moaned the sufferer. "I seen the hex-fires in the woods last Friday."

Dr. Gail Murchison bustled importantly in. "My patient, Doctor," he said to Horace.

"Take him and welcome, Doctor," returned Horace.

"Don't go," begged Donie, clutching him. "Give him some medic. Save him."

As Murchison bent over the bed, a dreadful convulsion racked the man. His back arched in an incredible curve until heels and head nearly touched.

"Ah!" said the old physician in a tone of satisfaction. "Foul play. The man has been poisoned."

To Horace it seemed at first only too probable. The symptoms were identical with those of *nux vomica* poisoning. But he had never heard of delayed action from strychnia. And how would the jailed man have had access to the drug? Donie, her face ashy, was plucking at his sleeve.

"The love potion," she whispered. "It couldn't have been! Could it?"

"When did you last give it to him?"

"Three nights ago."

He breathed a sigh of relief. "Have you any of it left?"

"Yes. Three powders."

"Keep them for me."

The sick man was trying now to throw himself out of bed. Horace jumped to help his colleague. In the struggle the bandage on the wounded wrist was displaced, revealing a furiously inflamed area. Horace stared at it in quick enlightenment.

"I think, Dr. Murchison, that your patient has tetanus," he said.

"Huh? Tet . . . Oh, lockjaw!" He peered into the strained face. The jaws were firmly clamped. "Perhaps he has," he grudged.

"If you have no opium," said Horace smoothly, "I shall be pleased to place mine at your disposal."

Having thus adroitly suggested the line of treatment, he watched until the drug took effect and the patient's agony eased. Murchison fumbled about a dressing for the wrist, applied a sinapism to the back of the neck, and brought out his lancet. Instinctively Horace started to intervene, then shrugged his shoulders in resignation. It probably did not matter.

Horgan died at dawn.

There was a tremendous to-do along the waterfront; talk of arresting Donie Smith; talk of arresting Quaila Crego; dangerous mutterings of violence toward the two women. It might have come to that but for Horace's prompt action. He made a chemical analysis of the love-medicine. No strychnia or allied drug was to be found, nor evidence of any other poison. For his further satisfaction, the physician administered a whacking dose to a tomcat that had been haunting his premises. Though evincing evidence of a strong dislike for the flavor, the tom exhibited no untoward symptoms. He did not even manifest any enhanced fervor on the prowl. By Horace's guess, Mistress Crego's stimulant was not as advertised.

All this he set forth in a lucid report for the village trustees. Dr. Murchison was induced to sign a certification of death from lockjaw. The two women were exculpated in the general mind. But suspicion against the witch of Poverty's Pinch still rankled in the hearts of the canallers.

At midnight of a Saturday which had been notable (and should have been suspicious) for its comparative peace and quiet, Horace was roused by a frenzied hammering at the office door. He had long reconciled himself to that peculiarity of pregnant womanhood which leads it habitually to start childbirth at the most inconvenient hour possible. He drowsily reached for his trousers, divided in surmise as to whether this would be Mrs. Seth Howard with her seventh, conveniently near on the next street, or the young wife of Sam'l Terry (Heaven forbid!), a primapara and two miles the other side of the ropewalk, at that.

"Coming," he yelled crossly. "Quit that pounding."

He opened the door. Tip Crego staggered in. The boy had been cruelly mishandled. He was soaked and muddied from head to foot.

"Come quick!" he panted. "They're trying Aunt Quaila."

"Who?" said Horace stupidly.

"The canallers."

"What for?"

"Witchcraft."

"Where is she?"

"They've got her on the *Anna Maria.*"

This was bad business. But the physician's immediate concern was with the boy, whose hand half covered his face. Horace drew it way. "Here! Let me look at that eye," he said.

Tip fought him off, sobbing. "Oh, come! Please come!"

Horace pushed him into a chair, dressed the eye, and plugged the nose which he judged to be broken. Through the window, as he worked swiftly, he could see a reddening of the low clouds above the Pinch.

"They're getting ready to burn her," wailed the boy.

It shocked Horace into action. Instinctively he reached for his fowling-piece, but reconsidered, a counsel of caution which he had reason to regret presently. On a sheet of paper he scrawled a dozen names.

"Get these men," he directed. "Tell 'em the canallers are out and there's going to be trouble at the Pinch."

Daggett, Jessup, Cronkhite, Turnbull Lay, Billy Dorch, Jed Parris, Carlisle Sneed, he could rely upon them. Even Silas Bewar, the Quaker of the smithy, could be counted upon in a case of saving human life. For good measure he added Tom Daw and Bill Simmons, the town drunkard and a willing fighter. Not all would be available, but those who were would rally others to them. If only they got there on time! He heard Silverhorn Ramsey's bugle in the distance, and ran.

As he crossed the little rise beyond which there was a drop to Ganargwa Creek at the point nearest the canal, the scene spread before him, lighted by a glowing brush fire. Gesturing men were clustered on the deck of Captain Job Gadley's freighter. Some were laughing, some talking eagerly, others bending above the hatch to listen to what was going on between decks. The trial, then, was still in progress. Boldly he advanced to the gangplank. A slim figure rose lazily from the coaming.

"Hullo, Young Æsculapius."

"Hullo, Ramsey. What's going on here?"

"Private doings. You'd better go home."

"Thanks for the advice. I think I've got a friend aboard." He was resolved to match the other for coolness.

"She's in good hands. She'll be looked after."

A screech of abject terror followed by a babble of pleadings from below cut him off. Horace started up the plank, to be confronted by Silverhorn's ready knife. Bitterly he regretted that he had not brought his gun. With that threat he might have held the self-constituted "court" helpless on board until aid came. As it stood, he was one man, unarmed, against a mob.

"That's far enough," warned Silverhorn.

"Will you come down and fight it out, man to man?" invited Horace.

"It would be a pleasure," replied the other. "Later perhaps. Duty first. I'm on guard."

"Are you going to stand by and see a woman burned?"

"There's no question of burning her. What d'you take us for—Choctaws? We'll just give her a bit of ducking at the end of a fender-pole."

The wretched woman, pealing shriek on shriek, was bundled to the deck, gagged, and neatly spliced to a stout twelve-foot pole.

"Take her to the swimmin'-hole," directed a voice. "'Tain't deep enough here for the job."

Horace recognized a small, wiry, chin-bearded Down East ruffian named Cambling who, it was said, had fled Massachusetts after kicking to death a discharged tow-boy for asking his wages.

"Ramsey," said Horace earnestly, "if they duck her with the gag in her mouth, she'll drown."

"Witches don't drown. Not that I believe in 'em. Now, you take a friend's advice and vammy. What can you do?"

Nothing, Horace perceived. Yet, to leave the unhappy Quaila to her tormentors was unthinkable. It was a question of how effectually Tip was raising the town. There came to Horace's mind an expedient of delay.

Above the deep hole to which the court was now conducting its prisoner the current rippled over stony shallows. The strand was covered with cobble-sized rocks as sweetly rounded as if nature had fashioned them for handy missiles. Horace flexed his throwing muscles.

"I'll hold you responsible for any harm that comes to her, Ramsey," said he crisply, and vanished into the shadows.

Keeping to their shelter he crossed the creek at a bend, skirted the far side, and scrabbled together a supply of the stones back of a bush where he hid. The mob appeared, with Quaila Crego in the midst. No sound came from her. She had fainted. The canallers lined up along the shore. All was to be done in order.

"What is the court's pleasure, Judge, your Honor?" humorously piped one of the attendants.

The harsh nasality of the Yankee answered, "Duck her three times till she confesses. Duck her three more till she recants. Then cast her loose to sink or swim."

And this—thought Horace—is the Nineteenth Century, the golden era of Science, of Christian Enlightenment, of Progress and Democracy, of Internal Improvements and the Grand Canal. The captive, reviving, began to moan. Several men laid hold on the pole, half-lifting, half-shoving the writhing form toward the water. One of them loosed his grip with a surprised grunt. Another combined a yelp with an oath, and toppled over.

"Hey! What the hell is this?" shouted Cambling.

Horace let fly with a sidefling, missed him, tried again and felled Gadley. His right arm had lost nothing of its prowess.

"There he is," yelled one of the assailed, spotting the dark figure insufficiently shielded by the shrubbery. "Get the son-of-a-bitch!"

The time was come for retreat. Running at his swiftest to escape being cut off from the shallows, the fugitive saw that it was going to be a tight thing. Four pursuers had drawn ahead of the rest. Here was the danger. Horace paused for a hasty shot to check them. By the splash in the water he knew that it had gone wild. So, he was the more surprised to hear a thud and a cry. On the opposite bank a bulky form emerged from cover. It stooped, rose and flung. Thump! Yelp! The check saved Horace; he splattered through the ford.

"Well, young man," said Genter Latham's heavy voice, "bigger targets, these, than bottles. Eh?"

"Are the others coming?" panted Horace.

"Look up the hill."

The slope was dancing with lanterns.

"We'd better run for it," said Horace.

Too many of the canallers were already pushing toward them. Now the towpath was dotted with hastening figures, summoned by the rallying cry of "Lo-o-o-ow bridge!" joined to the urgent peals of Silverhorn's bugle. In response to the summons, coffee-house, ginnery and brothel had spewed forth reinforcements. The two doughty stone-throwers withdrew under cover of their own fire, plunged through the canal, and met the advancing townfolk on the far bank.

"The witch-boy told me," Genter Latham imparted to his companion. He was in jovial humor. "Haven't had a fight for years," he chuckled.

"You'll have one now," prophesied Horace. "The captains are out for blood."

Tip Crego, it appeared, had gone on after encountering the magnate, to spread the alarum, and the result of his effort was seen in relays of hurrying villagers, half-clad or less, among whom Horace made out O. Daggett, Carlisle Sneed, T. Lay, Decker Jessup, Billy Dorch, Jed Parris, and, for good measure, Bezabeel Fornum with a hammer, L. Brooks, M.D., with a hop-pole, L. St. John with his stout bat, and the alcoholic Simmons appropriately brandishing an earthen gallon measure. It was a doughty enough band, full of fight, adequate perhaps to hold off the superior forces of the Erie men with the barrier of the canal to help, but insufficient for the business in hand which was the rescue of Quaila Crego.

Always for offense, the boatees now reconnoitered the stretch of canal water. Fresh accessions were arriving every minute, as Horace noted with dismay. Silverhorn, jaunty on his gangplank, seemed to be directing the strategy. A well-directed cobble to the ribs, from the hand of Genter Latham, brought him down, and he rose, raging, from the shallows to head a charge. The town group was forced backward. It looked as if they might be surrounded, captured and be subjected to the rite of "Erie baptism" as enthusiastic voices suggested. Horace, fighting at one edge of the group, was downed and found himself being dragged toward the brink when a calm and familiar voice, hazily heard, said,

"Stopper thy nose, Friend Amlie."

Then a prolonged "Squissh–ssh–ssh–sssshhhhh!"

Strangled yelps and moans from the four men who had him down followed. He was, himself, half-choked in stifling fumes when the powerful Quaker heaved him to his feet. Through tear-dimmed eyes he saw Silas Bewar brandishing an ungainly implement over the groveling forms of several human beetles who were aimlessly crawling about.

"Does thee wish any more?" inquired the peaceable voice.

Apparently no more was needed. Silas lowered the nozzle of the long squirtgun which he employed in his veterinary practice.

"I made free of thy firkin of hartshorn," he explained to the rescued man.

As the potent fumes of the ammonia dissipated, Horace perceived that the battle had entered a new phase. The mariners now were being pushed back under pressure of a compact force of new arrivals from the village. To the dim eyes of the observer it seemed that a familiar figure had taken charge of operations, but he could hardly believe his ears when Silas told him that the authoritative commander was the Rev. Theron Strang. Horace had not known it, but the lanky Doctor of Divinity was not only a mighty man of his hands, but had served as one of Andy Jackson's captains at New Orleans. Fighting was no novelty to him. Standing to his orders were Tom Daw, Cassius Moore, a dozen tannery lads, puffy, stocky old Simon Vandowzer, a likely group from the mintery, and a general representation of stable, store and warehouse. Though less mature and weighty, man for man, than the enemy, they were ready and willing.

Dominie Strang came to Horace and asked if he was able to go on. Receiving an affirmative, he set an apprentice lad to gathering rocks, and stationed the marksman at one corner of the attacking corps. On the other wing, Genter Latham was similarly supplied with an ammunition helper. The clergyman seemed to know instinctively just what each man was best fitted for. The sharpshooters were to harass the foe until the final charge came, and then join it.

As Horace took his assigned position, a form almost as impalpable as the night mist flitted past him. It was Tip Crego. The boy held what seemed to be a slender rod in his hand. Horace recognized the blowgun and thought it poorly selected for the tough encounter in prospect.

Silverhorn's bugle was sounding again, with a note of urgency. Cambling, Job Gadley and a couple of other captains were exhorting their followers with the foulest of objurgations and threats against the Palmyrans. The canallers about-faced and formed up between canal and creek, with their captive at their protected rear. As Dominie Strang made his swift dispositions, it was apparent that the juncture of battle would be in the canal bed itself, and Lord help the man that went down.

Of that melee Horace remembered little afterward and that little dimly. Early in the clash somebody hit him a handsome clip back of the ear causing a mental confusion through which, however, he could recall with satisfaction chin-butting an ambitious opponent who was trying to thumb out his eye after the approved Kentucky fashion. Horace disposed of him with a kick not countenanced by even the most liberal rule of the ring—this was no time for formalities—and waded to shore to retrieve his breath. Weaving on the bank and staunching his gory nose, he found time to admire the man of God as he smote the hosts of Midian hip and thigh in the forefront of that confused war. Genter Latham was doing valiantly, backed by Carlisle Sneed, Bill Simmons and a dozen mintery men in a rush which carried them to the side of the pole-bound Mistress Crego who had swooned again, this time in the stout arms of Silas Bewar.

A savage charge of the Erie men bore back Quaker, drunkard and magnate, and Horace was fain to rejoin the rescue squad. The brush fire had died down. Men fought, hand to hand, in the darkness of the rising mists, scarcely able to distinguish friend from foe. Horace's head was still ringing merrily, but he was valuable in the close work, being something of a wrestler. He presently found himself battling on one side of the reverend commander-in-chief, while Jed Parris, spouting his best line of profanity, upheld the other. A piercing call arose, downstream from them.

"Hey, Doc! Dr. Amlie! Where's Doc Amlie?"

Some overtone of terror in the cry gave pause to the struggle. Horace elbowed himself free from the ursine embrace of a large and drunken helmsman and splattered his way to where a little group was dragging a burden to the towpath. He bent over an inert form.

"Fetch a light," he ordered.

All the lanterns had been doused in the fighting. Not a man had a dry flintbox. While volunteers ran to the Pinch for torches, Horace dropped to his knees and loosened the fallen warrior's collar. His hand touched something small and hairy, projecting from the throat. His heart checked. Without sight, he knew it for one of Tip Crego's darts. He plucked out the lethal point and concealed it. So small and light a thing to have taken a strong man's life. There was no blood, hardly a mark. To all appearances the man had been drowned.

Lights arrived. In the glow the mean features of Captain Cambling were revealed.

"He's dead," said Horace.

"My God!" shivered a voice from the shadow.

"Let us pray," said the Rev. Theron Strang.

For an instant Horace glimpsed Tip's terrified visage in the circle above him. It vanished.

"Fire! Fire!"

The shout came from the Pinch. A torch had been dropped, or perhaps some vengeful canaller had started the flames. A rising wind whipped them to fury. Townsmen and canal folk, forgetting their feud in the shock of a fatality, combined to fight the holocaust. It was a hopeless attempt. In an hour there was only scattered ash where Poverty's Pinch had sprawled.

Just as well for Palmyra, the respectable said. Just as well, too, that Witch Crego and her bastard had relieved decent folk of their contamination by vanishing from the scene. It was easy for the humble and obscure to disappear, leaving no trace and little injury. Nobody cared except Horace Amlie, who had a warm affection for Tip, and the frail ones of the Settlement who, lacking Mistress Crego, now had none to turn to in trouble.

Not before dawn did quiet rest upon the battle scene. High o'er the field a lonely cadence grieved, as Carlisle Sneed mourned an eye, gouged out by a person or persons unknown in the heat of conflict. Happily it was his glass eye. But he could not be dissuaded from the search until Horace had promised him a new and better one.

For the young physician there was no sleep. The wounds of his own faction he patched up on the ground. Having thus fulfilled his immediate obligations, he boldly boarded the canal boats, offering repairs. The boatees welcomed him. They respected a lusty fighter, and readily displayed their own damages, courteously inquiring after his, and paying on the nail.

"That was a poxy fine turn-up," they said. "Too bad about Cap Cambling. But he was a pizen skunk, anyway."

Not only was no rancor cherished, except by that surly soretail, Captain Job Gadley, but Horace found himself endued with a new popularity. Specially admired was his dexterity with a rock, attested by an impressive list of stomach bruises, rib and arm contusions, and one minor concussion of the brain, all of which he treated. As an aftermath of his spreading repute, he was officially invited to become an honorary member of the Rochester Baseball Club which, fifty strong, met of weekday afternoons in Mumford's Pasture.*

After Sunday service Squire Jerrold accosted Horace while his wife passed on, nose in air.

"I hear you wrought mightily last night," said he with a twinkle.

"It was an active fight," answered Horace. "You should have seen our man of peace, Elder Strang."

"Dinty left good-bye for you."

Horace looked blank. "She's gone? Already?" He would never have believed that she would leave town without bidding him farewell.

"Unexpectedly. Colonel and Mrs. Hopkins were called to New York and stopped to take her for a visit to the Moses Rogers mansion on the Battery. She will see New York society at its finest and most fashionable," said the father with satisfaction.

* Nearly a generation before General Abner Doubleday "invented" baseball at Cooperstown.

It was on Horace's lips to protest that she was too young for such heady dissipations. Some instinct checked him. He was unreasonably depressed.

Her letter came by the first post. It began "Dear Dr. Amlie" and expressed polite regrets that there had been no opportunity for her to pay her respects before departure, and she was his Obedient Servant and Well-wisher, Araminta Jerrold.

The P.S. was more Dintyish. "I cried."

-23-

You Never can Tell till you Try.
(AN APOTHEGM FREQUENTLY
REPEATED IN DINTY'S DIARY)

THAT minor Neptune who holds sway over artificial waterways withdrew the light of his countenance from the Ganargwa Valley. In spite of favorable rains, the canal level in that stretch of navigation slowly diminished to a scant two feet. Optimistic Palmyra shut its eyes to the threat. Then came disaster.

The blow fell in the night, as July merged into August. The village, waking, looked out upon a vista of sodden mud patches between dreary pools, where clear water should have rippled. A few boats canted at unsightly angles while their captains raged upon the decks. Opposite the scaler's office a four-ply raft carpeted the canal floor.

There had been a breach in the berm toward East Palmyra, but this, in itself, could not account for the suddenness of the decrease. Others there must be to have caused so catastrophic a leakage. Urgent appeals were sent to the Canal Board for engineers. Contractors were dispatched to round up labor gangs. Plans were advanced for further tapping of the Genesee River. Prayers for rain were offered in all the churches. Palmyra, repentant of the pride and arrogance which had led it vaingloriously to exalt itself above less fortunate communities, abased itself in sackcloth and ashes.

Rumors and reasons for the misfortune were freighted about. One had it that Exhorter Sickel, notoriously a foe to the Erie, had prayed the water away. Another opinion held that an outraged Heaven had wrought the calamity in reprisal upon the political cabal which was scheming to oust Governor Clinton from the Commission, a plot which subsequently succeeded. The canallers ascribed it to the vengefulness of the Powers of Darkness.

Drunken Bill Simmons was their chief witness. Having unobtrusively borrowed a batteau on the creek to sleep off a spree, he had cast off and waked to find himself far downstream, staring up into a livid sky wherein bat-winged apparitions performed a hideous saraband. One figure which bore a striking likeness to the corporeal form of Witch Crego, had plunged like Lucifer down upon the very spot where the berm had given way.

The brotherhood of the towpath was for hunting down Mistress Crego. But even the most militant lost countenance when it became known that Elder Strang and Dr. Amlie had rescued her from a cave, helpless from shock and exposure, and had taken her to the Strang home, where the parson defied all the hosts of evil to touch her. The hosts of evil had no stomach for the job; one experience at the hands of the formidable man of God had sufficed them. Counsels of peace prevailed; let the hex be!

Tip Crego was nowhere to be found. Nor would his "aunt" be prevailed upon to give any information. She was fearful of everybody now, including Dr. Amlie. As soon as the Pinch rose from its ashes, which it quickly did in character hardly less noisome than before, she went back there to live. She commanded the respect of fear.

Public responsibilities pressed upon Horace. Thus far the season had been unusually healthy. Now, with the pools festering in the heat, anything might be expected. As the physician frankly admitted to Genter Latham, he was not yet satisfied as to whether the flies or the mosquitoes were the chief agents of disease. Other forms of insect life might be guilty, also; stink-bugs, snake doctors, hellbenders, even the innocent-appearing butterflies and moths, all were under suspicion.

"Go after 'em, my boy," said the great man good-humoredly. It was no skin off the end of his nose, whatever the fanatic might do to the premises of his neighbors. "Clean 'em all up."

"Yours, too?"

"So long as the town pays," grinned his sponsor.

By virtue of his constabulary authority, Horace organized inspection squads. His cronies of the smithy rallied to him, not that they harbored any passion for cleanliness, but for the sport of it. It developed into a sort of game; who could find the most and worst smells on his neighbor's premises; and though some ancient feuds engendered new heat, surprisingly little rancor attached to the instigator of the campaign. With practically no opposition he invaded privies, abolished garbage heaps, limed casual waste-water, and soaked up the foul mire of the canal bottom with acidulous refuse collected from the asheries. When, after three weeks of this, he appeared at town meeting to report both ague and intestinal affections below normal, he was cheered. The spirit of the place was chastened.

To the mind of the inhabitants this matter of health was secondary to the all-important question: when would the water come back? Lower and lower drooped the communal optimism, as week succeeded week and no keel moved between Clyde and Rochester. Even the sturdy *Wayne County Herald,* which was the old *Canal Advocate* renamed, drooped in print. Unless the leaks were located and staunched, would all the projected increase in supply suffice to restore navigation before the season closed? Ye Scribe darkly doubted it. In that case, what would befall the town? It would stagnate like the scum of its canal-bed.

Relieved of his specific preoccupations, Horace remembered that he had never answered Dinty's letter of farewell. He sharpened two quills, mixed himself a fresh well of ink by his best formula—no soot-and-water for his personal correspondence—sat in to his desk at nine of the evening and at ten had completed a labored composition which suited him so ill that he crumpled it and threw it into the fireplace. His second attempt was different. But when he came to read it over, his face turned a surprised and uncomfortable red. What kind of missive was this for a man of his age to be sending to an unfledged schoolgirl? Suppose someone else read it, the school authorities, for instance; they might almost mistake it for a love-letter, so warmly was it couched. Most assuredly, that was not what it was meant to be. He tore it into strips and went to bed in very ill-humor with himself.

Dinty was now back at school, having gone there direct from her New York visit, and writing her parents weekly that she had had enough of it. Wealthia was coming home at the end of the term; why could not she come, too? She implied that she knew practically everything that was to be learned from book or blackboard, an assumption which brought an indulgent smile to the mouth of her father and a thinning of her mother's lips.

"I daresay she knows too much about some things that are no part of a young girl's education," said Mrs. Jerrold.

"Nonsense!" said her husband. "What's on your mind now?"

"I hear things from Albany. There is too much license in that school. Half the young gentlemen in Albany follow Wealthia Latham and our daughter when they appear on the street."

"No wonder!" remarked Squire Jerrold, which as a contribution to family amity was far from successful.

"You're too weak with her, Mr. Jerrold. She can twist you around her finger. You don't understand her."

Mr. Jerrold might have retorted that Mrs. Jerrold not only failed to understand Dinty, but had never made any attempt to. To her narrowed-in mind, Dinty was an incomprehensible and unmerited affliction, a contumacious and high-minded little upstart who needed taking down. If parents could not do it, a husband might. So much she said to the Squire. It startled him.

"Why, my dear, she hasn't finished her schooling yet."

"She knows more than I did at her age."

Squire Jerrold thought it likely, but was too tactful to agree. "She is so innocent and unformed in many ways," he objected.

"Innocent!" said Mrs. Jerrold darkly.

"Well, about marriage and—and all that sort of thing," stumbled the father. "Do you suppose she knows anything about it?"

Mrs. Jerrold tossed her ringleted head. "She thinks she knows all about everything."

"What leads you to suppose that, my dear?"

"I've tried to tell her but she only gets fretty and fidgety and won't listen to me."

"That doesn't necessarily prove anything." The Squire had a juster view than his wife of Dinty's reticences. He sensed a frightened delicacy, a reserve for which Mrs. Jerrold had only impatience.

"Then you tell her," said she maliciously.

"God forbid!" was the hasty reply. "Let her find out when the time comes. Is there anyone in particular?"

"Oh, she has plenty of aspirants," answered his wife in accents indicating that she could not understand why. "Young Philip Macy and the Barnes youth, and a handful from Albany, and the Devereux cousins from Utica, and two or three young blades from New York, so I am informed. My choice is Marcus Dillard."

The manly Squire pulled a wry face. "A frippery fop," he observed.

"You're hard to please, Squire," complained his wife. "He's the catch of the town. With mint prices going up, his father will be a millionaire-man yet. Araminta will have all that her heart could desire."

Squire Jerrold sighed. A rich marriage would not be amiss. His own affairs had not been prospering. Those troublesome lawsuits over the canal damages had forced him to borrow heavily from his friend, Latham, and the twelve percent interest was wearing him down.

"What does Dinty think of him?" he asked.

Mrs. Jerrold sniffed. "How should she know what she wants? Miss Betsy Uppish! A husband will tame her."

By Squire Jerrold's guess, if young Mark Dillard were the husband, the taming would more likely be the other way around. However, there was no doubt that the match would be an advantageous one. But what about the Dillards?

"First catch your hare," he remarked.

"La! There's no hindrance there. The young fool is dowzened over her. He's taking the packet to Albany next week to see her. Mrs. Dillard—she's another ninnyhammer—fears he will go into a decline if he is thwarted. She was here to see me only yesterday."

"Have you talked with the child about it?"

"I shall when she returns." Dorcas Jerrold's curved lips straightened to an uncompromising thinness. "For once she will do as she is bidden, unless you support her obduracy."

The Squire sighed again. "Very well, Dorcas. I shall not interfere. This is woman's business. But be gentle with my little girl."

Dinty and Wealthia came home by coach. On one point, the Jerrolds found their daughter on the verge of rebellion. She could not bear to go back to the academy. Anything rather than that. She would run away. Or teach school. Or—or get married. Why must she learn any more? Why shouldn't she stay home, as Wealthia was going to do, and enjoy life? Palmyra was such fun!

There were two dark spots in Dinty's visit home. She sorrowed for Tip Crego, from whom no word had come. And she was deeply offended and puzzled by her erstwhile Uncle Horace. He had never answered her letter. He had ignored her existence. Very well, she could do some ignoring, herself. But not without one naive attempt at re-establishing the old comradeship. As a reminder she slipped into his office in his absence, and left on his table a fresh nosegay of the mixed white polly-whog and Indian pink. Could it be three years since Wealthy and she had enlivened Mrs. Harte's dull ménage with a similar bouquet? Would the recipient remember?

If he did, he made no sign. For, on the day before he found the floral offering, he had met Dorcas Jerrold who had informed him, with a smile of delicate malice, that Araminta was going to marry

Marcus Dillard. It was still a secret; she was telling him because he had always exhibited such a *special* interest in the child.

The scion of the Dillards had, indeed, been manifesting zeal. The formidable rivalry of the contingent from the eastern counties spurred his ardor. Nor was he without local competition. The handsome and elegant Philip Macy had deserted Wealthia's standard for Dinty's; De Witt Evernghim, Arlo Barnes and Jared Upcraft were now definitely of her court, with the result that the damsel's days and evenings were filled with engagements. Horace hardly more than glimpsed her, riding horseback with one or another of her visiting suitors, embarking on the Dillard pleasure barge for a canal party, or driving behind Philip Macy's matched roans. In those lists he felt that his age would render him absurd. In fact, Mrs. Jerrold had let fly a barbed hint to that effect.

Late one evening when Dinty was returning from a gay party, she remarked a light in Dr. Amlie's window and thought that it could not be good for him to work so hard. Having bidden her several escorts good night at the door of the stone mansion, she went to her room, took off her dainty party gown and hung it carefully in the press, but felt no desire for sleep. The half-open window lured her with the old, imperious call. She got out her house-hussey's dress, in which she used to help on cleaning days, and slipped into it. It was short-skirted and half-sleeved. A pair of stout boots completed her outfit. She let herself lightly down from the window and was off.

No special plan was in her mind; she merely felt restless and adventurous. Why wasn't Tip at hand? She would peek in at Dr. Amlie's window, perhaps hoot like an owl to give him a good startle, then make herself one with the night.

Arrived at his gate, she hesitated. It might squeak. Most gates squeaked. Anyway, what need had she for a gate? In that dress her childhood had come back upon her; she felt hoyden-free. She vaulted the fence and crept, cat-footed, to the window. What she saw within caught her breath and disarranged her lighthearted plan.

Her Dr. Amlie sat, staring across an opened pamphlet at an absurd object which she had long forgotten, but recognized on sight. Years before—they seemed very long to her now, those three years—a traveling artist with a camera obscura had visited Palmyra. She could even recall his name; it was Willoughby, and he had blond, inadequate whiskers and looked ill-fed. Through the medium of his frosted glass he had sketched Wealthy Latham and herself, only a shilling for the pair because, he said, they were young and pretty. Wealthia's portrait was successful; she had instinctively assumed the most advantageous pose; but Dinty had sat on a fence, whereupon Mrs. Jerrold had banished the work as Tillie-Tomboyish and Dinty had presented it to Dr. Amlie in a frame which she wove of willow-withe and labeled "Friendship's Guerdon."

This it was which now stood on the work table distracting the physician's attention from his proper toil. Beside it the nosegay of swamp-blooms withered in their vase.

Emotion overcame Dinty. She gulped. With a startled motion Horace swept the penciled picture into a drawer.

"Who's there?"

"It's me," said Dinty.

"Has anything happened?"

"Nothing but me. I just happened to see your light."

"It's an untimely hour for little gir—for you to be about."

"I couldn't sleep."

"Why not?"

Dinty put her elbows on the sill and her chin on her arms. "You're mean to me."

"Nonsense."

"You are. You never answered my letter."

"I did. But I—forgot to mail it."

"What did you say in it?"

"I don't remember."

"Oh, Uncle Horace!"

"There it is," said he glumly. "Uncle Horace!"

"What else is there to call you? Except Dr. Amlie."

He grunted.

"Aren't you going to ask me in?"

"Why, I suppose so."

She reversed her hands on the sill, preparatory to entry by that route, but changed her mind and walked sedately around to the office door which he held open for her. At his bidding she sat down, but not in the patient's chair which he advanced, preferring to perch on the high table.

"I want your advice," she said. "Your very par-tic-cu-lar advice."

"These aren't precisely office hours." At last he was smiling as he studied her. "You look well enough," he observed.

"Thank you for so overwhelming a compliment," she returned demurely. "I'm well in my health."

"How else would you expect to be well?"

"Please don't make fun of me. It's very serious. I've nobody else to go to but you."

"Is it Wealthia again?"

Dinty pouted. "I think you might stop worrying about Wealthy and worry about me."

"Well, stop swinging your legs and tell me about it."

"Do you think I ought to marry Mark Dillard, Uncle Horace?"

"Why shouldn't you?" he returned in a voice intended to be judicial.

"There's loads of reasons why I *should.*" She ticked them off, fingerwise. "He keeps pestering me to. And Ma picks on me to. And the Dillards want me to. And he's got a boat of his own and a gig, newer than yours with a tandem instead of just a mare, and Deacon Dillard will build us a stone house with leaded eagles in the door-sides and I shall insist on a separate room for me because I must always sleep with my window open—my doctor told me to—" (with a sideglance) "and we'll have a hired hussey to do the house-cleaning and wine Saturday evenings, and if I want to read in bed there'll be nobody to stop me." She looked at him speculatively. "Were you going to build a separate room for Miss Agatha, Uncle Horace?"

"Never mind Miss Agatha."

"I do mind. I've always minded," declared Dinty vehemently. She calmed down. "Ma says the sooner I am wedded, the better for all concerned."

"What does she mean by that?"

"I'm sure I don't know. Do you?"

"You've left out one point," he said. "How do you feel about it?"

Dinty's gaze wandered to the window. Little furrows of consideration appeared between the troubled eyes. "He's a very superior young gentleman," she recited. "He'll be cruel rich. He adores the ground that my foot presses, the flower that rises and falls with my breath, the air that parts my lips, the . . ."

"Stop it!"

"He's got six suits of elegant apparel, and a bay tandem, and a pleasure boat . . ."

"You mentioned the boat before."

"Did I?" she murmured vaguely. "It's an awfly dicty boat. I've always liked boats."

"Then you do want to marry him."

"I haven't made up my mind."

"Then why don't you make it up?"

"Because."

"That's no reason, my dear."

"You needn't call me your dear in that uppity way," she fretted. "Anyhow, it's the best reason I've got. And I think you're being dumb, dumb, *dumb*. You're no help to me at all," she concluded plaintively.

"What chance have I? You do and you don't. You will and you won't. How can I advise a weathercock?"

"Now you're being mean to me. D'you remember the day I took the spots out of your coat?"

"No."

"You do so! And how you cussed when Mark Dillard interrupted us at the Eagle ball?"

"Keep to the subject."

"Well, why don't you *say* something?"

"I did. I asked you if you want to marry him?"

She reached over to remove a petal from the spire of Indian pink leaning toward her, sniffed at it, and wrinkled her nose in disgust. "I ought to come back and take care of your house," she said.

"Do you want to marry him or don't you?" asked Horace patiently.

"I like him well enough. But it isn't the tender passion. Not like in books and poetry." Her shoulders rose and fell with the elaborate breath of her sigh. "Do you suppose, if I waited, I'd ever feel the tender passion?"

"You've time enough left yet," he suggested.

"I don't want to wait till I'm old-maidish. Like Miss Agatha. She was almost twenty."

"Are we discussing Mrs. Sickel or Marcus Dillard?"

"What do you think of him?"

"I think he is all you say." Horace deemed that admirably diplomatic.

She studied his expression, which was strictly noncommittal. "I don't believe you like him. Shall I tell you something, Uncle Horace?" A dazzling smile illuminated her. "Neither do I. Not truly."

"Why not?"

"He's so daffy-down-dilly." She made languorous, elegant and disparaging motions with hands and arms. "Besides," she added, reverting to an earlier grievance, "he always smells of mint extract. I think of it as soon as he comes near me. Just as I always think of arnica when I see you. Arnica is such a nice, clean smell." She pleated folds across her knee. "So you advise me not to marry Mark."

"Nothing of the sort. It isn't for me to advise."

"How can you say that! I wouldn't be here at all if you hadn't cut my throat." She arched up her rounded chin to give him full view. "Doesn't it look nice?"

It was, indeed, a workmanlike scar in which any surgeon might have taken proper and professional pride. But Horace's sentiments, as his eyes rested on that delicate contour, were not those of pride nor were they wholly proper and professional.

"Very nice," he assented.

"You aren't looking at it," she complained. "Feel. There's hardly any mark at all."

She caught his hand, pressed it into the soft hollow, and nuzzled down on it like an affectionate little animal. Horace freed himself abruptly.

"So that makes you responsible for me. My family are awfly set on it," she went on, reverting to her former thesis. "I sometimes wonder if they want to get rid of me." Her essay at melancholy was unconvincing. She hopped to the floor and stood by his side, drooping, again the appealing little maid of the earlier years. "Don't you think I'm awfly young, Uncle Horace?"

"You do seem so, in a way," he admitted uncertainly.

"Then couldn't you give me a certificate or something?"

"A certificate?" he repeated uncertainly. "What kind of certificate?"

She was vague about it, herself. "You know. Something with a seal on it to say I'm not old enough yet to marry Mark. Something I can show Ma. You're my doctor, aren't you?" she argued.

Thus recalled to the professional aspect of the situation, Horace said bluntly, "That's nonsense, you know, Dinty. The law of New York State establishes fourteen as the marriageable age for females."

"I'm more than that," she admitted lugubriously.

"I should think so, indeed." He rubbed his nose. "How old are you, anyway, Dinty?"

"Sixteen," said Dinty in a defiant voice. "Almost seventeen," she appended, recklessly helping herself to some ten months.

"Then you didn't tell me the truth when I first met you."

"I might have fibbed a little," she conceded, not looking at him. "Ma didn't like my getting to be grown up. Neither did I—then."

"Seventeen," he muttered with a kind of incredulity.

"Almost," she qualified. "I never wanted to be grown up for you because—well, because I thought you'd rather have me a little girl. I was afraid that when I grew up you wouldn't like me so much. And now I do want to be grown up, only I'm kind of afraid. That's funny, isn't it? D'you remember how I used to try and find out things in your medical books? Anyway, I don't like being old enough to marry Mark. Not a bit. *Now* will you help me?"

Horace summoned his resolution. "I can't give you any such certificate," he declared. "You are certainly old enough for marriage."

"Do you think so?" she said in a half-breath.

"It isn't a question of what I think. It's a question of fact and law."

"But *do* you think so?" she persisted.

"Yes, I do."

She said in a mouse's whisper, "Then why don't you marry me, yourself, Uncle Horace?"

He stood up, feeling dizzy. "Me?" he said.

"Don't you like me as much as you did Miss Agatha?"

"That dish of water gruel!" he said.

She gave her small crow of delight. "Oh, I *did* want you to say something like that!" She was twisting the third button of his broadcoat now. "After you found out she was like water gruel and stopped thinking about her, didn't you ever think about me? Not just a little? That way, I mean."

"I wouldn't let myself," he said with difficulty.

"Why not?" She was aggrieved.

"I've never been able to get over the idea of you as a child," he confessed.

She lifted her eyes to him, and there was something in her look—the immemorial guile of sex—that made her seem for the moment as old as the wellsprings of life.

"Not even after we danced together?" she whispered.

The tilted face with half-closed eyes and tremulous mouth was a passionate invitation. He bent to her and it was a woman who came, warm and sweet, into his arms.

"Do you think I'm a little girl now?" she said triumphantly as she drew her lips slowly, reluctantly from his. "Do you, Uncle Horace?"

"What! That again?"

"Now you're laughing at me. I don't care. Do you know what I used to call you to myself?"

"No. What?"

"Doc. May I call you that after we're married? When there's nobody else around?"

"You may call me anything," said the enamored young man.

Dinty reflected. "Ma is going to be awfly mad," she decided. "Pa likes you, though. He'll be glad."

"So am I," said Horace with fatuous fervor. "You'll never know how glad. Though I don't quite see why you want to marry me."

"Don't you, truly?" Again she reckoned the points on her fingers, reclaiming her hands from his for the purpose. "To get out of having to marry Mark. And to show the family I can't be told off. And because I think it will be very pompous to be Mrs. Doctor Amlie. And because you're going to be rich and successful—now you're looking like a bear with a sore tail. Oh, well," she grinned elfishly, like the old Dinty, "because it gives me the shivers to even think of marrying anyone else. And besides you're cruel handsome and I—I guess it must be the tender passion, after all. Now, are you satisfied?"

Having been convinced that he was, she drew away again. "Think of being married before Wealthy," she purred.

"Lord save us! It's a child, after all," said Horace.

"Wait till you see me running your house. We'll have banquet parties and sociables and entertain the Commissioners when they come to Palmyra." She gave him a sidelong glance. "Will you build a room for me to have for my very own?"

"No," said Horace.

"I don't care," said Dinty.

It was to be a short engagement. Dinty was deaf to parental suggestions that they wait until her seventeenth birthday. "I'm quite old enough. My doctor says so," said she complacently.

Was she really that old? Sometimes he found it hard to believe. There was, for example, the evening when, calling on his little betrothed, he found her immersed in a solid tome which she at first tried to conceal, then put on the parlor table with an affectation of ease, before lifting her face for his kiss.

"More Gilpin, sweetheart?" he asked.

"No. I'm trying to learn something."

He scrutinized the title: *A Reproof to Heedless Youth, together with a System of Correspondence Tending to Matrimony,* by Dr. G. B. Champlin.

"Are you Heedless Youth?" he inquired fondly.

"No," replied Dinty, making a prim mouth. "I am studying to become a helpful and prudent wife to you, Dr. Amlie."

"Helpful and prudent," he repeated suspiciously. "Is that you or Dr. Champlin?"

Dinty reverted to type. "He's a silly writer. It's a cheaty book. It doesn't tell you anything about matrimony except how to get a husband and I've already done that for myself." She gave him an enchanting smile.

"What did you expect? What did you want to find out?" he asked.

"Nothing," said Dinty hastily.

On the morning of the wedding ceremony, which was celebrated pompously, as the *Herald* put it with many other flattering characterizations, Dinty had a brief moment with her groom. They exchanged commonplaces. Last-moment, pre-marital conversations are usually of that order. But, as he said good-bye with an attemptedly humorous request that she would not be late, she looked down at her new prunella shoes and said in a strained voice,

"It's kind of scary. I don't know much of anything about this, you know, Uncle Horace."

So he was "Uncle Horace" to her still!

Seated very upright beside her bridegroom in the freshly painted gig, Dinty bade a brave farewell to family and friends. It would take them three hours to reach Canandaigua, which was to be their stopping place for the night. They arrived in good time for supper, washed up, and went down to what proved a neurotically conversational meal. Horace insisted upon her eating everything on the list with a solicitude which inevitably brought to mind an almost forgotten narrative about the last meal of a condemned criminal.

After prolongation could extend the rite no further, Dinty remarked in a high-pitched, mannery trill that Canandaigua was noted for its scenic beauties and this would be a fine opportunity to enjoy them. Horace agreed. They made a slow tour of the town and exchanged views upon the charm of the lake in the moonlight.

Even the most improving interchange of ideas eventually exhausts itself. The Presbyterian clock was announcing nine, in what seemed to Dinty unusually solemn tones, when they found themselves back at the inn. They ascended the steps in military unison and silence. It was broken in the hallway by the bride who stopped, absorbed in a wall placard which, in ordinary circumstances, would have lacked fascination, since it was no more than an announcement of improvements established by a new and enterprising proprietor.

"He hopes," stated the poster, "to Merit the Favor of his Friends and the Publick generally, by his Conduct to one and all. No noisy Rabbles will be allowed in his House whereby the Rest of the Weary may be Disturbed."

Below this reassuring message, a long-fingered hand pointed blackly to the word SPECIAL.

"A Bath with Fixed Tin Tub has been Installed on the Second Floor for the Refreshment of Patrons. Hot Water and Towel on Request."

"Isn't that dicty!" exclaimed Dinty with bright ease of manner. "How fortunate that we're on the second floor! I'm awfly dusty. I think I'll take a bath."

"Why don't you?" said Horace with equally studied nonchalance. He yawned elaborately. "And I'll go to bed."

Hot water and towel were commanded. Dinty went out into the hall, closing the door behind her. At her left hand a window opened invitingly upon a porch roof. Subconsciously she had noted from outside its slender pillars, easy of access and quite simple for an active little girl to shin down. Little girl? What little girl? She sternly reminded herself that she was a married lady.

In her bath she gave herself over to perturbed and inconclusive speculations. One could not remain in a Fixed Tin Tub all night. She climbed out and dried herself with particularity. Somehow, by a process which was quite apart from plan or volition, she found herself completely re-clothed even to her serviceable traveling shoes. They were fine, stout gear, fit for any road, sturdy enough to walk all the way home in. She could get there before daylight.

She tiptoed back the length of the hall and paused before the window, listening. No sound from behind the door. Perhaps he was asleep already. A perfumed breeze bellied out the paper curtain which subsided with a motion like a gesture of invitation to the world of freedom and escape. The well-loved world of night and the open tugged at her nerve-strings. She could be out and down to earth and safe in a minute, a half minute.

And Unc—and her (gulp) husband?

Dinty drew her knee back from the window ledge. She fetched a long, tremulous breath. Her favorite apothegm fortified her soul.

"You never can tell till you try," she murmured resolutely.

Her eyes lambent, her chin high, she opened the chamber door and made a valorous entrance.

For their honeymoon trip they made a conscientious survey of the state as far east as the capital. They visited the highest span in the world across the chasm at Portage, the wonders of Niagara, the mighty Aqueduct over the Genesee, the Bishop Museum in Rochester, the Longest Bridge in America, spanning the Cayuga marshes, the Hamilton College campus, overbrooding the majestic Valley of the Oriskany, the Capitol at Albany, and the State Prison at Auburn. In all they covered four hundred and fifty-five miles and their expense account, as set down in the bride's conscientious ledger, came to twenty-one dollars and sixty-five cents, which was extravagant, indeed, but perhaps not too much so considering that it included, besides the tolls and hotel bills, three attendances on the drama, admittance to a circus, tickets to a benefit cotillion where Dinty, much in demand, would dance with nobody but her bridegroom, sixpence apiece for a visit to the prison, a medical lecture at Fairfield, and the shillings for two successive Sunday contribution plates. It was on the day of return that the bride summed up her impressions in a line which she did not show to her husband until long afterward.

"Marriage is an Honorable Estate but full of Surprizes."

It is the last entry in Dinty's Diary.

Part Two

1

SCANDAL attached to the Amlie household before the marriage was a sixmonth old. It was common talk at the sewing bee that the couple acted toward one another more like a pair of flighty lovers in a drama than like decent wedded folk. Mrs. Amlie frequently addressed her husband by his given name when company was present. In private, it was alleged,. she called him "Doc." They had been heard to exchange endearing epithets, such as "darling" and "my sweet." Their laughter at meals was audible to passers-by.

"She jests with him," said Mrs. Van Wie.

"Worse! She coquettes with him," charged Mrs. Dillard.

"As if wedlock were not a serious matter," said Mrs. Levering.

"Not to her," said Mrs. Upcraft. "At least, there's no sign of it yet." She glanced with pride at the distended frontage of her daughter-in-law, Happalonia, whose marriage antedated the Amlie nuptials by less than three months.

"A high-minded and uppity minx," declared Mrs. Harte. She had never forgiven Dinty for improving upon her housewifery in the days when the young physician was her lodger. "Piano lessons at ten dollars a quarter!"

"And tachygraphy," put in Mrs. Sam'l Drake. "She's taking instructions in the Gurney Method of Swift-Writing. They say she's learning both the Angular and the Waving-Running hands."

Mrs. Upcraft sniffed. "So's she can assist her husband in his medical writings. I'm told some of his notions are very queer."

"And she reads all his medical books," said Mrs. Dillard with pursed lips.

"Indecent," snapped Mrs. T. Lay. "That's what I call it."

"It'll do his name and practice no good," darkly prophesied Mrs. Upcraft.

The meeting solemnly decided that flighty little Araminta Jerrold's influence had wrought in her husband an alteration such as nobody would have believed, and that such brazen levity of conduct on the part of the couple was a shameful example for the young. Old Miss Bathsheba Eddy alone lifted a dissenting voice, if, indeed, "lifted" be a proper term for the wistful murmur in which she said,

"They do seem so happy."

"What's being happy got to do with it?" barked Mrs. Upcraft. "As if folks married to be happy! Why doesn't she ever come to the sewings and help the heathen?"

"Oh, she's 'too busy,' " minced Mrs. Drake.

"Busy at what, I'd admire to know," said Mrs. Levering. "No good, I'll be bound."

A glimpse of the young wife at that very moment would have confirmed the circle's unfavorable opinion. She was perched upon the office table, one leg tucked beneath her, the other swinging free.

"Six months," said she. "Six months since I've been a respectable married lady."

"You don't look it," said Horace. Which was true. She suggested, rather, a cheerful and dainty young gnome.

"Sometimes I don't feel like it at all. Then, again, I do. It isn't so bad, once you get used to it," she added in the manner of one making a concession.

"Oh, it isn't, isn't it!" he commented. "Well, this is my busy day."

"Who'd have thought it!" Dinty looked pointedly about the empty room. "Oh, I know there'll be a passel of patients crowding in on the overworked doctor pretty soon." Her regard passed to the tall clock with real brass works, making its solemn measurements. "But you've got ten minutes yet." She leaned forward to rub her cheek against his. As he cast an apprehensive glance at the door, "Oh, there's nobody there. And what if there was?"

"We must remember our position."

Dinty's curved lips produced a sound delicately reminiscent of Silverhorn Ramsey's gardaloo. "Is it against the law in Palmyra to be in love with your husband?" she demanded.

"No. But . . ."

"Oh, Doc! Don't be so *dumb*. Do you love me or don't you?"

"That's a highly improper question," said Horace, "considering that I promised to. In church, too. I'm a man of my word, but . . ."

"I don't want any more 'buts' and I won't have any." She kissed him firmly. "Oh, I know what the old comfit-munchers say about us. I just don't care. Do you?"

"Not a deacon's damn," grinned Horace.

She looked at him sidewise. "Do they joke you about it? The men, I mean."

"Sometimes."

Indeed, among his cronies of the smithy, there had been for a time the customary nods and becks and wreathed smiles, all of which he took in good part, until Carlisle Sneed unleashed a decidedly ill-advised witticism on the subject and was disagreeably surprised to find his jest and his head submerged in Silas Bewar's waterbutt.

Subsequent humor was of a more subdued nature. Horace had taken on bulk and muscle since his advent in town, without corresponding lack of activity. He was now a fair match for any man of that sturdy company, except perhaps the mighty 200-pound Quaker, himself.

"Let 'em all tend their own pigs," said Dinty comfortably, hopping to the floor. "Now that *that's* settled, I shall be Mrs. Doctor Horace Amlie, M.D., with all the frills and furbelows. How's the state of our barter this morning?"

"That's your department. Go and see."

Market-book and crayon in hand, young Mrs. Amlie let herself into the storeroom which she had insisted upon her husband's building to accommodate his receipts in kind. There she noted down seven bushels of wheat, four of rye, as many of oats, a firkin of pickles, another of whisky, a keg of hard cider, three bags of feathers, a horn of powder, ten pecks of that always movable commodity, flaxseed, four dozen eggs, and three yards of coarse homespun. There were also potatoes, pumpkins, squash, a ripe melon, a hollowed log filled with hickory nuts, some pelts from trapper patients, herbs from the Pinch, a brace of fine, fat, live geese, and eight dead blackbirds which she set aside for a pie. The lot should tot up, if properly marketed (and there were few folk shrewder at knowing and getting the best price than the young wife), to close upon twenty dollars. She went back into the office.

"Doc, we're getting rich."

"We're not doing badly."

"Will you build me that round-stone house?"

"Some day."

"With a carved oaken door and leaded eagles in the sideglass?"

"What pompous ideas we're getting!"

"I've always had 'em. What d'you think I married you for?"

"Lest a worse thing befall you," he chuckled.

"If you mean Marcus Dillard, I'd have had my stone house already. But when I get it, I'd rather have you in it than him."

"Thank you!"

"And we'll have a glass flower-porch, and a pianoforte, and I'll put Gibson's Balm of Roses on my face every day to smell sweet, and we'll have wine for Saturday supper, and dine the bigbugs when they come to town. Darling, how much do you owe at Mr. Latham's bank?"

"Not very much."

"I'll wager it's a pizen lot. A thousand dollars?"

"No-o-o."

"Well, how much?" she persisted. "Seven hundred? Eight hundred?"

"There or thereabouts."

"Say nine hundred and interest," said she shrewdly.

He sighed. "I thought I'd married a wife, but it proved to be Professor Montgomery's Marvelous Computing Machine; Ten Cents Admittance."

"I'm going to pay it off twenty-five dollars every month," said she firmly. "I don't like debt. Doc, I'm afraid Pa owes Mr. Latham a lot of money. I know he's worrying over something. He doesn't look hearty at all. I wish you'd go and see him."

"And have your mother freeze me out of the house, as she did last time I went there without your protection? No, thank you!"

"You married trouble when you married me, didn't you, darling?"

"Well, I expected it," said he with a martyred air which changed to one of bland magnanimity as he added, "Not but what I consider you worth it at times."

"Thank you for nothing." She bobbed him a curtsey. "Sometimes I don't feel married to you a bit. It all seems so queer."

"Sometimes," he capped her, "you seem to me like the bad little Tillie Tomboy who made me blush by asking me questions about *Burns on Abortion*."

"I don't have to ask you any more. I've read Burns and De Weese and Rush and Hosack and all of 'em." She flourished a gesture toward the rows of learned volumes above. "I know all about my insides and your insides and everybody's insides," she bragged.

"Maybe you'd be willing to take over my practice, Miss Wise-eyes."

"I'll warrant I'd make more money out of it than you do," retorted the practical Dinty. "Look at that advertisement you inserted in the paper about vaccination. 'Immigrants and Indigents Inoculated Free.' Is that the way to build a stone house with an oaken door?"

He sighed. "If they can't pay, they can't."

Instantly contrite, Dinty gave him a quick hug. "I know, darling. You can't help being that way. I wouldn't want you any other way. But I truly think it would have been better for you to marry a rich lady."

"Which one?" asked Horace with animated interest.

She looked solemnly up at him beneath the long, dark lashes which accentuated the blue of the eyes below. "Why didn't you fall in love with Wealthy instead of me?"

"What chance did you give me?" said Horace reasonably.

"Now you're trying to shame me. Well, you needn't to try! I'm not ashamed and you can't make me be. How else would I have got you, I'd like to know! You never would have asked me first, old Slowpoke. And if you ever say you're sorry I'll—I'll take all the medicines in the chest and die in horrid convulsions."

"Come, now!" protested Horace. "Medicines cost money." Observing signs of a gathering storm, he decided that he had gone far enough. "When I feel symptoms of regret coming on," said he, "I'll write you a letter in the palsied hand of extreme age—I'll be ninety or a hundred by the time I start getting tired of you—and tell you so."

Dinty made a small noise like a contented cat. "Think of my being married before Wealthy!" she remarked. "Why, Doc, she's eighteen!"

"She's certainly getting on. I didn't realize she was that old. What about that young Southerner?"

"Kinsey Hayne? Oh, he's quite mad over her. I do think she's stupid if she doesn't marry him. I've told her so. I've told her that being married is wonderful after you get used to it. She is betrothed to him. But that's a secret."

"That settles the matter then, doesn't it?"

"Not necessarily."

"Doesn't Wealthia want to marry her young man?"

"Not for a year, anyway, she says. That's funny, *I* think. When I was betrothed to you, I wanted to be married to you right away."

"Ah, but think how fascinating I am," said Horace blandly.

"You needn't be so vainglorious. You aren't as handsome as Kinsey Hayne, and not *half* so pompous." Her brows narrowed upon him. "Horace Amlie! I hope you don't think you're going to receive patients in that neckcloth. Why, it's all rammidged along the fold. Take it off at once and give it to me to mend and put on your tartan one with the silver pin to hold it."

Properly abashed, Horace withdrew to carry out the command. When he came back Dinty said, "There's a grown man, swinging on our gate."

Horace peered out. "That isn't a man; it's a teapot."

"A teapot?"

"Yes. That's poor old Dad Hinch. His nose is the spout and I have to look after him to make sure that it doesn't get stopped up and steam him to death."

"Why, he must be crazy."

"No! Do you think so? That's what the cookee on the *Gypsy Maid* thought when he brought Dad in and said that every time the galley fire was lighted he tried to sit on the stovelid. And now you confirm the opinion. Well, well! What a talent for diagnosis!"

"Horace Amlie, I hate you! And I'm sure he isn't safe to have around. He ought to be put away."

"Where, Dinty?" Horace's face had become grave. "Do you know what happens to the insane poor? Either they're chained up like wild animals or put in jail with nobody to look after them or feed them. There's no other provision for them in this highly civilized age. Now would you like for me to enter complaint against Dad with the village trustees?"

"No," said Dinty hastily. "Do you think he's hungry, Doc?"

"No," said Horace incautiously. "I'm sure he's not."

She scrutinized his face with suspicion. How could he be so certain?

"Horace Amlie! Are you supporting that man?"

"Now, look, darling," he pleaded. "The poor fellow is a war veteran. The nation he fought for won't do a thing for him. My father was killed in Fourteen, you know. I can't stand by and see a man of his regiment starve. He costs me almost nothing. And he mounts guard over Fleetfoot to see that the horse thieves don't get her."

Dinty still felt that she must be stern about it. "First Unk Zeb and now this poor zany."

"Unk Zeb? Why, he's worth his keep twice over."

"He's a pig-headed old blackamore," asserted Dinty who had not won the Battle of the Kitchen and established her authority without a grievous struggle.

She opened the door and beckoned in the Human Teapot. He came to a stand, rigidly erect and with a military salute.

"Respects, Missus," he said. "Mornin', Capting. Pressure's down a bit this mornin'. If the steam gits too high," he explained to Dinty in confidential tones, "I explodes. If it gets too low, I poofs out like a pricked bladder."

"This is Mrs. Amlie, Dad," said Horace.

"My obedience to you, ma'am. You got the finest man in seven counties and I hope you vallies him proper."

"I'm sure I do, Mr. Hinch," said Dinty demurely and withdrew in response to her husband's privately slanted eye.

Though she had fought hard for the privilege, it was not permitted her to sit in on Horace's consultations. Wise Dinty knew just about how far she could safely go with her usually amenable husband. Everything else in his life was open to her, but from his professional activities she was rigorously barred. Woman's place, as she well understood, was in the parlor, church, ballroom, shop, kitchen, market, garden, anywhere but in the office. His utmost concession was that he would sometimes condescend to talk over his cases with her after the fact, though, even there, he employed that superior tone which man affected toward woman and the medical faculty toward the laity. He would have been scandalized to learn how much she really knew about his practice.

Whatever criticism Araminta Amlie's marital exuberances might have evoked among the sisterhood of the comfit, there was no question of her efficiency in the household. She was a housewife, born and bred. Her rooms were fresh with the fragrance of seasonal bloom, or spicy with the odors of roseleaf, bay and verbena. Her kitchen was immaculate, this being the principal *casus belli* between her and Unk Zeb, who adored her but could not be made to understand "Why mus' she finnick 'bout a speck of dirt dat wooden' make a gnat cry if you shev it into his eye, long as de food is tasty." Tasty the product of Unk Zeb's cookery certainly was; she had little to teach him there. Nevertheless it was her pumpkin pies that won an award at the town fair, that first fall.

Withal she led a luxurious life. Seldom out of bed before seven, in the dark of winter mornings she would draw down the frosted window, light the fire in the new and costly hot-air stove, heat a copper kettle of water, drag her tub behind the modest concealment of a side curtain, in case her husband might be awake, which was improbable, have her bath, put on her rough crocus housework gown, and not until then rouse her sleeping partner.

"Get up and take your bath, darling."

Grumbling—for he pretended not to appreciate his pampered state—Horace would roll out of bed into a pleasantly warmed atmosphere, and distrustfully contemplate the steaming tub. He was a firm believer in cleanliness, but he was no fanatic. Not another man in all Palmyra took a daily bath, except the Reverend Theron Strang who was of Spartan habit and was supposed to perform the rite as a mortification of the flesh. Horace had pointed this out to Dinty: why make a fetish of this soap-and-water business? Dinty made no reply in words; she merely sniffed the air like a hound dog. Horace gave in.

On the theory that a man cannot do his proper day's work on an empty stomach, she gave him a well-rounded though not extravagant breakfast: steak, sausage, ham, scrambled eggs, wheatcakes with syrup, muffins with butter and honey, pickles to spur digestion, and, when the weather was below zero, a dram of whisky in his Java. After that he might, on Sunday, have one cigar, but he must brush his teeth with chalk and powdered root afterward to get the odor off before church.

Unk Zeb's matutinal task was to clear the path to that chill and austere edifice which stood two rods back of the woodshed. Having warmed up a blanket and filled the footwarmer with red coals, Dinty wrapped her spouse's shoulders against the wind, placed the heater in his hands, and gently impelled him into the winter morning.

On his return he would find his beaver slicked to a nicety of gloss, his boots fresh greased, his fur gloves heating above the fire, and the full-skirted, richly sober coat of the professional class carefully brushed. His wife looked him over with critically approving eyes, adjusted his neck-pin at the correct angle, kissed him three times for luck on nose, chin and mouth and sent him forth on his visits, satisfied that no better-arrayed male, were it Silverhorn Ramsey himself, would grace the streets of Palmyra that day.

After making the bed, redding up the house, and going over the household linen for blemishes, she went to the kitchen to let Unk Zeb understand that she had an eye on his dishwashing, an activity for which he had little enthusiasm. Her next task was to bring her barter list to date. A—Those duck eggs must be marketed by the end of the week; B—L. St. John might take the whisky off her hands at a price; C—She could make Unk Zeb a greatcoat out of that swatch of homespun, and what of it if it didn't exactly fit; D—Mem. to inquire the store price of goosedown, and the warehouse rate on flaxseed. Now she must change her gown, bearing in mind the dignity of her married status, preparatory to the tour of Main Street.

She called Unk Zeb. With a shilling wickerwithe on his arm, and his ears, which were tender, wrapped in red flannel, he opened the door for her and toddled along, a respectful two paces in her wake. Later, but probably not until afternoon, he would attend her on her visits of charity or take her orders for homework while she attended some function of church aid. This was duty, but marketing was fun, a social diversion as well as a daily routine. At butcher's, baker's, maltster's or chandler's one met all one's friends.

Most of her contemporaries at the Polite Academy had married before Dinty, who was the youngest of the coterie, and were now quite obviously carrying out the Scriptural injunction as to fertility. On this crisp February morning, she met Happalonia Vallance Upcraft and Freegrace Fairlie Barnes, both bulging in loose garments. They told her that Clarissa Van Wie who had married De Witt C. Evernghim, was expecting any hour now, and that Bathsheba Levering was having a hard time keeping her breakfasts down. Dinty could feel their eyes fixed upon her with speculation. Or was it accusation as against one who was shirking her obvious duty? It annoyed her. What dratted business was it of theirs, anyway?

She refused to admit to a conviction of guilt or evasion of obligation. She knew, as well as the next, what was expected of her, of all brides. Expanding America needed the increase; child-bearing was patriotism. The wife who faithfully produced, nine months from the wedding day, was esteemed as having made a worthy start on a promising career. The Reverend Strang, now the father of ten, had made cautious reference, lest he shock his hearers, to the Scriptural injunction, "Increase and multiply," only last Sunday. Was he looking at the Amlie pew? Let him look! Dinty had her own views.

"Hullo, Dinty!" That sweetly hoarse voice could belong to nobody other than Wealthia Latham.

Dinty's half-frozen little nose perked about as she looked for the source.

"Here," said Wealthia from the dark stairway leading up to Miss Deborah Blombright's Emporium of Style. "I'm just going up. Come on."

Wealthia had returned from a visit to Syracuse whose salt works were building up a phenomenal population now that the canal opened up facilities for transportation. She was, her friend thought, looking unusually lovely, though a shadow of discontent lurked in the lustrous, dark eyes.

"Oh, Wealthy! What a pompous pelisse!"

"Seal's fur," said the rich man's daughter complacently. "I'm tired of mink and ermine and those common, home-grown pelts."

"Is it awfly costly?"

"Pa paid a hundred dollars for it in New York."

Dinty sighed. She had been wondering how long she would have to save her bee-money to have one like it. But—a hundred dollars! There was the note at the bank to be paid off before she could start the fund for the cobblestone house which would absorb all their possible savings for years. Sadly she put away the vision of herself, superb in a seal's-fur longcoat, stalking regally through the carved oaken door. By that time she'd probably be old and withered and shapeless from the annual baby. Life was hard on the poor. Not that they were really poor; that was an ungrateful and sinful thought. Horace was going to be rich some day. Why, already his takings were more than a thousand dollars a year. She had much to be thankful for, thought Dinty, striving to force herself to a virtuous contentment.

Wealthia's trying-on having been completed with enviable elaboration, she said,

"They've got a new stock of soda-powders at Stone-Front Sarcey's. Let's go have a fizzy syrup."

Mr. Sarcey proudly named his list of flavors: lemon, orange, currant or raspberry shrub, and the vanilla bean extract. Wealthia, always for the latest thing, chose vanilla; Dinty took raspberry. The fresh powder was of special potency and bubbled so high in the beautiful pale green glasses from the Royal Glass Factory at Deerfield that the froth got up their noses and impaired the elegance with which they had addressed themselves to the partaking. The proprietor left them to wait on another patron.

Dinty asked her companion, "Did you see the girls outside?"

"Yes. Disgusting."

Dinty laughed. "Natural, though."

"You, too?"

"Not yet." She crossed two fingers surreptitiously.

"Aren't you lucky!"

The young wife's smile might be taken to mean almost anything.

"Does your husband want 'em?"

"Oh, I suppose so. Some time. We don't talk much about it."

"Men always do."

"Well, it's no trouble to them," said Dinty philosophically.

"Let's take a walk," suggested Wealthia. "I don't know what's the matter with me. I feel so restless all the time. The village seems so small."

"We're not small," refuted Dinty indignantly. "We're growing every day. Going on visits has given you uppity notions. You ought to be married."

"I suppose I shall, one of these days."

"You don't seem very crazy about it. What's the matter? Aren't you sure of Kinsey?"

"Oh, as for that!" The beauty tossed her proud head.

"What is it you want to be sure of, then?"

"Not looking like Happalonia and Freegrace," answered Wealthia with a sort of sullenness. "I want to be pretty and have beautiful clothes and see people and places, and not settle down to being a bulgy old baby-factory."

"Wealthy!"

"Well, look in there." They had reached the bare grove in which the headstones of the Presbyterian churchyard thrust up through the snow. "Did you ever notice the arrangement of the family lots?" She went on passionately, "Look at them! One big stone for Father, three or four smaller ones for his wives, a lot of little markers. Deacon Smith and his wives, Sarah, Jane and Ann; Squire Jones and his lot of breeders, Ann, Jane and Sarah; Trustee Brown and his quartette, Mary, Jane, Sarah and Ann. All used up. Kill one with babies and take another. Wear her out and some other fool is ready and waiting. I hate marriage."

"Whatever's got into you, Wealthy?" marveled her crony.

"Oh, nothing much. I've been having too good a time, I presume." She raised her face and the velvety luster of her eyes swept the slope at the foot of which huddled and smoldered Poverty's Pinch. She lowered her voice. "Do you go to see Witch Crego?" she asked.

"Once in a while. She's a friend of mine."

"You know what I mean."

"No, I don't," denied Dinty, purposely obtuse.

"Do you believe she knows as much as people say?"

"About what?"

"You know. What we were talking of."

"People talk a lot about things they don't know anything about."

"You needn't be so superior just because you're married," complained Wealthia. "Oh, well, I suppose I'll marry Kinsey and take my chances like the others," she continued, reverting to her characteristic insouciance. "He is cruel handsome, isn't he!"

For some reason, obscure to herself, Dinty had not been wholly frank with her best friend. She had been to see Quaila Crego, shortly after her marriage. Quaila, with whom the girl was a favorite because of her friendship with the vanished Tip, had offered to read her fortune without pay. She began with the cards.

The subject, she said, would be very happy in her marriage with Dr. Amlie, who was a stout man and kind of heart. Riches would be theirs, but only after a struggle. Yes, there was trouble intervening, bad trouble. A woman."

"A woman!" said Dinty wrathfully.

"A dark woman. Dark and beautiful."

"Pooh!" said Dinty.

"There's no love card with her. But her influence is wove in with the hard times. Poverty follows close after her."

"I'm not afraid of poverty," declared Dinty sturdily.

"You better not bear any children. Not at first. Not till the dark years are past. Life would only be that much harder."

"I'm in no hurry. But how can I help it?"

"Did you ever hear of Satch Fammie?"

The bearer of that curious name which Horace, in a moment of etymological inspiration had surmised to be a corruption of *sage femme*, was an itinerant midwife, alleged to be a Belgian gypsy and intermittently attached to one of the tenker bands that roved the roads. Dinty had heard of her as the possessor of unhallowed feminine lore.

"She'll be here soon," pursued Quaila. "She knows all the secrets."

"More than you do?"

"Certes. She'll impart them to me for"—her shrewd, black eyes contemplated her visitor with speculation—"for five dollars, lawful money."

"Why don't you pay it to her?"

"Where would poor old Quaila find such a sum? Unless a rich, kind friend lent it."

"Two," said Dinty who had foreseen this.

"Four," said Quaila.

"Two-and-a-half," said Dinty, "and that's my last word."

The bargain was struck. Mistress Crego would buy the valuable lore to be passed on to her patroness.

"Then you must come to me at the turn of each moon," she directed. "But not a word to anyone, specially not to your husband, or I'll have no truck with it."

"I promise," said Dinty, impressed.

She was not unduly superstitious. But when all three portents explicitly coincided, how could one be wholly skeptical? As to the dark woman, she was more interested than alarmed. Already she was serenely confident of her hold on her husband. And he was quite enough to fill her life without any accessions to the family.

2

Every lock-keeper was, by virtue of his opportunities, a purveyor of waterway news and gossip. Jim Cronkhite, his day's duties at the upper lock completed, dropped in upon Horace after Dinty had gone to bed and to sleep. He had a gathering in his ear. After receiving directions for the placing of a hot cataplasm, and pocketing a bottle of medicine, he remarked, "Yawta been around Tooseday, Doc. What a turn-up!"

"Someone try to run your lock?"

"No, siree! None o' that with me. It was the rafters."

"Have a jam?"

"Nope. They don't jam no lock of mine. This was a four-horser from Wampsville way. Fence rails for Spencer's Basin. Creepers. Mile an hour and they consider they're doin' fine."

Horace nodded. "I saw them going through town."

"Mebbe you seen the *Jolly Roger,* too."

"What's that? Is Silverhorn Ramsey here?"

"Reckon he went right on through. He was here, sure-*ly.*" The lock-keeper chuckled. "The first section of the rails was just edgin' in towards my lock when I heard his bugle. I looked up and here comes the *Jolly Roger,* doin' all of five mile, the hoggee whalin' hell outa his hosses and Silverhorn standin' in the bow tootin' for a clear way."

Horace quoted a canal saw. "Back of a raft, you might as well take Sunday off and go to church."

"You don't know Silverhorn. In all my born days," said Jim with relish, "I never heard handsomer cussin'. Even my old woman kivered her ears, and she's used to towpath talk. And the *Jolly Roger's* deck passenger, she ducked below like a rabbit. The double team bein' off at the side eatin' the grass, the *Jolly Roger* hosses came right along, the boat followin' till it like to shove the fence rails clean through the berm. Out pops the raft-boss howlin' for blood. Silverhorn makes a leap like a stag, fifteen foot across open water, and damn me if he didn't walk the big rafter right off'n the path. I opened up for him and he went through cockadoodlin' on his instroomeut. Tossed me a handful of segars like they was so much stinkweed. A right free-handed gentleman, Captain Ramsey."

"Has Silverhorn gone into the passenger trade?"

"Not ginrally." The lock-keeper winked. "I don't reckon this passenger paid much fare."

"No?" Horace looked at him hard.

"No. Some folks would be supprised to know how she was travelin'. Special her pa-pa."

Horace did not pursue the topic. He would sound out Dinty in the morning.

Dinty was not present when he awoke. The titillant aroma of grilled pork kidneys apprised him that she had taken over from Unk Zeb, for this was a dainty which she always prepared with her own skilled hands. As he swung to the floor, he heard from below her happy lilt in a familiar measure.

> Lavender's blue, diddle-diddle.
> Lavender's green.
> When I am King, diddle-diddle,
> You shall be Queen.

Horace dressed thoughtfully and with some apprehension. Experience had taught him that the gay ditty upon his wife's lips was a song before action, presaging some project which might or might not contribute to domestic tranquillity—generally not. His first glance at the animated countenance back of the coffee urn put him further on guard. Deep beneath Dinty's wifely amiability lurked an ineradicable imp, jocund, perverse and unpredictable. Her first remark after her "Good morning" apprised him that the sprite was in temporary possession.

"How are Dr. Horace Amlie's standards of professional conduct holding up?"

A cautious grunt from Horace.

"You have solemnly sworn," she pursued, "that you 'will honestly, virtuously and chastely conduct' yourself in the high profession to which you are privileged. Darling, are you honest and virtuous? *And* chaste? You'd better be, except with me," she added savagely.

"I'm a notorious rakehell," asserted Horace. "In fact, a second Silverhorn Ramsey."

"What made you think of him?" demanded Dinty with narrowed scrutiny.

"He had a woman passenger coming in from the eastward day before yesterday. Isn't that the day that Wealthia got back?"

"Yes."

"In my opinion," said he magisterially, "the sooner that young lady is safely married, the better for all concerned."

His wife offered no comment.

"Well, are you finished catechizing me?"

She came back from a sojourn in the realm of thought. "I've been figuring on something."

"Anything that's proper for an honest, virtuous and chaste husband's ears?"

"Doc, we've got a lovely spare chamber, real pompously furnished, that's never even been slept in."

"Well, we can sleep in it if you've a taste for travel."

"Don't be so dumb. I don't mean us. It's Kinsey Hayne."

"Hullo! A handsome young blade about the house? I shall be jealous."

The quip did not even bring a smile to her grave eyes. "I think he's cruel miserable, darling. I've had a letter from him. A very respectful letter."

"I should hope so, indeed! Strange young men writing to my wife! Unk Zeb, oil up my musket."

"Don't tease me, Doc. I'm truly worried over Wealthy."

"Have him, of course, my sweet. Have anybody you like. I dare warrant you find life dull at times."

"Dull?" said Dinty. "With you? I never knew what living was before."

"When shall we have him?"

"He's to be in New York the middle of April to place his plantation's indigo crop. We might ask him then. Wealthy hasn't done anything at all about him. Don't you think that's funny, Doc?"

"How should I interpret that willful young lady's whims? I can't even keep pace with yours."

"You don't really like Wealthy, do you?" It was a statement rather than a query.

"I do. But she expects the earth and all that's in it, as of her natural right."

"Why not? She was brought up that way. I'll write Kinsey, then."

Wealthia received information of the project with an inscrutable countenance. She had been a smiling observer of the Amlies' glowing happiness, sometimes amused, sometimes wistful.

The grave and handsome young Carolinian proved a charming guest. He brought to Dinty, on his arrival from the metropolis late in April, sweetmeats, scents and the latest perfumed soaps, and to Horace, a box of choice segars. On acquaintance he proved himself not only an ornament to local society, but a sportsman, a master of horsemanship and a crack shot. Driving Fleetfoot to the gig at the weekly races, he handled her so cleverly that the Amlie stone-house fund, as Dinty called it, was the richer by fifty dollars. To Wealthia he was the ever assiduous swain, full of all courtesies and observances, and, Dinty thought, too much humility toward the imperious temper of his enchantress.

Wealthia accepted all the homage as her queenly right. That she was proud of her conquest was evident. She paraded him blatantly, for all her pretense of indifference. They were everywhere together. Was it pride alone that she felt? Dinty could not be sure about it. At times the beauty was in gay, even wild spirits. Again, she would shut herself away from her adorer for several days at a time. Whether she was happy was a question in the mind of her crony.

Those were the days of long visits. Urgent business calling Kinsey back to New York after a fortnight; the Amlies pressed him to return and stay a month, at least. Taking his hostess aside, he said,

"If Wealthia seconds the invitation, I'll be infinitely delighted to accept."

"Isn't anything settled?"

"Nothing. At times I suspect there is someone else."

"I'm sure there isn't. She finds more pleasure in your company than in anyone's. She told me so."

He brightened. "Then I shall hold to my hopes. But she refuses to give me any definite promise."

Wealthia wrote kindly to her suitor in New York, a letter which brought him back to Palmyra before the set time. She was in one of her accesses of feverish gayety. Any merrymaking within a ten-mile radius she must attend. Young Hayne was only too happy to be the preferred escort.

Spring was now warm over the valley. There were barn-bees and roof-tree raisings every other evening. To one of these at Manchester, the local belle and her Southern beau were bidden. There was a straw-load of the young folk going over, but Wealthia petulantly declared that she couldn't endure being mussed up and jolted, and her suitor was more than ready for the long intimacy of the drive alone with her. He called for her in a smart, light wagon with borrowed Fleetfoot between the thills. At five o'clock Dinty, a little wistful, saw them from her gate and waved to them as they approached.

"Won't you bear us company?" asked Kinsey, the ever-courteous.

"No, thank you," said Dinty. "Be good children and don't stay too late. I fear it is going to storm."

A distant note rose and soared and was stilled. Wealthia quivered.

"What's that?" asked her escort.

"Nothing," said she hastily.

"Some canaller signaling the lock," supplemented Dinty.

"He blows a right pretty note," remarked Kinsey.

They drove away. Dinty went in to direct Unk Zeb. After supper, the night turned thunderous and by bedtime there was a wild wind from the black southwest. Always a lighter sleeper than her husband, Dinty was up several times to bar windows, look to latches, make fast a slatting blind. She was sure that their guest was not abed when the clock struck three. Long after she thought that she heard him moving cautiously along the hall. She glanced toward the window. Stormy dawn was glowering in the east.

Thereafter she slept only fitfully. Earlier than her wonted hour she was up, set Unk Zeb in motion for breakfast, and slipped down to the stable. Dad Hinch, the Human Teapot, was on guard and saluted her in military style. She spoke to Fleetfoot, who appeared jaded, examined the wagon, and returned to rouse guest and husband. The former made his entry, a few minutes late for breakfast, which was contrary to his usual punctilious custom, freshly shaved and pomaded as always, but heavy-eyed. Only *force majeure* on the hostess's part kept the table talk from bogging down. After the meal, she followed Horace into the office, closing the door after them.

"Something has happened, Doc."

"Right! Your damned cat has been fishing in my leech jar again."

"I hope she caught 'em. I hate the wriggly things. But that isn't it."

"What is?"

"Kinsey—and Wealthy."

"What about 'em? Have they finally hit it off? High time."

"Do you know what hour he came in last night?"

"No. I go to bed to sleep, not to snoop."

"Well, it was daylight."

"What of it? There's no curfew in this house, is there?"

"Horace Amlie, I hate you! You don't even pretend to be interested. I don't believe they ever went to the barn-bee."

"Of course they did. What fairy-tale are you making up for yourself, now?"

"Then they went farther. Go and look at the wagon. There's dark red mud on the spokes. There's no such soil between here and Manchester."

"That's true. It begins farther along the Canandaigua Road," said Horace who had more than once been stalled in it. "I've got a clever wife. But what would they be doing in Canandaigua?"

"The Marrying Parson. Five dollars and secrecy."

There was no lack of interest in his face now. "Why, it's crazy! Why should Wealthia do a thing like that?"

"I don't know. Once she made up her mind, she might do anything. She's like that."

"I shall ask Kinsey," said Horace. He frowned. "No, I can't do that. I can't cross-question a guest. Maybe you can get it out of Wealthia."

"I'm going straight up there," said his wife.

Although it was almost nine o'clock when she arrived, Wealthia was still abed. Dinty yoo-hooed from the garden path. A slumber-heavy face appeared at the window.

"Ah-h-h-h-h!" yawned the slugabed. "Oh, dear! Why did you wake me?"

"I'm sorry."

"Well, come on up."

She was washing the sleep out of her languorous eyes when the called appeared. "What time is it?"

Dinty told her.

"Did you hear Kinsey when he came back?"

"Yes."

"We didn't mean to stay so late." She laughed artificially. "We had a spat."

"A quarrel? You and Kinsey?"

"Yes. Oh, I expect I did most of the quarreling. I hate to be questioned," she added querulously.

Dinty approached her. "Stand still a minute. Let me get that out." She loosed a small object embedded in the glossy hair above the nape of the neck.

"Ouch! What is it?"

"It's a windlestraw. Look."

Wealthia's face underwent a change. It became subtle and secret. "I went to our barn when we got home to have a look at the filly," she said. "She's been ailing."

"Oh," said Dinty.

"What do you mean by 'Oh'?"

"Nothing."

"Where's Kinsey?"

"Gone for a walk."

"Have you seen him this morning?"

"Yes. At breakfast."

"How did he seem?"

"I don't know. Jumpy, I think."

"Did he say anything about last night?"

"Not to me."

"No, I suppose he wouldn't. It's part of what he calls his code, whatever he means by that."

Dinty resented the touch of callousness. "D'you know what I think, Wealthia Latham?" she broke out. "I think you ought to be peacock-proud to have as fine a young man as Kinsey Hayne in love with you. I think you ought to take shame to yourself, the way you treat him."

"Pooh!" returned Wealthia calmly. "I'm never ashamed. If it's done, it's done. Why waste time pining over it?" She poked at the floor with the tip of her bed slipper. "Dinty, has anybody said anything about the party last night?"

"Not to me."

She laughed a little. "You'll hear. But they don't know what they're talking about. Shall I give you a note for Kinsey?"

"You needn't. Here he is."

The Southerner was walking up the sidepath, his head bent, his carriage a slump of depression.

"Good morning to you," Wealthia called in her throaty, caressing voice, leaning out of the window. He whirled and looked up, his face alight.

"Oh, Wealthia! Oh, my darl—"

"Dinty's here. Were you coming to take me riding?" Her smile was carefree.

"I thought you said . . ."

"Never mind what I said. I never said it. And, if I did, I didn't mean it. Will you fetch the horses?"

"Oh, yes," he cried, radiant. "You won't run away from me again, will you?"

"Hush!" she warned, arching her brows toward the third person who was pretending not to hear. "Anyway, you found me, didn't you?" Again she laughed. To Dinty, who was growing more and more puzzled, the laughter seemed unmirthful, almost cruel.

Across the fields from the high garden they could see a squad of the Palmyra Horse Artillery gathering for a drill. A metallic blare from the bugle came harshly to the ear. With that sound, the embryo of thought in Dinty's brain took on definite form. She drew her friend aside.

"Wealthy," she said, "was Captain Ramsey there last night?"

"At the party?" Wealthia's eyes shifted. "No, he wasn't at the party."

Later Dinty verified this. But she was still perturbed.

It was barter day for the young housewife. Followed by Unk Zeb and the two-wheeled cart, she went along Main Street. Several of the young married women were in a group around Tom Daw.

"Gone a good two hour, they were," said he with relish.

"In all that storm?" asked someone.

"Wealthy and her Southerner," explained Amelia Barnes for the benefit of the late arrival. "Didn't anyone see them leave?" she asked the hunchback.

"That's the funny part. They didn't leave together. Folks missed Wealthy first and somebody asked Mr. Hayne and he harnessed up and druv, licketty-split, and after a while they come back together in the rig. She wa'nt wet, neither." He leered about him. "I dunno where they mought-a been, outa the weather."

"You'd better be careful what you say, Tom Daw," warned Dinty hotly. "If Mr. Latham hears about your loose tongue, you'll be in a pretty kittle."

"I didn't say nothin'," he disclaimed hastily.

Dinty quit the group and sauntered down to the waterfront. Snugged up against the Evernghim wharf, with Silverhorn Ramsey directing operations from his foredeck, the *Jolly Roger* was taking on the last of a mixed cargo of pork, whisky and pickled eels in kegs.

It was a vast relief to her mind when, two days later, Wealthia told her that she had decided to marry Kinsey Hayne.

"When?" asked Dinty eagerly.

"Oh, not till fall. Pa doesn't want me to."

Six months was an exorbitantly long period for an engagement of marriage.

"I think it's fustian," declared Dinty. "You act as if you didn't *want* to get married," she said.

"South Carolina is so far away."

"I'd go to Europe with Horace and never think twice of it."

"Pa is going to miss me cruelly."

"So are we all. But think of Kinsey."

"I do think of him. Who could help it? He's so kind and heedful," said Wealthia with more warmth. She sighed. "South Carolina is so distant from Palmyra," she echoed herself. "When shall I ever see you or—or anybody again."

"There ought not to be 'anybody,'" said downright Dinty.

"I mean everybody," was the listless reply.

During his return visit to the Amlies', Hayne had no cause for complaint in his fiancée's attitude. Gone were her former coquetries with any attractive male who came within eyeshot. All her time and interests were his. Indeed, the pair were so constantly and intimately together, and often at such untimely hours, that the "sharp-clawed Abigails" as Dinty termed them, pursed their lips over the association and darkly whispered that if Genter Latham knew what was going on or the half of it, he might accelerate rather than retard the marriage.

Only one person in all Palmyra was bold enough to approach the great man on the matter. Elder Strang, with a lively distaste for his errand, called at the Latham mansion. Genter Latham listened to him with a darkening face, but patiently, for he respected the parson.

"Are you impugning my daughter's modesty?" he asked.

"Say, rather, her light and capricious carriage, about which there has been much talk."

"Send the talkers to me."

"That would profit nothing. Wealthia is of my flock. I hold myself responsible for her soul's welfare." There was no doubting the clergyman's sincerity and concern.

"My daughter's virtue is safe in her own keeping," said Mr. Latham courteously but firmly. "She has been carefully and modestly brought up. Mr. Kinsey Hayne, moreover, is a gentleman of honor."

"I make no doubt of it. Nevertheless, youth and hot blood," said the Reverend Mr. Strang sadly, "are an ever-present snare."

There the matter ended. The pastor had fulfilled his responsibility. As long as the father apprehended no harm from the association, the pastor loyally did what he could to stifle the talk.

The day came for the Southerner's long departure. He would not see his lady-love again for at least three months. Wealthia came to the Amlies' to bid him good-bye. They walked long in the garden. When she came in, her eyes were reddened.

"I wish he were taking me with him," said she to her chum.

"Would you have gone?"

"Oh, so willingly!"

"You've changed your tune, Wealthy."

"Everything will be so different with Kin gone."

Dinty hummed pensively, "What's this dull town to me?"

"As long as he's here, I feel so safe."

"Safe against what?" asked Dinty, wide-eyed.

"Nothing. I don't know why I said that."

"You are afraid of something, Wealthy."

"No, I'm not. What should I have to be afraid of? What are you doing this afternoon?"

"Taking some medicines and victuals to old Gammer Pennock down at the Pinch."

"I'm feeling blue-spirited. I'll walk along with you." On the way, she said, "Remember the Little Sunbeams? Do you come down here often?"

"There are a few people Horace likes me to look after."

"Have you ever seen the gypsy woman they call Satch Fammie?"

Dinty stopped short. "What do you know of Satch Fammie?"

"Nothing. But I'd like to."

"Why?"

The beauty smiled. "Well, I'm to be married and it might be convenient to know some of the things they say she knows."

This seemed reasonable enough. "She doesn't stay at the Pinch," said Dinty. "Only stops over to see Mistress Crego."

"Ask Crego to let you know when she's coming again."

Dinty nodded. "But don't you want to have children ever, Wealthy? I do."

"Oh, I guess so," was the careless reply. "But not for a while. I want to stay pretty and show the Southern belles what we York State young ladies are like."

She went on to chat about plantation life as Kinsey had described it to her, and to outline an elaborate wardrobe, calculated to take the wind out of the feminine sails of South Carolina. In the middle of a sentence, she stopped. A distant bugle was blowing a flourish to the lower lock with the purity of tone which only one mouth could achieve.

Blood surged up beneath the girl's dark skin to the roots of the luxuriant hair, only to recede as swiftly. The lovely face became blank, blind, rigid. The lips were stiff, from between which issued a soundless whisper. Not until the clear melody had died in echoes from the far hills did she regain self-control.

"I'm a fool," she said. "Don't mind me. I'll be all right now."

Dinty said soberly, "Wealthy, I'm worried."

"You needn't be. Forget all about it. I'm going to forget." She became vehement. "I love Kinsey. I do love him. I'm going to marry him. I wish we were married now. I'm going to marry him and go to South Carolina where I'll be safe, and never come back."

"Never come back!" cried Dinty in dismay.

"I mustn't." The pallor returned to her face, which again grew rapt, lost. "For, if I heard his bugle at night," she whispered like one speaking with a power upon her, "I'd leave my marriage-bed to go to him. I'd rise from my grave to answer his call."

– 3 –

NEVER of a studious bent, Wealthia Latham now evinced a tendency to bookishness which amused and puzzled Horace. Her interest was specifically medical. While Dinty was doing her housework and Horace was out on calls, the girl would curl up in the office chair and pore over the pages of De Weese, Burns, Gregory, Hosack, and other authorities on female derangements.

"What's she doing it for?" the physician asked his wife.

Dinty passed along the explanation given to her by her friend. "A Southern lady has to look after the health of the whole plantation," she said. "Wealthy's got to know how to take care of the blackamore women when there's no doctor handy."

"Very praiseworthy," commented Horace, but he said it dubiously.

The matter was still latent in his mind when Genter Latham's manservant came with a message; would Dr. Amlie call, at his convenience?

Never before had Horace seen the great man in such mood. He was nervous, depressed, uncertain of himself, and strangely reluctant to approach the matter for which he had summoned Horace.

Horace waited. After several lapses in the conversation, Mr. Latham rose, went to the window, then beckoned the visitor over.

"Look at her!" he said, his voice vibrant with pride. "Can you show me her like in ten counties?"

Wealthia Latham, shears in hand and wicker-weave on arm, was gathering blooms for the house. Her exquisite face, half shaded by the broad straw "scoop-shovel," was somber. When she came to the little pavilian at the entrance to the rose circle, she set down her basket and, leaning against a pillar, stared out into nothingness. With her face in repose, its likeness to her father's was accentuated; that same arrogance and self-will, the same pride and passion, gross in the man, refined to beauty in the girl.

"Is that like her?" muttered Mr. Latham. "What makes her look that way, Amlie? What ails her?"

"I am not prepared to give a professional opinion," said Horace.
"Why not?"
"I have no basis for a diagnosis."
"That's true. I won't have her worried. As I am," he added.
"Are you sure you're not magnifying unimportant indications, Mr. Latham?"

The great man left the window and let his bulk slump heavily into the desk-chair. He drummed with a pencil. Without raising his eyes he said,

"Her mother, my beloved wife, died of lung fever. It began at exactly her age."

"Have you observed any symptoms?"

"She coughs at night."

"Probably a touch of the influenza."

"When I ask her, she says it is nothing. Sometimes I have thought she was weeping."

A vision, at once ludicrous and pathetic, came to his hearer's mind; this rugged, undemonstrative man, in carpet slippers and nightcap, creeping to the beloved child's door, listening, dreading what he might hear.

"Has she anything on her mind that you are aware of?"

"She knows about her poor mother. I think she fears that she is going the same way, but is too brave to tell me."

"Isn't it possible, sir, that you are allowing your affection for Wealthia to exaggerate your fears?"

"She is all I have."

"There are no external signs of the decline," pronounced Horace, using the euphemistic term in preference to "the consumption."

"What do you think of her? The truth, Amlie."

"She has seemed to me very gay and spirited."

"You saw her just now. Was she gay and spirited?"

"No."

"That is how I see her when she is not on her guard."

"Mr. Latham, the vapors of a young girl in love, when separated from the object of her passion after the excitements of close contact, often manifest obscure phases. I am speaking plainly."

"That is what I expect of you. You are convinced that that is all?"

"Not convinced. Lacking a thorough examination, I can offer only theory."

"Then make an examination."

"Very well. Send Wealthia to my office at five o'clock this afternoon."

"Do it now. Here."

"It will be more satisfactory at my office."

"Who's paying for this?" Mr. Latham was his autocratic self again.

"You are paying for the best opinion I can give," returned Horace patiently but with firmness. "If you want a superficial diagnosis, call in someone else."

"By God, I will!"

"Good day, Mr. Latham."

"No, no! Wait." The black humor drained from his face. "There's no one else here I can trust. You're pigheaded, damn you, but you're honest."

"Mr. Latham," said Horace earnestly and kindly, "you are causing yourself needless suffering. I can all but warrant that there is nothing seriously amiss with your daughter's lungs."

"I'd like to believe you, Amlie. I'd give half my fortune to believe you. I've got such a dread of it." He tapped his great chest. "She shall be there at five o'clock."

Certainly Wealthia showed no evidences of wasting disease when she presented herself at Horace's private consultation room. She was in one of her gayer moods and laughed at the physician's professionally serious mien.

"There isn't anything the matter with me," she asserted. "Not a thing."

"Your father . . ."

"Oh, Pa! Pa's an old fussbuddle where I'm concerned. If I sneeze, he thinks I'm dying."

"You don't appear to be losing weight."

"Of course I'm not."

"The night-cough of which he speaks . .

"There isn't any night-cough."

He put further and more intimate questions, under which she became at first restive, then resentful.

"I don't know why I should be pestered and harstled this way," she complained.

"I don't mean to harstle you, Wealthia. I am merely trying to carry out my instructions."

"What are your instructions?"

"Among other things, to make a physical examination, if I think it needful."

"Well, you shan't," she flashed. "I think it's horrible of you to mention such a thing."

Blocked here, Horace could only report to the father that, as far as he could ascertain, there was no cause for alarm. He could tell that Mr. Latham, though relieved, was not wholly satisfied. Horace's own opinion was that Wealthia, in an impressionable and nervous state from her betrothal, had been reading too many medical treatises and, under their influence, had magnified some petty functional derangement out of all reason. For treatment, he resorted to the usual tonic of spring herbs: saxifrage, rhubarb and colewort.

There remained another source of diagnosis, Dinty's powers of observation and analysis.

"Has Mr. Latham always fretted over Wealthia like this?" he began.

"Ever since I can remember."

"Do you think there's anything really wrong with her?" he asked bluntly.

"No; I don't. Why should there be?"

"Is she worrying about herself?"

"Where do you get your funny ideas, darling? There's nothing for her to worry about."

"She could read herself into almost any symptoms out of those medical books of mine," said he thoughtfully.

"I don't believe there's a thing in it," declared Dinty.

She assumed more confidence than she felt, for she was sensible of an indefinable change in her friend. It seemed to her to date from the night of the barn-raising at Manchester. This was at the back of her mind as she added thoughtfully,

"If I were Kin Hayne, I'd come back here quickly and fetch a wedding ring with me."

Horace laughed at her. "The bride's panacea."

"Don't be horrid," said Dinty loftily.

It developed that Kinsey Hayne was coming back, though not with the appurtenance which Dinty had suggested. Some business had unexpectedly summoned him to Albany, and he was continuing his way west in time for the first large social function of the summer, the Canal Ball at the Eagle Tavern.

This, while a very high-toned affair, had a commercial angle. It was given by the warehousemen and shippers in honor of the Erie captains, upon whose good will they depended for careful handling and prompt delivery of their consignments. It was to be a fete of great formality and elegance. Even the experienced Wealthia was agog about it, and looked forward to Kinsey Hayne's escort with as much apparent eagerness as the most jealous love could demand.

Dinty, to her vast satisfaction, received her first official honor as having attained the estate of matronhood, by being appointed to the Ladies' Receiving Line. She wheedled Horace, who was quite unable to resist her persuasions, into letting her order a new gown at Miss Blombright's, and spent her spare moments in practicing languor of demeanor.

It was difficult to maintain this studied neutrality in the face of the splendors and gayeties of the occasion. Not only was all the local aristocracy present, but the uppercrust of the Erie had crowded the basins to capacity and, with their womenfolk, contributed the luster of their various uniforms. Now that Dinty was *hors de combat,* Wealthia Latham was undisputed queen of the spinsters, and was looking, so thought her admiring friend, a picture of careless and confident loveliness.

That was at the outset. A few moments later Dinty, catching a glimpse of her face, saw that all life and gayety had drained out of it. Puzzled and alarmed, she feared that the girl might have been taken ill or faint. A familiar and gay voice from down the line distracted her attention, and, turning, she recognized the reason for Wealthia's discomposure.

Captain Silverhorn Ramsey was advancing along the line. On his arm was his new wife, an elderly crone (to Dinty's young eyes) who would never again see thirty-five. She was arrayed in an overpowering elegance of black satin and lace, and sparkled with gems. The voice in which she acknowledged the committee greeting was a throaty caw, and the eyes which she kept fastened upon her handsome spouse glittered with suspicion and possessiveness. Silverhorn, plainly on his best behavior, appeared quite subdued, but his glance was vagrant, and Dinty knew too well the object of its range.

Wealthia had noted his presence before he discerned her in a group of ardent admirers. He made no effort to break in upon it, but devoted himself exclusively to his wife. Soon Wealthia recovered her gayety which waxed to a quite reckless pitch, as she distributed her smiles and little coquetries broadcast. Was she trying to make her fiancé jealous? Or did her purposes go farther afield? Dinty suspected that the courtly Southerner, for all his infatuation, would hardly be a safe person to play fast and loose with.

Soon or later the Ramseys were bound to come into some contact, were it only the most casual, with Wealthia. The encounter occurred in the middle of the evening and on the floor. Silverhorn had been dancing with his wife. Up to this time he had partnered no one else. At the close of the measure, he came face to face with Wealthia. He bowed low and gracefully. The girl barely responded, but Dinty saw her eyes swerve and was shocked to read in them a sort of desperation. Mrs. Ramsey put a query in a not-too-subdued squawk and he replied offhandedly. The episode was over.

At the intermission Wealthia escaped from her court and drew Dinty aside. Her face was strained, her regard unsteady.

"Dinty, you've got to do something for me."

"What?"

"I want to speak to Captain Ramsey."

"I shan't have anything to do with it," pronounced Dinty with matronly severity.

"Please! It's terribly important. Just for a minute."

"Don't be a silly goose. What would Kinsey think? Why must you see him?"

"He's been writing me letters. I—I want to tell him to stop."

"I'll tell him."

"No. That wouldn't do any good."

"How could you talk with him here? Be reasonable."

"Then you must give him a message. Tell him I've got to see him some time, somewhere, right away."

"I won't do any such thing."

"I hate you," said Wealthia. "I hate everything. I wish you were all dead."

Dinty, waiting for her to recover her poise, came to a decision. She would take matters into her own hands. Why not? Was she not, as an experienced married woman, in duty bound to protect her ignorant and reckless friend? Wealthia was now looking contrite for her passionate outbreak.

"Let's go get a glass of the elderberry punch," said Dinty. "That will refresh your spirits."

She led her friend to the "ladies' bowl," where, while she was about it, she took two small glasses to Wealthia's one, by way of fortifying her soul for the coming interview. As the Entertainment Committee had augmented the light, sweet wine with a considerable admixture of cordial, Dinty, who was little accustomed to spirituous experiment, felt a gently pleasurable tingle in her nerve-ends.

By the exercise of major strategy Captain Ramsey had managed to slip the custody of his wife and was talking to Dr. Amlie about a threatening manifestation in Rochester of a malady of typhous nature which he thought might prove the dread spotted fever. Up came Dinty.

"You haven't asked me to dance once," she accused her husband, with her best combination of pout and smile.

"I didn't venture to abstract you from your official duties," he replied.

"Let me repair the negligence," put in Silverhorn gallantly. "Will you honor me with the next dance, Mistress Amlie?"

"With great pleasure, if my husband permits." This was working out well.

Captain Ramsey's dancing was a model of decorum. At the end of the number he suggested a bit of refreshment, which fell in perfectly with her ideas. What she had taken of the punch, while pleasant and invigorating, had fallen short of its full duties as incitement to positive action. She was glad to see that her escort, returning to the quiet corner which he had found for them, bore in either hand a jorum of extra capacity. Thanking him prettily, she drew at the straws with dainty appreciation which was mingled with surprise as she observed how much character the beverage had taken on since her earlier sampling. She reduced the contents of the glass by a good quarter.

Absently she realized that Captain Ramsey was paying her some pretty compliments. Pleasant enough, but her mind was on matters weightier than flattery. How to open this delicate and difficult subject? He saved her further trouble.

"You have a message for me. Haven't you?" he asked silkily.

"Yes," said Dinty. "That is, no."

"I'm sure you mean yes."

Another cool and delicious pull at the straws inspired her to the attack direct. "Captain Ramsey, why can't you let Wealthia alone?"

He said dolorously, "She hasn't so much as looked at me, the whole mortal evening." Then, below his breath, "I can't stand it."

"You are a married man, sir," said Dinty, the married woman in the role of Stern Duty.

"You needn't remind me."

"I *will* remind you. I'll remind you and remind you and remind you," declared Dinty whose thoughts were becoming markedly circulatory.

"Let me remind *you* that you have a message for me."

"How do you know that?"

"From the way you sought me out. I could hardly flatter myself that my charms had alienated your affections from young Æsculapius."

"I should think not, indeed!" returned the wife, indignant and unflattering. "I have a message," she admitted.

He leaned forward, his eyes alight. "What is it?"

"Oorp!" said Dinty.

"I beg your pardon."

"I didn't mean that," said Dinty and giggled. "What makes me feel so funny?"

"It must be the scent of the flowers," answered her partner, who knew better, having, for his own purposes, liberally spiked her glass from his brandy-flask.

"I presume that it is. Oorp!" She tried to clarify the message in her mind. "She wishes you to stop writing to her."

"I haven't written to her," returned Silverhorn in obviously genuine surprise.

"Why haven't you? That isn't what I meant to say," said poor Dinty. "What I mean is *oorp*."

"Take three slow swallows," prescribed Silverhorn. "That will stop the hiccups."

Dinty did so and immediately felt an added sense of responsibility. "You should remember," she admonished her escort, "that Miss Latham is an affianced bride."

Silverhorn's scowl was feral. "You mean she's promised to marry that Southern whippersnapper?"

"He isn't a whippersnapper. He's a very fine young—oorp!—gentleman."

"I'll kill him."

"Maybe he'll kill you first," said Dinty brightly.

"By God, I wouldn't much care!" said he wretchedly, and Dinty found herself being foolishly sorry for him. Her brain was crystal-clear now. She remembered everything and had only the one desire to get it off her mind.

"Wealthy wants to see you. She wants to tell you that all is over between you. But I think it is more seemly and in accord with propriety that you should not meet. You may accept my word," she continued, enunciating with great particularity, "that she has no desire for further association with you."

Silverhorn ignored it all. "When and where?" he demanded.

"When and where wha-at?"

"Am I to see her?"

"You can't see her."

"Will you give me your word of honor that she doesn't want to see me?"

"No, I won't," she answered uneasily.

"Thank you, Dinty."

"Oorp!" said Dinty. "Oh, dear! Oorp! Please take me back to my place, Captain Ramsey."

"I don't believe you'd better go there," said Silverhorn, after contemplating her. "You sit still and I'll fetch your husband to you. Better not drink the rest of that."

He took the glass from her faltering hand and left. When she roused from a brief, unpremeditated snooze Horace was standing beside her.

"Well!" said he. Dinty decided that she liked his tone as little as his grin. It implied that she had been drinking. When Horace smilingly suggested "Home," she returned a brisk "Why?" followed by an even brisker "Oorp!"

"That's why," answered her husband.

"It's no reason at all," asserted she. "I want to dance. I want to go outside," she amended on second thought.

"That's why," repeated Horace, five minutes later, mopping her face with a bar towel.

"D'you mean I'm intoxicated?" asked Dinty viciously.

"Just a little."

"You're a very vile fellow," said she, weeping, "and I shall sleep in the guest chamber."

Horace grinned again. "You'll be sorry."

"I shan't."

"You'll be lonely."

"I shan't."

"You'll wake up in the middle of the night and want to come back."

"I shan't! I'll never come back."

It was their first quarrel. That is—as Dinty, waking at early light guiltily qualified—if that can properly be termed a quarrel which is promulgated by one party alone. If only Horace hadn't grinned so hatefully like a monkey!

Oorp!

4

Dinty was wrathful and unhappy. Dinty wished to die and be laid away in her mossy tomb for a remorseful widower to weep over. Would Horace weep, though? It was now a whole week since she had withdrawn the grace and comfort of her presence from his bed, and he had offered no comment upon it. She did not expect him to plead on bended knee for her return; Horace's knee-joints were not hinged that loosely.

But to have him simply and cheerfully ignore her absence was intolerable. Each morning he brought to the breakfast table his amiable smile, his lusty appetite, his polite solicitude regarding her night's rest. In vain did she develop an alarming cough. It failed to alarm. Upon having it called pointedly and pathetically to his attention, he listened at her chest and prescribed slippery elm and molasses, recommended as an alleviant. Dinty could have hurled the nauseous mixture at his head.

No; she doubted whether early demise would serve her ends. Horace might marry again. Widowers always did. It would be just like him! Whom would he choose, she asked herself in glum surmise. Not Wealthia, who was already bespoken; Dinty couldn't have stood that. Perhaps that pretty little Vandowzer chit who had shot up so abruptly into womanhood, much as Dinty herself had. Or he might take up with one of those mopsies at the Settlement. That Donie girl had been to the office several times lately. Dinty had heard that when husbands began to neglect their wives (thus she put it to herself) it was a sign of some interpolated passion. There was a touch of the rake about Horace, she reflected, apprehensively remembering Miss Sylvia Sartie. Dinty decided that it was her duty to live and suffer.

In her melancholy disillusionment, she even hinted to Wealthia Latham that wedded life was woman's martyrdom. Wealthia was not impressed. She was now in one of her calmer and more adjusted phases. She had settled the date of her marriage to Kinsey Hayne for October 15th, and was already planning a celebration the like of which Palmyra had not yet witnessed. Kinsey had left, quietly happy, for his affianced had been, toward the close of the visit, her most affectionate and demonstrative self.

"Wealthia seems quite recovered from her megrims," said Horace at the supper table on Thursday.

"She has no sorrows in her life," said Dinty darkly.

"That is what puzzled me about her," said he, helping himself lavishly to rabbit pudding. "I shall be late this evening," he added.

"Shall you?" The indifference of her response was meant to indicate that it would matter less than nothing to her if he stayed out all night.

"Horse Thief Society," he explained. "After that, I've a couple of professional calls to make."

"Expectings?"

"One of them. The other's a fever I don't like the looks of."

His wife yawned. "I have an entrancing book. The new Waverley. I shall read myself to sleep."

She had no such intention. The spell of vagrancy had returned upon her. It was the first stirring of the old impulse since she had fallen in love with Horace. Quaila Crego, laughing, had told her, "Marriage will cool the itch in your feet." Quaila was wrong. The night called and her blood answered.

The stair-clock struck ten. Dinty jumped from bed and got into her roughest costume, with the short, dark skirt and long, heavy boots. Long out of practice though she was, she let herself down from the window with gymnastic adroitness. To have made exit by the commonplace door would have belied her mood.

It was a wind-fretted night with clouds now revealing, now shrouding a shriveled moon. Dinty's quivering nostrils smelt rain to come. It exhilarated her. A whippoorwill, unseen in a thicket, rehearsed his insistent monotonies. Farther away, a hoot owl repented a misspent life in liquid and hollow measures. Dinty answered him, and he paused in some uncertainty, then resumed his penitential routine. A fox barked. The silent shadow of a mink, hunting, weaved across her path. Dinty was happy.

It had not been her conscious purpose to spy upon her husband. But, as she skirted the back fences, she heard the loud good nights of the Horsethievers as they poured out from meeting. Why not check up on him? At the end perhaps give him a surprise? To pick him out was easy; she could distinguish the loose, even swing of his gait in a thousand. He was with Decker Jessup, O. Daggett, Silas Bewar and

Elder Strang, but soon parted company to cross the street. To pick up Fleetfoot, doubtless. No; Fleetfoot, she recalled, was suffering a slight attack of the epizootic; so Horace would be going afoot. Good! Following afoot would be simplicity itself for the experienced Dinty.

If he had told her the truth (and why should she suspect otherwise, since he never lied?) he would be calling first on the expectant Happalonia Vallance Upcraft. Drifting beneath the window, she eavesdropped the conversation. Happalonia's pains had not yet set in. False alarm. Horace left, saying that she might expect him in the morning, and the tracker picked up the trail which now led to Poverty's Pinch. There the doctor spent twenty minutes in one of the huts at the water's edge. The sleuth heard a voice which she identified as Quaila Crego's, asking some question; then Horace's decisive instructions.

"Keep her as cool as you can, and wash your hands well in vinegar whenever you leave. It isn't spotted fever, but it might be scarlatina anginosa or even maligna."

Now, Dinty thought, he would turn homeward. He did not, but took the lower path toward the Settlement. Why should he be going there at such a time of night? It could not be an emergency call; nobody had sent any messages that day. Still they might have caught him at the meeting. Just the same, Dinty didn't like it. She followed along, keeping to cover, and, near the long shack which housed the demimonde, lurked in a thicket. There she got into trouble.

The dog was a mean, little, yappy cur. Not content with raising an embarrassing row, he snapped at her feet, giving her cause for thankfulness that she had on stout boots. There was no club available; the brute's fervor, instead of abating, increased. She must do something about it. Tip Crego's instructions of other years came to her aid. Stepping out into the clear back of the copse, she stood perfectly rigid, waiting her opportunity. The cur rushed her legs with swift, snapping advances and retreats, leaving the score of his teeth on the leather more than once, until overconfidence was his undoing. He stood, growling threats of further attack, when the expert kick landed fair and square in the vulnerable spot. Dinty grinned as her assailant faded away in a series of grievous yelps, to trouble her no more.

Creeping back to her point of vantage, she descried a familiar shadow against the paper curtain. It bent above a bed. A female voice shrilled "Darling!" and followed the endearment with a satisfied chuckle. Dinty's blood went first ice-cold, then boiling hot. She became a mixture of injured spirit and avenging virago. Running to the creek bank, she seized a small boulder, with which she crept close beneath the window. If she now heard or saw what she expected . . . !

Gwenny Jump's cheery voice said, "She'll be like that one time, Doc, and then it'll take three of us to hold her."

"See that she gets no more liquor," directed Horace. "This is opium. If the horrors come on again, give her two pills."

"Darling!" shrieked the creature on the bed. "Brush 'em off me! Brush 'em off!"

Dinty sneaked away, blushing hotly in the darkness. How could she ever have suspected her Horace! He might be dumb about understanding her; he might treat her like a silly child; he might make fun of her; but, at least, he'd never be guilty of such treachery as she had basely suspected. She fled up the hill and stopped to breathe in the churchyard. Remembering his assignation there with the fair and frail Sylvia, Dinty grew hot again with reminiscent resentment. She'd give him a scare.

She hid behind a tombstone and waited. When Horace approached, she arose with her skirts over her head for whiteness, and gibbered realistically. Horace paused without evidence of trepidation.

"Come out of there," said he.

Dinty, following her Shakespeare, added a squeak to her gibber.

"Or I'll haul you out by the scruff of the neck."

"Peep-bo!" said Dinty, disappointed. "Weren't you scared a bit?"

He was not even specially surprised, or, if he was, he concealed it.

"So, it's you," he remarked. "Night-walking again."

"It's such a lovely night," she returned, disregarding the raindrops that trickled coldly down her neck. (Now he would scold her and she would be prettily penitent and he would take her in his arms and all would be well between them forever after.)

"You know the way home, I suppose," he suggested mildly.

"Aren't you coming?" She could not keep the hurt surprise out of her voice.

"Not yet."

"Horace! It's after midnight. Where are you going?"

"Back of Winter Green Knob. Colicky baby."

"Ipecac, cohush and jalap," recited she glibly. "Poor baby! Take me with you, Doc."

"Come along, then. You can sit in the smokehouse."

Bella Griggs's wailing sixth was soon attended to. Dinty hooked her arm through her husband's as he emerged.

"I know a short cut," she said, and guided him across the rump of the knob and around a swampy thicket to the Lathams' sheeprun. Thence the way led along the back garden for a space.

"Someone up late," remarked Horace, peering at an upper light in the mansion window. "Why, the old goat!" he exclaimed involuntarily.

"Who?" asked Dinty, pausing to peek through the interstices of the privet.

"Genter Latham. Who else would be coming from his house at this hour of night?"

Dinty was not sure whether the figure, dimly seen through the rain, had come from the house or the stables. It was now locked in embrace with another and slighter form which had moved from the summerhouse to meet it. Hence Horace's ejaculation.

"Sarah Dorch," he whispered disgustedly. "So that's begun again. Come along."

They plodded home, Dinty, however, was not satisfied in her mind.

"Take off those things at once," commanded her lord and master. "I'll get out one of your flannel nightshifts and fix your bed for you."

Stirring up the kitchen fire, he filled two pickle-bottles from the kettle, inserted them into woolen stockings, and tucked them in at the foot of the bed—the spare chamber bed! Dinty could have wept with chagrin.

"There!" he said with cheery and detestable kindliness. "Can't have you coming down with peripneumonia."

Dinty morosely told herself that she wouldn't give a darn. Ten minutes later, evidence of her husband's untroubled slumber was rhythmic in the air. Sleep was not for the exasperated soul of the young wife. She lay, open-eyed, pondering what they had seen in the garden, for her woods-trained observation had noted more than her companion's less keen eyes had perceived. While she could not be positive of her theory, she was worried.

The moon came out. Dinty, warmed now, rose, dressed in dry clothing, and again slipped out into the night. She intended to make certain, one way or the other.

She made her cautious approach to the Latham premises from the rear. No light shone in the mansion. The summerhouse was empty. The lovers' tryst was over. Creeping in the shelter of the hedge, she made her way to the spot. In the rain-softened gravel, the trail stood, plain as print. The man's course had led, not from the house, but around its corner, indicating that he had presumably hidden in the stables while he waited. It was the smaller footprints that had come from the house and returned thither, while the midnight cavalier had taken a side-path back in the direction of town—and the canal.

Dinty did not need to visit the basin in order to be certain that the *Jolly Roger* was still moored there.

Fever broke out in Brockport and Horace Amlie was sent for. Dinty thrilled with pride over this evidence of his extending reputation. As he planned to spend a night with Dr. Vought in Rochester, he figured on an absence of at least four days. It was the first separation for the Amlies. Dinty went down to the packet landing to bid her husband farewell with wifely admonitions. Evening had set in when she got back to the house, after having supper at the Lathams'. A tubby figure rose from the front steps and saluted, military style. It was Dad Hinch, the Human Teapot.

"Sarvint, ma'am," said he.

"Good evening, Mr. Hinch." Dinty made it a point to be courteous to the least of her husband's patients. "The doctor is away."

"Yes, ma'am. I'm here."

"He won't be back before Monday."

The visitor scrutinized the lay of the land. "I can bivouac under the bush yonder."

"Bivouac? Here? What for?"

"Sentry duty, ma'am. Capting's orders." He had taken to regarding Dr. Amlie as his superior officer.

"Very well." It was thoughtful of Horace to provide her with a guard. Unk Zeb was not much protection. And the streets were full of rough characters from the canal on pay night. "I can fix the pallet in the woodshed for you."

"I'm used to outdoors, thank ye kindly, ma'am." He picked up a musty blanket, near which his musket leaned against the wall.

Dinty felt a little better over this evidence of husbandly care. Maybe Horace wasn't growing tired of her, after all. Why, then, did he permit this irksome separation to continue?

To mitigate her deserted child's loneliness, Mrs. Jerrold paid her a daily visit with which she could well have dispensed. Horace's absence was duly sniffed over.

"Only once in ten years did my husband quit me overnight," said the mother. "I knew better than to let him. Men!"

"Horace was specially summoned as an expert," said Dinty with pride.

"Expert! Smff! Does it take four days to discover a fever?"

"He plans to stop in Rochester to consult with the great Dr. Vought."

"Four days! Hmph! And four nights as well, I doubt. Has he separated your beds yet?" The young wife looked so glum that the maternal tormentor added triumphantly, "I warrant he has."

Each day she produced a new variation upon husbandly errancies. The evening of the fifth day brought Horace home. Dinty's welcome was carefully cordial. She was determined to play her cards cannily. Mr. Latham being away again on some banking errand, Dinty had endeavored to persuade Wealthia to remain for the night, which would have automatically precipitated a solution of the bed problem. But her chum manifested that strange, new awkwardness toward Horace which she had already noticed. It being after nightfall, Horace assigned the Teapot as a military escort to the departing guest. As soon as they had left, Dinty turned brightly to her husband.

"What did you do in Brockport?"

"Poked my long nose into all their nasty corners," he answered with his amiable grin.

"Did you get into rows?"

"Some of 'em don't exactly love me," he admitted.

"Was the fever bad?"

"It'll be worse."

"Then you really didn't get anything done."

"Nothing but give 'em some good advice which they won't take."

"And you left me for five whole days on a wasted errand," she pouted.

"Four," he corrected. "You were safe enough with Dad Hinch watching over you in case you were plotting any more nocturnal excursions."

"So that is what you put him here for!" returned Dinty, nose in air. "I could slip him like a weasel."

"Don't be too sure," he advised her. "Dad was a scout in the war."

"Suppose I put a watch over *you*," said Dinty. "Would you like that? What were you doing all that time in Rochester?"

"Taking in wisdom and encouragement from old Vought. We talked the night away."

"And neglecting your patients," said she severely. "You've got slathers of calls waiting. There's an erysipelas, and four boils, one of them malignant, and Mr. Pardee's deep rheumatism is going deeper. Little Simeon Daggett has been bitten by a dog. Freegrace Barnes tried to wait for you, but couldn't and Old Murch birthed her baby and it nearly died. There's a smallpox thrown off the *Buttery Maid* that they put into the jail-house because there wasn't any other place for him. David Stone has his rupture tied in with twine where his off ox gored him, and Mr. Sneed got a sprained wrist trying to handle the ox. T. Lay burned his eye with a flying cinder from the smithy forge and says he'll sue Silas Bewar if he loses the sight. There's a list of baby-colics on your desk. And I've put away seventeen dollars, two shillings and thruppence from the barter since you've been off gallivanting. And that's all and I'm perishing for sleep." She yawned elaborately.

"Trot along, then. I'll catch up with my work."

She lingered hopefully, awaiting a further move from him. Perhaps she wouldn't insist on an apology. If he would simply assume that she was coming back! He only looked absently in her direction, as if wondering why she was still there. At least, so she inferred. If that was a grin tugging at his upper lip, if he was reading her mind —a detestable and wholly unreckonable habit of his—nothing was too bad for him!

"Oh! A light," he said.

Taking out his pocket tinder-box, he flipped the wheel, expertly caught the spark, nursed it amidst the dry flax, and blew it to activity. With this he lighted the wick floating in the shallow pewter bowl half full of Seneca oil.

"Go ahead," he directed, and followed her up the stairs.

The second-floor hallway to the left led between the two bedchambers. Dinty, her heart thrumming, stood aside for him to lead the way. He passed her and stopped between the doors, holding the light high, the better to see her face. His manner was casual, but his eyes were dancing, and wrinkles played at the corners of the generous mouth. She could read *his* mind without difficulty. He was saying silently, "You started this silliness; now you must finish it." Why, darn him, he was laughing at her, *damn* him! So she was to come to heel like a chastised puppy. The Jerrold spirit rose, rampant. Not Dinty!

"Thank you," said she with a dignity so gracious that it was painful, as she took the lamp from his hand and opened the spare-room door.

"Good night," he said.

"Good night," she echoed in a steady but faded voice.

Inside, she sat down on the bed and bit the sheet. She would leave him. She would go back to her loving parents. She would turn Romanist and enter a nunnery. First, though, she would burn down the house. This it was which brought to her mind the Great Thought. *That* would bring him to his senses.

Very quietly she removed the summer-and-winter mulberry coverlet from the bed, substituting a cheaper and rougher pine-tree design in blue. The pillows were extra-selected gosling down. These she tucked away in the linen press, bringing out an everyday pair. Her clothing she prudently disposed in a far corner, well out of range. There was always some Improving Reading on the bedstand. She settled back with the volume in her hand, but it could not be said that her selection, *The Olive Branch,* however great its intrinsic merits, improved its reader in any phase of temper or morality. It was little to her mood.

After an interminable wait, during which she gritted her teeth and fortified her determination, she heard Horace's quick tread mount the stairs and move along the hallway. There still remained a chance, short of her planned expedient of desperation. If he now showed an inclination to come half way by opening her door and bidding her good night again, she would be cool and reserved until—well, as long as she thought it safe. It was so hard to tell, with Horace.

He did not pause for the fraction of a second, but lifted the other latch and entered their room—*his* room.

Dinty waited three full minutes. She sat up, let her feet down cautiously upon a floor which could not be trusted not to squeak in loud betrayal, carefully drew her nightgown about her, and manipulated the light. She then uttered a thrilling shriek.

"What's the matter?" shouted Horace. She felt the impact of his weight shudder along the floor.

"Fire! Fire! Fire!"

With the presence of mind of one accustomed to face emergencies, Horace snatched his water ewer from the stand as he passed and ran across the hall. There was no doubt as to the fire. The oil which Dinty had carefully applied to the bed clothing was burning merrily. Horace dashed his burden upon the spot and Dinty, having darted across the room, contributed a second ewerful. The flame died down to a nasty smudge. There was no further danger, but the bed was as plainly unsleepable as Dinty had planned that it should be. Everything was going as plotted. Nevertheless, her housewifely spirit quailed as she reckoned that five dollars would scarcely repair the damage.

"How did it happen?" asked Horace.

"I must have fallen asleep over my book."

"So it would seem," he said, staring hard at her.

Dinty peered down beneath her garment. "Maybe I'm burned," she said, adding in a tremulous whisper, "fatally."

Horace made the briefest of surveys. "Don't see any signs of it."

"Internally," she said, but he was busy with a vagrant spark which was trying to start something on its own account.

"My nice bed!" mourned Dinty. "Where can I sleep now?"

"There's the woodshed," suggested Horace.

"It's buggy," she whimpered.

"Well, I'll move the pallet into the big room."

"Way downstairs?" faltered she, almost choking.

"Or, I can make you up a nice bed on the landing."

"You're mean to me, Horace Amlie," said Dinty, weeping.

He picked her up then like a feather, and she snuggled into his neck with a bear-hug which he had to pry loose in order to deposit her in her proper, legal and wifely spot. Dinty's last intelligible word for that night was a stifled murmur, "Just the same, I think you were awfly mean to me."

5

Two crones hovered over gently simmering liquids in a kettle above a slow fire. About them hummed the night life of Poverty's Pinch. Their heads, one gray-patched, the other bald with age, drew together.

"Has she been to see you again?" asked the gray one.

"Yes. This very day."

"For the same?"

The aged one nodded.

"Is it what you suspicioned?"

"Who's to say? She tells little and admits naught."

"What have you to complain of? Her money's good."

The bald head nodded sagaciously. A clawed hand reached into the oven to pluck out a brand for the pipe which dangled from a mouth with but a single tooth. Rancid smoke, a blend of dock, cheap twist and the dried fiber of bitter-willow tainted the air. The crone spat.

"She's a kittle bitch to handle," she croaked.

Quaila Crego leaned closer. "Suppose it's *that.* Who's the spark that lit her?"

"Wasn't there a Southern gallant here a few months back?"

"Seek further. She could marry him tomorrow."

The smoker took several meditative puffs. "Would it be the canaller?"

"Silverhorn?"

Satch Fammie smirked. "They've been seen together. But not in church."

"She'll get no good by him."

"What she could get by him is already well gotten, for my guess."

"There'll be blue hell and red murder when her father finds out."

"Don't talk of that man to me." Satch Fammie shivered. "I had his black look once and I want no more of him."

"For all her fix, you'll see young Miss Uppity queening it, come

Independence Day, with all the young blades at her feet," said Quaila.

Her prophecy was wrong. Gala plans had to be altered because Wealthia Latham, who was to have worn Liberty's coronet in the pageant, had taken to her bed. All that her distressed father could get from her was that she was tired out and not feeling well. No, she didn't want a doctor. She would be all right. Pa mustn't fret himself over her.

Genter Latham did fret. Over her protests he summoned Dr. Amlie. Wealthia received the physician, sitting up in bed. Languor had touched her darkly sensuous beauty with fragility. She looked quite saintly. Her temper did not support the appearance.

"Why must you fuss over me?" she demanded with asperity. "There's nothing the matter."

"Your father thinks there is. Why are you in bed?"

"I'm tired."

"Bristol Sulphur Springs is well thought of as a recuperative resort. The waters have a salutary effect . . ."

"I don't want to go to Bristol Springs. I don't want to go anywhere. I want to be let alone."

Nevertheless Horace recommended to Mr. Latham a change of scene. The father shook his head.

"She's better at home. Do you know what I think, Amlie? I think it's this marriage."

"Is anything amiss between Wealthia and Hayne?"

"I think she doesn't really want to marry him."

"That might account for her low spirits," answered Horace cautiously. The explanation did not satisfy him. If Wealthia had changed her mind about her betrothed, she would have little hesitancy in jilting him. She always did as she pleased. The reluctance, he guessed, was Genter Latham's.

"She can't abide the thought of leaving her home and me," pursued the father. "Make no doubt of it; that is what is grieving her."

"Has she told you so?"

"Not in so many words. But I know my daughter. She hasn't a thought that I don't share. I can read her like a book."

"What's your objection to Hayne?" inquired Horace bluntly.

"Mine? No objection except that he lives so far away."

"But you'd rather this marriage didn't take place."

"No, no! I don't say that. I've offered the young man an advantageous position in my bank if he will settle here, but he doesn't seem disposed to accept. A pigheaded young sprig," he concluded gloomily.

Anyone who did not fall in with the Latham pattern of life was, by that mark, a pighead.

"See here, Mr. Latham," said Horace. "I think you're making a mistake."

"I never make mistakes, sir."

"You are trying to break off this match. That, in my opinion, is a mistake."

Genter Latham stiffened. "I pay you for medical opinion, not family advice."

"Take it for medical opinion, then." Horace declined to be intimidated on his own ground. "Something is making your daughter unhappy and unsettling her state of health."

"As you're taking so much on yourself," glowered the father, "suppose you ask her whether she still wants to marry Hayne."

"Have I your authorization to do so?"

"You have."

Horace remounted the stairs and put the question to her straitly. The result discomfited him. She hunched down beneath the sheet and sobbed convulsively. Only one response could he get out of her.

"Go away! Please go away."

After preparing a soothing potion, he set the glass by the bedside and left.

At home he found Dinty, her hands stained as with murder, going through the final process of making pokeberry ink for marking the linen.

"Do you know anything about Kin Hayne?" he asked.

She looked up from her skimming. "He'll be in New York soon again."

"Did Wealthia tell you?"

"No. I had a letter from him."

"Again?" For a second the treacherous thought flashed into his brain that Kinsey had fallen in love with Dinty and jilted his fiancée. "You didn't mention it."

"It came last week. You weren't being nice to me then," said she blandly.

"I see. You disapprove of my actions and take it out in carrying on a clandestine affair with your best friend's young man. A nice wife! The law permits me to beat you, in case you don't know it."

"So do," said Dinty calmly. "And do you know what then? I'll mix up your medicaments and *all* your patients will die instead of only part."

"What do you mean, 'only part'?" retorted Horace, outraged in his professional sensibilities. "Except for old Mrs. Dobell who was over eighty, I've only lost . . ."

"Never mind, darling," she interrupted sweetly. "What did you want to know about Kinsey?"

"When is he coming up?"

"He doesn't know. He hasn't heard from Wealthy for the last three posts. I think she's acting like a little slink."

"Wealthia is ill."

Dinty gave her refined rendition of the vulgar gardaloo. "She's no more ill than I am. She's after something."

"What?"

"I'd like to know. I'll find out. I always do."

The beauty, however, had turned uncommunicative. The day after Horace's call she rose, dressed and mooned around the garden for a time, but neither on that day nor for several days following did she visit the Amlie house. When, at length, she appeared late on a misty afternoon, Dinty, lifting an intent face from her rose vines, said,

"Go in. I'll be through in five minutes."

"I've come to see Horace."

"He's busy with patients. Office hours."

"I'll wait till they've gone."

She looked tired and depressed and, Dinty thought, as if she had been through a struggle to reach a determination. Instead of going in, she lingered, watching her friend.

"How is Kinsey?" asked the housewife, fishing for clues.

"All right, I guess."

"You guess! Don't you know?"

"Of course he's all right. Why shouldn't he be?"

"Don't be uppish with me," Dinty admonished her. "What ails you lately, anyhow, Wealthy?"

The beauty showed signs of impending tears. "You'll be sorry when you know," she faltered. "You'll be sorry you treated me so brutishly. Maybe I'm going to die."

"Tara-de-diddle-de-dee!" said the other briskly. Nevertheless she was concerned. "I'm going to fix you a nice, cool raspberry shrub and then you can rest until the doctor is free." In professional communications Dinty was particular always to refer to her husband as "the doctor."

It was a white and tremulous girl who was ushered into the private office.

"Well, Wealthia, what is it?" asked Horace.

She struggled for utterance. When the question came, it was barely audible.

"Do you tie people when you cut?"

"I don't understand."

"When you cut for the stone. And—and other things. You do it, don't you?"

Horace had. He hoped he should never again have occasion to. The dreadful contortions, the blood and shrieks and agony, the writhing sinews and tortured nerves made up a memory which he was eager only to hold aloof.

"What leads you to suppose that you have the stone?" he demanded.

"I don't. It's worse," she muttered. Her mind swung back to its original terror. "Tell me whether I must be tied."

"You are tormenting yourself with needless fears," he told her.

"I'm not! I'm not! Won't you answer me?"

To calm her he went into a detailed description of the technic of internal operations, presenting it in as mild and reassuring a form as his conscience would permit. No, he did not believe in binding the patient. It was much safer to have assistants carefully hold the sufferer's limbs to keep the body steady. Thus was obviated the danger of ruptured muscles or dislocated joints. Liquor could be given to inspire fortitude; opium was employed liberally to deaden the pain; local administration of ether paint did much to assuage the nerves. As he put forth his soothing euphemisms, he observed covertly her effort to keep herself under control. There was a reserve of courage in the spoiled and pampered daughter of fortune which he would hardly have expected. Quite calmly she said,

"I know what I've got."

"Self-diagnosis is seldom reliable," he returned.

"It's the cancer," she breathed.

"What leads you to suppose that?" he demanded, startled.

"I can feel it."

"Where?"

"Here." She pressed her hand against her slender body; not so slender as formerly, he now noticed for the first time.

"Why haven't you spoken of this before?"

"I've been afraid to admit it to myself."

"Take off your clothes."

She shrank. "Must I?"

"Would you like me to call Dinty?" he asked tactfully.

"Oh, yes, please."

Dinty entered, very businesslike, very serviceable, very much the physician's helpmeet. Wealthy mustn't think of her body, she explained. It meant nothing in that office; nothing more than one of the medical drawings she had studied or a wooden model of an arm or leg. She helped arrange the patient on the table, then withdrew to make up her barter lists.

Horace's examination was exhaustive. It was also shockingly conclusive. Wealthia kept her eyes tight shut throughout, only gasping now and again. He helped her down to the floor.

"You may put on your clothes now," he said.

"When will you cut?" she asked in a hard-breathed whisper.

"I shall not cut."

"Why? Why?" she cried shrilly.

"I think you know very well why."

"I don't know what you're talking about," said she woodenly.

Horace busied himself making up some powders slowly, with the purpose of giving her time to compose her mind. Sifting them into a glass of water, he handed it to her. It was a placebo, the powders being quite inert. After she had swallowed the potion, he said gently,

"Don't you think you'd better be honest with me, Wealthia?"

"I don't know what you mean."

"How can I help you if you take that attitude?"

"I'm not taking any attitude. I don't know what . . ."

"Who is the man?"

She broke. "No! No! No! It isn't that. It couldn't be that." She babbled out certain physiological details.

"I know, I know," he said. "But these minor manifestations are apt to be misleading."

Her voice rose hysterically. "It can't be. I won't let it be. It's cancer. It must be cancer. Take it away from me, Horace. Take it away! Take it away!" She beat upon the table with clenched and frantic hands.

"Quiet!" he warned. "Try to control yourself. Now answer me. When were you exposed?"

"Exposed?" she repeated. Then, as his meaning became clear to her, she began to weep, quietly and desperately. "What shall I *do*? What shall I *do?*"

"I will see you tomorrow for further consultation," he promised.

Calling Dinty to help her, he sent Wealthia home. He wanted

time to think over this revelation. Was the girl deliberately attempting to deceive him, with her talk of cancer? Or, more probably, had she succeeded in deluding herself with false and forced hopes?

Dinty, who accompanied the caller to the gate, returned to the office.

"Wealthy says she is going to die. She isn't, is she, darling?"

"No," said Horace.

Experience had convinced her of the futility of further questioning when opposed by that tone. No direct reference was made to the matter again that day. After dinner Horace asked his wife in a casual tone,

"Do you remember the date of Kinsey Hayne's visit to us?"

"April sixteenth," she answered promptly. "Why?"

"Nothing."

There was a knock at the office door. Unk Zeb brought in a note. It was from Genter Latham. Doctor was to come to the house at once. Horace was not surprised. He wondered what had happened. Had Wealthia confessed to her father? If so, there would be the devil to pay. But he doubted it. For that matter, had she confessed to him? Not categorically.

He found the great man pounding up and down his library, cursing as he strode. Bewilderment always translated itself into wrath in his autocratic soul. Anything beyond his comprehension he resented as a personal slur upon his power.

"I don't know what's come to that girl of mine," he growled without troubling to acknowledge the caller's good evening. "She's gone to her bedchamber and won't come out."

"Shall I talk to her?"

"If she'll see you. I doubt that she will."

The two men climbed the stairs. Wealthia's door was bolted. Mr. Latham knocked sharply.

"Dr. Amlie is here, daughter."

"I don't want him," returned the petulant voice. "Tell him to go away."

"Open at once."

Silence within.

"You see." The father turned upon Horace a visage dark with wrath and concern. "Never before in her life has she dared disobey me. I'm well-minded to smash in the door."

"If you do," threatened Wealthia's hysterical voice, "I'll jump out the window."

"She's like a crazed person." The father spread helpless hands.

"Leave this to me," said Horace.

Mr. Latham clumped sullenly away. Horace approached his mouth to the lintel.

"Wealthia?"

No reply.

"Wealthia, don't be so foolish. I only want to help you."

Through the crack beneath the door he could see the flicker of the approaching candle. Wealthia's low voice asked, "Is my father there?"

"No."

"You say you want to help me."

"Believe me, I do."

"There's only one way you can help."

"You must know I can't do that."

He heard a sob. Then, "It's all lies, lies, lies, what you think. And if you tell my father, I'll kill myself."

He heard her receding footsteps and the creaking of the bed as she threw herself upon it.

Slowly and thoughtfully he descended to the parlor where Mr. Latham was awaiting him. In the ten seconds of his passage he had come to a decision of which neither Hippocrates, Æsculapius, or the N. Y. State Board of Medical Censors would have approved. He was about to overstep his proper province of medical advice to proceed upon the cloudy assumptions of family friendship.

"Has she come to her senses?" demanded the father.

Horace shook his head. "Mr. Latham, I should like your authorization to go to New York on your daughter's case."

"Is it as bad as that?" asked the father, his sanguine face paling.

"It is complicated rather than serious," replied Horace, choosing his words with reference to effect more than exactitude. "There are eminent medical authorities in the metropolis who are concurrent with the latest developments of science, and always prepared to help a younger practitioner."

"When can you go?"

"Tomorrow, if you wish."

"I do. Spare no expense. If you want any of the bigbugs to see her, fetch 'em back. I don't care what it costs."

"That will hardly be necessary, I think. Good night, Mr. Latham."

Dinty received the news of the projected trip with delight.

"Oh, Doc! How grand! I've been perishing to go to New York."

"I'm afraid not this time, Puss."

Her delight turned to dismay. "You're going without me?"

"I must. There are special reasons."

"What kind of a loving husband are you?" she demanded sorrowfully. "Leaving me behind to pine!"

"You won't have to pine very long, darling. I shall be there only one night, then back by the next packet. Ten days in all."

6

Canal packet to Albany, steam packet down the Hudson brought Horace Amlie to the metropolis with speed and comfort. He put up at Mr. William Syke's favorably known hostelry and at once sent his name to Kinsey Hayne.

"The young gentleman is in the dining room, Doctor," said the clerk. "Will you join him there?"

"I'll wait," said Horace.

He found a chair in the lobby, from which he contemplated the pageant of business, politics and fashion that filled the pillared room with noise and color, sitting there until the spare and elegant figure of the young Southerner appeared. Kinsey Hayne was smoking an imported Cuban segar, and swinging a gold-banded malacca cane with a costly and artistic knob. At sight of his erstwhile host, his face which Horace thought rather haggard, lighted up. He came forward, his hand outstretched.

"This calls for a libation," he said.

Horace shook hands. "Where can we talk privately?" he asked.

"Follow me," said his friend and led the way to the taproom, where he found an empty booth. "What may I offer you to drink?"

Horace made a negative gesture. "I want you to come back to Palmyra with me."

If Kinsey was startled he did not show it. "When?" he asked.

"By tomorrow's boat."

"Impossible. Or, at least, most inconvenient."

"It isn't a matter of convenience, but of urgency. I think you have no choice."

The other's eyes narrowed and hardened. Horace thought that they became wary, too. Well, if this was to be a fencing match, there would be no buttons on the foils.

"I shall answer that after I have had an explanation," said Kinsey.

"Wealthia," said Horace.

His companion rose. "This is not the place to bring a lady's name into the conversation."

"Where you please," returned Horace.

"My rooms are on the floor above."

He led the way to what Horace guessed to be the most expensive suite in the tavern. Again he offered a drink, with more formality this time. Horace might have been a business caller or a casual stranger. The change in manner confirmed suspicions which hardly needed confirmation.

"Is Miss Latham ill?" he asked.

"You should know. You've heard from her, I presume."

"Your presumption is your own concern. Did she send you here?"

"No."

"Then I fail to understand your status."

"Would it help if I remind you that I am the Latham family physician?"

"Then Miss Latham is ill?"

"She is pregnant."

Kinsey turned very white. "I think you lie," said he with cold deliberation.

"Upwards of three months, as I estimate."

"I think you lie," repeated the Southerner.

"Four months ago you were in Palmyra."

"Are you going to swallow the lie from me?"

Horace's patience cracked. "Damn you and your 'lies.' I'm thinking of my patient."

"You are speaking of the young lady I hope and expect to make my wife and I say to you categorically that you lie. My friends will wait upon you this evening."

"They can save themselves the trouble. You can't shoot away your accountability with a pistol."

Kinsey said impassively, "You have me at a disadvantage, Dr. Amlie. I am a gentleman, bound by the code which gentlemen observe. Must I cane you publicly on the streets?"

An unholy light burned in Horace's eye. "I'd like to have you try it." At a swift gesture from the other he added, "Wait! I haven't taken a five-day journey to brawl with you. Do you deny that you are responsible for Wealthia's condition?"

A veil of blankness, of secrecy and caution overspread the handsome features. "I deny nothing and affirm nothing," was the stiff rejoinder. "Your preposterous accusation is unworthy of further discussion. I repeat my belief that you lie."

"God give me patience! What possible object could I have in lying?"

Kinsey Hayne scanned him, frowning. "It is possible that you are under a delusion. Your conduct is equally infamous in impugning the virtue of my betrothed."

"Will you come to Palmyra?"

"At my own convenience, sir."

"Listen to me, Kinsey Hayne," said Horace with such sincerity that the Southerner's set face altered. "Your own convenience may be too late. She can't hope to conceal her condition much longer."

"Does anyone else know of . . ." began the other and checked his utterance, his face flaming. "Have you spoken of this to anyone?"

"Certainly not!"

"Then I must solemnly warn you not to."

"Oh, for Heaven's sake, stop talking like the hero in a drama!" cried Horace in exasperation. "I shall certainly tell Mr. Latham in due time."

"I forbid you."

"Save your breath. Someone must tell him, and Wealthia will not."

"But it can't be," muttered the young man, as if arguing to himself. "Wealthia would have con—would have confided in me. Her last letter was full of high spirits."

"Because she is still cozening herself with false hopes."

"Then she has admitted nothing?" said Hayne quickly.

"Not in so many words."

"Because there is nothing to admit. There must be other causes for—for whatever symptoms have led you to your monstrous conclusions," said Hayne with reviving spirit.

"There might be," admitted the physician reluctantly. "It is always possible. But, when I tell you that she practically . . ."

"Then I am well convinced of your error," broke in the other, "though I now admit that it may have been kindly in intention." His manner was gentler now, but still aloof. "I shall visit Palmyra as soon as my business commitments permit." He rose. "I bid you good day, sir." He did not offer to shake hands.

On the return trip Horace had ample time to ponder over Kinsey Hayne and his attitude. He read Kinsey's character as that of the

Southern puritan, conscientious in principle, exact in honor, wholly dependable where he considered that responsibility involved him. If he had seduced Wealthia, of which Horace had no doubt, it must have been in an irresistible gust of passion which swept them both off their feet, and for which he would unhesitatingly make amends by marriage. Why, then, his violent resentment toward Horace's errand?

That, too, the shrewd analyst could answer to his own satisfaction. Shamed by her misstep and, deep in her soul a little afraid of her fiancé despite his slavish devotion, Wealthia had concealed the truth from him. It was quite within the bounds of her self-delusive capacity that she should write, assuring him that all was well with her. To that thesis she would cling until hope and concealment alike should have become impossible. On his part, the Hayne code would bind Kinsey to suppress the facts of his relations with the girl and protect her good name at any cost. Further, his confidence in her would incline him to take her word as against the doctor's assumptions. Hence his angry and obstinate rejection of Horace's statement.

The whole picture was a plain pattern to Horace's logical mind.

Dinty's welcome to the returned traveler proved that she harbored no resentment over his desertion. Except that he had seen Kinsey Hayne, who would soon be coming upstate, he said nothing of that phase of his trip, descanting upon his interesting call upon the famed Dr. Hosack (whom he had, in fact, visited) and his reading in the medical libraries. Horace's conscience regarding professional secrecy was acute. On no consideration would he have breathed a hint of Wealthia Latham's plight, even to Dinty.

To Genter Latham he reported that he had availed himself of the highest medical advice on his daughter's case, and that there was no cause for alarm. Meanwhile Wealthia was up and about again and insisting to her father in lifeless tones that she had never felt better. She shunned Horace, pettishly refusing to submit to further examination or to answer questions. Speculating as to how far his eye was prejudiced by his knowledge, the physician thought her already visibly gravid, and was fearful that Genter Latham must soon notice the alteration in the lines of her body or, worse, that it might become a topic for the clattertongues of the feminine populace.

Days passed, but Kinsey Hayne did not arrive. A post came in from New York City by coachmail. There was no letter for Dr. Amlie.

One afternoon Dinty, who had been to the stone mansion to see her friend, greeted Horace with the small and sly smile which always put him on guard.

"Have all you M.D.'s a mission to run the world, darling?" she began.

"Only the extra wise ones," he answered warily.

"Like my wonderful husband. Why don't they keep their wisdom for their practice?"

"What have I been doing now?"

"Poking your long, red nose into other people's private affairs." She lightly kissed the tip of the maligned feature.

"Has Wealthia heard from Hayne?"

She nodded. "By yesterday's post."

"When is he coming up?"

"What makes you so sure he's coming?" she teased.

"He gave me his assurance."

"Kin is a man of his word. But I doubt it will be soon."

"It should be soon," said Horace with emphasis.

Dinty's strong and delicately arched eyebrows went up. "Still bossing the world," she murmured.

He attempted to cloak his error. "When a young female becomes low-minded and vaporish and fails to correct her spirits," he explained, "it is sound medical practice to employ non-medical agencies for her recovery. I consider Kinsey Hayne to be in that category."

"What if your patient doesn't like the prescription?"

Horace hunched half way out of his chair. "Doesn't like the man to whom she's bespoken? What's all this?"

"That isn't what I said. Certainly she likes him. But that doesn't mean that she wants to see him right now."

"Why not?"

His wife regarded him with pitying condescension. "You don't know much about females, do you, Doc?"

"I'm sitting at the feet of wisdom," he returned with grim patience.

"A very proper place for you, sir. Now you shall have your lesson. Have you noticed a change in Wealthy?"

"Am I stone-blind?"

"All beauties have their ups and downs," pursued the little oracle. "Wealthia isn't at her best, and knows it."

Horace was relieved. So that was all that Dinty had observed.

"Do you think Kinsey would mind that?" he asked.

"He wouldn't show it. But he'd mind. Men always do. If I wasn't pretty any more," she added with an impudent tilt of the face, "you'd put me out in the woodshed to sleep. You tried once."

"Vanitas vanitatum," said he. "I thought we were discussing Wealthia."

"It's vanity with Wealthy, too. She doesn't want Kin to see her looking like this. Isn't that natural? You just fix her up like herself; then she'll send for him quickly enough." Her expression took on gravity. "Doc, how worried are you about Wealthy?"

"Not at all."

"You are, so. I can tell it. It isn't lung-fever? Or—or anything bad?"

"Nothing of the sort. There's no cause for worry, I keep telling you."

"You don't know what it is. That's what makes you so cross. I can tell you one thing: she's timid about marriage."

"Nonsense. Why should she be?" he amended.

"Why should anyone? Girls are, though. I was, myself."

"It didn't keep you from getting married," he pointed out. "It doesn't keep most girls if they get the chance."

"It won't keep Wealthy," said her friend. "Wait and see. I'm sorry for poor Kin, though. D'you think it would do any good if I wrote and explained to him?"

"Explained what? No, don't interfere with what you don't understand," he said hastily.

"Neither do you," she retorted. "You look mad as a bear with a sore tail," she added irreverently. "You always do when things puzzle you. It's a grave flaw in your character." This last was so accurate an imitation of the Reverend Theron Strang in his more personal approach to sinners, that Horace grinned as he politely invited his wife to leave, on the ground of office hours impending.

Some days later, Dinty met him at the gate, a waxed and sealed letter in her hand, a dancing light of curiosity in her face.

"From Kinsey Hayne," said she.

He took it to his office, leaving her in a pout. Here was he, gone all day and forgot to kiss her when he returned! He must be expecting something important from Kin Hayne. Well, soon or later she would find out what.

Hardly waiting to seat himself, Horace slit open the overflap. The date was July 17, six days before. There were only a half-dozen lines in Kinsey's small, strong, regular handwriting.

Sir,

This is to inform and assure you that the suspicions which you expressed to me are wholly baseless. This I state on the authority of the person most involved. I swear this on the honor of a gentleman and a Carolinian, and I bind you on your own honor to the silence of your profession.

Yours respectfully,
Kinsey Hayne.

What could it mean? Had he overestimated Hayne's quality. Was he no more than a conscienceless backslider? Had he got Wealthia with child and, too cowardly or too dishonorable to meet the issue, chosen this method of evasion? Or had Wealthia, in writing to her affianced, persisted in her desperate and hopeless course of denial? Or could his own diagnosis possibly be in error? He put the chilling thought from him hastily.

What had Wealthia written to Kinsey? All depended upon that. That, at least, Horace could and would find out.

It did not then occur to him that Kinsey might be perjuring himself, like the gentleman he was.

7

Horace was bending over what Dinty called, with invincible distaste, his leechery when she came dancing in. At first she did not notice his occupation.

"When I am queen," she warbled, taking unwarranted liberties with the text, "you shall be king."

Her husband straightened up with a corpulent bloodsucker carefully suspended between thumb and forefinger. To the end of stimulating its appetite for its next feast, he proceeded to strip it of blood, the crimson stream trickling into his spittoon.

"Awgk!" retched Dinty, turning white.

Horace cocked a swift and eager eye at her. "Hey?" said he. "What's this?"

"Nothing," said she, reddening. "Those awful creatures. They always make me sick."

"Hmph! Any other symptoms?"

"No!"

"No need to be violent about it. I've thought once or twice that I noticed indications." He eyed her with speculation. "Though I must say I don't see any signs."

"No fault of yours," she retorted impudently.

"Well, you ought to know," he admitted, lifting out another squirming blob.

"Do you want me to be sick on your floor?" she demanded.

"I shouldn't mind. In a good cause." He abandoned his task.

"Husbands are always 'expecting,' " said she with disdain. "Aren't I trouble enough in the house?"

"Heaven is my witness," he answered, raising pious eyes.

She sat down. "Of course I want babies, Doc. Lots of 'em. But not yet. Will you think I'm silly if I tell you why?"

"Probably. But that needn't stop you."

"I never want a baby of ours to come to a house we don't own."

"We own this one," said he, astonished.

"Not while there's a dollar left unpaid on it. Pa's always been in debt and pretending not to worry about it. I hate it. Is it awfully dumb of me, darling, to feel that way?"

"I don't know that it is. It won't take long to clear the note at our present rate."

"Then we'll save for our cobblestone house with the carved oaken door and the leaded sidelights with eagles. Won't it be dicty!" she purred. "And I'll start right in having a baby every year. Ten of 'em. Maybe twelve. Doc, the day the note is paid, I'm going to feel so lucky that I'll march right down to the Literature Lottery and buy a whole chance, and I'll warrant it'll win one of the Grand Prizes. And there's our cobblestone house! No trouble at all."

"Lord help me! I've got a gamester for a wife," lamented Horace, who occasionally, in secret and with consistent unsuccess, took a modest flier, though nothing like the full-chance twenty-five-dollar ticket which Dinty proposed.

"You ought not to object," she pointed out. "The lottery supports your old college that you're so dozened on." Which was something of an exaggeration, though not without a basis of truth. "We'll have a boy first, so you can send him there," she concluded indulgently.

He changed the subject. Observant as Dinty was, he felt sure that she must soon become suspicious of her chum. He asked,

"How does Wealthia seem to you lately?"

"Quieter than usual. It's something about Kinsey, I believe. She hasn't told me yet."

"I thought I'd drop around there this evening."

He found Genter Latham smoking with an expression of unusual amiability. "Your treatment is proving successful, my boy," said the great man.

"You think that Wealthia is improving?"

"Don't you?"

The physician chose his words discreetly. "I see no deterioration."

"She talks of going away for a time."

"Where?" Horace's uneasiness must have shown in his expression, for his host waved aside the cloud of tobacco smoke, the better to observe him.

To Albany. A visit to friends. Any reason why not?"

"Would you accompany her?"

"Do you think it advisable?"

As Horace made no reply, the great man pressed the question.

"Do you consider that necessary, Amlie?"

"I think it desirable."

"Why?"

"Wealthia should not leave town without someone to—to watch over her."

"Is it as serious as that?" Latham's face was seamed with anxiety. Pity almost but not quite undermined Horace's resolution. Wealthia must not, on any account, be allowed to take her case of "cancer" to some practitioner who might be free from Horace's professional and moral scruples.

"Mr. Latham," he said, "I have something grave to tell you."

The father shaded his eyes with his left hand. The hand shook. "Is my girl going to die?"

"No."

A bursting sigh came from the compressed lips. There was exasperation as well as relief in the next question.

"Can't you speak out?"

"Your daughter is pregnant."

"Pregnant," echoed Genter Latham so mechanically that Horace doubted whether he had taken in the full significance.

"She is going to have a baby."

The effect was startlingly different from Horace's expectations. Genter Latham laughed with unforced contempt. "You fool!"

Horace tautened. "You think me a fool? Ask her."

"I'll not insult her with any such blackguardly folderol."

"The visit to Albany is a pretext. She hopes to be rid of the child."

"A fool and a liar."

"Why should I lie to you, Mr. Latham?"

"To veil your own ignorance. You haven't the science to understand her case, so you fall back upon this foul pretext."

"If you won't believe me, take her to some other reputable physician."

"And soil her good name by telling him of your filthy suspicions?"

"Have *you* had no cause for suspicion?"

"No, by God!" shouted the father.

"And I'm the fool," said Horace quietly.

"Before I turn you out," said the autocrat, leaning forward to probe the other's face with his glance, "give me one reason for your foul charge against a virtuous girl."

"She as much as admitted it to me."

Horace observed with a sort of awe the phenomenon of a man's eyes turning red under stress of fury, as the veins of the iris suffused with blood. For the moment he feared apoplexy. Hastily filling a glass with water from the pitcher on the desk, he held it out.

"This is a shock, I know," said he placatingly. "Take a slow swal——"

The tall tumbler, struck from his grasp, crashed against the wall.

"Get out before I treat you the same," gasped Genter Latham.

"I'll go out as I came in," returned Horace, thin-lipped. "And I leave you one word of warning. Six months from now . . ."

A swift change in the glaring face before him checked the speech. He turned his head. Wealthia Latham stood in the doorway, her lips parted, the velvety fire of her eyes unearthly bright in the pallor of her face. She was in a loose robe, thrown over her nightdress.

"I heard something," said she, thrusting at a fragment of glass with her fur-shod foot. "What have you been telling my father?"

"Go back to your bed, my dawtie," said Latham tenderly. "A political dispute. Not for your little ears."

"What have you told him?" she challenged Horace.

"The truth."

She shook her lovely head. "Not truth. Imagination."

"Do you know what he has been saying to me?" demanded Genter Latham.

"I can guess." She seemed incredibly composed.

"Then tell me—tell him that he's a cowardly and malicious liar," he begged with pathetic confidence.

Again she made a sign of negation. "Not a liar. Too obstinate to admit that he doesn't know what is wrong with me."

"For God's sake, what *is* wrong?"

The girl, her eyes cast down, spoke with a commiseration and composure which astonished Horace who only now had begun to perceive that he had to do with a consummate actress playing a shrewdly devised role.

"I didn't want you to know, Pa, till it was over."

"Till what was over? Christ! Will someone give me facts?"

Wealthia turned upon Horace. "I asked him, I begged him to cut for the cancer."

"Cancer?" breathed her father. "The cancer? You, my dawtie?"

"That cancer," put in Horace bitterly, "is alive. It will come away of itself in December."

"You see," she sighed. "I have sworn to him that I am innocent. What more can I do?"

"Will you have the opinion of another physician?" asked Horace.

Too late he perceived his mistake. The only other physician readily available was Gail Murchison. That time-serving old quack would take any risk, lend himself to any deception to oust his supplanter from the favor of Palmyra's richest family.

"No," said Wealthia, and he breathed easier.

"Yes," said her father, and Horace essayed to mend his fences. "Let me call in Dr. Vought from Rochester. Nobody can deny his qualifications."

Wealthia appealed to her father with a maidenly shudder. "A stranger! I couldn't, Pa. It would be so horrid!"

"But, dawtie," he cried in anguish. "If it should be what you think."

She turned stricken eyes upon him. "Do you doubt me, Father?"

"No, no! Not as to what this blundering impostor claims. But the —the cancer"—he could hardly force himself to utter the word—"surely something can be done."

"To cut for cancer is death," pronounced Horace.

Genter Latham flinched. But Wealthia showed the courage of her breed.

"He's even ignorant on that. There are cures. The medical journ— I have heard of cures. Can you deny that there have been cures?" she challenged Horace.

"Claims," he replied. "Doubtful."

"If I am to be submitted to another examination," said the girl with meek patience, "let it be kind, old Dr. Murchison."

So there it was! Old Murch would provide the diagnosis that was expected of him. Too experienced to mistake a condition so obvious, he would, if Horace correctly read his unprincipled character, agree to perform an operation for the alleged cancer and remove it, though not by the desperate expedient of incision. Thus Wealthia would be relieved of the burden of her misstep. He could not but admire her courage and resource. How cleverly she had turned his revelation, which she must have long foreseen as inevitable, to her own purposes!

Not that Horace had any intention of standing inertly by and permitting an illegal operation to be performed. Unless he was the more mistaken, he could block that little game!

"I should like to be present when Dr. Murchison sees the patient," said he stiffly.

"I will go fetch him, myself," said Genter Latham, cutting short what his daughter had started to say.

She waited until his footsteps on the flagged path beneath the window had passed, then turned upon Horace. At that moment she looked like her father in his blackest mood.

"You saw Kinsey Hayne in New York."

"Yes."

"What did you tell him?"

"Everything."

"You—you false devil! Haven't you any honor or decency? You violated your oath."

Horace could not deny that this was technically true. "I acted as your friend and your father's," he defended himself.

"Friend!" she retorted bitterly. "A fine friend! You only made a fool of yourself. You couldn't make Kinsey believe you."

"He tried loyally not to."

Her face softened. "He is loyal, loyal and fine. He wouldn't betray a confidence."

"When is he coming?"

"Not at all."

"Not after what I told him?"

"I wrote him it was all a mistake," she said calmly. "I told him not to come."

"Wealthia," he said persuasively, "tell him the truth. He is an honorable gentleman. He will make amends. Have him come up here quickly. Or, better still, do you go down there and marry him quietly."

She gazed at him fixedly. "What if I don't choose to marry him?"

"The choice is no longer yours. What else can you do?"

"Remain a maiden."

"A *what?*"

The thrust was cruel. She took it without flinching.

"You have told my affianced and my father. Neither of them believes you. Who else are you going to tell?"

"No one."

"On your honor?"

"Yes."

"If you have any," she qualified. "Does Dinty know?"

"Not yet."

"What does that mean—not yet?"

He made a gesture of impatience. "Wealthia, I can't for my life understand you. Everybody must know before long. Can't you face facts?"

She said clearly, "What difference if I do die under the knife? The cancer is eating away my life day by day."

Horace frowned, seeking a clue to this change of attitude, when their foregoing talk had been based on her tacit admission of her pregnancy. He had the answer when the door opened and Genter Latham appeared. For a man of his bulk, the magnate could walk lightly. He was alone.

"Murchison is in East Palmyra," said he. "I've left word for him to call in the morning."

"I can be here at any hour," said Horace.

"No," protested Wealthia. "Don't let him, Pa. I don't want him. Not two of them. Please, Pa!"

"Why should it be necessary for you to be present, Amlie?" demanded the father.

"It is customary."

"I don't care a fip for your custom. You can see Dr. Murchison after his call if you like."

"Let me have this clear, Mr. Latham. Am I dismissed from the case?"

"Yes," snapped Wealthia.

But some modification of doubt and caution remained to the father. "You are dismissed when I tell you you're dismissed," he said tartly.

Horace swallowed the affront. He was now resolved to maintain his hold upon the situation as long as possible, the better to thwart the skulduggery which he knew to be impending. That he was upon his defense, he well realized. If he was in error, or if it could be made to appear that he was, his career in Palmyra was ended.

All Dinty's blandishments failed to rouse her husband from his somber preoccupations when he got home. He barely answered her anxious inquiries about her friend. No, the condition had not changed. No, Wealthia was not in danger. No, he could tell her nothing further; she'd better go to bed; he had some reading to do in his office. Dinty went, nose in air.

At breakfast he was hardly more amenable. Afterward he called in Dad Hinch to whom he gave low-voiced instructions, before withdrawing to the office. At ten o'clock the Human Teapot returned. Dinty, in her garden, heard him say,

"He's there now, Capting."

"At Mr. Latham's?"

"Yes, sir."

"Get back to your watch. Let me know as soon as he leaves."

The Teapot presented arms with an imaginary musket and marched away in military formation.

An hour later he was back again. Horace sought out Dinty.

"If anything urgent comes in, I'll be at Dr. Murchison's."

Dinty gaped. "At Old Murch's? Why, Doc! I thought you weren't on terms."

"This is not a social call," returned her husband.

Horace had decided to let the older man set the tone of the interview. If he was hostile, it would be hammer and tongs from the start. If he was reticent, the caller would know how to force his hand. If he was amiable, the other would match him in courtesy as long as developments permitted.

The Murchison office was frowsty with dust and faint, bad odors when Horace was ushered in by the feeble old housekeeper. The doctor, said the beldame, had gone upstreet to give his opinion on a pipe of Hollands gin just arrived by freighter. Soon Old Murch came in. His beard was carefully parted; his hair gave off the delicately greasy redolence of pomatum. His smile was all suavity.

"Good morning, good morning," he effused. "It is, indeed, a pleasure to see a colleague here."

"Thank you, Doctor," returned Horace, shaking hands.

"Yes, yes! We may have had our little differences in the past. But now, I venture to believe that our interests are one."

"I am sure they are."

"I have just come from the bedside of my patient—of our patient, Miss Latham."

"Did you make an examination?"

"Er—yes." Horace was sure that he had not.

"And you found?"

"The condition is less grave than the patient believes."

"Self-diagnosis always exaggerates."

"Always. Always. Cancer is not present. I am confident of it."

"I agree."

"Some sort of growth is responsible for the condition."

"I agree."

"Shall we predicate a soft tumor?"

"Again I agree."

Dr. Murchison beamed. "An operation is plainly indicated."

"What sort of operation have you in mind?"

"For the removal of the growth, certes, before it becomes occlusive." He set his long, soiled fingers together by the tips and regarded Horace over the tops of his octagon-rimmed spectacles benignly. "Will you perform it, or shall I? Your young hands are steadier than my old ones."

"Thank you, Dr. Murchison. But I think we may confidently trust to the growth to remove itself."

The cheery confidence, born of Horace's amenity, died out of Old Murch's hirsute visage. "I do not apprehend you, Doctor."

"There are soft tumors and soft tumors. It would be unfortunate for the operator if this one turned out to be a foetus."

The old man reared back like a scared horse.

"Surely the likelihood must have occurred to you, since you made an examination," proceeded Horace blandly.

"Sir! Doctor! You unman me. The daughter of our leading citizen!" babbled Old Murch.

"What has that to do with it?" said Horace impatiently.

"Sir, I decline, I positively refuse to entertain an idea so abhorrent."

Horace's tone changed. He spoke now with quiet but chilling emphasis. "Dr. Murchison, I put myself on record as warning you to perform no operation upon Wealthia Latham."

"Intimidation," blustered the senior. "This is unworthy of our noble profession."

"Abortion," said Horace clearly. "How do you like plain English?"

Without waiting for the reply, he left. His last impression of his colleague was that of a shriveling figure, a pendulous, bearded jowl, and hands that fumbled for a support that was not there. He was satisfied of having put the fear of God into the Old Fraud's soul.

A note from Genter Latham was awaiting him at home. It was in the imperative mood. Dr. Amlie was to expect a call from the writer at two P.M. and was to be alone in his office.

On the previous evening the young man had been agreeably disappointed at his patron's self-control. As to what lay back of it, he was in two minds. At times he thought that the father must surely suspect the truth. Again, he was ready to believe that the man's arrogant pride and hardly less arrogant love would reject any suspicion of his daughter's inchastity, short of irrefutable proof. Well, proof would be unhappily forthcoming in due period. During that encounter, Horace had forced upon himself an attitude of patience and diplomacy. Now, he decided, he would accept no further affronts from Genter Latham.

The clock was between stroke and stroke of two when the office door opened. Genter Latham strode in and stood, legs solidly planted far apart, his tall beaver unremoved from his head, little trickles of sweat making their way along the furrows of his brow.

"Your bill," he grunted.

"Sit down, Mr. Latham."

"Your bill," I said. "You're dismissed."

"You shall have the bill in due time. There is still a matter between us."

"I'll have no further dealings of any kind with you."

"Sit down, Mr. Latham," repeated the physician imperturbably. "Believe me, it will be better for you to listen to me."

"I can listen, standing. Say your say and be done with it."

"I stand by my diagnosis. Wealthia will bear a child, probably in December."

"God damn you for a liar!"

"Dr. Murchison knows what is wrong with her as well as I do. As well as, I think, you do in your heart."

"God damn you for a liar and a fool!"

Horace came out of his chair in a single, lithe movement, crossed to the door and threw it wide.

"Keep a civil tongue in your head or get out," he said.

Amazement paralyzed Genter Latham for a space of seconds. In a quarter century of waxing power and hardening tyranny neither man nor woman had spoken to him after that fashion. His eyes flickered. He wiped his forehead with his coat sleeve and stared stupidly at the dark stain on the blue cloth. Horace, who was holding himself ready for a rush, thought, for a moment, that the bulky form was about to topple. He hurriedly pushed forward a chair into which the other let himself slowly down, still with an expression of incredulity on his swarthy countenance.

"What—what? What—what?" he muttered.

Horace reflected. "Then I am wrong," he said. "You don't know. You must, however, be aware that Wealthia expects Dr. Murchison to perform an operation upon her."

"For the internal growth."

"A criminal operation."

"You're a . . ."

"Wait! Dr. Murchison will not perform any operation."

At this, Mr. Latham recovered himself. "So much for your cockahoop assurance," he sneered. "He told me, himself, that an operation was necessary."

"When did you last see him?"

"This morning. After his call upon my daughter."

"I have talked with him since. I assure you, Mr. Latham, that he will not touch your daughter. He dare not. I have warned him. Now, sir, I extend that warning to you. Procure an abortion upon her, and I will have you in a court of law the day she recovers—or dies."

The big man quivered from head to foot. "Dies?" he whispered.

"The operation is dangerous as well as criminal. Do you wish me to quote authorities?"

"No." Genter Latham pushed himself to his feet. "Now I will warn you. Speak one word against my daughter's character and I'll wait for no courts of law. I'll kill you."

"My professional oath binds me, not your threat," returned the young man calmly. "If anything becomes public prematurely, it will be through yourself."

"How through me?"

"I shall use every means to prevent the commission of a crime. If you take Wealthia away, I shall know why and shall take measures to trace her movements."

"I have no intention of taking Wealthia away," said the father heavily.

"Is that a bargain, Mr. Latham?"

"I will have no bargains with you, sir. My best advice to you is to leave Palmyra at once. Your usefulness here is ended."

"Not my usefulness to myself. Or, perhaps, to others."

"To everyone. I'm going to run you out of town."

"Nobody is going to run me out of town till I get ready to leave," retorted Horace, and his face was as ugly and dogged as his antagonist's.

"Then stay and starve."

"Tell me that in December," said Horace.

Again he half expected an attack. But he could not resist the temptation of reprisal for what he had endured. The other's reaction was quite unforeseen. His massive head went up. There was pride as well as wrath in his bearing as he said quietly,

"Wealthia is my daughter and her mother's. I put my hand in the fire for her. If she—if what you have imagined about her should prove to be anything but the vapors of a foul invention, I will swallow my words and publicly apologize to you. Good day to you, sir, and may it be my last word."

As he stalked out, Horace was moved to a reluctant admiration for his unshakable loyalty, his stupid and touching faith.

8

No great intelligence was required to tell Dinty that all was not well between Horace and his most important family. How deep the breach was she did not know until he said abruptly across the dinner table,

"I'm out of a job with the Lathams."

"That's too bad," said Dinty.

"A difference over diagnosis."

She held her peace.

"Mr. Latham called in Dr Murchison."

"That old noodlepate!"

"Noodlepate or not, his diagnosis was preferred to mine."

"I think you know more than any doctor in the world," said Dinty defiantly.

"Genter Latham doesn't. He dismissed me like a lackey."

"Because you wouldn't knuckle down," said she shrewdly.

"We'll manage without 'em, Puss," said he.

"Wealthy's acting queerly," observed Dinty. "I don't understand her lately."

"Be patient with her," advised Horace. "Nerves," he added vaguely.

In the fortnight after this talk, Dinty saw her friend only on the street. Being forthright by nature, she marched herself up to the stone house to make an issue. Wealthia came down, pale, languid and queerly apprehensive.

"Why haven't you been to see me?" Dinty demanded.

"Pa wouldn't like it."

"Much that would stop you! You always do as you please."

Wealthia's deep eyes dimmed with tears. Dinty ran to her; threw comforting arms about her. "Wealthy! Dearie one! Are you so sick?"

"No. I'm—I'm better. What has your husband told you?"

"Nothing. He doesn't talk to me about his cases."

Wealthia detached herself and sat down heavily. "He and Pa have had a quarrel."

"I know that much. They'll make it up."

"They'll never make this up. Never."

"Wealthy, you're frightened," said her friend pityingly. "Don't you want to tell me what it is?"

The girl put her hand to her side. "Nobody will help me," she said wretchedly. "Horace won't. And now Old Murch won't. They'll be sorry when I die!" She began to sob.

"Darling! You're not going to die. Horace says you're not."

"I don't care whether I do or not. Oh, Dinty, let's not talk about it."

"No, honey," said Dinty soothingly. "But I do think you look better than when I last saw you."

"Do you? Do you truly? Sometimes I think I feel better. Then—I don't know."

"What do you hear from Kin?"

"He keeps begging to come here."

"Naturally. Why don't you let him?"

"I can't bear to see him," she answered somberly. "I can't bear to have him see me. Not when I'm looking like this."

"You're *lovely*, Wealthy," averred the loyal friend, not too untruthfully. "You've changed. Your face is thinner. But you're just as beautiful. More so."

"Faugh!" gulped the girl. "Sometimes I hate myself."

"Write to him to come," urged the caller. "It'll do you good to see him."

A strange look, which seemed to the startled Dinty to have in it the gleam of sheer, desperate terror, distorted the face before her.

"I have written."

"When did you tell him to come?"

"He can come when he likes. He won't come."

"Of course he will!"

The other shook her head. "I'm tired," she complained. "Most of the time now, I'm tired."

Dinty rose and kissed her. "Come and see me," she said. "You needn't see Horace if that's the way you feel."

"Maybe I will, now that I'm feeling better," was the listless reply.

Trouble in her mind was apt to drive Dinty to the woods. She could think better in the leafy solitudes. Back of the garden, the abrupt northern declivity of a drumlin overhung the Latham premises. Dinty made a detour to climb the gentler slope and reach a sheltered spot where she could sit and review the unsatisfactory and puzzling encounter.

Thanks to Tip Crego's training, she could move through brush almost soundlessly. Having reached the summit she turned and was threading her way amidst a sparse scattering of whitethorn, when she halted, stiffening to attentiveness. A whiff of rank tobacco smoke had drifted downwind to her nostrils. She edged back of a thorn-clump and peered out.

A few rods ahead of her a sumach thicket extended to the brink of the hillock. At one spot the foliage was abnormally congested. She wormed her way, bellywise, toward it. As she suspected, the hand of man had been at work. The slender, gray boles were bent and interlaced, the leafage above plaited to form an effective shelter against sun and rain. Beneath the cover, a man sat, puffing an ash-knurl pipe. It was Dad Hinch, the Human Teapot.

Dinty's first thought was to withdraw as secretly as she had approached. A dull gleam of metal changed her mind for her. The Teapot's service musket was propped within reach of his hand. Nothing in the way of game would be moving in the vista below. Therefore, to Dinty's logical mind, it appeared alarmingly plain that if the ex-soldier intended to shoot anything from his hiding place, it must be a human and presumptively a Latham. That she might, herself, be courting danger did not occur to her. In her view, the Teapot was no more than an irresponsible looby. She stepped out into the open, whistling. Dad Hinch jumped to his feet, stared about him, caught sight of her, and stood to attention.

"'Day to you, Mistress," he said.

"Good day, Dad. What are you doing here?"

"Capting's orders, ma'am," said he importantly.

"Who are you going to shoot with that gun?"

"Nobody, Mistress. A good sojer allus carries his weepon."

A flicker of white caught her notice. The Teapot had looped a length of string over a convenient twig. Knots at intervals indicated a pattern. Dinty required no exegesis to explain its purpose. This was a familiar recourse of gypsies, tenkers and other unlettered folk to keep record of fact, time and persons. The whole layout was patent enough to her now. Dad Hinch, an experienced scout and a faithful henchman of her husband, had been set on sentry duty to maintain a watch on the Latham family, make a record, and report to his principal. But what did it mean? What could it mean?

To attempt secrecy with her husband on this matter would be futile. The Human Teapot would assuredly have knotted her into his string. At supper she said,

"I saw Dad Hinch today."

"Where?"

"On the knob, back of the Lathams'."

He scowled. "What were you doing there?"

"I'd been to see Wealthia."

"It's a roundabout way home."

"I felt like being alone."

"Why?"

"Oh—to think."

"It's nothing for you to meddle in, Dinty."

"But . . ."

"Mind you say nothing of this. Not a word to Wealthia, to anybody. You understand?"

Not by habit of mind a meek wife, Dinty understood her Horace well enough to know when she must go cannily. Covering her resentment with what dignity she could muster, she returned,

"When have I ever interfered with your professional affairs, Horace?"

He softened. "Never mind, Puss. You'll understand some day."

"Speed the day," said Dinty.

Since their marriage she had seen little of her mother. Horace and she had dined a few times at the big house, always over his protests. Squire Jerrold frequently dropped in to see her on his way to the Eagle for his social dram which was now a daily ceremonial. But Dorcas Jerrold's animosity had mollified little. Dinty had made her choice between her family and "that upstart"; let her abide by it.

So the young wife's eyes widened, not altogether with pleasure, at sight of her mother entering the garden gate alone. There was a malicious smile on Mrs. Jerrold's delicate mouth.

"That husband of yours has fashed his prospects well, this time," she began.

"How?" said Dinty, instantly defensive.

"By his quarrel with Genter Latham."

"If they have quarreled, it is Mr. Latham's doing."

"So he tells you, doubtless."

"He doesn't need to tell me. I know it."

"Mr. Latham has sworn to chase him from town."

Dinty's small and resolute chin went up. "Let him try!"

"Do you know what the trouble was about?" asked the mother curiously.

"No."

"I believe you do, but you won't say. Just like your high-minded uppishness."

"I don't. But if I did, I wouldn't tell."

"My poor child! Wedded to a pigheaded and reckless young nincompoop. When he has lost his practice and been driven from Palmyra in disgrace, you will be glad to find a home with us."

Dinty's small chin set solidly. "Where my husband goes, I go. Don't fret yourself, Ma. It will take more than Genter Latham to drive us from home."

"Wait and see," was Dorcas Jerrold's parting shot.

Apprehension sharpened the young wife's powers of observation. She noticed, or thought that she noticed a change of bearing on the part of some of the leading citizens toward her husband. Cordiality was waning. There was an attitude of caution. Genter Latham's enmity, though not yet overt, was beginning to tell. All the town knew, of course, that there had been a split between Dr. Amlic and the Latham family; that Dr. Murchison had supplanted the younger man. This, of itself, was a detriment to the Amlie prestige.

Horace's efforts on behalf of the communal health were impaired. Hostility toward his clean-up measures, never wholly eliminated, stiffened now that the great man was presumptively no longer backing them. Ephraim Upcraft, always a barometer of public feeling, drove a scavenging crew from his premises. Augustus Levering, whose compost heap had waxed in fragrance with every humid spell, threatened legal processes. There was talk of a memorial to the village trustees, protesting against the invasion of property rights by the special constable. Horace's uncompromising reply to criticism was that Palmyra could take its choice between filth and health. Anyone who wanted to stink and die, let him go elsewhere and do it. The suggestion, while liberal, did not make its proponent more popular.

Try as he might, Horace could not conceal his increasing concern from his wife. He announced one morning that he was taking the boat to Rochester to consult with Dr. Vought on public matters. Dinty suspected that one very private trouble might be thrashed out between them. She knew her husband's respect for his old mentor's judgment.

"It'll do you good," she approved. "You're working much too hard."

While he was gone, the post brought a letter in Kinsey Hayne's handwriting. Dinty could hardly believe her eyes when she saw, large, blue and oval in the upper center, the impress of the post office of mailing. It was Port Royal, S. C. Kinsey had gone back home, then, and without seeing Wealthia. Less than three months from the date set for the wedding. The thing was inexplicable.

Horace returned from his two-day stay looking refreshed and with the gleam of battle renewed in his eyes. Dinty handed him the post.

"Kinsey has gone back south," said she.

Horace stared at her as if not fully comprehending. "Surely not!"

"Look at the post-office print-mark."

He examined it, forced the overfold with care so as to avoid damage to the writing on the reverse, glanced at the inside, and went into his office, closing the door behind him. Two minutes passed. Dinty did not consciously listen, but she heard a sound interpretable in only one way, the *spitt* of steel against flint. Horace might be lighting his pipe to facilitate thought. Or . . .

The door opened. Horace appeared. His face was heavy with thought; distress, too, it seemed to Dinty. He was not smoking. He said,

"Dinty, is Wealthia still betrothed to Kinsey Hayne?"

"I don't know."

"Hasn't she said anything to you about him?"

"Yes. She said she had written to him."

"When?" he asked quickly.

"The last time I went there."

"Anything else?"

"She said that she didn't want to see him until she was feeling better and she thought he wouldn't come up."

"Apparently she was right."

"You're worried about it, aren't you, Doc?" she ventured.

"If I am, it mustn't go any further."

Plainly that was all that she was going to get out of him on the subject. After he had left on his rounds, she entered the office and scanned the fireplace. On the otherwise clean hearth there was a black, curled ash, and a thick, unconsumed fragment of the outer sheet which had carried the address. Dinty thought lugubriously that her husband might have trusted her with the substance of the letter, at least. Why must he be so secretive? She felt put aside, set apart from his interests and concerns.

Sorrow for Wealthia, disappointment in Kinsey Hayne, and a

sense of uncertainty and frustration over the whole affair, seethed in Horace's mind, as he wen about his calls. The Southerner had written:

> Owing to information recently received, I have now to tender you my humble and heartfelt apologies for my erroneous aspersions upon your veracity and character. I beg, sir, that you will not think too harshly of an unhappy man, and I invoke your charity toward an unhappy woman.
>
> We shall not meet again. I trust implicitly to your honor to destroy this letter at once and to hold its content inviolably secret. Believe me, sir, the brief friendship which I was privileged to enjoy with your lovely wife and yourself has been a bright spot in an existence which can end only in darkness. I am, sir, with profound respect,
>
> Your humble servant,
>
> KINSEY HAYNE.
>
> Post Scriptum—May I say, without offense, that an answer to this would be unavailing?

For some reason not clear to himself, the final sentence had struck a chill to the reader's heart.

9

THE first sign of waning popularity noted by Dinty was a diminution of cash receipts in ratio to barter. Several prominent names were crossed off her books. The Dillards and Fairlies now canalled to Rochester or coached to Canandaigua for their ordinary doctoring. George W. Woodcock belched his dyspeptic complaints in the sympathetic ear of Old Murch. Mrs. Van Wie bore her fourth baby with the aid of a midwife. L. St. John had his neck-boils lanced by L. Brooks, M.D., the barber.

In all this the hand of Genter Latham was patent. It did not extend to the brotherhood of the smithy, which stuck staunchly to Dr. Amlie. His canal and backwoods practice increased steadily. This was somewhat less remunerative than the best of the village patronage. Though total receipts were less, the little financier was still able to set aside a substantial sum toward the satisfaction of the note at the bank. When the fight should come into the open, she did not want her Horace beholden to the great man in any degree.

Mr. Latham no longer spoke to her when they met on the street, but restricted his acknowledgment of her existence to a dour jerk of the head. After two or three repetitions, Dinty went him one better by haughtily gazing over his head. With Wealthia, however, her relations remained affectionate. The two chums visited back and forth freely, though both chose hours when the men-folk would be absent. By mutual and tacit consent, the matter of the quarrel was avoided.

It was still a mystery to Dinty. Her mother's theory failed to satisfy her.

Further elucidation, if such it could be called, came from Mrs. Jerrold who stopped in, market basket on arm, for another chat. Two visits within a fortnight! Was it an overture for family peace? At the expression of petty triumph on her visitor's face, Dinty dismissed that idea and set herself on guard. Something unpleasant was coming.

The conversation opened with conventional housewifely complaints as to the dearness of market staples. Eggs had gone to a penny apiece. One could not be sure of good salted butter at less than fifteen cents a pound. A rise in butcher's meat was threatened; presently they would all be reduced to living on venison and wildfowl like penniless woodcutters.

"You'll feel the pinch, my poor child, in your straitened circumstances," prophesied the mother.

Dinty's eyebrows elevated themselves delicately, a manifestation which could be relied upon to annoy Mrs. Jerrold. "I'm sure I don't know what you mean, Ma."

"You're not going to tell me that your husband isn't losing all his patients!"

Dinty chose to present her own interpretation. "People do die, naturally," she said. "We've lost a few. But new patients come in to fill their places."

Mrs. Jerrold sniffed. "If Dr. Amlie lost them only by death! Having them quit him is so much worse. Though I'm sure I don't know what else he could expect."

"Pa's asthma is improving, isn't it?" said the daughter brightly if inconsecutively. "Horace has always been so successful with respiratory complaints."

Mrs. Jerrold's eyes snapped. "I suppose he was treating Wealthia Latham for asthma."

"Perhaps I forgot to tell you, Ma, that the Doctor doesn't discuss his patients with me."

"Then you don't know what's being freighted about?"

"I don't want to," valiantly lied Dinty.

"It's high time you did, for your own sake. People are saying that your precious husband told Mr. Latham that Wealthy is in the family way."

Dinty flushed furiously. "It's a lie. How could she be? I mean, Horace would never make such a vile accusation."

"Ask him."

"I won't."

"You're afraid to. Or you're so dozened on him still that you wouldn't, anyway."

"I never heard anything so wicked and silly in my life," said Dinty, recovering her poise. "Wealthy have a baby! Why, she isn't even married yet."

"Did I say she was going to have one? Nobody says that but your husband. Dr. Murchison, when he was called in, exposed the pretensions of ignorance finely."

"I suppose the old blab-mouth breached it to you," said the wife contemptuously.

"Never mind where I learned it," retorted Mrs. Jerrold, who did not care to admit that she had been listening to servant-maid's gossip. "Now you know what sort of a man you've married."

"I don't believe a single word of it," declared Dinty stoutly. "And you can just tell whoever told you that if she doesn't stop her mouth, we'll have the law of her."

"There'll be lawing before all's said and done maybe," returned the matron darkly. "But it won't be you that calls for it."

In spite of her doughty disclaimer, Dinty's heart quavered. Could Horace have committed himself to so disastrous an error? Something deadly serious had arisen between him and Mr. Latham. The quality of the autocrat's fury attested to that. With sickening realization, she admitted to herself that her mother's version would go far toward explaining the crisis; the sudden violence of the feud; Genter Latham's silent vengefulness; Horace's secrecy. If the thought flashed to her mind that Wealthy might, indeed, be "in the family way," she dismissed it instantly as being against the evidence. For, whatever had ailed the girl, she was quite plainly getting better, not worse. If the old insolent charm and careless gayety had not wholly returned, at least she was improved and steadily improving both in spirit and body. How could that be if she were carrying an illegitimate child? It was absurd. And Horace must know it. The whole thing was foul gossip and idle malice.

Nevertheless, she meditated long as to going to her husband about it. What good would it do? If she tried to lead up to the subject, she would only lay herself open to being told, tartly or indulgently according to his mood of the moment, to mind her own business. Tartly, in all probability. Horace's temper had been growing more and more uncertain lately.

On his part, Horace had marked with incredulous astonishment, that betterment on the part of his ex-patient which had so impressed his wife. The improved ease of body he could account for readily enough. This would be, by his reckoning the fifth month. Normally the physique should by now have adjusted itself to the new demands. But only by enlargement. The puzzling, the inexplicable feature was that while Wealthia's gravidity had been evident enough to his expert eye a month or so earlier, it now seemed to be lessening or, at worst, stationary.

Naturally he lacked opportunity of satisfactory observation, since the girl shunned him. Such casual encounters as those of the public streets, however, convinced him that there was something abnormal about the case; it was not apparently taking the course which he had so confidently forecast. Over-confidence? He refused to admit that possibility. It added nothing to his comfort to mark Dr. Murchison's smug smile when they met. On one such occasion, the hirsute physician brought the matter to speech.

"Do you still maintain your diagnosis in a certain case of mutual interest, Doctor?" he inquired slyly.

"I do."

"The symptoms hardly bear you out."

"Depends on who interprets 'em," growled Horace.

"You will admit that I am in better position to judge of my patient's state than you are."

"I don't count your judgment for *that.*" He rudely illustrated with a finger-and-thumb snap.

The old fellow was unperturbed. "The growth is abating under my medication."

Horace snorted and passed on. Abating, was it? A very gradual, almost imperceptible abatement. Too gradual for a miscarriage. Besides, Wealthia had not been bedridden for so much as a day. The Human Teapot's watchfulness assured him of that.

For further evidence, he fell in back of the girl when next he saw her on Main Street, and followed unobtrusively noting her figure and gait. There could be no doubt on one point; the slender grace of her form had thickened; not to the point of incipient unwieldiness, but still unmistakably to an eye familiar with her earlier outlines. His uneasy cogitations were interrupted by a small hand, slipped through his arm.

"What are you glooming about, Doc?"

"Oh! Hello, Dinty. Coming home?"

"No. I'm meeting Wealthy at Miss Blombright's."

"The dressmaker's?"

"Don't look so dumbstruck. Why not?"

"Is Wealthia interested in new clothes?"

"Isn't every girl?"

"She must be feeling better."

"Oh, she is! Heaps," replied his wife with enthusiasm.

Horace became Machiavellian—or so he considered himself. He drew his wife aside. "I'm still interested in Wealthia as a case," said he. "Could you get me her waist and bust measurements? Then I'd like to know what they were—well, say last winter. Miss Blombright keeps her patterns, I suppose. Could you find out without Wealthia's knowing? Pretend that you're going to knit a sickroom jacket for her."

Dinty eyed him sorrowfully. "Oh, Doc!" she murmured. "Are you still nursing that crazy idea?"

His chin jerked up. "*What* crazy idea?"

"Nothing," said she hastily.

"What have you been hearing?"

"I don't know what you mean." It was a sadly feeble disclaimer.

"This is no place to talk. Come home."

Dinty pulled away from him. "I can't. I've got an agreement for three o'clock with Wealthy."

"It can wait. Come with me."

Miserable and scared, she trotted along beside him. She was in for it now! He held the office door open for her, and closed it behind them.

"Now, Araminta," said he.

"Are you going to be mean to me?" she asked doubtfully.

"I'm going to have the truth out of you."

"Because if you're horrid, I'll run away."

"What is this crazy idea you accuse me of harboring?"

She drew a long breath. "That Wealthy was going to have a baby."

"So she is."

"Doc! I don't believe it."

"Don't you? Where are your eyes? And you, a doctor's wife."

"It can't be true. It must be something else."

"So she told her father. He believed her lies. That is why I was turned off."

"But—but—but, I don't understand. How could she be . . . ?"

"In the usual course of nature," was the grim reply. "It began when Kinsey Hayne was here in April."

"Oh, no! Not Kinsey!" she cried.

"Who else would you suspect?" he asked sardonically.

"No one," she hastened to assure him. "But—but if it were so, wouldn't he know?"

"He does know. He's run away from it."

"Never!" exclaimed Dinty. "Not Kin. He'd never do that."

"I wouldn't have believed it of him, myself," Horace admitted. "But Wealthia is here and he's in South Carolina. What else can you make of it?"

"That you're wrong," she said solemnly. "Oh, Doc, I can't help it if you hate me for it; I *know* you're wrong. Why, look at her now."

"I don't hate you for it, Puss," he said more gently. "Suppose I told you that she as much as admitted her condition to me? She told Hayne about it, too. He wrote me."

"Is that the letter you burned?"

"Yes. I've no right to be telling you these things, Dinty. But I want you to understand. I can have the whole village against me and stand up to it. But I can't have my own wife against me."

"I could never be against you, darling. You know that, don't you? No matter how wrong and pigheaded you were."

"If I'm wrong in this, I'll never believe in myself again. Now, Dinty, where did you get this precious bit of gossip?"

She shook her head. "Please don't ask me, Doc."

"I can guess. Has it gone far, do you think?"

"I—I'm afraid so."

"If it reaches Genter Latham there will be hell to pay."

"Are you having the Lathams watched still, Doc?"

"Yes. Dad Hinch reports to me every day."

"What for?"

"To let me know of any preparation for their going away."

"Why shouldn't they go away if they want to?"

"Try to get it through your mind, Dinty. I'm fighting for my professional honor; for everything in the world that I've got. You can see how it will work out. If Kinsey Hayne won't marry her . . ."

"She doesn't want to marry him," broke in his wife.

"Did she tell you that?"

"No-o-o. Not exactly. She's been peskily queer about him."

"It's possible that she's turned against him," reflected Horace. "Pregnant women sometimes take strange fancies. Whatever the reason, if marriage isn't in the offing, there is only one recourse left her. If she leaves Palmyra now, it will be to have a criminal operation performed. That I am determined to prevent if I have to follow her to the world's end."

"Horace! You scare me when you look that way."

"Nobody is readier to admit it when he's in the wrong than I am. What did you say, Dinty?"

"Nothing. I coughed. Can't I cough if I have to?"

He glared at her, then continued, "But I'm right on this. And you're going to be forced to admit it."

Saturday morning's mail was a heavy one. Horace stuffed a medical journal, two newspapers and a half dozen letters beneath the cushions of the gig, and went on about his professional duties. Several cases of special interest so absorbed him that when he reached home, he had quite forgotten everything else. When he came in empty-handed, his wife asked,

"Didn't the post come in today?"

"Eh? Why, yes. Yes, of course it did."

"Nothing for us?"

His brow wrinkled. "I'm sure there was. Now, what did I do with it?"

"Doc, do you realize how absent-minded you're growing?"

"Am I?" He passed his hand across his forehead. "I suppose I am."

"You're brooding. You mustn't, darling. I can't bear to have you worried."

He shook his shoulders as if disburdening himself. "I remember about the post now. It's in the gig."

"Sit still." She pushed him back into his chair. "I'll get it. I'll fetch you a nice refreshing drink, too. There's a jar of shrub cooling in the well."

She gathered the mail, carefully drew up the bucket, spiced the innocuous shrub with a lacing of elderberry cordial and a handful of mint sprays, and made him drink a tall glassful before she would give him his letters. One of the papers she held up.

"Dr. *and* Mrs. Amlie," she read. "Why, it's from Kin! How nice!" Her expression clouded as she opened the copy of the *Charleston Courier*. "Doc, you don't suppose he's gotten married?"

"Probably," grunted her husband, tossing aside a Literature Lottery solicitation sent him from college.

"I don't see anything marked," she said, running her eye down the columns. A moment later she added disgustedly, "It must be this medical article on the front page. You and your old fevers!"

She tossed it to him and he dipped into it. "Interesting. Very interesting," he remarked. "They've appointed a committee to investigate the new outbreak of agues along the Santee Canal."

"I don't believe that's it, at all," declared Dinty. "What does Kinsey Hayne care about the shakes? And why should he address it to me? I'll warrant there's something else. Let me look again when you're through."

He returned the weekly to her and lost himself in the pages of the *Medical Repository*. His reading was interrupted by a choking sound. He looked up. Dinty's face was pale and convulsed. Tears coursed down her cheeks. The hand holding the journal shook so that the paper rattled.

"Oh, Doc! Oh, Doc!" she gasped.

He jumped up, ran to her, caught her in his arms. "What is it, darling?"

"Kin. He's dead. It's in the paper."

She could scarcely control her hand to point to a small paragraph without caption, on an inner page. He read it.

> As we go to press we learn of the tragic death of Kinsey Hayne, Esq. of Beaulieu Plantation, Beaufort County. Mr. Hayne was hunting wild turkey when his fowling-piece was accidently discharged. Death was instantaneous. A wide circle of friends will mourn this highly esteemed young gentleman, scion of our state's proudest old aristocracy . . .

He let the paper fall. Dinty was moaning, "Oh, poor Kin! Poor Wealthy!" Her eyes widened; her jaw dropped. "Doc! It was in his handwriting. How could he send us the paper when he is dead?"

"Are you sure it was his?"

Both examined the cover. There was no room for doubt. Horace's face became stern. His logical mind had reached the solution.

"It was no accident, Dinty," he said slowly. "It was suicide."

"How do you know? Why should he?"

"I suspected that he had it in mind, from his last letter. He must have laid his plans to kill himself and left directions that the next issue of the *Courier*, which he knew would report his death, should be mailed to us. With the directions, he wrote out the address. His agent pasted the address on the paper and mailed it. It's perfectly clear."

"Yes, so far. But, Doc, why should he kill himself?"

"You don't know what those old plantation families are, my dear. To marry a pregnant girl and bring her home would have meant ostracism for both of them. He couldn't face it. Wealthia had kept it from him as long as she dared. When she gave up hope finally and faced her condition, she wrote him, probably begging him to come back and marry her. This is his answer, poor devil!"

Dinty's lower lip, still tremulous, nevertheless protruded in the familiar aspect of obstinacy. "I don't believe it and I won't believe it. Nothing shall persuade me but what Kin Hayne was brave and true and honorable."

"And you still don't believe that Wealthia is pregnant?"

At this Dinty broke completely. "Oh, poor Wealthy!" she wailed. "What's to become of her?"

"God knows!"

"Darling, you've got to save her."

"How?"

"There's a way. You know there's a way."

"Not for me."

"How can you be so hard!"

"Would you rather have me a criminal?"

"Yes," said Dinty defiantly.

"Women have no moral sense." He regarded her with a sort of awe.

"What good will it do you to let her be disgraced? What good will it do anybody?"

He sat down heavily, leaned his elbows on the table, and put his head in his hands. "The old, old argument," said he wearily.

"I suppose you want *her* to kill herself now."

He was silent.

"If she does, you'll hate yourself forever."

Still silent.

"And I'll hate you," she whispered.

He lifted his head and stared at her. She ran to him, sobbing. "I won't. I couldn't. You know I couldn't. But, oh, darling, give her a chance!"

"What kind of chance?"

"Let her go away. She can find someone, do something. I know she can."

"I'm beginning to think that you know too much."

"I'm not asking you to do anything, yourself. Only give her a chance," she pleaded.

"And if she dies, taking that chance?"

"That would be better than the other."

"Have you thought that, if she has the operation and comes back here, clear, I shall be made to look a criminal fool in the eyes of Genter Latham? It's ruin for both of us, my girl."

"I've considered that, too," said Dinty. "You must get a signed paper from Wealthia admitting the truth. That will fix Mr. Latham."

Horace gave in. "It's wrong, wrong, wrong. But I can't stand out against you."

Dinty hugged him. "Bless your heart, darling! I'd have *died* if you had refused me."

"It's for you to tell Wealthia about Kinsey."

Dinty shrank. "Don't you think she knows?"

"I doubt it. Kinsey had the paper sent to us so that we could break it to her."

"I'll do anything you want," said Dinty, "now that you're so good. Shall I go there now?"

"Yes. And bring her back here with you. Don't say anything about the—the other matter. I'll attend to that."

The two girls came to his office by the back paths in the first darkness. Wealthia displayed a frozen immobility. To Horace's expressions of sympathy on the death of her lover she returned a dull acknowledgment. Upon a silent signal from her husband, Dinty left the two together. Horace said, "Wealthia, if for any reason you wish to leave town, I shall make no objections and ask no questions."

"Why should I leave town?" she returned defiantly.

"I think there is no need of my answering that question," said he with dignity. "At the same time, I am bound to warn you that there is grave danger in the course which you are contemplating."

"I am not contemplating anything."

"Then you intend going through with your pregnancy here?"

At the word, she winced. A faint touch of color stained the pallid face. "I am not pregnant. I swear it."

"Stand up," he commanded. As she hesitated, he repeated more sharply, "Stand up."

The confidence of professional authority brought her to her feet.

"Lift your arms."

Again she obeyed.

He said, "Have you been taking drugs?"

"No."

"There may have been some arrestation. It has that appearance. The phenomenon is not without precedent. But there can be no reasonable doubt of your condition." More gently, he added, "As long as poor Kinsey was alive, you could still hope for honorable marriage."

Still in the same deadened accents she said, "There has never been anything of that kind between Kinsey Hayne and me. I swear it."

He ignored the denial. "What are you going to do?" he inquired.

"Nothing." With sudden savagery, she added, "You're the one that must leave town, Horace Amlie. And in disgrace. Good evening to you."

Dinty, waiting, heard the outer door close. Wealthia had left. But Horace did not emerge. She went in. He sat, sprawled in his chair, his face upturned.

"What did she say?" she demanded eagerly.

"Nothing."

Dinty stamped her foot. "Horace Amlie! Tell me."

"Very good. If you will have it, she as good as notified me that the Lathams are going to drive me out of town."

Dinty's soft mouth set to an uncompromisingly grim level. "She's siding with her father?"

"What would you expect?"

She said steadily, "Wealthy is my best friend. But you are my husband and my love. I'm never going to speak to her again."

The anger died out of his face. He shook his head. "No, Dinty. I don't want that. She's going to need you. You can't quit her that way in her need."

"Now you're being a noble Christian," retorted Dinty, her lips taking a disdainful quirk. "Well, I'm not noble. And I'm not *that* Christian."

"Neither am I, altogether," he returned and, as she gazed at him questioningly, added, "It's partly a matter of policy. I don't ask you to spy on Wealthia, but if you stay on friendly terms with her, you may pick up something that will be useful to me."

"How can I stay on friendly terms with her when she hates you?" said Dinty hotly.

"She doesn't. Poor child—she isn't herself. Try to keep that in mind, Puss. No pregnant woman is quite normal. And consider what poor Wealthia has on her mind."

Once more she ventured to express the doubt that still gnawed her. "Doc, are you certain, live-or-die sure?"

"Absolutely."

"Then I believe it. When is she going away?"

His face changed. "She isn't going."

"Doc! Not going? What else can she do? What does it all mean?"

"God knows," he answered dully. "God only knows."

10

No other reputation is so vulnerable as a physician's. A whisper, a rumor, an unfounded hint may compromise the confidence of his community. Horace now understood well enough that a campaign, informulate as yet, but none the less malign, was under way. While there was no way of tracing the innuendoes, he knew pretty well what was being said of him.

His heterodoxy of method and open contempt for old-school practices was attacked on all sides. Doubtless Old Murch was influential in this. According to that authority, the young harebrain had let Gammer Needham die of a dropsy rather than bleed the excess out of her. Parson Messenger of the Baptist church would have succumbed to a bloody flux when Dr. Amlie dogmatically refused to abate the evil with further purges, had not Dr. Murchison taken over the case and cured it by the classic treatment of calomel, more calomel, and still more calomel, fortified with squills and tartar emetic. To be sure, the parson had not left his bed since. Nevertheless he was indubitably alive. Dr. Amlie advocated wholesale throat-slitting for swollen tonsils (this being an echo of the fight for Dinty's life); what mother would be so reckless as to put her child at the mercy of such barbaric practice? His mosquito and fly fiddle-faddle was the laughing stock of older and wiser medicos: had not a leading New York journal published an editorial ridiculing "this addled, western upstart who had 'foisted such absurdities upon a helpless community'?"

Nor was his personal character immune. He was the chosen attendant of the malodorous Settlement. Who could know what secret malpractices he performed there for such money as stank in the nostrils of the righteous? Then, too, there was that scandalous private consultation room of his, to which lady patients were taken alone and compelled to disrobe, on the specious pretext of diagnosis. What devilment went on there? One story had it that he had attempted to abuse his professional privilege with the beautiful Wealthia Latham and that, when she rejected his dishonorable advances, he made foul accusations against her. Araminta Amlie, it was pointed out, sided with her friend against her husband. Were not the two girls constantly seen together?

"My daughter is too proud to complain," Dorcas Jerrold confided to her intimates, "but if all were known . . ." It ended in a maternal sigh.

"Genter Latham threatened to shoot him," Mrs. Levering whispered into the nearest ear at the sewing bee, thereby insuring a general circulation. "Watch him slink when they meet on the public thoroughfare."

The watchers were disappointed. Slinking was not in Horace Amlie's character. In fact, he was beginning to bear himself defiantly, which was the next worst thing.

The first overt move against him was when the village trustees voted away Special Constable Amlie's badge. That marked the revocation of official effort to keep Palmyra clean.

"All right," said Horace to his wife, through thinned lips. "Let 'em rot. Wait till the August rains fall. See what they'll make of the fevers then."

The rains fell in profusion. Muck-heaps and garbage piles gave forth their effluvia. Flies swarmed. Mosquitoes bred and bit. By one of those phenomena which still confound medical science, the village escaped the natural penalty of its negligence. It was an exceptionally healthy fall. Dr. Horace Amlie and his theory were thoroughly discredited.

"Never mind, my darling," said loyal Dinty. "They'll be dying like flies next spring. I hope they do," she added viciously.

"Where will we be next spring?" muttered her husband.

"Is it as bad as that?" she asked, wide-eyed.

"I'm losing patients every week."

This was partly the fault of his prickly pride. One of his earliest clients, Jim Cronkhite of the locks, sent him a note asking him to visit his daughter who had broken out in a rash. And would he mind coming under cover of dark?

"Why should I?" demanded Horace, meeting him across from Stone-Front Sarcey's.

"Sshh!" cautioned the canal man nervously. "Come over here." He led the way into a vacant lot.

"Well?" said Horace.

"My lock's a political holding," explained the keeper.

"What of that?"

"Mr. Latham got me the place."

"I see. Understand this, Jim. I make my visits openly or not at all."

"That's no way to keep your friends," returned the politician. "I'll call in Old Murch."

A more hurtful blow was a late evening call from Jed Parris, who hauled up his trouser-leg to exhibit a tetter on the knee.

"These aren't my office hours," said Horace suspiciously.

"I know it, Doc. I couldn't get around earlier."

"You were in town all afternoon."

The big teamster squirmed. "Look, Doc. I got the teamin' for Old Man Latham's oats and rye. You know how it is. I dassen't be seen comin' here. You and me are good friends, Doc. I wouldn't want to quit you. You can see how it is, can't you?"

"Did Genter Latham threaten you with loss of your teaming?"

"No. He ain't spoke a word. But everybody knows how it stands between him and you. It ain't healthy to go against Genter Latham."

"I'll treat you this once," said Horace. "But not again unless you come like a man."

"Don't say that, Doc," pleaded the big fellow. "Livin's hard in the freightin' line since the goddam canal. I gotta think of myself."

It was an ugly foretaste of the Latham power. If, by the mere tacit influence of his hatred, the autocrat was able to blackmail Horace's patients away from him, what would it be when that potent enmity was exercised in the open?

A more insistent preoccupation now obsessed Horace's mind. Wealthia Latham was evincing no signs of approaching maternity. Changed she certainly was, but she was changing no further. This was obvious beyond denial. The possibility of error forced itself upon him. If he had thus fatally misinterpreted the situation, how could he ever absolve himself from responsibility for Kinsey Hayne's tragic death? He was ready to resolve that never again would he overstep the strictest limitations of medical privilege. Yet, in moments of calm reasoning, he could find no reason for changing his opinion. Aside from the inescapable physiological evidences, Wealthia's earlier attitude had been tantamount to a confession. The grisly question was, would he be able to prove his case?

Through the rest of the summer and fall, the Amlie practice slowly dwindled. No longer could Dinty save out from the household surplus more than enough to carry the interest on the loan. Finances of the pickle-jar remained at the same level; new winter finery for her adornment was a vanished dream. A favorite evening diversion of the couple had been to get out her home-drawn plans of the projected cobblestone house and become absorbed—sometimes embattled—over such alterations, usually in the form of enlargements, as two lively and ambitious imaginations could devise. Her draftsmanship, for which she had a natural bent, now remained in the top drawer of the Butler desk by tacit consent, segregated but unforgotten.

In both minds one subject was uppermost; it was seldom mentioned. Wealthia Latham was back in full current of village life, but with a difference. She was now more given to good works, and less to adornment and coquetries. Nevertheless there was no lack of suitors, local and foreign. She was still the best match of the region; heiress of a rich man growing yearly richer, a powerful figure, gaining monthly in influence and authority. If her beauty radiated a less obvious allure, if it was less consciously seductive, it had lost little of its luster.

To all suitors she was equally and gently obdurate.

"It isn't natural," declared Dinty. "Wealthy isn't like that."

"Natural enough to her condition," returned Horace.

"Oh, her condition!" said she with a peculiar intonation. There was a long pause. "Satch Fammie is back again," she said.

"I saw the gyppos' pitch on the Jerusalem Road."

"She isn't there. She's staying with Quaila Crego at the Pinch. Why don't you go to see her?"

"What for?"

"I think she knows something."

"About Wealthia?"

"Yes."

"So do you, I suspect. More than you're telling me."

Dinty was silent, looking away from him.

"I'm not trying to force your confidence."

"There are things that I remember and put together since—well, since what you told me. I do think you ought to see Satch Fammie, Horace."

He assented. How much he could get out of the old crone was doubtful, he thought. He knew her to be friendly to him for services rendered once when she was mangled by a watchdog, and thereafter when she brought her rheumatic joints to him; he knew, also, the secretiveness of the Romany when dealing with the Gentile. Attack would be his best method. If he could frighten her, she might give up her secret, assuming that she had one.

Quaila Crego was absent when he reached the Pinch, and the gypsy was puttering over a cooking fire with a skinned muskrat dangling from the crossbar. She dipped him a curtsey, then squatted down, her black eyes glittering out from the stained parchment of her face.

"How are you, Satch Fammie?" he asked.

"Better of my misery, kind gentleman."

"Have you been taking the boluses?"

"They're all gone, kind sir."

"I'll send you more."

"Thank you gently. What can old Satch Fammie do for your service? Read the leaves and the stars for you?"

"Tell me the truth," he answered with sudden sharpness. "What did you do to the Rich Man's chal?"

The touch of Romany startled her. "No, no, kind gentleman, kind doctor. Nothing!"

"Don't lie to me, Satch Fammie. You performed an operation." This was pure venture but worth trying.

"No, no!"

"You tried to."

"No, no. By my God!"

"When did you last see her."

"I passed through in July. She came to me."

"You gave her a brew."

"Camomile tea," she quavered. "Only camomile tea, kind gentleman."

"Not seven-sisters weed?"

"No, kind doctor. By my God! I couldn't risk."

"Too far gone?" he asked, holding her eyes with his gaze.

She nodded mutely.

"You have said nothing of this to anyone?"

"May my tongue be drawn out and roasted on a fire."

"See that you don't. It would be better for you to drown yourself in the canal. The boluses will be delivered tomorrow."

"Thank you, kind gentleman. Bless you, kind doctor."

So much was settled, then. Wealthia had been desperate enough over her condition to appeal to the reputed Wise Woman for rescue. Satch Fammie was, he believed, telling the truth in claiming to have resisted the girl's importunities. Thus far his theory was borne out. But the mystery of non-progress in symptoms remained static.

He braced his soul for the coming attack by Genter Latham. December was the expiration date of their formal and hostile treaty.

The magnate, now assured of his unassailable position, did not wait. The first warning came to Horace late in November, from Carlisle Sneed. Dropping in at the smithy for the late afternoon confab, a practice which he had almost abandoned since his marriage, Horace was greeted by the village wit.

"Here comes Old Pestilence."

"I'm out of the pestilence trade since they stripped me of my badge," said the newcomer good-humoredly.

"Never thee mind," said the smith, handing him a freshly filled glass. "Thee will have the laugh of those sillyjohnnies yet."

"Him?" cried the jocund Sneed. "Why, he's the pest, itself, I've seen it in print."

"What's this?" demanded Decker Jessup. "What print? The paper isn't out for this week. Clap your clam to."

"It's not the paper. It's a broadside. Tom Daw showed me the printer's take. A rouncher!" He grinned at Horace.

"I'll go fetch one if I have to break that hunchback's neck," said Jed Parris.

He crossed to the newspaper office and presently returned, a single-sheet fluttering in his hand. In ink still fresh, a headline stood out blackly:

WARNING! A PEST IN OUR COMMUNITY

"The town'll be papered tomorrow," said he. "He's ordered one hundred and fifty struck off."

"Who?" cried a dozen voices.

"Guess for yourselves. There's only one would do this trick."

Horace read. It was a scurrilous screed of invective evenly divided against his professional capacity and his personal character. No signature was attached. The subject of the attack rose, impassive and deliberate, and took up his beaver.

"Where you goin' Doc?" queried Carlisle Sneed uneasily.

"On an errand."

Silas Bewar heaved up his bulk. "I'll go with thee, friend."

"No," said Horace.

The group sat silent for minutes after he left. O. Daggett shook an ominous head. Carlisle Sneed took a deep inhalation of the Superior Blend and sneezed convulsively. Decker Jessup plucked the broadside from Jed Parris's hand, twisted it into a spill, touched the end to the glowing ash of the forge, and lighted his pipe.

"Looks likely for rain," remarked the teamster, when the stillness had become uncomfortable.

"Now, as to Andy Jackson and his stringing up that Britisher," began O. Daggett in the contentious snarl appropriate to contemporary politics, "I say . . ."

What he was about to say was interrupted by a dozen voices, and the assemblage was off in full gallop of tongues on the hottest topic of the day, glad to get away from Horace Amlie and his peril.

Horace went straight to the stone mansion. Genter Latham was not at home; would Dr. Amlie come back later, asked the goggling house-hussey whom Wealthia had sent to answer the door. No, he would wait. He pushed past and took a chair. There he sat for two hours, supperless.

In an upper window, Wealthia waited for her father's step on the path. She ran to meet him.

"Pa! Horace Amlie is here."

"Where?"

"In the library. Since six o'clock."

"Go upstairs."

"Pa! You won't do anything—terrible?"

"Upstairs!"

She obeyed, but not at once. She stopped to gather his musket and fowling-piece from their rack in the hall and take them with her, to hide them in her clothespress.

The master of the house lighted a taper, walked into the dark library and set the flame to the two mantel-lamps. The caller rose. Genter Latham said, "What's your business in this house?"

Horace answered with an emphasis equally peremptory. "Your broadside."

"It will be on the street tomorrow."

"You don't disavow it."

"Why should I?"

"This is not December."

"You fool!" said Latham in black contempt.

"Fool I may be. I keep my given word."

"I consider myself released," retorted the older man negligently.

"I have not released you."

Latham dismissed that with a curt gesture. "Do you wish to remain in Palmyra?"

"I intend to remain in Palmyra."

Almost gently for him, Latham said, "It might be possible, on conditions."

"Unconditionally."

"I think not." The words were accompanied by an ironic smile. "Sit down."

Horace remained standing, while his host drew open the hinged upper of the chest-desk, established himself, and selected a pen. He wrote slowly and laboriously, crossing out, recasting, pondering. On a second sheet of paper he set down a fair copy. This he handed to Horace.

"Read it," he ordered. "Aloud."

Ignoring the second part of the command, Horace ran his eye through it, noting with grim satisfaction a wavery quality of the script, testimony to the writer's nervous tension. At what strain upon his self-command he was holding himself under control, the caller could pretty justly estimate. At any moment, upon any provocation it might break out in violence. Outmatched though he was in weight and power, in everything but courage and inner wrath, the visitor, while not there to provoke a fight, was in no mood to shirk one. His combative spirit was not ameliorated by what he read.

> I, Horace Amlie, M.D., by my hand herewith, do retract, withdraw, and confess as false my diagnosis of the physical condition of Miss Wealthia Latham. I further testify that any and all allegations by me reflecting upon her character, virtue and chastity are baseless and malicious lies, for which I humbly ask pardon. This statement I make of my own free will and conscience and without other compulsion.
>
> (Signed)

Horace lowered the paper from the lamp by which he had read it and faced the writer. Latham rose and motioned him to the vacated chair.

"Sign there," he directed, his finger on the sheet.

"If I don't?"

"You'll be sorry to the last day of your life."

Horace took the seat, cleansed and dipped the pen, crossed out three words and substituted one for the elision. With the alteration, the clause now read:

> . . . any and all allegations by me reflecting upon her character, virtue and chastity are baseless but unintentional error.

He handed it back to Latham. The magnate's eyes glittered.

"Squirming, huh?" said he. "Can't face it like a man. I'll give you that much leeway." He flattened the paper on the desk again. "Sign."

"There are two conditions."

"What are they?"

"First, it is to be dated January 15th."

Genter Latham's laughter was harsh with contempt. "Still hoping," he commented.

"Second, that your daughter undergo an examination by a competent medical expert, not Dr. Murchison."

"No!" roared Latham.

"You refuse?"

"Yes, by God!"

"For the reason that you're afraid of what an honest diagnosis would reveal."

In that moment he thought that the attack was coming. He could see the eyes redden, the muscles quiver. Again the autocrat mastered himself. He went to the door.

"Wealthia!"

Her voice, faint and scared, answered from above, "Yes, Pa."

"Come down here."

"I can't, Pa. I've gone to bed."

"Come down at once."

No word was spoken between the two men until she appeared. She paused in the doorway, one hand uplifted to the lintel for support. Her eyes met Horace's in what he was almost ready to interpret as appeal, before they shifted away.

"This man wants you to go through another medical examination."

"I wouldn't let him touch me," she said defiantly.

"Not by me, Wealthia," said Horace gently. "By any physician of good repute that you or your father may choose."

"But why, Pa?" she pleaded of her father. "Why should I? I'm well again."

"It isn't a question of your present health," put in the visitor. "You know what the matter is. Your father has put it in writing."

He held out the paper to her, but Latham intervened. The girl burst into sobs.

"He's insulting me again."

"There's your answer, Amlie. Sign and get out."

Horace deliberately tore the paper into four pieces which he let fall on the desk. Genter Latham, purple now, rushed into the hallway. They heard his furious cry:

"Wealthia! Wealthia! My weepons!"

She ran to Horace. "Go! Oh, please, go! I've hidden them. Go before he finds them. He'll kill you."

Prudence pointed out to Horace the reasonableness of the plea. Reluctant, but making no resistance, he let himself be half pushed out the side door. Until the gate closed behind him, he could hear the seeker raging through the house.

Palmyra had two sensations in the morning. The scurrilous broadside was everywhere, having been distributed before dayfall by the *Herald's* devil. Hardly less a subject of animated discussion was the news of Genter Latham's openly enunciated threat: if Horace Amlie ever set foot in his house again, he would get a charge of lead through his gizzard.

-11-

To Palmyra the Latham philippic was a declaration of war and boycott. In fact, it had concluded with a demand upon "all good and lawful citizens" to abjure the attendance and shun the "companionship and activities of this miscreant." The smithy debated it at length, recalling dire instances of the weight of Genter Latham's past disfavors. The general opinion was that Horace Amlie could not hope to stand out against the autocrat.

"He's a used-up man in this village," declared Bezabeel Fornum.

"I've got nothing against Doc," said George W. Woodcock. "But I've got my trade to think of."

"A man oughta consider his family first," said Jim Cronkhite.

"The Lathams are my best customers," stated T. Lay.

"They're everybody's best customers, mostly," added Billy Dorch.

"The bank holds my note," said Fornum.

"It holds a lot of notes."

"And Genter Latham is the bank."

"What's your view, Silas?" asked Woodcock.

"I tend my forge," answered the Quaker peacefully.

"You fellas put me in mind of young mead-larks in spring," remarked Sneed.

"How's that, Carly?"

"Yellowbellies," snickered the wit. The sally won no laughter.

"There's no yellow on my belly," averred O. Daggett, glaring sourly around the circle. "I stand by my friends."

Tom Daw piped up. "What's it costin' you?"

"You know too much," grumbled the sign-painter, discountenanced.

"Newspapers have to know everything," boasted the hunchback. "The bank's took an' h'isted his interest from twelve percentum to eighteen," he imparted to the gathering.

"Without so much as by-your-leave," confirmed the victim of this fiat finance.

"They say the devil gathers news with his tail," observed the humorist in not too subtle reference to Daw's humble position as press-devil.

The little fellow swelled pleasurably over the attention he was enjoying. "What about Mr. Latham's bespoken boots, Decker?" he asked.

"Canceled," grunted the cobbler.

"And with the leather already cut to measure, I hear."

"I ought to have the law of him."

"Who ever lawed against Genter Latham without getting the tar-end of the stick?" asked Jed Parris.

"That's what you must expect for being a friend to Doc Amlie," Woodcock warned the cobbler. "It'll cost you many a good dollar before all's said and done."

The gossip-freighter was not discharged of all his cargo yet. "They say Doc Amlie's mare slipped and fell with him yesterday."

"Will you blame that to Genter Latham?" came T. Lay's sardonic query.

"She needs re-shoeing," opined Billy Dorch.

"Will you do the job, Silas?" asked Parris.

"Why not?" said the smith serenely.

"Genter Latham might catch you at it," suggested Cronkhite.

"Up, Jenk!" called Silas.

The patient dog climbed to the treadmill. The forge glowed afresh.

Some days later Fleetfoot was left at the smithy while her owner made his calls afoot. The watchful Daw went scampering up the street, and shortly after, Genter Latham sauntered down, fragrant smoke from his segar benefiting the nostrils of the passers-by who gave him obsequious greeting. He paused at the smithy where Fleetfoot was waiting her turn while Silas Bewar tinkered with an oxbow. The great man removed his segar from his mouth and entered. The smithy was empty except for the proprietor and his dog.

"Good morning to you, Silas Bewar," said the caller affably.

"Good morning, Friend Latham."

"Is that Horace Amlie's mare?"

"It is, friend."

Latham walked around her, inspecting. "She's wearing down," said he disparagingly. "I've an ailing stallion at home," he added. "I'd like you to take a look at him."

The Quaker enjoyed something of a reputation as a veterinary consultant, but had voluntarily relinquished this practice to the more scientific M.D., who frequently found it more profitable than his human calls. Horses do not run up bills nor expect charity attendance.

"Thee had better call upon Horace Amlie," said the smith.

"I'll have no dealings with that scoundrel, and well you know it, Silas Bewar."

The smith continued his work.

"How long will you be?" asked the magnate impatiently.

"I've a nest of kettles to run over, and then to shoe the mare."

"Let the mare wait."

"First come, first served, friend."

The great man glowered. "I'm not accustomed to being put off."

The smith placidly tapped an iron band into place, surveyed his workmanship with care, and lifted the weighty apparatus aside. Genter Latham's veins swelled in his forehead.

"Did you hear me?"

"I heard thee, Friend Latham."

"Then why in hell and damnation don't you answer?"

"I'll have no profane swearing in my smithy, friend."

"You'll have no smithy this time next year, by God!" shouted Latham, now beside himself. "I'll drive you out of business. I'll break you."

The smith said, without altering his pacific tone, "The wrath of the ungodly wasteth as a vain wind. Peace be with thee, friend."

Genter Latham repaired to the Eagle to cool his fury in a jorum of iced, minted rum. His ailing stallion was largely a figment; there was nothing wrong with the animal worse than a swollen hock which he had used as a pretext to serve notice on the smith as to the disadvantages of continuing to do business with Horace Amlie. He had another errand for the morning in which he counted upon being more successful.

When the leading member of the congregation called, the Reverend Theron Strang was in his study, writing his sermon and taking care of the three youngest children while his wife was downtown trying to convert part of last week's contributions into cash. The magnate came to the point at once.

"Young Amlie's pew-lease is up at the month's end. I shall not renew it."

"Why, Mr. Latham?"

"He is a disgrace to the church."

"That is a grave accusation. With what do you charge him?"

"Immoral practices. Foul and slanderous speech. Irreligious conduct."

"I know nothing of this. Do you intend to prefer formal charges to the presbytery?"

"No." Genter Latham had no mind to air his grievances before a tribunal.

"By what right, then, would you deprive him of his place of worship?"

"Look you, Dominie; I've got the pew leaseholds for the church, haven't I?"

"This is the House of God," said the minister firmly. "Do you presume to dictate who shall worship here?"

"I've got the law back of me."

"The law of man. There is a law of God that is higher. If you turn a parishioner of mine out of his pew, I will seat him in the pulpit."

"So do, so do," growled the autocrat. "I won't be there to see it."

"Is this a threat?"

Genter Latham rose ponderously. "Take it as you choose. Good day to you."

He left the house. With him went one-fifth of the pastoral salary of $500 per annum, as the sturdy incumbent well knew.

It was worse than that. On Sunday morning not only the Latham sitting was vacant, but there was not a Levering nor an Evernghim to be seen in the congregation. Rumors were already circulating that a movement was afoot to vote the parson out at the close of the church year and supplant him with Exhorter Sickel. Elder Strang possessed many Christian virtues, but meekness under aggression was not one of them. That very evening the church rafters rang to a defiance based upon the text, "Thy money perish with thee." Dr. and Mrs. Horace Amlie were among the few edified listeners who appreciated the full meaning of the discourse.

Dinty now began to feel the hand of the oppressor heavy upon her barter operations. Prices withered before her. Several stores declined to deal with her on any terms, alleging that they were overstocked. T. Lay, after a shamefully low offer, put it frankly.

"That's my price. Take it or leave it. I'm running a risk in trading with you at all."

Unable to clear out her stockroom of its accumulation of fees in kind, Dinty borrowed her husband's wagon and mare, drove all the way to Macedon Village beyond the radius of the Latham power, and there made her sales. It was but a makeshift. Winter was close at hand. When the roads were clogged with snow, that market would be unavailable. She felt daunted.

Christmas was a meager festival for the Amlies. Dinty put a brave face upon it and set forth to the best effect such socks, mittens and tippets as her busy fingers had found time to knit secretly. Horace gave her a bangle from the whitesmith's which, he stoutly maintained, he was well able to afford. Of tasty food there was no lack; the stockroom was always good for that. The housewife graced the feast with a bottle of plum brandy which had been ripening in a charred keg. They dined alone. The had invited her parents, but they declined, Mrs. Jerrold tartly, the Squire with eyes averted and a timorous and miserable expression. Dinty surmised that there was truth in the rumor of his increasing involvement at the bank.

At dead of night, Horace Amlie awoke with the impression that something was wrong.

"Dinty!"

"What?"

"You're crying."

"I'm not."

He gathered her into his arms, feeling her whole slender body shake against his. "What is it, Puss?"

"Oh, Doc! I'm frightened."

"What about?"

"Here it is, past Christmas," she burst out, "and there's nothing. Nothing! I saw Wealthia yesterday. You said it would be in December. What are you going to *do?*"

"Have you lost faith in me, Dinty?"

"Doctors have been wrong before. I don't know what to believe," she answered distractedly.

"I'm not wrong," said he with passionate conviction. "Nothing on earth can persuade me that I am wrong. Something has happened. I don't know what. Something. I'll find out if it's the last thing I ever do."

"Another thing, Doc. We're living up every cent you make."

"Then we must cut down. Let Unk Zeb go. I can do the rough work."

"Unk Zeb won't go. He says he'd rather work for you, free gratis, than take a wage from anybody else."

"There must be other economies."

"Of course there are," said Dinty, rallying. "I can make do. We're always sure of our food and firing. Doc, have you got any bills out?"

"No. Well, maybe a few. The tailor. And the harness-maker. One or two others. Nothing much."

"Oh, Doc!" she wailed. "Haven't I told you we must always pay cash? Debt scares me so! It's my own fault for wanting you to look fine and pompous."

Upon her insistence, Horace withdrew from the Eagle post-board his announcement of free inoculation for immigrants and indigents, but he stubbornly refused to give over the practice. Vainly his wife proved by irrefutable arithmetic that he was losing not only time but money by this and other charities; he replied that when he had to turn away a patient for lack of cash, he would quit medicine and become a banker.

To her dying day Dinty could not recall without a shudder the first formal dun. It was in the form of a small dodger from the job press; a tasty bit of print in the best style of Burr Butler, poet and tailor, designed to jog the torpid consciences of his slow-paying clientele. It fluttered in, together with a whirl of snow, at the front door when Dinty opened it upon a blustery January morning. The legend read:

> We ask for our pay.
> Now make no delay,
> Or sue you we will
> And add costs to your bill.

Below was written in a stylish hand: "Aug. the 15; To one Brocade Waistcoat—$4.00."

Dinty quivered with mortification. Horace cursed.

"I'd forgotten all about the damned thing."

"How can we pay it?"

"We can't just now."

"Then you'll be sued and we can never hold up our heads again."

"I'll jostle up some of my overdue accounts."

"I made the rounds last week," said his wife. "Three shillings, cash. The rest, promises and excuses."

Unk Zeb set down the coffee pot which was steaming forth a dubious aroma of roasted Evans root, Dinty's home-made substitute for chocolate.

"I got fo' dollah," he said. "I got six dollah."

"Why, Unk Zeb! Where did you get all that money?"

"Neely's Lucky Office." This was the low-priced lottery which dealt in fractional chances down to one-fiftieth. "Lucky for Ol' Unk Zeb," he chuckled.

Husband and wife looked at one another. The exchange was a mutual negative, but Dinty could not repress a sigh of renunciation as she said,

"We can't take your money, Unk Zeb."

"Whuffoh you cain't?"

Both explained more volubly than satisfactorily to the old man, who retired to his woodshed, grumbling to himself.

Failing to elude Burr Butler in the street, a few days later, Horace was the astonished recipient of the tailor's thanks and apologies, together with a receipted bill. From the effusive explanation offered, it was not quite plain whether Horace was expected to regard the poetic dun as an error or a joke. What was clear enough (to Mr. Butler) was that Horace, like an honorable gentleman, had immediately sent around his "nigger" with cash for the bill. The poet-tailor solicited the honor of Dr. Amlie's further patronage.

There was nothing to be done about it. To spare Dinty further humiliation, Horace decided to keep the transaction secret.

A worse thing befell, which permitted no concealment. On the fourth day of February, Dr. Horace Amlie received a curt, official notification from the Board of Censors of the State Medical Society citing him for malpractice, unprofessional behavior, detrimental ignorance, and conduct prejudicial to the honor of his high calling.

-12-

By stated course of procedure Horace Amlie, M.D., should now have been cited by the District Attorney to present his defense before the Judges of the County Court. The roster for the session, however, was abnormally crowded. The bench had no time to devote to a long-drawn, technical and non-criminal process. Upon suggestion from Albany they appointed a three-man medical commission to convene at Palmyra, take testimony and report its recommendations. The accused was well satisfied; at least, he would be heard by a jury of his peers.

An angry letter from Dr. John G. Vought caused him to change his mind.

> A packed panel, my lad. I tried to get on it. Blocked by monkey-doodle politics in Albany. Someone is pulling the strings who does not like you. An ignoramus, a quack, and a doddering old sumph; that is the make-up of your precious commission. They intend to serve you for breakfast, fried and garnished.

Weather permitting, the commission would sit at the Eagle Tavern, March 15th, 16th and 17th. It was made up of Dr. Paul Bolger of Geneva, Dr. Thaddeus Smith of Rochester, and, to lend dignity and authority to two such dubious appointments, the old and respected Dr. Luke Avery of Oneida County in the chair. Inquiry convinced Horace that his friend's forebodings were well-founded. Dr. Bolger, having proved a failure in the enlightened village of Geneva, was known to be looking about him for a more propitious field of activity (and why not Palmyra if there should be a vacancy?). Dr. Smith was an aging, blustering diploma-less graduate of a six-month road-course as aid to a regular physician. Dr. Avery was eighty-two years old.

As sponsor of the charges, Dr. Gail Murchison would act as prosecuting counsel. Back of it all, as Horace well knew, was Genter Latham. But how to prove it? And of what avail, if proved?

On the afternoon of the day before the hearing, a small, robustious, bristly man, his reddish hair and beard flecked with gray, stamped up the steps of Dr. Amlie's office, kicked the mud and slush from his elegant boots, closed the door behind him with a bang, tossed his bearcoat upon a chair, and let out a lusty bellow.

"Pot-boy! Pot-boy!"

Dinty came in from the stockroom. She was in housework clothes, her hair was fluffily disordered, a slate pencil stood back of her ear, for she had been at her reckonings, and her azure eyes were wide and lovely with astonishment. Her natural assumption was that the author of the stentorian call was drunk. This inference was supported by the form of address adopted by the singular-looking person, upon seeing her.

"Chuckabiddy!" said he.

"Sir?"

"I want a drink."

"This is not the inn, sir."

"Listen, my ducky. My feet are damp. My nose is a freshet. I'm all a-shiver. I come to the house of a friend and the daintiest little kicksie-wicksie these old eyes have viewed for many a day advises me that this is not an inn."

"A friend?" said Dinty, beginning to wonder.

"The gaudy shingle without advertises this to be the office of Horace Amlie, M.D."

"Office hours, nine to eleven, two to four," she pointed out.

"These young medicos are an easeful lot. Not as in my day."

"Oh, my goodness me!" exclaimed Dinty in sudden enlightenment. "You must be the learned Dr. Vought."

"You recognize me," he said with satisfaction. "How?"

"By your gracious manners," answered Dinty demurely.

He threw himself into a chair, roaring with laughter. "My reputation precedes me."

"Your reputation for science, also, sir. Have you come to aid my husband?"

"Husband? At your age, child?" He regarded her short skirts and unruly hair with frank surprise. "Surely you're not . . ."

"Mrs. Dr. Horace Amlie, at your service."

"Pox and pestilence!" said the stubby little man, projecting himself from his seat. "And I took you for a pretty schoolgirl." He made her a low and not ungraceful bow. "*Apologia pro audacia mea.* Have you the Latinity, ma'am?"

"So much as academy schooling gives."

"*Aut potio, aut mors,*" he roared. "Translate me that."

"By the deed if not the word," she returned and made for the kitchen.

Presently she was back with a jorum of steaming rum toddy. "That should save you from death, sir," she said.

"We shall get along, you and I," predicted the great Dr. Vought, a moment later, lifting his dribbling mustache from a draught that would have scorched the lining out of a less hardy throat.

By the time Horace got back, the two were fast friends and the visitor had acquired a shrewd notion of the local cabal.

"So, it's Mr. Genter Latham that's back of this," he observed.

"There's no doubt of it," answered Horace.

"With Sir Pertinax McSycophant for his lackey. Our friend, Gail Murchison, M.D., save the mark! I've a rod in pickle for that sorry shyster."

"He has a strong following."

Dr. Vought snorted. "Our highty-tighty, high-and-mighty banking man might be due for a surprise, too. I have been making some investigations at home on my own account."

"Into his financial operations?"

"Not exactly that. Wait and see."

"Does this mean that you will assist me at the hearings?" asked Horace eagerly.

Dr. Vought thumped his chest, looking like a ruddy gorilla. "Is John G. Vought one to stand idly by and see the best pupil he ever taught set upon by a pack of medical wolves, and never lift a hand? Count upon me, my boy. I have visited Dr. Avery and demanded a public hearing."

"What for?"

"To get that old fraud of a Murchison into the open."

The lust of battle burned in his eye. Horace suspected that there would be more attack than defense in his method, that he would be as much concerned in holding up to contempt Murchison's ineptitudes as in exculpating the defendant. Very well. Since the case was evidently forejudged, they would at least give the other side a fight.

The hearings were well patronized, Palmyra having a keen scent for a free show. Genter Latham was there, looking stern, and surrounded by satellites, with Honest Lawyer Upcraft at his elbow. His daughter did not attend. On the other side a small group of Horace's supporters, made up chiefly of the smithy coterie, surrounded Silas Bewar. After the proceedings had opened, the Reverend Theron Strang arrived, pointedly went over to Horace to shake his hand and whisper a word of encouragement in his ear, then joined the blacksmith. Still later, Squire and Mrs. Jerrold entered. He gazed about him in painful indecision, but his wife plucked him imperatively by the sleeve and they seated themselves near the village mogul. Dinty, who was with her husband, clutched at his arm for a moment, before returning her attention to the jury which was to determine the future fate of the Amlies.

The chairman, a venerable and benign figure, divided his time between taking stuff to keep himself awake, and drowsing off between pinches. Dr. Bolger, a weasely, alert little man, entered squeaky notes on a slate. The rotund Thaddeus Smith fortified himself behind a rampart of volumes. Dr. Gail Murchison, ensconced at a special table, pored solemnly over a sheaf of papers.

Rapping for attention, Chairman Avery prepared to present the charges. Dr. Vought rose and addressed him deferentially.

"May I put a question, sir?"

"What is Dr. Vought's status here?" The interruption came from Lawyer Upcraft.

"What's yours?" snapped the redhead.

The lawyer ignored the question. Dr. Avery asked mildly,

"What is your question, Dr. Vought?"

"As medical counsel for the accused, am I permitted to call witnesses, sir?"

"For what purpose?" intervened Upcraft.

"Does the commission wish to know our purpose?" asked Dr. Vought pointedly.

The Chairman glanced uneasily at Mr. Upcraft. "It does," he answered.

"Very good. To show prejudice. To prove that this persecution is engineered by a person outside the medical profession." He slowly turned his body to face Genter Latham. "To support the honorable character of the accused."

Three committee faces converged, to be joined by the hairy countenance of Dr. Murchison, and the parched, lean features of the Honest Lawyer.

"You may call such medical witnesses as you see fit," decided the Chair.

"Since the prosecution enjoys the privilege of gratuitous legal advice from a lawyer privately retained, may we not avail ourselves of lay support?" inquired the Rochester man blandly.

"The point is, I think, well taken," said the old gentleman, and Vought whispered in Horace's ear, "He is going to be helpful if we can keep him awake."

The Chair was speaking again. "In due order the Chair will determine the competency of witnesses, as called. I will now read the charges, duly filed against Horace Amlie, M.D., of Palmyra in Wayne County, State of New York, and subject to the authority of the medical body which I have the honor to represent."

The indictment (drawn privately by Dr. Murchison with the aid of Lawyer Upcraft, and adopted in toto) was divided into eight heads.

Malpractice.

Soliciting patients away from established practitioner.

Self-advertising.

Advancing and supporting theories repugnant to medical science.

Ignorance prejudicial to the public weal.

Immoral associations.

Interference with private rights and infringement upon property.

Employment of dangerous medical methods.

"We plead innocence of one and all," said Dr. Vought. "We demand confrontation with our accusers, both overt and" (again the deadly pause and stare at Genter Latham) "covert."

"The commission will hear from Dr. Gail Murchison," said the Chairman, and incontinently dozed off.

The prosecutor opened with a semi-tearful disclaimer of any personal bias against his young associate and one-time friend, Dr. Amlie, notwithstanding that gentleman's notorious and baseless spite against himself.

"What says the learned Dr. Benjamin Rush?" inquired Dr. Murchison and answered himself, "That 'physicians in all ages and countries riot upon each other's characters.' I have been the humble and unresisting victim of such riot at the hands of the accused. Far be it from me, however, to make that the basis of the witness which I am compelled, however reluctantly, to bear against my young and misguided colleague. No! Protection of the health and welfare of my fellow townsmen alone constrains me to this painful duty."

"Was it protection of health and welfare that constrained you to maintain a nuisance in your back yard after Special Constable Amlie was relieved of his duties of guardianship?" inquired Dr. Vought mildly.

"I appeal to the commission for protection against such vile slurs," cried the prosecutor in distress of soul.

Awakened by the poignancy of the cry, the Chairman feebly clutched his gavel and called Dr. Vought to order.

Dr. Murchison continued his discourse with frequent references to his notes. It was evident that he had compiled a complete dossier on Horace Amlie, covering the events since the young physician opened his office. The presentation took up the entire session.

"He's a better lawyer than doctor," murmured Vought in Horace's ear. "But wait till I get at him."

Horace replied that Upcraft had undoubtedly prepared the case and would be at hand to pull the wires of its further conduct.

"I'll give him something to think about, too," promised the other.

The second session was taken up by witnesses to Dr. Amlie's civic offenses. Augustus Levering had surprised him "sniffing at my compost heap under cover of darkness, like a thief in the night, gentlemen; a thief in the night." T. Lay's three small offspring, although not patients of Dr. Amlie ("I wouldn't have him and his newfangled foolishness in my house") had been violently and illegally removed by him from a muck-pool where they were engaged in innocent play. He had barred from school the son of Michael Duryea because of a rash which had never been satisfactorily proven to be malignant, even though the child did die of it. He had invaded Simon Vandowzer's freehold and had without warrant captured and removed flies and other winged insects therefrom. "*My* flies," said Mr. Vandowzer grievously. He had wantonly threatened J. Evernghim in the matter of an alleged stench in his barnyard, which turned out to be nothing more unusual than a stray lamb, not very recently deceased. Among them they made him out to be a lawless invader of civic rights under the shallow pretext of conserving what he termed the public's health. Dr. Murchison punctured that flimsy bubble.

"The public's health!" he snorted. "The public's got no health. Has the public got disease? If it hasn't got disease, it hasn't got health. Health and disease are private business between the licensed physician and his patient." (Applause.)

Further testimony was adduced to show that Dr. Amlie had attended a performance of the farce, *Tricks of the Times,* and had, as Dr. Murchison put it, "laughed consumedly at its wicked and derisory slanders upon our noble profession" (Dr. Vought made a note); that he had stigmatized sundry valuable medical processes as "old wives' superstition" and "legalized witchcraft"; and that he had publicly and contemptuously made reference to remedies which were embodied in the newly appeared work *A Pharmacopoeia,* as "panaceas and catholicons, the fruits and symbols of medical knavery." His visits to the Settlement were brought out in the worst possible light, and the prosecutor hinted that in his private office, with immense stress upon the first word, he invited his female patients to disrobe for examination. (Dr. Vought, sotto voce: "How do you make *your* diagnoses? With a spyglass?")

It was over at last, leaving the accused with hardly a shred of character wherewith to bless himself. Dinty leaned over to whisper in his ear, "You're an awful villain, Doc, but I love you."

Dr. Vought arose, paid his respects to the commission, and addressed Dr. Murchison.

"You have referred to a farce, *Tricks of the Times,* sir."

"I have, sir."

"Did you attend the performance?"

"I did not. I would not so demean myself."

"Perhaps you are familiar with the subject of its sarcasms. I will read you a passage, descriptive of a species of M.D. which you may recognize as authentic." He drew out a paper and read from it:

> If one may believe his claims, he never loses a patient in any form or degree of fever, in croup, dropsy of the brain, or infantile flux. In his hands, even the pulmonary consumption is a manageable disease. Does he attend church of a Sunday? Through a servant or retainer he contrives to be called out once or twice in the session as if to administer to the wants of the sick, who must, we are thus led to suppose, incontinently die at once without his immediate care. He constantly exhibits himself in his gig or on horseback, hurrying from one quarter of the town to another, as if just called to apply the trephine, reduce a recent and painful luxation, control an alarming hemorrhage from a divided artery, or to minister in some other form of disease where delay and death would be synonymous terms. Thus, in the hands of such as he, are artifice and intrigue employed as substitutes for science and skill.

"What purpose has this wastage of the commission's valuable time?" demanded Upcraft.

"A portrait," replied Dr. Vought blandly. "Dr. Murchison ought to recognize it."

"Sir!" shouted the amateur prosecutor, exhibiting pre-apoplectic symptoms, "do you presume to attribute . . . ?"

"Excuse me," interrupted his tormentor. "I have not completed the selection. I resume." He continued:

> And the treatments: Bleed, bleed, bleed; purge, purge, purge; sweat, sweat, sweat. For every affliction which he fails to understand—and where is to be found one that he does?—he falls back upon his favorite recourse, wherewith he and his kind have slain their thousands; pepper potions, lobelia pukes, and one-to-six of the henbane muck.

Up rose Upcraft. "If this diatribe be directed at our honored fellow citizen, I beg to point out that Dr. Murchison is not upon his trial here."

"I propose, gentlemen of the commission," retorted Dr. Vought, "to show that this process, from which the defendant now suffers, takes its rise from the physician whose pen-portrait I have just presented; from his rancor against a younger, abler and more honorable rival who has already alienated from him numbers of his important and profitable patients; further, that this malpractitioner is supported in his nefarious designs by a powerful local influence whose enmity Dr. Amlie has incurred in the pursuit of his duty as a medical man. Will Mr. Genter Latham take the stand?"

There was a moment of petrified silence, shattered by Genter Latham's explosive, "No, and be damned to you!"

"You refuse?" The effect of surprise and disappointment were admirably feigned. "Surely, sir, you do not fear to submit to questioning which leads only to clarification. . . ."

"I fear nothing. I say to hell with you and your questions."

"If you decline, I must seek further," pursued the other. He stretched on tiptoe to scan the crowded room.

"What in tinkum is he up to?" whispered Dinty to Horace.

"I haven't a notion," he responded in the same tone.

The harsh voice inquired, "Is Miss Wealthia Latham present?"

"Oh, Doc!" shivered Dinty. "You put him up to this."

"I tell you I didn't! There'll be hell to pay if he goes on."

The silent tension of the room communicated itself to the Chairman to the extent of rousing him from torpor.

"What's this? What's this?" he said. "The young lady is not a competent medical witness."

"Am I, then, confined to medical testimony?"

"For the present. Until the commission has reached a decision."

"I bow to your authority, sir, and call Dr. Thaddeus Smith."

"What do you want of me?" asked that gentleman distrustfully.

"You are a certificated practitioner of medicine in Rochester?"

"I am."

"In April or May of last year were you visited in your office by a young lady who was at first reluctant to give her name?"

"I don't know what you would be at," blustered Smith.

"Look at Mr. Latham!" said Dinty under her breath. The magnate had hunched forward in his chair. "This is all new to him," she continued.

"And to me," muttered Horace.

"I am waiting," said Dr. Vought.

"Don't answer," vociferated Lawyer Upcraft. "What is the purpose of this outrageous line of questioning?"

"Merely to establish," answered the ever-bland Dr. Vought, "that Miss Latham, originally a patient of Dr. Murchison and afterward of Dr. Amlie, called professionally upon Dr. Smith; that the worthy doctor was thereby encouraged to hope for a profitable connection, or even for a foothold in Palmyra, should one of the two medical tenancies be vacated, which is, as I understand it, the purpose of this hearing. Self-interest in him is conjoined to revenge in Dr. Murchison, to operate to the prejudice of my client."

While he was speaking, Lawyer Upcraft had crossed over to mutter in the witness's ear. Dr. Smith now said with vast dignity, "I decline to answer a question which is improperly put to seduce me into violating a professional confidence."

"Then I request an adjournment," said Dr. Vought, having planted his barbs.

Horace could hardly wait to get him alone before asking, "What's this about the visit to Smith?"

Vought nodded sagely. "It's correct. Early last spring."

"How do you know?"

"I have my ways," chuckled the other.

"How much more do you know?" frowned Horace.

"Take the witness stand yourself. You haven't told me the whole truth. What's the row between you and Latham?"

Horace made no reply.

"Professional confidence again? Better tell me."

"I think you know too much already."

"I think I know it all," returned the other crisply. "No thanks to you. Wouldn't I have been a fool to come here without planning out my campaign! It began before I knew anything about your trouble; before you had any, I guess. It's Smith. We've been watching him in Rochester. He's been under suspicion for several years. Ladies' relief." He winked a wicked eye.

"An abortionist?"

"We lack full proof. He had a scare that made him cautious. Maybe that is why Miss Wealthia's visit had no result. Or did it? She didn't go there for her complexion, you know."

Horace heaved a sigh of relief. "If you know that much, I can tell you the rest," said he, and did.

Dr. Vought took full time to digest it. "It's a nasty mess," he pronounced. "You staked your reputation on December?"

"I did," said Horace with a wry face.

"And you stick to it?"

"How in hell can I stick to December when it's now March?"

"Don't bark at me, young fella. You stick to it that she's still in that condition?"

"I do."

"Then she got rid of the first one."

"The first one?" repeated Horace in a maze.

"Certainly, the first one. Ladies have been known to get pregnant twice. Even unmarried ladies," twinkled the rubicund doctor.

"I'll swear there's been no tampering since last summer. I've had her watched."

"Then what is your theory?" asked his senior curiously.

"You've had far more experience in that line than I. But couldn't there be a delayed process?"

"Once in a blue moon. No, my boy; you'll have to do better than that."

"By the way," said Horace, "I don't remember any such passage in *Tricks of the Times* as the one you quoted."

"Good reason why," sniggered his mentor. "It isn't there. I was saving up that blast for Murchison, waiting to find an opening, and when he gave me that one, I took it."

"Why are you so hot on his trail? And why antagonize Smith? I don't understand it," complained Horace.

Dr. Vought became sober. "They're going to strip you, my boy.

May as well take the diploma down from the wall. We're fungoed from the start. I'm building up a case of prejudice for appeal to the full board. We can't stop this, but we might get you reinstated. It will take time, though."

"How much time?"

He shrugged. "A year. Maybe more. Maybe two. Large bodies move ponderously."

"And what am I to do in the meantime?" demanded Horace angrily. "Turn quack with a bell and a bottle and vend cure-alls from the tail of my cart?"

"There are other states. A New York writ runs only for the lands within its bounds."

"Leave Palmyra?"

"If you can't live here you must leave here."

"Let Genter Latham brag he's run me out of town? By God, I won't!"

"Good lad! I wouldn't, in your place. Stay and fight it out. I only hope you're right."

"I'm right."

The other reflected. "Could I see this Latham wench?"

"Professionally? I don't see how."

"Not professionally. Not even to meet her. Observation, merely."

"I'll ask my wife. She knows Wealthia's ways."

Dinty reported that the girl would be attending the Missionary Society meeting at three o'clock the next afternoon.

The two doctors were free at that hour. The final session had closed with a single sitting, devoted to Dr. Murchison's summing-up, a performance so lawyerish that the Upcraft coaching was apparent in every sentence. Dr. Vought's rebuttal was a diatribe, vastly enjoyed by the audience but frowned upon by the commission, which then withdrew for a secret session, fortified by a liberal order from the taproom.

Mid-afternoon saw the visiting expert, escorted by his host, strolling down Main Street in casual enjoyment of the sights. As they dawdled along, Wealthia Latham, arm in arm with Happalonia Upcraft, passed them. They accelerated their pace to keep close behind the pair for a block. Dr. Vought's scrutiny was unobtrusive but careful. He expressed himself as satisfied and in need of a pipe. Seated beside the Amlie fireplace, he asked abruptly,

"Who's her lover?"

Horace's eyes brightened. "Then you agree with my diagnosis?"

"I'll stake my reputation on it. There's something about the gait of pregnancy. I couldn't describe it to a classroom, but I'd swear to it anywhere. Yes, lad, your town beauty has been carrying more than her prayer-book."

"You think she's still carrying it?"

"I hardly know what to think. Last April, you say?"

"All the evidence points to that date."

"Except the final proof."

"Which should have come in December."

"Ah, yes. Too far overdue, eh? You didn't say who the lover is."

"He's dead."

Dr. Vought whistled. "It's a pickle, ain't it! No help from him, then. And where's your proof?"

"I'll get it," answered Horace doggedly.

"How?"

"I don't know. But I'll get it."

"As it doesn't promise to prove itself, I reckon you'll have to. Well, God speed you, lad."

Before the commission caught coach from town, the gist of their report had leaked. They had recommended cancellation of Dr. Horace Amlie's diploma and withdrawal of his privilege of medical practice within the bounds of New York State. Three weeks later, at the spring meeting, the State Medical Society adopted the report without change.

Horace Amlie was a practitioner without a practice.

-13-

THE fourteen-foot batteau skimmed briskly westward along the canal, under the impulsion of a beam wind. Its leg-of-mutton sail, sagging unhandily at the leach, testified to amateur fitting. The boat itself was of rough, sturdy construction, equipped with oars as well as a mast, and held against sidewise drifting by leeboards. Amidships a strongbox, covered with sow-hide against the weather, occupied the breadth of the bottom, except for a narrow space where was stowed a small tent. In the stern, sheet in one hand, tiller in the other, Horace Amlie, M.D., smoked his pipe.

June was high in the land. Horace contemplated with lazy pleasure the vista of lush woodland and flowering swamp. He was hard and lean and weather-brown. His face, grown older than his years, was set in lines of endurance and obduracy. A reader of character would have said at a glance that Horace Amlie was a hard man. Many a sufferer along the Erie route would have given him the lie.

A Durham boat, light in cargo, hove in sight around the bend. As the two craft neared, the captain's whistle shrilled in signal to the hoggee on the towpath, who obediently whoaed his tandem. At the same time, the sailor luffed up against the berm and let his sail slat in the breeze. A hail came from the high deck.

"Ahoy, Doc!"

"Ahoy, *Genesee Rover!*"

"How's trade, my boy?"

"Can't complain. How's freights?"

"I'm light, as you see. Taking on planking at Bushnell's Basin. Got some calls for you."

The physician opened a locker and brought out a ledger. "Let's have 'em."

"Woman in labor near Batt's Landing."

"How long?"

"Since yesterday noon."

Horace made a note. "If the wind holds, I'll be there in two hours."

"Won't be none too soon, I guess. There's been a free-for-all at Malkey's Tavern."

"Shooting?"

"Yeah. And knifing. One fella got it through the belly. Plenty bumps and chewed ears for you."

"That's a foul ken," commented Horace, making another entry. "Anything else?"

"Usual shakes along the bank. They're waitin' on you. Behind your runnin' time, ain't you, Doc?"

"I had an amputation ten miles back. Tree jumped. Smashed the leg like a ripe pippin."

"Them woodcutters never learn. Could you fix him?"

Horace shook his head sadly. He wanted to forget that ugly experience of blood, agony, shrieks and writhing under the knife. And the smell of burning flesh when he applied the cautery to the stump. All useless, probably. Nearly all those comminuted fractures died of gangrene. A too familiar backwoods tragedy. Poor Tim Harkness! A stout young fellow of twenty-three with a wife and two babies. Well, there was always a chance that the strong young blood would prevail against the deadly rot. In any case, he had done what he could.

"Thank you, Cap," he called.

"Good luck, Doc."

The sail bellied out again. The prow piled up a little white wavelet, and with that bone in her teeth the boat made a handsome six knots. The four-knot passenger packets and the slower Durhams, heavy in freight, slacked their tow to give her free passage. Even the clumsy rafts, perennially at feud with all that went down to the canal in ships, nosed the bank in favor of the itinerant physician. For Horace Amlie, M.D., after two months of this new and experimental practice, was a recognized institution along the western reaches of the Big Ditch and the wild lands contiguous. The toughest of the canallers gave him consideration if for no other reason than—well, how could they tell when they, themselves, might be in sore need of his ministrations?

At Craven's Creek Lock the keeper passed him through without toll, which was strictly illegal, accepting the gift of a segar with aplomb, and requesting and receiving a soothing ointment for his piles. Two miles below, a man came running up the berm toward the sloop.

"Godsakes, Doc! Hurry on. She's almost gone."

"I'm coming as fast as the wind'll take me. Hop aboard."

He ran in close, and the woodsman leapt to the gunwale, almost upsetting them. His story was a familiar one. Alarming symptoms as labor drew near; no aid except a slovenly and dirty squaw; so the husband had brought his wife jolting over six miles of corduroy road in his oxcart, and she now lay under an improvised shelter of boughs, waiting and hoping.

Arrived at the spot, Horace went to work. He did not dare have the patient carried aboard the boat, as was his custom to evade the prohibition which forbade his practicing anywhere upon terra firma in New York State. In this case he must take the risk of prosecution. The husband and the squaw carried the sow-hide chest of medicines and instruments to the bedside.

Three hours later, Horace had the reward of knowing that he had saved two lives. It was his only reward. The woodsman had no money, not so much as a fip. He offered payment in stored grain or stock on the hoof, but bulky barter was of no use to the itinerant. He could not transport it. The debt was entered in his running account where Dinty would later discover it and scold.

Better returns attended his call at the tavern. The roisterer with the bullet through his belly was beyond help. But Horace patched up several stab-wounds, removed the pendent remains of an ear which had suffered an expert mayhem, treated a half-dozen contusions of varying degrees, and went on his way with six shillings cash besides a gallon of rum and two horns of gunpowder.

Sundry stops along towpath and berm followed. The friendly breeze sank with the sun. Horace bent to his oars, for he was now in a marshy stretch where he had no mind to spend a mosquito-tormented night. Four miles farther there was an inn. But inns cost money. He traveled on a rigidly economical basis. He rowed until the land lifted from the valley in shaly hills. There he pitched his tent and lighted his fire. His all-purpose woods-knife extracted several white, fat grubs from around the roots of a maple. With these as bait he had no difficulty in catching a couple of plump bullheads which, roasted on an iron prong, served him well for supper.

The useful blade was now turned to cutting hemlock boughs for his bedding. His keen nose directed him to a clump of wild pennyroyal with which he anointed himself carefully in case any vagrant winged creatures might be about. He took a swallow of his rum, set his rifle within hand-reach, pulled his blanket to his chin, and sank into well-earned slumber after a full day's work.

Between Rochester and the developing townlet of Black Rock, there was but one physician, a rheumatic, ague-shaken, undereducated, overworked wreck, already old at forty-two, who lived at Lock Port. The rest of the field was free for Horace. Could he have had full range, he might have prospered well in that wide opportunity. But restriction to the breadth of the canal limited his resources. Even here, his legal status was questionable.

The state medical authorities, prodded by Genter Latham and his subservient politicos, had already attempted to make trouble in Albany, only to be roundly told by the Canal Commission that Erie Water was no affair of theirs and that Dr. Amlie was free to practice as he chose anywhere between path and berm. Back of this stiffnecked attitude was the powerful clique of captains with whom Horace was a favorite.

Not only their moral support, but their active aid was at the young doctor's call. Against adverse winds, a tow would usually be offered to him. When the weather turned violent, a freighter would slack up, swing out a crane and tackle, and swing his craft and himself bodily inboard, where he could smoke comfortably in the captain's deck-cabin until his next port-of-call was reached. Tactfully the rough canallers would manage to develop a sore throat, an inflamed joint, a more or less imaginary temperature so that the popular but touchy "Doc" might feel that he was earning his passage.

With all these favors, it was still a hard life. Horace was toughened to it and would have enjoyed it, but for the separation from Dinty. He was lucky if his duties left him four days out of the month at home.

The wife's was the harder part. She must hold the fort, served by Unk Zeb and watched over by the faithful Teapot, facing a life which daily constricted about her. For now the wearing punishment of ostracism was being visited upon her for her husband's sins. Inevitably the essential truth about the Latham-Amlie feud had leaked out. It was bruited about boldly that Dr. Amlie had perpetrated a false and slanderous diagnosis; that, without evidence or warrant, he had declared Wealthia Latham to be in the family way; that when time refuted his disgraceful error, he had stuck to it and defamed the character of an innocent maiden to her own and her father's face. Public opinion held that Genter Latham would have been justified in getting down his musket and shooting the slanderer on sight.

Horace's stauncher friends stood by the Amlies. Silas Bewar, not to be intimidated by any man, was a frequent visitor, with his prim Quakeress. O. Daggett and Decker Jessup refused to have any part in the anti-Amlie campaign, and suffered in their trade from the ill will of the town magnate. The Reverend Theron Strang was an unswerving ally. To Horace's surprise, that volatile and light-minded humorist, Carlisle Sneed, made a practice of dropping in to ask if he could be helpful, and frequently was. Several others of the smithy coterie stood by loyally. But most of the Best People of Palmyra turned a cold shoulder upon the young wife. They got little satisfaction of it.

Dinty's bright beauty took on pride and courage under the petty persecution. She held her head high. She returned hauteur with hauteur, sniff for sniff. If at times she suffered from loneliness, she never permitted her husband to see it. Of each homecoming, she made a little, loving festivity, with something special of her own cooking or brewing. It became the central principle of her management to maintain an unchanged front.

The best she could do was not quite good enough to fool Horace. Adversity had made him more perceptive. He sensed the strain under which Dinty was living. In the face of her valor and cheerfulness, his determination weakened. At the close of a particularly unremunerative tour, he came home to find that she had quarreled with her mother. She airily refused to give any details, merely remarking that Ma was a fussbudget and said things she didn't mean. Horace knew that she was hurt. Loosing his cash-bag from his belt, he slammed it down on the office table, with a sadly thin effect, threw himself into his chair and glowered at the wall.

"This won't do," he said.

"What won't, darling?" Dinty smiled at him with the maternal aspect which an indulgent mother bestows upon a difficult child.

"All of it."

She lifted the bag, thoughtfully weighing it. "Didn't you do well, this trip?"

"Seven dollars, scant, and one of those an uncurrent note."

"Why, I think that's pretty good!" said she brightly.

"Good enough to live on?"

"Oh, well! You'll do better next time."

"Damn this town and all its people!" he burst out. "God damn them for a lot of Pharisees! God damn them . . . !"

"Doc! Doc!" She stopped his speech with the pressure of her own soft lips. "Don't. It isn't like you. You frighten me."

"I've had enough of it. I can earn a living for you elsewhere."

"You're earning it here."

"What kind? How long since you've had a new gown?"

"How long since you've had a new coat?"

"That doesn't matter. It's you."

She cocked an impudent head at him. "Don't you like me the way I am?"

"I love you like hell. That's what hurts."

"Don't let it hurt, darling. I'm happy."

"Happy!"

"I am," she insisted. "The only unhappy part is our being separated so much."

"There's an opening for a qualified medical man in Pennsylvania. At Bethlehem."

She gaped at him. "Pennsylvania? Way down there? Leave Palmyra?"

"Are you so enamored of it?" he asked harshly.

"I ha—" She swallowed the word. "Why do you want to go?"

"I told you. I'm sick of this."

"On my account."

"What of it? Isn't that reason enough?"

"Horace Amlie," said she clearly, "I know you. If you quit the town now, everyone will say that Genter Latham drove you out. And that'll fester inside you the longest day you live. You can't give up, that way. Not unless you were wrong."

He regarded her intently. "Suppose I were wrong?"

"Then you must go to Mr. Latham like a man and beg his forgiveness and Wealthy's," she said instantly.

"I'll see him in hell first."

"Then you don't believe you were wrong."

"I know I'm right."

"Then we stay right here."

"On seven dollars a week?"

"On seven cents!"

Horace's most pitiful and least profitable clientele was that of the towpath. Here plodded the hoggees, the friendless apprentice boys, taken on under indenture for the season, neglected or maltreated, and turned off at the close of traffic with ten dollars for their total wage—if, indeed, they were not mulcted of that by pretext or bullying. Whatever the weather, they must trudge behind their tandem, permitted the respite of an occasional ride only by the more humane captains. They were orphans, foundlings, bastards, halfbreeds, ranging from a precocious fourteen to a backward twenty-one years of age. On their watch off, they slept in foul and infested corners of the hold.

A more straitened and wretched existence would be hard to conceive.

One hoggee, whom he had once or twice seen but never treated or spoken to, enlisted his curiosity by reading a book as he drove. The lad was tallish, stringy, emaciated and unusually dark for an Indian, as the observer judged him to be. He worked on a small freighter of no special model, engaged in short-stretch pick-up traffic on the western run. It was a cheap outfit with a bad name. Horace asked his friend, Captain Ennis, about the lad.

"Hoggee on the *Merry Fiddler?* You mean the halfbreed? That'll be Whistlebone."

"Who is he?"

Ennis shrugged. "Who are any of 'em? Nobody knows about a hoggee. Why?"

"I noticed him reading a book."

"Never heard of a hoggee that could read. Captain Tugg'll take that out of him with a rope's end."

"Has Tugg got the *Merry Fiddler?*"

"Yes. Got jounced from the line boats. Drunk too often."

Horace knew Eleazar Tugg only by reputation, which was unsavory. He was one of those who gave canalling a bad name. "Grouncher" Tugg, a grouncher being one who worked his hands to exhaustion and paid them only under compulsion of the law. In worst case of all with such an employer was the hoggee who received no pay until the end of his term. Under such brutality, the unhappy lad was generally too browbeaten and cowed to stand for his rights. If he exhibited that temerity, he was only too liable to meet a trumped-up charge of incompetency or insubordination, and to be flung into the canal as the final argument, while the captain pocketed his wage.

A favoring wind carried the Amlie batteau past the slow-moving freighter one bright morning. Captain Tugg, acting as his own helmsman, gave a malicious touch to his tiller, to threaten the little craft with a squeeze. Knowing his evil disposition, the watchful navigator eluded the menace, and gave him a civil good day, to which the canaller responded with a grunt and a spurtle of tobacco-juice overside. His suffused face indicated a hard night.

Drawing abreast of the team, Horace slackened sail. He saw that the driver was limping painfully. One of his shoes, hardly more than a rag of leather, was bound on with a thong. Horace hailed him.

"Hi, sonny! Sore foot?"

The lad nodded, half averting his face. Horace thought that he had a stealthy, scared look. Then he noticed the swollen redness of recent tears in the eyelids. He was surprised. Indians do not cry. He edged in closer and got a second and shocking surprise. The hoggee was Tip Crego.

"Tip! What are you doing here?"

The hoggee said fearfully, "Don't tell them! Don't tell them!"

"Tell them what?" For the moment Horace was puzzled.

"Don't tell them about me," the boy besought again. "They'd put me in jail."

It came back with a rush now; the dead man with Tip's feathered dart in his throat, whence Horace had plucked it. He said gently, "Nobody is going to put you in jail, my boy."

"The man's dead."

Horace told a simple, straightforward, and effective lie. "Drowned," he said. "You had nothing to do with it."

A light of hope gleamed in the reddened eyes. "Can I come back home?"

"Any time you like."

Depression settled again on the thin face. "He won't let me. I ran away once. They caught me and he beat me nearly to death."

The captain's whistle shrilled furiously behind them, followed by a raging voice. "God damn and blast you, you pocky pillmonger! Leave my boy be or I'll come ashore and heave you both in the drink."

Horace paid no heed. He asked Tip, "Where do you lay off next?"

"Lock Port. Overnight."

"I'll meet you there."

"Don't let the captain know. He'd kill us."

The sail filled. The small craft drew away. Another burst of savagery rolled downwind to Horace's ears. The hoggee hunched his head between his shoulders and limped on.

Lock Port's basins were well occupied that evening. The *Merry Fiddler's* spavined horses brought her in at a torpid two-and-a-half mile rate, several hours after Horace's arrival. Captain Tugg, after seeing her snugged to the landing wharf, went ashore to get drunk. Thus Horace had a clear way to Tip.

He found the boy's body sore with contusions, the ugliest being on the right knee where the captain kicked him because he had asked for a dollar of his wages to buy shoes. A bandage would support it, but it needed rest. He told the patient so. Tip said,

"He won't lay me off."

"He's got to under the law. I'll certify you unfit."

"What does he care for the law?"

"I'll talk to him."

The boy said fearfully, "You'd better not, Dr. Amlie. He's a hard man."

"I'm not a soft man, myself," returned the physician, and Tip, scanning his face, wondered what had happened, so to change him. "Will you go home with me if I get you free?"

"Oh!" Poor Tip began to cry. By that more than from his emaciated body, Horace could judge how his spirit had been brutalized and weakened.

He got the boy's story. Tip had hunted, trapped and "yarbed" for a time, worked for an Ontario sturgeon fisherman until the man was drowned, gone hungry and cold on the road, finally, under fair promises, signed on with the *Merry Fiddler*. Since Captain Tugg took over, his life had been a hell. Through Satch Fammie he had kept in touch with Quaila Crego, and had once visited her under cover of night. She thought that it might be safe for him to remain, but he had the free woodsman's horror of confinement. The thought of jail made his bones quake; the briefest imprisonment would, he was sure, kill him. He dared not take the chance. So long as he shunned the vicinity of Palmyra, nobody was likely to recognize him, especially since one of Satch Fammie's gypsy kin had dyed his face to a deep hue with a lasting tribal preparation of green walnut juice.

Horace knew that to take Tip back to Palmyra without due process would be futile. Every newspaper issue carried advertisements offering six cents' reward for the return of runaway apprentices. They were liable to arrest on sight, and the courts always honored the claim of indenture against them. Tip would not remain unmolested for a week at the Pinch. To help him effectively Horace must deal with Grouncher Tugg.

The most likely place to find Captain Tugg, he learned, was in a towpath coffee house—which, to the cognoscenti, meant boozing ken—called the "Hearty Swallow." Having refreshed himself with a snack and a mug of ale in a more respectable resort, he made his way to the place.

Entering, he was enveloped in an atmosphere heavy with smoke and rich with the reek of split liquors. A jocund baritone was raised in a lay familiar to his ears.

Randy-dandy-dandy, O!
Randy, my dandy.
With a rangdang, dingdang, dandy-O!
My name is Randy.

The singer drew breath with an exclamation of surprised greeting.

"Young Æsculapius, by the bowels of Beelzebub! Well met. What's your fancy?"

Horace shook hands with Silverhorn Ramsey, but declined the offered drink.

"I'm looking for Captain Tugg of the *Merry Fiddler,*" he explained.

Silverhorn cocked a roguish eye toward the upstairs floor, where the blowzy nymphs of the establishment carried on a sideline of recognized but unlicensed traffic.

"He'll be a good few minutes yet, I reckon. Sit down."

"What brings you here, Silverhorn?" inquired Horace, taking a chair opposite. "I thought you were in the lake trade."

"I laked it for nigh a year. Smart little schooner as ever you saw. Wrecked off Oswego in last month's gale. One hand and I are all that got ashore. Now I'm back to the *Jolly Roger.*"

"And Mrs. Ramsey? How is she?" asked Horace politely.

The handsome face twisted wryly. "Still got her death-grip on the purse-strings." He eyed his companion interestedly. "What's come to you, Æsculapius? You look more of a man than you were."

"I'm in the canal trade, myself."

"I heard something of that. Got into a mess with Sharkskin Latham, didn't you?"

"Yes," answered Horace, wondering how much he knew.

"And got run out of town, huh?"

"No!"

"Stirred your bile, have I?" grinned Silverhorn. "Didn't sound likely to me when I heard it. You ain't that kind. Not if I know you."

As Horace's vision accustomed itself to the surcharged air, he studied an altered Silverhorn. The gay and careless face was puffy. The lips were nervous at the corners, the eyes restless and, he thought, unhappy. But the old, confident, raffish charm still radiated from the man, and the elegance of the beau's get-up shone in that dingy environment. A jeweled ring glowed as the hand that wore it tapped the table in an irregular rhythm. Silverhorn said, with an affectation of ease, "The girl: I suppose she's about?"

"Yes."

"I heard she was ailing."

"She's recovered."

"She didn't marry her Southern cavalier."

"No."

"Jilted him, I reckon."

"You reckon wrong."

"Maybe he jilted her."

"He's dead."

"Dead? I didn't know about that."

Horace sensed a repressed excitement which pricked his curiosity. He said with deliberate experimentation, "Kinsey Hayne killed himself."

The hand that held Silverhorn's glass jumped so that the liquor slopped over. "Good God! The poor devil! What made him do that?"

"You're asking a lot of questions, Silverhorn."

"I'll ask you another. Are you sure Wealthia is all right?"

"To all appearances. I'm no longer her physician, you know."

"Doc, will you take a letter to Palmyra for me?"

"I will not."

"You would if you knew everything."

"I would not in any conditions."

"I can't be sure that my letters reach her," complained Silverhorn. "She hasn't answered."

"Why should she?"

"There are reasons."

"A girlish infatuation," said Horace sternly. "One thing I can tell you; she's well over it."

"Damn you! You lie!" He controlled himself with an effort, and spoke with a queer sort of appeal, "Doc, I've never believed much in this love talk. But I can't get the girl out of my mind. I'd divorce my old hag at the drop of a hat and marry that girl tomorrow if she'd give the word. Or I'd carry her off with me and to hell with all of you."

"You'll always be a ruffian, won't you, Silverhorn?"

The other smiled complacently. "I'm no finicky daffodil," said he. "There's your man," he added, motioning toward the stairway with a hand not yet quite steady.

It was a formidable figure that lounged out into the room, hoarsely shouting its demand for a beaker of brandy-and-egg, a gangling ape of a man, with corded arms and thick, knuckly hands. His face seemed to be composed mostly of a huge jaw, equipped with yellow buck-teeth, above which a long and leathery upper lip underhung a beaked nose. Strabismic eyes squinted out from beneath absurdly feathery brows. Although he wavered slightly, Horace judged that he was not yet drunk. He would be capable of understanding what was wanted of him.

"Captain," began the physician with a civil intonation, "I'd like a word with you."

"I don't know yah," growled the captain. "What's it about?"

"Your hoggee. The one that is injured."

"Whistlebone? What about him?"

"He isn't fit for the towpath."

"Who says so."

"I do. I'll be glad to explain."

"And who the hell are you?" He peered through the murk. "You're the God-damn gut-flusher that stopped my boy on the towpath 's mornin', aincheh?" He approached the table, thrusting forward his toothy countenance.

"Look out!" warned Silverhorn sharply.

Horace, watchful, stepped lightly back. He felt a sharp aversion for that proximity, were it only because of the rank breath that befouled the air. Captain Tugg, having put his question, now answered it.

"I'll tell you who you are. You're one of those softmouths. A smoocher. A sneaker. A goddam churcher. I've booted the bum of better than you and left 'em screechin' their prayers in Erie muck. You keep your hands off'n my boys."

"I am a physician," said Horace, "and I tell you that the boy is liable to lose his leg if he doesn't keep off it."

"What the hell do I care for his leg!"

"Do you care for a report on your boat to the Canal Commission?" demanded Horace, beginning to lose temper.

"God damn the commission and you, too!"

That jutting jaw seemed again to be advancing, as if under some vicious impulsion of its own.

"Look out!" said Silverhorn Ramsey again.

A motion so swift and deft that it was barely noticeable brought to sight his ready knife. He toyed with it, gazing speculatively at the man above him. Captain Tugg eyed the weapon with respect.

"What's *your* trade here?" he asked sulkily.

"Fair play. The Doc is my friend."

The intervention cooled the bellicosity of the captain. He addressed Silverhorn. "What call's he got to stick in his clam?" he growled, jerking his chin toward Horace. "I got the boy indenched, ain't I? Wanta see the paper?"

"I'll buy it of you," said Horace.

"My price is twenty-five dollars."

"Nonsense! Your indenture is only for ten."

"Twenty-five's my price. But I'll tell you what: I'll fight you for it."

This was a contingency which Horace had foreseen but hoped to avoid. He scrutinized the challenger coolly. The captain topped him two inches in height and probably two stone in heft. As against this advantage, he was perhaps forty years old and, on the evidence of his sallow skin and sour breath, not in the best of condition. Horace, trained in sparring, was no mean man of his hands, and, thanks to the regimen of his life on the water, was iron-hard in every muscle. Under prize-ring rules, the contest should be fairly equal. But would this ruffian respect any rules? Silverhorn's thoughts were running along the same channel, for now he put in,

"Fair fighting?"

"Fair!" gibed the apish captain. "Fair! I'll show him fair, when I get his nose betwixt my teeth."

Now Horace understood Silverhorn's warnings. He recalled with a sick qualm, several grisly facial repairs to which he had been called after taproom free-for-alls. This creature before him was a rough-and-tumble fighter, a biter, a gouger, a maimer. In such a battle he would have all the advantage. Yet to draw back now would incur for Horace a disastrous loss of prestige in the canal world where lay his sole chance of livelihood. There was one other chance, though a more perilous one. He said steadily, "I'll fight you with any weapon you pick."

"No weepons," the other grinned. "What God gave a man to fight with like a man, and naught else."

He was within his rights. There was nothing for Horace to do but to accept the conditions.

"You're met," he said quietly. "Fetch your indenture to the path opposite Stannard's meadow at eight o'clock tomorrow morning. We'll pick a stake-holder on the ground. I'll put my ten dollars in his hands. The man who is on his feet after half an hour claims the pot."

"Twenty-five," objected his opponent.

"Ten, or no fight. Take your choice."

Captain Tugg gave surly acquiescence. He had been taken aback at the matter-of-fact acceptance of his chosen type of combat. Nevertheless it was with a cocksure grin that he said, "Ten dollars and ten minutes—if you live that long."

Silverhorn now spoke softly. "I'll be in the Doc's corner. And if you so much as reach a finger to your pocket, you big son-of-a-bitch, you'll get my knife through your guts."

To Horace's surprise, the ruffian swallowed the insult. Evidently Silverhorn had him cowed; evidence that his courage was not beyond proof. As for the threat, Silverhorn explained as they went out together, that foul fighters sometimes held in reserve a species of spiked brass knuckles which could gouge out an eye or punch through a cheek at one thrust.

The mentor further delivered sage instructions on the enemy strategy and tactics, adding, "If he gets you in close, give him this." He brought his knee up in a fierce lunge.

"He isn't going to get me in close."

"No? How are you going to stop him?"

"You know how to use your hands, Silverhorn."

"Enough to keep my head," admitted Ramsey in the ancient phrase.

"Have you ever sparred with the pads?"

"Not me." The mustached lip curled.

"The bare knuckles are the trick, if you want to cut a man up. If you want to settle him, the pad's the thing. I had the tip from the sparring champion of a wandering fair who gave me some lessons."

"It don't sound reasonable."

"Principle of the sandbag," explained Horace. "You can knock a man colder with that than with an iron bar."

"I'd admire to see it," said his second skeptically.

"Come with me to the cobbler's."

That artisan was abed, but obligingly got up when he learned that a sporting event was in question. Selecting his softest piece of doeskin, he worked it under his customer's directions, stuffed it with horsehair and dried milkweed fluff, and sewed it into a rough but serviceable right-hand glove. Silverhorn viewed it with undisguised derision.

"I'll give you a free punch at me with that pillow," he offered.

Horace shook his head. "I don't want to spoil a good second. Try it, yourself."

"On you?"

"No, thank you," grinned his principal. "Let's find a subject."

It being now past nine o'clock, the respectable element was in bed, but this was not the type that Horace sought. A two-hundred-pound gauger rolled up the street, singing merrily. They stopped him.

"Friend, do you want a free dram?"

"Who wouldn't? What's your lay?"

"Stand up and give my friend one crack at your jaw with this," invited Horace, exhibiting the glove, before fixing it on his friend's fist.

The big fellow scrutinized it, felt of it, and guffawed. "Two, if you like."

He folded his arms and stood, smirking. As Silverhorn's hearty swing landed, the smirk quivered and faded. The eyes fluttered. The knees buckled. He wobbled gently to earth.

"Be-dam; be-dam; be-dam," he murmured in dolorous amaze.

"Be damned, myself!" echoed Silverhorn. "I didn't give him my best, either."

They hauled the victim to his feet, escorted him to the nearest tap, and revived him with the promised drink and an extra for luck.

"Come back to the Hearty Swallow," said Silverhorn to Horace abruptly.

"What for? I want my sleep."

"Bets. I smell money."

At the coffee house Captain Tugg was accepting treats from his admirers and roaring out offers to bet on himself at two to one, five to one, ten to one, by God! if he could find a fool to take him up.

"Cover that," invited Silverhorn, planking down a five-dollar gold piece.

The captain stared at it as if mesmerized, but recovered swiftly. "I ain't got the cash on me," said he. "Fetch it with you tomorrow and I'll cover it and as much more as your weaselskin holds."

There was Tugg money and to spare, when Horace and his backer appeared ten minutes early, at the meeting place. There was also a goodly crowd. Matters proceeded with the formality proper to so important an event. To each principal was assigned a committee of three in support. Besides Silverhorn, Horace was attended by Captain Ennis and Old Bill Shea, who happened to be in town arranging for barreled winter fish, in his capacity as factor. The challenger's staff consisted of Sandy Clark, a horse coper, a town tough named Miley and Captain Gadley of the *Starry Flag*. The two bodies chose Deacon Levi Bardo, a highly respected village trustee, as stakeholder with power of decision on moot points of etiquette. As anything short of murder was in order, the arbiter's duties were not onerous.

The terms were substantially as Horace had outlined them in his reply to Tugg's defi; the contestant who, at the end of half an hour of fighting, was on his feet to claim the stake, got it. Fifteen minutes' grace was allotted for wagers. Though the physician's popularity easily surpassed that of his ugly opponent, few cared to back it with cash. To be sure, the gauger was there with two dollars in his hand, and a secretive and knowing smile on his lips, but, except for him, Silverhorn seemed to be the only bettor on that side. To his bland inquiry about Captain Tugg's ten-to-one, that gentleman responded with a hasty denial of such offer. As a substitute, he suggested doubles, which some of his backers raised to triples. Captain Ramsey got his fifty dollars covered in no time.

As the contracting parties tightened their belts, rolled their sleeves, and stood forth on a dry and level sward below the towpath, the disparity in weight and reach more than justified the odds. Tugg's face was congested, his eyes bloodshot, but there was plenty of vigor in his lank and powerful frame as he flexed his ropy arms, leapt in the air, and clacked his hobnails.

"Hey! What's this?" demanded Captain Gadley as Silverhorn prepared to lash on his principal's odd handgear.

"My man has a sore finger," suavely explained the second.

"Lessee that thing. What's into it?" growled Miley.

Silverhorn tossed it over. The Tugg committee poked and prodded it, finally passing it to Deacon Bardo who judicially pronounced that, while he had seen nothing like it before, a combatant had the right to safeguard an injured member.

"Better tie it on his nose," sneered Tugg to Silverhorn. "Is he goin' to fight or ain't he? He don't look like he wanted to."

Horace ignored the taunt, his ear attentively bent to his second who was now imparting his final admonition.

"He'll reach with his right. When you feel his fingers, let him have it. If he draws you in, butt him."

Horace nodded and stepped out. Tugg flailed his arms, let out a blood-curdling howl, and charged. Some object which he had not noticed interfered with his plunge, so that he stumbled and all but fell. The obstacle was the enemy's foot, cleverly interposed as he swerved from the rush. Roaring again, the canaller repeated his advance, only to be evaded a second time. He stood, shaking his head like a furious bull.

"Close in! Close in!" shouted Sandy, the horse coper. "Grip um."

The big man moved forward with deadly deliberation this time. Horace maneuvered along the foot of the slope until the morning sun was in the captain's eyes. Was he going to be trapped? Captain Ennis and Old Bill shouted warnings. Tugg's great right hand was opening and contracting. It darted forward. It clutched. Horace, set for it, put all that he had into his swing. The spectators heard a *Pop!* such as small boys achieve by inflating a bladderwort leaf to bursting.

Captain Tugg, with a mildly disappointed expression, wavered to earth.

It would have been within Horace's privilege, under the rules, to kick his ribs in. He had other designs. Slowly the gladiator got to his feet, waggled his head to clear it, and lunged again at his opponent. Yells of derision sounded from his faction, as the smaller man warily retreated up the bank to the path.

"Clinch um! Clinch um!" howled Miley, dancing.

The temporary daze had passed from Tugg's brain. He pursued. His first experience had taught him nothing. That nervous right hand stretched forth once more, the apish fingers crisping. Horace withdrew, slowly, more slowly, hardly moving now in a sidling curve. The hand settled, gripped, half encircled the other's neck. Tugg uttered a yelp of triumph, cut short by a second *Pop!* a shade solider than the first. This time the kindly earth was not there to receive the tottering warrior, for, as he gave back, his opponent's head took him under the chin with all the spring of lithe knees in its drive, and a mighty splash marked the spot where three-and-a-half feet of Erie water closed over the distorted features.

Erie mud is slithery-soft. The fallen man wavered to his feet, choking with fury and slime.

"Stay there! Stay there!" howled his committee, perceiving the peril.

If he heard them he paid no heed. Clawing his way forward, pawing the ooze of the incline like a dog on a treadmill, he lurched on, bent half double. As soon as he was within reach of the bank, he received a neat clip under the chin and collapsed backward. Bubbles rose. Uproar filled the air. Miley, Clark and Captain Gadley rushed to succor their man, but were met by the embodiment of authority in the redoubtable person of Deacon Bardo. If aid were given to either contestant, warned the arbiter, that man's stake would be forfeited forthwith.

"You goin' to leave um drown?" shouted Miley.

This was rhetoric, as the extreme depth was no more than four feet. The stakeholder drew out his watch. From the face of the troubled waters a convulsed and streaming visage emerged. It coughed, strangled, retched. Horace, with an intent expression, waited on the bank.

"Keep away! Keep away!" Tugg's committee unanimously yelled to their man.

The canaller hawked water from his pipes, squeezed it from his eyes, dribbled it from his sinewy frame. Hoarsely he cursed, in language so choice that the toughest water rat within hearing marveled and admired. Now he backed toward the berm. In a foot depth he bent and groped. He straightened and let fly a great rock at Horace's head, less than thirty feet away. It was the mistake of his career.

Horace swerved lithely, but not enough for full avoidance. The missile struck him on the shoulder, fortunately the left one. It sent him rolling down the bank.

As he stopped, he whipped off the glove. Near by was a pile of stones. His cool mind perceived the opportunity; the enemy had made the choice of weapons; it could not have been a better selection for Horace. Climbing to his feet, he picked out two rounded rocks, one double the size of the other.

Shouts and cheers apprised him that the foe was floundering back to terra firma. He set himself, the heavier missile in his right hand. He must take no chance of missing with the first shot. Certainly Tugg's body was a fair enough target.

The rock took the canaller full in the chest. It staggered him. His arms went down. Before he could raise them in protection, the cobble smashed into his face. His most formidable weapon of offense, the great horse-teeth, caved in in a welter of blood. He fell, groaning, pawing, twitching.

The fight was over.

14

Horace's return to the village was a triumphal progress. Shaking off his admirers, he sought out the *Merry Fiddler*. Tip Crego limped out on deck to meet him.

"We heard about it," he said joyously. "A canoe just came past. Where's Captain Tugg?"

"At the doctor's. He wouldn't let me patch him up. Make up your bundle."

"Can I quit?" cried Tip.

"Here's your indenture. We're going home."

Tip's joy over his release overbore the natural reticence of his Indian blood. He laughed, and would have danced but for the damaged knee. The doctor examined and rebandaged it as soon as they were aboard.

"Now I can go to college," the boy exulted. "I've kept up in my books."

Horace was glum. "I can't help you, Tip. I can hardly make my living."

"I heard about that, sir," said the boy.

"Did you? How?"

"I meet up with the gyppos sometimes. The gyppos know everything."

Horace suppressed the temptation to ask how much the gyppos knew about Wealthia Latham. A bugle-catch outside brought him to the path. Silverhorn beamed brightly upon him. Silverhorn was pleasurably drunk.

"I've been standing drinks," said he. "Topside, downside and alongside. If I was in Albany, I would be elected mayor of Albany. If I was in Utica, I would be elected mayor of Utica. I could also be mayor of Syracuse and maybe New York, if I wanted to take the pains. Name your potion."

Horace declined the drink. The jaunty sportsman removed his

neckcloth, spread it carefully upon the ground, and proceeded to discharge his pockets into it. Gold, silver, copper, notes current, notes uncurrent, a watch, a compass, a jeweled brooch, a table knife, a gilt ring and a fistful of geegaws made up the sum of his takings.

"One hundred twelve dollars and the extras," he reckoned. "And the half of it is yours, young Æsculapius; the half of it is yours."

"Thanks, Silverhorn. But I can't take your money."

"Now, by Noah's navel, you can and shall! Didn't you win it for me? Pop!" said Silverhorn delightedly. "Pop! And over he keeled. The big son-of-a-bitch! Made a fine hole in the water." Scooping up a double handful of the specie, he extended it to his companion.

In the interests of comity, Horace compromised by accepting the compass for himself and the brooch for Dinty. Silverhorn stowed the remainder in various pockets, and said, "I did you a turn today, didn't I, Æsculapius?"

"You did, surely. Without your advice I shouldn't have known how to fight him."

"Now you can do me a turn."

"What is it?"

"Be my post office."

Horace frowned. "That's your price, is it?"

"Carry a letter. Just one little letter."

"What good will that do anyone, Silverhorn? Let the girl alone."

"What if she doesn't want to be let alone?"

"You've no right to assume it. I'll do anything else for you, but I can't carry messages in that quarter. For one matter, I'm not on terms with Miss Latham."

"Your wife is," returned the other who seemed to be surprisingly well informed in the premises. "Will you do this much, then? Will you take a message from that quarter, if there is one for me? Leave it to the girl, herself. Does she know that I'm back on the Ditch? She'll know anyhow, come spring, for the *Jolly Roger* will be on the Main Haul by then. My respects to your lady wife, and will she ask her friend whether she ever got my letter and is there an answer? Is that too much to ask?"

"I'll go that far," agreed Horace reluctantly.

Silverhorn seemed quite sober now. "You can reach me at the Lock Port Inn. Good-bye and fortune's luck to you, Æsculapius. You're a likely man of your hands." He turned away, but came back at once, his face both morose and exultant. "Hell and all its fires won't keep me from her," he said deep in his throat. "You can freight that along to her or not as you choose, Æsculapius. It won't matter. She knows it."

As the straight, slender back disappeared, Horace lost himself in surmise. What would Ramsey do if ever he learned that the girl had conceived a child by another man? Go murder-mad perhaps. One day he must know it. Everybody would know it. For Horace still cherished the ineradicable conviction that eventually that somber truth would out, though it might not be through any procurement of his.

Three days of alternate sailing and towing, neither wounded occupant being fit for the oars, brought the batteau to home port. Dinty welcomed her old playmate joyously, exclaiming over his emaciated condition and insisting that he must stay with them until he was recovered. Quaila Crego's claim, however, took precedence. The boy went back to Poverty's Pinch. He made daily visits to his benefactor, bringing in, as before, roots, plants and berries for his medicaments. His account of the towpath battle turned Dinty breathless. By his worshipful saga, second-hand though it was, Horace was a superior composite of David, Ulysses, Richard Coeur de Lion and George Washington. She proudly wore Silverhorn's brooch, as an incentive to acquaintances to ask her for the story, but in private admonished the hero that henceforth he was to eschew combat as, in the terms of her informal Latin, infra his professional dig.

"No worry," Tip told her. "There's not a tough on the Ditch that would tackle him now. Not even Silverhorn, himself."

Dinty gathered her courage for another attack. "Doc, could you be mistaken about its being Kin?"

"I'm so certain that I'm writing to Colonel Hayne."

"Kin's father? Oh, Doc!"

"Somebody has to help her if Genter Latham kicks her out when the truth is forced on him. The Haynes ought to do it."

"You mustn't write them, darling," she pleaded.

"I must and shall."

"Haven't his people had enough suffering? You don't really *know* that it was Kin."

"It was somebody. Are you suggesting that Wealthia has been promiscuous?"

"No," returned Dinty indignantly.

"Yet you won't allow that it was Hayne."

"In my heart I've never believed it."

"Who's your candidate?" he inquired sardonically, and answered himself. "Silverhorn Ramsey, I suppose. Well, my darling romanticist, you're one hundred percentum wrong, and science proves it."

"Pooh for your science!" retorted Dinty.

"Silverhorn couldn't be the father of Wealthia's child. He couldn't be the father of anyone's child."

"Why not?"

"Professional secret."

"I know he had the bad disease, if that's your professional secret. Witch Crego told me that long ago. But that wouldn't prevent him making a baby."

"Wouldn't it?" he retorted condescendingly. "Undoubtedly you keep abreast of the latest discoveries of Science, but a few things may have escaped you."

For the moment, however, she was more concerned with the Hayne family. After much and specious cajoling, she extracted a promise that he would hold the projected letter, at least until there was a change in the Latham status.

At the first opportunity she set herself to prowl through the files of the professional journals which Horace read with such religious faith. A year-old volume of a defunct publication calling itself the *Physician's Eclectic* turned up the information. Therein a prolix writer proved, to his own satisfaction, that men afflicted with venereal ailments were sterile for at least three years after the incidence of the disease, and bolstered his theory with impressively tabulated figures.

Like so many physicians of that day (and not a few of the present) Horace Amlie believed in the immaculate conception of statistics. Dinty knew how trustingly his mind would accept those serried numerals. It did appear, she confessed to herself, as if the laborious compiler must know what he was doing. And yet . . .

Silverhorn's message was now in her keeping.

"I can't force you to deliver it if you don't want to," Horace informed her with an enigmatic glance and half-smile.

"I'll deliver it. Not for Captain Ramsey, but for Wealthia."

"Do as you please. I see nothing but trouble in it."

"Maybe she won't think so."

"You're still possessed of the idea that she is enamored of him?"

Dinty's lips formed the thin, red line of obstinacy.

"How could she have been?" he argued. "If she were, would she have gotten herself into the mess with Kinsey Hayne?"

"You're a very wise and wonderful medico, Doc," his wife observed, "but you don't know quite everything about women."

Dinty found Wealthia in the garden and bluntly discharged her errand. The girl whitened.

"I—I don't want to see him."

"Shall I tell him that's your last word?"

"No, don't."

"Did you get his other letters?"

"Yes."

"He had no answer, he told Horace."

"I was frightened. I'm frightened now."

"That's dumb. I never was afraid of any man in my life," boasted Dinty, and qualified it. "We—ell, perhaps a *little* of Doc when he gets very mad with me. What will you do when Captain Ramsey comes back on this run?"

"I'll go away," said her friend wildly. "I won't stay here."

"Wealthy, you ought to get married. You've had heaps of chances."

"Oh, I have chances enough," returned the girl dully.

"Why don't you, then?"

"I'll never marry."

"Because of Kinsey?" asked Dinty softly.

Wealthia flinched. "Don't! Talk about something else or go home. I hear Tip Crego is back."

They discussed the returned fugitive, and out of that conversation Dinty took back to her husband a surprising bit of news.

"Doc, what do you think?"

"I think you've probably been making a sentimental ninny of yourself."

"Wait till you hear. Wealthy wants to send Tip to Hamilton."

"Good Lord! What's got into her?"

"It seems to be a sort of thank-offering to Heaven, by what I can make out."

He pulled a sour face. "What has she got to be so thankful about? Attempted infanticide?"

"Aren't you cruel! She'll pay all his fees. Does he still want to go?"

"He'll jump at the chance."

So it was arranged that Tip should share the physician's voyages as assistant, receiving tuition as opportunity offered. Thus, under the lax requirements then prevailing, he would be qualified to enter in the winter term. It was a satisfactory arrangement all around.

With a capacity for piecing information together, the boy, while in town, picked up enough from old associates at the Pinch and from village gossip to gain a pretty good notion of his doctor's dilemma. One day he came to Dinty.

"Dinty, I've got something I want to ask the Doctor."

"What about?"

"Wealthy."

"He won't talk about her."

"Maybe he would to me."

"Not to anyone."

"There's something I could tell him that might help him."

"Tell me."

Tip looked embarrassed. "It isn't something a fellow would talk about to a lady."

"I'm not a lady. I'm Dinty. And I'm married. To a doctor. There isn't much I don't know. Don't be dumb."

"Dinty, why did that Mr. Hayne kill himself?"

"Why do you think? And how much do you know?"

He hesitated long before replying. "I know that Wealthy was in trouble. I think the Doctor knew it, too, and told Mr. Latham and Mr. Latham wouldn't believe it and that's what caused all the row."

"How do you know Wealthy was in trouble?"

"She went to Satch Fammie."

"I know that. I was with her."

"Not that time. This was later."

"Did Satch Fammie do something to her?"

"She didn't dare. She was too far gone."

"That must have been before Kinsey Hayne knew anything," reflected Dinty, reckoning dates.

"Mr. Hayne? How would he know?"

"I know I can trust you, Tip. Doc believes that Kin Hayne got Wealthy that way and couldn't face it. That's why he killed himself."

"Mr. Hayne? He didn't get her that way."

"Tip! Do you know what you're talking about?"

"Certes, I do."

"Who do you think it was?"

"I don't think. I know. Silverhorn Ramsey."

"And I know it couldn't have been."

"Why couldn't it? He took her to Satch Fammie himself and offered a lot of money. Would he do that unless he were the one?"

She pressed her hands over her eyes. "But—but—there's something else; another reason. Oh, Tip! Are you *sure?*"

"Hasn't she always been mad over him? Have you forgotten that day under the hill? Aunt Quaila knows when this happened. It was a year ago last spring."

"The barn-raising at Manchester!" exclaimed Dinty. She remembered that telltale straw embedded in the black tresses.

Tip nodded. "Wealthia ran away from the party and met Silverhorn in a loft. It had been fixed up between them beforehand. Mr. Hayne followed and brought her back. I don't know where he found her nor what kind of story she made up for him. Wealthy's slick as a mink when she's so minded. He couldn't have known about Silverhorn."

"Oh, poor Kin! Poor, poor Kin!" mourned Dinty.

If Tip was right, in what a different pattern the whole involved and pitiful tragedy unrolled itself! Kinsey guiltless, Wealthia at first afraid to confess to him, though too honorable to marry him while carrying on the intrigue with the canaller, for doubtless the intimacy had been repeated. Cornered because of Horace's quixotic and ill-inspired visit to Kinsey with a view to setting matters aright, she was forced into her confession. It drove him to suicide.

"But Silverhorn couldn't . . ." No, she was not going into that with Tip. "Where's the child?" she demanded.

"Maybe she went away and had it fixed. There are others besides Satch Fammie," said Tip darkly.

Dinty bethought her of the Syracuse visit. But Horace had discovered her condition since then.

"She hasn't been away," she asserted. "And she couldn't have it done here in Palmyra without somebody knowing."

"I don't understand it then," he confessed. "But you can see now why I want to tell the Doctor about it."

"Never! You mustn't. I won't let you."

"Why not?" he asked, amazed at her vehemence.

"Tip," she said tightly, "if you breathe a word of it to Doc, I'll never forgive you. You don't know how awful it would be."

"No, I don't. You'd better tell me."

"Tip, Doc has made a terrible mistake. When he found that Wealthy was pregnant, he went straight to Kinsey Hayne to make him marry her. When Kin denied it and called him a liar for scandalizing Wealthy's good name, there was an awful row. Then she must have owned up to Kin or anyway told him she couldn't marry him. He wrote a letter to my husband."

"What did it say?"

"I never dared ask. Doc burned it. It made him very sad. I think he was disappointed in Kin. You see, he was so sure that Kin was the father."

"But wouldn't Mr. Hayne have denied it?"

"You never can tell about those Southerners. They're so lofty-minded about women. Maybe he thought it would be easier for Wealthia if he took the blame. I don't know just how much he did know, but Wealthia must have told him *something*. Enough to drive him to suicide. So, when he killed himself, that was absolute proof to Doc that he was responsible for Wealthy's condition and wasn't man enough to marry her. If Doc learned the truth now, I don't know what it would do to him. He'd blame himself for poor Kin's death."

"There's no sense in that," objected Tip. "Wouldn't Mr. Hayne have done it, anyway?"

"Of course he would. He was so mad over Wealthy. But you don't know my Doc. Nothing would ever persuade him that it wasn't his fault. With all the rest he's got on his mind, it would drive him crazy."

Impressed, the boy said, "You know best, Dinty. I'm sorry I told you."

"No. It's a good thing you did."

"Why?"

"I can have it out now with Wealthy. I've been wanting to get the truth out of her for ever so long."

At the stone house she found her friend packing a hamper of charities, to take to Poverty's Pinch, one of the good works to which she was increasingly devoting herself. Dinty said,

"Can anyone hear us?"

The girl's eyes widened in alarm. "No. What is it? Has something happened?"

"Nothing." She set her two strong young hands on the other's shoulders. Of the two she seemed now immeasurably the older and firmer. "Wealthy Latham," she said, "I want the truth from you."

The beauty cringed away, twisting in the grip of the hands, turning her face to avoid the solemn and searching eyes.

"This is dead secret," Dinty went on. "I'll never breathe a word." She reverted to the formula of solemn childhood. "Cross my heart and double-die. I won't even tell Doc. But I'm going to have the truth from you, Wealthy. Was it Silverhorn Ramsey?"

Wealthia quivered like an animal. "Yes," she whispered.

"Where is the baby?"

"There isn't any."

"Don't lie to me. Or"—her voice softened—"did it die?"

"No. There never was any."

"Wealthy!"

"There wasn't! There wasn't! There wasn't! It's God's truth. I thought there was. I was sure of it. For months. Oh, Dinty, what a hell in life I lived! I wanted to die. Then—nothing."

"You didn't get rid of it?"

"I swear in God's name, I didn't. Nobody would help me. I was almost crazy. And then—it was all a mistake. God was better to me than I deserved," she went on humbly. "Oh, Dinty! I've been such a wicked little fool! But I couldn't help myself. I'd do it all again if he came back. That's why I must never see him again. How can I make you understand?" She broke the hold of those imperative hands and threw herself into a chair, convulsed. "I don't care whether you believe me or not," she sobbed. "It's true, every word of it."

Dinty had to believe her. She was appalled. Where did that leave her adored Doc? And what of that theory of sterility to which he had pinned his faith? Dinty's brain whirled.

-15-

WINTER loomed, a grisly threat to the Amlies. With the closing of canal traffic, Horace's source of income stopped. They could still live. Unk Zeb had accumulated a noble woodpile; there was no danger of freezing. Dinty's industrious chickens, the family cow and sundry barrels containing salted pork, pickled eels and Lake Ontario sturgeon, insured them against hunger. But other expenses must be met with cash. They faced a harshly straitened future.

Horace was fretful. He had tried his hand at odds and ends of employment, only to find himself blocked by the Latham influence. Dinty found him one day in his empty and chilly office, poring over an advertisement clipped from the local weekly.

> We are in want of a good post rider to circulate our paper through Macedon, Port Gibson, etc. We seek an apprentice who is disposed to be industrious—to abhor and shun the haunts of vice and the company of obscene and pilfering youth—and who would detest the idea of *embezzling* his employer's money. Opposite characters need not apply. We are heartily sick of them and will not keep them. Good encouragement will be given to the right individual.
>
> GRANDIN & TUCKER, Props.

"Just the thing for Tip!" said Dinty enthusiastically.

Horace looked hastily away from her smile. "I wasn't thinking of it for Tip."

"Doc!" she cried in dismay. "You couldn't."

"It's honest employment," he pointed out. "It would fetch in cash, not much, but regular. And—" he forced a grin—"Fleetfoot needs exercise."

"But, Doc," she wailed. "Post riding! A man of your learning!"

"We've got to live, Puss. The question is whether they'll give me the job."

"They'd better be proud to have you."

"Genter Latham owns a share in the paper."

"I wish he was dead!"

"Unfortunately, I've never seen him looking better. He is now forwarding a movement to vote Dominie Strang out of his pulpit."

"Because he stuck by us," said his wife bitterly. "How hateful! Can he do that, Horace?"

"He can do almost anything in this town," returned he gloomily.

Her chin went up. "Except drive us out."

"He'll never stop trying."

In his shiny coat, but with boots polished, and neckcloth trimly set, Horace called at the newspaper office. Messrs. Grandin and Tucker exhibited surprise, succeeded by caution. Dr. Amlie's application would be taken under advisement, and he would be informed later. Horace understood with a sinking heart that they wished to assure themselves against objections by their backer.

No such objections were advanced. Mr. Latham remarked, with his grimmest smile, that it was just about what the young squib was fit for, and added that if he were found some morning in a snowdrift, Palmyra would be none the worst for it.

Horace entered upon the rigorous duties of post riding, growing thinner, hardier, more withdrawn from everyone but Dinty, day by day. Tip Crego had been dispatched to Hamilton College where, thanks to his mentor's tutelage, he was admitted without difficulty.

February of 1824 was a terrible month. Blizzards closed the roads for days at a time. Horace's earnings declined to the vanishing point. Unable to cover his route on horseback, he took to snowshoes. He was stormbound in an abandoned woodcutter's hut overnight and came stumbling home, burning with fever. He made his own diagnosis—pneumonia. To Dinty's terrified plea that she be allowed to call in Dr. Murchison, he returned a flat negative.

"I'd rather die with my blood still in my veins," said he, and when she failed to suppress a frightened cry, added with grim determination, "I'm not going to die, Puss. Not and leave a certain bit of business unsettled."

No explanation was needed as to what the certain piece of business was.

Before he fell into unconsciousness he gave her full directions for his care. Friends rallied to them. Quaila Crego moved in, bag and baggage, to act as nurse. Gwenny Jump, prosperous on the traffic of the Settlement, brought daily delicacies and was hurt when Dinty, as tactfully as she could, declined the offer of a loan. The brotherhood of the smithy was represented openly by the more upstanding element, such as Silas Bewar, O. Daggett, Decker Jessup and Carlisle Sneed, and secretly by the timider souls whose offerings Unk Zeb found on the doorstep of mornings. That stout old son of God, Elder Strang, was a regular visitor and helped buoy Dinty's spirits when the prospect looked blackest.

Between devoted nursing, exemption from medical attention, his hardy constitution, and a dogged determination to survive, Horace pulled through. Convalescent, he was a handful. Although the disease had left him much depleted, it took all his wife's management to prevent his going back on the road. If he did not work, he argued, how were they to manage. There was the interest on the note to meet, and after that the town tax. Could they live without money? Dinty answered that she could but that she couldn't live without him, and that she wasn't going to let him go out and work himself into a relapse. He must be patient and wait for the opening of the canal. Then they would be all right again.

What galled him worst was the constant appeal of old patients. They crawled or tottered to his door, the sick, the injured, the frightened, begging his aid. It was futile to refer them to Murchison; they had faith only in their Dr. Amlie. So he took the most importunate or unfortunate of them back. He could treat them, gratis, and still be within the law. But how could he afford to dispense the medicines that they so needed? Driven to the risk by their necessities, he accepted pay for some of his drugs. An information was laid against him. Upon the procurement of the Board of Censors he was haled into court and mulcted in the considerable sum of five dollars, with an alternative of ten days in jail.

Dinty quivered from head to foot when haggardly he confessed his imprudence and its direful consequence. Five dollars! Where was she to find it? There was but one recourse, the picklejar which in the days of their carefree prosperity had grown heavy with her pin money, now the hold-all of the household finances. It contained barely enough to cover the interest which came due with such shocking and pitiless regularity.

"I may as well go to jail," said poor Horace in the depths of contrition. "I'll be just as much use to you in jail as out."

She cried out at that. Let Genter Latham gloat over him? For she had no doubt that the magnate was the one who had fomented the charge. Not while there was a dollar in the hoard!

A week before the due-date Horace, still weak and crotchety, was summoning resolution to crawl out of his warm bed into the dank chill of the room, Dinty having long been busy about breakfast, when his heart stirred to the lilt of her voice in that little, absurd song of happiness which he had not heard for long.

Lavender's blue, diddle-diddle.
Lavender's green.
When I am king, diddle-diddle,
You shall be queen.

He dressed in haste and came out to find his wife smiling behind the coffee urn which was exhaling a not very coffee-like aroma of parched and roasted oats.

"What are you so cheery about?"

She jumped up, slipped around the table, and kissed him. "I've had a—er—communication," said she importantly.

"Who from?"

"Guess."

"I can't guess," he said dispiritedly.

"Neither can I," she returned with a trill of laughter. "Look!" She flaunted before his incredulous eyes five greenbacks.

"What are those?" he demanded.

"Forty-two dollars, lawful money," she gurgled. "Enough for the interest and four shillings over to buy you a new neckcloth."

He scowled. "Where did it come from?"

"I—don't—know. There's the cover they came in. Unk Zeb found it under the door this morning."

Horace peered at the oblong of folded paper with the broken wax along the edge. It bore, in stiff, unidentifiable capitals, the legend, "Mrs. Horace Amlie, Present."

"So there's no mistake about it." She caroled,

Lavender's green.
When I am king, diddle-diddle . . .

"Charity," he said hoarsely.

She stopped dead. "I don't care. It's money."

"Not our money. You must send it back."

"Where?"

That stumped him. "We haven't fallen that low," he said, but with less conviction. "Whom do you suspect?"

She looked as innocent as a baby. "I haven't a notion to bless myself with."

This was not the precise truth. On the previous night, she had heard soft footsteps. And in the morning she had found clear footprints. The heels were delicate and fine; finer than anything of Decker Jessup's facture. But why follow up the clue? Look so timely a gift horse in the mouth? Not Dinty! Nor would she mention her suspicion to Horace, who was in one of his resentful and stiff-necked moods. It was a boon from Heaven, that benefaction. To question or refuse it would be akin to impiety; certainly base ingratitude. If Wealthia Latham chose to appease her conscience by secret offerings, far be it from Dinty to thwart so helpful an intent. Horace, though, was still feebly conscientious or, as Dinty put it, pernickety.

"We'd better set it aside till we find out," said he.

At this, Dinty's wifely spirit of obedience broke. There was an unwonted fire in the blue depths of the eyes that were turned upon him.

"And what about the interest?" she asked with ominous quiet.

"Haven't we enough for that?"

"You know we haven't. Not since your fine was paid."

"I don't care," he shouted. "Throw the damned things into the fire."

She caught the precious notes to her bosom and stood at bay. "You'd let your wife be turned into the street by Genter Latham's bank?"

"Oh, do as you like!" he groaned.

It was well along in April when the Amlie batteau, extra-loaded with equipment and medicaments, took the water when there was barely the depth to float its shallow draft.

Harsh spring weather beset and slowed the trip. Dinty, worrying at home, grew anxious as a week passed into ten days, and ten days into a fortnight with no Horace and only such casual word of him as she could cull by frequent visits to the locks which were the circulating media of canal news.

On the seventeenth day he stamped up the steps, whistling untunefully, a manifestation which lifted the wife's heart. It was a token of satisfaction with life which she had not heard for weary months. He bustled in, enveloped her in a bear-grip which heaved her slight form clear of the floor and kissed her hungrily a dozen times. Reaching for the cash-bag at his belt, he tossed it blithely into the air. It fell to the table with a heartening bang and jingle.

"Count that," he ordered, turning again to her.

"How can I when you're hugging me?" she protested. "Behave yourself, darling."

With his arm still around her, she sorted out bills and specie.

Wonderment grew to awe as she passed the twenty-dollar mark. At thirty she stopped and kissed him again. At thirty-three she detected a dollar-note which, she suspected, was less current than it should be, and set it aside. Without it the count came to an imposing total of thirty-six dollars and some odd coppers.

"Darling," she said with a catch of the breath. "We're rich."

"We're liable to be."

"And you're well again. And happy. Aren't you?"

"Who wouldn't be, with such a wife! I feel like my own man again."

"You're not," she retorted jealously. "You're mine. Oh, Doc! Isn't it dicty to be alive! Let's go and throw a rock through Genter Latham's window."

"Have you seen Wealthia?"

"Twice. She's been here."

He looked at her with lifted brows of interrogation. She shook her head. That was as near as they now approached the subject which lay, imbedded and irritant like a foreign substance, in both minds.

Prosperity continued to smile on the Amlies, while politics worked underground. Genter Latham had acquired influence in the reconstituted Canal Commission. Early in June the blow fell.

Homeward bound, of a Tuesday, Horace had accepted a tow for the last five miles from the lordly packet-boat, *Chief Engineer.* As they approached the upper lock, Jim Cronkhite descended to the berm, hailing the captain.

"Hey! I can't lock you through."

"What's the matter?"

"Orders."

"Orders out against the *Chief Engineer?"* said the stupefied navigator.

"I can lock the *Chief Engineer,"* said Cronkhite, "but I can't take your tow."

Captain Ingram struck an attitude worthy of Nelson at Trafalgar.

"You can't take my tow! You can't take the *Chief Engineer's* tow! Why, you shrimp! You mudchick! You stinkfish! Do you know who the hell you're talkin' to? I'm the Erie Canal Navigation Line."

Horace cast off and slewed in to the berm. "What's this, Jim?" he asked quietly.

"Commission's instructions, Doc. Sorry."

"What are the instructions?"

"You and your boat are henceforth barred and proscribed from all waters, banks and locks appertainin' to the Erie Canal. Papers just come in. Want to see 'em?"

"Stick your damn papers up your pants-leg," roared Captain Ingram, tempering his language to the attentive ears of the passengers on his deck. "Swing out your tackles," he snapped to the crew.

They sprang to the work. The ropes were affixed and the batteau snugged smartly inboard.

"Now, you puddlepup! Do you refuse to take my freight?"

Cronkhite hurried back and bent to his handlebars. Horace and his batteau were freighted home on what he knew to be their last voyage.

A few weeks earlier so stern a reversal of fortune would have shattered him. Now he had regained the old fighting spirit. His only dismay was over the effect upon Dinty.

"They're going to be sorry for what they did to you in this town," she declared when she heard the news. "There's a lot of sickness."

"Since when?"

"Since you left on this last trip. It came with the warm spell. Old Murch can't handle it alone. And that fat pig from Geneva who thought he was going to step into your place, got drunk and mixed his doses and nearly killed a lot of people. So he can't come till they let him out of jail, and I hope that's never."

"I'll just sniff around after supper," he said.

His nose told him much. Freed from the nuisance of his officious and impertinent interference, the village had lapsed into its old, typical slovenliness; once again it was foul and contented. Warm aromas rose from drainage, pools and offal piles. Along Main Street manure had been washed into the gutters and shoved into conical heaps which sweated and stank. In sunlight they would be reeking with life. Perhaps with death, as well.

Horace wagged his head ominously. It was none of his affair. He had been officially discharged of all authority and responsibility in the matter. Nevertheless every instinct within him revolted at the peril which he foresaw. He prophesied dire things to Dinty, who tossed her head and said it would serve 'em right.

In the middle of the night, she awoke to the uneasy feeling of being alone. She put out a hand to where the partner of her bed should have been; the hollow in the goosedown mattress was empty though still warm. She hopped out and threw a wrap over her shoulders. Someone was moving in the office below. She went to the stairhead.

"Doc! Horace! Dr. Amlie!"

The door opened. "A call, Dinty."

"Where?"

"The Pinch."

"Do you have to go at this hour?"

An urchin whom she recognized as a canal-rat thrust forth his head.

"It's the twins, ma'am," he piped. "One's dead an' t'other's twitchin'."

"You see," said Horace.

"You'll be arrested again."

"They'll have to jail me, then. I can't stand by and do nothing."

Argument against that mood was waste of breath. She ran down, carrying his coat, helped him arrange his medicines, and saw him out into the night, accompanied by the ragamuffin.

It was broad day when he returned. He was haggard. To his wife's inquiry he shook his head.

"Too late," he said. "And they'd been sick less than forty-eight hours. There's a twelve-year-old girl down, too. I think I've checked her case."

"But what is it?"

"Intestinal. Filth and flies. It strikes like cholera."

"Oh, Doc! It isn't the cholera!"

"Might almost as well be. Give me a bite of breakfast, Dinty, and I'll get some sleep. I'm a used-up man."

So peacefully was he sleeping at noon that she at first refused to rouse him at the urgent instance of Sam'l Drake, whose fifteen-year-old son, Adam, had been stricken.

"Get Dr. Murchison," she said with a degree of saturnine satisfaction, for the wheelwright was one of those who had testified against Horace.

"He's sick with it, himself. For the pity of God, Mrs. Amlie!" His voice rattled, high and hysterical in his throat. "My boy looks like dying."

"Tell him I'm coming," shouted Horace from above.

He hurried away with the father and was able to check the deadly drain of the dysentery with blackberry brandy and Jamaica Ginger. Two other calls were on the slate when he got back; one from the Eagle, the other a maltster's apprentice in Vandowzer's brewery. By nightfall he had attended eleven patients. It was an epidemic. Dinty said, with unaccustomed hardihood, that Palmyra was getting what it deserved and that her Doc was a fool to lay himself liable to further prosecution.

"May as well be hanged for a sheep as a lamb," he retorted. "I'm taking no fees. So far, I'm clear."

"Working yourself to death for nothing!" she returned wrathfully.

The disease spread on wings. Children fell to it quickest and with the least resistance, but no age was exempt. The village fathers, convened in emergency meeting, voted to bring in outside help. But whom?

Private exchange of ideas brought out the fact that most of them wanted Dr. Vought but hesitated to suggest it before Genter Latham. The autocrat, however, made no objection when the subject was timidly broached. Although he lost his case before the commission, the Rochester man had impressed the clearheaded business element of Palmyra with his decisiveness and capacity. An appropriation from village funds were agreed upon. They invited the veteran to make an inspection and advise what was to be done.

Dr. Vought made his inspection mainly with his nose. At least, this was the impression of the special sub-committee which accompanied him on his rounds. He wrinkled his nostrils disgustedly all over their fair village. Chairman Levering offered a half-hearted apology for conditions, allowing that they had grown a little careless, maybe, but smells did not mean much, anyway. The visitor fixed him with a glassy stare.

"Death stinks," he observed succinctly.

"Do you consider this visitation a miasmatic disease, Doctor?" asked Deacon Dillard.

"Home-grown miasma," barked the visitor. "What do you folks think God gave you noses for?"

As nobody had a theory to offer, he continued, "To scent danger. If something smells bad, that's a warning. Even your dog's nose knows that much."

"But what is the nature of the disease?" asked Mr. Van Wie anxiously.

"False cholera."

There was a breath of relief. J. Evernghim thanked God audibly and was transfixed by an eye like a red bead.

"You've had deaths, I believe," said the physician.

"Three thus far."

"And they're just as dead as if they'd died of true cholera, ain't they?"

The fact, being undeniable, was tacitly allowed.

"Then don't talk like a dithered lunk," said Dr. Vought.

"Dok-tor Amlie vos alvus pesterin' us to clean up," volunteered Simon Vandowzer.

"Ah! Amlie. There's a man with brains in his head." Dr. Vought looked about him as if challenging his hearers to produce any other with such desirable equipment. "I shall need his professional aid."

The escort glanced at one another uneasily.

"Well, what's the matter now?" snapped the visitor.

"I fear the gentleman is no longer available," said Mr. Levering. "There are reasons."

"Such as?"

"*Mister* Amlie is no longer an M.D. He is prohibited from practicing here."

"Well, well, well!" said the other, elaborately sardonic. "You tell me that! Hark ye, village fathers of a bastard community, I want Dr. Amlie and I propose to have Dr. Amlie. No Horace Amlie, no John G. Vought. Is that clear?"

It was as clear as silence could make it.

"No dissenting voice? Good! We shall now proceed."

A messenger was dispatched for Horace and the tour was resumed. At its close the consultant delivered his opinion.

"The type is unmistakable. Not Asiatic cholera. Bad enough, though. You're going to suffer for your sins, my friends. Fetch me four stout laborers with shovels and picks and we'll get to work."

Palmyra accepted the cleansing as meekly as an urchin before the Sunday morning washtub. The two physicians worked night and day, aided toward the end by Murchison who had made a good recovery. Within ten days the number of new cases was on the decline; in a month the onset was over, with a total of thirteen deaths, mostly young children. The last case was a dubious one; that of Tim Mynderse, the constable, who washed down a quart of black cherries with ale followed by whisky, went to bed, writhed and died, leaving the office vacant.

In his farewell meeting with the trustees, Dr. Vought addressed to them some admonitions in very unpalatable terms, told them that they were unfaithful curators, and departed with his considerable fee in his pocket. His last call was at the Amlies' and was signalized by his plunking down upon Horace's desk the handsome sum of twenty-five dollars, representing a fair half of his emolument. More moved than he cared to show, Horace refused it, whereupon the old gentleman cursed him in seven categories for the seven different kinds of fool he was, went out the front gate and in the back and found Dinty.

"Your husband," he pronounced, "doesn't deserve you."

"He's the best husband in the world," said Dinty with conviction.

"He's the fool of his conscience. I'll warrant you're more sensible."

Dinty dimpled. "Thank you."

"Well, are you or ain't you?"

"I don't know until my conscience has the facts."

"Twenty-five dollars," said the old gentleman, and waved the bills before her dazzled vision. He supplemented the action with explicit facts. "What about your conscience now?"

"It's asleep."

"Wise child. I thought you'd see it my way."

"I wouldn't if I didn't think Horace had earned it."

"He's earned it, and better." He regarded her intently. What was coming now, Dinty wondered.

"Watch that Horace of yours, my dear."

"You think he's liable to do something foolish?" asked she, astute and alarmed.

"I'm afraid of it. He's in a dangerous frame of mind."

"Who wouldn't be!" said the wife, her eyes snapping. "They've turned him out of his profession."

"He's got the gristle to stand up to that, because he knows he's in the right. It's the Latham affair."

"I know," said she miserably. "He talks of it in his sleep."

"Therein he's afraid he's wrong," pursued the mentor. "That's rank poison to a man of his temper. He's a mind possessed, Dinty."

"Sometimes it scares me," she admitted.

"What? You don't look easy to scare."

"The fear that maybe he is wrong. Dr. Vought, *is* he right or wrong?"

"Damned if I can figure. But he mustn't do anything without consulting me."

"What kind of thing?"

"How can you tell, with a man like him? Kidnap the girl, maybe, to make an examination for himself. He's surely brooding something. I wish he could ease his brain of it."

"So do I," said the wife fervently.

He scrutinized her concerned face. "What else have you got on that restless mind of yours, child?"

For reply she got the *Eclectic* from Horace's office and presented it, opened to the significant page.

Dr. Vought read, snorting as his brisk mind assimilated the purport. "Well? What of it? What's the relevancy?" he demanded.

"I want to know if it's true. It's very important for me to know."

The little physician stared. "What! You don't mean to tell me that Horace . . ."

"No!" she blazed. "How dare you think such a thing, you—you wicked-minded old man!"

"Hoity-toity! I'm a medical practitioner. Don't try to bullyrag me, young lady. What's your concern with this? Out with it."

"I can't tell you. Is it true or not?"

"Passel of damned lies backed up with fraud. This man, Dorpener" —he tapped the paper with a horny finger—"writes himself down an ignoramus, a quack and an impostor. Why, he isn't even an M.D. Everything in his silly article has been blown to bits by better men with fuller data. Still," he added with an attempt at justice, "a-plenty of sound medical men believed his trumped-up figures. Your Horace ain't any worse than a lot of better men."

Dinty received this extraordinary statement with disfavor. "There aren't any better men," she averred stoutly. "Good-bye, and thank you, dear Dr. Vought. And I'm sorry for what I said about your mind being wicked. Would you mind not telling Horace about his mistake? Not yet, anyway."

She secreted the twenty-five-dollar honorarium (as she chose to consider it) in a place more private than the pickle-jar. It was to be their final recourse in the thin times which she saw in prospect.

Politics fermented beneath Palmyra's placid surface. There were private convocations at Simon Bewar's smithy, conferences among the elite of the ninepin alley, strategies in the inner circle of the Horse Thief Society. Shortly before the special election for the office of constable, Tom Daw, with a healthy bribe in his pocketed, manned the foot-treadle Ramage press of Messrs. Grandin & Tucker under cover of night, and ran off a batch of broadsides and ballots. Thus set in motion, the campaign gathered too much headway for the Latham-Levering-Vandowzer faction to head it off.

Horace Amlie, ex-M.D., was elected town constable by the notable plurality of fifty-seven votes. That meant a dollar a day for the tenure. It was not luxury, but it was a living.

16

THROUGH the spring and summer a further change was evident in Wealthia Latham. It manifested itself in the outer as well as the inner woman. Though her figure had never recovered its old butterfly poise and lissome slenderness, her beauty, so long subdued, glowed again. She ordered the newest and costliest modes. She coquetted gaily with her swains. Her good works fell in arrears. That shell of reserve which she had put on for a defensive armor was abandoned. No longer did she trouble to avoid Horace Amlie. When they met on the streets, she greeted him politely, though with what seemed to him a remnant of timidity.

Observant Dinty thought and feared that she knew the reason for her friend's revived spirits. The *Jolly Roger* was back on the old run. Once she was walking with Wealthia on Winter Green Knob when the peal of Silverhorn's bugle, serving notice from afar on the lock-keeper, stirred the echoes. The girl stopped in her tracks; her eyes became heavy, her mouth tremulous. Her breath quickened. Had she confessed in so many words that she and the canal man were meeting once more, Dinty could not have been certain. Before this she had noticed that the fancy boat laid over in the Palmyra basins more frequently than other craft, and that it specialized in the local freights, hemp, mint and merino wool.

On other occasions Wealthia would come out of a dreamy silence to make some obscure remark, quite unconnected with what had gone before.

"It's silly to let things frighten you," was one of them, and "If you let yourself be scared by what others think, what do you get out of life?"

Dinty took that up. "I wouldn't presume that there's much you're afraid of, Wealthy."

"Not any more. I've had my bad time."

Again, she said, "Dinty, do you realize I'm almost twenty?"

"How cruel old that used to seem!" smiled the other.

"When I'm twenty-one, I'll have my own money. That isn't long to wait."

"For what?"

"Nothing," was the hasty rejoinder. Too hasty, Dinty thought.

Promise-bound, she must not relay her apprehensions to Horace. She did, however, skirt the subject.

"Doc, do you see anything of Captain Ramsey nowadays?"

"Every time he's in town. Why, Puss?"

"Is he still married to his rich widow?"

"Very much so. She doesn't let him forget it, I gather."

"You've become quite friendly, haven't you?"

"He did me a good turn, you know, in what you are pleased to call 'that disgraceful brawl,' " he returned with his provocative grin.

On his constabulary wage, the Amlies were making ends meet, though only by virtue of Dinty's most expert economies. Powerful friends and allies were at work trying to get the ousted physician's case reopened before the full State Board: Dr. Vought with his fellow townsman, the influential Dr. Levi Ward, Dr. Hosack, the honored Dr. Alexander Coventry of Oneida County and now old Dr. Avery who had become convinced that his commission had wrought an injustice. Genter Latham was finding it more and more difficult to hold his political opposition in line.

Meantime Constable Amlie was doing a good job and, profiting by experience, doing it tactfully and almost inoffensively. Opposition dwindled. The false cholera had been a stern and salutary lesson. Palmyra made a discovery which, in a century of subsequent experience and education still fell short of universal acceptation, that it is cheaper to be clean than dirty; more profitable to be careful and healthy than careless and sick. Carly Sneed, that gay wag, paid O. Daggett a dollar to fabricate a sign which they put up at the head of Main Street.

Village Limit.
Flies, Bugs and Skeeters,
KEEP OUT!
This is Doc Amlie's Home Town.

Illness fell well below normal for the hot season. Regular elections would be held in the fall. There was little doubt that Horace's incumbency would be continued. Genter Latham himself would hardly fly in the face of public opinion to the extent of opposing it.

Labor troubles afflicted the region, as fall approached. The destructive influence of the high-wage canal-building era persisted, working like a slow poison through the body economic. Field hands were asking fifty cents a day and their keep. Something had to be done about so vicious a threat to prosperity. The wool-growers, the mint-pressers, the ropewalk owners and the hemp cultivators got together, on call from Banker Latham (who had his finger in all their enterprises) and raised a fund to fetch in a corps of immigrants.

Mint was still the standard money-crop of the region, but hemp was crowding it close. Prices were high; the market was assured; the canal allowed a favorable freighting rate; labor alone was the stumbling block. The hemp plantations called for only the lowest grade of work in the fall. No skill was required for the harvesting; any Dutchman with a hemp hook or Irisher with a peat knife could qualify with a little instruction. The stalks were cut close to the ground, left to dry, and then shocked. Through fall rains and winter snows they would slowly rot, the processes of nature loosening the fiber from the woody portion and rendering it easy of removal.

Employment in this field was therefore temporary. The approved method was to bring in a corps of migrants, house them roughly, feed them well for the sake of the long and exhausting work, pay them as little as possible, and ship them out as soon as the crop was shocked.

Communication was established with the toughest and most reliable labor factor in New York City, who contracted to supply sixty mixed Irish and Dutch immigrants. They would be brought up by Hudson River and transshipped at Albany to Erie Water, at one cent per mile per head. Only the fly-by-night casuals of navigation would take on so mean a traffic.

Wages? They would take what was given them. Few of them spoke English enough to make a protest, anyway. Delivery was to be in September when the spikes of the mint were in the purple and the leaves rich with juice; when the cannabis shrubs wanted stripping, and the sheep would be foraging the lowlands.

Word of the enterprise leaked out to Horace. It worried him. These indentured laborers were of the lowest and most degraded type, poverty-stricken and filthy of habit. Too often, strange diseases broke out where they set foot. Officially he could not interfere unless danger to the community were established. He could only be ready.

Barracks were prepared, some near the Pinch, others on higher land, one unit being back of the Latham pasture lot. This was the first intimation that the great man had reached out into the hemp industry and acquired an adjacent plantation, taken over by his bank for debt.

Wealthia was singing in her garden when Dinty walked up that way on an early September afternoon. There was in the girl's face that strange look, at once withdrawn and radiant, which her friend had learned to interpret, though, in this instance, she needed no enlightenment. She knew that the *Jolly Roger* was unloading at the warehouse.

"Come up and look at our bunkhouse," Wealthia invited.

They walked through the fields to the place. The building was primitive but clean and well-ordered.

"I'm in charge," said the heiress importantly, exhibiting first the sleeping quarters, then the cooking shack with its outdoor ovens of brick with cranes, kettles and spits. "Think of me being a wage-earner! Pa is paying me to look after his two dozen wild Irishers and dumb Dutchmen."

"When are they due?"

"Any day now. Captain Ra— I mean, a canaller who passed the *Merry Fiddler* this side of Lennox brought in word."

"The *Merry Fiddler*," repeated Dinty. "That's the awful man that Horace fought. It's a vile boat."

"Those creatures won't know the difference," said her friend disdainfully.

Captain Ramsey was in Horace's office. "Something in your line, Æsculapius," said he.

"What have you been up to now, Silverhorn?"

"Not me. It's our friend, Tugg."

"Is he looking for me?"

"Oh, no! He's had plenty of you. He's Palmyra bound with a hold full of labor." His delicate nostrils wrinkled. "Spoiled in transit, I should say."

"Redemptioners?"

"You might call 'em that. More like slaves, under their contracts. There's sickness aboard."

"Of course. There always is on those floating privies."

"Doc, they said in Utica it was the spotted typhus."

Horace sat up abruptly. "And they're going to discharge here?"

"That's the contract of delivery."

"I won't allow it."

"Then, by the bellybutton of Barnabas, you'll have your work cut out for you," grinned the canaller. "Every bigbug in town has a finger in that pie."

"Where's the boat now?"

"Ought to be just beyond Port Gibson. Tugg's underfed horses played out on him and he bought a span of old oxen. Two miles an hour."

This gave Horace ample time to arrange a reception. Harnessing Fleetfoot to the road wagon, he set out to pick up volunteers. Without difficulty he enlisted Carlisle Sneed, who brought his blunderbuss, Dad Hinch with his war musket, and Decker Jessup who, being a man of peace, was lightly armed with an ax. The quartette drove to the eastern boundary of the village, and there waited on the towpath.

Presently the ox-team hove in sight. It was guided by a wretched travesty of a youth, whose sore toes protruded nakedly from their rag-wrappings, and whose scarcecrow garb flapped in the breeze.

"Whoa!" he quavered, finding his progress blocked by an armed wagon.

The oxen stopped, drooping their great heads sorrowfully. One hundred feet back, the helmsman began to shout as the boat, losing steerage way, drifted toward the shallows. Furious bellowings reinforced his efforts. Captain Tugg, aroused from his siesta, charged up on deck.

"Whash shissh?" he roared, his enunciation having been liquidated by the rock which ended the classic duel of Lock Port. "Who the damnation hell issh shtoppin' my boat?" Horace stepped forward. "Oh, my Gawd!" said the Captain in enfeebled accents and ducked below.

At a point opposite the cabin Horace halted and hailed. A jabber of outlandish voices answered. Strange, bearded faces popped into sight. Arms flailed and gesticulated. The jabber rose to a clamor. The helmsman's petulant query cut through the babel.

"What's all this hubble-loo?"

"Don't let anyone ashore," Horace directed.

"Who says so?"

"The law." He exhibited his badge.

"Hey, Captain Tugg, Captain Tugg!" bawled the helmsman.

Setting his companions on guard, Horace jumped aboard. Tugg's ugly face appeared in the hatchway. "Ish you, you shunnabish," hissed the Captain through his dental vacancy. "Get offa my deck."

He emerged, bearing a huge horse-pistol. Musket and blunderbuss immediately converged upon his head. The pistol muzzle drooped.

"Shree to one," said Captain Tugg reproachfully.

"This is business, not ill-will, Captain," said Horace civilly.

"Whash the bisshnish?"

"Have you fever aboard?"

"Goddam lie," said the mariner sulkily. He had had his troubles in Utica, where he had informally dropped two corpses overside.

"You have sick men. Take me to them, please."

Four hairy creatures lay in unspeakable filth between-decks. Horace hardened himself to make the examination. There was little doubt concerning the nature of the disease. The high fever and telltale spots were evidence enough. The medical constable had a problem on his hands.

His first act upon disembarking was to buy a gallon of vinegar at the nearest farmhouse, strip to the waist, and disinfect himself with jealous particularity. On returning to the towpath, he gave his orders: no one was to leave the *Merry Fiddler* until further notice.

"Hey!" said the helmsman grievously, "I gotta gal waitin' on me in town."

"I'm afraid she will have to wait."

"How long?"

"Until the fever is over."

The Captain shrieked, "Like hell! Whoosh goin' to feed ush?"

"The village, I suppose," answered Horace, to whom this question had already presented itself with unpleasant force.

There was a splash in the water, astern. The helmsman had unobtrusively gone outboard, gained the berm, and was now running like a deer for safety.

"Tell Genter Latham," yelled Captain Tugg after him. The runner waved and went on.

"Trouble coming," observed Decker Jessup.

"You don't have to be the Prophet Isaiah to tell me that," retorted Horace gloomily.

It materialized within the hour in a cloud of dust, from the midst of which a speeding gig appeared, discharging first Genter Latham, then Lawyer Upcraft. The magnate advanced upon Horace.

"By what right do you stop this boat?" he demanded. It was the first word he had spoken to the other since the quarrel.

"There is a malignant and catching disease aboard, Mr. Latham."

"Let it stay there. I'll take the sound ones." He raised his voice. "Captain, muster your passengers."

Horace's lips thinned to a hard line. He reached back and took the Human Teapot's musket from him. "I'll shoot the first man that sets foot ashore," he announced.

The outlanders, who had crowded to the rail armed with hemp

hooks and peat knives, though probably failing to understand the language, had no doubts about the musket. They backed away.

"Why, you . . ." began Latham, when the lawyer's hand upon his shoulder stopped him.

They withdrew to confer in low tones. Both climbed into the gig. Genter Latham laid to with his whip. The gig whirled dustily away.

"Doc," said Carlisle Sneed, "the trustees'll never pay to feed these cattle."

"They'll have to," said Horace, but without conviction. "I'll go back and ask for a meeting."

Leaving the Human Teapot on military guard, he drove the other two back. It was not necessary for him to request a meeting. The meeting was waiting for him, having been urgently convened by Genter Latham. Horace stated his case briefly, asking an allowance to provide food and medicines for the marooned men.

The storm broke. The village fathers were outraged. Not only was the labor sequestrated for which they had paid transport in advance, but they were now expected to shoulder the expense of maintaining it in idleness at "the whim of a swollen and crazy fool" (Genter Latham's contribution to the amenities of the occasion). The session was of one mind. Constable Amlie was ordered to lift the embargo forthwith.

"I am responsible for the safety of this community," said that official firmly. "You have no authority to direct me and I refuse to obey the order."

"Vere's Lawyer Upcraft?" shouted Simon Vandowzer, and received a glowering side-glance from Genter Latham's warning eyes.

The magnate knew well enough where the lawyer was. He was on his way, with all speed, for Canandaigua, where court was holding.

One of those many banquets whereby the small communities of the period lived and were made glad convoked at the Eagle Tavern that evening. Early among the toasts, and before the diners became too cheery and optimistic to be impressed, Horace secured the floor and delivered a brief disquisition upon Typhus. All good citizens, he told the assemblage, would shun the vicinity of the pest-ridden boat. One fugitive, he warned them, was already in their midst; the runaway helmsman was a threat, to be apprehended on sight and returned to the *Merry Fiddler*. (Nobody, however, got sight of him, as, after a visit to the Settlement, he took to the road and subsequently turned up in Rochester, having prudently made the twenty-two-mile journey on foot.)

With the painful memory of the false cholera still tweaking at their bellies, the guests were well inclined to heed Horace's words. Several volunteered as guards. He held a session afterward and divided them into watches. In vain did the more conservative citizens pooh-pooh the danger. Word came in opportunely that one of the redemptioners had just succumbed. The village was ready to accept the medico-constable's views in toto.

With matters well under control, as he supposed, Horace rode out to the boundary after breakfast next morning. The *Merry Fiddler* was snugged to the bank. The passengers lolled on deck in the morning coolness. Aft of his cabin sat Captain Eleazar Tugg, woebegone and subdued. At sight of the constable a mighty clamor arose. The prisoners thronged to the rail, jabbering vociferously and pointing with unmistakable significance to their open jaws. They were hungry.

Barbarians they might be—and certainly looked—but to hold them imprisoned and unfed would be more than barbarous. It was Horace's immediate responsibility. If the trustees would not feed them, the contracting employers who brought them there must. Distasteful though the errand might be, Horace could think of no other course than to lay the problem before Genter Latham and his associates. He was about remounting Fleetfoot when he was hailed from the water. A dugout drew in from which emerged Ephraim Upcraft. He addressed Horace in his best courtroom manner.

"Oyez! Oyez! Oyez!" said he, and tapped the constable's shoulder with an official document, which he delivered into the other's hand.

It was a court order, under seal of the State of New York, prohibiting Horace Amlie, constable of the town of Palmyra, or any other official or private citizen from interfering with, preventing, or hampering the free disembarkment and importation of such passengers as were aboard the packet-boat, *Merry Fiddler*, Captain Eleazar Tugg, upon the berm, towpath, or territory adjacent to the Erie Canal in all its length and span. The injunction had been issued upon the plea of Genter Latham, Esq., of Palmyra, N. Y. Horace read and returned it to the lawyer.

"This is the worst day's work you've ever done in this town," he pronounced slowly.

"*Majestas legis,*" returned the other. "I call upon and summons you to respect the honorable court's order."

"Oh, I'll respect it," answered Horace, and advanced upon the lawyer. "And for two red cents I'd ram it down your gullet." Upcraft fled.

Horace withdrew his guard. No other course was open to him. At once the immigrants came streaming off the boat, the sound supporting the sick, and were marched to town to be parceled out among the various employers.

Attempts to inspect living conditions in the shacks were checkmated by the Honest Lawyer, who produced a new and more sweeping injunction. It was rumored, denied and rumored again that two new cases had appeared in Genter Latham's squad, and three among the workers in the mint meadows. The employers declared that the ailment was no more than the "canal shakes" to which all newcomers were liable.

Under Horace's persuasion, Elder Strang preached a powerful sermon on the care of the body and the duty incumbent upon a good Presbyterian to guard his household against the contamination of disease. It had one good effect. People shunned contact with the foreigners as far as possible. The discourse was regarded as settling the old clergyman's hash. He was "giving a bad name to the town." Owing to Genter Latham's hostility, his incumbency was already precarious. Now it was practically certain that the next church meeting would throw him out upon the world, after thirty years of devotion and sacrifice.

About this time, Gail Murchison's practice began to increase. It was whispered that Genter Latham's clique were subsidizing the whiskered physician. He went about proclaiming that fears of a pestilence were all hunca munca, that the slight increase in sickness was due to the fact of the imported workers being unused to the climate, that there was nothing malignant about the cases and that he had cured all of those under his care without complications.

It was freighted about that Horace Amlie's warnings were the vapors of a professional alarmist. What standing had he, anyway, a discredited physician? Horace, himself, fell a prey to doubts. So little was known as to "the spotted manifestation of the typhoid disease," as the erudite medical pamphleteers termed it. Such data as he could elicit from his reading were meager and contradictory. Nothing conclusive could he find regarding the "catching" period. Had it already passed in Palmyra?

Such was the official opinion of the Board of Trustees. They issued a manifesto, certifying the village free of all but normal and seasonal sickness.

Under cover of night Quaila Crego came to Horace's office.

"There's two cases at the Settlement," she said in a fearful undertone.

"How do you know?"

"Gwenny called me in. She was afraid to send for you for fear of getting you into more trouble."

"Did you see them?"

"Yes. It's the spotted death, for certes. My craft is useless against that. I'm going away, Doctor, before it reaches the Pinch."

"Tell Gwenny I'll look in tomorrow."

Another caller was before Horace at the Settlement. Dr. Gail Murchison looked up with a sour face from Donie Smith's bedside. The girl was delirious. To avoid a sickroom squabble with his confrere, Horace moved on to the other patient, a girl known as the Peach. Hers was a newer case, but the maculations were well defined and typical. While Horace was examining them, Old Murch entered.

"Are you treating this case, *Mister* Amlie?" he asked with intention.

"No," said Horace.

Gwenny Jump came to the door. Murchison gave her some directions, ignoring Horace. "The measles should abate presently," he concluded.

Horace almost shouted, "The *what?*"

"Measles," repeated the other, looking annoyed.

"Good God Almighty, man! Have you ever seen rubeola spots resembling those?"

"Rubeola patrida," said the physician blandly. "An unusual type. Anomalous. Anomalous."

Horace said to the proprietress, "These girls have typhus. They are very sick. Donie will probably die."

To him, not to his senior, Gwenny said, "What must I do?"

"Pay no attention to him, Mistress Jump," puffed Murchison.

"Send the other girls away," directed Horace. "Let nobody come here. Are you going to look after them?"

"Who else would?" said she simply.

"Don't touch them any more than you can help. Keep yourself washed in vinegar. Dr. Murchison will treat the cases," he added with an unpleasant grin directed at that gentleman.

"Harr! Hummh!" grunted the practitioner. "Here's a great todo about a small matter."

"Small matter, eh?" snapped Horace. "Tell me that in a couple of days."

Murchison had nothing to tell in that time. Nor would he answer questions when Horace accosted him on Main Street. The constable called again at the brothel, to find it closed, barred and void of life. The sick girls had been spirited away. The next day two suspicious cases were reported from Poverty's Pinch. There were grisly rumors about conditions in the Latham labor quarters, but Horace was not allowed near the place so he could neither verify nor disprove them. He even went so far as to approach the camp at dead of night, whereupon a guard testified to the explicitness of Genter Latham's system by firing a musket at or toward him.

Returning thoughtfully homeward, he heard a sound of muffled hammering back of Bezabeel Fornum's shop. Never the most industrious of men, the cabinet factor was not prone to nocturnal labor. Horace made his way by path to a rear shed where he beheld Fornum, by the light of two candles, busily engaged.

"Hello, Bez," he said.

The factor looked up, hammer poised above an oblong pine box. " 'Lo, Doc," he responded. "You kinda scairt me."

"You work late."

"Yup."

"Special job?"

"Yup."

Horace glanced about the dim interior. Two other factures, similar in size and shape to the one in hand, leaned against the wall.

"What do you call those?"

"Feed troughs," answered Bezabeel without a blink.

"For worms," said Horace.

"Cute, ain't ye?" commented the toiler.

"Where are they going, Bez?"

"Don't know and ain't inquirin'."

"How far wrong would I be in guessing that the trustees are paying for this job?"

"Not fur mebbe."

"How many more besides these have you made?"

The factor set down his hammer, removed a chaw from between his jaws and regarded his visitor earnestly. "Now, look, Doc. You and me is good friends. I'm bein' paid extry money for this, so I'd just as ruther you'd go back to your bed and mind your own business. Good night to you."

"Good night, Bez," said Horace.

He was up early, making a rough canvass of the village. Though many doors were closed against him as a troublemaker, he had gathered enough information for his purposes when he presented himself at the Board meeting that afternoon with a request for a hearing.

To a growing uneasiness among the members he owed his admittance. While they had adopted and officialized the Murchison pronouncement of measles, there was a feeling among some of them that much was being concealed. They allowed Horace five minutes.

For once in his life he was diplomatic. There might be, he admitted, a question as to the exact nature of the disease in their midst, but there could be no doubt that it had assumed epidemic proportions. There had been at least four deaths since the previous meeting, perhaps more (several of the members blinked), and Dr. Murchison could testify to an abnormal amount of sickness. The town was endangered. Something ought to be done.

"Vot?" asked Trustee Vandowzer.

"Vote a fee to Dr. John Vought and bring him up from Rochester. He is experienced in such matters."

Angry protest came from Dr. Murchison, backed by Lawyer Upcraft. But there were influences working against them. Deacon Dillard's eldest son lay mysteriously ill; the "measles" which Old Murch had diagnosed in the Drake household resembled no eruption with which the experienced Grandma Drake was familiar, and Constable Amlie's confident statement as to deaths had impressed Chairman Levering (who did not like having been kept in the dark) and several others. Out of their alarms the Board found courage to withstand the Latham influence, voted fifty dollars for Dr. Vought, and deputed Horace to procure his attendance. To Horace's surprise, the magnate offered no objection.

The old gentleman arrived, full of spunk and fire. He made a tour of the village in company with Horace, brusquely declining the offered escort of Dr. Murchison, after which he addressed the Board in such terms as that dignified body had never before heard vented upon itself. Numskulls and nincompoops were the milder terms of his characterization. As for that looby who called himself Doctor Murchison. God save the mark! professional courtesy prevented a proper description of a man who could not distinguish the bright red of rubeola from the dull purple of typhus. For typhus it was, and the honorable Board could swallow that or puke it up, just as they liked. For the rest, he demanded that the ban on medical practice be at once lifted from his young and valued colleague. This was done by tacit allowance, Dr. Murchison hoarsely protesting that it was illegal, as, in fact, it was.

Dr. Vought's presence was a vast relief to Horace. The Rochester physician had experienced one typhus epidemic, as a medical student in New York City. No better expert could have been found. Taking up his domicile in the Amlie house, on Dinty's pressing invitation, he settled in to see the battle through.

In such conditions, it was impossible for Dinty to refrain from contributory activities. With Wealthia Latham and Happalonia Upcraft, she rallied the alumnae of the now defunct Little Sunbeams Cluster to the standard of Good Works. Entrance to the danger spots was interdicted to them, but they found helpful occasions in distributing medicines, acting as messengers for those autocrats, Drs. Vought and Amlie, canvassing houses for suspicious illnesses, and bearing food and encouragement to the poor.

Another and an unexpected aide joined Horace. Tip Crego had formed a determination to follow in his benefactor's footsteps and become an M.D. As he could not qualify by "riding" with the unlicensed ex-Doctor Amlie, he had been putting in his vacation by acting as factotum for the eminent Dr. Alexander Coventry of Oneida County who, learning of the affliction under which Palmyra lay, gave the lad a leave of absence to study an epidemic at first hand. Dinty welcomed her former playmate with delight.

"How do you like being a collegiate young gentleman?" she asked.

Tip liked it enormously, all but one feature. "I have to sleep between stone walls, even in the warmth," he complained. "Like a jail. I almost smother."

"Dr. Vought has our guest chamber," she smiled. "And I could hardly offer a learned scholar like you lodgment in the tool-shed. But there is shelter in the garden."

"I'll do finely there," he said. "Aunt Quaila is off gypsying."

He rigged himself a cunning lodge and settled in to act as man-of-all-duties for the two overworked medical men.

Ominous symptoms were reported from scattered localities, mainly households having some connection with the imported labor. Within a few days, Dr. Vought had identified five well-developed cases and two doubtful ones. The townsfolk had no acquired immunity in their blood; the pest felled them where it struck. Marcus Dillard died a week after being stricken. Cole Barnes lost his wife. J. Evernghim's youngest daughter was at death's door. Rumor spread that two more corpses had been removed by night from the Pinch. Secrecy surrounded the labor camps.

Although he foresaw an angry reaction, Horace placarded the infected houses, a measure hitherto reserved for smallpox. As the labels bore the word, TYPHUS, in conspicuous lettering, this was flying in the face of officialdom. The Board of Trustees ordered the offending papers removed. But the damage was done.

Rochester, Auburn and other newspapers published the bad news. Stage coaches canceled their victualing arrangement with Mine Host St. John. Packet-boats refused to take on passengers from the vicinity. Business suffered. Horace Amlie became Palmyra's most unpopular citizen. The *Sentinel* denounced him in a sizzling editorial. Tar, feathers and rail were too good for this ill bird who befouled his own nest. Horace went about his business with grim determination. There was plenty of work for him, for, despite his new unpopularity, the frightened citizens preferred to trust his skill rather than the pretentious ignorance of his rival.

"You'll live it down," said Dr. Vought, rubbing his hands. He enjoyed a fight in a good cause. "Have you noticed that we're being weasled, lad?"

Horace had. He had observed a slinking fellow clumsily spying upon their night rounds.

"Who is he?" asked the old gentleman.

"A poor rat from the Pinch. He does Lawyer Upcraft's dirty work for him."

"He isn't working for Upcraft this time. It's Murchison," said Dr. Vought, who had a surprising way of finding out things for himself. "That old muckworm is after evidence."

"What kind of evidence?"

"Illegal practice, I presume."

"On my part?" Horace grinned. "I'm 'riding' with the learned Dr. Vought. Nothing illegal in that."

"All very well," grunted the learned one, "but how many times have you gone ahead on your own hook?"

"Only in emergency cases, sir."

"Well, they're hoping to get something to hang you on. That's certain. Don't give 'em any more openings than you can help, lad."

"I wonder if Genter Latham isn't back of it."

"I'll tell you something about Genter Latham, my boy. That man is scared."

"I've never known him to be."

"He is, just the same. Of the typhus. There's more and worse of it in his camp than anyone but himself knows of, by my guess. You don't notice him taking any stand against us."

"That's true," admitted Horace thoughtfully.

"Nor won't till the run of the fever is over. He don't know when he mightn't need us." This time it was the old gentleman who grinned. "That pus-brain of a Murchison isn't getting favorable results from his bleed-and-purge treatments. We're stealing his patients every day. After you're reinstated, they'll be your patients. That's why he's so hot after your scalp. He'll stop at nothing to get it."

The epidemic dwindled. No more did Bezabeel Fornum's muffled hammer sound at night. A full week passed without a new report. After the evening rounds, the eminent Dr. Vought addressed his assistant.

"I believe on my sinful soul we've got it under, my boy. Give me a drink, a smoke and a bed, and let me sleep the clock around, for by the moldering bones of Galen, if you wake me up before my time I'll gut you with your own scalpel."

Informed of the good news, Dinty climbed the slope next morning to bear it to Wealthia. Turning the corner of the Latham porch, she came upon father and daughter in quiet talk. Genter Latham stood up abruptly. That expression of smiling tenderness which he kept for Wealthia alone was supplanted by a black glower. He turned his broad back upon the visitor and entered the house. The girl flushed an unhappy red.

"You mustn't mind him, Dinty," said she. "He's been under a strain, with all this trouble."

"I know," sympathized her friend. "Hadn't I better stay away for a while?"

"No. You mustn't. I want to see you as much as I can while I can."

"But you can any time," replied Dinty, puzzled.

Wealthia gazed out across the garden. "I may be going away."

Scrutinizing her, Dinty was struck with something new in her loveliness: a soft excitement, a look of adventure and expectancy such as, she thought, an explorer might wear at the start of a voyage into the unknown.

"When?" asked Dinty.

"I don't exactly know. It's a secret. Promise."

"Cross my heart and double-die," swore Dinty.

"I've been wanting to tell you something for a long time."

"I've always told you everything," said Dinty. "Well, pretty near."

"I know. This is about Silverhorn."

"I think it's desperate you're still seeing him."

Wealthia looked away. A smile hovered on her lips. "I was with him last night."

"Where?"

"On the *Jolly Roger*. All night."

"Oh, Wealthy!"

"I don't care," burst out the girl with defiant passion. "I'm tired of all this pretending and concealing and waiting. I'm going away with him."

"Oh, *Wealthy!* Where?" cried Dinty, and again her friend said, "I don't care. Anywhere he wants to take me."

"Aren't you afraid?"

"Yes, but I can't help myself."

"But—but, Wealthy. Mrs. Ramsey. His wife."

The quick, angry, lovely color warmed the dark face. With appalling simplicity and sincerity, Wealthia said, "She isn't his wife. I am. He had me before he had her. And since. More times than I can tell you."

"Wealthy, I do believe you're out of your mind."

The smile returned to the curved lips. "I believe so, too. I've got no mind or soul or body that doesn't belong to him."

"It's terrible." Dinty was near to weeping.

"It's terrible, and it's wonderful."

"You'll be a Lost Soul."

"I tried to be good. I tried for a while to keep myself from him. It's no use."

One more matter was on Wealthia Latham's mind. She made her confession with courage.

"Dinty, I'm sorry about getting Horace into such trouble. You must tell him so after I'm gone. He thought he was right about me. So did I. He might so well have been! I—I don't understand it even now. When Pa knows that I've gone away with Silverhorn, he'll realize that he was in the wrong, and that I acted as I did because I was afraid to face him with the truth. It will be all right between Horace and him then."

"I don't believe it will ever be all right between them," said Dinty with profound depression.

Wealthia's desperate resolution weighed upon Dinty's spirits. Horace rallied her over holding something back from him, but abandoned this process when he saw that she was genuinely troubled. One Wednesday evening, the publication day of the *Sentinel*, he sat across the table from her, reading by the smudgy light of the Seneca oil lamp. He lowered the paper and whistled.

"Listen to this, Puss." He read a flattering description of the Elegant Durham Cargo Boat, *Jolly Roger*, sold to Captain Stillwell of the *American Spy,* with all appurtenances, for the round sum of thirteen hundred dollars. "So Silverhorn sold out," he observed. "Wonder what's up."

He was astonished beyond measure when Dinty, after struggling for a moment against some mysterious emotion, jumped to her feet and bolted from the room.

-17-

Greatly refreshed by his twelve-hour repose, the learned Dr. Vought announced his intention of extending his visit for a few days with a view to writing a brochure for his favorite medical journal.

"I'll give you a title for it," said Horace. "The Triumph of Science, or How the Pest was Eliminated."

Lowering his cup of coffee, the guest eyed his erstwhile disciple with dark suspicion.

"What might that mean?" he demanded.

"Nothing at all, sir." Horace's aspect was innocence itself. "All treatises on epidemics conclude with the triumph of medical science over the disease. Isn't that true? So I assume that yours will."

"Damme! I believe on my soul the boy is making sport of me."

"Oh, no, sir!" said Horace, full of shock.

"Of medical science, then. That's worse."

"Every disease, properly understood, yields to its ordained remedy," recited the young man woodenly.

"Who said that?"

"Every lecturer I ever listened to."

"Not me, you young yahoo!"

"Well, perhaps not you. But it's accepted medical doctrine."

"Have you kept case records of this epidemic?"

"Yes, sir. Dinty has them copied fairly for you. You might begin with Big Shawn."

"Which is he?"

"The red-headed Irisher in Mr. Latham's lot. He was one of the first."

"What was the treatment?"

"Brandy, opium and Peruvian bark," said Horace consulting the neat entry.

"Recommended by the highest authorities on typhus. It recovered him, I believe."

"Something did."

"And we exhibited that same remedy in the case of the Dutchman who came down next day."

"Piet Vroot. He died."

"So he did, now that you mention it. Odd. We tried a different method after that, didn't we?"

"Bark-and-wine and volatile alkali. Three of those cases recovered and one died."

"I've always leaned to that regimen, myself."

"So did I until that fourth death at the Pinch. We were giving it down there, if you remember."

Dr. Vought swore in his beard. "I suppose you think oil of peppermint, elder-root decoction and the blisters are better."

"I don't believe there's any difference," returned the young man boldly. "The disease runs its course, and if we can fortify the system to resist it, we've done about all that science can do."

"And what becomes of medical practice on that theory?" roared the veteran. "Not that I believe all that's in the books," he added, moderating his tone. "Not half, for that matter. In fact, I'd like some of the treatises I've written blotted out and forgotten," he admitted ruefully. "Ah, well! The people die and go the way of all earth, but the race is preserved. Small thanks to science, say you. We live and learn. But our books live after us and perpetuate our errors. *Littera scripta manet*. I think I won't write that article after all, my lad, and be damned to you for an interfering and undermining young heretic." He finished his smoke and tossed the stump into the fireplace. "I saw our friend, Latham, yesterday."

"Does he still hold out for measles?"

"Pretends to. I told him when the spots came out on his belly to fetch 'em around to me. He cursed me and stamped away."

"He's a hard man to move."

"You should know. Anything more about the girl?"

Horace shook his head morosely.

"Look at it sensibly," said his senior. "The girl has been pregnant. That much I allow as probable though unproven. She is no longer pregnant. Ergo, there has been an abortion or, more likely, a miscarriage."

"Then I shan't rest until I've proved it to Genter Latham."

"And ruined the girl's life?" said the old man gently.

"It needn't go any further."

"You know Genter Latham. He'll turn her out like a strumpet."

Horace's face was haggard. "Haven't I a right to think of my own future and my wife's?"

"Ah, that's a nice question. If it were a fair issue betwixt the two, I'd say yes. But I'll be open with you, lad. It would be an uphill fight as long as you stayed here, with the most powerful element of the community against you." He set a persuasive hand on the other's arm. "Come to Rochester," said he. "We're a growing village with golden prospects. Already we have forged ahead of your Palmyra. There's a brave opening for a knowledgeable young physician. Levi Ward is growing old. Thaddeus Smith is a discreditable and discredited scamp. I'm not as young as I was. We'll get you reinstated by the State Medical in Genter Latham's teeth. There lies your future, lad."

"I won't accept reinstatement on those terms. If I'm rounched out of here at the toe of Genter Latham's boot, so help me God, I'll never again practice medicine."

Dr. Vought snorted like an enraged bullock. "Of all the double-damned, pigheaded, mush-brained sapwits!" he stormed, and stamped out into the garden to find Dinty and relieve his mind.

He had little comfort of her. Horace, she said with resignation, was that way, always had been that way, always would be that way. There was no use trying to change him. She ought to know, she added, having tried with uniform lack of success. Moreover, she didn't want him changed. The old man snorted again and opined that there wasn't one of 'em to mend the other.

Two days later she was up before the household and had gathered a dozen fresh-laid eggs for the breakfast omelette when a movement in the boundary hedge drew her attention. Silverhorn Ramsey's face appeared. It was white and lined.

"I want the Doc," he said.

"He isn't up yet."

"Get him up."

"What's happened?"

"She's taken."

"The fever?"

"Yes. It came on before daylight."

"Are you sure it's the fever?"

"The spots are all over her." He shivered.

Dinty considered. "Does her father know?"

"How could I tell him? How could I let him know I'd been with her?"

"My husband won't set foot in that house," said she decisively. "You should know that, Captain Ramsey."

"She may be dying," he said brokenly.

Dinty took a resolution. "I'll come, myself," she said.

Silverhorn hesitated. "It's dangerous," he said with an effort.

"Somebody must tell Mr. Latham. Then, if he sends for Horace I might persuade him to come. Or Dr. Vought. He's here, too."

"That would be better," said Silverhorn. "For God's sake wake him."

But Dinty knew her medical ethics too well for that. In the circumstances of strained relations, she explained, either physician would have to be called in by the head of the household. She set out for the stone house on the rise, accompanied by the canaller, who, as they approached the spot, slipped into a thicket to await further news.

An open window on the ground floor afforded the caller easy entry. Dinty tiptoed up the stairs and down the length of the hall, lifted the latch on Wealthia's door, and pushed gently. It resisted. Bolted! Of course. It would be, since Silverhorn had been there. He must have made his exit by the porch pillar. Access by that route, however, would be too difficult even for Dinty's practiced skill. She knocked on the door, at first lightly, then more insistently. There was no response. Setting her ear to the woodwork, she could hear a dim babbling.

Genter Latham must be called. She ran to his door and hammered with both fists. The bolt slipped; the door was swung wide. He stood before her in shift and nightcap, massive, surly, his eyes heavy with slumber."

"What is it?" he demanded.

"Wealthy. I'm afraid she's ill."

He stared at her stupidly. "How come you here?"

Dinty was deft at improvisation. "Our dun heifer strayed. I followed her here and heard Wealthy crying out."

He strode to the door and shook it, calling on his daughter's name.

"Break it in," Dinty urged. "She won't answer you."

For the first time, fear showed in his face. The woodwork crashed before him. Dinty followed him to the bed. Its occupant lay, sprawled and half nude. Between the firm, young breasts was a scattering of angry spots. The eyes were glazed, and only partly open. Genter Latham bent over the tossing figure.

"My dawtie! My dawtie!" he murmured. She gave no sign of hearing him.

"Don't touch her," warned Dinty, moistening the hot brow and neck.

The great eyes, sunken and red-rimmed but still lovely, opened wider, though with a vacant gaze. The lips parted to a sigh which would have merged into a name.

"Silv—" she began when Dinty's swift hand pressed upon her mouth.

Genter Latham, distraught, asked not so much of Dinty as of any kindly powers that might aid, "What shall I do? What shall I do?"

"Dr. John Vought is at our house," said Dinty.

It recalled him to practicality and authority. "Go and fetch him. Quick!"

"I am better here than you," she returned calmly. "Do you go."

Genter Latham ran from the room. Dr. Vought returned with him. One look sufficed the expert.

"It's the true typhus," he pronounced.

Genter Latham could hardly force his lips to form the words of his agonized question: "Will she die, Doctor? Will she die?"

"That no man can say yet."

"I'll give you a thousand dollars to save her," he babbled. "I'll give you two thousand, five thousand."

"Man, man!" said the old physician pityingly. "Do you think your money can buy the life?"

On her way home, Dinty diverged to speak a word to Silverhorn Ramsey in his hiding place. He begged for a chance to see his love, if only for a word, but she pointed out the impossibility.

"It wouldn't do you any good, anyhow," she told him. "She wouldn't know you."

She tried to harden her heart against the groan that she heard as she moved on.

Horace received her angrily. He insisted, against her protests, in scrubbing her, himself, with contra-infectants until she thought her skin was coming off, and, as he scrubbed, he scolded.

"Haven't the Lathams harmed us enough without your risking your life?" was the burden of his wrath.

"Oh, Doc, she's so sick!" said Dinty. "I wish you'd go and see her."

"I'll go when I'm called and not before," he retorted.

He was called. On the fourth day, Dr. Vought who had been unremitting in his devotion to the case chiefly on account of Dinty's grief, said to the father, "This is going badly. I should like a consultation."

"Send for anyone you want at any cost."

"I should like to have Dr. Amlie."

"No, by God!"

Dr. Vought shrugged. "Very well."

In an hour the fever-scorched girl began to toss and babble again. Genter Latham broke down.

"Get Amlie," he snarled.

Horace came with a divided mind. He hoped to save the patient. He hoped also and ardently that, in the delirium which possessed most of her moments, she might reveal her secret in such unmistakable and definite form as to convince her father.

By the heroic and, as it was generally deemed, desperate resort of tepid baths, Wealthia's temperature was reduced. She recognized those around her, and even had a weak smile for Horace. But at night the fever burned more hotly, and in the morning she was a desperately ill girl. Both physicians were there and the father when, in one of those accesses wherein "the intellectual power, through words and things, goes sounding on its dim and perilous way," she began to speak clearly, coherently, consecutively under the stress of an unforgotten dread. She had been staring stony-eyed at Horace Amlie. Now she closed her eyes and spoke with a piteous intensity of defensiveness.

"It isn't true! It isn't *true!* It couldn't be true. Don't believe him, Pa. You don't believe him, do you? You couldn't believe that of me, not of your dawtie. How could he know? Nobody could know . . . Poor Kin! Poor Kin! He told Kin. Why did he tell Kin?" It died out in a rapid, muttering repetition, "Lies—lies—lies—lies . . ."

Horace's face was ghastly. Dr. Vought was gazing at him with pity in his expression. Genter Latham twitched all over his powerful frame with the latent lust of murder.

A voice from the dead had accused the living. Wealthia Latham died as the sun went down.

-18-

PEOPLE passing the stone mansion on the night of Wealthia's death, heard Genter Latham's dreadful voice crying out upon man and God. The two domestics fled the place in terror. By their report, the master was circling the floor of the room where his dead daughter lay, with a loaded musket on his arm, cursing and mouthing threats that he would kill Horace Amlie on sight. Squire Jerrold, his nearest friend, was turned from the door with brutal words.

The servants refused to return. All that night the light burned in the dead girl's room where the father watched. In the morning a shawled and veiled figure walked up the kitchen path. Sarah Dorch quietly built the fire, put on a kettle to boil and got breakfast. She went to Wealthia's chamber.

"Come, Genter," she said. "You must eat."

He stared at the ravaged face, rose and with a strange docility followed down the stairs. The meal finished, he returned to his vigil. Sarah ordered the house as best she was able and went to see Dominie Strang. Though Genter Latham had left the Presbyterian Church in dudgeon when its pastor sided with Horace Amlie, he had formed no other affiliation; accordingly the clergyman deemed himself still responsible for that racked soul.

"I'll come at once," said he.

He was received at first with dull hostility, then apathetically permitted to pray over the death bed, and to make arrangements for the services and burial.

In the Amlie home, after the return, there was hardly less unease than in the house of mourning. Dinty's grief was distracted by her alarms for her husband. Through all their close-knit association, she had never before seen him in such a mood; so distraught, so possessed of dark and lost ruminations, so hedged away from her love and anxiety. Was he sickening for the pestilence? Frightened, she appealed to Dr. Vought. He relieved her more immediate fears.

"No, not the typhus," he said.

"What is it, then?"
"It's the mind, not the body."
"He won't talk to me," she said pitifully.
"Nor to me," said the old man. "I think he's trying to nerve himself to some course of action."
"But what?"
"I don't know."
"Do you have to go back to Rochester, Dr. Vought?" she made appeal.
"No. I'm staying over."
By that she knew how seriously worried he, too, was. She was profoundly grateful.
At ten o'clock the guest yawned, consulted his watch, said he was for bed, and advised his junior to follow his example. Horace shook his head. He had some work to finish up, he said.
Dinty saw the old physician to his chamber and went to her own. Exhausted, she soon fell asleep. A cold splatter across the bed woke her. She ran to close the window against the storm and stood, stiffened. A broad, flickering sheet of radiance illuminated the path below. Upon it, Horace, bareheaded and coatless in the furious lash of the rain, paced with bent head. She stifled her instinct to call him. Some inner, wifely wisdom warned her that it was better to let him alone.
Lowering the window cautiously lest the sound of it reach his ears, she put on a wrap, drew up a chair, and sat watching in the intermittent revelation of the skies. Up and down he strode, up and down, heedless of the encompassing turmoil. A small, dead branch, torn loose by the gale, struck and staggered him. He threw it aside and resumed his patrol. She thought fearfully of him now as a creature possessed who, if he were startled, might well run away from her in panic and never return.
Soon his steps began to falter and slow down. Dinty crept downstairs, stirred the banked ashes in Unk Zeb's oven to heat, and set on a pannikin of fresh water. It was steaming when Horace came into the house through the side entry. She mixed a toddy with the hot water and met him with it. He took and drank it gratefully.
"What are you doing up, Puss?" he said.
Voice and manner were relaxed, near to normal now. He was, she thought, like a man who, after wandering in mazes of doubt, had at last emerged upon the known road of decision. She kissed him and said in the best approximation to everyday tone that she could manage.
"Aren't you silly, darling! You're soaked to the skin. Come to bed."

They woke to a day of freshness. The air had been vivified by the storm after heat. Dinty, correctly garbed in full mourning, visited the Latham mansion. She saw Genter Latham, but he would not talk to her. From Sarah Dorch she learned the time of the funeral, eight o'clock that evening. It was to be private. Nobody was invited. This was Genter Latham's decision.

Dinty returned, a sad little figure in her habiliments of mourning, and took the safety-bath of vinegar-and-alcohol which Horace had ready for her.

"You couldn't help but be sorry for Mr. Latham, Doc," she said. "He looks like a man that has died inside."

"Does he?" said Horace with a peculiar intonation.

"He's so pitiful. I think he's softened. If you want to see him soon, I believe it would be all right."

"Do you?" said Horace. "Read that."

He pushed a letter across the table to her. It was from Lawyer Upcraft notifying him that, unless he immediately delivered a formal undertaking to quit Palmyra within one week from date, he would be prosecuted to the extreme rigor of the law for malfeasance in office and the illegal practice of medicine. Appended was a list comprising every house visited by Horace during the epidemic. Dinty's tearful eyes cleared and snapped.

"How hateful!" she cried. "Is that what's been worrying you so, darling?"

Instantly his expression became closed, secretive. He did not answer. But she knew well enough that this was not the source of his troubles. He never brooded over a fight.

"Don't you think I ought to go to the burial, Horace?" she asked, half expecting an objection.

"I thought it was private."

"Mr. Latham won't mind. I think he'd like to have me there. Tip will want to go, too."

"Very well."

Come death, grief and bereavement, nonetheless household routine must be maintained. Downtown on her marketing tour, Dinty picked up fragments of gossip. People were saying that Dr. Amlie had better look out for himself now. The dead girl, they said, had exerted a moderating and restraining influence over her father, and, because of her old friendship for Mrs. Amlie, had dissuaded him from extreme measures. Now, with that ameliorating factor gone, his ruthlessness would have no check. Taproom bets were offered that Horace

Amlie would leave town or be in jail within the week. Seething with indignation, Dinty bore her modest provender home.

That afternoon and evening packed more trouble, uncertainty and apprehension into a few short hours than would have sufficed to Dinty for a lifetime. The worst of it was that she could find no clue to set her upon any identifiable trail. Yet there was plenty to harrow her wifely soul with forebodings. For one thing, the normally chatty and contentious Dr. Vought either wandered in the garden or sat in glowering silence. And what was the matter with faithful Unk Zeb? But for lack of premonitory symptoms, Dinty would have diagnosed it as St. Vitus's dance. It came on shortly after Horace had gone into the kitchen and held a brief, low-voiced talk with the old Negro. Thereafter Unk Zeb withdrew at intervals to mutter, shiver and finally to pray. At supper he dropped two plates and broke a water goblet.

The meal was a dreary function. Horace and his fellow practitioner were on prickly terms. Tip did what he could to enliven the occasion with sprightly discourse about life and learning in the classic shades of Hamilton College. It was a monologue. Had not her responsibilities as hostess restrained her, Dinty would have liked to jump up, give a loud yell and vanish into the evening shadows.

A sharp rat-tat-tat on the office door almost lifted her from her chair.

"Sit still," Horace said sharply to Tip, who had risen to answer.

The host went out. They heard him giving directions of some sort. A hoarse voice responded,

"Right you are, Capting. I got my orders."

Dad Hinch! But what part had the Human Teapot in these secret brewings?

At a quarter before eight the two young people set out for the cemetery. Only one carriage attended the body. It bore Genter Latham, the Reverend Theron Strang, Lawyer Upcraft and Sarah Dorch. The services were brief. Dinty's quick eye caught a movement in a thicket above the grave. The coverage was too thick for identification of the furtive mourner, but Dinty thought that she knew who it was.

The clergyman spoke the solemn final words, crumbling a clod between his fingers. He bent his head silently, then took Genter Latham by the arm. The father released himself and directed the others to leave. Two spademen shoveled the loose earth in upon the casket. The last sight that Dinty had of Genter Latham, he was towering above the grave, his clenched fists raised to the sky. It was not a gesture of sorrow, but an imprecation of vengeance.

On the decorously slow walk back, Tip said to his companion, "Dinty, what's wrong with the Doctor?"

"You've noticed it, too."

"Anybody would notice it. You haven't been doing anything to worry him, have you?"

"Don't be dumb!" said Dinty indignantly. "Why should it be me?"

"Well, it's somebody or something. I've never seen him like this before."

"Do you think I haven't worried about it?" cried Dinty passionately and broke down.

He slipped a brotherly arm about her. She pressed to him. He could feel her trembling.

"Dinty, you're scared."

"Of course I'm scared."

"What at?"

"I don't know. That's what scares me so."

"Won't he tell you?"

"No. I've got a feeling that something awful is going to happen."

"I'm here if you want me."

"I know, Tip."

As Dinty entered the side gate, she paused beneath the lighted window of the private consultation room. Dr. Vought's harsh voice emerged.

"Do you hanker after Auburn Prison, you young fool?" it demanded angrily.

Dinty was not conscious of having cried out or made any other noise. But she heard footsteps crossing the floor and Horace's challenge:

"Who's there?"

Before he could reach the window, she had scuttled around the angle of the house.

"Who's there?" repeated Horace.

"It's me, Dinty." The effort to keep her voice natural took every resource of her will. "May I come in?"

"No. We're busy."

It was so unlike him, that curtness. "Aren't you coming to bed soon?" she asked anxiously.

"Yes. Before long. You go up."

"I shan't be able to sleep. I'd rather wait for you."

"No. Go up."

Not since she was an unruly and interfering child had she heard that tone from him. In a moment he would call her "Araminta" and she would burst into tears.

"Good night, darling," she said, trying to keep the fear and desolation out of her throat.

"Good night," he answered more gently.

"Good night, Dr. Vought."

" 'Night," he growled. He was in a *very* bad temper.

Dinty ran upstairs, entered their room, and, pausing only to kick off her shoes, crawled cautiously through the south window to the roof of the porch. Lying flat and projecting her head over dark space, she could make out Dr. Vought's tart speech without difficulty. Horace's calmer tones were less plainly audible. The colloquy had apparently been resumed where she interrupted it.

"Ten years," shrilled the old man. "Think of that."

What Horace thought about it was too quietly expressed for the eavesdropper's ears.

"What can you gain by it?" persisted the old gentleman.

Another subdued answer.

"Your own satisfaction, eh?" The reply crackled. "You'll have plenty of time to enjoy that in your cell."

Dinty cringed. Why must he keep harping on that? What had Horace done to hazard ten years in jail?

The gate hinges creaked. Dinty flattened herself against the roof as a figure threaded the light mist. Horace came to the window. There was a whispered colloquy. The man saluted and left. By that gesture Dinty knew him for Dad Hinch. Happily for Dinty's overstrained ears, Horace did not return to his desk, but remained looking out of the window.

"What do you expect to find?" insisted Dr. Vought.

Horace's reply astonished her by being, as she thought, in a foreign language. Latin perhaps? Or Greek? Whichever it was, it stirred his mentor to contempt.

"Medical fairy-tales, my boy."

"It does happen."

"Once in a million times."

"Are you familiar with the report of Dr. Little * to the Albany County Medical?"

"I have heard of it."

* David Little, M.D. (1768–1832) of Cherry Valley, N. Y. A factual account of this case appeared in *The New Yorker* for Dec. 10, 1938.

"Was that a medical fairy-tale, sir?"

With less assurance the old gentleman said, "David Little is a reputable and skilled physician."

"What happens once can happen twice. This is either a" (again the unfamiliar term) "or a case of abortion."

Dr. Vought repeated the word with such a stress of fury that Dinty now got it clearly. "Lithopedion! Lithopedion! And you persist in staking your whole career on this mad assumption."

"I see no other way."

"You were always the stubbornest young fool alive."

"Sorry, sir."

That response was deadly quiet. It was also, as the listener above well knew, deadly resolute. Nothing that anybody could do would move Horace Amlie an inch. The old physician probably realized this, for he sighed, though still persisting.

"You won't reconsider?"

"No, sir."

"And you won't take a little more time to think it over?"

"No."

"Then, damme! I'll go with you."

"That I won't have," cried Horace.

"How are you going to stop me?"

"Be sensible, sir. You couldn't do any good. You'd only involve yourself with Genter Latham."

"I'm not afraid of Genter Latham or twenty Genter Lathams."

"I know that, sir. But this is my risk. You can't lessen it by sharing it."

"If I insisted, I suppose you'd simply put it off until I left for home."

"I would."

"Go ahead and ruin your life, then," he snapped. His tone softened. "Whatever comes of it, you know I'll stand by you, my boy."

"I know that, sir," answered Horace gratefully.

"Then I'll be off to bed."

Dinty eased herself back through the window and undressed, thinking hard. The net produce of her analysis was that her Doc had planned a visit to Genter Latham, so fraught with grave probabilities that Dr. Vought, unable to dissuade him from it, had offered to accompany him. But for what purpose? To confess some crime, a crime punishable by State Prison? And the mysterious lithopedion; what conection had that with the danger? And how explain Unk Zeb's ashen terror?

At least, there was no immediate action to fear. Horace would not seek out the bereaved father at this hour of the night. She resolved to stay awake until her husband came up, and, if she judged it expedient, question him tactfully. She propped herself on her pillows, where she could see the office light pallidly reflected from the top of a lilac bush.

Anxiety could not keep so healthy a young animal as Dinty awake indefinitely. She had been through an emotionally exhausting day. She dozed—roused herself—dozed again—slept more heavily—came awake with a shock to see the dull splotch of leaves above the window unillumined. There was no sound from below. Where was Horace?

She leapt from bed and pattered out into the hall. Beneath the guest chamber door a thready gleam showed. He must be in there, talking further with the guest. She rapped.

"Ugh! Hullo!" grunted Dr. Vought's voice.

"Is my husband there?"

"Wassat? Must ha' fallen asleep at my reading."

"Is Horace there?"

"Eh? No. No. Of course he isn't here. Why should he be here?" return the testy voice.

"Where is he?"

"What? Where is who?"

She stamped her bare foot. "Where is my husband?"

"Oh—er—he went out on a call, I believe."

"Where?"

"How should I know?"

You old liar! thought Dinty savagely. She ran back and dressed in frantic haste. Noiselessly she made her way to the floor below and out into the night. Tip Crego materialized from a shadow. She had forgotten, in her turmoil of mind, that he was on watch. She clutched him.

"Oh, Tip! He's gone."

"There's nothing to worry about in that, Dinty. He's often called out at night."

"Then what makes you look so white and queer?"

The boy gulped.

"I'm going after him," said Dinty.

"Where?"

"To Mr. Latham's."

"The Doctor hasn't gone to Mr. Latham's." (But what was the

matter with Tip that his voice should be so unnatural, his eyes so strained and evasive?)

"Where has he gone?"

"I don't know."

"You do know. I'm going to Genter Latham's."

"You couldn't do anything worse."

"What are you holding back from me? Tell me. You've *got* to tell me, Tip. It's something to do with the Lathams," she cried wildly. "If you don't tell me, I'll go straight and ask him."

At that his will broke before hers. "They've gone to the churchyard," he said very low.

"They? Who?"

"Unk Zeb and Dad Hinch are with him."

"What for? What are they going to do?"

"They—they took pick and shovel."

At that, the truth blazed into her mind. "Oh, Tip! How hideous!"

She turned to run, but he caught and held her. "Dinty, you mustn't go."

"I'm going to go."

He gave up. "Not by the road, then. Dad Hinch will be on watch. Around through the beech wood."

They set out at the fast, steady Indian lope, gained the knob beyond the churchyard, and paused at the summit for breath. The mist had dissipated before a wind which was now subsiding in fitful gusts. Directly overhead a lopsided moon shouldered its way through the opposition of pale cloud masses. All the world of branch and leaf was stirring about them. The night was alive and uneasy.

Dinty panted, "How long have they been gone?"

"Not long. Fifteen or twenty minutes."

"What time is it?"

He gave a quick upward glance. "Close on midnight. Let's crawl into that brush."

From that shelter they could overlook the Latham lot. The raw earth was undisturbed.

"They haven't begun yet," whispered Dinty.

"Something must have stopped them," he replied in the same tone.

Dinty clutched him. *"Look!"*

From the shadow of a shrub a lone figure moved into the fitful light. It stood before the grave, motionless as a headstone. Then an arm slowly lifted and the glint of moonglow on white metal turned it whiter. There welled into the darkness Silverhorn Ramsey's lament for his dead love, rising and sinking in unquenchable beauty, heart-searching, heart-breaking, the song of grief and farewell.

Dinty's breast swelled to bursting. She pressed her hands to her throat. She leaned out, her eyes fixed on the dull earth-heap, stark amidst the greenery. There came to her the despairing passion of Wealthia's avowal.

"I'd rise from my grave to answer his call."

Was not the raw earth stirring above the dead?

The final diapason fulfilled itself in unearthly beauty. The mourner's head sank. His lips moved. Now he was threading the tombstones, skirting the foot of the hill where the watchers lay. Gone was the old gallant strut. He shambled forward on leaden feet and vanished around the shoulder of the hill. Dinty covered her face and wept unashamedly.

Waiting for the paroxysm to exhaust itself, Tip said, "That might rouse the village. They'll wait now to see if anyone comes."

"Where are they?"

"Dad Hinch is under the oak by the gate. The others must be in the angle of the church."

Dinty stood up. He seized her and dragged her back beside him. She struggled.

"Tip, there's time yet. I've got to stop them."

"You can't," he said.

"They're going to do a crime. My husband can be put in jail for this."

"Listen to me, Dinty," he said. "Do you want to ruin everything? This is the Doctor's one chance against Genter Latham."

"How? Why?" she demanded wildly.

"Quiet! If there was an abortion done on Wealthy, this will show it. If you try to stop it now, you'll be sorry the last day of your life."

Impressed by his vehemence she faltered, "Are they trying to steal the body?"

"No. They'll do it here. The Doctor brought his instruments."

She shuddered so violently that he could hardly make out her words: "I can't bear it! I can't bear it!"

"The only chance," he repeated.

Two figures, bearing shovels, rounded the corner of the building. Horace's voice cautiously raised, said, "All clear, Dad?"

"All clear, Capting."

"Stay where you are."

Excavation in the loose earth was easy and swift. Dinty quivered throughout her body at the thud of iron on wood. Ropes were adjusted. The oblong box came slowly up. She heard the shriek of protesting nails as the cover was pried loose. A light flickered, casting a patterned glow. Dinty's vision clouded.

"Are they taking it out?" she breathed.

"Yes. Don't look."

She did not mean to look. Imagination drew the grisly picture for her; the pitiful body of the friend she had loved; the pitiless knife, the dreadful process which had sickened her when she read about it in Horace's book.

But for what occurred next she was wholly unprepared. A stertorous gasp came to her ears. Involuntarily she opened her eyes. Horace was bending above the inert body. He straightened up, as Unk Zeb, with a howl of pure animal terror leapt in the air like one shot through the heart, plunged forward, kicking the lantern into darkness, and dashed wildly through the underbrush until the sound of his panic flight died away.

From a vast distance, Tip's voice came to Dinty's ears. "My God! What did he see? What *did* he see?"

"I want to go home," moaned Dinty.

He had to lift her to her feet.

"Stand still!" he said sharply.

"What's the matter?"

"Dad Hinch is looking this way. I think he saw us."

He eased her back into the shrubbery. Safely screened, she started to run with the instinctive desire to leave that horror behind her, but her knees were loose. She could make but slow progress. It did not matter. The accomplices could not return, as Tip pointed out, until they had reinterred the corpse and obliterated their traces. At the gate he anxiously studied her face.

"Dinty, are you going to tell the Doctor?"

She shook all over. "No. I wouldn't dare."

"I think you're right."

"Maybe some day, when we're both very old," she qualified. "If I told him now, I don't know what he'd do to me. He'd hate me. He'd send me away from him and I'd die. I'd *die,* Tip."

"I don't believe he'd do that," said the boy. "But I guess it's better for him not to know. Better for both of you."

Dinty said dolorously, "How'm I going to live with this between us?"

"You look terrible," said he. "I'll get you a sleeping draught from the cabinet."

"I'll never sleep again," said Dinty.

She lay, tense and rigid, for a long hour, listening to the broken grief of Unk Zeb below, moaning, weeping, calling upon the name of his Jesus.

The gate swung. Dinty crept to the window. Horace was walking up the path, his head erect, his shoulders squared. Behind him plodded Dad Hinch with a bulging bag of coarse cloth slung across his shoulder. They entered the office.

The guest room door opened and closed. So, she was not the only sleepless one in that house of fear. Dr. Vought pattered nimbly down the stair. She could hear but dimly the exchange of a word between him and her husband. The three men went into the private consultation room. Eavesdropping there was too risky. Dinty crawled back into her bed.

In the closed room Horace pointed to the bag.

"There it is," he said to his guest. "Look at it."

The old gentleman peered within. "By God Almighty!" he swore excitedly. Then, professional admiration supervening, "What a lovely specimen!"

"I doubt if Mr. Genter Latham will agree."

"You're not going to take it to him!"

"Why else do you think I risked jail?"

A shade of anxiety darkened the sagacious, old countenance. "Lad, I ought to have warned you, but I thought of it too late."

"What about?"

"Are you sure that Upcraft's weasel wasn't snooping after you?"

Horace struck his forehead. "What a damned fool! I forgot all about him." He brightened. "Dad would have seen him, though. Dad sees everything. You didn't notice anyone following us, did you, Dad?"

"No, Capting." The next instant he struck consternation to their souls. "Somebody was on the hillside whilst we was at work," said he.

"Somebody? Who? Why in hell didn't you tell me?" cried Horace.

"Dunno who," answered the Human Teapot stolidly. "Wouldn't have done no good to tell you. I didn't see 'em till they was leavin'. I think there was two on 'em. Mighta been three."

"Get out," said Horace. "And if you ever breathe a word of tonight I'll cut your throat from ear to ear."

"Orders is orders, Capting," said the Teapot, unmoved, saluted, and left.

The two physicians stared at one another. "Now what?" asked the senior.

"I'm going to Murchison's."

He was back in ten minutes. He had not been to his rival's, for, on the way, he had spied a light in Ephraim Upcraft's front room, and, gaining a viewpoint, had seen within the Honest Lawyer and the bearded physician in absorbed consultation. Dr. Vought heard his report with a sickened visage.

"I guess that spills the beans from the nosebag," he muttered. "Will you still see Genter Latham?"

"Yes. First thing in the morning."

"I'll go with you." He saw only disaster ahead.

-19-

Sarah Dorch answered the Latham knocker. She cowered when she saw the two men.

"Oh, Dr. Amlie! You didn't ought to come here."

"I want to see Mr. Latham."

"He won't see you. He won't see nobody."

"Is he up?"

"He ain't been to bed."

"Where is he?"

"In Miss Wealthia's room." She began to snivel. "All night he's been walkin' the floor. If you speak to him, he don't so much as look your way. I don't believe he knows I'm here. Reverend Strang came back from the grave with him. Lawyer Upcraft, too; he wouldn't even notice 'em when they spoke. Squire and Mrs. Jerrold was in after the buryin' and . . ."

"Stop chattering," said Horace sternly. "We shall not leave this house without seeing him."

With a little startled cackle of dismay she scuttled off. The massive figure of Genter Latham appeared at the stairhead. Horace spoke.

"Mr. Latham, we want a word with you."

The banker descended stiffly, treading step by step with the gait of a marionette. His face was fixed and expressionless. He advanced between the two men, and flung the door open with a powerful heave which sent it thudding against the wall.

"Out!" he said.

"Mr. Latham," began the old physician. He got no further.

"Out!" Murder was latent in the dull undertone.

Horace stepped forward. "We'll go when we've completed our errand," he said solidly.

"You have no errand with me."

"Your daughter."

In accents of mingled hate and desolation the father said, "I have no daughter, sir. She is dead and buried beyond the reach of your calumnies."

"They are not calumnies."

"Will you go—now—before I kill you!"

In a tone at once authoritative and soothing, Dr. Vought said, "Let there be no talk of killing. We stand for the truth. Are you man enough to hear it?"

Genter Latham passed his hand over his eyes. "Say your say," he muttered.

Horace spoke quietly. "Your daughter conceived a child by her affianced husband."

"You told me that lie before."

"I now offer you proof."

"And I substantiate it," added his companion.

The father rocked on his feet. He groped behind him, encountered the solid support of the wall and straightened up. His lips moved puffily. It seemed to Horace that he was repeating the words spoken to him, without comprehension.

"Do you understand us?"

"Proof. A child. A baby," whispered the lips.

"Yes."

A gust of rage shook him all through his bulk. "A lie! The same lie! The same God-damned lie."

"Will you see the proof?" said Dr. Vought.

Again the chill quietude of the old man prevailed. Doubt flickered in the savage eyes.

"A baby! Where is it?"

"It was never born."

"Where is it?" persisted the father.

Horace answered deliberately. "It was removed from Wealthia's body, after the body was taken from its grave."

"Grave-robbery! You?"

"You left me no other recourse."

The man's laughter shocked them like a blast. "I'll see you rot in jail for this. No, by God! I'll do more. I'll rouse the village and have you hanged to the first tree."

"And your daughter's good name?" said Dr. Vought.

The frantic glee of vengeance died out of the face before them. It withered into uncertainty.

"Proof!" he gasped. "You claim proof. Where is your proof?"

"Will you see it?" said Horace.

The older physician intervened. "Do you think, Doctor," said he in professional form, "that, considering the nervous strain to which Mr. Latham has been subjected, he is in condition . . . ?"

"I can stand anything," brusquely interrupted Genter Latham.

Horace moved forward into the library, followed by the others, crossed to a window, opened it, and called out an order. Unk Zeb appeared. His face was gray. He was shaking from head to foot. Reaching out, his master took from the trembling hands a misshapen bag which bulged at the bottom. Unk Zeb turned and ran. Horace lifted the burden across the sill, and set it down beside him. Genter Latham's stare fixed upon it. His breath was fast between pouted lips.

"Just a moment, Dr. Amlie."

The old physician's tone was coolly professional. He went briskly out, and spoke to Sarah Dorch, shivering in the kitchen. Returning, he set a glass of brandy on the mantel. "I will elucidate this matter for Mr. Latham." He spoke with the authority of the pundit toward the neophyte. Horace breathed a sigh of gratitude and relief. The matter was out of his hands, for the time.

Dr. Vought might have been back in his professorial chair, so composed was his manner. It was admirably adapted to mollifying the grisly business in hand.

"We have here," he began, "a phenomenon of rare and obscure occurrence. That has befallen the late Miss Latham which occurs perhaps once in a million times. A woman becomes pregnant"—Genter Latham started, twitched, but controlled himself—"and for some reason the process of gestation is checked. Science is not yet prepared to say why. The foetus dies. Again obscurely the mechanism fails to expel the burden. What occurs? Nature, ever self-preservative, sets about saving the mother's life. The calcium in the system infiltrates the unborn child, calcifies it, by a slow, sure process, turns it to harmless stone. Thus it may be carried within the mother's body, indiscernibly, for years, for a long lifetime. I have, myself, seen one of these monstrous and rare lithopedia in the museum at Edinburgh University, where I enjoyed the privilege of finishing my medical studies. I never expected to see another until my learned and respected young friend, Dr. Amlie, correctly diagnosed this strange and tragic case.* Did you speak, Mr. Latham?"

"I don't believe you," said Genter Latham hoarsely.

The old gentleman's voice grew crisper. He gestured toward the

* The actual lithopedion upon which this episode is based is now in the Museum of the Albany (N. Y.) Medical School.

bag. "Do you insist on ocular demonstration? I must advise you . . ."

An imperative gesture checked him.

"Show."

Dr. Vought lifted the black bag. As he grasped the object within it, Genter Latham visibly braced himself. Momentarily he closed his eyes. When he opened them a small image rested on the stand near by.

There was nothing horrible about it. It was merely grotesque. More than anything else it suggested a small Buddha which the sculptor had roughed out but had lacked time to finish. Genter Latham regarded it intently.

"Is that a human child?"

"Look at the hands and feet," said Dr. Vought.

The autocrat leaned forward. He stretched out his arm. His finger tremulously touched the object. He shuddered profoundly throughout his great body.

"Are you convinced, sir?" asked Vought.

"Yes," he answered thickly.

The older man shot a swift glance at him and reached for the glass of brandy. "Take some of this."

Genter Latham swallowed slowly and with visible effort. Horace restored the weird image of unfinished humanity to its covering. The master of the house lifted his head.

"Have you any further business with me, gentlemen?"

Answering for both, Dr. Vought said, "No."

"I will ask you to leave me. I am very tired." He spoke with pathetic gentleness and dignity. The two doctors questioned one another with their eyes. The senior asked, "Don't you think I'd better stay with you, Mr. Latham?"

"I must be alone."

They found their hats and canes and walked slowly down the peony-bordered path, Horace carrying the stone baby.

"He's taking it hard," he said.

"Harder than he shows. He'll break."

"He might. I doubt it, though. It's tough fiber."

"You'll have no further trouble from him."

"Not from him perhaps."

"There's Murchison, to be sure."

Horace nodded.

"Would he dare go against Latham's wishes?"

"He never has. That doesn't prove that he mightn't."

"He hates you enough for anything short of murder," admitted the old gentleman.

"And, as you said, this might finish Mr. Latham. Then Murchison would be free to act."

Horace deposited his burden in the wagon. Unk Zeb cramped the wheels for them to get in. They drove home in gloomy silence. At the gate, Horace gave the Negro low-voiced instructions and sent him to the barn. To Dr. Vought he said, "My wife mustn't know about this."

The old gentleman looked dubious. "Aren't you going to tell her anything?"

"Not until I have to."

"Sure you aren't making a mistake, lad? That's a canny child you married."

Horace broke out grievously, "Why burden her heart with it? Dr. Vought, I'm a coward. I just haven't the gristle to face this thing. Oh, it isn't for myself! I can stand state prison if I have to. But what's to become of my Dinty?"

"Her family," began his friend, when Horace cut him short.

"You don't know Dinty's loyalty. Her mother hates me. Dinty would never go to live under the same roof with her."

"There'll be others to look after her, lad," the old man assured him kindly. "To my mind, you're taking too black a view. Suppose Murchison does know about your—your . . ."

"Crime," put in Horace bitterly.

"Crime, if you will. That doesn't prove that he's going to take action."

"Do you think he and Upcraft were discussing crops at two o'clock this morning?" railed Horace.

The other pulled a wry face. "That's a kittle point."

"I'm not going to make Dinty miserable before I have to," continued the husband with determination.

"Now you're showing sense. I'll be going back tomorrow, lad, but you can get me at call."

Main Street was seething like a maelstrom meanwhile, with rumor and counter-rumor, when, in due time, Mrs. Horace Amlie appeared upon her morning errands of housekeeping. She was mobbed by a wave of women. Horace Amlie was a prickly customer to tackle when in the wrong mood, but nobody was afraid of friendly little Dinty. Friendly though she was, she now proved as reticent as her husband.

Surges of curiosity beat upon her as against a rock, and fell back in a spume of resentful disappointment. Her own mother could get nothing out of her, and proclaimed her for an ungrateful and undutiful daughter before the attentive ears of the Hepzibah Sewing Circle. Dinty did not attend. She was as prickling with curiosity as any of her questioners, but, from her demeanor, one would have inferred that, beneath that calm appearance of information, she carried the secrets of fate.

Both her husband and her guest had been infuriatingly uncommunicative. There remained Unk Zeb. When the menfolk were clear of the house, she put him to the question. Downtown she had heard excited commentary about a mysterious cloth bag which had figured in the still more mysterious proceedings at the Latham mansion. She began, "Did you bring the bag back with you, Unk Zeb?"

"Do' know nuffin', Miss Dinty," he mumbled. His affirighted eyes refused to meet hers.

"Did you leave it in the barn?"

"No'm. Po' ol' niggah don' know . . ."

"Don't lie to me, Unk Zeb."

"I call my Jesus to say . . ."

"What was in it?"

He uttered a cry of terror and misery and began to retch. When she went to him, he slumped to the ground.

"I wanna go home," he wailed. "I wanna go home to No'th Cahlina. I do' wanna stay heah no mo'."

"You lie quiet on your bed and I'll fetch you a calming potion," said Dinty. As she held it to his lips, he faltered.

"The Doctah say he sen' me home if I do like he tol' me las' night."

"If the Doctor promised you that, he'll do it," she assured him. "Now lie back and rest."

The "calming potion" was considerably more than that, being as strong an opiate as the amateur practitioner dared administer. The patient, still fuzzily lamenting, dropped off.

With him disposed of, Dinty went to the barn. First she carefully explored the wagon and its box. Nothing there. A search of the stable was barren of results. She mounted to the loft. In a far corner the hay showed signs of having been disturbed. She burrowed and felt against her fingers the rough crocus of the bag.

Steeling herself, she bore it to the light, loosed the thong which bound the neck, and peered within. Her first reaction was one of pure astonishment. A block of stone, blackish and vaguely fashioned to human likeness, met her eyes. Then she noticed the faintly modeled hands and feet. An illustration in a book rose vividly from the depths of her memory. *Burns on Abortion!* Now Dinty knew. She thrust bag and contents back and covered them.

Now that she possessed the knowledge, what use could be made of it? Dared she consult Dr. Vought? She sought counsel from Tip Crego who had come in after dinner. Tip vehemently besought her to say nothing.

"I wish we'd never gone to the churchyard," he shivered.

"I don't," said the more resolute Dinty. "No matter how bad it is, I'd rather know."

The doctors came back for early supper. At sight of her husband's wan and weary face, Dinty's heart swelled with pity. Whatever was harassing him, she would, as she guessed, only make matters worse by questioning. Wisdom taught her that, with Horace, it was always best to wait and let him take the initiative.

The usually talkative Dr. Vought proved a sad disappointment to her when she got him alone. He was totally unresponsive to her broadest hints. In his aspect there was a sort of pity which worried her, as he assured her with superfluous warmth that she could always depend upon his friendship when needed. Why should she specially need support? What had occurred between Horace and Genter Latham?

The two men were deep in talk behind the door of the inner sanctum when the *Sentinel* came. Dinty perused it with no special interest until she came upon a local item which was worth retailing. She waited for the consultation to come to an end, then said to Horace,

"Here's something about Old Murch."

"In the paper? What is it?"

"He left for Albany by today's packet."

"Albany!" repeated Dr. Vought. He looked across at Horace.

"To be gone for a week or two," pursued the reader. "What do you s'pose that means?"

"I haven't the faintest notion," answered Horace steadily.

In his heart he had no doubts. Murchison was going to lay the case before the State Medical Society and solicit their backing for the prosecution.

-20-

The pattern of impending disaster worked itself out in Dinty's mind. In his mad prepossession to prove himself in the right, Horace had confronted Genter Latham with the strange object, the lithopedion which he had taken from Wealthia's body. Thus, self-convicted of a crime, he had delivered himself into the hands of an enemy. What form would Genter Latham's vengeance take? She remembered miserably Dr. Vought's angry protest when he was trying to dissuade Horace from the venture, "Do you hanker after Auburn Prison?"

How long would they keep him there? Two years? Five years? Ten years? Dinty's soul quivered within her. She could wait; forever, if need be. But what would life be without her Doc? There was nothing to be done meanwhile, until he chose to speak, but guard herself against betrayal of her dire knowledge.

The carefully constructed logic of her fears endured for barely a day before it came crashing down in bewildering ruin.

On the morning following Dr. Vought's departure, Horace received a summons and left his office. Having redd up her housework, Dinty, with market basket on arm, repaired to the meat-shop. In the midst of an animated chaffer with Butcher Mays who had the effrontery to ask seven cents a pound for a prime cut of beef—sheer extortion, as she pointed out in the most explicit terms at her command—she became aware of a commotion outside. People were running as to a fire, exchanging excited comments as they ran. She caught Genter Latham's name and her husband's. With tripping heart, she hurried to the door and stopped, stricken to immobility by the amazement of what she saw.

Genter Latham and Horace Amlie were coming down Main Street, arm in arm.

Quiet fell, as if a spell had bound the busy street. All heads were turned to the one focus. A span of oxen stood still in the middle of the road, their driver furling his whip and staring. A stray cur barked, shockingly loud in that hush.

The older man was leaning heavily on the younger. Genter Latham's face was stony and colorless. He looked straight ahead of him. Passage cleared to the front, the people edging against the buildings or stepping aside into the gutter. Some few spoke in greeting, obsequious or timid. Mr. Latham made no reply. Dinty doubted whether he even heard them. She tried to catch Horace's eye. He was intent upon his charge and did not see her.

The two men entered the Latham office. A messenger came hustling out and ran up Ephraim Upcraft's stairs. At once the Honest Lawyer bustled importantly down, emerging upon the street with a tin box which he carried into the bank.

No citizen of Palmyra would have had the effrontery to listen in upon the trio back of the locked door. But the bank's normal traffic swelled to special proportions. Little reward did the hopeful ones reap. Only once was anything overheard from within, Genter Latham's imperious basso.

"Tell them? Tell them nothing. Let 'em swallow their own spittle."

For a long hour the three consulted. The Reverend Theron Strang was sent for, came, remained for five minutes, and emerged with a face both grave and happy. He had nothing to say except that Mr. Latham had renewed and increased his subscription to the Presbyterian Church. The parson's salary would be paid again in full.

Rumor ran wild. It was said that Genter Latham was drawing a new will. It was said that he had professed repentance of his sins and would join the church as full communicant. It was said that he had instructed Lawyer Upcraft to secure Horace Amlie's full restoration to medical practice and privilege. It was whispered that, knowing himself to be a stricken man, and in fear of death, he was doing what he could to right a grievous wrong inflicted upon the young physician.

Lawyer Upcraft came out. He had nothing to say. His face was so sour that Carlisle Sneed observed that he looked like he'd bit into a green pawpaw.

All that morning the magnate was closeted with the physician. At noon Horace sent for his gig and drove him home, remaining for dinner. Later he sent out for Aunt Minnie Duryea. It became known that the effort had been too much for Mr. Latham's overstrained powers and that he had suffered a stroke. On leaving to obtain some remedies from his office, Dr. Amlie relaxed his reticence enough to admit that much. Mr. Latham might live or he might die; he would never again be the man he was.

Straightway the attitude of the village toward the Amlies radically altered. Mr. Latham's open and deliberate advertisement of his restored favor to Horace reinstated them as by fiat. Solicitous attentions surrounded Dinty. The older women went out of their way to shower her with courtesies. Comfit-munchers paid visits to the house, putting sly and eager questions which elicited a minimum of information. It all made Dinty queasy. She had no taste for a fawning Palmyra.

Horace's practice boomed. In the wake of the epidemic, now safely past, there came an outbreak of minor ailments, largely nervous. The office slate filled up. The physician recklessly accepted every call. It was blatantly illegal, but what did that matter now? As well be hung for a sheep as for a lamb. He was avid to lay up all the money possible for Dinty against the time when his support should be removed. For he did not deceive himself as to the immediate peril of his position. Genter Latham was a broken man. Even though he lived, his protection must soon become ineffectual. There would then be nothing to restrain Murchison from instigating Horace's prosecution for the violation of Wealthia Latham's grave. That the purpose of the Albany trip had been to report to the State Board and enlist their aid, Horace had not the slightest doubt. He was living beneath a suspended sword.

What made life continuously difficult was his resolution to deceive Dinty and protect her happiness to the last possible moment. For she was happy again.

> Lavender's blue, diddle-diddle.
> Lavender's green . . .

she sang at her work in the kitchen over which she now held undisputed sway, Unk Zeb having carried his secrecy and his terrors back to his No'th Cahlina.

Everything was lovely in a fair and friendly world for Horace Amlie's wife. The threat of Mr. Latham's powerful enmity was removed. If Horace chose to be close-mouthed about the reasons, she refused to let that disturb her renewed satisfaction with life. One fine piece of news she had: the note at the bank had been forgiven, principal and interest. They were free of debt. All their surplus, which had taken a most enheartening spurt, could now be devoted to the cobblestone house fund.

Never had Horace been more tender, more solicitous toward her. In all ways he was perfect except for his secretiveness. With wifely instinct she felt always that understrain of concealment. Or was that her own conscience, guilty by reason of her unconfessed spying? Then, too, he had taken to sitting up late in his office, arranging and docketing papers, like a man in expectation of death. But he laughed off any suggestion of impaired health. Indeed, he seemed in the pink of condition, except that he slept uncertainly, tossed and sometimes muttered unintelligible plaints. Frequently she caught him unawares, gazing at her with a regard so wistful, so hungry, yet so grievous that her heart stirred.

The explanation came to her in a flash. It was his disappointment over their childlessness. He had always wanted a family. Very well, that lack was easily remedied; he should have it. Now that they were debt-free and her fancy could see the little leaden eagles, beckoning with uplifted wings from the side-glasses of the cobblestone house, there was no reason for further delay.

> Lavender's blue, diddle-diddle.
> Lavender's green.
> Babies are sweet, diddle-diddle.
> Five—Ten—Fifteen.

warbled Dinty in a crescendo of ambition.

Daily Horace visited Genter Latham, who was up from his bed in a week but kept to his house except to totter about the garden upon two canes. The shock of that interview in the library, well though he had supported it at the time, had undermined him. It was doubtful, Horace told Dinty, whether he would outlast the year.

Two weeks passed, and three, and Dr. Gail Murchison was still absent from his diminishing practice. The strain of waiting wore upon Horace Amlie's nerves. Learning from the *Sentinel* that the absent physician had indicated the probability of an early return, Horace set Dad Hinch on watch for the westbound packets as they arrived.

On a thundery Tuesday morning the Human Teapot brought the expected news: Dr. Murchison had debarked from the *Chief Engineer*. Carpetbag in hand, he had gone direct to Lawyer Upcraft's office. The pair were still in consultation when Dad reported.

All Horace's resolution was needed to hold him to his professional engagements that day. He had now but one desire: to face Murchison and know the worst. Quite probably, he thought, there would be an offer of compromise, a bargain whereby he would be permanently exiled from town as the price of his rival's silence. None of it for him! Even for Dinty's sake, he could not accept so cowardly a composition. To accede to such terms would be to put himself under the threat of further blackmail. If prison it must be, and separation from Dinty, he would find the fortitude to face it. After all, they were young. There would still be time to build a life together.

Having taken care of his crowding office calls and with an hour left before supper time, Horace washed up, donned his broadcoat and beaver, took his silverheaded cane, and called at the Murchison office.

Dr. Murchison was out.

When would he be back?

The house-hussey who did for him could not say.

The next call was at Ephraim Upcraft's house. The Honest Lawyer was also absent. Was he expected back soon? No, not until next day probably. Mrs. Upcraft vouchsafed the information that her husband and Dr. Murchison had set out for Canandaigua some hours before, in the Upcraft rig. Was there a leer on her face as she imparted the news? Horace thought so. She had never liked him.

It was clear enough now. After hearing Murchison's report on his interview with the State Medical Society representatives, the lawyer had taken his client to see the district attorney in Canandaigua. Horace assumed that the State Medical authorities had fallen in with the Murchison plan and agreed to support the prosecution. What else could they do? Grave-robbery was a dire offense. Similarly there would be but one course for the district attorney to follow. Horace's respite was over. He might expect arrest any time within the next few days, possibly on the morrow.

Up to a point, his reasoning was correct. The purpose of the Canandaigua trip was to inspire criminal action against Dr. Horace Amlie though not, of course, upon the grounds which he assumed. Nor were the two agents over-sanguine of success. For the State Medical Society had received Dr. Gail Murchison's request that it officially procure the arrest of Horace Amlie for the illegal practice of medicine with a chilling lack of enthusiasm. Thanks to the militant advocacy of Dr. Vought, that body was well informed as to the accused medico's "unsparing, heroic and successful efforts to save Palmyra and its vicinage from the devastations of a horrible scourge" (the rhetoric being the Rochester man's) and was heartily disinclined to any punitive measures. In fact, the flea with which Dr. Murchison left after his protracted and abortive efforts whispered in the ear which it occupied that the Board was preparing to reinstate the brash flouter of its former edict.

Notwithstanding, Lawyer Upcraft, upon consideration of the status, gave opinion that they might still incite young Hedges, the prosecutor, to take action on his own initiative. Just about the time when Horace was going wretchedly home to his supper, Mr. Hedges was informing the two emissaries that he wouldn't touch the case with the charred end of a hickory poker unless the medical authorities made the first move. Thereupon the callers repaired to the Hardy Angler on the bank of the outlet and so effectually drowned their disappointment that, driving home by moonlight, they up-ended two logs of the corduroy pike, tipped over the rig, and broke Old Murch's arm, which Horace set the next day and never charged him a penny out of professional courtesy.

But before that, much had happened.

Still resolute to tell Dinty nothing—poor child! she would know soon enough—Horace went home to his supper wearing a mask of determined cheerfulness. He heard Dinty singing as she dished up the meal. It was a particularly tasty supper, directed to Horace's special appetites and garnished with a pint of currant wine. Dinty was celebrating the return of prosperity. Through the repast, the master of the house maintained his air of light-heartedness. Only when his helpmeet had left to wash up did he lapse into a blue reverie.

He did not hear her come in from the kitchen until she was standing before him with a challenge.

"What makes you look so glum, darling?"

"Eh? What's that? Glum? I'm not."

"You are. And you're trying to hide it from me. Is one of your cases worrying you?"

"No, no, indeed!"

"You needn't be so hearty about it," she observed, eying him with suspicion.

"Don't you think we might have another bottle of that very tasty wine?" he insinuated, clinging to the note of festivity.

"Later, maybe. I want to talk to you seriously." She came and perched lightly on his knee. "Doc, I've been thinking."

He rallied to the point of cautioning her against mental excess. She stuck out a small, pink tongue at him, retracted it, and employed it in saying with slightly smug satisfaction,

"We're getting to be people of substance, aren't we, darling?"

"You might say so."

"Well, I've been thinking," she repeated. "I think it's time we had a baby."

The sudden contraction of his muscles almost dislodged her. She stared, aghast, into his face which seemed to have frozen.

"You dont want me to have a baby?" she faltered.

"No." It was a cry of pain.

"Why not?"

"We—we can't afford it. It isn't—it wouldn't . . ."

She rose and stood, looking gravely down at him. "Darling, what is it? There's something. Tell me." As he kept silent she added softly, "Is it terrible?"

"Yes."

"Have you stopped loving me?"

"God! *No!*"

"Then it can't be very terrible."

He drew her back into his arms, pressing her face against his. "Dinty, I may have to leave you."

"Why? Where are you going?"

"To prison."

She gave a little gasp, pushing herself back from him. "Is it Genter Latham? It can't be! I thought that was all over, all made up. Isn't it?"

"It isn't Latham. Dinty, I've committed a crime."

In his misery and his absorption he did not heed her half-whispered "I know." Carefully and with such suppression of the horror as he could compass, he told her of the exhumation and the result of the autopsy.

"That's what you took to Mr. Latham's house," she murmured.

"Yes."

"But, darling," she cried, "that wasn't a crime. Nobody could blame you for that. Not Mr. Latham, anyway. You said, yourself, he wasn't going to do anything to you."

"It is a crime," he insisted. "I'd do the same thing again in the same circumstances. But that doesn't alter the fact that I'm a criminal."

"I don't understand," she said piteously. "Nobody knows but Mr. Latham and Dad Hinch. You can trust Dad, can't you?"

"Yes."

"Who's going to send you to prison, then?"

"Murchison. He was spying—he or his man or both of them—and saw it all. Next day he started for Albany."

"Oh, Doc! Are you sure about it?"

"Dad Hinch saw them moving on the hilltop."

"Where?" she gasped. "What part of the hill?"

"Just above the steeple."

"Nobody was there. There couldn't have been."

"There was, I tell you. Dad went up next day and found where the shrubbery was broken. He thought there were two people."

Dinty said in a small, broken voice, "There were. Tip and I." Then, at the look on his face she quavered, "You aren't mad with me, are you, Doc? I'd never have followed you, only . . ."

She stopped because she was being violently shaken and, presently, as violently kissed. Again and again he made her repeat that no other person could possibly have been on summit or slope without their discovering him. Assured at length, he said,

"Where's that bottle of wine, Puss? I need it."

As they sipped it, they went through the entire course of the tragic events from the first. Dinty regarded her husband with something like awe.

"It must have been dreadful," said she, "having to face down Genter Latham with that Thing."

"I never in my life so hated to do anything. But it meant our whole future, yours and mine. How else could I convince him?"

She pondered. "Do you think Wealthy knew what had happened to her?"

"How could she? After the terror of being pregnant, think what a blessed relief it must have been when nothing came of it. No, she was honest in her denials at the last, whatever she may have been at first. How bitterly she must have regretted having told Kinsey Hayne . . . ! What's the matter, my sweet?"

Slowly, effortfully she said, "There's one other thing, Horace. I don't know whether I ought to tell you even now."

"Hasn't there been enough concealment? We'd better clear this up once and for all."

"Darling, Kinsey was never Wealthy's paramour."

"Not Hayne! Are you crazy, Dinty? Who else could it have been?"

"Silverhorn."

"I told you that it is medically impossible he should have been the father."

"But it isn't, darling. I read that article. Ask Dr. Vought. He's sent me another article proving that the man in the *Eclectic* didn't know what he was talking about." She ran to get it, thrust it into his shaking hand.

As he read, his face grew still and gray. "Ramsey," he whispered. "Then it was Ramsey. The bugle over the grave!"

"You wouldn't listen to me." Dinty was not above preening herself a bit. But at the twisted anguish of his expression, she ran to him.

"I'd have written to Colonel Hayne but for you. I accused poor Hayne. I'm responsible for his death."

"You aren't! You aren't!" she cried passionately. "Oh, I was afraid of that! It's not true. You're not to blame. Wealthy confessed to that. He was as infatuated with her as she was with Silverhorn. After that he didn't want to live."

There was a long silence. Horace sighed and said.

"Dinty?"

"Yes, darling?"

"Do you think we can put this out of our minds by never speaking or thinking of it again?"

She fell back upon her favorite apothegm. "You never can tell till you try," she said. "And now," she asked meekly, "can I have my baby?"

"You can have ten," said Horace.

Dinty did not have ten children. But she did have six, which was a respectable average for those days, and she raised them all to maturity, which was little less than a miracle. The Amlies never built their cobblestone house with the leaded side-glasses. There was no need to. Genter Latham's will left his mansion to, "My beloved and lamented daughter's loyal friend, Araminta Amlie," and Dinty put in her own eagles, to taste.

Horace prospered mightily, became dogmatic with riches and success, and laid down the medical laws for village, town and surrounding countryside with an authority hardly less autocratic than Genter Latham's own.

Once thereafter they saw Silverhorn Ramsey. He was aged beyond his years, seamed and sodden with debauchery, but preserving still some imperishable glamour of his vitality. He was again in the lake trade, had bought a smart and able two-masted sloop, and (as he told them with a wink) could deliver them the finest old-country goods from Canada without the burden of import taxes. When the *Dark Beauty* was wrecked in one of Ontario's furious gales, her master brought an injured sailor ashore on his back, and himself perished, exhausted among the rocks.

Westward the star of empire shimmered along the reaches of Governor Clinton's Ditch. Rochester took pre-eminence over Palmyra, then Buffalo. There came a day when, incredibly, the Grand Canal, that utmost achievement of Man the Engineer, diminished to a negligible agency of the nation's traffic, as the swift trains sped, hooting disdainfully, across an expanding land. Today Palmyra fulfills its quiet destiny, toiling and sleeping beside its inland waters, one of a thousand small communities, pioneers and monuments of a past in which they played an ardent part in the growth of a new America.